Kate Charles, a past Chairman of the Crime Writers' Association and the Barbara Pym Society, is well known as a fictional chronicler of the Church of England and an expert in the field of clerical crime fiction. She is co-organizer of the annual St Hilda's Crime and Mystery Conference and a member of the prestigious Detection Club, as well as an occasional contributor to the *Church Times*. She has published twelve novels to date, including the popular Book of Psalms series, three standalone suspense novels and a series featuring curate Callie Anson.

Kate lives on the English side of the Welsh Marches with her husband and her Border terrier.

Also by Kate Charles

A Drink of Deadly Wine
The Snares of Death
Appointed to Die
Evil Angels Among Them
Unruly Passions
Strange Children
Cruel Habitations
Evil Intent
Secret Sins
Deep Waters
False Tongues

A DEAD MAN OUT OF MIND

KATE CHARLES

First published in Great Britain in 1994 by Headline Book Publishing

This edition published in 2015

Marylebone House
36 Causton Street
London SW1P 4ST
www.marylebonehousebooks.co.uk

British Library Cataloguing-in-Publication Data
A catalogue record for this book is available from the British Library

ISBN 978–1–910674–13–0
eBook ISBN 978–1–910674–14–7

Typeset by Graphicraft Limited, Hong Kong
Manufacture managed by Jellyfish
First printed in Great Britain by CPI
Subsequently digitally printed in Great Britain

eBook by Graphicraft Limited, Hong Kong

Produced on paper from sustainable forests

For Jacquie, who has demonstrated the value of women's ministry to so many

The Book of Psalms mysteries: looking back, looking forward

It's difficult for me to believe, but it has been 25 years since I began writing *A Drink of Deadly Wine*, the first novel in what would become 'the Book of Psalms mysteries'. Contrary to what readers may believe, in my experience writers of fiction don't very often reread their own books – they are too focused on the future to have time for the past, too concerned with what comes next to worry about what has been. So the republication of this series of novels, 25 years on, has provided me with a rare opportunity to revisit a world I once inhabited totally, the world of the Church of England in the early 1990s.

In so many ways, the early 1990s belong to a long-gone past. Young readers today might find that past laughable, if not totally incomprehensible. Those years provide the context of the books: my characters live in a world which is, first and foremost, uncontrolled by technology. There are no mobile phones, and certainly no smartphones; phones are mostly attached to walls. No one listens to music on anything other than a radio or a record player, unless they're very modern and have adopted CDs. Televisions are large and bulky things. Home computers are non-existent, as are Kindles and other e-readers – not to mention iPads. People carry address books and use telephone directories. If they need information, they go to a library, and if they want to travel to somewhere unfamiliar, they look at a map.

Other differences are cultural, reminding us of how many things have changed in our society. In those books, supermarkets closed their doors by 5 or 6 p.m., and were never open on a Sunday. Pub licensing hours were strictly regulated. People smoked in pubs, restaurants and workplaces. Fox hunting was pretty much unquestioned. Laura Ashley represented the height of fashion. And 'British Rail tea' was unfailingly undrinkable.

And yet . . .

And yet, when moving into the sphere of the Church of England which these books so firmly inhabit, not so much has changed.

Yes, I can report with a joyous and thankful heart that women are now acceptable as priests in much if (sadly) not all of the Church, and by the time these new editions are published, women bishops will probably already be consecrated, or at least appointed. *Deo gratias*.

But so much remains the same, and not in a good way. Power struggles, judgemental attitudes, 'them' and 'us', gossip – it was true then, and I still see these things going on in parishes everywhere. It is the stuff of which mystery novels are made: the base human nature which puts self above others, and which manifests itself at its worst in the Church.

People often ask me why there are so many crime novels set in the Church, and this, I believe, is at the heart of it. The Church is the perfect setting for a crime novel precisely because human nature at its ugliest is most evident set against the ideal which the Church represents. And because church people are usually aware that a higher standard of behaviour is expected of them, when they are unable to live up to the ideal they have a better reason for concealment. Concealment leads to secrets, and secrets provide the perfect scenario for the crime novelist.

So when I embarked upon the series 25 years ago, I was but following in the steps of a long line of writers such as G. K. Chesterton, C. A. Alington, Victor L. Whitechurch, Ellis Peters and P. D. James, and writing in a tradition which would grow to include D. M. Greenwood, Phil Rickman, Andrew Taylor and James Runcie, among so many others.*

Why, though, the 'Book of Psalms'?

As a member of a parish choir for many years, I have had the weekly privilege of singing the psalms, and have found them a source of incomparable richness. Especially when sung to Anglican chant, in the BCP Coverdale translation, they are replete with every human emotion, from sublime joy to utmost despair. In spite of – or perhaps even because of – their archaic language, they have a timeless resonance which speaks to me on so many levels. I have come to love them more than practically anything else in the liturgy; this series aside, there are only two of my subsequent novels which don't also bear titles from the psalms.

---

* For further information on the history and tradition of clerical crime fiction, see my feature article/cover story 'The Chief Suspect? Chesterton' in the *Church Times*, Issue 7588, 22 August 2008.

When I began the first book, the title was a part of it from the beginning (Psalm 60.3), inextricably bound up with what I wanted to say about the characters, and about their relationships to each other and to the Church. I'm not sure why I set myself the task of finding an appropriate psalm verse as an epigraph for each chapter, but that became a challenge I enjoyed as the series progressed, and I now think it is one of the things about the series which has caused it to endure.

Another factor contributing to the longevity of these books is the fact that they are not in any way typical crime novels: yes, there are crimes in each of them, but the books are not *about* the crimes. The books are at heart about *people*, with the crimes providing a particularly potent way to set events in motion and put the characters under pressure, allowing me to explore their motivations and their actions. For this reason I find the American term 'mystery', with its additional theological overtones, to be more appropriate than the preferred British usage of 'crime novel'.

In my novels I have attempted to create and depict a consistent world, with characters who move in and out of story lines and sometimes reappear in unexpected places – much in the tradition of my favourite novelist, Barbara Pym. This presents a challenge for a writer who must also be concerned with plot: one of the unspoken rules for writing a series of crime novels is that they should be able to be read in any order, so that something in one novel does not give away the solution to a crime in another. This can be tricky with a cast of ongoing characters, but I do believe that people come to know and care about those characters.

For whatever reason, these books continue to be popular with readers. Scarcely a week passes when I don't receive at least one email from someone who has just discovered them, or loved them for a very long time and is desperate for another. I'm hoping that these new editions will bring 'the Book of Psalms mysteries' to a whole new, untapped, group of readers who will find something about them to enjoy.

A Dead Man Out of Mind, revisited

I can vividly recall the exact moment that I decided to write this book: it was a November day in 1992, and I had been watching the live television coverage of the historic General Synod vote on the ordination of women as priests. When they announced that the measure had passed in all three houses, I burst into tears of joy, and Rachel Nightingale came into being as I suddenly grasped the ramifications of this momentous and somewhat unexpected decision. The Church of England, I realized in that moment, would never be the same again. And I wanted to write about that.

The writing took place over subsequent months, while the shock waves were still reverberating, and the book was actually published just a few weeks after the first ordinations, in the spring of 1994, addressing the consequences of women's ordination both for the Church and for individuals. Because of this historical context, *A Dead Man Out of Mind* is in some ways the most dated of my books. It is tied to a specific point in time, when women could be deacons but not yet priests (let alone bishops!), and the IRA still disrupted London transport. Yet in spite of that it remains one of my own firm favourites among my books.

I've been trying to analyse why that is the case. It's partially, I suspect, because women's ordination is one of the issues which has passionately interested me over the years, and was by no means settled by the vote on that November afternoon. Also, I think that the book is inhabited by a number of strong and interesting characters, including two of my very favourites: Rachel Nightingale and Ruth Kingsley.

On rereading, *A Dead Man Out of Mind* stands up very well as an exemplar of the traditional detective story. It has a dead body at the very beginning with more to follow, a pair of amateur sleuths reluctantly investigating a crime that the police aren't interested in, a bunch of suspects with varying motives, a colourful setting, a great number of plausible red herrings and an equal number of clues displayed in plain sight yet invisible to all but the cleverest reader.

The primary theme of the novel is the potential cost of love, weighed against its rewards. Is it possible to love too much? Is it worth the risk? These are questions which ultimately confront David and Lucy: questions without easy answers, and ones with which they must grapple as their relationship enters its next phase.

Kate Charles

Acknowledgements

I would like to thank everyone at Marylebone House, especially editor Alison Barr, for giving this book a new lease of life. Retrospectively, I offer my deep gratitude to my incomparable editor, the late Sara Ann Freed of Mysterious Press/Warner Books. I would also like to thank MJO; my debt to him is beyond words.

Author's note

As in the past, I have taken certain liberties in creating churches: St Margaret's and St Jude's, as well as St Dunstan's, are as much a product of my imagination as the people inhabiting them. I have also created the post of Archdeacon of Kensington, to avoid any possible confusion with actual clerics.

Dramatis personae

At St Margaret's Church, Pimlico

Fr Julian Piper	The late curate
Fr William Keble Smythe	Vicar of St Margaret's and St Jude's
Martin Bairstow	Churchwarden
Vanessa Bairstow	His wife
Norman Topping	Churchwarden
Dolly Topping	His wife
Stanley Everitt	Parish Administrator, St Margaret's and St Jude's
Joan Everitt	His wife
Mrs Goode	Housekeeper for Fr Keble Smythe
Robin West	Sacristan
Rachel Nightingale	New curate, St Margaret's and St Jude's
Dr Walter Bright	Parishioner
Vera Bright	His daughter
Nicola Topping	Daughter of Norman and Dolly Topping

In London

David Middleton-Brown	A solicitor at Fosdyke, Fosdyke and Galloway, Lincoln's Inn
Lucy Kingsley	An artist
Ruth Kingsley	Her niece
Mrs Simmons	Secretary to David Middleton-Brown
Sir Crispin Fosdyke	Senior Partner, Fosdyke, Fosdyke and Galloway
Henry Thymme	A solicitor
Justin Thymme	His son
Colin Nightingale	Husband of Rachel Nightingale
Francis Nightingale	Brother of Colin Nightingale
Cindy Lou Nightingale	His wife
Gabriel Neville	Archdeacon of Kensington
Emily Neville	His wife

Pamela Hartman	An immigration officer
PC Huw Meredith	A policeman
Russell Galloway	Senior Partner, Fosdyke, Fosdyke and Galloway
May Thymme	Wife of Justin Thymme
Mr Atkins	Dealer in antiques

Elsewhere

Miss Morag McKenzie	Fiancée of Fr Keble Smythe
Fr Desmond	Spiritual director of Rachel Nightingale
Hamish Douglas	Friend of Fr Keble Smythe
Alistair Duncan	Housekeeper, St Dunstan's, Brighton

PROLOGUE

What profit is there in my blood: when I go down to the pit?

Psalm 30.9

It was a clear case of a burglary gone wrong; the police at the scene were in no doubt about that. They'd seen plenty of these church burglaries – an increasing number in recent years, and not just in rich London parishes like this one. Invariably they fell into two categories of crime. The professional burglar knew what he was looking for, often stealing to order; he would be in and out of the church quickly, leaving a minimum of mess behind. In these cases, the stolen items – silver mostly, and antique ecclesiastical furniture – would be on a boat to the Continent before they were even missed. The other sort of church burglary was of the opportunistic kind, and usually left chaos in its wake.

From the shambles in the sacristy, it was apparent that the burglary at St Margaret's Church, Pimlico, was in the second category. Papers and documents, evidently from the open safe, were scattered around the floor, a table had been overturned, an empty communion wine bottle smashed, and in an act of wilful and mindless vandalism, the purple chasuble which had been laid out for the next celebration of the Mass had been slashed to ribbons. But there was one significant difference from the usual pattern: by the safe lay the body of a clergyman, the back of his head caved in.

'He must have caught them in the act, poor devil.' Detective Inspector Pierce touched the arm of the young uniformed constable who had been the first officer on the scene; the man looked distinctly green round the gills, thought Pierce with compassion. They couldn't do any more until the police pathologist arrived to certify death – not that there was any doubt about it, but procedures must be adhered to – so Pierce began talking to take both their minds off the gruesome sight before them.

'I suppose it was kids,' he said with a detachment he didn't feel. 'These sorts of crimes usually are. Unpremeditated. They break into a church looking for something they can turn into a bit of ready cash. For drugs, you know – that kind of thing.'

The PC's Adam's apple bobbed up and down as he gulped convulsively, grateful for the distraction. 'And what do they do with… with the stuff they take, sir?'

'Oh, they flog it for a few bob. It usually turns up down the Portobello Road in a day or two.'

'And do you usually catch them?'

Pierce smiled grimly. 'Sometimes we do, and sometimes we don't. Most of them are pretty stupid, you know. At least in this sort of crime. With the pros we don't have much chance of catching them, but the kids are a different story. The pros never leave prints, of course, but often the kids do. They wipe the obvious things and then leave a clear set of prints on a door handle. Or they wear surgical gloves and then peel the gloves off and leave them at the scene – with their prints inside.'

'So you think you'll catch whoever did… this?' The PC's eyes returned without volition to the bloody mess that was the priest's head, and he gulped again.

'I'd say we've got a damn good chance,' Pierce reassured him. 'They're sure to have slipped up somewhere. They probably panicked after the priest surprised them, and when he ended up dead I imagine they got out in a hell of a hurry.' He fell silent for a moment, contemplating the body on the floor.

Pierce was undecided about the dead man's age; his black cassock gave no clues, and while his face was young and almost boyish, his dark hair was peppered with grey in virtually equal measure. That youthful, unlined face was turned towards Pierce, its blue eyes staring at him in a final look of sightless surprise. 'God, I wish that doctor would get here,' the inspector muttered, jamming his hands in his coat pockets.

A moment later his wish was granted. The police pathologist shoved his way into the room, made a quick examination, and nodded curtly. That was the signal for the scene-of-crime officers to begin their detailed work; as the specialists moved in to bag the hands of the corpse and gather evidence, Pierce led the PC out of the cramped and overcrowded sacristy and into the church.

'Can't you tell me what's going on in there?' The man who hovered outside the door looked terrible, his face as bloodlessly white as that of the dead man in the sacristy. In fact, thought Pierce, he had something of the look of a death's head about him, with a cadaverously gaunt face, sunken eyes in deep sockets, a high bony forehead, and a balding crown with a few lank and lifeless strands of hair brushed across the top. 'I'm the one who found him,' he added, wringing his hands. 'When I came in this morning. He must have surprised some intruders. Thieves, robbers. Oh, it's just too terrible! That's what happened, isn't it?'

'You know just about as much as we do at this point, but it seems likely.' Pierce looked the man up and down. 'And who are you, sir, if you don't mind my asking?'

'Oh, sorry. Sorry.' The hand-wringing ceased as the man raised a hand to smooth the strands on the top of his head. 'Stanley Everitt. I'm the Parish Administrator.'

'So you work here?' It had never occurred to Pierce that people other than clergymen worked in churches.

'Some of the time.' The man's voice, with its unpleasant sibilance, took on a pedantic tone and he almost seemed to forget why the policemen were there as he explained. 'I'm actually the Administrator of St Jude's. You know, the big church up the road. St Margaret's is a satellite of St Jude's, so it comes under my jurisdiction as well. Most of the time I'm based at St Jude's, but I spend one day a week here. Fridays. I always come here on a Friday.'

'But this is Saturday,' interposed the constable, a stickler for details.

'Yes, of course, but there's a wedding today, and the Vicar asked me to—' Everitt broke off, suddenly recollecting what had happened. 'The Vicar! Oh, how am I going to tell the Vicar?' The hand-wringing resumed with increased agitation. 'He'll be shattered. He's so over-worked already – however will he manage now?'

Pierce frowned in puzzlement. 'You mean that bloke in there isn't the Vicar?'

'Oh, good heavens no. He is . . . was . . . the curate. Father Julian Piper.'

'The curate?'

'Technically the curate of St Jude's *and* St Margaret's, of course,' Everitt explained. 'It's a combined benefice. Father Keble Smythe, the Vicar of St Jude's, is Priest-in-Charge at St Margaret's. But he's far too busy at St Jude's to have much time for St Margaret's, so Father Julian usually takes – or rather took – the services here. Oh, dear. I just don't know what's going to happen . . .'

Pierce, tiring of the man's rather prolix officiousness, interrupted the flow. 'Mr . . . um . . . Everitt, as soon as they're finished in there, I'd appreciate it if you'd take a look and let me know what, if anything, is missing. It will help us in our enquiries. Unless you'd rather that I asked the Vicar—'

'Oh, no, you mustn't disturb Father Keble Smythe!' Everitt pursed his lips and squared his shoulders self-importantly. 'I'll do all I can to help, of course. That's what a Parish Administrator is for.'

'Thank you.' Pierce's eyebrows lifted in unconscious irony but his voice was without inflexion.

'And I'll break the news about Father Julian's . . . death to Father Keble Smythe,' Everitt added. 'He'll be so upset. It wouldn't do for him to hear it from a stranger.'

An hour later, the scene-of-crime officers had collected their evidence with meticulous precision, and the body had been removed to the mortuary. But the chaos remained, and Stanley Everitt flinched as he surveyed the wreckage of the normally tidy sacristy. 'Why did they have to make so much mess?' he moaned.

'Pure maliciousness, most likely,' the policeman at his side explained dispassionately. 'But this isn't bad, Mr Everitt. You should see some of the scenes of crime that we get called to. You wouldn't believe the unpleasant things some burglars do to . . . leave their mark, let's say. I won't go into details.'

Everitt turned a startled gaze on him, then opened and shut his mouth soundlessly. 'Really?' he said at last.

Pierce nodded. 'So if you wouldn't mind having a look round . . .'

The inspection didn't take long; Everitt was evidently familiar with the contents of the sacristy. 'The chalice is missing,' he proclaimed at once. 'It would have been set out ready for early Mass, so they would have seen it straightaway.'

Catching the eye of the constable, Pierce nodded meaningfully. 'Anything else?'

'I don't think so.' He stuck his head in the safe. 'The other silver is still here, all wrapped up – the alms dish, the ciborium, the candlesticks, the altar cross, the thurible, the monstrance, the ewer. I suppose they were in too much of a hurry to look any further after . . . well, you know.'

With his toe, Pierce indicated the papers which were scattered about the floor. 'What about this lot? Anything important missing?'

Everitt frowned. 'I can't imagine why there would be. These are just things like insurance forms and faculty documents – no reason to steal them. And the registers haven't been damaged – they're still in the safe.' He patted the leather-bound volumes reassuringly. 'Of course I'll have to sort through everything and get it back in order. What a lot of work!'

Patiently, Pierce tried to return his attention to the matter at hand. 'So as far as you can tell, only the chalice has been taken.'

Stanley Everitt straightened up and looked slowly around the sacristy. 'There's just one other thing . . .'

'What is that, Mr Everitt?'

'One of the brass candlesticks seems to be gone. See, there's just the one, there on the vestment chest. Its mate is missing. Why would someone steal one brass candlestick?'

Pierce smiled grimly. 'Oh, you don't have to worry about that, sir. We know exactly where that is. It's on its way to the lab, sealed in a polythene bag.'

'But . . .'

'Evidence.' He took perverse pleasure in spelling it out. 'You see, Mr Everitt, that candlestick was used recently for something other than throwing light. That candlestick was used to smash in the back of your Father Julian's head.'

Everitt closed his eyes. 'Excuse me a moment, Inspector,' he said faintly, heading for the door.

Part 1

CHAPTER 1

He shall call upon me, and I will hear him: yea, I am with him in trouble; I will deliver him, and bring him to honour.

Psalm 91.15

Liucy Kingsley frowned thoughtfully at the letter. It seemed a somewhat odd request for her brother to make. Odd, too, that the letter had come from her brother, rather than from his wife. She and her sister-in-law corresponded intermittently, but Lucy couldn't remember ever having received a letter from Andrew.

The letter had come in the post, interrupting her painting. Now she returned to her studio, re-reading as she climbed the stairs the lines written in Andrew's upright, unfamiliar hand.

'I realise that this is rather short notice, but I hope that it will present no problems. Ruth's year at school has to participate in a work experience project this term, and as it is Ruth's ambition to be a solicitor, it seems sensible that she should spend her three weeks in a solicitor's office. Father tells me that your friend David is a solicitor in London, and I should be very grateful if you could arrange with him for Ruth to "shadow" him for her work experience. It seems an ideal arrangement, as she could stay with you for the three weeks (beginning the first week of March). Although Ruth is very bright, she is in many ways a young fourteen, and I would rest more easily knowing that you were looking after her. And you know how Ruth has always adored her beautiful Aunt Lucy!'

Lucy frowned again, absently twisting a curl of strawberry blonde hair around her finger. Flattery will get you nowhere, my dear brother, she said to herself, knowing in spite of everything that she would have to say yes. But David wasn't going to like it. He wasn't going to like it at all.

David Middleton-Brown, a pleasant-looking man in his early forties, was not having a tranquil morning. A letter had been waiting on his desk from the solicitor who was dealing with an estate in which David had a personal interest: when the estate was settled, he would inherit a very valuable house near Kensington Gardens. The letter was of a routine nature, asking a few questions which needed to be cleared up before matters could proceed.

The trouble was, David didn't want matters to proceed. It wasn't that he didn't want the house, or wasn't grateful for the generous bequest. But when probate was granted, and the house was his, there were issues that would have to be faced which David was not yet ready to confront.

Would he move into the house? And if he did, would Lucy come with him? He couldn't even bring himself to discuss it with her, for fear of what she would say. The last few months, since he'd moved to London, had been the happiest time of his life. Living in Lucy's house, coming home to her every night, was almost as good as being married to her. He longed to marry Lucy, longed for the security that marriage would bring. If they were married, he told himself, the house wouldn't be important. They would be together, whether in Lucy's little mews house in South Kensington or in the grand Georgian mansion that would be his. But Lucy stubbornly refused to marry him.

He still couldn't really understand it, much as he tried. She said that she loved him, and she could be in no doubt by now that he loved her. But Lucy had been married before, years ago, and it had been a brief but painful disaster. According to her, she'd been scarred so deeply by that early failure that she was unwilling to try again; she seemed incapable of realising how different it could be this time. David had by no means given up hope, but his proposals had been offered with decreasing frequency over the past months, as he tried to avoid the hurt that inevitably came with her gentle but firm refusals.

His living at her house was meant to be a temporary measure, just until the estate was sorted out. That had been the understanding when she'd invited him to move in, and they hadn't discussed it since then. One of these days Lucy was bound to ask him, he realised, but until then . . .

With a grimace, David slid the letter under his 'In' tray. He wouldn't reply to it right away; perhaps that would postpone the evil day for a bit longer. He could always pretend that he hadn't received the letter, or that it had been misplaced by his secretary.

Before he'd had a chance to sort through the rest of his post, his secretary, Mrs Simmons, popped her head around the door to report, with a suitably solemn face, that he was wanted by no less a personage than Sir Crispin Fosdyke himself, senior partner of Fosdyke, Fosdyke & Galloway. 'Immediately,' she added unnecessarily.

The summons from on high did not come very often, especially to one with as little seniority as David had at the firm, so he approached the heavy oak door of the inner sanctum with more trepidation than anticipation. 'Come in!' was the response to his diffident knock.

Sir Crispin's office occupied the corner of the firm's suite of offices in Lincoln's Inn, so it was well lit by windows on two sides. Its furnishings were discreet but obviously expensive; the chairs were leather, the chandelier was Georgian, and unless David was very much mistaken, the Monet on the wall was no reproduction. The great man himself, seated behind his massive desk, was every bit as impressive as the room, silver-haired and with his self-assured ruddy face dominated by a pair of truly awesome silver eyebrows.

'Oh, there you are, Middleton-Brown. Come in, come in.' David edged into the room and perched on the leather chair towards which he was waved. Sir Crispin wasted no time with preliminaries. 'I have a little matter for you to see to. Do you know Henry Thymme?'

'Henry Time?' David echoed, puzzled. 'I don't think so.'

'Thymme, pronounced Time, spelled T-h-y-double m-e,' explained Sir Crispin. 'Senior partner at Barrett, Peters and Co in the City. A member of my club. Known him for years.'

'Oh, yes. I *have* heard of him, but I don't believe we've met.'

Sir Crispin appraised David with ice-cold blue eyes, 'His son is in a bit of a scrape, and I'd like you to sort it out for him.' Concisely, he outlined the problem. 'And so you see, Middleton-Brown,' he concluded, 'there's no time to be lost. I'll be most grateful if you can take care of this with a minimum of fuss. I'm sure you understand me.'

Dismissed, David returned to his office, shaking his head. Young Mr Thymme had been picked up in the early hours of the morning on Hampstead Heath; he was, as official parlance would have it, engaged in an act of public indecency with another man. 'Caught with his trousers down,' David muttered to himself, bemused. 'And in the middle of winter!' The young man was now cooling his heels in the local police station, awaiting the arrival of a solicitor: David. Out of consideration for his father – or possibly in fear of his wrath – he had waited until morning to ring him, and Henry Thymme was obviously calling in a favour from his colleague Sir Crispin, thus keeping his own firm well out of it. It was clear to David why Sir Crispin had put him on to it: a case like this was distasteful in the extreme, especially for a respectable firm like Fosdyke, Fosdyke & Galloway. Under ordinary circumstances they wouldn't have touched it with a bargepole, he realised, but as a professional courtesy to a fellow senior partner, and a member of his club to boot, Sir Crispin could not very well have refused. David was the newest member of the firm, so it was only natural that the case should be shunted on to him. And perhaps, he said to himself, it was a sort of test, to see how well he acquitted himself. 'I'm afraid I've got to go out,' he said to his secretary, fetching his overcoat. 'I'll be back as soon as I can.'

David found Henry Thymme waiting for him at the police station. A large, bluff man, his thinning fair hair worn long enough to make him look younger than he probably was, he wrung David's hand gratefully. 'Awfully decent of you to come, dear chap,' he declared with feeling. 'I'm afraid the lad's got himself into a spot of trouble.'

David's manner was consciously professional. 'So Sir Crispin tells me.'

'Ah, well.' Thymme chuckled fondly. 'Boys will be boys, you know. And Justin's a good lad, really. The apple of his mother's eye.'

For a moment the professional coolness slipped. 'Justin Thymme?'

The older man laughed. 'You got it, then. Good, that, isn't it? A bit of fancy on his mother's part, and the lad has to live with it for the rest of his life! He was the last child, you see – after four girls. No more kiddies, she said. This is the end of the line. So the boy came just in time.' He laughed again with immoderate amusement, considering how many times he must have told the story.

David allowed himself a small smile. The scenario was all too clear: the spoiled young tearaway, indulged by his father and petted by his mother, and no doubt by all of those sisters as well. He was not likely to be an ideal client, and David longed to get it over with. 'I think I'd better see him now.'

'By all means, my boy, and the sooner the better. We'll have a word with the duty sergeant straightaway.' Thymme gave a wink. 'Not that it's done the lad any harm to wait – quite the contrary, I should think.'

When at last David was ushered into the interview room, into the presence of the young Mr Thymme, he found him not at all what he'd expected. Far from cutting a dashing figure, his client was small and pale and prim, and not so very young either, come to that: David judged him to be about thirty, with fine fair hair receding from his high forehead. He wore oval steel-rimmed spectacles, one of the lenses of which was cracked, and above which he sported a nasty purple bruise. 'How soon can I get out of here?' he demanded; his voice was deeper than his size might have indicated, and his accent was true to his public school education.

'Good morning, Mr Thymme,' said David pleasantly, as if the other man hadn't spoken. He introduced himself, then went on, 'How did you get the black eye, if you don't mind me asking?'

Justin's hand went to the bruise. 'The chap who arrested me. He gave me a thump with his truncheon – said I was resisting arrest.'

This seemed highly unlikely to David, but he decided to let it pass. 'And were you?'

He pursed his thin mouth prissily. 'No, of course not. I'm not that stupid.'

With a thoughtful nod, David sat down, folding his hands on the table that separated them. 'You've been in here for quite a few hours now. Have you made a statement, or allowed yourself to be interviewed?'

Justin looked at him with scorn. 'I told you, I'm not stupid. And my father's a solicitor – I know how these things work. I'm not likely to have said anything to incriminate myself, am I?' He drummed his fingers on the table. 'So when are you going to get me out of here? I'm hours late for work already!'

David told Lucy about the case over supper that night, deliberately making the story as amusing as possible. 'I was expecting an eighteen-year-old in skintight jeans, an earring, and a black leather jacket, and I walk into the interview room to find someone who looks like an accountant! And do you want to know the funniest thing about it – apart from his ridiculous name, that is? That's exactly what he is – an accountant!' He shook his head with a self-deprecating grin. 'That's what I get for making assumptions.'

'An accountant?' Lucy was making a great effort to concentrate on his story, dreading what she was going to have to ask him.

'A blooming accountant. With an upper-class twit of a solicitor for a father.'

She pushed a bit of salad around on her plate. 'Did you get him out?'

David nodded. 'He's out on police bail – that's the usual thing in these cases.'

'What will happen to him now?'

'Oh, I'll be able to get him off, I think. At least if I value my job, I will,' he added wryly. 'I wouldn't want to face Sir Crispin if his friend's darling son got a fine, and his name in the papers.'

Lucy looked puzzled. 'But isn't he guilty?'

'Well, of course he is! They caught him in the act, remember.'

'I don't understand. How will you get him off, if you know he's guilty, and the police know he's guilty?'

Choosing his words carefully, David tried to explain. 'It's all in knowing how to play the game. Now in this case, the young man tells me that the police gave him a gratuitous thump with a truncheon. I don't really believe him – these days the police are more careful than that – but that's beside the point. If I let it be known that my client is prepared to take the matter to the Police Complaints Authority . . . well, let's just say that the police don't need that kind of hassle, not to mention the adverse publicity if it were leaked to the press. I think they'll be prepared to drop the charges against him, in return for keeping quiet about what he claims the police did to him. After all, he's a respectable member of society – his word would carry some weight. And don't forget his father's clout.'

Lucy's full attention had been captured at last. 'But that's dishonest!'

'Oh, no, Lucy love. It's just using the system.'

'But you're saying that because he has the right connections, and a good solicitor, he'll get off scot free, whereas if he were some poor bloke who happened to get caught . . .'

David laughed without amusement. 'You've got it in one, love. It may not be fair, but that's the way it works.' She looked so distressed that he reached across the table and took her hand. 'I can't pretend to have much stomach for it, myself, but it's my job, and I've got to do what's best for my client, objectionable though he may be. Not to mention that Fosdyke expects me to get the miserable little toerag off.'

'Would you say,' Lucy asked slowly, 'that Sir Crispin will owe you one after this?'

'I don't imagine that he'd put it in quite those terms, but that's the gist of it, certainly.' David's generous mouth curved in a self-deprecating smile. 'I took an unsavoury case off his hands, and if I manage it well, and get my client off without attracting any unwelcome attention to him or to Fosdyke, Fosdyke and Galloway, I should think that Sir Crispin would be suitably grateful. It won't do me any harm, anyway. But if I don't produce the goods—'

'But you will,' Lucy interrupted him urgently. 'You said that you would be able to. And then Sir Crispin will be in your debt.'

David gave her a questioning look. 'What are you getting at?'

Unable to meet his eyes, she looked first up at the ceiling and then down at their clasped hands; with her free hand she pushed back her hair. 'Well, it's just that …' She took a deep breath and plunged into the story of her brother's letter and her niece's proposed visit.

For a moment David just stared at her. 'You want me to ask Fosdyke if a fourteen-year-old girl can follow me around for three weeks?' he exploded at last. 'Do you have any idea what you're asking?'

'Yes, I know it's asking a lot, but you just said that he'd owe you a favour …'

'A favour, perhaps, but this …!'

Lucy's head drooped despondently, her long curly red-gold hair falling forward to shadow her face, and David's heart melted. 'Oh, all right. I'll ask him,' he relented, with much misgiving. 'I can't promise that he'll say yes, though.'

'Oh, David darling, thank you.' Her smile was radiant. 'I know that you'll do your best to convince him. And why should he object, after all? She might even be able to help you.'

'You don't know Sir Crispin Fosdyke,' he retorted darkly. 'And I very much doubt that she'd do anything but get in the way. There are issues of client confidentiality to consider – I'd have to spend all my time finding fiddly little things to keep her busy.' After a moment he had another thought. 'And she's supposed to stay here with us? In this house? Where would we put her?'

'On the sofa bed, of course.'

David frowned. 'For three weeks? It would be all right for a night or two, I'm sure, but for three weeks? Rather in the way, I'd think. And she's bound to have great quantities of clothes, and other bits and pieces – teenage girls do, don't they? She'd probably leave her things all over the place. This house just isn't big enough for three people.' Lucy looked at him quizzically, and in an instant he saw the danger in that line of reasoning: it was after all *her* house, not his, and if he wasn't careful, he'd find himself the one without a place to stay for three weeks. 'Oh, never mind,' he muttered, then effected a rapid change of subject. 'More wine, Lucy love? The bottle's almost empty.'

CHAPTER 2

Nevertheless, when he saw their adversity: he heard their complaint.

Psalm 106.43

For the past several minutes, the only sound in the parlour of the clergy house had been the loud ticking of the longcase clock in the corner. Seated opposite each other on expensively upholstered chairs, the two churchwardens remained silent, regarding each other uneasily.

The two men had little in common, save their office – and their high churchmanship. Martin Bairstow, the younger of the two, was a wealthy man, having made his fortune in the City. Single-minded, he had early in life directed his energies to the amassing of wealth, and that accomplished most satisfactorily, he now devoted his time outside work to being the most conscientious and hard-working churchwarden that St Margaret's Church had ever known. He was still only in his mid-forties, and was possessed of looks that most women found handsome, if somewhat stolid: he was large and well-built, his thick dark hair was only slightly threaded with grey, and his features were pleasingly even, though dominated by a heavy jaw.

Norman Topping, on the other hand, looked the part of the amiable buffoon, with his peculiar bullet-shaped head and his comical jug ears; what little hair he had was in the form of colourless stubble. He was short and slightly flabby, and his deep, somewhat nasal voice betrayed his northern origins. Topping was good-natured and amiable, but completely without imagination. Nearly sixty, and approaching retirement from his career as a mid-level civil servant, he had been churchwarden of St Margaret's for a number of years.

The clock chimed four o'clock; Norman Topping jumped slightly, drawing a bemused and somewhat contemptuous look from his fellow warden. 'Sorry,' he mumbled. 'I thought he would have been here by now.'

Unnecessarily, Bairstow looked at his handsome gold watch. 'He's thirty minutes late,' he confirmed. 'It's not like the Vicar to be late.'

They turned expectantly as the door of the sitting room opened, but if they thought to see a contrite Father Keble Smythe, they were disappointed. Instead the housekeeper made a diffident entrance. 'It's gone four,' she said. 'I can't think what's keeping Father, but I thought that perhaps you might like some tea.'

Used to making decisions, Bairstow agreed instantly. 'Yes, thank you, Mrs Goode. That would be very nice.'

'Yes, a cup of tea would go down a treat,' Topping seconded.

'If it's not too much trouble, Mrs Goode,' added Bairstow with his most winning smile. 'It's most kind of you to offer.'

Martin Bairstow was a particular favourite with Mrs Goode, as he was with a great many middle-aged and older ladies in the parishes of St Margaret and St Jude: excellent and devout Anglican women every one, who appreciated his consideration and his various little kindnesses towards them, and who regularly confessed to Father Keble Smythe the unseemly – perhaps even sinful – envy they felt towards the fortunate Mrs Bairstow. Flustered now by his attention, Mrs Goode tried to cover it up with a show of efficiency. 'No trouble at all, I'm sure. China or India?' she asked, backing out of the room.

'China,' said Martin Bairstow.

'India,' said Norman Topping simultaneously.

'I shall make both,' Mrs Goode declared. 'And I'm sure that Father will be here any minute.'

The tea, served in thin china cups, was delicious, and accompanied by buttery fingers of Mrs Goode's homemade shortbread. The Vicar had as yet failed to appear; over their tea the men made some effort at conversation.

'Your family is well?' Bairstow enquired courteously. 'Avoiding the bugs that have been going round?'

'Oh, yes. Dolly is never ill – it's a point of pride with her. She says that she's never been ill a day in her life.'

Bairstow nodded. 'What is Dolly doing with herself these days, now that Ladies Opposed to Women Priests have lost their *raison d'être*? Has she found another cause?'

Chuckling, Norman Topping helped himself to another shortbread finger. 'They may have lost the vote, but they've by no means disbanded. Dolly will never give up hoping that some miracle will occur – that God will instantly strike dead all women who want to be priests, and any heretical bishop who's prepared to ordain them. But yes, she's looking to fresher pastures these days – she's getting involved with an anti-abortion campaign. And if I know Dolly, she'll be running the show within a few weeks.'

Martin Bairstow stroked his chin thoughtfully. 'The Church needs people like Dolly, who are prepared to stand up for what they believe. And she's absolutely right about women priests, of course. As we've often discussed before. Disaster for the Church of England, complete and utter disaster.'

'But as long as we don't get any of them here . . .'

Bairstow got up and went to the window. Already the days were lengthening, and it was not yet dark; he could see the austere Victorian edifice of St Jude's across the street in the deepening gloom. 'It would be out of the question – untenable,' he declared forcefully. 'I can't see it happening, quite frankly. But if it did . . . well, I'd have to re-think my position about staying in the Church of England. All of us at St Margaret's would. Dolly would be the first to—' He broke off at the sight of the Vicar's car turning into the street. 'Ah, here is Father Keble Smythe. At last. Now we can get on with this meeting.'

Father Keble Smythe, sweeping into the parlour in his great clerical cloak, was of course fulsome in his apologies for keeping his churchwardens waiting on a Saturday afternoon when they were sure to have other commitments. 'It was unavoidable,' he assured them. 'Even though I'm a bachelor myself, I am most conscious that you both have wives waiting for you at home, and I wouldn't have delayed you if it hadn't been of the utmost importance. But I'm so pleased to see that Mrs Goode has supplied you with tea. An excellent woman, Mrs Goode. The next best thing to a wife.' His voice was beautifully modulated, and his accent plummy in the extreme.

Accepting his apologies, they followed him into his study. Like the parlour, it was a well-appointed room, nicely proportioned and expensively furnished. Waving the churchwardens into chairs, the Vicar seated himself behind his desk and allowed himself a moment to glance at the silver-framed photo which had pride of place in front of him, then picked it up and handed it across the desk to Martin Bairstow. 'Have you seen this? A new portrait of Miss McKenzie, my fiancée. She had it done for me, for Christmas. Uncommonly good, don't you think?'

Bairstow studied the representation of the rather horse-faced young woman with a noncommittal expression. 'Very nice, Father.' An old-fashioned Anglo-Catholic, he disapproved of married clergy, and regretted the fact that St Margaret's affiliation with St Jude's in a united benefice had given it a vicar with rather different standards.

St Margaret's had certainly never had a married vicar before, and although Miss Morag McKenzie – so often spoken of – had yet to be seen in the parish, that looked set to change at some time in the future. It was the thin end of the wedge, as far as Martin Bairstow was concerned.

Father William Keble Smythe smiled at his wardens across the desk. Dressed in his black cassock with its thirty-nine buttons, he was everything that a young, upwardly-mobile priest should be: good-looking, personable, well-educated and evidently well-connected. He had been Vicar of St Jude's for something over five years, and in that time he had slightly, yet perceptibly, raised the churchmanship of that staid parish without alienating any of his wealthy parishioners: no mean feat. Three years ago when the benefices had been combined he had also been named Priest-in-Charge of neighbouring St Margaret's, where the churchmanship was traditionally far higher than at St Jude's; there he was admired for his avowed adherence to Catholic practices, though in actuality he rarely took a service at St Margaret's. Within the diocese of London it was acknowledged that Father William Keble Smythe had never put a foot wrong, had never rocked the boat, and was undoubtedly destined for bigger things.

'Do you know why we've asked for this meeting?' Martin Bairstow began.

The Vicar's cordial smile betrayed nothing. 'Why don't you tell me?' he invited.

Ignoring his fellow warden, Bairstow addressed the Vicar. 'You must know that the staffing situation at St Margaret's has become intolerable. To put not too fine a point on it, Father, we're absolutely desperate for a new curate.'

'You promised us a month ago that you'd do something as soon as possible,' Norman Topping put in.

'And things have got worse since then,' Bairstow continued. 'We've just about managed on Sunday mornings, with the goodwill of curates from neighbouring parishes. But the weekday Masses have been a real problem – I don't know if you realise.'

'I thought that Father Travis—'

'Father Travis means well,' said Bairstow, frowning. 'But he always was absent-minded, even when he was active. Now that he's retired – well, he just can't be relied upon. Last week he failed to turn up on three consecutive days. Three days without a Mass! You must agree, Father – that just isn't on!'

Father Keble Smythe put his fingertips together. 'No, that's not acceptable. But you must realise that I'm just as inconvenienced as you are – this is a very large parish – two parishes! – to run without the help of a curate. I've—'

'In January it's bad enough,' interrupted Norman Topping. 'But with Lent coming up soon, and then Holy Week and Easter, we just can't go on like this. Something has to be done. We've got to have a new curate, as soon as possible.'

Inclining his head, the Vicar went on in a somewhat pained voice. 'As I was about to say, gentlemen, I've made this my top priority. That is the reason I was late for this meeting – I've spent the afternoon seeing the Director of Ordinands, the Archdeacon, and then the Bishop.'

The two churchwardens' expressions changed in an instant to ones of hopeful expectation. 'And?' prompted Martin Bairstow.

Father Keble Smythe shook his head. 'I'm afraid it's all very difficult. As you would expect, curates are not that easy to come by at the moment. The next ordinations won't take place till Petertide, and we certainly can't wait until the middle of the year for a new curate.'

'But we don't want a deacon in any case,' Bairstow protested. 'We want a curate who's already been priested, one who can celebrate the Mass.'

'A second curacy,' contributed Topping.

Again the Vicar shook his head. 'Impossible, I'm afraid. There isn't anyone in the diocese who fits the bill. But as I said before, I just can't go on without a curate – I very badly need someone to help with the visiting, the sick communions, weddings, funerals, parish meetings . . .'

'Then what are you suggesting?' Bairstow demanded. 'You're not giving up so easily, are you?'

The Vicar waited a moment before replying, framing his words very carefully. 'I didn't say that I had been unsuccessful, only that it had been difficult.'

'You mean that you've found a curate?' The eagerness returned to Norman Topping's voice.

'Well, yes.' Now he picked his words even more carefully. 'The Director of Ordinands suggested a candidate – someone who has quite recently moved into the London diocese because of family circumstances, and who has been looking for a post.'

'Why, that's perfect!' Topping exulted. 'So he can start right away, then!'

'Within a few weeks, I hope.'

Martin Bairstow was more sensitive than his colleague to the nuances of the Vicar's announcement. 'There's a problem, though, isn't there? He's just a deacon, I suppose. That's fine for you, Father – he can help you with your parish duties with no problem. But it's not so good for us at St Margaret's, if he can't celebrate the Mass without using the Reserved Sacrament.'

Father Keble Smythe's expression was grave. 'Yes, I'm afraid that's so. Our new curate – for I've talked to the candidate, and offered the post – is a deacon, not a priest, though that will be remedied as soon as priesting is possible, with any luck in a few months' time. I've explained the circumstances – I'm sorry, but it's the best I can do at the moment.'

'Well, who is he?' Norman Topping demanded. 'I don't suppose we'll know him, but what is his name?'

For the first time that afternoon, the Vicar was not able to meet the eyes of his churchwardens; strong as were his personal reasons for the decision he'd made, he knew that they would never understand. Looking down at his hands, he spoke softly. 'Gentlemen, the name of our new curate is . . . Rachel Nightingale.'

A quarter of an hour later, after the explosion, the explanations, the threats, and the apologies, the two churchwardens stood outside on the pavement, looking at each other. At the end of the day, in spite of their protests and the Vicar's professed regrets about the matter, it was done, and it was too late to go back on it.

'A woman!' Martin Bairstow said in a dangerously quiet voice. 'I can't believe he's done this to us.'

'He said he didn't have any choice, but—'

Bairstow thought aloud. 'Someone put pressure on him, you can depend on it. Someone high up, who was trying to make a point, or do someone a favour.'

Norman Topping's concerns were closer to home. 'Whatever is Dolly going to say about this?'

'And not just Dolly, either. It might be all right at St Jude's, but St Margaret's will not stand for it!'

'But Martin! What are we going to do? What *can* we do?'

Bairstow's face was set. 'Oh, we'll do something, my friend,' he stated ominously. 'Believe me, we're not going to sit still and let him do this to us!'

CHAPTER 3

I stretch forth my hands unto thee: my soul gaspeth unto thee as a thirsty land.
Psalm 143.6

Late on a Friday morning at the end of January, Lucy returned home from her weekly trip around the shops, laden with bulging carrier bags of food. As she put her key in the lock, she heard the telephone ringing inside the house; she dropped her bags inside the door and made a frantic dive for the phone.

'Hello?' she gasped into the phone.

'Oh, hello,' said a tentative female voice. 'Is this Lucy Kingsley?'

'Yes, it is. I'm sorry – I've just come in from shopping, and I'm a bit breathless, getting to the phone.'

'I'm so sorry. If it's a bad time for you, I can ring back later.'

'No, not at all.' Lucy had by this time caught her breath, and she consciously warmed up her voice. 'What can I do for you?'

'My name is Vanessa Bairstow,' the other woman said. 'I'm interested in commissioning a painting, as an anniversary gift for my husband, and the Archdeacon's wife suggested that I ring you.'

For an instant, Lucy drew a blank, then remembered; even after over a year, she was unused to thinking of her friend Emily as the Archdeacon's wife. 'Oh, yes. Emily.'

'She said that you might be able to help me.'

'Of course.' Lucy never had a shortage of commissions, but she was willing to do whatever was necessary to squeeze in a friend of Emily's. 'Do you know my work at all?'

Mrs Bairstow was apologetic. 'No, I'm afraid not. But I'm sure . . .'

'Then perhaps the best thing would be for you to come by my studio and see the type of thing that I do. Before you commit yourself!' she added, laughing. 'We can talk about what you're looking for, and all the rest of it. When would you like to come?'

'Any time that's convenient for you, Miss Kingsley.' The other woman's voice had a curious yearning note. 'I don't work, so I could come any time. I wouldn't want to disturb your painting or anything.'

Lucy thought for a moment. 'Would this afternoon be too soon? I'm not actually doing any painting today, so it would be a good time for me.'

'Yes, that would be fine.'

They agreed on a time, and Lucy gave her directions. 'I'll look forward to seeing you this afternoon, Mrs Bairstow.'

'Oh, yes. Thank you so much.'

Lucy put the phone down thoughtfully and went to retrieve her abandoned shopping. She wasn't sure why, but she was looking forward to meeting Mrs Bairstow: there was something intriguing about her voice, some elusive quality that piqued Lucy's curiosity. Perhaps a bit later she'd ring Emily and ask her what she knew about Vanessa Bairstow.

Emily, in a rush to collect the children from school, didn't tell her much. Vanessa Bairstow was the wife of a churchwarden at St Margaret's Church, Pimlico, in her forties, well off, and had no children. She was a nice woman, Emily said – Lucy should get on well with her.

The woman who rang Lucy's bell some time later was very much in keeping with Emily's description, though Emily hadn't begun to convey Vanessa Bairstow's attractiveness. She was a strikingly good-looking woman, Lucy discovered, although perhaps best described as handsome rather than beautiful, with the kind of looks that improve rather than fade with age. Her wheat-coloured hair was thick, wavy and beautifully cut, and her figure, clad elegantly and expensively in the latest sophisticated fashion, was full yet firm, heavy-breasted and curvaceous. But her voice, when she spoke, had that same almost wistful note that had so intrigued Lucy on the phone. 'Hello, Miss Kingsley. It's so kind of you to see me on such short notice.'

'Please, call me Lucy. And do come in.' Lucy took her cashmere coat and hung it up carefully in the cupboard under the stairs.

'And I'd like it very much if you'd call me Vanessa.' She put a hand to her hair and took a surreptitious peek at herself in the hall mirror. 'I do hope my hair looks all right. I've just been to a new hairdresser – my old one was inconsiderate enough to move to Brighton – and you just never know, do you?'

'It looks lovely,' Lucy assured her. 'And you're right – there's nothing worse than having to find a new hairdresser!'

That shared female confidence established them on a footing of empathy immediately; after a few additional pleasantries, Lucy led

Vanessa Bairstow upstairs to her studio, a small room strewn about with artists' paraphernalia and paintings in various stages of completion.

'Oh, I say, Lucy.' Vanessa looked around her with lively interest. 'Emily Neville was right – your paintings are wonderful!'

Lucy smiled modestly. 'I'm glad you think so. But Emily would say that in any case.'

'Are all of these spoken for?'

'Most of them, yes. And the ones that aren't done on commission get sent to various galleries. You said that you wanted a painting for your husband?'

'Yes, that's right. To hang in his office – as a gift for our twentieth wedding anniversary.'

They spent a quarter of an hour discussing Lucy's techniques and theories of painting as well as various details of the commission before retiring downstairs for tea. Lucy settled Vanessa in the sitting room and went to the kitchen to boil the kettle; when she returned a few minutes later, carrying a tray, she found the other woman with a cat ensconced quite firmly in her lap, curled up and purring.

'Oh, I'm sorry about Sophie,' Lucy apologised. 'She can be a bit of a pest – throw her off if she's bothering you.'

'Not at all!' Vanessa stroked the small marmalade cat lovingly, and the cat responded with a blissful yawn. 'I love cats – I have one myself. Augustine is my pride and joy.'

Lucy pictured a sleek regal Siamese, a cat worthy of this elegant woman. 'I'll look forward to meeting Augustine some time.'

'Yes, you must come to my house soon.' Her voice was almost shy in its eagerness.

'I'd like that.' Lucy poured the tea. 'I didn't ask you – Earl Grey is all right, I hope?'

'Oh, yes. My favourite.'

'With lemon?'

'Perfect.'

After a few minutes, over tea and cakes, they were chatting like old friends; Lucy's natural warmth, and the gift she always had for drawing people out, seemed to have overcome Vanessa's shyness. In short order Lucy learned that Mr Bairstow was called Martin, that he had something to do with investments in the City, that he was a churchwarden at St Margaret's, and that his wife had little more to occupy her time than volunteer work, maintaining her wardrobe, and overseeing the running of their home. All of this was elicited without the least semblance of nosiness on Lucy's part; she was a good listener, and genuinely interested in other people. On the other hand, she was herself a very private person, and rarely revealed very much personal information.

'More tea?' Lucy lifted the pot invitingly.

'No, I mustn't. I should get home soon. Martin will be home from work early tonight – he has some church meeting this evening – and I'd better be there when he gets home. After all, this painting is meant to be a surprise, and I don't want to have to make excuses for where I've been, if I come rushing in after he's home! I'm not a very good liar, I'm afraid.'

Lucy smiled. 'He might think you were spending the afternoon with another man.'

Deposing Sophie, who departed with a displeased howl, Vanessa stood up abruptly. 'Oh, no, he mustn't think that!' She flushed and moved towards the door.

The remark had been meant to be humorous; Lucy could see instantly that it had been ill-judged. She covered over the awkwardness as best she could, fetching the cashmere coat. 'It's been such a pleasure meeting you, Vanessa. And I'll get to work on your painting as soon as I can.'

Vanessa seemed conscious that she had somehow spoiled the mood of friendly intimacy that had developed between them. At the door she turned and touched Lucy's arm. 'Thank you so much for everything. For the tea, and for . . . everything.'

'It was my pleasure.' Lucy spoke with such obvious sincerity that the other woman hesitated for a moment on the doorstep.

'Lucy . . .'

'Yes?'

'I wondered if I might ask you a very big favour.'

'Ask away.' She smiled. 'After all, I can always say no.'

'I just had an idea, that's all.'

'Sounds ominous!'

Vanessa was reassured by the bantering tone. 'It's just that we have this women's group – mostly women from church, from St Margaret's, and a few from St Jude's,' she explained. 'We get together once a month, on a Wednesday afternoon, and have a speaker of some sort, then tea. Very informal.'

Lucy's heart sank. It sounded absolutely dire, she thought: a flock of well-heeled church women with nothing better to do than sit around gossiping, and listening to some boring speaker talking about gardening or some such subject of interest to the idle rich. But she supposed she'd have to grit her teeth and go. 'And you wanted me to come?'

'Well, not exactly.' Vanessa gave an apologetic half-laugh. 'Actually, I was hoping that I could talk you into speaking to us next week – the meeting is at my house. We were meant to have a woman from the Royal Horticultural Society talking to us about "Preparing Your Garden for Spring", but she's cancelled – had to go into hospital.'

Lucy was astonished. 'But I'm no public speaker!'

'Oh, but you know so much about art! I'm sure that the others would be as fascinated as I was today to hear about your paintings – where you get your ideas, how you execute them, and so forth – especially if you could bring a few examples.' Vanessa flushed with enthusiasm. 'It would be so much more interesting than our usual speakers, I assure you!'

'Oh, I don't think . . .' she protested feebly. 'Surely you can find someone else?'

Vanessa shook her head. 'Well, Dolly Topping – she's one of our members – has offered to step into the breach with a talk about the evils of abortion, but I don't think anyone wants to hear it. Anyway, she talked to us last month, about "Christmas in Other Lands", so I think we've had enough of Dolly for a while.' She gave Lucy a beseeching look. 'Won't you at least think about it? Emily Neville usually comes,' she added cunningly.

Poor Emily, thought Lucy. The things one has to endure as the Archdeacon's wife. 'Oh, all right,' she capitulated, trying not to sound ungracious, and knowing that she would probably be sorry.

Vanessa's smile was radiant. 'Thank you so much. I'll ring you on Monday with the details, if that's all right.'

'See you next week, then.' Lucy shrugged philosophically as she closed the door, realising that in spite of everything she was rather looking forward to next week. She would enjoy seeing the Bairstows' house, and her curiosity about Vanessa Bairstow was intensified rather than assuaged by their face-to-face meeting.

Absently she returned to the sitting room to clear up the tea things; as she stacked the empty cups on the tray the phone in the hall rang.

It was David, at his most apologetic. 'I hope you haven't started fixing supper, love – I'm going to be rather late. A last-minute meeting.'

'I was just going to make a pot of soup, so it won't matter. Something urgent, is it?'

'I'm not sure. I must admit that I'm rather intrigued – the chap who rang me to set up the meeting was quite mysterious about the whole thing. All I know is that the meeting is at St Margaret's, Pimlico. It was the churchwarden who rang me – a chap by the name of Martin Bairstow.'

CHAPTER 4

Blessed is he that considereth the poor and needy: the Lord shall deliver him in the time of trouble.

Psalm 41.1

Martin Bairstow took out his pipe and fiddled with it, then decided it wasn't appropriate to light it in church – not even in the vestry – and put it back in his pocket. 'He should be here soon. Let me do the talking,' he instructed his fellow churchwarden, not for the first time.

'Where did you find this solicitor bloke?' queried Norman Topping.

'One of the wardens from St John's, North Kensington, recommended him. Apparently he did some work for them about a year ago, when they were threatened with closure unless they came up with the money to repair the roof,' Bairstow explained. 'He negotiated the sale of the school and the church hall to some property developers – really saved the church's bacon, apparently.'

'And we're . . . you're . . . going to tell him . . . ?'

'What we've discussed.' Bairstow's tone was brusque. 'It should suffice for the moment. Eventually we may have to tell him the whole truth, but I don't see why that should be necessary for a while, if at all.'

Topping furrowed his brow. 'And what about the Vicar?'

'What about him?'

'What are we going to tell *him*?'

'I've already had a brief word with Father Keble Smythe, and have explained what we intend doing – at least as much as he needs to know. I don't think he'll look into it too closely – he's got enough other things on his plate at the moment, without worrying about this.'

'Is he coming to this meeting?' Topping asked.

'I've mentioned it to him, but he may be too busy preparing for the service. Perhaps he'll drop in.'

'Surely, though, the solicitor will have to be instructed by the Vicar and churchwardens, and not just . . .'

Bairstow's heavy jaw was thrust out farther than usual. 'Just leave it to me, Norman. And let me do the talking.'

Leaving Victoria Underground station, David looked at his watch. The church was about a ten-minute walk from the station, he reckoned, and he'd told the churchwarden that he'd be there by six. He'd allowed plenty of time for the tube journey, but it was the Friday night rush hour, and he wasn't going to have much time to spare. He walked briskly through the busy commercial area around Victoria, soon reaching the quiet streets of Pimlico, where rows of white houses gleamed with austere prosperity in the chill, misty evening.

He'd been to St Margaret's before, in the church-crawling days of his youth. Though that had been twenty or more years ago, he now found the church easily, and spent a moment or two surveying the exterior. Built of soft Kentish stone, it had weathered rather less well than other churches of a similar age. But it had evidently been well cared for, and the window tracery showed signs of having been recently renewed. Lights shone welcomingly through the stained glass; David shivered in the cold and headed for the door.

The churchwarden had mentioned during their telephone conversation that there would be a service that evening – hence the early starting time for their meeting – so David was not surprised to find the church unlocked and well lit. He couldn't for a moment think what festival the service was to commemorate, but as he entered the church he discovered that pride of place for the evening had been given to a large oil painting of King Charles the First. It stood near the chancel entrance, attended by an arrangement of white lilies and a votive candle stand. Of course, he said to himself. The feast of the Martyrdom of King Charles. A church like St Margaret's *would* mark that feast.

David stood for a moment, assimilating the building's interior. It was a large Victorian church, built in an uncluttered Gothic style, with exceptionally wide side aisles and a lofty roof; the overall impression was of space and light. The chancel, with its polychromed vaulting, had evidently been re-done at a later date, and was ornately gilded and decorated with Pre-Raphaelite murals. As he moved towards the chancel, David realised that he was not alone in the church: a man in a cassock was kneeling in front of the altar. He turned at David's approach.

'I'm so sorry. I didn't mean to disturb your prayers,' David apologised.

The man laughed. 'Oh, I wasn't praying.' He held up a fine-tooth comb. 'I was smartening up the altar.' Demonstrating, he began running the comb through the silk fringe of the superfrontal. 'We've put the red martyrs' set on for tonight, of course, and they do get a bit *déshabillé* with handling.' He half turned and squinted up at David. 'Can I help you with something?'

'I'm meant to be meeting the churchwardens here at six,' he explained. 'They don't seem to be here, unless I'm not looking in the right place.'

The other man jumped to his feet. He was tall, with an ugly rubbery-looking face that reminded David of a frog. 'Oh, the wardens are in the vestry. Waiting for you, I expect. It's through that door on the north side, by the organ.'

'Thanks.'

David turned to go, but the man seemed reluctant to have him leave. 'I'm the sacristan, by the way. Name's Robin West.' He thrust out his hand – the one without the comb – so David was obliged to return and shake it.

'David Middleton-Brown.'

Robin West looked him up and down, taking stock. 'Are you staying for the service?'

'I hadn't planned to,' David admitted.

'Oh, do!' He made a sweeping gesture towards the portrait of the martyred king. 'It's one of the highlights of the year at St Margaret's! No one else in London does anything like it – there will be all sorts of visiting clergy, and the red copes, and lots of lace. Well worth seeing, I promise you! We're even using the 1637 Prayer Book service!'

'Sounds tempting.' While he was speaking, David looked at the altar furnishings; he was passionately interested in ecclesiastical silver, and was always interested to see what various churches possessed. The silver altar cross was disappointing, he decided: overly ornate, and not particularly well made. The six candlesticks were a mixed bag, one pair of which might be reasonably good. He wished that he could have a look at the hallmarks.

'And I shall be thurifer, of course. You really *must* stay.' Robin West smirked. 'You'll even have a chance to see the Vicar – not something that happens very often at St Margaret's, I can assure you!'

That caught David's attention. 'What do you mean?'

'Oh, our Vicar is *far* too busy at St Jude's down the road – where all the money is – to honour us with his presence very often,' the sacristan declared with an arch look. 'But tonight he'll be here – after all, this is the place to see and be seen on the Feast of King Charles the Martyr, if no other time.'

'I see.'

'Father Keble Smythe would like us all to think that he's such a good Catholic, after all.'

'And isn't he?'

Robin West twitched the skirts of his cassock. 'I really wouldn't like to say,' he stated demurely. 'Most people believe it. I suppose that's the important thing.' As David seemed about to move off, he reached out and touched his sleeve with a delicate finger. 'You *will* stay, won't you? Promise me that you'll stay?'

The man made David nervous, but he didn't know how to say no. 'All right, then. I'll stay.'

'Oh, you won't regret it. It's the best show in town. And if you're free for a drink after . . .'

David didn't stay to hear the rest of the suggestion, or to reply.

Martin Bairstow came straight to the point. 'What we're interested in, Mr Middleton-Brown, is some advice and assistance in selling a few bits and pieces. I assume that faculties will need to be applied for, and we thought that perhaps you could advise us on the best way of finding the appropriate buyers as well.'

This wasn't really what David had expected; he thought for a moment. 'Let's start at the beginning. Why do you want to sell these things, and what are they?'

'Just a few pieces of old silver,' the churchwarden explained. 'We want to raise some cash to refurbish a house in the parish.'

'Magdalen House, it's called,' Norman Topping interjected; he was quelled immediately by a look from his fellow warden.

'Magdalen House,' Bairstow repeated. 'It was founded by the Community of St Mary Magdalen, an Anglican sisterhood, back in the 1880s, as a home for what they so quaintly called "fallen women". But the last of the sisters died a few years ago, and the house is now under the jurisdiction of the parish.'

'I don't suppose there are so many fallen women these days, in any case.'

Bairstow didn't return David's smile. 'No,' he said seriously. 'In the recent past it has served as a curate's house, but it is no longer being used for that purpose.'

'Do you have another use in mind for it, then? That would require it to be refurbished?'

Bairstow's eyes flickered to Norman Topping, then back to David. 'My colleague and I feel that we have a responsibility to address the terrible problem of homelessness in London,' he stated solemnly. 'As trustees of Magdalen House, we agree that it should be converted into a shelter for the homeless.'

David nodded. 'That sounds entirely reasonable. But to sacrifice your church's silver, even for such a good cause . . . ?'

'Well, it *is* lovely stuff, especially the altar cross, but we think the cause is one that's worth the sacrifice,' Bairstow said, lifting his chin in a noble look. 'I'm not sure exactly what we might expect to get for it, but we're hoping that it will fetch a few thousand pounds. And we can replace it with some nice modern pieces.'

David kept his opinion of the altar cross to himself, and decided to reserve judgement on the value of the rest until he'd seen it. 'Would it be possible for me to have a look?'

Bairstow rose. 'Yes, of course. We were hoping that you'd be able to advise us on its value. My colleague at St John's said that you knew quite a lot about church silver.'

'Not at all.' David shook his head with customary modesty. 'I'm just an amateur. But I *am* very interested in it.'

'I don't suppose any of the clergy have arrived yet, so it's all right if we go to the sacristy,' Norman Topping contributed.

Martin Bairstow led the way. The sacristy was not, however, empty; the door was ajar, and a man with a face like a death's head was seated at a table, pen in hand. He looked up at them impatiently as they entered. 'I'm getting the service register ready for tonight,' he explained.

'We won't get in your way,' Bairstow assured him. 'We just wanted to have a look at the silver. Mr Middleton-Brown, this is Stanley Everitt, the Parish Administrator.'

The men exchanged pleasantries as Bairstow opened the safe with a long, old-fashioned key. 'Here we are.' He pulled out a cloth bag and unwrapped a chalice.

'Ah.' David assessed it in an instant: it was mass-produced, late in date, and of very little value. 'Interesting,' he said diplomatically.

'There's more.' Bairstow brought out a ciborium, an incense boat, a large alms dish, and an assortment of candlesticks. 'Then there's the altar cross, as well.'

'I see.' Searching for a tactful way to break the news, David picked up the incense boat. 'Nice.'

Norman Topping was watching him eagerly. 'Do you like it? Is it worth something, then?'

He didn't give a direct answer. 'Is this all you have? Don't you have a thurible, or a monstrance?'

'Well, the rest of the plate is only copper-gilt,' Bairstow explained with an apologetic shrug. 'There's a whole set of it, as a matter of fact. But it's really hideous Victorian stuff – not worth anything. After this is sold, we'll have to use it until we can get some new pieces.'

'Show it to him,' Topping urged.

Bairstow reached into the safe and pulled some pieces from the back. 'Here's the thurible.' He handed it to David.

'Oh, yes.' David turned the heavy thurible over in his hands with surprise and rising excitement. 'This is a lovely piece.'

The taller churchwarden straightened up and stared at him. 'It is?'

'It's very fine.' He pointed to the hallmarks. 'You see? It's not copper-gilt at all. It's silver-gilt. Very tarnished with age, but definitely silver-gilt.'

'Silver-gilt?' Topping echoed, his eyes lighting up at the implication.

'Yes. And unless I'm very much mistaken, it was designed by Pugin. The design is certainly very characteristic of his work.' David was trying to be cautious, but he couldn't help betraying a certain degree of anticipation in his voice. 'You say there's more? Could I see the rest, please?'

Bairstow lined the pieces up one by one on the counter. 'Two ciboria, flagon, monstrance, and processional cross.'

'It's a lovely set,' David stated. 'And the fact that it was probably designed by Pugin certainly adds to its value.'

'How much?' Norman Topping demanded baldly. 'What is it worth?'

'The market for ecclesiastical silver is rather depressed right now, but you should certainly get a few thousand for it. Possibly a bit more, since, as I say, it's by a prestigious designer like Pugin. And as it's a set.' Suddenly he realised that something was missing. 'But where is the chalice?'

The two churchwardens looked at each other. 'I'm afraid it's been stolen,' Bairstow said slowly. 'There was a burglary. A month or two ago.'

'Stolen?' David was dismayed.

'I'm afraid so,' interjected Stanley Everitt, looking even more lugubrious than usual. 'The police said that it happens all the time.'

'Oh, it does. But a silver-gilt Pugin chalice! Some thief got a bit more than he bargained for, I dare say. I hope that it was insured?'

Again the churchwardens looked at each other. 'It was insured, of course, but not for very much,' Bairstow confessed. 'To tell you the truth, I've always thought that this stuff was pretty hideous.'

David shook his head, despairing at the Philistinism which, in his experience, seemed to afflict churchwardens everywhere. 'Never mind. So what do you want to do, now that you know it might be worth a bob or two?'

'Sell it, of course,' Bairstow replied promptly, without even a glance at his colleague. 'How do we go about it?'

Rubbing his chin thoughtfully, David considered the options. 'If you don't need the money immediately, the best thing would be to put it into one of the sale rooms – Christie's or Sotheby's – for auction. That would take a couple of months, to get it into the catalogue. If you're in a great hurry, I could try a few dealers, but you're not likely to get nearly as good a price from them.'

'Oh, we want as much money as we can get,' Bairstow stated.

'But as soon as possible,' Topping added.

'Don't forget, though, that you'll have to get a faculty before you can sell it,' David reminded them. 'That means that your PCC will have to agree, and then the papers will have to be filed with the Diocesan Advisory Committee, who will have to approve the sale. I don't anticipate any real problems with that, but it will take a month or two, no matter what. You can't rush the diocese.'

Wringing his hands in a thoughtful way, Everitt spoke. 'That reminds me about that question you were asking me a few days ago, Martin. Did you ring the diocesan solicitor as I suggested?'

Bairstow seemed to want to change the subject. 'Yes, I did. Now perhaps we should think about—'

'And was I right?' Everitt droned on, oblivious. 'Is it right that if a congregation leaves the Church of England, the building and everything in it remains the property of the C of E?'

The churchwarden was saved the necessity of a reply by the arrival of the Vicar. 'Father Keble Smythe! I'd like you to meet David Middleton-Brown, the solicitor who's going to help us with the sale of the silver, as I mentioned to you. And you won't believe what he's discovered! The old stuff – what we've always thought was copper-gilt – might actually be worth something!'

The Vicar made the appropriate noises, then said, 'How kind of you to turn out on such an unpleasant evening, Mr Middleton-Brown.'

For the first time, and with great interest, David shook the hand of Father William Keble Smythe. He was younger than David had expected, and very good-looking. How would he describe him to Lucy, later on? Wavy dark hair, contrasting vividly with a pale complexion. Perhaps a bit *too* pale, he decided. In fact, everything about him seemed just a bit over the top: his hair in perfect waves and parted as if with a ruler, his accent perhaps a shade too posh, his cassock immaculate, his shoes polished to a blinding shine.

'I must begin getting ready for the service now, but I'd like to chat further with all of you after,' the Vicar said, taking in David and the churchwardens with his gesture. 'How about joining me at the clergy house for a drink after the service?'

'Sorry, Father,' Martin Bairstow demurred. 'I have to give several of the old girls a lift home.'

'And Dolly will have supper ready,' Norman Topping added. 'She wouldn't appreciate it if I were late.'

The Vicar turned back to David. 'Mr Middleton-Brown? You *are* staying for the service, I trust? How about a drink afterwards?'

David hesitated; Lucy would be expecting him, but on the other hand he felt that he ought to accept. It would help to learn as much about the set-up at St Margaret's as he could, and talking to the Vicar on his own could be a useful way of doing that. He admitted to himself as well that he was curious about Father Keble Smythe, especially in the light of Robin West's veiled remarks. And a drink with the Vicar would extricate him from the clutches of the repellent sacristan. 'A quick one, perhaps.'

'Jolly good. I'll see you after the service, then.'

The service was everything that the sacristan had promised, and more. Multiple clergy went through their paces, the proceedings obscured by copious smoke from the Pugin thurible, ably wielded by Robin West. The 1637 rite was suitably arcane for even the most hardened spiritual thrill-seekers. It was just a shame, thought David, that not more of them were present: as far as he could tell, there weren't more than a few strangers, who, like himself, joined the churchwardens, a sprinkling of devout elderly ladies, and a few others who were clearly regular members of the congregation, for an experience that was well out of the ordinary.

Some time later he found himself at the clergy house, transported there in great comfort in Father Keble Smythe's opulent car. Mrs Goode was waiting for them at the door. 'There's a nice fire going in your study, Father,' she greeted them. 'I thought you'd need it on a cold night like this.'

'Oh, excellent woman!' The Vicar removed his clerical cloak with a flourish. 'And is that your incomparable fish pie that I smell?'

The housekeeper nodded, gratified. 'It will be ready soon. Will the other gentleman be staying to supper?'

Father Keble Smythe turned to David. 'How about it, dear chap? Mrs Goode's fish pie is enough to make anyone look forward to Friday, believe me. I'd be delighted if you'd join me.'

The smell that wafted from the kitchen was enough to tempt David, and it had been a long time since he'd had a good home-made fish pie: since Lucy had become a vegetarian, nearly a year past, he'd been deprived of such fare, and at moments like this he regretted it keenly. But Lucy would be waiting for him, and her soup would be delicious, if meatless. 'I'm sorry, but I really can't.' He followed the Vicar into the study. 'I must get home, I'm afraid.'

'Are you married, Mr Middleton-Brown?'

David was instantly defensive, and not inclined to discuss his domestic arrangements with the Vicar. 'Not exactly,' he hedged.

Father Keble Smythe chuckled understandingly. 'I feel that way myself.' He swept the silver-framed photo off his desk and presented it to David. 'My fiancée, Miss Morag McKenzie,' he explained with a sentimental sigh.

'Very nice,' said David, feeling inadequate. 'She looks . . . nice.'

'A lovely young woman.' The Vicar's eyes were misty. 'But I honestly don't know when our marriage will be able to take place. Her father isn't very well, you see, and she's absolutely devoted to him. So all of my pleas to her to end my bachelor state are to no avail! I have Mrs Goode to take care of me, she says, and her father has no one else.'

'Does she live in the parish?'

'Oh, goodness, no. She lives in Scotland. Her father is a professor of classics at St Andrews University.'

David could empathise with the loneliness of separation. 'That must be very difficult for you.'

'It is. It is.' Father Keble Smythe sighed again, with great feeling, and took the photo back. 'But I've invited you here for a drink, not to talk about my sad situation.' He gestured invitingly at the tray which the housekeeper had prepared. 'As you see, Mrs Goode looks after me awfully well. What would you like? Sherry? Whisky? Gin?'

'Whisky, please.' While the Vicar poured the drinks, David took a moment to appraise the room in which he found himself. The study had been furnished with a great deal of taste, he thought, and at no little expense; he wondered if the Vicar had private means, or if he were just successful in loosening the purse strings of his wealthy parishioners.

'So,' said Father Keble Smythe when they had settled comfortably by the fire with their drinks, 'you've met with the churchwardens. And you've seen the silver. Pretty good, is it?'

David nodded. 'Not the bits they wanted to sell, but the old set. I don't know how much you know about Victorian silver, but it's almost certainly designed by Pugin, and that alone makes it well above average in interest and value.'

'That's splendid. You must get on, then, with applying for a faculty to sell it.'

'I'm surprised that you can bear to part with it,' David said frankly. 'It's lovely stuff. If it were *my* church, nothing would induce me to sell it.'

'My churchwardens seem to think that it's the right thing to do.'

'The shelter for the homeless is a worthy idea, of course, but . . .' David tailed off at the unexpectedly ironic laugh which erupted from the Vicar.

'That's what they told you, then? And you believed it?'

He stared at Father Keble Smythe, baffled. 'Of course I believed it.'

The genial, affected manner had gone in an instant, to be replaced by an air of knowing cynicism. 'Then you haven't known as many churchwardens as I have, Mr Middleton-Brown. Believe me, a shelter for the homeless is the *last* thing that money is intended for.'

'Then what . . . ?'

'Oh, I'm not sure about that, though I have a fairly good idea what they've got in mind.' The Vicar's chuckle was mirthless as he held his glass up and squinted through the amber liquid, and he spoke more to himself than to David. 'But I'm a step ahead of them. I shall let them hatch their little schemes, thinking all the while that they're putting one over on me. And then . . . well, my friend, I shall give them just enough rope to hang themselves!'

CHAPTER 5

They are inclosed in their own fat: and their mouth speaketh proud things.
Psalm 17.10

'You must admit, it was rather a coincidence.' It was Wednesday morning and Lucy was still in bed, sipping the cup of tea that David had brought her, while he got dressed. 'Vanessa Bairstow ringing me, the same day that Martin Bairstow rang *you*.'

'I suppose it was, in a way.' He frowned at himself in the mirror, which was at an awkward height for him to see his tie properly, and straightened the knot. 'But you've got to remember, love, that the Church of England is a small world. Mrs Bairstow rang you because of Emily, who happens to be the Archdeacon's wife in addition to being your friend, and her husband rang me because of what I'd done for St John's last year. Not really that amazing, when you think about it. Just one of life's funny little coincidences – the sort of thing that happens every day.'

'I think it was very clever of you to identify the silver as being by Pugin.'

David ran a comb through his hair – brown in colour, with just enough silver at the temples to give him an air of distinction. 'Not really – his stuff is quite distinctive,' he demurred modestly. 'I've got a book on Pugin somewhere, in one of the boxes in the loft – I'll try to find it this evening, if you like, and show you.' He turned to face her. 'What time are you going to the Bairstows'?'

'The meeting starts at half-past two. I'll go a few minutes before that, I suppose.'

Abstractedly, he shrugged his suit jacket on, then took a final glance at himself in the mirror. 'You're not going to mention me to her – to Mrs Bairstow, are you? About the coincidence?'

Lucy gave him an amused look. 'Good heavens, no. I don't imagine it will come up, quite frankly. And you know that I don't go about advertising our relationship. But why do you ask?'

'I wouldn't want her husband to think that I'd been talking about the case to other people. He might think it was unprofessional.'

'Don't worry, David darling,' she laughed. 'My lips are sealed.'

He moved close to the bed. 'That's not all they are,' he murmured, bending to kiss her goodbye.

Laden down with paintings, Lucy took a taxi to Vanessa Bairstow's house. It was in the exclusive heart of Pimlico, facing a black-railed, tree-shaded square. Now, at the beginning of February, the square was less than inviting, its trees bare under a grey sky, but already there were signs of life in the buds that swelled on them, and Lucy could imagine how pleasant it would be in the summer. The house was imposingly tall, pristinely white, with a shiny brass doorknocker in the shape of a lion's head.

Lucy wrestled the paintings out of the taxi and up the steps to the front door. She rang the bell and waited a moment, expecting Vanessa Bairstow to answer, or possibly a servant.

The woman who opened the door was most definitely not Vanessa, but she was clearly not a servant either. To call her large would be understating the case: her massive bosom jutted out like the figurehead of a ship, and her width seemed crammed into the doorway. Her face, under a rather fussy arrangement of permed grey curls, was strong-featured and bespectacled, and seemed unnervingly familiar to Lucy, who was nevertheless unable to think where she might have encountered her in the past. 'Oh, hello,' she said uncertainly. 'I'm Lucy Kingsley.'

'Yes, of course you are.'

This reply, and the tone in which it was spoken, reinforced the impression that she should know the other woman; as she struggled into the house with her paintings, she ventured, 'Have we met?'

'No.' The woman laughed. 'You've probably seen me on television. I'm Dolly Topping, from Ladies Opposed to Women Priests.'

Lucy remembered: Mrs Topping had indeed been an ubiquitous presence on television, during the General Synod debate on the ordination of women, the person who could always be counted upon to put the 'anti' point of view with force and conviction. 'A woman's place is at the kitchen table,' she had been fond of saying, 'not at the Sacred Table.' It was a good line, and it had been widely quoted at the time. 'Yes, of course,' Lucy acknowledged. 'It's nice to meet you, Mrs Topping.'

'Please, call me Dolly,' insisted the other woman. 'Everyone does. My name is really Harriet, but no one has called me that for years.' She waited for Lucy to ask her why, but when the question wasn't forthcoming she told her anyway. 'You might not believe it, but I used to be a tiny little thing. When I was first married, my husband Norman said that I was no bigger than a doll. His little Dolly, he said.'

There was no tactful response to that, so Lucy merely smiled.

'Vanessa is on the phone – it rang just as you arrived. She should be with us any minute,' Dolly went on, oblivious to the awkward silence. 'It's very kind of you to come and speak to us today, Miss Kingsley. Though as I told Vanessa, there was really no need – I could have stepped into the breach, if necessary. If I say so myself, I'm rather an expert on quite a few things – Ladies Opposed to Women Priests is by no means the only string to *my* bow,' she asserted.

Again Lucy was at a loss for an appropriate reply. 'Oh, I'm sure,' she said somewhat lamely, wondering where Vanessa Bairstow might be.

Vanessa appeared just then, carrying a cat. 'Oh, hello, Lucy,' she said with a shy smile.

'Who was on the phone?' Dolly demanded.

'Just Vera. She's not going to be able to make it this afternoon – her father isn't well.' She sighed. 'It's a real shame – she was so looking forward to it, she said.'

'I do hope that Dr Bright isn't seriously ill,' said Dolly, frowning.

'I'm sure he's not. Probably just one of these colds that's been going round.' Vanessa turned to Lucy. 'Are you all right?'

'Yes. Mrs Topping – Dolly – has been taking care of me.'

'This is Augustine.' She held the cat up for Lucy's inspection and admiration. 'My pride and joy.'

Augustine was no sleek Siamese; Lucy saw instead an evil-looking tom, battle-scarred, with a torn ear and a single malevolent yellow eye.

Lucy once again searched frantically for a suitable response. 'How ... um ... nice.' She reached out a tentative hand to stroke him, and was regally ignored. At least, she thought, he didn't rip my hand off.

'Sweetums kitty,' crooned Vanessa, enraptured.

Dolly snorted derisively. 'That's what happens to women who don't have babies,' she muttered to Lucy. 'They go daft over their animals.'

It was a monumentally insensitive thing to say, and judging by the flush on Vanessa's cheek, the barb had gone home. But to Lucy's great relief, almost immediately the doorbell chimed, and Emily Neville joined them.

Lucy and Emily embraced with genuine pleasure and deep affection. Their friendship was of long standing, dating back more than ten years to the time when Emily first occupied the vicarage of St Anne's,

Kensington Gardens, as the Vicar's brand-new wife. Lucy had been on the periphery of the congregation then, largely through her interest in music and her regular attendance at the weekly organ recitals, and she had befriended the shy young woman, teaching her to cook and helping her to redecorate the forbiddingly masculine vicarage. Through the years they had met often, routinely at organ recitals, and at other times by choice, and Lucy was godmother to Viola, one of Emily's twins. Now, though, since Emily's husband had become Archdeacon – and perhaps not coincidentally since Lucy's involvement with David – their meetings were less frequent, and required more planning, though they kept in touch often by phone.

'Em! You look wonderful!' Lucy spoke only the truth: Emily did indeed look every inch the Archdeacon's wife, her dark brown hair sculptured around her heart-shaped face, her delicate and small-boned figure set off by a trim navy blue dress. But Lucy couldn't help regretting the loss of Emily's own personal style. When she had first known her, barely down from Cambridge, Emily had dressed casually; Lucy had rarely seen her in anything but a pair of jeans and an oversized jumper. It was perhaps not what most vicars' wives wore, but Emily had been loved and accepted for what she was by the parishioners of St Anne's, and there had never been a word of criticism. Now, clearly, things were different, and Emily had to conform to people's expectations of an Archdeacon's wife. Poor Emily, thought Lucy. She hoped that she didn't mind too much.

'So do you, Luce. As always. Love evidently agrees with you,' she added with a teasing smile, and was rewarded by seeing Lucy's fair skin flush. 'How is dear David?'

'Oh, fine.' Lucy went on quickly, 'How about Gabriel? And the children?'

'All very well, thanks. Gabriel is rushed off his feet, of course, but that's to be expected.'

The bell chimed again, another guest was admitted, and soon it was time for the meeting to begin.

Lucy's talk was enthusiastically received, but afterwards her efforts to reach Emily for a chat were thwarted by all the other women who wanted to speak to her.

Self-importantly, Dolly Topping pushed ahead of them all with another woman in tow. 'This is Joan Everitt, the wife of our Parish Administrator,' she announced. 'She wants to know how much you charge for your paintings, but she didn't want to ask you herself.'

'That depends, of course,' Lucy hedged delicately. 'We could discuss it, if you like.'

'I think my husband would like one, but I don't suppose we could afford it,' said Mrs Everitt. A middle-aged woman with a bland, chinless face, she wore her hair in a style inappropriate to her age, long and straight with a black velvet Alice band. Her clothes, too, were far too young for her – not, though, as with some women of mature years who wear short, tight skirts or clothes in the latest teenage fashion. Instead her garb was schoolgirlish: a round-collared white blouse, a modest pleated skirt, and black plimsolls. The effect was mildly jarring.

'We could discuss it later,' repeated Lucy, before, to the disappointment of Dolly Topping, changing the subject. 'Your husband is the Parish Administrator? That must be an interesting job.'

'Oh, yes. Stanley likes it very much.'

'And how about you?' asked Lucy, wondering how to phrase the question without giving offence, one way or the other. The women at this afternoon's gathering were not likely to have – or even want – careers of their own, but to make that assumption could be equally dangerous. 'Do you . . . um . . . work?'

She needn't have worried; the tone of Joan Everitt's reply was complacent rather than defensive. 'No, not me. Not since the children came along.'

'I should think not,' interjected Dolly. 'A woman's place is in the home.' She managed to say it as though it were an entirely original phrase. 'Unless,' she added with a look of pity at Lucy, 'she's unfortunate enough not to have a husband to support her.'

Lucy couldn't help herself. 'And especially if she has the temerity to want to be a priest.'

The statement was taken at face value, irony being a quality with which Dolly Topping had scant familiarity. 'Absolutely,' she agreed. 'I take it you've heard about the announcement that was made last weekend?'

'No . . . ?'

Dolly seemed to swell with indignation. 'The Vicar, Father Keble Smythe, announced that there's to be a woman curate at St Jude's and St Margaret's! Can you imagine anything more ridiculous?' It was a rhetorical question; without waiting for a reply, she went on, 'I'm quite sure that it wasn't *his* idea – there must have been a great deal of pressure from higher up. After all, Father Keble Smythe is a proper Catholic – he's been a supporter of The Cause from the beginning.

Many times I've heard him say that women priests are unnatural, unscriptural, completely contrary to the unbroken tradition of the Church.'

'Then why did he consent to have a woman curate?' Joan Everitt put in. 'Not that I blame him, of course.'

'As I say, he must have been under pressure,' repeated Dolly. 'Mark my words, this female was foisted on him against his will. I, for one, feel sorry for poor Father. I won't hear a word against him.'

'Stanley says that it probably won't have much effect on St Margaret's – that things will go on much as before, with priests from other churches filling in for services. After all, she's only a deacon – she can't celebrate the Mass.'

Dolly glowered. 'For the moment, that is. But she wants to be priested, Norman says. And then what will happen? It will all end in tears, I can tell you. I, for one, will not stand still to see a female desecrate the altar at St Margaret's.'

Lucy had been following the exchange with a certain detached amusement, but the vehemence of the last statement startled her. Realising that the other two women had forgotten her presence, she seized the opportunity for escape, and turned towards the corner where Emily Neville nursed a cup of tea. But almost instantly she was waylaid by several other women who had been waiting their turns to talk to her.

At long last, though, she achieved her objective; Emily beckoned her into an empty chair. 'You made it,' she observed, smiling. 'Here – I got you a cup of tea. It's probably cold by now, though.'

'Never mind. I'm so thirsty I won't even notice.' Lucy took a gulp of the tea. 'I was beginning to think I'd never get to you – and I don't think I would have agreed to do this today if Vanessa hadn't promised me that you'd be here. Don't you have to pick up the children from school this afternoon?'

Emily looked at her watch. 'Not for a while yet. They've got music today, so they won't need collecting for nearly another hour.'

'Great. Then we've got time for a natter.'

'What's all the fuss about? Any idea?' Emily indicated the knot of women around Dolly Topping; the discussion was clearly a heated one, dominated by Dolly, who seemed to be lecturing about something.

'It has something to do with their new curate, who had the misfortune to be born female,' Lucy explained wryly. 'Mrs Topping doesn't seem very keen on women in holy orders.'

'To say the least!' Emily leaned closer to Lucy, to avoid being overheard. 'As a matter of fact, I know something about the situation.'

'Because of Gabriel, you mean? I suppose the Archdeacon's wife knows all kinds of things like that.' Absently, Lucy twisted a curl around her finger.

'No, he doesn't usually discuss diocesan matters with me. But it just happens that I know the woman who is going to be their new curate – Rachel Nightingale, her name is.'

Lucy couldn't help being curious. 'How did you meet her?'

'Actually,' Emily explained, 'I've known her for years. We were friends at Cambridge – we were at the same college, and we both read English. In fact, when I married Gabriel, and turned down that graduate fellowship I'd been offered, she was the one who took it up. She's remained in Cambridge ever since, living the academic life that I would have had if it hadn't been for Gabriel.' She smiled, without regret. 'We've kept in touch with Christmas cards and so forth, but I've only seen her a few times since I came down, mostly at college functions.'

'But if she's an academic, how did she get to be a deacon? And why is she in London?'

Emily sighed. 'It's a sad story. She married a young man whom she met at Cambridge – Colin Nightingale. He was a scientist, absolutely brilliant. I knew him slightly. Several years after they were married, when they'd practically given up hope that it would happen, they had a little girl.' She looked into her empty teacup; Emily's own efforts to have children had been traumatic, though ultimately successful. 'Rachel was thrilled, though it meant a few adjustments in her academic workload.'

'And?'

'A few years ago, they were all in a car crash, on a foggy road outside Cambridge. The little girl, Rosie, was killed instantly. Colin lived, though in some ways it would have been better if he hadn't – he's virtually a cabbage, and hasn't ever regained consciousness. He's been in hospital, just kept alive, ever since the accident.' She shook her head. 'Tragic – all that scientific genius lost. Not to mention the little girl, of course.'

Lucy found that her hand was clenched around her cup. 'And Rachel?'

'She was wearing her seat belt, and was only slightly injured. But of course the experience changed her life. She'd lost her family – lost everything. Not surprisingly, she had a crisis of faith, and at the end of it she decided that she was being called into the Church, to serve other people who were hurting. To be a priest, in fact.'

'How brave of her!'

'It was difficult, especially since at that time the legislation on women priests hadn't yet been passed by the General Synod. She was no strident revolutionary with an axe to grind or a flag to wave – just a woman who felt that God was calling her to the priesthood. So she went through theological college, was ordained a deacon, and started her curacy at a church in Cambridge. Then Colin's doctors decided that they could do no more for him – that he should be transferred to a hospital in London, where they've been pioneering new treatments for brain-damaged people. It was terribly hard for Rachel to leave her church in Cambridge, but she knew that she had to put Colin's needs first, and of course she wants to be near him. She visits him every day, even though he almost certainly doesn't know that she's there.'

There were tears in Lucy's eyes and tightness in her throat. 'Oh, the poor woman!'

'Financially she has no worries, of course. The chap who was driving the lorry that hit them had just come from the pub and was well over the limit, so she was awarded substantial damages. Colin is receiving the best possible care, and now that Rachel has moved to London, she's ready to get back to work.' Emily looked over to where Dolly Topping was still holding forth on the evils of women at the altar. 'It's just her misfortune,' she added with a bittersweet smile, 'that she has to do it at St Jude's and St Margaret's, on Dolly Topping's patch.'

CHAPTER 6

Who have whet their tongue like a sword: and shoot out their arrows, even bitter words.

Psalm 64.3

Supper had been eaten and the washing up had been accomplished; Lucy and David had learned from experience, during their months of living together, that unless the washing up was done immediately after supper, it was not likely to be done until the next day. Now, though, it was out of the way, and they were curled up together on the sofa in front of the fire, drinking their coffee and enjoying each other's company. Tonight Lucy had suggested accompanying the coffee with brandy: she felt that she needed it – and deserved it – after her afternoon with the women's club.

Through supper she'd told David about the experience, dwelling on the dreadfulness of Dolly Topping. He was entirely sympathetic. 'From what her husband said,' he confirmed, 'I got the strongest feeling that she rules him with a rod of iron.'

'I'm sure she does. She's really bossy – I found her absolutely terrifying. And she's unwilling to accept the existence of any point of view but her own.'

David grinned. 'And he is a bit of a wimp, I fear.'

She'd told him, as well, of Rachel Nightingale: her tragic story, and her imminent arrival in the parish. The woman's history, seen through Emily's sympathetic eyes, had touched Lucy deeply, and she found herself returning to the subject again and again. 'Poor Rachel. I can't imagine how they'll treat her at St Margaret's. Dolly Topping will be vile to her – she doesn't deserve that.'

'And I don't think that the churchwardens will be particularly gentle with her either.' David set his empty coffee cup on the table and put his arm around Lucy's shoulders. The room was cosy, the fire and the brandy were warming, and he was ready to progress to the next stage of the evening.

She twisted around to look at him. 'They didn't mention anything about her to you at all?'

'No, nothing.' He took her cup from her, putting it next to his. 'Though that isn't really surprising, if it wasn't announced till last Sunday. Presumably they were keeping it quiet until then.'

'Did they know about it, do you think?'

'Oh, probably. But I was there to talk about the silver, not the curate.' He kissed her. 'Can't we change the subject now?' he murmured. 'If I remember correctly, this is where we left off this morning.'

Lucy responded to him for a moment, then pulled away. 'The silver!' she said. 'This morning you promised to show me something about the silver, darling. A picture in a book – remember?'

David was loath to be interrupted. 'Can't it wait till later?'

But the amatory mood was broken, at least as far as Lucy was concerned; her curiosity was as aroused as David's libido. 'If you don't get up right now,' she predicted, 'there's no hope of you finding that book tonight.'

He acknowledged the truth of her statement, but failed to see it as the end of the world. 'Is that so terrible? Won't tomorrow do?' He kissed her again. 'Isn't this more fun?'

'Please? I'd really like to see it. Then we can go to bed.'

'Oh, all right,' David grumbled, sighing a martyr's sigh and disentangling himself from her. 'If it's that important to you.'

He went upstairs and pulled down the ladder to the loft, where his boxes of books were stored. When he'd moved out of his house, a few months previously, he'd put most of his books into store in Norfolk pending a more permanent arrangement, but he'd brought a few boxes of favourites with him. In the event, Lucy's tiny house, with its crowded bookshelves, couldn't absorb even these few essential volumes, and they'd been consigned to the loft.

As he looked over the boxes, his thoughts returned to their earlier conversation about Rachel Nightingale. The story interested him from a legal as well as a human point of view: he was sure that he remembered reading and hearing about the case, in which she had been awarded an astronomical amount of financial compensation, based on her husband's brilliant future in science and his subsequent reduction to a brain-dead condition. There had been something special about that case – it had set some legal precedent, or been noteworthy in some way. He wished he could remember what it was.

While his mind was thus engaged, David found the box with the books on Victorian churches, dusted it off, and in short order retrieved the book he was looking for, the catalogue from a V & A exhibition entitled *Victorian Church Art*. He took it back to the sitting room, where Lucy had put another log on the fire and was pouring out second helpings of brandy.

'That didn't take long.' She smiled and patted the sofa next to her invitingly.

Demonstrating his displeasure at her recent treatment of him, David instead took a chair. 'I knew which box it was in.' He flipped through the book, looking for the illustrations. 'As I said, Pugin's style was quite distinctive. Here, for example, is a ciborium, quite similar to the pair they've got at St Margaret's.' He began to hand the book across to her, then suddenly snatched it back and stared at the illustration. 'Good Lord,' he said.

Lucy was baffled at the look on his face as he rapidly scanned the text under the picture. 'What's the matter, darling?'

He didn't even hear her, so focused was he on the book. 'Good Lord,' he repeated softly. After a moment he looked up. 'It *is* like the set they've got,' he said with quiet assurance.

'What do you mean?'

'The silver at St Margaret's – the silver that they want to sell. I thought that it was fairly late, made to one of Pugin's designs after his death. But it says here that this set was extremely early. Lucy love, don't you see? St Margaret's set is almost exactly like this – that means it's very rare, and much more valuable than I thought.'

'Are you sure?'

He shook his head. 'I can't be positive until I've seen it again, and taken a closer look at the hallmarks. I'll ring the Vicar,' he decided. 'Perhaps he could meet me at the church.'

'Now? At this hour?'

He glanced at his watch. 'It's not that late – barely gone nine.'

Lucy forbore to say that he was the one who was ready to go to bed a quarter of an hour before; instead she gave him an arch look. 'Shouldn't you ring the sacristan? After what you told me about him, I'm sure he'd be more than happy to drop whatever he's doing and meet you. At the church. Alone.'

'Ha. Very funny.'

'Seriously, though – shouldn't you ring the wardens? They're the ones who contacted you in the first place.'

'Technically I'm taking instructions from the Vicar *and* churchwardens.' He went to the phone. 'So at the risk of incurring the legendary wrath of Dolly Topping, I suppose I'd better ring them as well.'

David rang the Vicar first, and was restrained in what he told him – he had reason to believe, he said, that the silver might be more important than he had at first thought, and he would like a chance to examine it again at the earliest opportunity, in the light of what he now knew. That was enough, though, to make the Vicar amenable to going out on a cold night, and on very short notice.

In the end five of them gathered in the sacristy some twenty minutes later. Both churchwardens had been only too eager to come, and the Vicar had brought along Stanley Everitt, with whom he had been having a meeting when David's call had come through.

They all watched in anticipation as the Vicar opened the safe and brought out the pieces of silver, one by one. As Martin Bairstow had done a few days earlier, he lined them up side by side on the vestment chest. 'There,' he commented. 'I always did think it was uncommonly fine silver. What are you going to tell us about it now, Mr Middleton-Brown?'

David opened the book to the page he'd marked and laid it down next to the silver; the similarity was unmistakeable. 'You see? It's very like the set he designed for St Mary's Church, Clapham – comparable in quality and design.' He picked up the thurible and scrutinised the hallmarks with the magnifying glass he'd brought along for the purpose. 'Yes. John Hardman and Co., 1850. It all fits!'

'Is that good?' Norman Topping asked naïvely.

'You told us the other night that it was designed by Pugin,' Bairstow stated, looking at his watch. 'Was this really worth bringing us out tonight for? Why does it matter that it's like the set in the book?'

David took a deep breath; there was no point getting annoyed, he told himself – they really *didn't* understand. 'Don't you see?' he explained patiently. 'It means that it's extremely valuable.'

'Valuable?' echoed Stanley Everitt, his face sharpening.

'Extremely valuable.' David reached out a finger and stroked the thurible with an unconscious gesture. 'It's much earlier than I thought it was, made in Pugin's lifetime. Most of Pugin's work was done for the Roman Church, of course, so for an Anglican church to have a set . . .'

'How much?' Bairstow asked bluntly. 'How much is it worth?'

'That's a difficult question. It always depends on how much someone is willing to pay, but I'd say that you're looking at a figure well over a hundred thousand pounds. Each piece on its own would fetch five figures, and as a set it's worth even more.'

'Cor,' breathed Norman Topping; Everitt drew in his breath, and Bairstow nodded in satisfaction.

Father Keble Smythe had been taking it all in; now he spoke thoughtfully. 'That's wonderful news, of course. But what are the implications, now that we know what it is?'

David had been thinking about that very question on his way to the church. 'Well, of course it will make the sale more difficult,' he admitted. 'For starters, the Diocesan Advisory Committee might not want you to sell it – they could quite legitimately claim that it's a unique treasure, and should stay here at St Margaret's. If the DAC throw up any obstacles, it will probably go to Consistory Court, and that will take time, and cost money – counsel will have to be briefed, and there will be other expenses. But at the end of the day, *if* you're allowed to sell it, you should have a small fortune on your hands.'

'Oh.' The Vicar stroked his chin. 'So it will take time, will it?'

'I'm afraid so.'

A significant look passed between the churchwardens. 'I think that we'd better discuss this between us before you take the matter any further,' Bairstow stated.

Everitt turned on him. 'But surely now that we know what it is, we can't just forget about it! It's unique and valuable – you heard what he said!' Wringing his hands, he pulled his normally lugubrious mouth into an approximation of a smile, revealing long teeth from which the gums had receded; this gave him an even stronger resemblance than usual to a skull. 'I don't know about you, but I think it's wonderful news!'

'What is the next step?' Father Keble Smythe put in. 'If we should decide to go ahead with the sale, that is.'

David lifted the thurible by its slender silver chains. 'In any case, whether you decide to go ahead or not, you should have it authenticated and valued. The V and A will do that for you, and they won't charge for it, but it will take a few weeks.'

'Do you have any doubt at all?' Everitt picked up the monstrance and held it protectively against his chest. 'I mean, is there a chance that they'll tell us that it's a later copy?'

'No.' David shook his head. 'I'm sure it's a very rare set of early Pugin silver. And in three or four weeks' time, that's what the V and A will tell you as well.'

The churchwardens exchanged another look. 'Then perhaps, Mr Middleton-Brown,' said Martin Bairstow, 'you would be so good as to see to that for us.'

'And I don't need to tell you all,' the Vicar added, 'that until this is settled, the matter is not to go any farther than these four walls. No one else needs to know.'

'What about the sacristan?' asked Everitt with an anxious look. 'Mr West will want to know where his silver has gone.'

'I'll deal with Mr West,' asserted the Vicar firmly. 'I'll talk to him tomorrow – leave it with me.'

Some time later, David walked home through the chill night, his hands in his pockets for warmth. It was very strange, he reflected, that the churchwardens, who had been so keen to sell the silver when they thought it was worth a relative pittance, now seemed reluctant to pursue the sale when it could bring them a very large windfall. He didn't deceive himself that they had any attachment to the silver itself – as he would have done – either for its intrinsic value, its historic interest, or its beauty. Even the Vicar had seemed subdued in the face of what David thought of as good news of the best possible sort. Only the Parish Administrator had seemed as overjoyed as he would have expected them all to be. It was most puzzling.

He wondered what Lucy, with her shrewd insights into people and their motivations, would make of it. In spite of the Vicar's injunction, he knew that he would discuss it with her: after all, she already knew what he'd discovered about the silver, so what was the point of keeping quiet about it now? And he knew that he could trust absolutely in Lucy's discretion.

The other question that fascinated him was that of the silver's origins. How had it come into the possession of St Margaret's in the first place? Who had commissioned it? And why had no one discovered it before? From what he had read, he thought he could make a fairly good guess. At the time St Margaret's Church was built, in the mid-nineteenth century, Pugin had been considered a dangerously popish designer. If an early benefactor – perhaps the first Vicar – had commissioned a set of Pugin silver for the new church, it surely would have been sailing close to the wind. No one would have publicised it; on the contrary, it would have been considered so naughty that its existence would have been kept as quiet as possible, and within a few years its origins might have been completely forgotten. It could very easily have happened that way, David realised.

Tomorrow he would collect the silver from the church safe, and deliver it to the V & A. For tonight, all he could do was talk about it with Lucy. She would have waited up for him, he knew, so it was with confident expectation and anticipation of a warm house, a warm bed, and an even warmer Lucy that he walked a little faster towards home.

Norman Topping's feet did not bear him quite so eagerly towards his house, not far from St Margaret's. He and Martin Bairstow had retired to the pub to discuss the latest development, and hadn't left till closing time, so he looked rather anxiously at his watch as he fumbled for his key and let himself into the house. He'd told Dolly that he wouldn't be more than half an hour – she wouldn't be pleased.

The house was in darkness, and she hadn't even left a light on for him. Holding his breath, Norman crept up the stairs and into the bedroom; perhaps Dolly would be asleep, and the moment of reckoning could be postponed until morning.

But as soon as he entered the room, Dolly sat up and snapped on the lamp on the table between the twin beds. Her appearance at night was even more terrifying than Lucy's daytime experience of her: her hair was wound around pink foam rollers, and covered with a loosely woven hairnet, and her face glistened with night-time potions meant to keep wrinkles at bay. 'Well?' she said; the word was invested with as much weight, as much meaning, as it was possible to squeeze into a single syllable.

'I'm really sorry, Dolly.' The coaxing propitiation of his tone didn't carry much conviction. From experience he knew that Dolly's wrath was as unpleasantly inevitable as a head cold, once the scratchy throat had manifested itself.

'You said you wouldn't be long!'

'It was important.' In a flash of inspiration he saw how he might distract her, deflect her ire away from himself and on to her pet hobby-horse. 'Because of the woman curate, you know. I told you about Martin's plan to sell the silver.'

Dolly's fleshy jaws quivered. 'And a good plan it is, too. It's just as well that there are people who aren't prepared to stand round and see the True Church delivered over into the hands of those heretics and their female so-called priests, lock, stock, and barrel. Thank God we've got *one* churchwarden with some sense!'

Norman bowed his head meekly at the implied criticism; now was not the time to defend himself.

But in a moment she was on the offensive again. 'So what does that have to do with this evening? I thought that you had that solicitor chap all set up, and that he told you the silver should fetch a good price. What's happened?'

'Well, now he says that the silver is much more valuable than he thought. I didn't really follow the whole thing, but what it boils down to is that it might be difficult to sell it – the diocese might object – and it will take longer than we'd thought. Martin and I had to talk it over afterwards, to decide what we're going to do.'

'Hm.' Dolly narrowed her eyes, short-sighted without her spectacles. 'And what did *Martin* decide?'

'That we should wait a while and see what happens. The solicitor is going to take the stuff to the V and A to see what they say about it.'

'And in the meantime,' muttered Dolly fiercely, pulling the bedclothes around her, 'we shall have that woman foisted on us. I never thought I would live to see such an outrage in my church!'

CHAPTER 7

Thy wife shall be as the fruitful vine: upon the walls of thine house.
Psalm 128.3

On the following morning, Thursday, David arrived at St Margaret's at the prearranged time to collect the silver. To his surprise, though, he was met not by the Vicar as he had expected, but by the sacristan. On their previous encounter the man had been wearing a cassock; today he was much more colourfully arrayed in a gaudy multi-hued jumper, adorned with a discreet enamelled pink triangle.

The expression on Robin West's ugly, frog-like face changed instantly from a sulk to a smile as he saw David. 'Oh, it's you, is it? *Quelle surprise!* The Vicar said that someone would be calling to collect the silver, but he didn't tell me that it was going to be *you*.'

David cringed inwardly, but managed to retain his outward composure. 'Yes. I hope I haven't caused you too much trouble.'

'Not at all. Not at all.' He turned and led the way to the sacristy. 'Though I wouldn't admit that to the Vicar. He expects too much of me, you know. Takes me for granted. Thinks I should be here at the drop of a hat. And he wouldn't even tell me what you're going to do with the silver.' Reaching the sacristy door, he swivelled and gave David an expectant look, tacitly inviting enlightenment on the subject.

'I'm afraid I can't really discuss that.'

The sacristan shrugged. 'Never mind. Not your fault, I'm sure.' He inserted the heavy key into the lock. 'Very hush-hush, it must be. Can't you even tell me what line of work you're in? Are you a silversmith, or an insurance valuer? Or does it have something to do with the robbery? Surely you're not a copper!'

'Oh, no. I'm a solicitor,' David admitted, somewhat reluctantly.

'A solicitor!' Robin West paused and looked David up and down. 'Curiouser and curiouser!'

'I really can't say more than that.'

'Yes, I know all about you legal types. The soul of discretion, I'm sure.' The sacristan tapped him on the arm with the safe key and favoured him with a broad wink.

David was relieved as the man turned to the safe and began fiddling with the lock, but the stream of speculation and conjecture never faltered. 'I can't imagine what a solicitor would be doing with the silver. Very interesting. There are of course other reasons why the churchwardens might employ you – to issue writs, if that's how you say it, to prevent the Vicar from bringing that woman in to this church. Now that *would* be useful.'

'Woman?' David wasn't really following the train of thought. 'You mean his fiancée, Miss McKenzie?'

'Fiancée!' Robin West snorted in derision. 'Fiancée, I'm sure! No, I mean the so-called curate – you've heard about her, haven't you?'

'Oh, yes, of course.'

'Not that I accept the validity of her orders, of course.' The sacristan swung the heavy safe door open. 'Not even her deacon's orders. Women have no place in the Sanctuary. The very thought is a sacrilege.'

'There seem to be quite a few people at St Margaret's who agree with you about that.'

'I should think so! This is a proper *Catholic* parish, always has been!' His voice had lost its customary languor as he went on, 'I can't imagine what Father was thinking of when he agreed to her appointment! He must have known that heads would roll, that people wouldn't just sit in the pews and accept it!'

David frowned. 'But what can people do? Apart from leaving St Margaret's in protest, and finding another church? I mean, people may not like it, but . . .'

'Humph.' The sacristan reached into the safe and brought out a candlestick. 'I can think of a few people who would rather see that woman dead than at the altar of St Margaret's. I, for one, will not serve in the Sanctuary, or even enter it, if *she* is there.' He nodded resolutely, as though that settled the matter. 'Here – is this what you want? You'll have to tell me which pieces you're taking.'

Helping David to carry the silver to his car, Robin West continued his litany of grievances. 'I don't know how we're meant to manage without the thurible or the monstrance. Or the processional cross, for that matter. Will you have them back by the weekend? By Sunday morning?'

'I'm afraid not. It may be several weeks, in fact.'

'Then what does Father expect us to do? Though Lent will be upon us soon, and we don't have incense during Lent, so the thurible won't be so critical.'

'Perhaps you can borrow some pieces from St Jude's,' David suggested. 'I think that's probably what the Vicar has in mind.'

If he'd been wearing a cassock, Robin West would have twitched his skirts. 'Oh, I'm sure *you* know more about that than I do. After all, I'm only the sacristan,' he said cuttingly.

Having stowed the silver with great care in the boot, David was anxious to get it to the V & A before anything happened. He faced Robin West with an awkward smile. 'Well, thank you very much for your help. I won't keep you any longer.'

The sacristan waved a dismissive hand. 'Oh, that's all right. I don't have to be at work for a while yet.'

David's curiosity got the better of him. 'What sort of work do you do, Mr West?'

'Please, call me Robin,' he smirked, then explained, 'I manage a restaurant. A bistro, really. In South Ken.' With a flourish he produced a card from his pocket and handed it to David. 'As you see. *La Reine Dorée.* Lunches and dinners, seven days a week. Why don't you call in for a drink one day? On the house, of course.'

Framing his answer carefully, David replied, 'Thank you very much. Perhaps I'll come in for a meal with my . . . um, girlfriend.' He realised that the word sounded faintly ridiculous coming from a man of his age, but the important thing was to establish the gender of the person involved; a more accurate term such as 'partner' could be dangerously ambiguous, and he wanted Robin West left in no doubt.

The sacristan took it well, with the equanimity of one who was used to rejection. 'Yes, of course,' he shrugged. 'But don't feel that you have to bring her if you don't want to,' he added with a grin, reaching out a hand to touch David's sleeve.

'Oh, there's the Vicar,' David said quickly.

Robin West's head swivelled to the direction David was looking, and at the same moment Father Keble Smythe saw them. He was leading a small, fair woman towards the church, gesticulating and talking, but when he spotted the two men at the kerb he changed course and started in their direction, saying something to the woman as they approached.

'It's *her*,' the sacristan hissed. 'He's actually had the nerve to bring that woman here! If he thinks I'm going to stand round and be civil to her, he's got another think coming!' And with that announcement he disappeared in the opposite direction.

In his astonishment, David had time for little more than a quick impression of the woman before they reached him. The dog collar on her light blue blouse confirmed her identity as the hated and feared Rachel Nightingale, but she wasn't what he'd expected. In the split second that he had to think about it, David realised that he wasn't sure *what* he'd been expecting her to look like – large and looming and hirsute, with feminist slogans tattooed on her forearms, or vampish and red-fingernailed? – but certainly not this. Rachel Nightingale was so slight that she seemed scarcely more than a child, though David knew that she must be approaching thirty-five. Her fine fair hair curled loosely around a china-doll face, a face without real beauty but possessed of character and great sweetness. With a small shock he recognised what it was that gave her face such character: a long, thin scar bisected her rosy cheek, running from the outside corner of her left eyebrow to her chin, the legacy and continual reminder of the accident that had robbed her of her husband and child.

'This is Mr Middleton-Brown, who is doing some legal work for us,' the Vicar told her, looking perplexedly in the direction in which his sacristan had disappeared.

She extended her small hand for a surprisingly firm handshake. 'Hello.' She smiled up at David, and her smile was friendly without being in the least bit coy. 'I'm Rachel Nightingale, the new curate.'

The Venerable Gabriel Neville, Archdeacon of Kensington, sat at his desk that Thursday morning, frowning at the telephone. A moment earlier he'd needed to place a call, but when he'd picked up the receiver he had realised that his wife was on the kitchen extension. Impatiently he tapped his pen on the foolscap sheet on which he was drafting some notes for a series of Lenten addresses which he had been asked to deliver at a prestigious Knightsbridge church. They hadn't made it clear whether there would be six addresses or seven, and he needed to know.

Gabriel Neville, at forty-one, was young for an archdeacon. He was also far better-looking than the average archdeacon, tall and slender with arresting sapphire-blue eyes and a full head of rich auburn hair. His blessings didn't stop with the purely physical, either: Gabriel was accomplished as a preacher, intellectually gifted, and possessed of a wife who adored him and who had borne him two – on the whole – delightful children. He had risen to his present eminent position largely due to his superior abilities and on the strength of his conscientious performance during ten years as the Vicar of St Anne's Church, Kensington Gardens, from which he had been promoted something over a year previously. In his more analytical moments, Gabriel realised that his wife, so very suitable, and his well-behaved and attractive children had done him no harm either when it came to promotion: a family man always makes a good impression on the powers-that-be.

At the moment, however, he was feeling slightly fed up with the demands of family life. He and Emily had argued at breakfast – though perhaps argument was too strong a word for the ongoing disagreement, or rather non-agreement, which had punctuated their life of late. Emily had mentioned that the twins were begging for a dog, and she was inclined to agree with them. At eight, she said, they were old enough to assume the responsibility for a pet. 'But what will happen when they go off to boarding school next year?' he'd asked. 'Who will look after the dog then?' Emily had been tearful, but stubborn as usual: no boarding school, she'd said. Why was it necessary to send their children away, when there were perfectly good schools in London, and when they could have places at the cathedral school? She didn't seem to understand that the Nevilles had a long tradition of Eton for boys and Cheltenham for girls; he'd put Sebastian and Viola's names down as soon as they were born. As far as Gabriel was concerned, it wasn't even an issue.

Now he sighed, looking at the telephone. Chatting on the phone, probably with Lucy Kingsley, on a morning when she knew that he had important calls to make. There were days when he entertained the fleeting notion that it would have been preferable to have remained a bachelor.

A moment later, however, Emily tapped on his study door and came in with a tray of coffee and biscuits for his mid-morning sustenance. 'I thought you'd be about ready for this,' she said.

Gabriel gave her a perfunctory smile. 'Thanks.'

Sensing his irritation, she hesitated by the door. 'Is everything all right?'

'Who were you talking to on the phone?' he replied elliptically.

It was Emily's turn to sigh. 'Dolly Topping.'

He made an involuntary face. 'Dreadful woman. Why ever were you talking to her? Didn't you talk to her yesterday, at that awful women's meeting?'

'It would be more accurate to say that *she* was talking to *me*,' Emily corrected him. 'On both occasions.'

'About the horrors of having a woman curate, no doubt.' Gabriel raised his eyebrows cynically. 'Foisted on them by some evil diocesan functionary like a bishop or even an archdeacon.'

Emily gave a dry laugh. 'The subject did come up, I believe. But that wasn't why she rang me this morning, as a matter of fact.'

Taking a sip of his coffee, he looked at her enquiringly. 'Yes?'

'It was something to do with the silver at St Margaret's,' she amplified. 'I didn't follow it very well, but apparently the churchwardens are hoping to sell some of the church silver, and they've just found out that it's very valuable.'

'Valuable?'

'Apparently so. Worth over a hundred thousand pounds, Norman told her.'

Gabriel frowned. 'They can't just sell it, you know. They'll have to apply for a faculty, and I'm not so sure they'll get it.' He put his coffee cup down with a decisive thump. 'Why haven't I been informed about this?'

Shrugging, Emily interpreted the latter as a rhetorical question. 'I thought you might be interested.'

As she slipped out of the door, Gabriel flashed her a genuine smile of gratitude. Wives could be very useful sometimes, he reflected wryly, finishing his coffee. But whatever were those churchwardens up to? The Venerable Gabriel Neville, Archdeacon of Kensington, resolved to find out.

CHAPTER 8

I have considered the days of old: and the years that are past.

Psalm 77.5

The voice on the loud-speaker was as muffled and incomprehensible as always, though in these days of customer service the announcements of delayed or cancelled trains were no longer stated baldly, but were couched in terms of feigned regret. 'We apologise for [crackle, spit, mumble, crackle],' David heard as he waited on the northbound Piccadilly line platform at the South Kensington tube station. He sighed; from experience he was able to decipher the garble, and the bottom line was that he would be late for work.

'Mr Middleton-Brown?' ventured a tentative voice.

David turned to see Stanley Everitt beside him on the platform. 'Oh, hello.'

'Did you understand what they said?' In his right hand he clutched a carrier bag; with his left he gestured vaguely into the air.

David's laugh was without humour. 'The usual. Security alert – that's London Transport-speak for yet another IRA bomb threat – at Gloucester Road has caused unavoidable delays to northbound service on the Piccadilly Line. They apologise for any inconvenience, rhubarb, rhubarb.' He looked up at the moving light display, which merely announced that no smoking was permitted on the London Underground. 'They're not even listing the next train. It could be a long wait.'

'Oh, dear.' Everitt tucked his carrier bag under his arm to facilitate his characteristic, if unconscious, hand-wringing. 'Did you know that there's been a bomb at Victoria Station this morning? I went there first, and it's all cordoned off, so I came here instead.'

In just a few months of living in London, David had become accustomed to such things. 'Was it serious, do you know?'

Everitt's voice dropped to a lugubrious whisper. 'I heard that one or possibly two people had been killed. Terrible.'

'Dreadful,' David agreed automatically. His mind was occupied with wishing that the train would come, to deliver him from this tiresome man. His contact with Everitt had been slight, but the man, with his nervous mannerisms, his peevish negativism and his cadaverous appearance, made him uncomfortable. In fact, he realised, the feelings elicited by the Administrator were rather similar to those he felt in the presence of the sacristan, albeit for completely different reasons.

'Do you take this line every day?' Everitt asked after a moment.

'Yes. My office is in the City. Lincoln's Inn.'

'I'm very lucky, really – I can walk to work. St Jude's is just round the corner from where I live, and St Margaret's isn't far at all. Of course I only go there one day a week, generally. That's all it really requires to keep things ticking over there. St Margaret's used to be a much more active parish, of course, in the old days. Very high, it's always been, but that sort of thing used to be more popular than it is now. Father Keble Smythe is a proper Catholic, of course, but he knows when to trim his sails. St Jude's requires a much more moderate approach. I've always preferred St Margaret's, myself.'

David gazed at the display, willing it to flash up the next train. 'I met your new curate yesterday,' he said, without thinking.

At least it stemmed the flow of self-important stream-of-consciousness; Stanley Everitt sucked in his breath, looking as though he'd just bitten into a lemon. 'Her.'

'You've met her?'

'Yes, of course. As the Administrator I was one of the first to meet her, naturally.'

'She seems very nice,' David stated, aware that he wasn't making himself very popular.

'Oh, I have nothing against her *personally*.' Everitt raised a hand to smooth the strands of hair across the crown of his head. 'I just don't understand what the Church is about, going against two thousand years of tradition. When there are so many qualified *men* who'd like to be ordained,' he added with a significant nod.

In an instant, David understood; Everitt's objections were not so much theological as the result of hurt pride and thwarted ambition. 'You'd like to be ordained?' he hazarded.

'Well, yes,' admitted the Administrator with some reluctance. 'I have put myself forward for ordination. I do feel that I have a real call to the priesthood, a true vocation. With my administrative skills, and my interest in all things spiritual . . . Well.'

'What happened?'

The sour-lemon expression intensified. 'I was turned down by the Board of Ministry. Three times. It's all right for *some*,' he added in a burst of bitterness. 'The first batch of women – just because they're women, they don't have to go to a selection conference. Different rules apply. It's just not fair.'

With relief, David saw on the display that the next train would be arriving in two minutes. It was bound to be crowded; perhaps he'd be able to lose Stanley Everitt and be spared travelling into the City with him. 'Ah. Our train should be here soon,' he declared.

The call from Martin Bairstow came later that morning, when David had barely had a chance to catch up with his post and to deal with the inevitable consequences of his lateness by rescheduling a few missed appointments. 'The Archdeacon wants to see us,' Bairstow announced. 'This afternoon.'

His heart – or was it his stomach? – gave a quite unexpected lurch. 'The Archdeacon? But why?'

Bairstow sounded distinctly unamused. 'He's got the wind up. Someone has told him about the silver – that we want to sell it, and that it's probably worth a lot of money.'

'Who would have told him?'

'He wouldn't say, and I can't imagine who would have done it, after the Vicar specifically mentioned that we should keep it to ourselves for the time being. But he had his facts right, and I couldn't very well deny it.'

David's first guilty thought, quickly dismissed, was that Lucy might have told Emily; he digested the information in silence for a moment. 'He's asked for a meeting, you say?'

'Yes. He wants the churchwardens to come and see him this afternoon, at three.'

'Me, as well?'

'I told him that we'd be bringing our solicitor.'

'Are you sure that you wouldn't do just as well without me?' David asked faintly.

'Nonsense,' was the robust reply. 'Bringing our solicitor along will show him that we can't be intimidated, that we mean business.'

'But . . .'

'I'll come to your office to collect you at half-past two,' Bairstow stated in a tone that would brook no argument, a tone that he had often used to great effect in his business dealings. 'See you then.'

David put the phone down.

The Archdeacon. Gabe.

This afternoon.

He looked at his desk diary for the afternoon's entries: only one appointment, at half-past three, for a consultation about revising a will.

Gabe.

He went out to find his secretary. 'Would you mind ringing Wing Commander Fitzjames and rescheduling him for next week? Something important has just come up.'

Mrs Simmons looked disapproving, but nodded and reached for the phone.

David returned to his desk and picked up the pad on which he was drafting a complicated brief; several times he read over what he had written, but the words didn't register.

Gabe. This afternoon. In just a few hours.

He wasn't sure that he was ready to see Gabe again. He hadn't seen him for over a year, not since before Gabe had become Archdeacon. They had parted on good terms, as friends, with their painful misunderstandings laid to rest, but they hadn't met again. David was convinced that his feelings about Gabe had been resolved – of course they had: Lucy was all that mattered to him now – but he still wasn't sure that he wanted to see him, to stir up what was for him a closed chapter of his life.

There had been occasional opportunities to see Gabe over the last year and a half, at various social occasions, but he had always managed to find some reason to avoid him. He told himself that it was out of consideration for Lucy's feelings. After all, she had never liked Gabriel Neville much, even when he was no more than the husband of her best friend. She'd been upset when David had confessed to her the history of his relationship with Gabe, which had ended suddenly and painfully almost twelve years ago when Gabe had disappeared from his life and then married Emily. Lucy's reactions had been complex, dominated by indignation at Gabriel's heartless behaviour, whatever its justification, and by compassion for David's suffering. David and Lucy hadn't really talked about it since, both of them preferring to put it behind them and to get on with building their own relationship; but by unspoken consent they had avoided social contact with the Nevilles. Lucy continued to see Emily, if somewhat less frequently than before, and her affection for her was unchanged, but she had no desire to see Gabriel.

Neither, David realised now, did he. There was Lucy and her feelings to consider, yes, but was he also afraid of his own reactions? Was he afraid that all those years of love could not so easily be dismissed, and that seeing Gabe again would bring it all back? In spite of Lucy, and in spite of his love for her? It was unthinkable, and yet it had to be faced. How would he feel, when he saw Gabe again this afternoon?

At least David knew what was coming; Gabriel hadn't the least warning of the encounter. Before either of the churchwardens had a chance to make introductions, Gabriel blurted out, 'David!'

'Oh, you've met, have you?' Martin Bairstow surmised, raising his eyebrows.

David had the advantage, but still it was perhaps surprising, given their respective characters, that he was the one who replied first. 'Yes, the Archdeacon and I go back a long way,' he said with an easy smile, stretching out his hand. 'How are you, Gabriel?'

Gabriel was grateful; it gave him an instant to regain his composure. He shook the proffered hand. 'Very well, thank you. And you?'

'Never better.'

It was true: David had never looked better, Gabriel realised with a small pang. The happiness he'd obviously found with Lucy had given him an air of contentment that became him well; the puffiness under his eyes that Gabriel remembered from their last meeting had subsided, leaving only the attractive laugh-lines at their corners, and he looked as fit and healthy as a well-fed cat.

David, returning his scrutiny, marvelled that he could do so without the least trace of self-consciousness. It was so strange, he thought in the split second as their eyes met. Once not so long ago Gabriel's very presence had had the power to reduce him to a quivering jelly. Now he saw him merely as a good-looking man, much like any other good-looking man who was past the bloom of youth. What a relief it was. 'How are Emily and the children?' he enquired calmly.

'Oh, they're fine.' Gabriel hesitated for a fraction of a second. 'And how is Lucy?'

David's smile lit his whole face. 'She's wonderful.'

And that was all. It had taken no more than a few seconds altogether, yet they both knew that the balance of power in their relationship had been altered for ever.

Gabriel turned to the churchwardens. 'Now, gentlemen. What is this that I hear about some silver?'

CHAPTER 9

O what great troubles and adversities hast thou shewed me! and yet didst thou turn and refresh me: yea, and broughtest me from the deep of the earth again.
Psalm 71.18

Rachel Nightingale wheeled her bicycle into the entrance hall, tucked it into a corner, and locked it just for good measure; in Cambridge she'd lost more than one bicycle by placing too much faith in the basic honesty of humankind. Then she let herself into her ground-floor flat and peeled off her coat and gloves as she headed towards the kitchen to put the kettle on.

It was still quite early on a chill Thursday morning in February, a morning on which it had taken more than the usual amount of discipline and determination to get her out of bed in the dark and launch her forth on her bicycle into the damp fog. But she'd never yet missed a morning of visiting Colin. She liked to be there early, when he woke up. Or rather when he would have woken – such terms denoting changes in state, or indeed indicating consciousness of any kind, were no longer applicable to Colin; he was in what the doctors called 'PVS', or persistent vegetative state, his bed surrounded by complicated monitors. But morning after morning Rachel ignored the medical paraphernalia and concentrated instead on the man in the bed. Invariably she sat by his side for half an hour, reading to him quietly from a scientific journal or a favourite novel, her voice low-pitched and soothing. When the half-hour was up, and the nurses began hovering about, anxious to get on with their day's routine, she would stroke his face, tell him that she loved him, and promise that she would return in the evening.

She spent up to an hour with him each evening, during which she would tell him about her day, describing all of the new people she had met. Rachel had a gift for mimicry; often, in the old days, she had made Colin roar with laughter at her spot-on impression of a fellow don, a difficult student or a well-known Cambridge eccentric. Now she included comical descriptions of her new parishioners in her monologue, believing that Colin would find them all very amusing.

The nurses told her that she was wasting her time, and wasting her breath: that Colin didn't know she was there, couldn't possibly understand her, and probably couldn't even hear her. But morning after morning and night after night she went, still trusting in spite of everything in the power of love to reach him somehow, perhaps in some manner or through some dimension that was known only to God.

Waiting for the kettle to boil, Rachel rubbed her hands together to warm them. Cycling in this weather wasn't very pleasant; though the exercise itself engendered enough heat to keep a well-clad body moderately warm, the hands and the face invariably suffered. Cycling had become a way of life for Rachel: since the accident, she had been unable to bring herself to get in a car again. Most of the time she didn't mind, but on this raw morning she was really looking forward to a cup of tea, hot and strong.

She turned on the hot-water tap and rinsed out the teapot, looking out of the window into the still-wintry garden. There had been a ground frost the night before, and the few brave daffodils which had poked swollen green heads through the grass were rimed with white. In the summer the garden would be pleasant, Rachel reflected.

She'd only been in the flat in Pimlico for about a week. She'd been lucky to find it: it was spacious and well-kept, and though it wasn't as near to Colin as she would have liked, its location mid-way between St Jude's and St Margaret's churches made it most convenient for her work. The previous curate had, she understood, lived in a house in St Margaret's parish that was owned by the church, but the churchwardens had made it clear to Rachel that the house was no longer available, and she would have to find herself a place to live. This she had done, and had moved in the week before. Already she was establishing a routine for herself: Colin first, and early Mass at St Jude's on the way home. A quick cup of tea, and perhaps a bite to eat, before a full day of parish duties. Then a simple supper – she knew that she was too thin, that she didn't eat enough, but it just wasn't a priority – and up to an hour with Colin at the end of the day. Sometimes, she knew, it would be necessary to attend parish meetings or carry out other responsibilities in the evenings, in which case she would have a shorter time with Colin. But she would never fail to go to him, even if she could spend but a few minutes at his bedside.

So far she was finding her parish work interesting. The people at St Jude's had welcomed her with a fair degree of warmth, and had made her feel that her work there was valued. St Margaret's was a different story, of course. It was ironic, she reflected: the Anglo-Catholic churchmanship at St Margaret's was actually much more to her taste than the middle-of-the-road blandness of St Jude's. Though her faith, reached through intense suffering and adversity, was deep and personal, she enjoyed the ceremonial of Anglo-Catholic liturgy and found that the appeal to the senses – incense, vestments, music – enhanced her ability to worship. It was a great shame that the people at St Margaret's seemed unable to accept her at face value, and to recognise the validity of her feeling of vocation.

Even within St Margaret's, though, she had met with a variety of reactions. Most of the parishioners were guardedly polite, in a typically English sort of way. She was learning early on which ones to avoid – though in some cases that was scarcely necessary. The sacristan, Robin West, disappeared in the opposite direction whenever he saw her coming, refusing even to speak to her, and there were a few others who behaved similarly. The churchwardens didn't have the luxury of avoiding her. Martin Bairstow treated her curtly, looking down on her from his superior height as though she were some lower life-form or perhaps a visitor from another planet. His wife, Rachel sensed, was in fact quite kindly disposed towards her; in their limited contact Vanessa Bairstow had been friendly, her manner inviting closer acquaintance. Norman Topping, too, seemed much less hostile than Rachel would have expected. On Tuesday evening at the Shrove Tuesday pancake supper, her first real introduction to parish life at St Margaret's, she had caught him more than once looking at her with something approaching a smile, and at one point she could have sworn that he winked at her.

The only person to treat her with blatant and deliberate rudeness was Dolly Topping. Rachel supposed that she shouldn't be surprised, given what she knew about Mrs Topping and her views on women clergy, but it hurt nonetheless. Her attempt at friendly conversation had been rebuffed; loudly, for all to hear, Dolly had made it clear that as far as she was concerned, Rachel was the worst thing that had happened to St Margaret's in its long history, and that once she was ordained a priest (or a 'so-called priest'), Dolly would no longer be able to worship in the church that she had loved for so many years. 'I don't know what you women are trying to prove,' she declared, 'but I hope you can live with the destruction of the Universal Church on your conscience!'

It made all the more curious the phone call which Rachel had received the previous morning, the day after the pancake supper. A tentative female voice had identified itself as belonging to Nicola Topping, and had requested a meeting at Rachel's earliest convenience.

Rachel had a vague memory of a rather large girl hovering somewhere in the background on Shrove Tuesday. 'I'm afraid today's not much good,' she had apologised. 'Ash Wednesday, you know. Father Keble Smythe has asked me to be at all the services, to assist with the ashings. How about tomorrow?'

They had agreed on a time on Thursday afternoon, after school. 'Would you like to come to my flat?' Rachel had suggested.

'Oh, yes, please. I couldn't possibly ask you to come to my house,' the girl had replied. 'I'm sure you understand.'

Now, sipping her tea at the kitchen table, Rachel wondered what Nicola Topping might want with her. At any rate, her curiosity would soon be satisfied – after a morning of calls on elderly parishioners, and lunch with her old friend from Cambridge, Emily Neville.

Her first call was on Walter Bright, a retired doctor who was recovering from a mild bout of the flu. Dr Bright hadn't felt well enough to make it to any of the Ash Wednesday services at St Margaret's, and had requested that the Sacrament be brought to him. Rachel hoped that he wouldn't mind receiving it from the hands of a woman.

Father Keble Smythe hadn't told her much about Dr Bright, other than that he had been in general practice in the area for many years, and that he was universally beloved in the community and in the parish. 'He's a splendid old chap, Dr Bright,' he'd said. 'A great character. His heyday was well before my time, of course, but there are still many people in the parish who were brought into the world by Dr Bright, or were looked after by him for much of their lives. He's a real institution in the parish, is Dr Bright.'

The door of the double-fronted house was opened by a small, spare woman with faded gingery-grey hair and a face etched deeply with lines of resignation. She was wearing a cotton housecoat and an apron; from her age, which she surmised to be around seventy, Rachel assumed that she was Dr Bright's wife, though she could possibly be his housekeeper. 'Mrs Bright?' she asked tentatively.

'*Miss* Bright, actually,' said the woman, taking in the dog collar and stepping aside for Rachel to enter. 'Vera Bright. I'm Dr Bright's daughter. And you must be the new curate.'

'Yes, I'm Rachel Nightingale. It's so nice to meet you, Miss Bright.' If this is his daughter, she thought, how old must Dr Bright be?

'My father is in the drawing room. It's so kind of you to come – he was very distressed to miss Mass yesterday. But this flu has left him rather weak – he's usually as strong as a horse, my father, but he *is* ninety-six.'

Ninety-six! thought Rachel. Born in the last century, when Queen Victoria was on the throne.

Walter Bright, dressed nattily in a tweed suit and club tie, rose to his feet without any evident effort when the two women entered the room. He was a short, wiry man, rather bird-like in appearance, with a beaky nose under small dark eyes and a round head covered with sparse downy hair. Putting his head to one side, he regarded Rachel with a welcoming grin. 'So! The Vicar has sent me his new curate instead of coming himself!'

'I'm sorry that Father Keble Smythe couldn't come,' Rachel began apologetically.

'Not at all! You're much better looking than he is, my dear. At least to my old eyes,' he twinkled. 'Come closer and let me see you.'

She moved up to him and took his hand. 'I'm Rachel Nightingale.'

'Is that Miss or Mrs? And what am I to call you, may I ask? I can't very well call you "Father", can I?'

'It's "Mrs",' she replied, keeping her voice steady as a momentary vision of Colin flashed through her mind. 'And you may call me Rachel, if you like. You don't have any objection to receiving the Sacrament from a woman?'

'Not if she's as pretty as you are, my dear,' he said with a wink. But his eyes were shrewd as he went on, 'Seriously, I don't see that it makes the slightest difference. I know there are some people at St Margaret's who get hot and bothered about it all, but I don't imagine that God cares.'

'In Christ there is no male or female,' Rachel quoted, smiling.

'Exactly.' Dr Bright sat down and addressed his daughter, who was still standing near the door, for the first time. 'Vera, why don't you go and put the kettle on? I'm sure that Rachel would like a cup of coffee, once she's given me the Sacrament.'

Rachel turned to see the other woman's hesitation. 'Perhaps you'd like the Sacrament as well?' she suggested. 'Or were you able to make it to church yesterday?'

'No, I didn't make it to church. I can't possibly leave Father when he's poorly,' Vera said. She shot her father an unreadable look. 'And I'd very much like to have the Sacrament, if you don't mind.'

'Well, come on then, girl,' Dr Bright ordered. 'Let's get this business over with first. Then you can make the coffee.'

On her long cycle ride to the Archdeacon's house, Rachel had time to think about the visits she'd paid that morning. There had been three of them altogether, but of all her jumbled impressions she found that it was Vera Bright to whom her thoughts returned again and again.

Vera had escorted her to the door. 'Thank you so much for coming,' she'd said.

Impulsively, Rachel had taken her hand. 'It was my pleasure, meeting you and your father. If there's any way I can ever be of help, please don't hesitate to let me know.'

Her sincerity must have communicated itself; for just an instant there had been such a look of yearning and hope on Vera Bright's face that Rachel had been taken aback. But then the shutters had come down again, leaving the customary lines of resignation firmly in control of her expression. The memory of that momentary slip haunted Rachel: she wondered how she could reach Vera, how she might help her. She resolved to try to meet with her alone at the earliest opportunity.

With anticipation she wheeled her bicycle up the drive to the impressive-looking stone dwelling that served as the Archdeacon's residence. She'd known Emily Neville – at that time she'd been Emily Bates – fairly well at Cambridge and had always appreciated her intelligence and her straightforward approach to life. Now she looked forward to renewing the acquaintance; it would be nice to have a female friend in London, especially one who had known Colin in happier days.

'Rachel! You can put your bike here around the corner if you like.' Emily came out of the house and embraced her with affection. 'Are you hungry?'

'Starved. Cycling this far really helps build up an appetite. Though,' she added, smiling, 'I'm fairly awash with tea and coffee – I've just done three pastoral visits.' She locked the bike and followed Emily into the house.

Emily laughed. 'Gabriel always says that's one of the clergy's greatest occupational hazards. You can't very well refuse when it's offered, can you?'

'No, though sometimes it's difficult to work up a proper semblance of enthusiasm for yet another cup of instant coffee or stewed tea. But offering and accepting hospitality is a great ice-breaker sometimes,' she added seriously.

'You must be freezing, as well. Come on into the kitchen – it's warm in there,' Emily invited.

The kitchen was indeed warm, courtesy of the Aga. It was also brightly lit and cheery, with a red quarry-tiled floor, blue and white tiles on the wall, and gleaming white worktops and kitchen units. The table was set invitingly with blue-and-white crockery, and delicious smells wafted from the Aga; another woman rose from the table as they entered.

Emily performed the introductions. 'Rachel, this is my friend Lucy Kingsley. Lucy, this is Rachel Nightingale, the new curate at St Jude's and St Margaret's. Gabriel is out today, so it will just be us women for lunch.'

They liked each other instantly, instinctively; by the time the food was dished up they were chatting away like old friends.

'The garlic bread isn't quite warm enough,' Emily apologised, 'but I think we'll start anyway.'

'This looks wonderful, Emily,' Rachel said as a steaming plate of pasta with a savoury-smelling mushroom sauce was put in front of her. 'I don't seem to remember that cooking was one of your accomplishments in your digs at Cambridge.'

Emily made a face. 'Your memory serves you well. Beans on toast was my chief speciality in those days.'

'Em is an excellent cook,' Lucy asserted loyally.

'But only because you taught me,' Emily reminded her, then went on to explain to Rachel. 'Lucy saved my life after I married Gabriel. She taught me everything I know about cooking. We've been friends ever since.' Lifting a bottle of Frascati, she poised it invitingly over Rachel's glass. 'Wine?'

It was Rachel's turn to make a face. 'I'm afraid not. Lent.'

'Oh, you disciplined people!' Lucy laughed. 'I'm glad to say that I'm not that holy. Yes, please, Em. Some for me.'

'I'm not that holy, either,' Emily admitted. 'Much to Gabriel's horror, I don't have to tell you. I'm giving up chocolate instead.'

Lucy groaned. 'I think that would be even worse.'

'Gabriel always gives up alcohol *and* chocolate for Lent.'

'Yes, he would.' Lucy tried to keep her voice neutral, to mask the acid hostility she felt. She must not have been particularly successful, as Emily gave her an odd look and quickly changed the subject.

'Rachel, how are you settling in to your new job?' She filled Rachel's glass with mineral water.

'It's going pretty well, actually. The most difficult thing is learning so many new names and faces all at once. Everyone expects you to remember *them*, even if you forget everyone else.'

'And how is the Vicar?' Emily queried. 'Are you getting on well with him?'

Rachel chose her words carefully. 'Father Keble Smythe is very . . . agreeable. A very able man – his parishioners think the world of him. But he's quite busy, of course. He doesn't really have time to come around with me holding my hand. He gives me credit for being able and qualified to do the job, and has more or less let me get on with it. With some help from the Parish Administrator, of course.'

'Ah, yes,' Emily said. 'Mr Everitt.'

'Yes, Stanley Everitt.' Rachel gave them a conspiratorial grin. 'Within these four walls, I must admit that he's driving me completely round the twist. What a relief it is to be able to tell someone! I have to be so polite all the time.'

'What has he done?' Lucy wanted to know.

Rachel shook her head. 'Nothing, really. He's just so self-important. He never misses a chance to tell me how much the Vicar relies on him, and how everything at St Jude's and St Margaret's would grind to a complete halt without him and all of his hard work. He's as much as said that a curate – especially one who's only a deacon and can't celebrate the Mass – is really surplus to requirements with an Administrator like him around.'

'Oh, dear.' Emily, who had encountered her fair share of self-important people in the Church of England, was sympathetic.

'And he has these annoying mannerisms – he wrings his hands, just like Uriah Heep!'

'Are you sure he doesn't just patronise you because you're a woman?' Lucy asked shrewdly.

'Oh, no. He's like that with everyone.' With a deft motion of her wrist, Rachel twisted a strand of pasta around her fork and conveyed it to her mouth. 'I'll tell you who *does* patronise me because I'm a woman, though – Martin Bairstow, the churchwarden. He's very polite, but it's the sort of politeness that some people use with small children or the mentally deficient, as a thin veneer of civilisation over their contempt. It makes me uneasy. And it's strange,' she added, 'because all of the old women absolutely sing his praises. I've been to see three elderly parishioners this morning, and every one of them has told me how wonderful Martin Bairstow is, and how lucky his wife is to have such a gem for a husband.'

'I've heard that, too,' confirmed Emily. 'Apparently he gives them all lifts to church functions, and even goes round to their houses to do little odd jobs, the sort of thing that is difficult to get done without a man about the house.' Belatedly she realised that her last remark might be interpreted as insensitive, given Rachel's situation, so she hurried on. 'And what about the other churchwarden, Norman Topping?'

'He's all right,' admitted Rachel. 'It's his wife who's really rude to me.'

'Oh, Dolly.' Emily rolled her eyes.

Lucy groaned. 'That frightful woman.'

'You both know her?' They nodded. 'Then I don't have to explain.'

'Not at all,' confirmed Emily. 'And now, if the mention of Dolly Topping hasn't completely spoiled everyone's appetite, I think that the garlic bread is ready.'

It wasn't until they were drinking their coffee after lunch that Emily steeled herself to ask the question that she knew had to be asked. 'How is Colin?'

Rachel looked into her coffee cup. 'Oh, the same as he's been for some time. I visit him every morning and every evening. I talk to him and read to him, but there's no change – no indication that he knows I'm there.'

'I'm sorry, I didn't mean to . . .' Emily said awkwardly.

'No,' said Rachel, raising her hand to her scarred cheek in an unconscious, poignant gesture. 'You don't have to be afraid to mention him. He's not dead, you know.' After a moment she went on, 'It's so good to be able to talk about him. I don't, as a general rule – people are embarrassed about it, so I don't even mention him.'

Impulsively Emily leaned over and squeezed her hand. 'Well, you can talk about him to us any time you like. Can't she, Luce?'

'Any time,' echoed Lucy thoughtfully.

Rachel had scarcely had time to make herself a reviving mug of tea before the doorbell rang, heralding the arrival of Nicola Topping. 'Come in,' she greeted the girl who stood, ill at ease, at the front door. 'There's fresh tea in the pot. Would you like a cup?'

'Oh, yes, please, Miss . . . Mrs . . .' Nicola fumbled.

'Just call me Rachel. That will make things easier.'

Nicola followed her into the kitchen. The school uniform emphasised the girl's size, the white blouse straining across her enormous breasts. Clearly she had inherited her mother's large frame, but her face was unexpectedly pretty, especially when she smiled, which she was now doing in a nervous manner: her small, pearly teeth were flawless, and she had attractively dimpled cheeks. Her complexion was good for a girl of her age, and her long brown hair was thick and glossy.

'There's a tin of biscuits somewhere,' Rachel went on. 'Let me see if I can remember where I put it.'

'Oh, that's all right. I shouldn't really have biscuits.' Those were Nicola's words, but Rachel could read the ambivalent yearning in her voice. 'My mum would kill me if she knew I was eating biscuits.'

'Well, your mum isn't here,' Rachel stated, pulling the tin out of a cupboard. It was a commemorative Royal Wedding tin, Charles and Diana vintage, battered with age and usage. 'Hobnobs and chocolate digestives,' she analysed, peering inside. 'I thought there might be some shortbread, but I must have eaten it.'

As Rachel poured another mug of tea, Nicola pulled out a chair, sat down and shamefacedly helped herself to a chocolate digestive biscuit.

Rachel settled down across from her. 'I think it's cosier in here than in the lounge,' she said in a conversational tone, cupping her hands around her tea mug; she could sense the girl's nervousness and was trying to put her at ease by behaving as naturally as possible. 'But if you'd rather, we can go in there and put the gas fire on.'

'No, this is fine.' Nicola, having polished off her first biscuit, reached for another.

Rachel waited, sipping her tea. It would all come out eventually, she knew, but she wouldn't push her. If she were a sociologist, she thought with detachment while she was waiting, she'd investigate what you could tell about people based on what they chose to drink their tea and coffee from. Cups or mugs? Bone china or stoneware? Decorated with what? Coffee at the Brights' had come in serviceable brown stoneware mugs; Emily had provided the after-lunch coffee in blue and white cups of contemporary design but impeccable English manufacture. Lucy Kingsley, Rachel was sure, would serve tea in thin bone china cups, probably antique. Her own mugs were a thoroughly mixed lot, collected over a lifetime. The one she'd given Nicola was, by coincidence, a Royal Wedding one, the two names linked forever, indissolubly, on the mug as they no longer were in life; her own tea was in a Beatrix Potter mug that had been a particular favourite of Rosie's. Rosie, now nearly four years dead. Why had she kept it?

'I suppose you're wondering why I wanted to see you,' Nicola began at last, after four biscuits and a cup of tea.

Deciding that it was safer to say nothing, Rachel inclined her head, a gesture that could mean anything Nicola wanted it to.

She interpreted it as an invitation to talk. 'I've got a problem,' she began, 'and I just didn't know who else to talk to. When I saw you the other night at the pancake supper, I could tell that you were nice. I hope you don't mind.' She gave Rachel a shy smile.

Rachel returned the smile. 'Don't mind you thinking I'm nice, or don't mind you talking to me?' Her mother is at the bottom of this somehow, she told herself. Depend on it – otherwise she'd be talking to *her.* 'No, of course I don't mind.'

'Well, then.' Nicola took a deep breath and another chocolate biscuit, which she held in her hand like a talisman while she talked. 'I'm in love. And Ben is in love with me, too.'

'That doesn't sound like such a problem,' Rachel said lightly.

'Oh, but it is!' Her tone was heartfelt and intense. 'You don't know my mum, or you wouldn't say that!'

Exactly. Rachel tried to keep her voice neutral. 'Your mum.'

'Yes. She's been just awful about Ben and me. We want to get married, you see. And Mum says absolutely not.'

'Well, you are quite young,' Rachel said. 'Is Ben older, then?'

'No, he's the same age as me – seventeen. He's in the sixth form with me at school. But that's not the problem!'

'It *is* a problem if your mother won't consent. You can't get married without your parents' permission until you're eighteen.'

'Don't you think I know that?' Nicola said bitterly. 'But the real problem is that Ben is . . . well, his skin is darker than mine. No big deal, right? But not to my mum! She calls him . . . a filthy wog!'

Just what she'd expect from the charming and tactful Mrs Topping, thought Rachel. She didn't trust herself to say anything.

'She says that he doesn't really love me – that he just wants to marry me so he can stay in this country. She's heard all these stories about people doing anything to get a British passport. But that's ridiculous – Ben is as English as I am! He was born in this country, and so were his parents. And she says that I can't possibly love him, that . . .' Here Nicola broke off, chewing her lip, as a tear escaped from each eye. She gulped and went on, 'That I'm just desperate, because I'm fat. That I think it's my only chance, and that no one else will ever want me. But I *do* love Ben,' she finished passionately. 'And he loves me. I'll always love him, no matter what my mum says!'

'What about your father? What does he think?'

Nicola's voice was scornful, dismissive. 'What he always thinks about everything – exactly what my mother tells him to.'

Rachel gave her a thoughtful nod.

'Have you ever read *Romeo and Juliet*?' Nicola asked.

She fought the urge to smile. 'English was my subject at Cambridge.'

'We did it at school, for our English GCSE,' explained Nicola. 'Well, it's just like that, isn't it? We love each other, but our parents – *my* parents – are keeping us apart. Tragic,' she sighed with melodramatic fervour. Absent-mindedly she nibbled at the biscuit she was clutching till it was gone, then licked the melted chocolate from her fingers.

'I'm not sure how I can help you,' Rachel admitted, after careful thought. 'You do realise that it will do no good my trying to talk to your mother? I'm not exactly tops on her list,' she added in an attempt at humour.

'Yes, I know that she hates you,' Nicola said frankly. 'Maybe that's one reason I wanted to talk to you – just to get back at her for being so horrible to me.'

'Then what—'

Nicola interrupted her in a flood of emotion. 'Say that you'll marry us, as soon as we're both eighteen. Ben will be eighteen next month, and my birthday is in May. Then we can be married, whether my parents like it or not. Promise me that you'll marry us. Father Julian said that he would, and my mum wasn't half furious at him, but he's dead now so he can't. Father Keble Smythe says that he won't, because he doesn't want to upset my parents, but Mum couldn't hate you any more than she does already, so it won't matter. Please say yes, Miss . . . Rachel. Please?'

CHAPTER 10

Nevertheless, when he saw their adversity: he heard their complaint.
He thought upon his covenant, and pitied them, according unto the multitude of his mercies: yea, he made all those that led them away captive to pity them.
Psalm 106.43–44

Pamela Hartman rolled off Huw Meredith with a satisfied sigh. 'Brilliant,' she said, when she was ready for talking.

'Brilliant,' he echoed, meaning it.

Pamela Hartman, employed by Her Majesty as an immigration officer, had met PC Meredith about a year earlier, in the course of duty: a young man arrested by PC Meredith for being drunk and disorderly had subsequently been discovered to be an illegal immigrant. The two had hit it off immediately, and had been meeting once or twice a week since for a bit of extracurricular fun.

He was a tall, black-bearded Welshman, just one generation removed from the coal mines. She was a sophisticated blonde, a few years older than he, and from a solidly middle-class background. Both were married, but that was irrelevant. Neither was interested in anything permanent or long-term. Their couplings were sometimes playful, sometimes rough, occasionally tender, but always enjoyable. It was an arrangement which suited them both admirably.

Usually, as now, they met on a Friday evening after work, in the flat of one of Pamela's colleagues who spent weekends in the country, thoughtfully leaving her keys behind for Pamela's use.

Pamela sat up in bed and reached for a cigarette on the bedside table with sinuous grace. She had a loose-limbed body, casually sensual in its movements, reinforcing the message of her heavy-lidded eyes, her full mouth, and her tumbled mane of honey-blonde hair.

'One for me too, love.' Huw Meredith's bass voice retained the sing-song cadence of the Welsh hills.

'Mm.' She lit two cigarettes, blew the match out with a sensuous puff, and settled back down beside him in the rumpled bed.

He took a long drag and exhaled slowly. 'Had a busy week?'

'So-so. I've got a fairly heavy caseload at the moment. How about you?'

'Just the usual sort of thing for February. A few cars pinched, and the odd burglary. Still a bit chilly for much hanky-panky on Hampstead Heath.' He grinned, displaying strong white teeth.

With her free hand she stroked the thick, curly black hair on his chest. 'Poor buggers, with no nice comfortable bed to do it in.'

His grin widened. 'Some people prefer it that way – adds to the thrill, you know.'

'I suppose.' She sucked on her cigarette thoughtfully. 'I can't see it, myself. I prefer all the comfort I can get.'

'Don't I know it. It's just a shame that our hosts aren't thoughtful enough to provide silk sheets for our Pam.' She tweaked his beard playfully in retribution. 'Ow,' he said, more for effect than from conviction, then gave her bare thigh a pinch that turned into a fondle.

Pamela, seeing in what direction things were moving, and regretfully conscious of the clock, searched her memory for some suitably entertaining anecdote to distract him. 'Your mum collects funny names, doesn't she? Well, I came across a good one for her this week. Justin Thymme.' She spelled it for him. 'Get it?'

'Justin Thymme.' He suddenly looked alert. 'What's he done, then?'

'Done? He hasn't done anything. Nothing except get married, that is. I had an application come across my desk this week for his wife to be granted residency status as a spouse.' She smiled, remembering. 'In fact, her name is a good one as well. May Thymme. Get it?'

Huw Meredith sat up straight. 'Justin Thymme has just got married? You're sure?'

Pamela was puzzled. 'Of course I'm sure. Why – do you know him, or something?'

'We've met.' He watched her face as he went on, 'On Hampstead Heath, as a matter of fact. A month or so ago. He had his trousers round his ankles at the time. Damn chilly, but there you are.'

Her brow furrowed. 'You mean . . . ?'

'Exactly. A fourteen-carat poofter.'

In spite of herself she laughed at the mental picture. 'But he can't be! It must be someone else.'

'Another Justin Thymme? Come on, Pam. Get real. It's him, all right. But it doesn't have to mean anything. You're a woman of the world – surely you must realise that even married men go cottaging.'

She narrowed her eyes at him. 'When did you say this happened?'

'Round the middle of January, I reckon.'

'But that's just about the time he was getting married, if I remember the application! I've heard of stag nights, but this is the first time I've ever heard of a man celebrating his marriage by having it off on Hampstead Heath! And in the dead of winter!'

He laughed. 'What are you going to do about it?'

In one fluid movement she stubbed out her cigarette in the bedside ashtray and got out of bed. 'I'm going to have Mr and Mrs Justin Thymme in my office first thing next week, or know the reason why,' she said crisply. 'You just can't imagine the lengths some people will go to for the right to remain in this country – including paying poofters to marry them – and I have the strangest feeling that Mrs Thymme might be one of those people.'

'Come back here. You can't do anything about it now, love.' He arranged himself to display his charms to their full advantage. 'The main course was lovely, but now I'm ready for pud.'

'Not now.' She was already beginning to get dressed, but avoided looking at him in case her resolution should fail her. 'We're going out for a meal tonight – I've got to get home.' In a few moments the transformation was complete: in prim navy-blue suit and pristine white blouse, and with her hair tied back in a modest ponytail, Pamela Hartman was once again the image of an efficient female civil servant, on her way home to her husband.

The call came through to David on the following Tuesday. It was Henry Thymme who rang him, on behalf of his son Justin. 'I'm afraid the boy needs you again,' he announced, with more amusement than chagrin.

'But the charges were dropped,' David said, confused. 'He hasn't done it again, has he?'

Thymme laughed immoderately. 'Oh, no. Not that. At least if he has, he hasn't got caught. But it seems that the immigration authorities want a word with him.'

David was more confused than ever. 'Immigration?'

'They want to see him with his wife, actually.'

'Wife?'

'Didn't I mention that the boy had a new wife?'

Unseen by the caller on the other end of the phone, David put his head in his hands in a gesture of despair. 'No, you did not.'

His tone must have communicated itself to the other man; for just a moment the persona of the amiable buffoon slipped to reveal the shrewd lawyer beneath. 'I'm sure that the immigration people must be thinking exactly what you are,' he said frankly. 'Though how they found out about it is beyond me.'

'Tell me about the wife.' David's voice was flat.

'She's Hong Kong Chinese. They married last month. A lovely girl,' Thymme added with his usual bluffness.

David sighed. 'I don't know that much about immigration law. If you can't deal with it yourself, can't you find someone who's an expert in the field?'

'The boy wants you,' Thymme said. 'He was impressed with the way you got him off over that other business. He's your client now,' he added by way of a reminder. 'You can't abandon him.'

David could think of a few things of a more violent nature that he'd like to do to Justin Thymme, but he refrained from telling his father so. 'You'd better give me the details, then,' he said with ill-concealed resignation.

Thymme's chuckle reflected his satisfaction. 'Justin will fill you in.'

Hoping to discover just what the immigration officer knew, and how he knew it, David arranged to have a short meeting with him before his client arrived. He needed all the help he could get, he admitted to himself as he entered the Immigration Office, located at Waterloo Station: his client, Mr Justin Thymme, had been as unhelpful as he'd expected during their initial conference on the previous afternoon, insisting that theirs was a love match and indignant that anyone could think otherwise. Mrs Thymme he had not yet had the pleasure of meeting.

In the event, the immigration officer turned out to be a woman, and an attractive one at that, though her manner was businesslike to the point of being intimidating. With a firm handshake she introduced herself as Mrs Hartman and escorted David to her office.

Ensconced behind her desk, she studied a file for a moment without speaking, before raising her head to meet David's eyes. 'Well, Mr Middleton-Brown. What can I do for you?' Her voice was as crisp and as self-possessed as her appearance.

David's manner showed more assurance than he felt in the presence of this rather formidable woman. 'As you know, my client's wife has applied for a change in her residency status due to her recent marriage,' he said in what he hoped was a firm voice. 'It is my understanding that in most cases this is granted routinely, upon proof of marriage.'

Pamela Hartman nodded. 'In general, that's true.'

'Can I take it, then, that there is some problem in this particular case? Or is there some other reason that you've asked for this interview with my client and his wife?'

She assessed him for a moment. She had met her share of belligerent and demanding solicitors, but this one seemed different: there was a gentleness and a sense of integrity about him, in spite of his assured manner, and though she was determined not to show it, she warmed to him. 'Let me be honest with you, Mr Middleton-Brown,' Pamela Hartman said; it was something she said often, but this time she meant it. 'In this case there may very well be a problem.' She hesitated just a second before continuing, 'I happen to be in possession of some information that has left me in some doubt as to the validity of this marriage.'

'But I can show you the certificate,' he asserted. 'They were married last month.'

'Oh, I don't doubt that the marriage took place.' She looked down at the file, afraid that her amusement would show in her eyes. 'But I do have my doubts about the . . . well, let's say the motivation behind this marriage.'

David's heart misgave him, but he kept his voice steady. 'I don't understand what you mean, Mrs Hartman.'

She answered him in a roundabout way. 'Do you have any idea what some people will do to get a British passport, Mr Middleton-Brown? Entering into a marriage of convenience is one of the easier ways to do it. I've seen people in this very office whose desperation has led them to do much worse things. Lie, certainly, and steal – there is a thriving trade in stolen marriage certificates at the moment – and practically anything else short of murder. Even that wouldn't surprise me, quite frankly.'

'Are you suggesting that my client and his wife have contracted a marriage of convenience?'

'That's exactly what I'm suggesting.' Pamela Hartman's eyes met his. 'As I said, I'll be honest with you. I can't reveal my sources, but I happen to know that getting married wasn't the only thing Mr Justin Thymme did last month.' She smiled, a cool and almost mocking smile, and was unable to resist adding, 'But as you're his solicitor, you probably know that already, don't you, Mr Middleton-Brown? Hampstead Heath, remember?'

'Bloody hell!' In his shock, David was sure – almost sure – that he hadn't actually said it aloud, but given the glint of amusement in

Pamela Hartman's eyes, he couldn't be positive. It was true: she was enjoying his discomposure, and even if he hadn't spoken, his thoughts were all too evident on his face. How on earth had she found out? And why had she chosen to reveal her knowledge? At least, thought David, he now knew where he – and his client – stood.

Justin Thymme and his new wife arrived a short time later. Even if he had not known what he knew about young Mr Thymme, David would have found them an oddly matched couple. He had a preconceived notion that all Chinese women were tiny; Mrs Thymme confounded that expectation by being several inches taller than her short husband, even in flat shoes. But she was slender and graceful, with a sweet, ingenuous smile and a manner that was eager to please.

And for once David could find nothing to criticise in Justin's demeanour: he was civil to David, courteous to Pamela Hartman, and showed every sign of loving devotion to his new wife, clinging to her hand and looking up at her adoringly. It was most disconcerting.

After the introductions they all sat down, the newlyweds inching their chairs closer together so they could continue to hold hands. Pamela Hartman caught David's eye and smiled in what he took to be a cynical way.

'There is something wrong?' May Thymme spoke first. Her English was good – she had entered the country on a student visa and was studying English at University College London – but heavily accented. 'Justin and I are married, since last month. We have papers. We can show you.' She seemed tense, and her dark eyes were large with worry.

Pamela Hartman studied her carefully before replying. Her instincts were usually good, but this was a difficult one to size up. Often in these cases it was all too apparent what had motivated the marriage, with the husband and wife treating each other as the virtual strangers that they were. But in spite of what she knew about Justin Thymme's sexual escapades, she wasn't so sure about this set-up. Either these two were better actors than most, or there was some genuine affection between them. It wasn't impossible, and she decided to give them the benefit of the doubt for the time being. There would be plenty of time later for getting tough, for interviewing them separately and asking them which side of the bed each slept on and how they squeezed the toothpaste tube. After all, this process of discovering the truth usually took months. If they were hiding something – and in spite of the appearances she was prepared to lay money that they were – it didn't hurt to be reassuring at this point, to lull them into a false sense of security in which they might betray themselves. 'This is only a preliminary hearing,' she said in a soothing voice. 'I'd like to see your papers, and then I'll ask you a few questions. With Mr Middleton-Brown's permission, of course,' she added with a nod of exaggerated deference in David's direction.

CHAPTER 11

And I lie even among the children of men, that are set on fire: whose teeth are spears and arrows, and their tongue a sharp sword.

Psalm 57.5

Lucy frowned, surveying her sitting room; absently she twisted a curl around her finger. Her niece would be arriving tomorrow. How on earth was she going to accommodate Ruth and all her possessions? David was right: the girl was bound to bring all sorts of things with her. And he was right, too, that the house wasn't big enough for three people.

Sleeping wasn't really a problem, with the sofa bed in the sitting room. But where would she put her things? Apart from the sitting room, the downstairs consisted of a small dining room and a good-sized, extended kitchen – but that was no help. Upstairs was a tiny bathroom, the bedroom and Lucy's studio. Perfect for one person, workable – just – for two, but three was stretching the house beyond its limits.

Ruth was only part of the problem, of course, Lucy realised. The other person in the equation was David. Whatever happened, Lucy didn't want him to feel surplus to requirements, or unwelcome in her house. For the first time she acknowledged to herself that she now thought of it as *their* house, hers and David's. She loved having him there, loved sharing her life with him. While she was working in her studio during the day, it was wonderful to be able to look forward to his return home, and a shared evening of good food and conversation. Not to mention what followed: she enjoyed the luxury of sleeping in David's arms almost as much as she enjoyed the lovemaking that preceded it.

Then why, she asked herself, wouldn't she marry him? It was by no means the first time she'd wrestled with the question. There was more to it than the aftertaste of a bad marriage, she admitted to herself in her more self-analytical moments. This relationship, after all, was in no way comparable to the one she'd had with Geoffrey, who had been so much older and had never let her forget how superior he was to her on every level. She and David had so much to offer each other; they were complementary equals.

Perhaps she was afraid that marriage would somehow alter that fine balance, and spoil the relationship. Certainly to legalise the union would endanger its spontaneity. Their lovemaking now was both frequent and spontaneous: would marriage make it routine and taken-for-granted?

But she didn't want to lose him, she knew. That would be an even greater evil. Self-sufficient though she was, Lucy hadn't realised how much she'd hated her solitary life until she'd found someone to share it with. Was she being unrealistic, hoping to have her cake and eat it, to enjoy the benefits of togetherness without the ossifying commitment of marriage? And was it fair to David, when he wanted to marry her so badly?

She dreaded the day when he would come home and tell her that he'd finally sorted out the inheritance, and could move into the house near Kensington Gardens. It would force them to talk about it, the subject that had become so painful for them both that it was now taboo. And ultimately it would propel her into some kind of decision. Until then, though, she would do everything possible to maintain the status quo.

That was what was so worrying about Ruth's visit, Lucy realised. It was a threat to the status quo. And, she asked herself, looking around, wherever would she put her things?

'The cupboard under the stairs was a great idea,' David complimented her the next morning as they waited at Euston Station.

'I had a sudden inspiration. It's always been a convenient glory hole, so I thought – why not?' She'd cleaned it out, had thrown out quite a bit of rubbish, and transferred the rest to the loft for the time being. 'It should work quite well – there's room for her to hang a few clothes, and shelves for her bits and pieces. You'll see. It won't be so bad.' She squeezed his hand, wishing that she felt as confident about it as she sounded.

'What is she like?' David squinted up at the arrivals board; her train was due at any moment. His contact with teenage girls throughout the course of his life had been minimal, and his apprehensiveness was increasing by the minute.

Lucy qualified her reply. 'I haven't seen her for nearly a year, but she actually reminds me quite a bit of myself at that age. Other people say so, too – my brother always says that it's like déjà vu.'

'Oh, well, that's all right, then.' His relief was evident.

She gave a wicked laugh. 'You don't know what I was like.'

'I know what you're like now, and you couldn't have been so very dreadful then,' David asserted loyally.

'I wouldn't be so sure about that if I were you.'

He exhaled on a sigh as the train from Northampton pulled into the station, and they waited in silence while the Saturday morning passengers trickled through the barrier. It was a different crowd from the Monday-through-Friday commuters: mostly parents with young children, coming to London for a day's outing, the children already whipped into hyperactivity by their train journey and the parents already showing signs of exhaustion. There was a sprinkling of well-dressed matrons with empty shopping bags, most likely bound for Knightsbridge, a few couples on their way to the West End for matinées at various theatres, and the inevitable rag-tag of international back-packers, young people weighed down with enormous rucksacks and large bottles of Evian water, jabbering to each other in German or Italian. David wondered inconsequentially what sights might have drawn them to Northampton; it didn't seem likely that they would be interested in shoe factories or even Eleanor Crosses.

'There's Ruth,' said Lucy, pointing. Near the end of the stream, just behind a harassed mother trying to corral three overexcited small boys, was a girl on her own, slowed down by the wobbling progress of an oversized suitcase on wheels, wearing the singularly unattractive uniform of her generation: faded jeans, a leather jacket over a T-shirt, and great clomping Doc Marten boots. At the barrier she straightened up and looked around anxiously, then spotted her aunt and waved. 'Hi, Aunt Lucy.'

David drew in his breath. To say that Ruth Kingsley resembled Lucy was not quite accurate. She was like her, yes, but in the manner of an out-of-focus photograph, or even more accurately like two paintings of the same subject executed in different media, by different artists. If Lucy was the watercolour, then her niece was the oil painting, altogether more vibrant in colouring and bolder in style. Where Lucy's hair was a pale, shimmery red-gold, the colour of ripe apricots, Ruth's was unashamedly red – almost orange – and cut short so that the curls were more pronounced, standing out around her face in an aggressive Afro. Ruth's eyes were a true green, rather than the blue-green of Lucy's; her skin was whiter than Lucy's peaches-and-cream coloration, and was demarcated by a sprinkling of freckles across her nose. Ruth's features, too, were reminiscent of Lucy's, but the overall effect was quite different: while Lucy was an attractive – some might say beautiful – woman, not even a fond parent could claim that Ruth Kingsley was other than a rather plain girl, though the charitable might add that she had the potential to grow into her looks. It was as if, thought David, she hadn't quite caught up with her face; her nose and her mouth seemed out of proportion to everything else, and the size of her mouth was only exacerbated by an awesome array of glinting hardware when she pulled back her lips in a smile. Poor kid, he found himself thinking.

Lucy stated the obvious. 'Ruthie, darling! You've got a brace on your teeth!'

The smile faded. 'Since last summer,' she admitted. 'I have to wear it for two years, probably. And please don't call me Ruthie,' she added. 'I'm not a baby any more, Aunt Lucy.'

The girl hung back awkwardly, but Lucy moved forward to embrace her. 'Darling, it's so good to see you. It's been so long!'

'Almost ten months,' Ruth stated in a voice that, even muffled in a hug, was clearly accusing. 'Not since the christening last May, remember? Aunt Lucy, why haven't you been to see us for so long?'

This evoked the very guilt it was meant to produce; Lucy had realised recently how little she had seen of her family, apart from her father, since her involvement with David. Her response was defensive. 'It hasn't really been that long,' she said, contradicting herself.

'Your Aunt Lucy is a very busy person,' David put in.

Ruth pulled away from Lucy to look at him, while Lucy performed a hurried introduction. 'Ruth darling, this is my friend Mr Middleton-Brown. David. You know, the one who's going to help you with your work experience.'

'Hi.' Ruth gave him a rather stiff nod as she tried to assess him. She didn't much like the way he was hovering around Aunt Lucy, and she definitely didn't like the way he'd spoken to her in Aunt Lucy's defence. She hadn't been talking to *him*, after all – who did he think he was? And why did he have to be here, anyway, when she wouldn't start her work experience until Monday morning? She'd been looking forward to having Aunt Lucy all to herself this weekend, without her parents or her brothers around to share the attention.

David could feel the hostility radiating from the girl, but was at a loss to understand the reason for it. Bewildered, he overcompensated with a false smile and a jolly manner. 'We're really pleased to have you, aren't we, Lucy? Now, let me take your case. It must be awfully heavy for a girl like you.'

Ruth pressed her lips together – a painful thing to do given the quantity of hardware in her mouth – and made a lunge for the handle of her case. In a complete contrast to Lucy's natural grace, her movements were gawky and graceless. 'No, thank you. I can do it myself. It's got wheels.' With a determined grunt, she pulled it into motion.

Before David could protest and take it from her, Lucy caught his eye and shook her head slightly. 'Well, at least I've brought the car,' said David ruefully, as they followed Ruth and the wobbling behemoth in a slow, awkward procession through Euston Station.

After Ruth had unpacked and settled her possessions in the cupboard under the stairs, and after they'd had some lunch, they moved into the sitting room to discuss the plans for the afternoon. Ruth scooped up a somewhat reluctant Sophie and claimed the spot next to Lucy on the sofa, relegating David to a chair. 'Nice kitty,' she crooned, ignoring Sophie's squirms.

'We wondered, darling, what you'd like to do this afternoon,' Lucy began. She and David had discussed it at length, and had a few ideas, but had decided to leave the final decision up to Ruth.

'I don't know,' Ruth said unhelpfully, her head bent over the cat.

'We thought that you might like to go to one of the museums – the Science Museum or the Natural History Museum,' David put in. 'They're not far from here, you know.'

Ruth looked up at him and wrinkled her nose. 'That sounds dead boring. I hate science, and I can't think of anything more boring than a load of old dinosaur bones.'

'Well, how about the Tower of London, then?' suggested Lucy.

'We went there on a school outing. Boring. Full of naff American tourists, all saying that they want to take the Crown Jewels home for a souvenir.'

'There's always the zoo, though it's still a bit chilly for that,' said David.

'Zoos are for little kids,' Ruth stated with an indignant scowl at him. 'I told you, I'm not a baby.'

'Of course you're not,' Lucy said quickly, giving David a warning look. 'He didn't mean to imply that you were. Lots of grown-ups enjoy the zoo, too.' Before Ruth could express her opinion of the sort of grown-ups who enjoyed the zoo, she went on, 'There's Madame

Tussaud's, or any of the art museums. Or we could even go shopping at Covent Garden, or Harrods, or the General Trading Company.'

'Him too?' she nodded her head in David's direction.

'Yes, of course.'

'I'd rather wait and go shopping with just you, Aunt Lucy. Shopping's much more fun without men around. Dad goes spare when he has to take me and Mum shopping.'

Lucy, fighting to curb her own rising irritation, didn't dare to look at David. 'Well, where would you like to go then, Ruth darling?' she asked sweetly, thinking to herself, Oh God, it's going to be a long three weeks.

Clutching Sophie to her chest, Ruth thought hard. 'How about Westminster Abbey?' she said at last. 'We've been doing Elizabeth I at school, and I'd like to see her tomb. I think she was pretty cool. And I'd like to go to Evensong.'

'Well, that's settled, then.' Relief and exasperation were mingled on David's face as he rose from the chair. The fact that the girl wanted to visit a church was something in her favour at least as far as David was concerned, and it redeemed her slightly in his mind. Though her affinity for Elizabeth I was no accident, he told himself wryly: it takes one imperious redhead to appreciate another.

They passed a few hours in Westminster Abbey, taking one of the supertours and then poking around the chapels on their own, paying homage to Elizabeth I. Ruth deigned to do a rubbing of a lady with a horned headdress and a supercilious expression in the brass rubbing centre, while Lucy and David strolled round the cloister, and then it was time for Evensong.

A well-sung cathedral-style Choral Evensong was one of the chief pleasures of David's life; by closing his eyes and losing himself in the music and the liturgy – the beautiful, time-honoured cadences of the Book of Common Prayer – he was able to forget for a few moments what a trial the next three weeks were likely to be. Thus Lucy was the first to notice a fellow worshipper on the opposite side of the stalls. During the first reading she nudged him gently. 'Look,' she whispered, 'there's Rachel Nightingale over there.'

Immersed in the tranquillity of the service, Rachel didn't see them until the very end, as the verger led the choir and clergy out of the stalls and the congregation stood. After the organ voluntary had finished, she crossed the chancel with a smile. 'Hello, Lucy. How are you?'

'Oh, very well. And you?'

'Not bad.' Rachel looked curiously at David, sure that she'd seen him before, but equally sure that it had had nothing to do with Lucy. 'Haven't we met?'

'Yes,' he said, smiling. 'At St Margaret's. Father Keble Smythe introduced us. David Middleton-Brown.'

'Yes, of course. I'm sorry, but you were out of context. The solicitor, wasn't it?'

'That's right.'

'Rachel, this is my niece, Ruth Kingsley,' Lucy interposed. 'She's visiting me for a few weeks.'

Rachel favoured Ruth with her sweetest smile. 'Hello, Ruth. How lovely for you, Lucy. You *are* lucky.'

'Hi,' said Ruth, returning the smile.

'Where are you from, Ruth?'

'Northampton. A boring town,' she stated dismissively. 'But I'll leave there as soon as I can. I want to live in London, when I'm qualified.'

'Ruth wants to be a solicitor,' Lucy explained. 'That's why she's here – she's doing a work experience project with David.'

'I see. And what about university?'

'That's a few years off,' Ruth admitted. 'But I'd like to go to Cambridge.'

Rachel looked off into the distance. 'Cambridge,' she said reflectively. 'You'll love it there. I spent over fifteen years of my life in Cambridge, and I think it's the most wonderful place on earth. Let me know when you're going up,' she added on impulse, 'and I'll come up to meet you and show you round, introduce you to a few people, that sort of thing. I'd love to show you around Cambridge.'

'Oh, yes!' Enchanted, Ruth studied her avidly, noticing the discreet dog collar that she wore with her sprigged blouse. 'Are you a woman vicar?' she asked.

Rachel laughed lightly. 'Not yet. But I will be one day soon, God willing. I'm only a deacon at the moment. Just an overworked curate.'

'And they let you off long enough to come to Westminster Abbey?' asked Lucy.

Lucy's tone may have been facetious, but Rachel's reply was serious. 'I don't have much free time, but Saturday is supposed to be my day off. I had a wedding this afternoon and two hospital visits in spite of that, so I felt entitled to take a little time to treat myself to Evensong. It's something I love, so I come here whenever I can – they do it so beautifully.'

'They let you do weddings, even if you're not a vicar?' Ruth wanted to know.

'Oh, yes, that's one of the things a deacon is allowed to do, and one of the things that curates often get stuck with – I've got one next week as well.' She looked at her watch. 'And that reminds me – one of the other things a deacon is allowed to do is preach, and I've got a sermon to finish up for tomorrow morning's 10.30 service at St Jude's, so if you'll excuse me . . .'

Ruth was fairly quiet through supper, but afterwards, when David retired to the sitting room to leave her alone with Lucy, she became animated. As they did the washing up, she began talking about Rachel Nightingale. 'I think she's wonderful,' Ruth pronounced. 'Where is her church, anyway? Didn't she say it was called St Jude's?'

'That's right. It's in Pimlico. Not too far away. She's got two churches, actually – St Jude's and St Margaret's.'

'Well, can we go to St Jude's tomorrow, Aunt Lucy? I'd really like to hear her sermon. I'll bet it will be great.'

Lucy looked bemused. 'Yes, I suppose so, darling. If you really want to.'

'Of course I want to.' Then she started asking Lucy questions about Rachel; Lucy told her what she knew about Rachel's tragic life and how she had managed to rise above her pain and eventually to bring good out of it. At the end of the story Ruth had tears in her eyes. 'I think that's the saddest thing I've ever heard,' she said with feeling. 'The most romantic story, with the saddest ending. Poor Rachel. And poor Colin. And poor Rosie. Oh, she must have loved them both very much. And now, to see him like he is . . . Oh, poor Rachel.'

Lucy nodded. 'And she's such a lovely person.'

'Oh, she is, Aunt Lucy! She's wonderful!' Ruth declared passionately. She fell silent for a moment, rubbing the tea towel round and round on a plate until it squeaked. 'I wonder . . .' she said in a thoughtful voice. 'I wonder if I could be a solicitor *and* a woman priest?'

Lucy stifled her desire to laugh, and replied seriously, 'I don't know why not, Ruth darling. But it does seem rather a lot to take on, doesn't it? They're two very demanding jobs, and with a family as well . . .'

'Oh, I shan't have a family,' Ruth stated. 'I'm never getting married.' Her expression was fiercely determined. 'Never.'

'I see.'

'No, I mean it. It may start out all right, but after a while you just start fighting, and then you end up hating each other,' she asserted with authority. 'You're much better off on your own. I mean, look at *you*, Aunt Lucy.'

A wet plate slipped in Lucy's hand and she caught it just in time. Ruth's statement had surprised her: her short-lived marriage had preceded in its entirety her niece's birth, and she wasn't sure whether Ruth even knew that it had happened – certainly she had never told her. Her cynical description of the course of a marriage described with devastating accuracy the few months that Lucy had spent as Geoffrey's wife, but how would Ruth know about that? And if not her, to whom was she referring? 'Yes?' she said neutrally, hoping that Ruth would elaborate.

'You're not married, and you have a wonderful life – living in London, in your own house, and with a successful career.' Her voice dropped. 'I've always wanted to be like you, Aunt Lucy,' she confided, almost shyly. 'You're proof that a woman can live life on her own terms, without some man telling her what to do all the time.'

Lucy realised that she didn't have the courage to disillusion her niece, either about the past or about her present situation. 'Well, you've got plenty of time before you have to decide about anything like that,' she said in a falsely jolly voice, hating her own cowardice as she said it; at Ruth's age, she had despised grown-ups who patronised her in that way. Seeing the disappointment on Ruth's face, she went on quickly, 'It looks like the washing up is just about finished. What would you like to do for the rest of the evening, darling? I've got a brand-new Cluedo set – how about a game or two?' In a moment of inspiration earlier in the week, Lucy had recalled the favoured activity on visits to her brother's family, long afternoons round the kitchen table with Ruth and her two younger brothers, punctuated with triumphant cries of 'Miss Scarlet in the library with the lead pipe!' or 'Colonel Mustard in the conservatory with the rope!' The idea had sent her off to the shops to buy a new set, in the hopes that it would help to keep her niece occupied for at least part of the three weeks.

Ruth frowned. 'I don't play Cluedo much any more – it's kind of babyish, I think. And it doesn't work very well with just two people. I like Scrabble better. But I've got a better idea – why don't we go out and get a video to watch?'

'I'm afraid I haven't got a video machine,' Lucy apologised. 'I don't watch much television. And I don't have Scrabble. But there are three of us for Cluedo – that would be all right, wouldn't it?'

Ruth's frown deepened, and she lowered her head. 'When is *he* going home?' she said quietly. 'He doesn't need to stay all evening, does he? Can he take a hint, or will you have to tell him to go?'

Lucy felt as though the breath had been knocked out of her; she put a hand on the worktop to steady herself. The emphasis that the girl had put on the word 'he' made Lucy realise that Ruth had not once, since she'd arrived, called or referred to David by name. Taking a deep breath, she forced herself to look at her niece. 'Ruth darling,' she said in a remarkably calm voice, 'David *is* at home. He lives here.'

The girl's mouth dropped open, and a scarlet flush spread up her neck to suffuse her face. 'He lives *here*?' she gasped. 'Do you mean that he sleeps in your bed, with *you*?'

Lucy took another deep breath. 'That's right. You're old enough to understand about things like that. As you keep reminding me, you're not a baby.'

'But that's immoral! It's . . . disgusting!' Her lower lip trembled.

Feeling sick, Lucy turned her head away. It hadn't occurred to her that a fourteen-year-old, growing up in a sexually aware and morally ambivalent society, would find such an arrangement unusual or blame-worthy. But Ruth *was* a young fourteen, as Andrew had said, and she had probably led a fairly sheltered life. 'We love each other,' she said. 'One day you'll understand. I'm sorry if you don't approve, if it upsets you . . .'

'Does Grandad know that you're living in sin?'

If Ruth had tried, thought Lucy, she couldn't have hit a sorer spot: she wasn't ashamed of her relationship with David, but somehow she didn't expect her unworldly father to understand it. 'No, he doesn't,' she admitted. 'And I'd be very grateful, darling, if you didn't mention it to him.'

'And Rachel – I bet you haven't told her, either. Rachel would never approve of anything so horrible,' Ruth went on with deliberate cruelty. But there were tears in her eyes as she added, 'Oh, Aunt Lucy – how could you?'

Much later, behind the closed door of the bedroom, with Ruth safely tucked up on the sofa bed at last, Lucy and David talked into the night. 'She hates me,' David stated, with as much bewilderment as resentment, as he got into bed. 'How on earth am I supposed to work with her, when she treats me like some lower life-form?'

Lucy, brushing her hair in front of the mirror, was determined not to tell him about Ruth's strong disapproval of their living arrangements, though she was afraid that it was already all too evident to him. 'She'll get used to you,' she tried to convince him. 'She just wasn't expecting to have to share me with you, if you know what I mean.'

'She thought that she and her Aunt Lucy would have a cosy time together, you mean? Just the girls, doing girlish things?'

'That's it exactly,' Lucy confirmed. 'She has two younger brothers at home, you know, and I think she was looking forward to getting lots of attention from me.'

'Well, too bad.' He didn't care if it sounded callous; he wasn't particularly in the mood to be charitable.

She slid in beside him. 'David darling, you've got to make allowances for her,' she said coaxingly, snuggling up against him. 'She's at a very difficult age.'

David gave a self-deprecating laugh. 'Then what's *my* excuse? I don't like sharing you, either.'

Things weren't so bad if David could still laugh at himself, Lucy decided. 'I'm serious, darling. I remember being fourteen, and I was absolutely frightful.'

'Not you.'

'Oh, yes I was.' She turned on her back and looked up at the ceiling, reflecting. 'It was an awful age to be. I remember when I was around that age, grown-ups were always telling me how lucky I was to be young, and I knew that it was a lie – that being fourteen is horrible, and that either they were lying, or they didn't remember. I said to myself then that I would never forget how absolutely awful it was to be fourteen.'

'And?'

'Oh, you *do* forget,' she said with a thoughtful sigh. 'Of course you do. It's like any kind of pain, a toothache or a stubbed toe – you can remember that it hurt, but not really how much. At least, though, I'll never underestimate the agony of being fourteen. That much I've held on to.'

'You're more charitable than I am, my love.'

'And of course,' she added in a matter-of-fact voice that masked great depths of unresolved pain, 'when I was about her age, my mother died. At least Ruth is lucky enough to have two parents to help her through being fourteen.'

David had his doubts that Ruth would be any less objectionable at forty than she was at fourteen, but he refrained from saying so. 'And lucky to have her Aunt Lucy as well.' He turned and put his arms around her. 'Just don't forget that *I* need you, too.'

'Oh, darling. It's only three weeks,' Lucy protested against his chest.

David's response was rhetorical but heartfelt. 'Why do I have the feeling that it will be the longest three weeks of my life?'

CHAPTER 12

The law of thy mouth is dearer unto me: than thousands of gold and silver.
Psalm 119.72

Vanessa Bairstow spread her toast with marmalade, looked at it without seeing it, then put it down on her plate untouched. 'I wonder where he could be?' she asked rhetorically, her normally tranquil forehead creased with concern.

Her husband sighed. That damned cat, he thought. If Vanessa spent half as much time worrying about the important things in life . . . But he made the dutiful, if impatient, reply. 'I'm sure he'll turn up soon. When he's good and ready. You know that cat has a mind of his own.'

'But Augustine has never stayed away *this* long before.' Absently she brushed toast crumbs off the table cloth.

Augustine's non-appearance was not affecting Martin Bairstow's appetite; he always declared that breakfast was the most important meal of the day, and he practised what he preached, deploring the fact that his wife limited herself to toast.

'Perhaps I'll stay at home today, just in case.'

Bairstow looked at his wife in surprise. As far as he was aware, she rarely left the house anyway, excepting the occasional shopping trip. 'Why, where were you going?'

'Oh, this afternoon is the monthly women's club. First Wednesday of the month, you know.'

'Hm.' That information was enough to satisfy his perfunctory curiosity on the subject; he put down his fork for a moment and picked up the copy of the *Financial Times* from the table to scrutinise a story on the front page which had caught his eye.

Desperate to retain her husband's attention, Vanessa went on, 'It's at Joan Everitt's house this month. Rachel Nightingale is the speaker – she's going to give a sort of travelogue about Cambridge, I believe.'

She had succeeded in capturing his attention. He looked up quickly, frowning. 'You weren't planning to go, were you?'

'Why, yes. Until Augustine went missing, anyway. Now I don't know.'

Martin Bairstow put his newspaper on the table for emphasis and leaned across the table to look his wife in the eye. 'I'd really rather you didn't. The more that woman is encouraged . . . well, let's just say I don't think it's a good idea. Surely Dolly isn't going?'

'Well, no,' Vanessa admitted. 'Dolly said that under no circumstances would she have any social contact with her.'

'Very wise, too. I certainly hope that you'll follow her example.'

Vanessa didn't dare tell him that in her limited contact she had found Rachel Nightingale to be a warm and sympathetic person, and was looking forward to seeing her that afternoon, and possibly even intended to encourage further meetings. 'Well, we'll see,' she prevaricated.

Her husband merely raised his heavy eyebrows in a way that conveyed his disapproval more clearly than words. Rolling up his napkin and restoring it to its silver ring, he rose from the table. 'I'll be a bit late tonight,' he announced. 'Norman and I have a meeting with the Vicar at six. So I should be home shortly after seven.'

'I'll ring you if there's any news about Augustine,' Vanessa promised to his indifferent back. 'I'm sure he's all right,' she added, more to herself than to him. 'He *must* be all right.'

'It's dead boring,' Ruth protested to David. 'Nothing but photocopying. Why can't you give me something interesting to do?'

He didn't try very hard to conceal his irritation. 'If you'd rather, you can collate and staple those reports. Or make me a cup of tea,' he added, knowing that the suggestion would infuriate her.

'I didn't come all this way to spend three weeks running the photocopier, or making tea!' she flared. 'I want to learn to be a solicitor, not a secretary!'

David took a deep breath, on the verge of retorting, 'Then I suggest that you begin acting less like a spoiled brat and more like the bright young lady that everyone tells me you are,' but he caught himself in time. It was only the third morning of the first week, and already he'd had ample cause, both personal and professional, to regret giving in to Lucy in the matter of Ruth's work experience. He'd tried, several times, to explain to the girl that client confidentiality prevented her becoming involved in any meaningful way in his work, but she seemed unable to accept the limitations, and resented the menial work to which she was relegated. He had known it would happen, and he had been right. Looking down at his desk in an effort to control himself, he saw the notes he'd been making during his last telephone conversation, and had an inspiration. 'Then you can go downstairs to the library, and see what you can find out about Canon Law and Consistory Courts,' he said in a mild voice. 'Take as long as you like.'

'Oh.' He had caught her by surprise, and it took her a little while to recover. 'All right. But don't forget that you said I could have the afternoon off,' she added. She was going to hear Rachel Nightingale speaking to the women's club. Lucy had been invited by Vanessa Bairstow, and had reluctantly agreed to go, along with Emily, to support Rachel; when Ruth had found out about it, she had insisted on going along, and David was only too willing to accede to her request for a few hours off.

'I haven't forgotten.'

'Well, I'm off to the library, then.'

As soon as she had gone, David picked up the phone and dialled Martin Bairstow's business number, passing through several layers of secretaries before reaching the man himself. 'I have some news about the silver,' he told Bairstow.

The other man's voice was eager. 'Yes?'

'It's not good news, I'm afraid,' David cautioned belatedly. 'I've just been talking to the secretary of the Diocesan Advisory Committee. He says that the DAC have turned down our application for permission to sell it. In view of its singular importance and great value, he said.'

'Oh.' Bairstow was silent for a moment, assimilating the information. 'What recourse do we have?'

'Well, Mr Bairstow, there's the Consistory Court, but as I explained to you before, that will take time and cost money. Counsel will have to be briefed, and it might take months.' He scanned his notes. 'And, to be perfectly honest, the DAC secretary said that he didn't think we stood a chance of overturning the DAC's decision. In similar matters, the Consistory Court has always backed the DAC – they're the experts, after all. Of course, it's up to you,' he added. 'And Mr Topping and Father Keble Smythe. I'm prepared to fight it, if that's what you decide you want to do.'

There was another, shorter silence. 'Thank you, Mr Middleton-Brown,' Bairstow said at last. 'I'll have to get back to you. As it happens, I'm meeting this evening with the Vicar and Norman Topping, and I promise you that this will be top of the agenda. I'll ring you as soon as I can.'

'No hurry,' said David. 'And I'm awfully sorry to have been the bearer of bad news.' As he put the phone down, he realised that in fact he was quite cheerful: the DAC's decision had affirmed his faith in the system. He had been uneasy all along about the sale of the silver, especially after the Vicar's veiled hints about the churchwardens' hidden agenda. In consequence he'd been feeling faintly guilty about his own role in doing something he didn't believe in, though he never would have admitted it even to Lucy. Now he hoped that the churchwardens and the Vicar would have the good sense to leave it, even if it meant that his fees would be considerably less than they might have been if it went to Consistory Court.

The Everitts' house was, compared to Vanessa Bairstow's mansion, a modest dwelling, perhaps a bit too near Victoria to be strictly considered Pimlico. But Joan had spared no trouble, or at least expense, in preparing for the meeting, offering her guests an impressive array of delicacies that had obviously come from the food hall of a famous Knightsbridge emporium.

For Rachel's sake, if not her hostess's, Lucy was glad she'd come: the turnout was embarrassingly small. She and Emily and Ruth made up nearly half the audience for Rachel's talk, in the absence of both churchwardens' wives as well as quite a number of the other women who had been at the previous month's meeting. Lucy could only assume that the snub was deliberate and possibly even organised, and hoped that Rachel didn't realise it.

Joan Everitt had no such compunction, as she circulated after the talk with cups of tea for her guests, looking more than ever like an ingenuous schoolgirl. 'I'm sorry about the poor turnout,' she said to Rachel, who had been cornered by an enraptured Ruth as soon as she'd finished speaking. 'We usually have loads more than this. Dolly wouldn't come, of course, and Vanessa rang earlier to say that her cat had gone missing, and she wanted to stay home in case he turned up.'

'Oh, dear. That will have upset her. Perhaps I should call by her house later to make sure everything is all right,' Rachel thought aloud.

'And Vera Bright had wanted to come,' Joan went on, 'but she didn't feel that she should leave her father alone. Then, of course, there are the rest of Dolly's crowd, who wouldn't come because of you.' Seemingly oblivious to the possible hurt she had caused, she passed on to her other guests, leaving Rachel bemused and Ruth indignant.

'Of all the insensitive . . . !' Ruth spluttered furiously.

Rachel, undecided whether it had been deliberate or merely naïve, gave her a philosophic smile. 'Don't worry, my dear. I'm used to it.'

'What do you mean?'

'I'm afraid that there are still quite a few people who haven't accepted the reality of women clergy in the Church of England – that's the problem with being the first generation. I don't consider myself a trailblazer, but somehow it's ended up that way. By the time that *you're* grown up, no one will think anything about it.'

'I'd like to be a priest,' Ruth confided on impulse.

Rachel was surprised. 'I thought you wanted to be a solicitor.'

The girl's face flamed, but she set her mouth in a determined line. 'I thought I did, but I'm not so sure any more,' she admitted. 'My work experience so far has been boring – dead boring. Your job seems *much* more interesting, even if there are people who don't appreciate you. I wish that I could do my work experience with *you*.'

Recognising the elements of hero-worship, and the unrealistic expectations that were driving the girl's new, as well as her former, career aspirations, Rachel had an idea. 'I wouldn't want to interfere with what you're doing with Mr Middleton-Brown. But you're free in the evenings, aren't you?'

Ruth looked at her eagerly. 'Yes.'

'Perhaps you'd like to come out with me one evening when I'm on duty, as it were.' That would disabuse her of any notions of glamour in the quickest possible way.

The prospect beckoned, infinitely more appealing than yet another endless evening of telly and Cluedo with Aunt Lucy and her awful boyfriend. 'Oh, yes, please.'

'Well, then . . .'

'Can't it be tonight?' Ruth suggested, unwilling to wait any longer than necessary. Her mind leapt ahead: perhaps it could even become a regular thing, for what was left of the three weeks.

Rachel took a sip of her tea and considered the idea. She had already decided to call on Vera Bright that evening, in view of her non-appearance at the meeting. Perhaps it would do both Vera and Ruth good to meet, across the generations. 'All right,' she said. 'But I'm afraid that it will have to be on foot – I don't have a car, and I don't think you'll fit on the back of my bicycle!'

'I don't mind,' Ruth assured her. 'Honestly, I don't.' For Rachel, no inconvenience was too great.

CHAPTER 13

Who say, Let us take to ourselves: the houses of God in possession.
Psalm 83.12

The Vicar hadn't yet returned home from saying Evensong, for which Martin Bairstow was grateful: it gave him an opportunity to discuss matters with his fellow warden before Father Keble Smythe became involved, as they waited in the vicarage study.

'Middleton-Brown says that the DAC have turned us down,' he stated baldly. 'And that he doesn't think a Consistory Court would take a more . . . liberal view of our request to sell the silver.'

Norman Topping thought of what Dolly would say, and he frowned. Though perhaps, he reflected, with all this business about Nicola to occupy her, Dolly wouldn't be so bothered. 'Then what can we do? Is there anything else we can flog off?' He began taking a mental inventory of the church's treasures.

'I've thought about that, and I don't think there's anything else that would raise the sort of ready cash that we'd need.'

'To refurbish Magdalen House, you mean?' Topping whispered. 'But how else will we manage when we go over to Rome? We've got to have a place to hold services, and since we can't take the building with us . . .'

Looking at his watch, Bairstow spoke urgently. 'Listen, Norman, there's not much time. Father Keble Smythe will be here any minute. I've been thinking about this all afternoon, and I'll tell you what I think we should do.'

'I'm all ears.'

'I think that we should forget about our original idea of going over to Rome, and consider opting out of the diocese instead. They've made some rather generous provisions for congregations that remain in the Anglican Communion with alternative episcopal oversight, you know. Then we could keep our building – no compromises like Magdalen House.'

'But that was such a brilliant idea of yours, Martin – to fix up Magdalen House, and then as trustees to hand it over to Rome, so we could use it as our church when we went over. Dolly thought that it was a wonderful idea.'

Bairstow fought to keep his impatience out of his voice. 'I'm telling you, Norman, it isn't going to work. Without the cash from the silver to refurbish it, Magdalen House is just a house. It's not suitable for use as a church. Rome wouldn't want it.'

Dolly's not going to be happy about this, thought Norman Topping. 'But how can we opt out of the diocese over the ordination of women, when we've got . . . her? The curate? She rather buggers things up, doesn't she?'

The door opened and Bairstow gave the other man a warning look. It was Mrs Goode, bringing in the drinks tray. 'Are you gentlemen all right?' she asked, ostensibly addressing both of them but fixing her attention on Bairstow. 'Father should be home any minute. But I'm sure he'd want you to help yourself to a drink.'

Bairstow favoured her with one of his patented charming smiles. 'Thank you so much, Mrs Goode. It's so kind of you to bother with us.' He was glad of the interruption: Topping had raised a point for which he had no easy answer. The existence of Rachel Nightingale as their curate was rather a challenge to their claim of doctrinal purity, even if she had not yet been ordained as a priest. If only the Vicar hadn't been conned into having her, he reflected, they would have so many more options. If only there were a tidy way of getting rid of her . . .

As Mrs Goode set the tray down, the phone rang; having been well trained not to pick up the extension in the study, she hurried off into the hall to answer it. Bairstow busied himself pouring drinks to avoid addressing Topping's question, and within a moment Mrs Goode was back. 'It was a message for you,' she said to Bairstow. 'Your wife. She said to tell you that the cat has just come home – she thought you'd want to know.'

He tried to summon some enthusiasm but failed. 'Thank you, Mrs Goode. Sorry for the bother.'

'Oh, no bother. No bother at all, Mr Bairstow.' She smiled at him and hesitated by the door, hoping for a little chat. 'I had a cat myself once. A fine black tom he was. Mr Goode used to say that I had more time for that cat than I had for *him*.'

He was once again spared the necessity of a reply by Mrs Goode's prompt reaction to the faint sound of a key in the front door. 'Oh, there's Father now,' she stated, making a quick exit from the study. 'I'll tell him you're here.'

Bairstow had time only for a whispered warning to Norman Topping before the Vicar entered, rubbing his hands together briskly. 'Chilly out there, isn't it? I see that the excellent Mrs Goode has taken care of your needs, with drinks and a nice cheery fire.'

'Oh, yes,' Norman Topping assured him with a chuckle. 'This whisky goes down a treat, all right. Keeps the chill out better than the fire.'

Pouring himself a drink, the Vicar sat down across from them. 'To your good health,' he said, lifting his glass.

Bairstow was in no mood for pleasantries. 'The DAC have said no,' he announced bluntly. 'We can't sell the silver.'

'Ah.' The Vicar's smile didn't falter, but he put his glass down and pressed his fingertips together in a thoughtful way. Unwilling to commit himself to further comment, he regarded his wardens and waited for them to speak.

Although Bairstow understood what game was being played, and would have preferred a more cautious approach, he was afraid of what Norman Topping might say if the silence continued too long, so he rushed to forestall him. 'It requires that we . . . re-think certain plans we'd made,' he said as circumspectly as possible.

'About the shelter for the homeless, you mean.' The Vicar managed to say it without a hint of irony in his voice or on his face.

Silently Bairstow cursed him; he was making it damnably difficult. He knew that they all knew exactly what was at stake, but he wasn't about to let the Vicar force him into spelling it out. Changing tack, he replied. 'Yes, that's right – it's a great shame, isn't it? The need is so great, even in this affluent part of London.'

'The solicitor said that a Consistory Court wouldn't go against the DAC,' Topping contributed. 'I was wondering if there was anything else we could sell instead. But Martin said—'

Bairstow interrupted him. 'I said that perhaps we'll have to put that idea on the back burner for the time being, and look at other priorities in the parish instead.'

'Yes?' The Vicar raised his eyebrows, inviting him to go on.

Taking a deep breath, Bairstow plunged in. 'It's that . . . the curate. She's got to go, Father.'

'Rachel?' The look of surprise on his face raised deliberate obtuseness to a fine art. 'But she's doing a good job. Works jolly hard, she does. It's been a great help to me in my parish work. And she's bright, as well – she's only been on the job a few weeks, but already she's picked up so much about the people involved, and the setup in the two parishes. Give her a few more months, Martin. It's early days yet. She'll shape up – you'll see.'

'Only if she's capable of changing her gender!' Bairstow exploded. 'Bloody hell, Father! I have nothing against the woman personally, but this is an Anglo-Catholic parish! Don't you read the papers? Don't you know what's happening in the Church of England?'

Long after the wardens had gone, Father Keble Smythe sat in his study, cradling an empty glass and staring into the dying embers of the fire. It didn't require a Martin Bairstow to tell him that he'd made a mistake in appointing Rachel Nightingale as his curate. But his concern was not for the parish, nor for the delicate sensibilities of Dolly Topping and her cronies. From his point of view the mistake was personal, with consequences that might damage his own prospects.

His piloting of his own career to date had been characterised by an unerring instinct for those things that would best enhance his image, and a certain amount of caution; together with good connections and a fair degree of ability those qualities had served him well, and had advanced him to a position where preferment seemed assured. But now he had made a potentially fatal error: he had allowed his short-term needs to overshadow his long-term goals. The loss of Father Julian as his curate had left him hopelessly swamped with parish work, and that, along with the desire to curry favour with those who had suggested it, had blinded him to the dangers inherent in Rachel Nightingale's appointment. His instincts had let him down, and that in itself depressed him almost as much as the consequences of his misstep.

Now that it was too late, now that he had tacitly allied himself with the pro-women camp, it had become evident that the Church of England was prepared to be more than generous with opponents of women's ordination who were willing to stay within the Anglican Church rather than joining the exodus to Rome. Fast-streaming promotion opportunities were available – deanships, archdeaconries and suffragan bishoprics were being offered to the best and brightest of the anti-women clergy. Bribes, perhaps, if one were being cynical, but those who were beneficiaries of such largesse were not about to put too fine a point on it.

It might have been him. William Keble Smythe groaned unconsciously, thinking about what might have been. He could have been a suffragan bishop, or even a London area bishop.

Then what was he to do? Going over to Rome, as he'd been aware all along was his churchwardens' intention, wasn't really an option for him. He had no illusions that a horde – or even a trickle – of rogue Anglican clergy would be received by Rome with open arms, bags of money, or opportunities for career advancement. Rome was a dead end. Even without the complications of a wife, he knew that it wasn't for him.

But what was left?

If only . . .

She had to go.

With a surge of resolution, Father Keble Smythe reached for the whisky decanter and refilled his long-empty glass. He didn't know how it was to be accomplished, but Martin Bairstow was right. Rachel Nightingale had to go. Changing horses in mid-stream could be a dangerous activity, but sometimes it was the only alternative to drowning. Somehow, some day soon, she had to go.

Walking along beside Ruth Kingsley, Rachel was glad that the girl was in an ebullient, talkative mood: it gave her time for reflection, and masked the fact that she was less than her usual cheerful self.

Her impromptu visit to Vanessa Bairstow had been cut short by Martin Bairstow's return home, and the resulting scene had not been a pleasant one. Accustomed as she was to rudeness, both subtle and direct, Rachel had still not been prepared for what the churchwarden had said to her. The experience had left her badly shaken.

But Ruth seemed unaware of her disquiet, chattering on about her boredom with her work experience. 'Dead boring,' she said yet again. 'Nothing but running the photocopier and making tea, although today he sent me to the library to look up some information. About Canon Law and Consistory Courts. Don't ask me why. It wasn't really much more interesting than photocopying, but at least it got me out of that boring office.'

'Canon Law?' For a moment Rachel's interest was caught, but soon Ruth was off on another variation of her complaint. 'And the evenings are just as bad. Sitting around playing Cluedo, just like I was eight years old. Aunt Lucy just doesn't seem to realise that I'm nearly grown up. And *him*.' She shuddered melodramatically. 'He's *awful*. I just don't know what Aunt Lucy sees in him.'

'Mr Middleton-Brown, you mean?'

Ruth nodded. 'Yes, *him*. He's so soppy about Aunt Lucy – it just makes me sick.' With a few gagging noises to demonstrate her disgust, she went on, 'Last night, I went into the kitchen before dinner and found them *kissing*. Ugh – it was nauseating! Before dinner, even!' She gagged again. 'Gross.'

In spite of herself, Rachel smiled in amusement. Poor Lucy, she thought. And poor Ruth, to have her delicate sensibilities so offended. 'Aren't you being a little hard on your aunt?' she suggested gently.

'Oh, no. Aunt Lucy used to be so . . . sensible. Before she met *him*,' Ruth declared, adding maliciously, 'they're living in sin, you know. And she doesn't want Grandad to find out. I told her that you wouldn't approve.'

Rachel decided that the situation wasn't really so amusing; she thought carefully about how to respond. 'It's not up to me to approve or disapprove,' she said as mildly as possible. 'And it's not up to you, either. Your aunt is a grown woman, responsible for her own decisions.'

'But it's so hypocritical,' Ruth declared with fierce intensity. 'If she wasn't ashamed of it, she wouldn't mind Grandad knowing about it.'

'Oh, Ruth.' Rachel shook her head. 'I'm afraid that people are often a lot more complicated than we'd like them to be. That's one thing I've learned in my job. There are so often conflicting motivations, and so many factors that someone on the outside can't possibly understand. When I realised that, I knew that I was halfway towards accepting people as they are, not as I wish they were.'

She wouldn't have listened to anyone else, but Rachel's words carried a great deal of weight with Ruth. 'Oh,' she said thoughtfully. 'Well, maybe. But still . . .'

'Now, here we are at Vera Bright's house,' Rachel interrupted in a brisk voice. 'She lives with her father, who is very old – nearly a hundred.'

That had the desired effect; Ruth turned to her with wide eyes. 'A hundred!'

'Well, nearly. Ninety-six,' she amended.

To Ruth, it was much the same; as far as she was concerned, anyone over thirty, even Aunt Lucy though perhaps not Rachel Nightingale, was terminally old. The woman who answered the door, with her wrinkled face and stringy body, looked to her young eyes as though she might have been a hundred as well, but common sense told her that if she was the daughter of the ninety-six-year-old man, she probably wasn't much over seventy.

'Hello, Miss Bright,' said Rachel with a smile. 'Have we called at an inconvenient time?'

The older woman's face lit up. 'No, not at all. Father and I were just watching the television. We do most evenings.'

'I wouldn't want to interrupt anything important.'

'Oh, no,' Vera Bright assured her. 'It's only a programme about the life cycle of the bee that Father wanted to see. He likes the nature programmes, though I'd sometimes prefer to watch a film. Or listen to the wireless. Please come in.' She looked curiously at Ruth as they stepped into the hall, but was too polite to say anything.

'This is my young friend, Ruth Kingsley,' Rachel introduced her. 'Ruth, this is Miss Bright.'

Vera Bright smiled at Ruth. 'How nice to meet you. You might not believe this, but you remind me a great deal of myself when I was a girl. My hair was just that colour.'

Ruth hoped that her face didn't betray her amazement. It was difficult enough to believe that this faded, drained-looking woman had ever been young at all, but that she should have been like her was beyond comprehension. 'Oh, really?' she managed.

The older woman gave a quick look over her shoulder in the direction of the room from which issued a barrage of sound, loud buzzing with an even louder voice-over. 'Come upstairs for a minute,' she whispered conspiratorially. 'I'll show you.'

Rachel and Ruth followed her up the stairs and into a room that was surprisingly small and claustrophobic for a house of that size. It wasn't that the room was cluttered – it was in fact almost bare in its simplicity – but it had an airless quality about it that both Ruth and Rachel found oppressive. 'Here,' said Vera, picking up a silver-framed photo from the table beside the bed and handing it to Ruth. 'See what I mean?'

The girl who laughed up at Ruth was young, probably in her late teens or early twenties. Though the photo was in black and white, the camera had captured the girl's essence: a face bursting with vitality and happiness, framed with vigorous curls that might have been red, her head held on a proud neck above a lithe, lively body.

'Oh!' said Ruth.

'She *is* like you,' Rachel declared, looking over her shoulder. She smiled at the older woman. 'Miss Bright, you were lovely.'

After a moment of staring at the girl in the photo, Ruth's attention shifted to the other inhabitant of the frame. Next to the young Vera Bright, his arm draped around her shoulders casually but possessively, was a good-looking young man in uniform. He had an open, guileless face with liquid dark eyes and a wide smiling mouth, under cropped hair that looked as if it might have been dark blond in colour. 'Who is he?' she asked with curiosity.

To her own amazement, Vera Bright's voice was steady; she hadn't spoken his name in years. 'Sergeant Gerald Hansen, his name was. Gerry. He was an American airman, in the war. We were going to be married. But he . . . he was killed.'

'Oh!' Stricken, Ruth looked up at her. 'Oh, I'm so sorry. How sad.'

'It was a long time ago,' Vera Bright said quickly, embarrassed. She reached for the photo.

Over the cacophony of the television below, a querulous, imperious voice made itself heard. 'Vera? Where have you disappeared to, girl? Who was it at the door?'

CHAPTER 14

Teach me thy way, O Lord: and lead me in the right way, because of mine enemies.
Psalm 27.13

The next two days were busy ones for Rachel, as Ruth returned to the tedium of the photocopier. In addition to her regular parish duties, there were several things that she needed to follow up on.

It was on Thursday afternoon that she paid another call on Vera Bright. The older woman had been much on her mind lately, but she'd found it extremely difficult to get to know her in any meaningful way with the old doctor always present. On Thursday, however, she was in luck: Dr Bright was taking a nap when she called, and she was able to have nearly an hour alone with his daughter before he returned to consciousness and began demanding his tea.

Afterwards, cycling home, Rachel wasn't sure whether it had been a good thing or not. Vera Bright had clearly needed someone to talk to, someone to listen to her, but it had been an emotionally draining – and troubling – experience for Rachel. Vera Bright had poured out her soul to her: where should she take it from there? Obviously some action was needed. It was the second time in as many days that she'd felt pastorally out of her depth, and it made her realise how inadequate her theological college training had been in preparing her to minister to people in the real world. Her knowledge of tidy textbook cases was extensive, but it was only now that she was becoming aware of how insufficient that was. People, and the lives they lived, *weren't* tidy – they were messy and complicated. She had a lot to learn, Rachel thought ruefully, and the realisation was both depressing and dispiriting.

The problem was, she didn't know quite where to turn for help. Father Keble Smythe wasn't the answer, she decided: he was far too busy with his own parish responsibilities. He might even think she was interfering, overstepping her brief as a curate, by getting involved with the parishioners in this way.

Father Desmond! she thought suddenly, as she came round the corner near her flat, wondering why she hadn't thought of him sooner. Father Desmond, her mentor, who had seen her through that terrible time after the accident, and had set her feet on the road to healing, faith, commitment and finally vocation. He had been her spiritual director through her time at theological college, a wise and holy man as well as an experienced parish priest. Dear Father Desmond – he would know what to do. Letting herself into the flat, she was overwhelmed with the need to see him, to draw on his compassion, his wisdom, and above all his experience.

She went straight to the phone and rang his Cambridge vicarage. He wasn't there. 'I'll have him ring you as soon as he gets in,' his housekeeper promised. She knew that she could have expected no more, but Rachel couldn't help feeling vaguely disappointed as she put the kettle on for a cup of tea.

Father Desmond rang back later. 'Come up and see me, my dear,' he said promptly. 'Come tonight, if you like.'

'I can't do that,' she protested. 'I have to visit Colin tonight.'

'Then come in the morning, on the train. You can be here in an hour. Name the time, Rachel dear – I'll meet you at the station.'

Frantically she reviewed her schedule for the following day. It would be tight, but if she put off one or two non-essential things she just might be able to manage it and still be back in time for her weekly late afternoon staff meeting with Father Keble Smythe, the Administrator, and the Director of Music at St Jude's. 'All right,' she said, making her mind up. 'But I'm not sure about the time – why don't I ring you when I get to King's Cross?'

Her visit to Colin the next morning was necessarily a brief one. She had to get to St Margaret's well before early Mass to prepare the register for Saturday's wedding, a task she'd meant to do later in the afternoon; now, given the uncertain timing of this trip to Cambridge, she decided that she'd better get it out of the way before she left. As soon as Mass was over she was on her way to the Victoria tube station to get the Underground to King's Cross.

When she returned home, a little after three, her answerphone was flashing. She filled the kettle and switched it on, then pushed the button to listen to her messages while the kettle boiled.

There were two messages. The first was from an almost incoherent Nicola Topping. The girl's voice was frantic, desperate: 'Rachel,' she gasped tearfully, 'I've got to see you. This afternoon. It's a matter of life or death. You can't reach me, but I'll come to your flat at four. Please don't let me down.' There followed a few seconds of uncontrolled sobs before the phone was put down.

Rachel barely had time to react before the second message began playing. It was, surprisingly, from Colin's brother Francis; Colin and his brother had never been particularly close, and Rachel's contact with him since the accident had been minimal. 'This is Francis Nightingale,' the brisk voice informed her. 'Please ring me at my office. I don't think it's anything to be alarmed about, but Colin's doctors weren't able to reach you so they've just rung me instead.'

Rachel wasn't alarmed. She might have been, but this sort of thing had happened before: periodically, Colin developed infections, and the doctors had to check with her before they started treatment. The only difference was that Francis had never before been involved; these new London doctors were evidently being ultra-conscientious.

She'd better ring Francis first, and reassure him, she decided, before worrying about Nicola and the staff meeting. Automatically she went about the soothing routine of making tea, pouring the boiling water on to the bags in the teapot, releasing their fragrance.

While the tea steeped she set about locating the number for Francis's London office; it wasn't one she had often required. Eventually she found an old address book in the bureau. She poured herself a large mug of tea and took a reviving sip; she hadn't realised until that moment how tiring her flying trip to Cambridge had been.

The secretary who answered put her on to Francis almost immediately. 'Hello?' he queried.

'Francis?'

'Oh, hello, Rachel.'

'Colin's doctors rang?' she prompted him.

'Yes. They couldn't reach you, and they had me down on their list as next-of-kin after you. It seems that he's developed a kidney infection, and they wanted to talk to you about treatment.'

'But the answerphone was on,' she said. 'Why didn't they just leave a message?'

'I suppose they thought that a message on your answerphone might alarm you.'

'Oh, I'm not alarmed,' Rachel reassured her brother-in-law. 'This sort of thing has happened before, when he was in Cambridge.'

'They don't just automatically start treatment, then?' he asked curiously.

Rachel laughed. 'It's all terribly discreet – they'd never come out and say so – but what it's all about is ... well, you know. Letting people die.'

'What do you mean?'

She took a sip of her tea. 'Sometimes, family members ... well, I suppose they find it difficult having someone like Colin to worry about. They might even consider it a burden in some ways. And when the person gets an infection, it's easy for the doctors to give them minimal treatment, in effect just to let them die of the infection. It happens all the time. The doctors always like to give the next-of-kin the chance to opt for that.'

'And what about you?' he probed.

'Oh, there's no question about it,' Rachel stated. 'The doctors in Cambridge stopped asking, after a while, because they knew I would always want them to do everything they could.'

There was a pause on the other end of the phone. 'Haven't you ever been tempted? I mean, it must be very difficult for you ... ?'

Rachel might have been angry, but she realised that her brother-in-law didn't know her very well. 'Good heavens, no,' she responded mildly. 'I love Colin. I've never considered him a burden.'

'Then what will you do?'

'Well, if you'll give me the number, I'll ring the doctors straightaway and tell them to go ahead with the treatment. And tonight I'll go and see him as usual.'

Francis gave her the number; there was another brief pause. 'Do you think that I might visit him some time?'

He had never before expressed any interest in seeing his brother, so Rachel was surprised and touched. 'Yes, of course. It would be lovely if you did.'

'When do you usually go?'

'Early in the morning, and again at night, at about half-past nine.'

'Every day?' Francis asked incredulously.

'Of course.'

After yet another thoughtful pause, Francis said, 'Well, perhaps I'll see you there one day soon.'

As she put down the phone, and before she rang the doctors, Rachel acknowledged an unhappy truth to herself: it wasn't quite as simple as she'd made it sound to Francis. One day the treatment wouldn't work; one day she would lose him. She said a silent prayer that it would be far in the future, and that when the time came, she would have the grace to let him go.

The doctors dealt with, Rachel looked at her watch. It was clear to her that she'd have to be here when Nicola arrived at four, but that would mean missing the staff meeting. She picked the phone up again and rang the vicarage.

Father Keble Smythe answered himself. 'Stanley's just arrived,' he said. 'I thought you'd be on your way by now.'

'I'm so sorry, Father, but I won't be able to make it this afternoon,' she apologised. 'Something very important has come up – an emergency with a parishioner.'

He masked his irritation quite well. 'Ah, well. Can't be helped, I suppose. Anything I should know about?'

'Not really, Father. Perhaps later.' Rachel hesitated. 'There is something else, though. Something I really need to talk to you about, and as soon as possible. I was wondering if you might have a few moments this evening, after the service . . . ?'

The Vicar gave a short laugh. 'Actually, that's one thing I wanted to speak to you about. I've got some problems about tonight, and I'd like you to take the service for me.'

He wasn't really offering her a choice, but Rachel thought carefully just the same. The service wasn't a Mass – it was St Margaret's Friday night Lenten observance of Exposition of the Blessed Sacrament and Devotions – so there was theoretically no reason why she shouldn't take it, but it seemed to her that there were a number of factors that made it not a very good idea. Her detractors at St Margaret's – how would they accept it? And she'd never done it before, so she was unsure about how well she would manage it. 'I don't know, Father,' she equivocated. 'Isn't there anyone else? I'm not so sure . . .'

'Nonsense,' he declared heartily. 'You've been there every week – you know the form. Just a few prayers, the usual stuff. You'll do just fine. Didn't you do that sort of thing at Cambridge?'

'Well, no,' she admitted. 'But that reminds me, Father. I had to make a quick trip to Cambridge earlier today, and while I was there I called in at my old theological college, and met someone who said he knew you at St Andrews – his name was Douglas. Hamish Douglas. He said to say hello to you.'

There was a brief silence on the other end of the phone. Oh God, thought William Keble Smythe. Not that. He felt a trickle of sweat on his brow that had nothing to do with the warmth of the fire which Mrs Goode had so efficiently provided in his study. 'So you'll take the service,' he said at last, in a jolly voice that sounded false to his own ears. 'Good girl. And I'll see you on Sunday.'

Aimlessly Rachel rearranged a few things on her kitchen worktop, then looked at her watch again. There was still nearly a quarter of an hour to go before Nicola was due, enough time to make another phone call, this time to the Archdeacon.

Emily Neville answered the phone. 'Oh, hello, Emily,' said Rachel. 'This is Rachel. I'd hoped for a word with the Archdeacon.'

Returning her greeting, Emily went on, 'I'm sorry, but Gabriel's not here. I don't expect him back much before supper time. Was it something urgent?'

Rachel, half regretting the impulse that had made her ring, hardly knew how to articulate it. 'Well, no, I wouldn't say urgent. But it's important, I think. I'm not even sure that he's the person I need to talk to, but there's something that's bothering me, something not quite right, and I thought perhaps I ought to tell him about it.'

'If you'll hold on a minute, I'll check the diary in his study,' Emily offered. After a brief pause she came back on the line. 'It looks as though he should be able to see you first thing on Monday,' she said. 'Say about nine. Will that be good enough?'

'Oh, that's fine.' Rachel was relieved; that would give her time to think out what she wanted to say to him, and perhaps to have a word with the Vicar as well. She switched gears. 'So, how are you, Emily?'

'Fine. We're all fine. How about you? Is the job getting to you?'

'Oh, it's not so bad,' Rachel said charitably.

'Even Dolly?'

Rachel laughed. 'Even Dolly. I stay out of her way, and she seems to be trying equally hard to stay out of mine.'

'I'm sure that's just as well.'

'We're both much happier that way, I'm sure,' Rachel agreed.

'And how is Colin?'

'Well, not so good at the moment, as a matter of fact. He's got a kidney infection.'

'Oh, dear.' Emily sounded genuinely concerned, prompting Rachel to go into more detail.

'He'll be fine,' she assured her friend. 'Once they get him pumped full of antibiotics. I was in Cambridge earlier today – I made a quick trip up to see Father Desmond – and when I got back I had a message that the doctors had contacted Colin's brother.'

'I didn't know that Colin had a brother,' said Emily curiously. 'And why did they contact him?'

'Yes, just the one brother, but we've never seen much of him. Francis is some sort of high-powered businessman in London, and Colin has never felt that they had much in common. Anyway,' she went on, the doctors needed permission from the family so that they could begin treating his infection.' She then explained matter-of-factly to Emily, as she had to Francis earlier, that some families might wish to have treatment withheld, and the reason why.

Emily was horrified. 'But that's terrible! How could anyone do that – just let someone die?'

'I used to feel that way about it,' Rachel said with a small sigh. 'I certainly couldn't do it, myself. But now I realise that other people's circumstances are different. For instance, I'm very fortunate – the financial side of it isn't a problem for me. But nursing care of the type Colin needs doesn't come cheap, and might be devastatingly expensive for someone who didn't have the money and who wanted something beyond the level of care that the NHS provides.'

'Colin is lucky that he has you,' Emily declared staunchly, then realised how it might sound to define as lucky a person who was doomed to spend the rest of his life in a hospital bed, completely unaware of his surroundings – especially to the person who seemed likely to spend the rest of *her* life looking after him in one way or another.

But Rachel didn't take it amiss. 'Well, yes,' she said in a facetious tone. 'If he didn't have me, Francis would be his next-of-kin, and he might decide to pull the plug!'

CHAPTER 15

When my spirit was in heaviness thou knewest my path: in the way wherein I walked have they privily laid a snare for me.

Psalm 142.3

At St Margaret's it would be remembered as one of the all-time great rows in the church's history, its causes and its aftermath discussed endlessly afterwards. Oddly enough, in all the postmortem analysis, no one ever thought to accuse Father Keble Smythe of deliberate maliciousness in sending his curate to take the service in his place, or indeed to attribute to him any base motivation or blame for what ensued from his opting out. And though the question of his whereabouts might have come up at the time, such minor matters were swept away by what happened, and later no one gave it a thought. Suffice it to say that Father Keble Smythe was not present at St Margaret's that evening, and never claimed to be; no one else would have admitted missing it.

Robin West, the sacristan, took credit for having seen her first. He was in the chancel when she came in through the church, and though the sole fact of her presence in the church was not a great shock, he was alarmed to see her heading towards the sacristy, his own domain.

His natural impulse, whenever he saw Rachel Nightingale, was to flee, but on this instance, for whatever reason, he decided to stand and fight. Moving in the direction of the sacristy, he intercepted her near the door, just under the stained glass window depicting the stoning of St Stephen. 'Where do you think you're going?' he demanded.

As it was the first time he'd ever spoken to her, she was understandably startled. 'To the sacristy, to vest,' she explained. 'The Vicar has asked me to take the service.'

The sacristan bristled in outraged indignation. 'That doesn't seem very likely. I'm sure that *Father* would never do such a thing.'

It was just the sort of reaction that Rachel had expected; she took a deep breath and stood her ground, and her voice sounded remarkably calm. 'Nevertheless, it's quite true.'

Robin West sputtered ineffectually for a moment and paused as Rachel continued on her way into the sacristy. Uncertain, he turned to find that Martin Bairstow, Stanley Everitt and the Toppings had arrived more or less simultaneously at the back of the church; he rushed to intercept them. 'It's that woman!' he announced dramatically. 'She claims that Father has sent her to take the service She's gone into the sacristy!'

In spite of her considerable bulk, Dolly was the first to reach the sacristy door, followed closely by the others. They met Rachel coming out, her face set in determination, carrying the veiled monstrance. 'Oh no, you don't,' Dolly bellowed. 'Not here. Not at St Margaret's. You're not ruining *our* church. Can't you see that you're not wanted here? Why don't you just go away and leave us alone?'

Stanley Everitt wrung his hands in an even more agitated manner than usual and begged everyone to stay calm, but his voice was scarcely heard in the fracas. Bairstow raised his voice in support of Dolly; Norman Topping nodded vigorously and emitted the occasional squeak of encouragement. In the midst of it all, Rachel Nightingale stood with her eyes closed, her scar standing out in angry relief on her pale cheek. She clutched the base of the monstrance, willing it all to end. I didn't ask for this, she said to herself, trying to think of a way to escape. It was clear that no service would be held that night: no matter the outcome of the battle, these people were in no fit state to worship God, to bow their knees and their heads before the presence of the Sacrament.

Incensed beyond rational thought, Dolly made a grab for the monstrance. She hadn't counted on Rachel's firm grasp; for a moment the two women seemed locked in a stalemate. Then, with a superhuman wrench, Dolly tore it away from Rachel, and the veil, dislodged by the violence of the gesture, floated downwards between them like a silent scream of protest.

It was only a short time later, though it seemed an age, that Rachel was on her bicycle, traversing the familiar streets that led her, every morning and every evening, to the nursing home and Colin. She made a very great effort not to dwell on the horrific scene that had just taken place, thinking instead about Father Desmond, about Colin, and about the unfortunate and unhappy Nicola Topping.

I do hope that I've done the right thing about Nicola, Rachel thought. Sending her to talk to Vera Bright – it could well be a great help for both of them. Then again, it could backfire, and make things even worse.

She was an experienced bicyclist; no matter how preoccupied she was with other concerns, or how familiar she was with the quiet backstreets, she rode cautiously and didn't take foolish risks. But she never saw the car coming. It caught her broadside, sent her flying, and the pavement rushing up to meet her was the last thing that Rachel Nightingale saw.

Quiet as the street was, it was only moments later that the off-duty PC Huw Meredith strolled along, feeling sated and more than a little pleased with himself after one of his regular Friday evening interludes with Pamela Hartman. This evening's encounter had been exceptionally satisfying, and Pam had promised to try to make some excuse to her husband and meet him on Saturday as well. Even after tonight, or perhaps especially after tonight, that was something to look forward to: a whole Saturday afternoon in bed – or on the sofa, or in the shower, or on the hearth rug in front of the fire – with the delectable Pam.

What caught his eye was the spinning bicycle wheel. Its rapid revolutions had slowed considerably, but still it turned with the click-click-click sound of a roulette wheel. Huw Meredith paused to investigate, wrenching his mind away from Pam.

The sight was not a pretty one: apart from the spinning front wheel, the bicycle was a mangled and twisted metal sculpture with no resemblance to its former state. With a small shock, PC Meredith saw that its rider had been a blonde, like Pam, and that she had probably been an attractive young woman. Probably – with the injuries she had sustained, it was difficult to tell. He was an experienced policeman, whose beat included some rather unsavoury areas of London, and he had seen hit-and-run accidents before. 'Bloody kids,' he muttered savagely as he looked round for a phone box, furious to have his enjoyable evening spoilt by a bit of juvenile tomfoolery gone wrong. 'Bloody joy-riding kids.' He would ring the nearest police station; it was clearly too late for an ambulance.

Part 2

CHAPTER 16

Out of the mouth of very babes and sucklings hast thou ordained strength, because of thine enemies: that thou mightest still the enemy, and the avenger.
Psalm 8.2

Few people in London truly mourned for Rachel Nightingale, but of those who did, Ruth Kingsley was inconsolable.

From the beginning – from the first shattering moment – she'd insisted that it had been no accident; nothing that anyone said could convince her to the contrary.

'But darling,' said Lucy in her most reasonable voice, one which she'd been called upon to employ consciously with increasing frequency since Ruth's arrival. It was a raw March Sunday afternoon, the day after they'd learned about Rachel's death; with no real will to do anything else, the three of them were in the sitting room of Lucy's house, waiting for the day to end. 'Darling, the police know about these things. They say that it was a hit-and-run driver who killed her. Another person was badly hurt in almost the same spot, just a few weeks earlier. By young kids, probably in a stolen car. It happens more often than you'd think in London.' David had checked with a policeman he knew, and he'd been quite definite.

'That's what they *say*.' Ruth's tear-stained face had a mulish expression. 'Maybe they believe that, or maybe they're just saying it. But I *know*. I know that someone at that church – at St Margaret's – did it, on purpose. They wanted to get rid of her, and they did. They ran her down in cold blood.'

'Aren't you being just a wee bit melodramatic?' David's patience with Ruth, always tenuous, had worn a bit thin of late.

The girl seemed even more gawky than usual, wrapping her thin arms around her body as she glared at him with undisguised hostility. 'I don't care what you say. I don't care what the police say. I know that they did her in, one of them.'

They'd been through it all before, endlessly, but Lucy, who was keeping a firm lid on her own emotional reaction, hoped that there might be something cathartic for Ruth in the process, and that it was better for the girl to talk about it than to bottle it up inside. 'But why, darling? They're church people. Church people don't go round murdering one another just because they don't like them.'

'Because she was a woman, of course. They were horrible to her. She told me so.'

Lucy lifted the lid of the teapot and peered inside. They'd been through a great deal of tea, but it looked like this pot might stretch to one more cup for someone, before she had to get up and boil the kettle again. Unselfishly she offered it to Ruth. 'More tea, darling?'

The girl shook her head in a listless negative, but Lucy poured the remaining tea into her cup anyway, then took the empty pot to the kitchen. Not touching the tea, Ruth sat very still, tears trickling down her cheeks. After a moment, she gulped, wiped at her eyes with the back of her hand, and said in a bitter voice, 'The police won't do anything, will they?'

David sighed. 'They'll try to find the hit-and-run driver, if they can. After all, it was more than the usual hit-and-run – someone was killed. The driver could be charged with causing death by reckless driving, and that's a criminal offence, with a prison sentence involved.'

'But how could they find them?'

He picked up his teacup and looked at the dregs in the bottom. 'Oh, the police have ways. If the car was stolen, it may be abandoned later, and it might have prints in it. And they check body shops for cars that have been brought in for repairs to damaged wings. I mean, unless someone was driving a tank, that sort of impact would have to do some sort of damage to their car,' he explained, with a feeble smile at the mental picture of a tank on the streets of Pimlico.

'If that's supposed to be funny,' snapped Ruth, 'I don't think much of your sense of humour.'

Deciding that defending himself would be counterproductive, David lapsed into silence. He wished that Lucy would come back with more tea; he wished that it weren't too early for something stronger. In his opinion it was by no means too early, but he was sure that the *enfant terrible* would disagree. *Enfant terrible*: that was how he had come to think of Ruth. Once or twice it had slipped out when talking to Lucy, who didn't appear to find it very amusing.

The intrusive chirp of the telephone interrupted his reverie, as it rang just once; obviously Lucy had been near enough to pick it up right away. It meant, though, that she might be a while in returning.

Clearing his throat, he tried again with Ruth, who had withdrawn into a bleak stillness. 'I know that you're upset about Rachel, but . . .'

'Upset?' She startled David with the intensity of her reply. 'Of course I'm upset! She was the most wonderful person I've ever known, and now she's dead, and the person who murdered her is going to get away with it, because no one believes me!'

'Murder is an easy word to throw around,' he said carefully. 'But I think you'll find that people don't very often murder each other because of their gender. There are plenty of reasons I've heard for murder, but that's not one of them.'

In spite of herself, Ruth was interested. 'Like what?' she demanded. 'What sort of reasons?'

'Money, for a start. If there were someone who was going to benefit financially from Rachel's death, I'd want to take a closer look at it myself. Or sometimes people commit murder to conceal a secret, something that they wouldn't want anyone else to find out. If Rachel had found out something like that . . .'

'Maybe that's it,' Ruth interrupted him excitedly. 'People confided in her, you know – she was that kind of person. Maybe someone told her something, and later regretted it. And then they murdered her so she wouldn't tell anyone else. I'm going to find out what it was,' she added with resolution. 'If the police won't do it, I'll have to investigate myself. *I'll* find out who murdered her.'

The vehemence of David's reaction surprised him almost as much as it did Ruth. 'Don't be so bloody stupid,' he said with quiet force. 'You can't just go round asking people questions, as though it were a game of Cluedo! You're not dealing with Mrs Peacock or the Reverend Green here – we're talking about real people, with real lives and real secrets. You could get yourself into a hell of a lot of trouble prying into things that aren't your business, murder or no murder.'

Shocked but stubborn, Ruth didn't deign to answer, pulling her lips over her mouthful of metal and withdrawing back into herself. She turned away from David and bit her lip as the trickle of tears started again.

Why did I do that? David asked himself. I've only antagonised her, and she's going to go ahead and do whatever she damn well pleases anyway.

He was comforted when, a moment later, Sophie appeared and jumped on his lap. And so Lucy found them – sitting in silence, Ruth with her tears and David with the cat – when she returned, bearing a fresh pot of tea and looking thoughtful.

'Who was on the phone, love?' David held his cup out.

'Emily.' She took the cup, filled it and handed it back to him.

He sniffed the steaming liquid gratefully, waiting a moment for it to cool. 'Anything important?'

She shook her head, but gave him a look which he rightly interpreted to mean that she'd tell him about it later.

Although David and Lucy generally favoured a rather leisurely approach to lovemaking, that night they made love with an unaccustomed urgency, fuelled by the inevitable sense of mortality in the aftermath of the death of someone they knew, someone younger than either of them. Afterwards, too keyed up to sleep, they talked for a long time.

'You don't think that Ruth could be right – that Rachel's death wasn't really an accident?' Lucy suggested tentatively.

David laughed. 'I know that our recent experiences have suggested otherwise, love, but sometimes people really *do* die by accident. Just because your charming niece has a fixation about Rachel Nightingale ...'

'That's not really being fair to Ruth,' she protested. 'There *were* people who hated Rachel, who wanted to get rid of her. If it weren't Ruth who was saying it, you'd be the first one to agree that her death is a little too convenient.'

He thought about that for a moment, then admitted with a self-deprecating chuckle, 'Well, you may be right about that. I *am* inclined to take a contrary position where the *enfant terrible* is concerned. But that aside, Lucy love, I just can't see that anyone had a strong enough motive to ... well, you know. Just because she was a woman who wanted to be a priest, I mean. I'd have to be convinced that there was some other motive before I even considered the possibility seriously. Like money, as I said to Ruth earlier.'

'According to what Emily told me,' Lucy thought aloud, 'Rachel must have had a lot of money. From the settlement after the accident, you know.'

'Not necessarily,' he cautioned. 'In the first place, the money might only just be enough to pay for her husband's personal care, assuming he lives for a good many years yet. And secondly, who would benefit financially from Rachel's death? Presumably only her husband, so that doesn't really lead us anywhere.'

The heat generated by their lovemaking had begun to dissipate; Lucy shivered slightly and pulled the duvet up under her chin. 'Colin has a brother, Emily tells me. Couldn't he benefit somehow?'

'I don't see how, as long as Colin is alive. Why – what does he have to do with anything?'

'Well,' Lucy explained, 'when Emily rang me this afternoon she told me that she talked to Rachel on the phone on Friday, just a few hours before . . . you know.'

'And?' he prompted.

'Rachel told her that Colin had a kidney infection, and that somehow his brother had got involved. Emily said that she made a little joke that she hoped nothing happened to her, or Colin's brother might decide to pull the plug. And a few hours later . . .'

'Hmm. Just a coincidence, I'm sure,' David stated as he drifted off to sleep. 'And not a very funny joke, as it turned out.'

But two days later, when he opened his morning paper to the obituary page, David read that Colin Nightingale had died at the age of thirty-five, of complications from a kidney infection.

CHAPTER 17

Thou hast turned my heaviness into joy: thou hast put off my sackcloth, and girded me with gladness.

Psalm 30.12

David read the obituary out to Lucy over their after-breakfast coffee, while Ruth was taking her customary extended shower. '"The young scientist, whose brilliant career was cut so tragically short by a road accident nearly four years ago, had survived in a vegetative state since then. By sad coincidence, his wife Rachel, a Deacon in the Church of England, was killed in another accident just last week in London." And then it goes on about his career, and the research he was involved in before the accident. Don't ask me to read it – I can't even pronounce most of the words.'

Lucy, still in shock at the news but fully aware of the implications, put her finger on the cogent point. 'But it doesn't say anything about the money? Or about any survivors or other family members?'

'Nothing. These things usually don't.'

'Is there any way you can find out?'

He shook his head, still unwilling to admit that there was anything in it. 'Not really. Why don't you ring Emily and see if she knows? If you're really that curious, that is.'

Lucy gave him a warning look as Ruth came into the kitchen, her face almost as white as her towelling dressing gown, the freckles standing out in sharp relief and her short, damp, copper curls providing a shocking contrast to her pallor; two days and nights of crying had taken their toll. 'I don't really feel like going to work today,' she announced. 'I think I'll just stay here.'

David was quick to agree. 'If you don't feel well, then you must stay home. Your Aunt Lucy will take good care of you.'

The look Lucy gave him this time mingled understanding with annoyance – now *she* was the one whose work would suffer – though her voice betrayed nothing but concern. 'Of course you must stay home, darling. I'm sure that David will manage without you somehow.'

He smiled wryly. 'Yes, I'll manage.'

'You'll just have to find some other flunky to make your tea,' the girl muttered, sitting down at the table in expectation of being waited on by her aunt.

Lucy did what was expected. 'Would you like some tea now, darling?' She got up and went to fill the kettle.

'Yes, please.'

'And how about something to eat?'

Ruth considered the options. 'I think I might be able to eat a poached egg. And some dry toast, perhaps.'

'And I'd better be off,' David stated, anxious now to escape in spite of feeling vaguely guilty about lumbering Lucy with the burden of Ruth for the day. But it was Lucy's own fault that the girl was here in the first place, he justified to himself.

Lucy walked him to the front door. 'Have a good day, David darling, and if you have a chance to find out anything about Colin Nightingale . . .'

'Not likely, my love.' He kissed her lightly. 'And you take good care of the *enfant terrible* for me.'

In spite of his scepticism, though, David found himself, during the course of the morning, thinking about Colin Nightingale and the unlikely coincidence of his demise just a few days after his wife's untimely death. Once again he remembered the feeling that had nagged him when Lucy had first told him about Rachel: there was something about that settlement that had been important.

Restlessly he left his desk in the late morning and wandered downstairs to the firm's library. From the shelves he pulled a few volumes of cases and precedents; based on the date of the accident, he could judge with a fair degree of accuracy when the legal aftermath was likely to have occurred. He settled down at a table with the weighty books and began flipping through them.

It didn't take him long to find what he was looking for. He read through it twice, just to make sure that he hadn't misunderstood; his eyebrows went up and his mouth rounded in a soundless whistle.

Lucy had been right about one thing: there was a great deal of money involved. Although the settlement that Rachel had been given in compensation for her own rather minor injuries was not large, nor was the amount awarded for the death of her daughter, that was only the beginning. She had also been awarded a generous settlement – much more generous than was usual – in compensation for the loss of companionship and financial support of her husband. That was in addition to the even larger sum bestowed on Colin, based on the curtailment of his brilliant future as a scientist and the likely cost of his medical care over his expected lifetime. All told it added up to an astronomical sum, in excess of a million pounds.

It sounded like a lot of money, but David realised that it was not over-generous: private medical care for brain-damaged people was cripplingly expensive, and over a number of years the money would be eaten away, even if the capital was carefully invested. But the settlement had been made less than a year ago, so little of the money would have been spent. That meant, thought David, that at the time of her death Rachel Nightingale had been in possession of a tidy fortune. On her death it would have gone to Colin, but now Colin was dead as well. Someone, he thought, has done very well indeed out of the two deaths, occurring as they had in that particular order and with such convenient proximity in time.

It was nearly time for lunch. During the past week, David had been encumbered with Ruth at lunchtime; in spite of his contention that the girl was perfectly capable of going round the corner for a sandwich on her own, Lucy had been firm. It was a part of her overcautious reaction to her position *in loco parentis* that had led Lucy to insist that Ruth was not to travel anywhere in London on her own, a restriction that Ruth resented every bit as much as David did. And so David had been reduced to eating his lunch in Ruth's company at a sandwich bar in High Holborn, thus missing out on the legal gossip on offer at the various pubs and wine bars clustered around the Inns of Court which catered to members of the bar, solicitors, and assorted hangers-on in the profession. Indulging in a bit of professional gossip over a drink at lunch was one of the things he most enjoyed about working in London, and after a week of bland sandwiches and even blander conversation – if you could call Ruth's peevish and non-communicative noises that – he felt out of touch; today, without her, he could catch up. He headed for El Vino's, perhaps the most venerable of the establishments frequented by lawyers, vowing to treat himself to a smoked salmon sandwich and a half-bottle of the house champagne in celebration of his unexpected freedom from the *enfant terrible.*

In the five or so months that he'd been in London, David had made quite a few contacts over lunchtime drinks. Entering El Vino's, he scanned the crowd for a likely source of gossip; to his disappointment, the only familiar face he saw belonged to none other than Henry Thymme. That was one person he definitely *didn't* want to talk to, he decided. He found a seat at a table with a view of the bar, ordered the champagne and sandwich, and retreated behind his newspaper, noting with interest an item about a forthcoming sale at Christie's, featuring ecclesiastical silver and other bits and pieces. It would be worth stopping by one day when he was in that area and picking up a catalogue – not because he was likely to buy anything, but just from general interest.

When his lunch arrived he put his paper down and glanced in the direction of Henry Thymme, curious to see what he was up to. Thymme seemed to be enjoying an uproarious drinking session with another man at the bar; his face was even redder than usual, and his voice boomed out across the room. 'Time for another, dear chap?'

His companion nodded, turning to the bar. He didn't look familiar to David; in fact, there was something about him – about the cut of his suit, perhaps, or the cut of his hair – that seemed to indicate that he wasn't a lawyer. Not that there weren't impeccably dressed and coiffured barristers and even solicitors, especially in this part of Fleet Street, but somehow David didn't think that this man was one of them. He was tall and thin, sharp-featured, with an artistic swoop of grey hair and a trim grey moustache to match, though he didn't look much over forty.

His curiosity satisfied, David returned to his newspaper as he sipped his champagne and ate his sandwich, becoming engrossed in an article about a church treasurer who had managed to embezzle a mind-boggling sum of money over a period of some twenty-three years before being found out when the new incumbent decided to have a look at the books. 'Ah, the good old C of E,' he muttered, shaking his head. But his cynical ruminations were interrupted by a cry of delighted recognition at his elbow.

'Middleton-Brown, my good man!' Henry Thymme hailed him. 'Why are you hiding behind your newspaper? Come and join me for a drink!'

'But . . .' David protested feebly.

'No buts, my friend. You're all alone, and that's not a good thing to be. In fact, it's not allowed at El Vino's, is it?' he insisted, addressing the last query to the waitress, who shook her head obligingly, mindful of a good customer. 'What are you drinking, my boy?' he went on, pulling up a chair across from David.

David swiftly calculated his intake. He'd finished off a half-bottle of champagne; he could safely have another glass or two and still be able to function in the afternoon. Realising that there was no escape, he capitulated. 'Well, I was having champagne.'

Thymme snapped his fingers at the waitress; he seemed to have trouble making them work properly. 'A bottle of your best champagne,' he ordered.

It arrived promptly, on ice, and was poured out with ceremony. David, whose budget didn't usually run to that particular brand, took an appreciative sip. 'Lovely stuff. Thanks.'

'I like a man who knows his champagne.' Leaning across the table, Thymme confided loudly, 'That's one of my disappointments with the lad. Young Justin. Never has developed a taste for good wine. Says he prefers lager, like some football lout. Or sweet sherry – even worse. A great disappointment.'

The subject of Justin Thymme was one to be avoided at all costs. Casting about wildly for a neutral topic of conversation, David observed, 'Are you alone? I thought you were with someone else.'

'*Was*, dear boy. He's gone now. Client of mine, just had some good news. Wanted to buy me a drink.'

'Yes?' David wasn't particularly interested, but any alternative subject was to be encouraged.

Thymme shook his head ruminatively. 'Just goes to show you how quickly things can change. You know what I mean?' David nodded his encouragement, and Thymme lowered his voice to a volume more appropriate for the delivery of confidential information. 'When I saw him a week ago, he was ready to cut his throat. Not literally, of course, but the man was pretty damn low. Lost a packet with Lloyd's. Not the only one, of course – hell, plenty have. But that wasn't all, poor sod. Rich wife. American. She's just left him. Left him or chucked him out, I'm not sure which. Found out he's been screwing his secretary. Found out how much money he'd lost. Can't really blame him about Lloyd's, of course. But between you and me, my friend, he's got a weakness for the ponies, as well. He's in rather deep to a few unsavoury types. When his wife left him, he didn't know how he was going to raise the cash.' He shook his head again. 'Life's funny, isn't it?'

David was fascinated in spite of himself. 'What happened?'

'Oh, didn't I tell you?' Thymme's voice dropped to a whisper. 'He's come into an absolute fortune. A million at least. His brother died, and he'll get everything. Even after death duties, it's a hell of a lot of money. Now it's up to me to get the divorce settlement pushed through before the will is settled, so his bitch of a wife can't get her filthy little hands on any of the dosh.'

'Francis Nightingale?' whispered Lucy in amazement; they had to keep their voices low so that Ruth, languishing in the sitting room, wouldn't hear them. 'But how clever of you, darling!'

'Not clever at all,' David replied with a self-deprecating but pleased smile. 'You might say that it was handed to me on a plate – or more accurately, in a glass. Thymme was so legless by that point that he didn't care how indiscreet he was being. He told me everything I ever wanted to know about Francis Nightingale, including the fact that he's due to get all of his brother's money. And that he needed it pretty badly.'

They were in the kitchen, preparing supper. David related the gist of Thymme's revelations under the cover of running water as he washed the lettuce.

Lucy's verdict was swift and succinct. 'He sounds like a complete sod.'

'Absolutely,' he agreed. 'Just like his solicitor. But the point is, Lucy love, that I should have trusted your instincts. Francis Nightingale had a hell of a motive to run his sister-in-law down and make it look like a random hit-and-run. Rachel dying when she did, before Colin, saved his bacon – if Colin had died first, Francis would presumably not have seen a penny of all that money.'

'But how could he have known that Colin was going to die? If, like Emily said, he'd had these infections before, why should anyone think that this one would kill him?'

David turned the water off and shook the lettuce vigorously. 'You're forgetting the other thing that Emily said. That after Rachel was dead, it was up to Francis whether he pulled the plug or not – whether Colin received treatment for the infection.'

'And you think . . . ?'

'I think,' said David, 'that if the police aren't going to take a closer look at Francis Nightingale, someone else is going to have to do it.'

CHAPTER 18

Plead thou my cause, O Lord, with them that strive with me: and fight thou against them that fight against me.

Psalm 35.1

The next morning, David sat unproductively at his desk, trying to think through the puzzle of Rachel Nightingale's death. He was by no means convinced, even yet, that it had been anything but accidental, but he admitted to himself that there were some circumstantial grounds for suspicion. It certainly would have been possible, in any case, for her brother-in-law to have been involved. Rachel went to see her husband every night, presumably at a regular time. From that supposition it took only a small leap for David to arrive at the conclusion that anyone who knew of her routine, and that surely included her brother-in-law, would have been able to lie in wait for her to cycle past. It really had nothing to do with him, he acknowledged, though he was curious nonetheless. Would it be possible to make some discreet enquiries, just to satisfy himself? If so, how might he go about it? Before he'd had time to formulate a plan, a call came through from Henry Thymme. It was an occurrence that David had come to dread, heralding as it always did some further problem with 'young Justin', so he picked up the phone with trepidation.

Thymme sounded unusually subdued; perhaps, thought David, he was just hung over. He certainly deserved to be, given the quantity of alcohol he'd consumed in the early part of the previous day, let alone what he'd probably drunk later. 'I've realised, my dear boy, that I might have been just a touch . . . ah . . . indiscreet in our conversation yesterday. From what I can remember, anyway,' he added with a more characteristic chuckle.

'Think nothing of it,' David assured him.

'The thing is, old chap, I could use your help.'

'Oh?' He tried to keep his voice noncommittal, but he was afraid that it sounded as dismayed as he felt. Here it comes, he thought. The latest escapade of Justin Thymme. The immigration office's investigation into the validity of the younger Thymme's marriage was still in progress;

had the fool done something idiotic to jeopardise that? Surely he hadn't been back to Hampstead Heath . . .

'I think I mentioned that I was handling my client's divorce, and that I wanted to expedite it as much as possible.'

'Yes, you did mention that.'

Thymme cleared his throat thoughtfully. 'Well, I've remembered that the wife's solicitor is a partner at your firm – Russell Galloway.'

'One of the senior partners,' David amplified.

'Yes, of course. The thing is, I was rather hoping that you might do me a great favour and have a word with him.'

'Oh, yes? About what, exactly?'

Thymme's voice took on a wheedling tone. 'About this divorce settlement. Try to get him to speed it up at his end. Without telling him what I mentioned to you yesterday about the money, needless to say.'

David was astonished at the man's effrontery. 'And why should I do that? Why should I want to do something against the best interests of a client of one of the partners in my firm?'

There was a pause on the other end of the phone as Thymme chose his words carefully. 'I like you, my boy. You've done well by me and the lad so far, and I think you're a damned good solicitor. And with all due respect to Sir Crispin and Fosdyke, Fosdyke and Galloway, I also think that you could do better for yourself. I could use a smart chap like you in my firm. I could offer you a partnership straightaway, with a substantial financial incentive, and unlimited potential for advancement. What do you say, Middleton-Brown?'

'I say,' David stated quietly, 'that I'm going to forget that we ever had this conversation, and I suggest that you do likewise. And that I wouldn't work for you, Mr Thymme, if you were the last solicitor in London.' Before Thymme could reply or even react, he put the phone down, gently but with great satisfaction.

Mastering his fury, after a few minutes he was able to think coherently about what Thymme had said to him, and about its implications. Mrs Francis Nightingale, a client of his own firm: this might be an avenue to explore. Perhaps he should have a word with Russell Galloway.

It was Russell Galloway who had been instrumental in David's move to Fosdyke, Fosdyke & Galloway. David had met the senior partner the previous year when acting in a volunteer capacity on behalf of a London church, in a successful effort to save it from redundancy and possible demolition; Galloway had been impressed with David and the job offer had resulted. David liked and respected Russell Galloway, finding him more approachable and less intimidating than Sir Crispin.

Now he went through the corridors to Galloway's office, pondering how best to handle the matter. If he told Russell Galloway what he'd learned, Thymme would certainly know where the information had come from, and would undoubtedly be prepared to make David's life difficult in future. Since 'young Justin' was still his client, whether he wanted him or not, and was currently under investigation by the immigration office, that could be awkward. But his first loyalty was to his firm; he'd have to find a subtle way to let Galloway know about Thymme's interest in the case.

Russell Galloway was behind his desk, which as usual looked as though it had a life of its own, piled high with papers, briefs, files, empty crockery and other assorted items. David had learned, though, that the impression of chaos was illusory: Galloway knew exactly where everything was, and could instantly put his hands on anything required. Russell Galloway's own appearance was equally deceptive. He had none of Sir Crispin's polished elegance, instead possessing a distinct resemblance to an unmade bed: his suit was always rumpled, and his tie was always askew. With his lack of sartorial style and his broken nose he looked more like a prize fighter than a highly-paid solicitor, and though he also lacked Sir Crispin's underlying ruthlessness, he was a pragmatic man with a great deal of integrity; David had learned early on that it would be a mistake to underestimate him.

Looking up to see David hovering at the door, Russell Galloway grinned. 'Come in, my friend.' He returned David's liking and esteem, perhaps recognising in him some of his own qualities of gentleness underlaid with strength and integrity.

'Are you busy?'

Galloway laughed and ran his fingers through his greying hair, short and as crisply waved as corrugated cardboard. 'I'm always busy. But always ready for an excuse for a break. Pull up a chair and tell me something I don't know.'

Deciding that the direct approach was best with a forthright man such as Galloway, David plunged straight in. 'The grapevine tells me that you're handling a divorce for a Mrs Nightingale.'

Galloway groaned. 'Yes, for my sins.'

'Difficult?' David probed.

'God, yes,' was the heartfelt reply. 'She's a twenty-two carat bitch, that one, and she knows exactly what she wants.'

'What *does* she want?'

'She wants to get shot of her worthless philandering spendthrift husband as quickly as possible, before he can spend any more of her money,' he said succinctly.

'But won't he be entitled to some of it when they divorce?' asked David.

Galloway shook his head. 'She's been far too clever for that. Or rather Daddy's smart American lawyers have been. It's her father's money, really – he owns a chain of supermarkets in the southern United States. So he's got the money all tied up for her in neat little legal knots. Prenuptial agreements and all that. The husband can't touch it.'

'Interesting,' David commented. 'So where do you come in?'

'My job, pure and simple, is to produce the divorce. Nothing more, nothing less. Fortunately it shouldn't be too complicated – no kids involved, and clear evidence of his adultery. His wife found letters from the secretary, and they didn't leave much doubt, or much to the imagination. I don't think he's contesting – he'd like to get his hands on some of Daddy's American bucks, I'm sure, but if he's got any sense he'll realise that there's no hope – so it should go through on the nod.' He turned curious eyes on David. 'Why do you ask?'

David shrugged. 'I just wondered.'

Galloway scratched his head with an elaborate display of nonchalance, then said casually, 'I don't suppose I could talk you into standing in for me at a meeting with her?'

This was better than David could have hoped for, but he matched Galloway's casual disinterest in the tone of his reply. 'Why?'

'Oh, it's nothing really. But I'm supposed to see her on Friday morning, and the wife is giving me hell about missing some school play that I promised a long time ago that I'd go to. The kid has a starring role, apparently.' Russell Galloway produced the half-embarrassed smile of a proud father. Though he was some years older than David, with grown children, he was in a second marriage to a younger woman and was raising a young family, with the generally successful intention of doing a better job of it than the first time around; complications like this one caused him more mental anguish than he'd care to admit.

'Why can't you just see her another time, then?'

'Not that simple, I'm afraid. She's been in Paris for the last few weeks, and is only stopping over in London on Friday, on her way back to the States, and presumably the comfort of Daddy's loving arms.

Not to mention his bank account.' Galloway rummaged around on his desk and came up with his diary, then checked the entry for Friday. 'Here it is. I'm supposed to meet her in the Concorde lounge at Terminal 4, Heathrow. Friday morning at half-past nine.'

David had no intention of missing out on this opportunity, but he didn't want to appear too eager. 'Well, Russell, I don't know. What is the meeting supposed to be about? Won't she mind if you don't come yourself?'

'It's really just to get her to sign some papers – nothing more complicated than that. And believe me – as long as she gets her divorce, Cindy Lou Nightingale won't give a damn who turns up! If you could see your way clear to helping me out, I'd be more than grateful.'

There was such pleading in his eyes that David could hold out no longer. 'Well, all right. After all, I wouldn't want to disappoint your wife.'

Russell Galloway sighed gratefully. 'Thanks, David. You're a real friend.'

CHAPTER 19

Or ever your pots be made hot with thorns: so let indignation vex him, even as a thing that is raw.

Psalm 58.8

Rachel Nightingale's funeral was to be held at St Jude's Church on Friday morning. Incongruously, the day had dawned clear and sunny and almost warm, after nearly a month of chill grey skies. David thought about the irony of it as he drove along the A4 at the end of the morning rush hour. He had expected Lucy to be disappointed that he couldn't go with her to the funeral, but she had taken altogether a more pragmatic view. 'It's more important for you to take advantage of this opportunity,' she'd said. 'Besides, you didn't know Rachel as well as I did, so it won't really matter if you miss it. Ruth will go with me. And maybe it's even better this way,' she'd reflected. 'The people at St Margaret's still don't know that there's a connection between us, and perhaps it's not a bad thing to keep it that way. Some of them may well be at the funeral.'

So while Lucy was putting on her best black dress, he was on his way to Heathrow Airport. Perhaps it was just as well, he reflected. Ruth had shown signs of incipient hysteria before he'd left, and he felt unequal to dealing with her.

In his briefcase were the papers for Cindy Lou Nightingale to sign, papers that would set into motion the machinery of law that would ultimately result in her divorce. Signing the papers wouldn't take long, but David hoped that the soon-to-be-former Mrs Nightingale would be inclined to chat with him, in spite of the impression he had formed of her as being difficult and temperamental. His plans hadn't been formulated beyond that: meeting Mrs Nightingale, and encouraging her to talk. Anything that she might add to the picture he was building up of her husband could be helpful.

He'd never been to Terminal 4 before, so he followed the signs carefully to the multi-storey car park. There was plenty of time, he noted on his watch. But it took more time than he'd planned to find the Concorde lounge, tucked away discreetly in a corner of the terminal, and he had to do some fast talking – and to submit to repeated and thorough inspections of his briefcase – to get through the security checks without a ticket or a boarding pass in order to gain entry to an area of the terminal which was intended for departing passengers only. That he hadn't anticipated, so it was just about half-past nine when he finally arrived at his destination.

David sank nearly up to his ankles in thick carpet as he looked round the lounge for Mrs Nightingale. It wasn't difficult to spot her; most of the passengers were businessmen, in a hurry to get to New York for morning meetings, beavering away on their lap-top computers or reading the *Financial Times*, and there were one or two wealthy dowager-types, be-ringed and bejewelled. Only one inhabitant of the lounge looked a possible candidate. She sat alone in the centre of a luxuriously upholstered blue sofa, sipping a glass of champagne: a stunning brunette clad in a flame-red and lime-green ensemble that had obviously just come out of the door of one of the more famous Paris fashion houses, tailored to fit her statuesque form to perfection. Her jewellery was not, like that of the dowagers, flashy or ostentatious, but instead was discreet in the extreme: gold button earrings and a thin gold chain. No wedding ring, David noted with interest – not even for the purpose of discouraging unwanted attention from her travelling companions. Then he realised that such help was scarcely needed; her demeanour was such that not even the dimmest businessman could fail to get the message that she was not available, and not to be approached.

It was all he could do to approach her himself. She looked up as he neared and frowned, a small crease of displeasure between her perfectly plucked brows. 'Mrs Nightingale?' he said in a voice that sounded more confident than he felt. 'I'm David Middleton-Brown from Fosdyke, Fosdyke and Galloway. Mr Galloway sent me to see you.'

'Why didn't he come himself? I've always dealt with Mr Galloway in the past.' Her southern drawl was as thick as a slab of shoo-fly pie and as viscous as blackstrap molasses.

Good Lord, David thought. She thinks she's Scarlett O'Hara. 'I'm afraid that Mr Galloway had a . . . family emergency,' he exaggerated, summoning up his most appealing smile. 'He's briefed me on your case, and I'll do my best to look after you as well as he would have done.'

Cindy Lou took in his appearance with practised rapidity: not exactly a heart-stopper, but more than presentable, and an improvement on the unprepossessing Russell Galloway in any case. She decided that there was nothing to be gained by being difficult, so she may as well be as charming as only the flower of southern womanhood could be. She dimpled fetchingly and indicated the chair across from her. 'Oh, I'm sure you'll do just fine, Mr Middleton-Brown. Why don't you sit down over there?' (She pronounced it 'ovah theyah'.) He sat, and she added, 'Wouldn't you like some champagne?'

Having prepared himself for at least some degree of hostility, David was taken aback. Oh, why not, he decided. It was never really too early for champagne, and the *enfant terrible* wasn't around to disapprove. 'Yes, please.'

As another glass materialised, he took the papers from his briefcase. 'Do you want to go ahead and sign these papers now?' he asked. 'Get it out of the way? Or is there anything you'd like to discuss first?'

She waved a languid hand in the air. 'All in good time. There's no hurry, is there? My plane doesn't leave for another hour.'

'Fine.' Uneasily David settled back in his chair and took a sip of champagne. Now that he was here with Francis Nightingale's wife – and she was behaving much more pleasantly than he'd expected – he hardly knew where to begin. 'You've been in Paris, I understand?' he ventured.

'Yes. Buying a few new clothes, trying to cheer myself up.' She assumed a tragic expression and sighed deeply. 'But I think it was a mistake. Paris is no place to be on your own, Mr Middleton-Brown. Don't you agree?' She didn't really expect an answer, continuing with the trembling lower lip of an ill-done-by faithful wife, 'Frankie and I went to Paris on our honeymoon. It's full of such bittersweet memories for me.'

David, whose only trip to Paris had been on his own but who now entertained fantasies of taking Lucy there one day, nodded sympathetically. 'If you feel that way,' he said, 'perhaps you ought not to rush into this divorce. Give it a little more time, perhaps. You might be able to work things out between you.' That sort of advice would infuriate Henry Thymme, he realised with satisfaction.

Abruptly her mood and her demeanour shifted. 'Frankie is a worthless, no-good piece of shit,' she snapped. 'A dog turd. Lower than a rattlesnake's belly. I wouldn't have him back if he were the last man on earth, and came crawling to me on his hands and knees. The way that man treated me . . .' Then the tears welled up in her luminous dark eyes, demanding more sympathy. At a loss for words, David produced a clean handkerchief and leaned across to put it in her hand.

Cindy Lou's manicured fingers lingered on his for a moment as she took it from him; she dabbed at her eyes in a delicate way so as not to smudge her make-up, and gave him a watery smile of gratitude. 'Oh, you're very kind,' she murmured. 'I'm sorry. I don't know what's come over me. But Frankie hurt me so bad that sometimes I just can't help myself.'

'He did?'

'I gave that man everything. Everything I had! And how did he repay me?'

David shook his head.

'By sleeping with his slut of a secretary.' Her anger flashed again for an instant as she thought about it, her Frankie and that unspeakable girl who, apart from her youth, could surely have nothing to offer a man like Frankie, who was used to the better things of life. The letters that she'd found had been written in a childish scrawl and were badly spelled, if sexually explicit; it was an unforgiveable insult to *her*, his wife, that he should have transgressed with someone so unworthy. This time a tear actually did spill over; she let it roll down her cheek for effect and said in a piteous voice, 'And she's not even pretty! I just don't understand how Frankie could do it. It wasn't a gentlemanly thing to do. Oh, Mr Middleton-Brown – you'd never do anything like that to your wife, would you?' She regarded him searchingly.

Disconcerted, he tried to pass it off as a joke. 'My secretary is sixty-two,' he mumbled with an unconvincing smile.

She looked hurt, as if she had expected a more gallant reply. 'You know what I mean, Mr Middleton-Brown.'

He gazed into his champagne, hoping to be forgiven for his gaucherie. He had expected Mrs Nightingale to be indifferent towards her husband, or possibly even vindictive, but from what Russell Galloway had said he hadn't anticipated this combination of outrage and misery.

'I gave that man everything,' Cindy Lou repeated bitterly. 'Frankie was happy enough to have my money – my daddy's money – to spend. And he was glad enough for the lifestyle that money gave him, and the doors it opened. Do you think he ever would have made it as far as he has in business without my money behind him?'

'But I thought that the money wasn't at issue,' said David, glad to be back on firm ground. 'Mr Galloway said that your husband wasn't seeking any sort of financial settlement . . .'

She gave a scathing laugh. 'He'd better not even try it, the rat. My daddy's got lawyers who can run circles around Frankie's lawyers.

Daddy never did like Frankie. He made sure before we got married that there was no way Frankie would ever be able to touch my money if we split up, or if I didn't want him to have it.' Downing the rest of her champagne in one gulp, she held out her glass for David to refill it, adding, 'Now let's see how he likes being poor again, like he was before he met me.'

At last the conversation was beginning to go the way David had hoped. 'You mean he doesn't have any money of his own?' he probed.

'Hardly a red cent,' she declared with satisfaction. 'In fact, between his gambling debts, and all the money he's lost with Lloyd's, he's so far in the hole that he'll *never* dig himself out. Not unless he manages to figure out a way to kill off his sister-in-law and his brother, in that order, and get away with it!' she added facetiously. 'Not that I'd put it past him, mind you!'

David was stunned; he stared at Cindy Lou Nightingale for a moment as he realised that she'd been abroad and wouldn't have known about the two deaths. She misunderstood his reaction, and went on to explain, 'His brother has millions, but it's not doing him any good, poor guy. He was in an accident, and will be a vegetable for the rest of his life. But even if he dies, Frankie won't get any of his money unless the wife dies first – otherwise she'll get it all. Poor old Frankie – two inconvenient people in between him and all that money.'

'But it's been in all the papers,' David blurted out. 'You wouldn't have seen it. They're both dead. Rachel Nightingale was killed in a traffic accident last week – a hit-and-run driver. And her husband died a few days later.'

Cindy Lou's laughter was tinged with hysteria. 'Then he's done it, the greedy little bastard. He's finished them off somehow. I know him, better than anyone, and I know what he's capable of, especially when that much money is involved. Mark my words – those deaths may have looked accidental, but Frankie was behind them.' She raised her glass with a smile of grudging admiration. 'Here's to Frankie. May all that money bring him nothing but misery. And I hope he gets caught.'

CHAPTER 20

Their throat is an open sepulchre: they flatter with their tongue.

Psalm 5.10

St Jude's Church was full for Rachel Nightingale's funeral, as two congregations of parishioners turned out to pay tribute to their curate; now that she was no longer a threat to them in any way, they were prepared to be generous to her in death as they never would have been in her life, and to mourn her with every evidence of sincerity.

Father Keble Smythe delivered an eulogy that was both stirring and profoundly touching in its evocation of a Godly life cut short by cruel fate. That, combined with the beautiful singing of the choir and the heart-rending words of the Order for the Burial of the Dead from the Book of Common Prayer, ensured that Ruth Kingsley was not the only person in the congregation to shed tears that morning.

Ruth wept noisily; beside her, Lucy's tears trickled in silence as she clutched Ruth's hand. In her own quiet way, Lucy mourned as deeply as Ruth: in the short time she'd known Rachel, the other woman had made a great impression on her, chiefly for the manner in which she had managed to transcend unspeakable tragedy and rebuild her life so positively. Lucy had looked forward to getting to know her better, to discovering the secret of her inner strength. Now she would never have that opportunity.

After the funeral there was no interment, or even a committal; in due time there would be another service in Cambridge, in the church where Rachel had begun her clerical career, and afterwards she and Colin would both be laid to rest beside their young daughter, in a Cambridge churchyard. So the proceedings rather fizzled out at the end, and the mourners adjourned to the vicarage, where, in the absence of a close family to do the honours, Mrs Goode had surpassed herself in providing a plentiful cold feast for anyone who chose to come. Needless to say, no one stayed away, and soon the vicarage was crammed full of those who had come to mourn, to eat, or to gossip – or any combination of the three. They filled the sitting room, then spilled over into the dining room, where the food and drink were on offer, and even eventually took over the kitchen and the Vicar's study.

In a remarkably short time, and by virtue of her untimely death, Rachel Nightingale had seemingly achieved the status of sainthood. So Lucy surmised from the conversation in the kitchen, where Dolly Topping and her cadre of women gathered. 'I, for one, won't hear a thing said against her,' Dolly pontificated. 'We may not have always seen eye to eye, Rachel and I, but she was a lovely young woman. And so devoted to her poor husband.'

'Oh, she was,' Joan Everitt agreed. 'You remember, Dolly? – I always did say so. Last week, when the meeting was at my house – you didn't come, Dolly, remember? – I was so impressed with the way she spoke. Afterwards I asked her about her husband, and it nearly made me cry, the way she talked about him.'

'Terribly sad,' confirmed Dolly, who insisted on having the last word on all matters. 'And I'm so sorry that I had to miss that meeting. I heard that her talk was fascinating.'

Sickened, Lucy turned away. Ruth had already disappeared; Lucy was very much afraid that the girl, who held doggedly to her belief that Rachel had been murdered, might be engaged on a misguided fact-finding mission. Before she found her niece, though, she ran into Emily. 'Oh, there you are, Luce. I've been looking for you,' Emily greeted her.

Lucy looked around for Emily's husband. 'Gabriel's not here?' The Archdeacon had assisted with the funeral service and might have been expected to attend the post-funeral reception.

'He's around somewhere,' confirmed Emily. 'The last time I saw him, that creepy Administrator was dragging him off into a corner for a chat about something. That's when I decided to leave him to his own devices and find you instead.'

'Have you seen Ruth?'

'I did, a little while ago. She seemed to be coping all right.'

'Poor kid.' Lucy sighed. 'She's taken it very hard, you know. She didn't know Rachel long, but she really got attached to her. How are *you* coping, Em?' she added.

Emily shook her head reflectively. 'I thought I was doing all right, until today. But I just can't deal with all these endless eulogies by people who would have gone a mile out of their way to avoid her a fortnight ago.'

'Horrible, isn't it?'

'Obscene,' Emily stated with force. 'Apparently there was a huge row at St Margaret's, everyone ganging up on Rachel, last Friday evening just before her . . . accident. And now no one will admit that they took part in it – just innocent bystanders, they all claim.' Her voice sounded bitter.

'Well,' said Lucy, who hadn't heard about the row before, 'at least it may explain some of what's going on now – all the denial and so forth. Though no one would ever say it, I'm sure they feel guilty about it. I mean, it's possible that she was so badly upset about the row that she wasn't being as careful as she might have been on her bicycle – and in that case, all the people who were involved might feel a little bit responsible for her death. Does that make sense?'

'There might be more to it than that.' Emily lowered her voice cautiously. 'Listen, Luce. Gabriel thinks that there's something funny going on. I can't really explain it now, but he has reason for thinking it. And we wondered . . . well, you and David have had experience with this sort of thing before. I know it's short notice, but could the two of you come to supper tomorrow night, just to talk about it?'

Lucy hesitated. She was reluctant to speak for David, especially given the situation. And she wasn't particularly keen on an evening with Gabriel herself; in the best of circumstances it would be awkward, and this was far from the best of circumstances. But Emily's dark eyes were fixed on her with a pleading look, and the demands of friendship prohibited a negative answer. Besides, she said to herself, they owed it to Rachel. David might not be very happy about it, but he would agree that it had to be done. 'Yes, all right,' she said. 'What time would you like us to come?'

In an effort to redirect her grief over Rachel's death, Ruth resolved to carry through with her intention to do a bit of investigation. To that end she had slipped away from her aunt, and tried to make herself inconspicuous on the edges of various groups of people, eavesdropping on conversations. But she heard little more than the sort of valedictory comments about the dead curate that had so upset Lucy.

'Oh, hello,' said a tentative voice at Ruth's shoulder; she turned to find Vera Bright, her face splotchy and her eyelids swollen. Recognising the signs of a fellow sufferer from genuine bereavement, Ruth gave the older woman a quick, impulsive hug.

'Hello, Miss Bright. I was looking for you at the church, but I didn't see you.'

Vera Bright clutched Ruth's hand. 'How nice. We were a little late, I'm afraid.'

'Your father came too?'

'Yes. He's gone off into the other room to talk to the men, and I just didn't feel like being on my own, so I thought I'd have a word with you.' She fumbled in her pocket for a handkerchief, which she produced to dab ineffectually at her eyes. 'I'm sorry, my dear. I can't help myself. This has been such a shock.'

'Oh, I know.' Ruth looked around and spotted a pair of vacant chairs against the wall of the sitting room. 'Why don't we go over there and sit down?' she suggested.

Vera complied readily. 'This is very nice, my dear. And it's most kind of you to keep an old lady company.'

'Not at all,' Ruth protested. 'Can I get you anything? A cup of tea, or something to eat?'

'Oh, no. I don't feel that I could eat a thing. I haven't really eaten properly since . . . well, you know. Since it happened,' she confided.

'Me neither,' admitted Ruth. 'I haven't had any appetite at all. I just can't believe it. I can't believe that she's really . . . gone. It's too horrible to contemplate.'

Vera sighed. 'You're the first person I've talked to who really understands. There are a lot of people here saying nice things about Rachel, but somehow they don't sound as if they really mean it. I believe that you do.'

'Oh, yes,' Ruth declared passionately. 'I loved her – she was the most wonderful person. I've been devastated. Shattered. And I just can't stand listening to all those hypocrites who were so horrible to her when she was alive.'

'There was *one* other person who cared about Rachel,' said Vera. 'But I haven't seen her here today. Nicola Topping – do you know her? She was very fond of Rachel – I can't imagine why she's not here.'

'Topping? Is she related to Dolly Topping?' demanded Ruth with an incredulous look.

'Her daughter. She's a few years older than you, my dear. But you can take my word for it that she never shared her mother's opinion of Rachel. In fact, I don't think her mother ever knew how much she relied on Rachel's advice, or how much time she spent with her.'

Ruth was still suspicious. 'How do *you* know?'

For the first time in their conversation, Vera looked uncomfortable. 'I'm not really at liberty to say. But I promise you that it's true. I hope her mother didn't find out and keep Nicola away today.'

'Is Dolly Topping around?' asked Ruth. 'I've never met her. I'd like to know who she is.'

'I think she's in the kitchen. I'll let you know if I see her.'

Ruth folded her arms across her chest and regarded the room full of chattering people with something approaching loathing. 'I wish I knew which one of them killed her,' she muttered, almost to herself.

'What did you say?' Vera turned a startled face on the girl.

'I said I wish I knew which one of them killed her,' Ruth repeated defiantly. 'One of them did, you know. I'm sure of it. They said it was an accident, but I don't believe that for a minute.'

'Oh, my dear!' Her voice fluttered with dismay.

'Don't you believe me? There's no reason why you should, I suppose – no one else does. Not my aunt, or anyone else.'

'Oh, if it were true . . .' Vera faltered, looking down at her hands.

Standing near the food table in the dining room, Emily introduced Lucy to the churchwarden Martin Bairstow. 'A sad occasion to bring us all together today,' Bairstow said with lugubrious gravity. 'And a great loss for us at St Margaret's.'

Father Keble Smythe chimed in, 'She gave of herself so unstintingly to all of us. Rachel Nightingale was a rare young woman. Not that the principle of women clergy is one we can all subscribe to, of course. But Rachel was different.'

'Different,' echoed Norman Topping. 'Even Dolly always said so.'

Stanley Everitt wrung his hands. 'The Church of England is the poorer for the loss of such a one.'

'And she was a pretty little thing, as well,' twinkled old Dr Bright, drawing horrified looks from the others. 'Well, she was,' he insisted, unrepentant. 'Pretty as a little rose. And always as charming as could be to me, when she came to bring me the Sacrament or to see my Vera.'

Lucy edged away from them and over towards the food table, where she contemplated the array on offer. As a vegetarian, her choices were necessarily limited, but there were cocktail sticks with cheese and pineapple, and what looked like a cheese and onion quiche, as well as a number of salads. She had just picked up a plate and begun to help herself, giving the sausage rolls a wide berth, when Ruth flew up to her in a state of high excitement. 'Aunt Lucy!' she hailed her in a shrill voice that carried much more penetratingly than she realised. 'I'm not the only one who thinks that Rachel was murdered! Miss Bright thinks so too, but that's not all! She won't tell me, but I'm sure she knows who did it!'

CHAPTER 21

I am wiser than the aged: because I keep thy commandments.

Psalm 119.100

'But I don't see why I can't go!' Ruth whined. 'It's not fair for you to go off and leave me by myself – you're supposed to be looking after me, Aunt Lucy. I don't think my parents would be very happy if they knew that you were abandoning me.'

'Ruth, darling.' Lucy struggled to keep her voice even. 'You're continually telling us how grown-up you are, and keep reminding us that you're not a baby. This is your chance to prove it. It's only for a few hours – I think you're quite capable of amusing yourself for one evening. Surely you can read a book, or watch the telly.'

'But I don't *want* to stay here by myself! You're going to talk about Rachel, and I should be there! After all, I've said all along that someone did her in, but no one believed me.'

Lucy looked at David, hoping for moral and verbal support, but he was too busy counting to ten – repeatedly – to notice her unspoken plea for help. Going to Emily and Gabriel's for supper was the last thing he wanted to do that evening; Ruth's intractable whingeing only deepened his gloom.

In the end the grown-ups prevailed and Ruth, protesting to the end, was left behind. They were able to talk more freely in the car en route than they had at home. 'I still don't see what this is all about,' David stated. 'I can't see that it has anything to do with the church. *If* Rachel's death was something other than an accident, I think it's fairly clear that her brother-in-law was behind it. He was the one who had everything to gain.'

'You're being as stubborn about this as Ruth,' Lucy pointed out. 'Don't you think you should keep an open mind until you hear what Gabriel has to say?'

David bristled at the comparison, while acknowledging to himself that there might be truth in it. 'I'll listen to what he has to say,' he conceded grudgingly.

His underlying apprehension about the evening was dispelled somewhat by the spontaneous warmth of Emily's greeting, as she embraced him unreservedly. He had always got on well with Emily, in spite of factors that should have made them adversaries; the fact that he hadn't seen much of her during the course of his relationship with Lucy didn't seem to make any practical difference, and she seemed willing to pick up their friendship where they'd left off.

Gabriel's greeting was slightly less enthusiastic, if only in comparison. He kissed Lucy's cheek and shook David's hand, masking any discomfort in a way that a clergyman well practised in such social niceties should find well within his powers. He asked the time-honoured question for smoothing over social awkwardnesses. 'What can I get you to drink?'

'I'll have a glass of white wine, if that's on offer,' said Lucy, taking a seat in their handsome sitting room.

'Gin and tonic, I think,' David replied, perching next to her on the sofa.

Gabriel poured generous measures of gin into two glasses while Emily went to the kitchen for the wine. There was a fractional moment of silence, then the three of them began talking at once.

'My niece wasn't very happy about being left at home tonight,' said Lucy.

'Have you had this room redecorated?' was David's contribution.

Gabriel said, 'We missed you at the funeral yesterday, David.'

They all laughed, the ice was broken, and Emily returned a moment later to find the atmosphere considerably eased. Over their drinks they settled down to inconsequential small talk about the weather (improving), the twins (thriving, though the vexed topic of their schooling was assiduously avoided), Lucy's paintings (selling well), David's new job (challenging) and Ruth's visit (trying).

It wasn't until they had moved to the dining room and were into the first course that Gabriel broached the subject on all of their minds. 'I apologise for having brought you here at such short notice,' he said, 'but I thought that it might be a good idea for us to put our heads together.' He flashed an ingratiating smile at Lucy, then at David. 'The two of you have had some experience at this sort of thing, I believe.'

'*What* sort of thing?' David asked with deliberate obtuseness.

'Informal investigation, if you'd like to call it that.'

'Gabriel thinks that Rachel's death might not have been as accidental as it's been made out to be,' Emily intervened. 'And from what Ruth said yesterday at the vicarage, he's not the only one to feel that way.'

Mentioning Ruth was not a good move in trying to enlist David's support. 'And why should I believe the fantasies of a hysterical, hero-worshipping teenager?' he snapped. 'Why should *you*, Archdeacon? I would have thought you'd have more common sense.'

Gabriel took it with a smile, including the almost insulting use of his title. 'I was about to tell you that,' he said gently.

David, unwilling to admit or to share the basis of his own suspicions of the dead woman's brother-in-law, subsided into silence.

'Rachel talked to Emily on the phone just a few hours before she died,' Gabriel began.

'Yes, Emily told me,' said Lucy. 'Rachel was telling her about Colin's illness.'

'But that wasn't the reason why Rachel rang. She didn't ring to talk to Emily – she wanted to talk to *me*.'

That announcement took David by surprise; he raised his head from contemplation of his avocado vinaigrette.

'To *me*,' Gabriel repeated for emphasis. 'Not personally, but in my official capacity. She said that she wanted to discuss something with me. What were her exact words, darling?'

Emily's brow furrowed as she called on her excellent memory. 'She said that she wanted a word with Gabriel – the Archdeacon, she said. I asked her if it was urgent, since he wasn't at home, and she said something like, "No, not urgent, but it's important, I think. I'm not even sure that he's the person I need to talk to, but there's something that's bothering me, something not quite right, and I thought perhaps I should tell him about it.'

'"Something not quite right",' echoed Gabriel. 'And a few hours later she was dead.'

'What are you implying?' David asked slowly.

'That she might have uncovered some funny business at St Margaret's – something she wanted to discuss with me – and that someone was sufficiently concerned about the consequences of discovery to want to stop her. With a convenient accident.'

'It could have happened, quite easily,' Emily added earnestly; evidently the two of them had discussed the possibility at some length. 'David, did you hear about the row at St Margaret's just before the accident? I mentioned it to Lucy yesterday.'

'What row?' He took a fortifying gulp of wine and tried to concentrate on what was being said. 'I don't know about any row. What happened?'

Concisely, Emily described the circumstances of the unfortunate encounter in St Margaret's, as gleaned from the accounts of several who had been present. 'And so Rachel left early, and apparently was on her way to see Colin when the accident happened. Anyone who'd been at the church that night could have followed her by car and knocked her off her bike.'

'She went early?' David picked out the relevant fact and caught Lucy's eye with a slight grimace; his *de facto* case against Francis Nightingale was based entirely on the supposition that Rachel's nightly visit to her husband took place every night at a regular and verifiable time. This new piece of information seemed to make that impossible: her brother-in-law couldn't conceivably have known that she'd go early that night.

But anyone who had been at St Margaret's would have known. David pressed his fingers to his temples and admitted to himself that he'd been on the wrong track all along.

'Quite early, as a matter of fact. The service didn't take place, so she was probably an hour and a half earlier than usual,' said Emily, demonstrating that she had thought it through.

David made one last attempt to preserve his neutrality. 'But perhaps you're overreacting to what she said on the phone, in the light of what happened afterwards. It might have been just some small incident – Dolly Topping being rude to her or something else minor. Archdeacons must get curates complaining to them all the time about trivial things like that.'

'Rachel wasn't like that,' Emily defended her friend. 'She was sensible, and she was used to being badly treated. I'm sure she wouldn't have even thought of bothering Gabriel unless it was something really important.'

Lucy, who had been absorbing the unfolding story in silence, nodded her agreement. 'Emily's right. I'm sure it's relevant. It's certainly consistent with what we know about Rachel.'

'And about St Margaret's,' added Gabriel.

'What do you mean?' queried David.

'I was concerned about that church well before Rachel died. As I said, there are some rather peculiar things going on there.'

'Do you mean Dolly Topping and her opposition to women priests?' David challenged. 'It's not the only church in the diocese to have outspoken opponents of the ordination of women in the congregation. I really don't see how that can be turned into a motive for murder.'

'That's not really what I meant.' Gabriel looked thoughtful as he framed his words carefully. 'You've been involved with them – with the churchwardens and the Vicar – on this proposed selling of the silver.'

'Yes?'

'Well, you must admit that it doesn't add up. All that holy claptrap about providing housing for homeless people. Does that square with what you know about those two churchwardens? Or the Vicar either, for that matter?'

For the first time that evening, David laughed. 'Not at all,' he admitted. 'I never believed that that was their true intent – in fact, the Vicar hinted as much, the first time I met him.'

'He didn't happen to say what they were *really* up to?'

'No.' David picked up his wine glass and twirled it by the stem. 'He wasn't in on it, that much I know. It was the churchwardens who were scheming, and he was trying to out-guess them.'

'A nice little setup.' The Archdeacon gave an unamused laugh.

Emily hopped up. 'Just a minute. The casserole will be all dried out if we don't eat it soon.' There was a pause while she cleared the plates and served the main course.

'So,' said David as they resumed eating. 'The churchwardens were playing a little game with the Vicar and the diocese, and had something to hide. But they'd given up on the plan to sell the silver, once the DAC ruled against them.'

'That doesn't mean that they didn't have something else up their sleeves,' Gabriel pointed out.

'No . . .'

'And then there's the Vicar, our friend Father Keble Smythe himself,' Gabriel went on. 'I don't think he's exactly as pure as the driven snow, either.' Automatically he lowered his voice. 'This isn't to go beyond these four walls, of course, but he's written me a most peculiar letter. When he came to see me a while ago, absolutely desperate to have a replacement for his curate, I told him that there was no one available but Rachel. A woman. I expected him to refuse outright, given the presence of people like Dolly in his congregation. And the fact that he likes to be known in the diocese as a Catholic, albeit a fairly moderate one.'

'But he didn't refuse?' Lucy put in.

'No, he didn't. He was desperate, of course, but he actually seemed rather keen to give it a try. Don't ask me why. I was surprised at his position – I even tried to talk him out of it. I pointed out that a parish like St Margaret's would probably not take very kindly to a woman curate, that it wouldn't be fair on her. But he insisted.'

'What about this letter?' David prompted.

'Yes. The letter. It came last week, just about the time that Rachel died. In it he said that the appointment *I'd* insisted on had been a mistake, and he wondered if anything could be done to rectify it.'

'Don't you see?' Emily interrupted her husband. 'In the first place, he must have known that nothing could be done to *un*-appoint Rachel at that point. And Gabriel *hadn't* insisted on their having her.'

'Curiouser and curiouser,' said Lucy, pushing her hair back from her face.

David added a comment in a somewhat flippant tone. 'I don't understand why he was so desperate in the first place. Didn't he know that he was going to lose his previous curate? Why hadn't he made arrangements for a replacement before the old curate left? That doesn't sound like our friend Father Keble Smythe at all!'

Gabriel looked at him as though he'd just told a joke in rather bad taste. 'That's not really very funny.'

'Why? What happened to him?' David asked idly.

'You don't know?'

'Don't know what?'

'You don't know what happened to Father Julian? Honestly?'

David was baffled at his tone. 'I'd rather supposed he'd got his own parish somewhere. Not that I'd given it all that much thought.'

'Father Julian was killed in the burglary at St Margaret's last December,' Gabriel said with appropriate gravity. 'The burglary in the sacristy. Surely you've heard about that.'

'Killed?' David stared at him for a moment, trying to absorb it. 'Good Lord.'

Lucy stopped with a forkful of food halfway to her mouth. 'You mean he was murdered?'

Gabriel shrugged. 'Accidentally. It would seem that he was unlucky enough to surprise the burglars, and had his head smashed in for his pains.'

That horrific fact, so casually delivered, made Lucy wince. 'But have they caught the people who did it? Surely the police have tracked them down somehow.'

'No, they haven't, as a matter of fact. He was under my jurisdiction, of course, so they've kept me informed. And so far they haven't managed to find anything – no prints at the scene of the crime, so they didn't really have much to go on.' He shrugged again. 'I think that after a few weeks they just gave up and shoved it into the files. A sad thing, but I'm sure it happens all the time.'

While he was speaking, David was engaged in serious re-evaluation of the situation, in the light of this second death. 'It just doesn't wash, you know,' he interjected suddenly. 'Two curates at the same church, dead within four months. Accidentally. It's statistically impossible.'

'Oscar Wilde might have said that to lose one curate could be counted as unfortunate . . .' said Gabriel, waiting for David to complete his thought as he had done so many times in the past.

'But to lose two is careless,' David finished. 'I think that in this case it's gone a bit beyond careless. Don't you agree?'

It was the previously undisclosed fact of Father Julian's murder – for surely it could be called nothing short of murder – that finally turned the tide in David's mind, and convinced him, in spite of his prejudice against Ruth and her intuition, that Rachel Nightingale's death could not have been an accident. Nothing else would have persuaded him to agree to Gabriel's request for his – and Lucy's – help with a discreet investigation into the circumstances of a death on which the police had closed the book, apart from a desultory search for the driver of the hit-and-run car.

Once that agreement had been obtained, they proceeded to make more detailed plans. 'It must have been someone who was at St Margaret's that night, when they had the row,' David thought aloud. 'No one else would have known that she would be going at that particular time.'

'That doesn't really narrow things down too much,' Emily pointed out. 'From what I've heard, everyone was there.'

'Except Father Keble Smythe,' Gabriel added slowly.

'Well, that lets the Vicar out, then,' David stated. 'The one person with an alibi.'

'But it leaves us with quite a few others as possibilities,' said Lucy. 'I should think that the churchwardens would have to come top of the list.'

'Martin Bairstow, yes,' David agreed. 'But not Norman Topping. He wouldn't have the bottle.'

Lucy smiled. 'Unless Dolly told him to.'

'Lady Macbeth, handing her wimpy husband the dagger,' said Emily the English scholar. 'Or Dolly might have done it herself,' she added.

'Let's not be sexist here – a woman could have done it just as easily as a man.'

By this time they had moved back to the sitting room for their coffee; Gabriel added a dollop of cream to his and stirred it thoughtfully. 'It seems to me,' he said, 'that the first thing you need to do, David, is to talk to the churchwardens. With or without the Vicar – I don't think it makes much difference, unless you think he might be able to shed any light.'

'But how can I do that?' David protested. 'I don't have a credible excuse. As far as they're concerned, my usefulness is over. I discovered that their silver was valuable, but I wasn't able to persuade the diocese to let them sell it. I can't just ring them up . . .'

'Oh, but you can,' Gabriel interrupted smoothly. 'What if you were to ring Martin Bairstow and tell him that your old friend the Archdeacon – and you made a point of our long-standing friendship, if you'll remember – has had a change of heart about the silver? That he's willing to consider recommending to the DAC that since there are two ciboria, one of them might be sold to the V & A?'

David sighed. 'Yes, I suppose that would work. I could ask them to come to my office to see me, to talk about the details.'

'It would be better to see them at the church, surely?'

'Yes, all right,' David gave in. 'I'll talk to them.'

Gabriel got up and went to the drinks tray. 'Can I offer you a drink with your coffee? Cognac, or a liqueur, Lucy?'

'I'll have a Cointreau, thanks.'

He dispensed it, then lifted a bottle of single-malt whisky. 'And is this still your favourite tipple, David?'

'Yes, thanks. How kind of you to remember.'

No one in the room, least of all Gabriel, could have been unaware of the irony in his tone, but he poured the drink and passed it to David without further comment.

Lucy put down her coffee cup with an abrupt movement and a clatter of spoon and saucer. 'I think there's something we're overlooking,' she stated. 'You may be disinclined to believe anything that Ruth says, David darling, but don't forget what she said about Vera Bright.'

Gabriel turned towards her. 'Oh, yes. That business at the vicarage yesterday. What was that all about? Who *is* Vera Bright?'

'Vera Bright is a member of the congregation at St Margaret's,' Lucy explained. 'Ruth met her through Rachel. Yesterday at the vicarage Ruth was talking to her, and she said something that made Ruth think that she not only believed Rachel had been murdered, but that she knew who was behind it. Based on something that Rachel had said to her, apparently – though she wouldn't tell Ruth what it was, or whom she suspects.'

'Just another of Ruth's fantasies, I expect.' David waved his hand dismissively.

Gabriel, however, got up and paced across the room. 'I don't think we can afford to ignore it out of hand, David. There may be something in it. Does anyone know this Vera Bright? Besides Ruth, that is?'

Lucy nodded. 'Well, I've met her, anyway, though I don't really know her. Do you think I should have a word with her?'

'If you would,' said Gabriel. 'At least you might be able to get some feeling about whether she really knows anything, or if it's all in Ruth's mind.'

'All right. I'll go on Monday.'

'Shouldn't someone talk to the churchwardens' wives?' suggested Emily. 'To Dolly Topping, anyway?'

'I've got a good excuse to see Vanessa,' Lucy admitted. 'The painting she commissioned is just about finished, and I could deliver it to her this week. But I can't really think of any plausible way that I could talk to Dolly.'

Emily sighed. 'I suppose it's my turn to be noble. Much as I loathe the woman, I'll invite her round for a cup of tea this week, and get her talking about Rachel.'

'Will she come?' David wanted to know.

'Oh, she'll come.' Emily smiled smugly. 'In her circle, one doesn't turn down invitations from the Archdeacon's wife. If you understand me.'

'Yes, of course.' David lifted his glass and squinted through the pale straw-coloured liquid. 'I'm thinking,' he said slowly, 'that it might be a mistake to concentrate on Rachel, without considering this Father Julian as well. Perhaps the two deaths are actually connected in some way.'

Gabriel gave him a sharp look. 'What do you mean?'

'Well, maybe they both died because of something they had in common. And as far as I can tell, that's only one thing.'

'Yes?' With one raised eyebrow, Gabriel invited him to continue.

'I mean, it doesn't seem that there was much commonality there. He was a man and she was a woman. She was married, and he was . . . ?'

'Not.' Gabriel's voice might have conveyed a trace of disapproval or even distaste.

'She was a deacon, and he was a priest. But . . .' David looked around at the three of them. 'They were both curates of St Jude's and St Margaret's. That's the link, and that may be important.'

'So what are you implying?'

David continued with some reluctance. 'That we won't really be doing everything we can to discover the truth about Rachel's death unless we find out something about Father Julian as well. About who he was, first of all, and then about how he died, and why. And there's only one person I can think of who could almost certainly tell us the answer to at least the first of those questions.' He paused, and forced himself to say it. 'Robin West. The sacristan at St Margaret's.'

'Ah.' Gabriel's mouth twitched in what might have been a suppressed smile; clearly he had run across him in the course of his official duties. 'I think that talking to him is just the job for you, David.'

'Can't someone else do it?' he pleaded without much hope. 'Gabriel, how about you?'

'Oh, no. That wouldn't be the done thing at all. I'm afraid it's got to be you, David.' He smirked. 'Pull up your socks and take your medicine like a man.'

'That's the whole problem,' David muttered miserably.

'Well, then.' Gabriel rubbed his hands together in a brisk manner. 'We all know what we have to do within the next week or so. I suggest that we meet again next weekend to compare notes and see where we've got. Emily, you're to chat with Dolly Topping. Lucy, you've got Vera Bright and Mrs Bairstow to talk to. And David, you need to see the churchwardens and the sacristan.'

'Wait a minute,' said David. 'What about *you*?'

'Oh, I'm the Archdeacon. It wouldn't be proper for me to get involved directly. But,' Gabriel added, 'let me know if there's anything at all that I can do to back you up. That's what I'm here for.'

CHAPTER 22

Let his posterity be destroyed: and in the next generation let his name be clean put out.

Psalm 109.12

Lucy rang Vera Bright on Monday morning, reminding the older woman that she was Ruth's aunt, and asking if it might be convenient for her to call and see her a bit later. Vera agreed readily; any visitor was a welcome change from her father's sole company.

'What time would be best for you?' Lucy asked, mindful of the intrusion.

'Any time. Any time at all. It's such a nice morning that I thought I might venture out into the garden for a bit, but I'd be happy to see you whenever you can make it. For coffee, perhaps? Around eleven?'

'If that's not putting you out.'

'Not at all. I'll look forward to seeing you later, Miss Kingsley. And may I say,' she added shyly, 'that I find your niece a delightful young lady. Absolutely delightful. A credit to you and your family.'

'Oh. Thank you.' Nonplussed, Lucy put the phone down; it was the first time since Ruth's arrival that anyone other than Rachel had said a good word about her.

It was indeed a beautiful morning, the air mild and fresh and promising real warmth as the day progressed. So spring has come at long last, Lucy reflected as she walked the short distance to Vera's house. On a day like this she could almost believe that somehow, one day soon when Ruth had gone, things would return to normal, in spite of the trauma of Rachel's death.

She found the Brights' house without difficulty. It was in a street that was respectable rather than prestigious, but it was freshly painted and beautifully maintained on the outside. Lucy rang the bell. There was no reply, so after a few minutes she pushed it again, holding it in for a rather longer time; Vera might be in the garden, she realised, and might not have heard the bell.

After a delay, Lucy heard sounds from inside the house: heavy footsteps and a querulous old voice. 'Vera!' said an old man's scratchy grumble. 'Are you deaf, girl? Can't you hear the bell?' Then, as he got nearer, 'Hold your horses, out there. I'm coming.' The door flew open, and the old man from the post-funeral gathering peered out at Lucy. Ever susceptible to a pretty face, Walter Bright transformed his scowl into an approximation of a smile, baring a mouth full of surprisingly sound teeth. 'Oh, it's you! I saw you at the vicarage, didn't I?'

'That's right. I'm so sorry to bother you, Dr Bright. I'm Lucy Kingsley, and Vera is expecting me.'

'Well, you'd better come in then, hadn't you?' The old man stepped aside to let her in. 'I don't know where the damnfool girl has got to, though.'

'She said that she was going to do some gardening,' Lucy suggested. 'Perhaps she's out in the back and didn't hear the bell.'

'I was taking my nap. I always have a nap in the mornings, and then Vera brings me my coffee.'

'I'm so sorry to have disturbed your nap,' Lucy apologised again.

The old man grinned. 'I don't mind being disturbed by someone as pretty as you.' Walter Bright's eyes dropped to Lucy's chest and seemed fixated there. Embarrassed, Lucy spared a moment of empathetic pity for generations of his women patients. She was not to know that during his many years of practice, Dr Bright had been the model of rectitude and upright behaviour; it was only in his dotage that he had begun to ogle young women, to his daughter's immense mortification.

'Should we look for her in the garden?' Lucy suggested.

'I'll go. You stay here.' He tore his eyes away from her chest and shuffled off towards the back of the house.

His shriek, a moment later, was unearthly in quality, a banshee's wail that struck Lucy to the bone with intuitive terror. Without any volition or conscious thought she followed the sound, and found herself standing next to the old man in the kitchen. Out of some primitive instinct of self-preservation, her eyes looked everywhere but in the direction of the old man's trembling finger. In some corner of her brain she took in the cheery sprigged wallpaper, the angle of the sun streaming through the window on to the counter, the serviceable brown coffee mugs – three in number – set on a tray near the old-fashioned metallic electric kettle along with a plate of biscuits, the two identical brown mugs on the draining board, the muddy-fingered gardening gloves thrown carelessly on the table, the open door into the garden. Then she could avoid it no longer; her eyes followed his finger.

It was a strangely peaceful sight, with no blood and no signs of violence, but it was all the more horrible for that. Vera Bright was sitting in a chair, slumped over the table. One thin arm was flung across the table, palm up, in a beseeching gesture. And over her head was a green plastic bag with an unmistakeable gold logo, tied round her neck with a piece of garden twine.

Somehow Lucy managed to do the right things. She removed the old man from the kitchen, rang the police, told them the facts in a concise manner, then calmed Dr Bright down with a mug of strong, sweet tea, being careful while making it not to touch anything that might be important.

Ensconced in his customary armchair in the sitting room with his tea, the old man talked incessantly and seemingly at random as they waited for the police to arrive. 'It's the bag I don't understand,' he said over and over. 'My Vera didn't give herself airs. She never set foot in a shop like that in her life. She wasn't that kind of girl. But who would have done such a thing? To my Vera? She may have been useless, that girl, but she never hurt a fly. Who would want to harm her?' He wrapped his arms around himself and rocked back and forth. 'And what am I going to do without her? I'm not going into some home, where they'll tie me down and leave me to die. I don't understand about the bag. Why would anyone want to hurt Vera?' He repeated it over and over, in various permutations, like some kind of litany of misery. Lucy let him talk, realising that he wasn't really asking for answers.

The police arrived, a uniformed PC first and then a number of plainclothes officers and the police doctor. Lucy could hear them in the kitchen, going about their choreographed routine, but she blocked out any conscious speculation about what they were doing. For some little while they left her alone with the old man, who continued to ramble in the same vein. After a time, though, a neatly-dressed man with kind dark eyes and a large square jaw joined them in the sitting room and introduced himself. 'I'm Inspector Shepherd.' He looked at Lucy expectantly.

In a few words she told him who she was and why she was there, then indicated Dr Bright. 'This is Miss Bright's father. I'm afraid he's a bit incoherent at the moment – as you can imagine, Inspector, this has been a great shock for him.'

The policeman leaned over and addressed the old man. 'I'm very sorry about your daughter, sir.'

'Oh, my poor Vera. She was a good girl. Careful with her money. Not like some of these young things who go off shopping all the time.

She never was like that, my Vera. Never been inside that shop in her life. And why should she be?' The last was said on a belligerent note.

'No reason at all, sir,' said the policeman soothingly; he was used to dealing with people in shock, and the irrelevant things they often said. He turned back to Lucy. 'He found her, did he?'

She nodded. 'But I was right behind him. I'm sure he didn't touch anything. And I tried not to disturb anything either, though I didn't think it would hurt if I made a pot of tea. I thought he could use it.'

'No problem. We'll need to take your fingerprints, of course. And his as well, just for purposes of elimination.' He took out his notebook. 'Do you mind if I ask you a few questions, Miss Kingsley?'

'Not at all.'

'Did anything in the kitchen look out of place, or unusual?'

Regretfully she shook her head. 'I'm afraid I can't really help you. This is the first time I've been here, so I wouldn't know.'

'So you also wouldn't know if anything in the house were missing?'

'No. Sorry. You'll have to ask Dr Bright.'

The policeman looked at the old man without much hope. 'Sir,' he said, 'it looks like your daughter might have surprised a burglar. At some point, when you're feeling like it, I'd like you to have a look round and tell me if anything is missing. Silver, jewellery, appliances like video recorders or tellies.'

Walter Bright gestured scornfully at the box across from him. 'There's the television. Still there. No modern do-dads like video recorders in this house. And none of that other rot – I told you, my Vera was a simple girl.' He fixed the policeman with a belligerent glare. 'Don't you dare say otherwise. She might have been useless, but at least she was no spendthrift.'

Hastily Inspector Shepherd turned back to Lucy. 'You'll be wanting to get on, I expect. I don't think there's anything else we need from you at the moment. If you'll just let me know how we can get in touch with you, if necessary . . .'

'Dr Bright shouldn't be left alone,' she protested. 'He's very upset.'

'Don't worry about him – I'll get a WPC to sit with him,' the policeman assured her.

'Yes, just go off and leave me. Just like my Vera,' moaned the old man. 'How could she desert me like this? All alone. I'm all alone.'

Suddenly the horror of the situation – and the reality of it – descended on Lucy like a black curtain; she put her hands over her face and sobbed. 'I'm sorry. I know I shouldn't be like this. But it's just so . . . awful. Poor Vera.'

The policeman, who had seen far too many scenes like this, let her cry for a moment. 'Do you have a car, Miss Kingsley, or can we take you somewhere? I know that this has been upsetting for you.'

After a time Lucy regained control and lifted her chin. 'I'll be all right. If I could just use the phone and ring someone to collect me . . . ?'

'Yes, of course.'

Fortunately the phone was in the hall rather than in the kitchen. It was the old-fashioned sort with a dial; somehow she forced her fingers to push the dial around.

'Fosdyke, Fosdyke and Galloway,' announced a solemn female voice. 'May I help you?'

Lucy's voice sounded remarkably calm. 'Mr Middleton-Brown, please.'

'I'm sorry, but Mr Middleton-Brown is not in his office. Would you like to speak to his secretary, or can someone else help you?'

She took a deep breath as she felt the panic rising again. 'No, thank you. But if you could tell him that Lucy rang . . .'

The receptionist did not feel that conveying personal messages was part of her job. 'Very well,' she said repressively. 'I'll tell him.'

Putting the phone down, Lucy leaned her head against the wall and thought about what to do next. Emily, she decided gratefully. Emily would come for her. She dialled again.

'I'll be there in a few minutes,' Emily promised, when she'd had a brief outline of what had happened. 'Just hang on, Luce.'

'Thanks, Em.'

Before she left, Lucy had her fingerprints taken, efficiently and without fuss, then returned to the sitting room to say goodbye to the old man. She took his hand and leaned over him. 'I'm going soon, Dr Bright. But I'm sure they'll take good care of you.'

He raised his eyes, glanced over at the placid form of the WPC on the sofa, then beckoned Lucy closer. She bent down, and he cupped his hand over her ear to whisper, 'Those damned police don't believe me. They think I'm daft. But I know it was no burglar that killed my Vera. She would never go to that shop. And what about those two cups on the draining board? How do they explain those, hey?' For an instant the belligerence left him and his eyes were those of a vulnerable, pleading old man. 'Please,' he said softly. 'You're a good girl. Please find out who killed my Vera. Don't let them get away with it.'

CHAPTER 23

Their priests were slain with the sword: and there were no widows to make lamentation.

Psalm 78.65

Monday morning seemed to go very slowly for David. Ruth was being more than usually stroppy with him, causing him to reflect that five days was after all a very long time – time enough for God to create a fair chunk of the world. And hanging over the sunny morning like a black cloud was the prospect of his visit to Robin West. Having made up his mind of the necessity to interview the sacristan, he had determined to do it straightaway – that very lunchtime, in fact. It would be less suspicious – and undoubtedly safer – to meet him at his restaurant, as if by accident, and to have an informal chat. After all, he *had* been invited to stop by for a drink. He was sure that West would take his visit at face value, and that with the sacristan's penchant for gossip, there would be no difficulty in getting him to talk.

First, though, he wanted to ring Martin Bairstow. The younger churchwarden, ruthless in his business dealings and temperamentally suited to eliminating his opponents, seemed to David to be the most logical suspect, though a clear-cut motive eluded him. Perhaps it was as Gabriel had suggested, and Rachel had found out what the wardens had hoped to accomplish by the sale of the church's silver. Was there any way that the two of them could collude to skim off some of the money? But Bairstow didn't seem in any need of money, so there must be something else in the equation that David didn't know about.

Consulting his files for the number, he rang Bairstow's office. 'I'm sorry,' said his secretary, 'but Mr Bairstow isn't in at the moment. I expect him back at any time – can I have him return your call?'

'It's not urgent,' David said, but he gave his name and number to the secretary, and towards the end of the morning Mrs Simmons put through a call from the churchwarden.

'How can I help you, Mr Middleton-Brown?' Bairstow sounded slightly more brusque than usual.

David adopted an apologetic tone. 'I don't know how you feel about this,' he said, 'but if you're still interested in selling some of your silver, the Archdeacon has indicated to me that he would support the sale of one of the ciboria to the V and A. A privately negotiated sale, to keep it in the national collection. I realise that's far short of what you originally had in mind, but it would still bring in a tidy sum. Fifteen or twenty thousand, at a guess.'

There was a pause on the other end. 'I'll have to think about it,' was the eventual cautious reply. 'And speak to Norman Topping and Father Keble Smythe, of course. Can I get back to you in a few days?'

'I thought that perhaps we might meet to discuss it. At St Margaret's, if that's more convenient for you.'

Bairstow, who had seen his share of inflated solicitors' bills, wasn't so easily convinced. 'I'll get back to you as soon as I can,' he repeated. 'By the end of the week, if possible.'

David had to be satisfied with that. 'Very well, Mr Bairstow. I'll look forward to hearing from you.'

He looked at his watch; it was getting on for lunchtime. Realising that there was at least one advantage to his visit to *La Reine Dorée*, he went out to Mrs Simmons's desk to ask her if she'd mind very much taking Ruth to lunch with her, as he had an urgent lunchtime meeting.

Having been subjected to Ruth for the last fortnight, Mrs Simmons inevitably *did* mind very much, but she couldn't very well say so. 'No problem at all, Mr Middleton-Brown,' she replied bravely.

Good woman, he said to himself, resolving to pick up some flowers for her on his way back from lunch.

La Reine Dorée was located in South Kensington, not far from the tube station but in the opposite direction from Lucy's house. It was much as David had expected it to be: rather dimly lit, its walls adorned with a mixture of old French cigarette posters and framed black-and-white glossy photos of 1930s' screen goddesses, and patronised by a glittering array of decorative young people exemplifying various permutations of sexual preference but with a predominance of men.

Robin West, who was leaning in a cultivatedly insouciant pose near the door, stood to attention when he spotted David's entrance. 'My dear chap!' he beamed, putting out both hands. 'So you've finally come! I knew that you wouldn't be able to stay away for ever.' He gave David an exaggerated wink. 'Where's the girlfriend?'

'Oh, she . . . couldn't come today,' David said lamely.

West turned down the corners of his mouth. '*Quel dommage!*'

Overcoming his distaste, David forced a smile. 'Yes, well. How about that drink you promised me?'

'Absolutely, my dear. What will you have?'

For a split second David considered whether he would be better off staying sober and keeping his wits about him, or blotting out the pain of this ordeal with as much alcohol as possible. Prudence prevailed, and he chose the first option. 'Just mineral water, thanks. With ice and lemon.'

'How *boring*. Wouldn't you rather have a G and T? Or even champagne? It's on the house, remember?'

It was tempting, but not tempting enough. 'Sorry, no. I've got to go back to work this afternoon,' David explained, adding, 'I'll have to come back another time for the champagne.'

'Promise that you'll leave the girlfriend behind again and it's a deal,' West smirked, going behind the bar for the mineral water. He poured it out with a flourish, added an artistic twist of lemon, then concocted a gin and tonic for himself, before leading the way to a corner table. 'Are you having some lunch?' he asked.

'I thought I might.'

West went off for a moment and returned with a menu. 'The breast of *poussin* in cream and Kirsch sauce is quite nice,' he advised. 'Or if that's too rich for you, I recommend the warm salad with *goujons* of duck and rocket in balsamic vinaigrette.'

David studied the menu. 'Actually, I fancy the steak sandwich,' he said firmly. And he wouldn't tell Lucy about it afterwards, either; although he of course ate no meat at home, her attempts to woo him into committed vegetarianism had thus far failed, but he didn't go out of his way to confess to her his occasional and enjoyable lapses into meat eating. 'And some chips, if you do anything so plebeian,' he added in a defiant tone.

West looked shocked, but refrained from voicing his disillusionment with David's taste. 'If that's what you want, then that's what you shall have.' He flagged down a waiter and gave the order, choosing the *poussin* for himself, then settled back and grinned at David. 'I suppose you've heard about all the excitement at St Margaret's,' he said with relish.

'You mean about your curate's death?'

'That woman, yes. I never acknowledged her as the curate, as you know. Her orders were invalid.'

'You're not one of the people who's praising her to the heavens now that she's dead?'

West snorted in derision. 'Not I. I didn't want her at St Margaret's, and I'm not sorry that she's gone, though I might have settled for a less drastic method of removal. I wasn't alone in either of those sentiments, as I'm sure you're aware, but you'd never know it from the way people are talking now. Even Dolly Topping. That particular brand of hypocrisy doesn't appeal to me, my dear. No, I'm not ashamed to admit that I'm glad she's gone.'

'Still, it must have come as rather a shock, so soon after Father Julian's death,' David ventured.

'Father Julian.' Robin West sighed gustily and shook his head. 'Now that was a great loss to the church. Not just to St Margaret's, but to the Holy Catholic Church. He was a true Catholic. With a brilliant feel for liturgy, as well.'

'Did you know him well, then?'

'Oh, quite well. He used to come in here often in the evenings with Alistair. I'd usually have a drink with them if we weren't too busy.'

'Alistair?'

'He always called Alistair his "lodger", of course.' West gave him a knowing wink.

'You're telling me that this Alistair was Father Julian's . . . lover?'

'Of course. What else? You know and I know that it goes on all over this diocese. I think that there are more priests with "lodgers" than without, my dear. But our blessed Archdeacon takes a dim view of such things,' West said cuttingly. 'A good family man, our Archdeacon. So it has to be "lodgers" and "friends".'

Gabriel? thought David in astonishment. That was rich. To cover his confusion, he asked quickly, 'This Alistair chap. He lived with Father Julian in . . . what's it called? Magdalen House?'

'That's right. They'd been together for quite a while – he came to London with Julian.' If Robin West thought David's questions were odd, he gave no indication. Obviously David had not misjudged his voracious appetite for gossip.

'And where is he now? I mean, surely he had to move out of the house? Does he still come in here?'

Robin West shook his head. 'He's left London, I'm afraid. Gone to Brighton. Gone off with one of my other regular customers, as a matter of fact. Father Gilbert, who was at St Benedict's, Earl's

Court – he's just moved to a church in Brighton. St Dunstan's – do you know it?'

'Yes,' said David. 'Yes, I do.'

'It's supposed to be a real spike shop,' West declared with a certain amount of envy. 'No nonsense about women in a place like that.'

Suddenly David knew that he had to go to Brighton, to talk to this Alistair. He needed to find out as much as he could about Father Julian, and Alistair was the obvious person to talk to. 'But St Dunstan's has a clergy house,' he thought aloud. 'Father Gilbert can't have a lodger there.'

'Why not, dear?' West waved a careless hand and giggled. 'He's turfed the curate out, I hear. But the curate didn't mind. Now he can go into digs with his boyfriend.'

The food arrived, and David ate his sandwich with enjoyment. The sacristan chattered on through the meal, mainly about Father Keble Smythe and the ludicrous charade of his fiancée Miss Morag McKenzie, but David was no longer interested in the gossip. He had found out about the existence and the whereabouts of Alistair; that was enough.

Refusing a sweet, he made his escape with as much speed as was possible – with promises to return in the near future for that champagne. There was still time to get to Brighton that afternoon, if he hurried. He stopped at a call box and rang Lucy's house to let her know his plans, but there was no reply; knowing that she'd planned to visit Vera Bright that day, he wasn't unduly worried at her absence. He could ring her again later, he decided, hurrying to the tube station to catch the Circle Line to Blackfriars, where he transferred to the Thameslink train to Brighton.

It was a relatively quick journey; David arrived in Brighton by mid-afternoon. From the station he made another unsuccessful attempt to reach Lucy, then hailed a taxi; 'St Dunstan's clergy house,' he instructed. In the taxi he reflected upon the possible folly of his precipitate journey: there was no guarantee that this Alistair would be there. In fact, given that it was a Monday afternoon, the chances were good that Alistair would be elsewhere, most likely at his place of employment.

This line of thought, distressing as it was, kept him from brooding on the irony of returning to St Dunstan's clergy house in these circumstances. He hadn't been back there since Gabriel's days as curate of St Dunstan's, years ago. It was inevitable that there should be memories associated with the place, even now. Not that he had ever lived there with Gabe – there had never been any question of that. They had always been painstakingly discreet about their relationship. And in those long-ago days, neither curates nor incumbents seemed to flaunt their 'lodgers' more or less openly, as they clearly did now.

Arriving at the clergy house, he paid the cab driver, then took a deep breath, went to the door, and rang the bell.

In the old days, it would have been the dragon of a housekeeper who answered the door. Now it was a thin young man in his late twenties, casually dressed, with fine straight sandy hair which hung nearly to his shoulders and grazed his eyebrows in a sideswept fringe. 'Hello?' he said questioningly, his open face displaying no suspicion.

'Are you by any chance called Alistair?'

'That's right. Alistair Duncan.' His voice had a heavy but pleasing Scots burr.

David produced the story he'd decided upon during his train journey – one that was very nearly the truth. 'My name is David Middleton-Brown. I'm a solicitor, acting for St Margaret's Church in London. I understand that you . . . knew . . . Father Julian, their former curate, and I wondered if you'd mind my asking you a few questions.'

A guarded, tense expression clamped down on his face. 'Have they caught the bastards that killed him yet?'

'No,' said David seriously. 'That's why I'm here, really. There are several people who are interested in finding out the truth about what happened to Father Julian, and they don't think that the police are doing enough. They've asked me to come along and see you – if you're prepared to talk to me, of course. You might be able to tell us something important, something that we don't know, that will help us find the killer.'

The young man relaxed, shrugged, and smiled an attractive lopsided smile. 'Why not?' He waved his arm. 'Come on in, why don't you?'

They went into the drawing room. Amazingly, it had altered hardly at all in the years since David had last been there; the ancient and massive furniture was a bit more frayed around the edges, and the oriental carpet was rather more threadbare. But the gloomy wallpaper, of indeterminate pattern and colour, was the same, with its even darker rectangles hinting at long-departed pictures that once must have occupied the walls. Those walls sported the same dreary engravings that David remembered: ugly continental churches, and the odd simpering saint. He couldn't understand why someone hadn't got rid of them years ago.

The drawing room was definitely dustier than it had been in the regime of the dragon-housekeeper (whatever had her name been?), the windows admitted the light through a film of grime, and the vast fireplace showed signs of a recent fire. *She* would never have allowed such a thing, he was sure, not even in the dead of winter – let alone on the cusp of spring.

'Could I get you a cup of tea?' Alistair offered hospitably.

That sounded wonderful, but David made the polite response. 'I don't want to put you to any trouble.'

'No trouble. I was about to have one myself.'

'Then I'd love a cup.'

Tea was produced in short order, and properly: on a tray with a cloth, poured from a silver teapot into bone china cups, and served with thin triangles of bread and butter. David, having expected somehow to be presented with a mug of tea, was glad to see that standards at the clergy house had not entirely slipped. 'How nice,' he said.

The young man grinned engagingly. 'It's the one thing I've been well trained to do. Jules wasn't particularly bothered, but Gil likes his tea done properly.' He waved his hand around at the room. 'I may not be much of a housekeeper, but at least I can serve up a proper tea.'

'You're the housekeeper, then?'

'In a manner of speaking.' He grinned again. 'As you can see.'

David found himself liking this open and honest young man very much. 'That doesn't seem like a very exciting career,' he remarked, smiling.

'It's all I've got at the moment,' Alistair explained. 'Since I came to Brighton, I haven't been very successful in finding work in my own profession.'

'Which is . . . ?'

'I'm a hairdresser. And if you know anything at all about Brighton, you'll realise that hairdressers are quite thick on the ground here.'

David laughed: yes, they would be.

'So until something comes up, Gil has said I can be his housekeeper. The patience of a saint, that man has, to put up with me and my slovenly ways.'

'You weren't Father Julian's housekeeper, then?'

'Oh, Lord, no.' Alistair laughed at the idea. 'Jules had a woman who came in twice a week. He was a bit fussier than Gil. And I was just the lodger. In a manner of speaking.'

David leaned forward. 'I hope you don't mind talking about Father Julian. After all, it must be rather painful for you.'

The young man looked out of the window and brushed the fringe from his forehead absently. 'A wee bit,' he confessed. 'Jules and I were together for a long time, you know. He was my first real love, and that's always special.'

'Yes,' said David.

'And of course I never had any official status in his life, which made it more difficult. His lodger, that's all I was.' His voice had become bitter.

'You weren't a member of the congregation, then?'

'Me? You've got to be joking! I have no use for the bloody Church of England.' His face was as congested with pain as his voice. 'A church that put up so many barriers between me and the man I loved, that forced us to live a lie just so a load of old biddies wouldn't have their delicate sensibilities offended! It's mad – a church that would rather turn a blind eye to its priests cottaging in public loos than encourage them to form stable, loving relationships like the one that Jules and I had.' He shook his head. 'Most of the people in Jules's churches didn't know that I existed. And it had to be that way. Not because I wanted it to be a secret, but because of their own bloody hypocrisy.'

David was stunned; he framed his next question carefully. 'If you feel so strongly about the Church, then why have you become involved with another priest?' And so soon, was the unspoken corollary.

Alistair pressed his lips together, then twisted them into a semblance of a smile. 'It must seem hardhearted to you, and even calculating. After what I've told you about what Jules and I meant to each other. That I could take up with Gil so quickly, I mean. But I didn't really have much choice.' He ran his long fingers through his fringe. 'I don't know why I'm telling you all this,' he confessed, 'but somehow it seems like you understand. And I haven't really had anyone to talk to about Jules. Gil doesn't like it when I go on about him all the time.'

'What did you mean, that you didn't have much choice?'

The young man shrugged, and answered baldly. 'I had to move out of Magdalen House after Jules died, didn't I? I was having trouble finding new digs that I could afford. Gil had been offered this new post here in Brighton. He'd always fancied me, even when I was with Jules, so he said I could come along and be his housekeeper.' He shrugged again, looking down into his tea cup. 'It's not so bad. Gil's all right. We rub along well together. But it's not like it was with Jules . . .'

'Why don't you tell me about Jules, if you feel that you can,' David suggested gently.

Alistair's voice changed as he talked about him. 'Oh, Jules was special, he was. Ask anyone at that bloody church and they'll tell you the same. A caring man – he got involved with people. He really cared about them, and their problems. And he was good at his job. Conscientious. All that bloody paperwork that some priests can't be bothered with – he did all that, too. It seemed like he spent half his time doing things that that useless bugger of a vicar didn't want to deal with.'

'Father Keble Smythe?' asked David, smiling at the description.

'Him.' His dismissively scornful tone indicated what he thought of the Vicar of St Jude's and St Margaret's. 'Jules wouldn't hear a word against him, but I thought he was a waste of space. And I know a few things about him, through the Scottish grapevine, that I don't think he'd want his precious congregation to know. They think he's some bloody saint or something.'

'Did Father Julian get on with the churchwardens?' David probed, mindful of his mission.

'Oh, aye. Jules got on with everyone. There wasn't a soul who didn't like Jules.' A small smile twitched at the corner of his mouth. 'And I know what you're thinking – that I'm just saying that because I loved him. But it's true. Jules was a grand lad, with a heart as big as a house. Or a church. He loved all those people, just like they loved him.'

And one of them had killed him. The thought popped unbidden into David's head, but as he articulated it to himself he knew that it was true. One of them had killed him, and made it look like a bungled burglary. The same person who had cut Rachel Nightingale's life short. What dangerous knowledge had the two curates of St Margaret's shared? Knowledge so deadly that it had cost both of those loving and gentle people their lives . . .

'Do you by any chance have a photo of Father Julian that you could show me?' requested David.

'Oh, aye. I have to keep them well hidden from Gil, you understand.' The young man left the room for a minute or two, after providing David with a fresh cup of tea; he returned bearing a heavy photograph album. 'This goes back a long time,' he explained, sitting next to David on the sofa. He opened it to the first page and pointed. 'Here's Jules. Years ago, when we first met.' A fresh-faced, happy young man, little more than a youth, grinned at the camera. He had straight dark hair, worn rather long, and honest blue eyes. 'And here I am.' A younger version of Alistair, with the same lopsided smile, inhabited the next photo, equally young and equally happy as his friend.

Alistair flipped through the pages of the album, lingering over some pages with nostalgic melancholy, providing occasional explanations or commentary for David when it seemed called for. Most of the photos were of the two young men, separately as they turned the camera on each other, formally posed or candid, and sometimes together when they found a third party to press the shutter. Some of the most hilarious were, Alistair explained, experiments with the camera's self-timer: the two young men together in absurd and antic poses, with various humorous props. 'Oh, we did have a grand time,' he said, and David could believe it.

As the pages progressed, the young men matured. Julian's face lost some of its fresh innocence, but none of its gentle good humour. Premature threads of grey emerged in his dark hair even before the dog collar appeared. Eventually the grey replaced the dark in almost equal measure, adding a certain air of gravitas that was not at all unattractive.

Then, suddenly, they were at the last page, or at least the last page with pictures on it; a number of blank sheets followed, poignant testimony to holidays never to be taken and occasions never to be shared. 'Last summer, on our holiday in Scotland,' Alistair said, his voice bleak. 'There may be a few more in the camera, as a matter of fact. I haven't used it since . . . since Jules died.' No antic snapshot sessions with Father Gilbert, then, David thought. He was moved: Julian Piper looked like a man who would have been worth knowing.

'Your Jules looks like a lovely man,' he offered inadequately, but it was enough.

'I have some other things I could show you, if you were interested,' Alistair suggested in a tentative way.

David turned to him with eagerness. 'Yes, of course. I'd like to see anything you've got.'

'Actually, I've got all of his things. Most, anyway. His family took a few things, but the house had to be cleared, so I took what was left.'

'And you have it? Here?' He tried to control his excitement.

'In a chest in the loft.' Father Gilbert again. 'Most of it wouldn't mean much to anyone but me, but there are a few bits you might find of interest.'

He disappeared for a few more minutes, returning with an armload of scrapbooks and other ephemera of a life, left behind like a butterfly's discarded cocoon. Perched on top was an item of even less use than most in the next life, but one upon which David's attention was immediately fixed. 'Can I see that?' he asked eagerly.

'Oh, aye. I thought you might like to look at his diary.' Alistair put down his burden and handed David the diary, the date of the previous year stamped in gold on the cover.

As David took it, the clock chimed six. 'Good Lord, is that really the time?' he said with a start.

'I'm afraid so. Gil will be back from saying Evensong soon, so we don't have long to look at Jules's bits and pieces. Would you like to join us for supper?' he added diffidently but sincerely. 'It won't be much, but you're welcome to stay.'

'Thanks, but I really can't.' David checked his watch in disbelief. 'Listen, would you mind awfully if I used your phone to make an important call? It's to London, I'm afraid. But my girlfriend doesn't know where I am.' It was amazing how easily the word tripped from his tongue once he was used to it.

'No problem.' Alistair grinned. 'Talk as long as you like. The diocese pays the phone bill.' He led David to the phone in the hall, then withdrew discreetly.

Whatever would Lucy be thinking? David worried as he dialled the number. She would be expecting him home by now. He prepared his apologies as it started to ring. The phone was picked up on the third ring, but it wasn't Lucy's voice which answered.

'Hello?' said Ruth.

Ruth. Good Lord, thought David, stricken. He'd forgotten all about the *enfant terrible*. 'Oh, hello,' he said casually, deciding to bluff it out. 'Can I have a word with Lucy?'

'She's not here.' Ruth's voice was outraged. 'And I don't know where she is, either. What's going on around here? What's happened to everybody? First you go off and leave me without a word, and then Aunt Lucy disappears. It's just a good thing that I've got a key to this place. My parents aren't going to be very impressed when I tell them how you've neglected me. I waited for you,' she added accusingly. 'I waited until half-past five at the office, and then I had to come back here by myself. Anything could have happened to me. I could have been mugged on the Underground, or even murdered, and you wouldn't have cared.'

No, I *wouldn't* have cared, he thought savagely. All he cared about at the moment was Lucy. Where the hell was she?

'And the cat is starving as well,' she went on in an excess of gratuitous malice. 'I'm sure that the RSPCA would like to hear about that.'

'Just stay there,' he told her with as much civility as he could muster, which wasn't a great deal. 'Fix yourself something to eat. I'll be home eventually.'

He took a deep breath and tried to apply logic to the situation. Who would know where Lucy was? Emily, he apprehended in a flash of inspiration. If anyone knew where Lucy was, it would be Emily.

Of course he didn't have the number. But that was one advantage to being in a clergy house: on the desk in the hall, sticking out from under the Brighton phone directory, was a copy of the *Church of England Year Book*. He pulled it out, opened it to the section on the London diocese, and found the number for the Archdeacon of Kensington.

Emily answered the phone on the second ring. 'David, thank God,' she said in a heartfelt voice when he'd identified himself.

His heart rose to his throat. 'Lucy?' he choked.

'Oh, she'll be all right. But we've been trying to reach you all afternoon. Something terrible has happened. I won't go into it on the phone – I'll tell you all about it when you get here. But hurry, David. Lucy needs you.'

CHAPTER 24

Why art thou so heavy, O my soul: and why art thou so disquieted within me?
Psalm 43.5

The trip between Brighton and London had never seemed longer, as David's fevered imagination ran riot over all the lurid possibilities. Lucy injured, or ill. Perhaps she'd been attacked by someone who knew that she was getting close to the truth about Rachel's death. That possibility couldn't be underestimated, he realised: after all, two people had already died to protect whatever secret someone was hiding. Emily had said that it was something terrible. Oh God, what could it be?

He didn't have much recollection of getting from the clergy house to the station, or indeed of anything after the phone call, but after a time he became aware, sitting on the train, that Father Julian Piper's diary was still clutched in his hand. Either Alistair had given him permission to take it, or hadn't realised that he still had it – David couldn't remember which.

To take his mind off his painful but ultimately fruitless speculations, he opened the diary and flipped through it. It was the sort with a week to a page, so there was little space for detailed annotation. Father Julian, with the busy life that he had obviously led, had developed a kind of shorthand to squeeze as much information as possible into each daily square. David applied his brain to cracking the code.

Some of it was easy. A single 'M' quite clearly stood for Mass, as there was one noted for each day, with a time and either 'SJ' or 'SM': St Jude's and St Margaret's, and far more of the latter than the former. A single 'S', usually on a Sunday, most likely indicated a sermon. On Saturdays there often appeared a 'W' – weddings, thought David. And there were 'F's as well, sprinkled throughout. Funerals, both at SJ and SM. Other double letters were probably initials, indicating people with whom he was meeting for pastoral counselling or various other reasons.

Interested in spite of himself, David turned through the months to December. What had Father Julian been doing around the time of his death? He tried to remember the exact day that the priest had died, deciding that perhaps Gabriel hadn't told him more than that it had been at the beginning of December.

Advent, the start of the Church's year. The season of penitence as much as of anticipation. 'Lo, he comes with clouds descending', but also 'deeply wailing', and 'That day of wrath, that dreadful day'. In the diary, the usual daily 'M', an 'AP' on the first Sunday – Advent Procession, translated David – and a 'W' on the following Saturday. Unusual to have a wedding during Advent, since flowers were not normally allowed in the church, but it wasn't unknown.

Then his attention was truly caught by a notation on the Friday of that week. 'VB, 2', it said, and right under it, 'NT, 4'. 'Vera Bright,' he said aloud, drawing a dubious look from the woman across from him. Father Julian had seen Vera Bright right around the time he had been killed, as Rachel Nightingale had done just before her death. And then, seemingly, he had seen Norman Topping on the same day, before Solemn Evensong.

If he hadn't been so worried about Lucy, he would have been jubilant. He wondered, though, if Lucy had managed to talk to Vera Bright, and if so what she had found out. This was convincing evidence, if such had been necessary, that Vera Bright might well hold the key to the two curates' deaths. Galling as it was to admit it, Ruth might have been right in her belief that Vera knew who had killed Rachel. And Father Julian, David added to himself, tucking the diary into his pocket for safekeeping.

Emily met him at the door. 'She's all right, really she is,' she assured him. 'Just a bit shaken up. But she was in no fit state to be on her own, so I brought her here.'

'But what happened? Has she been hurt? You said something terrible . . .'

'Nothing like that. Vera Bright is dead, and Lucy found her body,' Emily told him bluntly.

David experienced a jumble of conflicting emotions: relief that Lucy wasn't hurt, dismay about Vera Bright, and a great sense of powerlessness and frustration. 'Dead?!'

'Murdered.'

'Oh, God. Where's Lucy?'

'In the drawing room.'

With two strides he was at the door to the room. In the back of his mind David registered the fact that Gabriel was there, and somehow

Ruth had appeared as well – presumably Lucy had remembered her and someone had fetched her. But Lucy was the only one he saw. She rose from the sofa as he appeared at the door, her eyes huge in a white face. 'David,' she said as he crossed the room to her and crushed her against his chest.

'Oh, my love,' he murmured with great tenderness. 'Lucy, my poor love.' He didn't care what Gabriel thought; he didn't care what Ruth thought. Lucy was all that mattered.

'Vera's dead.'

'Emily said.'

'Oh, David. It was so horrible. I can't tell you how awful it was.' Her body trembled in a convulsive spasm as she remembered the scene vividly once again in every dreadful detail.

He held her tighter. 'Oh, love. Don't think about it.'

'How can I forget it?' Lucy raised her eyes to his face. 'I'll *never* forget it.'

Emily had held the meal until David's arrival, so after a while, the twins tucked into bed, they adjourned to the dining room for a simple, subdued meal.

It was inevitable that there should be one primary topic of conversation: Vera Bright's murder, and the light that it cast on the previous deaths.

There was no question this time of excluding Ruth. She was very much a part of the discussion; in fact, wallowing in guilt, she very nearly stole the limelight from Lucy.

She'd been very quiet for a few minutes before her initial outburst. 'It's all my fault,' she wailed suddenly. 'I practically killed her myself!'

'Don't be ridiculous,' David snapped, being in no mood for her histrionics.

'But don't you see? She'd still be alive now if I hadn't said what I did after the funeral!'

'What do you mean?' Gabriel asked slowly.

'You were there – you heard me. I told Aunt Lucy that Miss Bright knew who killed Rachel.'

Lucy nodded. 'I'm afraid that nearly everyone heard you.'

'That's just the point! I was so excited that I didn't realise how loud my voice was, and everyone heard me. Including the murderer, and then he knew that he had to kill her, too. To stop her telling anyone what she knew.'

There was an appalled silence around the table, as everyone acknowledged the probable truth of her reasoning.

'How could I have been so stupid?' Ruth said shrilly. 'I should have known that the murderer would have been there, and would have heard what I said. But I thought it was Dolly Topping, and she wasn't in the dining room.'

'Her husband was,' Emily pointed out. 'He could have told her quite easily, or so could a number of other people. As you said, you didn't exactly lower your voice.'

'Oh, I'll never forgive myself. Poor Miss Bright – she didn't deserve to die. She didn't deserve what I did to her.'

David looked across the table and saw Lucy's expression of distress. 'Stop it!' he said sharply to Ruth. 'Can't you see that you're upsetting your aunt?'

Ruth wasn't about to let up. 'At least now everyone will believe that Rachel was murdered,' she stated. 'I mean, Miss Bright's death wasn't exactly an accident, and no one could say that it was. Now maybe the police will start looking for the murderer.'

Lucy shook her head suddenly. 'No,' she said. 'The police think that Vera Bright was killed by a burglar who'd broken into her house. That's all they'll be looking for – a burglar like the one who supposedly killed Father Julian.'

'Father Julian?' Ruth hadn't yet heard about the previous curate. Between them, they explained.

The girl was incensed. 'You mean that *three* people have been murdered, and the police still aren't doing anything?'

'That's about the extent of it,' said Emily.

David stood up. 'I'm going to ring my contact on the police,' he announced. 'I want to see what they have to say about what happened today. Surely they *can't* think that it was a burglar.'

He returned a few minutes later. 'You were right,' he told Lucy. 'Her father, the old doctor, insists that it couldn't have been a burglar, but they've dismissed him as a senile old man. The way they reckon it, the burglar came through the back door into the kitchen. Either she was there when he came in, or else she came in from the garden a few minutes later and caught him red-handed. He panicked, grabbed a plastic bag that was lying in the kitchen, popped it over her head, and, as he so colourfully said "Bob's your uncle". Sorry, love,' he added contritely at the look on her face.

'It's all right.' She gave a brave smile. 'We have to talk about it, don't we? It's clear that the police aren't going to do anything.'

'No, they're not,' he confirmed. 'No more than they did for Father Julian.'

'Or Rachel,' put in a loyal Ruth.

'They didn't really listen to Dr Bright, but what he said made perfect sense,' Lucy said. 'He told me – just like he told the police – that Vera never shopped at any of those smart Knightsbridge shops. That may have sounded like an old man's nonsensical ramblings, but what he was trying to say was that whoever killed her came into the house armed with that carrier bag.'

'What do you mean?' Emily asked.

Lucy gulped as she visualised the green bag. 'The bag that suffocated her came from a shop she never went to, so the murderer must have brought the bag with him.'

'Or her,' David amended.

'Or her. And there was other evidence that she knew the murderer, and probably let him, or her, in herself.'

She had their undivided attention.

'Her father was taking a nap, so someone might have even rung the bell and come in through the front. Apparently he takes a nap every morning, and probably everyone at the church knows that, so it wouldn't really be taking any chances to come quite openly while he was asleep. And I believe he's a bit deaf as well.'

'But what's the other evidence?' demanded Ruth impatiently.

'The mugs. There were three mugs on a tray, ready for morning coffee – one for me as well, since she was expecting me. But there were also two mugs on the draining board, rinsed out but recently used. I saw them myself, and Dr Bright mentioned it to me later.'

'Couldn't they have been left over from their breakfast?' Gabriel asked.

'Apparently not, according to Dr Bright. He told me that she always washed up and put away the breakfast dishes straightaway. He'd watched her do it this morning, as usual, so those mugs had been used since then.'

'By Vera and the murderer,' said Emily slowly. 'But didn't he tell the police about the mugs?'

'Yes, of course he did. More than once, probably. But again, they didn't understand the significance. They thought that he was just rambling.'

'So,' David summed up. 'It looks as though it's down to us.'

* * *

It was odd that no one had thought to ask before, but in the drama surrounding Vera's death it scarcely seemed to matter. Not until they were eating the fresh fruit that served for a dessert did Gabriel enquire, 'And where were *you* today, David, by the way?'

'Brighton,' David said deliberately, watching Gabriel's face.

With an effort Gabriel controlled his expression, betraying emotion only with a flicker of his eyelids. 'Oh?'

'But that's the end of the story, really, rather than the beginning,' David went on. 'I had lunch at Robin West's restaurant, and had a little chat with him about Father Julian. He told me, with great relish, that Father Julian had had a lodger at Magdalen House.'

'Oh?' This time it was Lucy, giving David a warning look as she kicked him under the table and indicated Ruth with a slight inclination of her head.

But Ruth, peeling a banana, was oblivious both to her aunt's concern and to the subtext of David's statement. David looked at Ruth and the banana with equal distaste, but resolved to couch his story in terms that would not offend or corrupt innocent young ears. 'It turns out that this lodger, a chap by the name of Alistair Duncan, is an unemployed hairdresser, currently living in Brighton and acting as housekeeper for the new Vicar of St Dunstan's.'

'A man housekeeper – that's funny,' Ruth said scornfully. 'I don't suppose he's very good at it.'

Her comment covered the sound of Gabriel dropping his fruit knife. He picked it up again, hoping that no one had noticed. 'St Dunstan's? What a coincidence,' he remarked in a hearty voice. Turning to Ruth, he explained genially, 'I was a curate at St Dunstan's, a long time ago.'

'Oh, yes?' She didn't try very hard to sound interested. It must have been a *very* long time ago, she thought, since the Archdeacon was now so elderly. Forty, at least. As old as her father.

'And your Uncle David was there at the same time, as a server.'

'Don't call him my uncle,' she muttered fiercely. 'He's not my uncle. He's living in sin with my aunt, not married to her!'

There was a long, embarrassed silence, then Gabriel turned back to David. 'So you actually went to St Dunstan's, then?'

'To the clergy house.'

'And how was it?' Gabriel would have given anything at that moment if he and David could have been alone having this conversation, launching into a reminiscence of old times, reaffirming the ties that had never completely disappeared. As it was, he fought to keep the yearning and the enthusiasm from his voice.

'Very much the same.' David's tone was dry. 'Though Ruth is right – Alistair Duncan *isn't* a very good housekeeper. Everything was a bit dusty and grimy.'

Gabriel produced a chuckle. 'Wouldn't old Mrs Ellison turn over in her grave, then?'

That was her name, thought David. 'I dare say she's spinning even as we speak.'

Emily was growing impatient with all this nostalgic chat, from which she rightly felt excluded. 'So what about this Alistair Duncan? Did he tell you anything useful about Father Julian?'

'Oh, yes. He gave me a great deal of background information, which I won't go into now,' he said; the flick of his eyes in Ruth's direction was immediately understood by the others. 'And,' he went on, 'he gave me Father Julian's diary for last year.' With a flourish he produced it from his pocket.

'His diary!' Lucy looked up at last from the extended examination of some satsuma peel to which Gabriel and David's exchange had driven her.

He opened it up to the first week in December. 'Did you ever tell us, Gabriel, exactly what day he was killed?'

'It was on a Friday night or Saturday morning at the beginning of December, that first week. He was found in the sacristy on Saturday morning, but they're not sure exactly what time he died, because of the effect of the cold temperature of the church in delaying rigor mortis,' the Archdeacon explained with technical precision.

'Well, that makes it the fourth or the fifth. And look,' David stated triumphantly, pointing to the entry in the diary. 'This is what I think is significant. On Friday the fourth of December, Father Julian had an appointment with VB at 2 o'clock. That must be Vera Bright! Don't you see? Rachel talked to Vera Bright the day before she died, and so did Father Julian!'

Ruth practically bounced up and down in her seat with excitement. 'So I was right! They both told her something, didn't they? She *did* know who killed them!'

'It certainly looks that way,' David agreed. 'And look what else I think is interesting. Right after he saw Vera Bright, he had a meeting with NT. Norman Topping – what do you think of that?'

* * *

Not surprisingly, Lucy didn't sleep very well that night. Vera's death, and the circumstances surrounding it, had hit her hard, intensifying the distress that Rachel's death had aroused in her. She tossed and turned, dozing intermittently, but every time she dropped off it was to a gut-wrenching dream of that outstretched, pathetic hand, a slumped body with a green bag where a head should be, or alternatively the pleading eyes of an old man who begged her, 'Find out who killed my Vera.'

Vera Bright. Vera Bright. Vera Bright. The name pounded in her head like an unwelcome mantra, impossible to exorcise. In a desperate effort to counteract it, she tried to project her thoughts into the future rather than the past. After all, they were a long way from knowing who had murdered Vera Bright, even if they did know why. And the motive for the other two deaths was still unclear.

What could they do – *she* do – to find out? She had failed signally, it must be admitted, in the task assigned to her, to talk to Vera Bright. She had been just a little too late, and because of that, Vera had died, and her knowledge with her.

Was there anything else she could do? She had intended, she remembered, to deliver the finished painting to Vanessa Bairstow, and have a chat with her. Vanessa Bairstow, as different as could be imagined from Vera Bright, beautifully coiffed and elegant. Vanessa Bairstow. Vera Bright.

She sat up in bed and shook David's shoulder urgently. 'David darling, wake up!'

He had been sleeping rather better than she – he, after all, had not found a dead body that day, but had done some fairly tiring travelling – so it was surprising how quickly he came to life. 'What's wrong, love?'

'Vanessa Bairstow. It might have been Vanessa Bairstow.'

'What are you talking about?'

'Listen, darling. It was natural that you should have thought that Father Julian went to see Vera Bright on the day before he died, since we know that Rachel did. But it could have been Vanessa Bairstow. VB – don't you see?'

He grasped her point. 'Oh. But I don't . . .'

'And that's not all. I just remembered something that she said, the first time I met her. She said that she had a new hairdresser, because her old one had just moved to Brighton.'

'But . . .'

'We've thought about her husband as someone who might be involved in the deaths. But what if *she* has something to do with it, directly or indirectly?'

'It's possible, I suppose,' David admitted sleepily.

'I'm not sure how it all fits together, but there could be some connection. I'll go and see her tomorrow.' She thought for a moment, then added, 'But there's something you can do, as well – you can ring your friend Alistair, and see if he knows anything about Vanessa Bairstow.'

'All right,' he agreed, yawning. 'If you'll promise to stop worrying about it for now, and try to get some sleep. On second thoughts,' he amended as she lay back down beside him, 'I think we could both use a cuddle. Come here, Lucy love.'

She allowed him to take her in his arms, and didn't resist when his caresses became more insistent, but for the first time in the history of their lovemaking she was just going through the motions; though her body was engaged most pleasurably, her mind was elsewhere, and her heart was gripped in a chill ache that was beyond comfort.

CHAPTER 25

There is no health in my flesh, because of thy displeasure: neither is there any rest in my bones, by reason of my sin.
For my wickednesses are gone over my head: and are like a sore burden, too heavy for me to bear.

Psalm 38.3–4

After seeing David and Ruth off to work on Tuesday morning, Lucy washed up the breakfast dishes, fed Sophie, then moved about the house restlessly, feeling that she should be doing something of a constructive nature. The sitting room was a mess: Ruth had left the sofa bed unfolded, so Lucy removed the bedding, folded it up and stashed it in the cupboard under the stairs, then restored the innards to their hidden state inside the sofa. Her niece had also left an assortment of sweet wrappers and empty crisp packets on the table and even the floor. With an unconscious sigh she collected them all up and transported them to the bin in the kitchen, then took a cookery book off the shelf and located a recipe for that evening's meal.

She went upstairs, took a leisurely hot bubble bath, washed her hair and dried it, got dressed, then went into her studio. Vanessa's painting was on the easel, completed and ready to be wrapped up and delivered. Lucy was pleased with the painting, and thought that Vanessa would be as well; in keeping with the importance of the occasion which it was to mark, it had been executed on an ambitious scale, and it had worked. She had used Christian motifs, including a variety of crosses, repeated and combined in innovative ways, and the result was pleasing to the eye, devotional without being in any way sentimental.

Lucy looked at her watch. It was late enough to ring Vanessa, so she went into the bedroom to use the phone there.

Vanessa answered promptly, and seemed eager to see both Lucy and the painting. 'Do you want me to come and fetch it?' she offered.

'Oh, no. That's not necessary. I'll bring it to you. I can come by taxi.'

'I can't wait to see it. And I can't wait to give it to Martin.'

'Your anniversary is this weekend?'

'That's right. Twenty years.' Vanessa sighed. 'It doesn't seem possible that it's been that long.'

'Well, I hope that you'll both like the painting. Is this afternoon convenient for you?'

'Of course. Do you want to come around teatime?'

'That would be nice,' agreed Lucy. 'I'll see you then.'

David rang a short time later, his voice conveying suppressed excitement. 'You may well be on to something with this Vanessa Bairstow business, love,' he informed her. 'I've just had a chat with Alistair, and Vanessa *was* one of his hairdressing clients.'

'And where does that take us?'

'He told me something very interesting. He said that women tell their hairdressers things that they'd never tell anyone else, except maybe a psychiatrist or a priest. Do you think that's true?'

'Yes,' said Lucy thoughtfully. 'Yes, it's true, in a sense. There's something impersonal about a hairdresser – they just listen, and don't really engage with you like a priest would, or a psychiatrist. But I suppose that's the attraction for a lot of women. A nonjudgemental, listening ear. Something they don't get anywhere else.'

'Especially not from their husbands,' David added with a dry chuckle.

'Well, exactly. That's just the point. I've heard women sitting in the next chair to me, and whilst the scissors are snipping away they're chatting on in the most astonishingly intimate detail. The hairdressers never bat an eye. They'll just say, once in a while, in a bored voice, "Oh, yes, dear? And what did he do then?" It's amazing. Don't men do that too, at the barbers'?'

'You've got to be joking, love. The barbers are the ones who do all the talking – every one of them is a self-proclaimed expert on cricket, football, and politics. In fact,' he said, 'I think that this country would be in much better shape if we sacked the government and put the barbers in charge.'

Lucy laughed, then recalled the purpose of the call. 'But what about Vanessa? Does she have a deep dark secret that she confided to her hairdresser?'

'You've got it in one, you clever girl. Did I ever tell you that I adore you?'

'Once or twice. But what was it?' she demanded. 'Did he tell you what it was?'

'No,' David admitted. 'He said that as far as he's concerned, he's in the same position as a priest. The sacredness of the confessional, you know. He listens, but he won't repeat anything that a client tells him. He'd like to help us, he said, but if we want to know, we'll have to find out some other way. You've got to admire his integrity, though it's as annoying as hell.'

Thoughtfully Lucy twisted a red-gold curl around her finger. 'But what about Father Julian?' she asked after a moment. 'Did *he* know Vanessa's secret?'

'It would seem so,' David confirmed. 'Alistair admitted that she'd been to talk to Father Julian – she'd actually come to the house to see him. That's how Alistair knew the connection, that one of his clients was also one of Julian's parishioners.'

'Ah,' said Lucy. 'It's all beginning to make some sense, I think. Anyway,' she continued briskly, 'I'm going to deliver her painting this afternoon. So we'll see what I can find out.'

'You're good at getting people to tell you things,' David encouraged her, adding with a chuckle, 'And if all other methods fail, can't you offer to cut her hair?'

Later that afternoon, Lucy balanced the unwieldy painting on the top step and pushed Vanessa's bell, with a terrible sense of déjà vu from the day before.

Vanessa opened the door a little way, then swung it wide. 'Oh, hello, Lucy. Come in,' Her voice, normally deep-pitched and rich, sounded flat.

'Where would you like me to put the painting? Somewhere in the light, where you can look at it properly?'

She gave an indifferent shrug. 'It doesn't matter. Put it anywhere. I'll look at it later.' Vanessa turned and walked towards the drawing room, moving woodenly.

Puzzled, Lucy followed her. There was something wrong, she realised quickly: gone was the enthusiasm that Vanessa had shown on the phone that morning. And though Vanessa was dressed as elegantly as always, her face, under its layer of perfect make-up, seemed almost *too* perfectly arranged.

But whatever was wrong, she remembered her manners, gesturing to a chair. 'Please, sit down, Lucy. Can I offer you some tea?'

'If you're having some.'

Without another word, Vanessa went off to the kitchen, coming back a few minutes later with a tea tray. She set it down carefully on the table, her movements controlled in an unnatural way. 'Lemon or milk?' she asked.

Concerned, Lucy stood up and went to her, putting a hand on her arm. 'Listen, Vanessa. Something's wrong, isn't it? Can't you tell me what it is?'

The other woman tensed, then consciously relaxed. 'I'll show you,' she said in a lifeless voice. Again she turned, and, moving almost like an automaton, led Lucy up the stairs and into a beautifully appointed bedroom – the sort of bedroom that she would have expected Vanessa to have, with lovely Georgian furniture, Colefax and Fowler wallpaper, and coordinating quilted spreads on the twin beds.

'There,' said Vanessa, pointing to one of the beds.

Again Lucy experienced a painful sense of déjà vu at the pointing finger, but she forced herself to look. There, stretched on the bed, was a large yellow cat, with no apparent injuries but unmistakeably dead, its limbs extended stiffly and its mouth slightly open. As unmistakeably dead as Vera Bright, thought Lucy with an involuntary shudder.

Vanessa sensed the shudder, and turned to face her. 'It's Augustine,' she said unnecessarily and with studied calm. 'I found him a little while ago. He's dead. It looks like poison.'

'Oh, Vanessa, I'm so sorry!' With impulsive but genuine empathy and pity, Lucy put her arms around the other woman, feeling her as rigid as the dead cat in her embrace.

This unexpected evidence of human warmth was all it took; in an instant Vanessa was wracked with tearing dry sobs of agony. 'Oh,' she gasped. 'Oh, he's dead! My baby – he's dead!'

Lucy knew that it was better for her to cry, healthier to express her grief than to suppress it. 'Yes, yes,' she murmured.

Vanessa cried for a long time, clinging to Lucy, the dry sobs giving way to tears which thoroughly soaked Lucy's shoulder and wrecked her own perfect make-up. Eventually, with an effort, she controlled her sobs and pulled away from Lucy, revealing a face all the more human for the runnels of mascara and the smears of iridescent eye shadow. She reached for a tissue from the bedside table, then sat abruptly on the edge of the other bed, dabbing at her eyes.

'Who could have done such a thing?' she said almost to herself.

'Do you think that someone did it on purpose?' Lucy asked, horrified. 'Put down poison?'

'Oh, yes, I'm sure of it. The neighbours didn't like Augustine much, you know. They didn't like the way he killed birds, or . . . you know . . . in their gardens.' Vanessa wrapped her arms around her body and began rocking, forward and back, on the edge of the bed. 'But how could they have done it?' she said softly. 'The neighbours all have children. But he was all that I had. My darling Augustine, my beautiful cat. He was all that I had to love.'

Lucy knelt beside her. 'That's not true,' she protested. 'You might not have any children, but you have Martin.'

'Martin.' Her laugh was low and without humour as she continued her rhythmic rocking. After a moment she began speaking, softly and quickly, almost as if to herself. 'He's never loved me, you know. Not even at the beginning. If he had, surely he would have wanted me to be a true wife to him. It didn't matter so much to me at first – I loved him so much, and thought that the other would come in time. But later I wanted it – not just because I wanted children, but because I needed to know that he loved me. I wanted to be held, I wanted to be loved.' She bit her lip, choked, and went on. 'He never even wanted to try. Whenever I suggested it, he would turn away from me, as if I were something . . . filthy. Unclean. Sometimes I was so desperate that I even got into his bed with him. Usually he just pushed me out. Once or twice he . . . tried. That was the worst.' She squeezed her eyes shut; tears trickled from their corners. 'He just couldn't do it. He didn't find me attractive, he said. It was my fault.' Lowering her head, she whispered, 'I've tried so hard to be attractive for him, to make him proud of me, to make him love me, to make him . . . want me. But it's no good. Now he can't even bear to touch me.'

Lucy took her hand and pressed it comfortingly; there was nothing she could say.

'They all think he's the ideal husband, of course,' Vanessa went on in a noticeably more bitter tone. 'All those old women at St Margaret's. They all envy me – can you believe it? But why shouldn't they? In public he always treats me like a cherished possession. And why shouldn't they think he's wonderful? There's nothing he wouldn't do for them – he gives them lifts to church, wires their plugs, prunes their hedges, helps them balance their chequebooks. He has more time for them than he's ever had for me. Sometimes I wonder what they'd say if they knew what he was really like.' Her mouth twisted in a sour smile. 'Sometimes I just feel like standing up in the middle of church and shouting it out: "This man is a fraud – twenty years of marriage and he can scarcely bring himself to touch his wife, or even look at her, let alone make love to her!" What a fine churchwarden he is.'

Then she raised her head and looked at Lucy as though she were seeing her for the first time. 'Oh, God, what have I done?' she breathed in an appalled whisper. 'Please, you mustn't say anything, and you must never let Martin know that I've told you. There's no telling what he'd do if he found out.'

'But this isn't something that you should have to deal with alone. Haven't you ever talked about it with anyone before?' Lucy asked, knowing the answer even as the question was spoken.

Vanessa sighed and looked down at her clasped hands. 'Sometimes I feel desperate, as though I have to tell someone or I'll burst. Once I tried to say something to Father Keble Smythe, but he didn't want to know. So I talked to Father Julian. He was wonderful. He made me realise for the first time that Martin is the one with the problem, and that I'm not really as repulsive and . . . unnatural . . . as he always tells me I am, just because I want a normal married life. But then he died. And Rachel. She stopped by to see me a couple of weeks ago. Augustine had disappeared, and I was so upset. I said more than I should, and Martin came home in the middle of it and went mad. He loves playing the part of the perfect husband in front of everyone at St Margaret's – it would kill him if people knew the truth. Please,' she repeated with unmistakeable urgency. 'Please forget that this ever happened. Promise me that you'll never tell a soul!'

Lucy hadn't been home long when David and Ruth returned from work. 'Hello, my love,' David greeted her, and was pleasantly surprised at the warmth of her welcoming kiss; she'd been more shaken by the day's events than she was willing to admit.

'Ugh – gross,' gagged Ruth, but they'd learned by now to ignore her.

He lifted the lid of the casserole on the hob, sniffed and nodded in approval, then said, 'How about a drink while you tell us what happened at Vanessa's this afternoon?'

'Alcoholic,' muttered Ruth, but this too they'd learned to ignore.

'The drink sounds good – supper won't be ready for a bit. But I'm afraid that I don't have anything to tell you.' She flicked her eyes in Ruth's direction.

'You mean that you don't want me to know, don't you?' the girl challenged her in a shrill voice. 'Well, I think that stinks. I'm not a baby – there's no reason why I shouldn't know what's going on! Emily would tell me – I know she would. You're just being horrible to me on purpose, Aunt Lucy.'

Lucy sighed but said nothing. There was no way that she was going to be bullied into telling Ruth, and by now she'd discovered that arguing with the girl didn't work – a dignified silence was by far the best approach. At first David had automatically jumped to Lucy's defence in these encounters, but he too had finally realised that it only made matters worse.

So David had to contain his curiosity throughout supper, and afterwards, when he would have expected Ruth to disappear and leave him to help Lucy with the washing up, the girl stubbornly refused to leave.

While they were washing up – David washing, Lucy drying, Ruth spectating – the phone rang. 'I'll get it,' offered Ruth in a moment of unusual helpfulness.

She was only gone for a few seconds, afraid that they'd say something important in her absence. 'It's Emily,' she announced. 'She wants to talk to you, Aunt Lucy.'

'Thanks, Ruth darling.' Lucy went to the phone in the hall, leaving Ruth looking thoughtful.

With studied nonchalance she said, 'I think I'm going to go up and take a bath now. Is that all right?'

'Fine,' David responded in amazement; it was the first time that he could remember her asking his permission for anything. 'But there won't be much hot water at the moment, while we're washing up.'

'Oh, it doesn't matter. I like cold baths,' she said over her shoulder. Her progress up the stairs was stately, but once out of Lucy's vision she made a dash for the bedroom and lifted the receiver of the extension phone silently, with the expertise born of long practice.

She was in luck: they were still exchanging pleasantries. 'Well, I'm glad that you're feeling better today, at any rate,' said Emily in a concerned voice. 'That really was a dreadful shock for you, Luce.'

'I didn't sleep very well last night,' Lucy admitted. 'But the person I really feel sorry for is her father. He's a bit of a selfish old man, but that's what makes it so difficult for him. He'll miss having a live-in slave, I expect.'

They chatted in that vein for a few minutes. 'Have you made any progress today?' Emily asked at last.

'As a matter of fact I have. I realised last night that David was jumping to conclusions when he assumed that "VB" had to be Vera Bright – it might have been Vanessa Bairstow instead.'

'That was clever of you,' Emily said approvingly.

'So today I went to see her – Vanessa. It was pretty horrific. Not on the same scale as yesterday, of course, but I got more than I bargained for.'

'Well, tell me!'

Lucy paused and Ruth held her breath. 'I can't, Em. Not on the phone. It's not the sort of thing you can talk about on the phone. I'll see you later in the week and tell you about it.'

'All right, then.' Emily accepted it equably. 'I'm afraid that I don't have much to report from this end. I decided to get the martyrdom bit out of the way as quickly as possible, so I had Dolly over for coffee, but she didn't tell me anything that I hadn't heard from her a dozen times before.'

'Such as?'

'Oh, just all the usual twaddle about women priests, and about poor dear Father Keble Smythe, and what a saint he is. Somehow, though, it almost seemed as if she were just going through the motions, as if her heart wasn't really in it. She seemed almost distracted.'

'That doesn't sound like Dolly.'

'I think,' said Emily, 'that she may have family problems of some sort. She said that she couldn't stay long as she had to get home to her daughter.'

'I didn't know that Dolly had a daughter.'

'Just the one – she's a teenager, I think.'

'Oh, well,' Lucy said with heartfelt conviction. 'Say no more. Family problems is probably putting it mildly, if that's the case.'

Ruth scowled and put her tongue out at the phone. But as she scurried to the bathroom to run the taps, she was already beginning to make plans of her own.

It wasn't until they were in bed that Lucy was able to tell David about her visit to Vanessa. He listened in silence and a large measure of disbelief as she outlined the nub of the Bairstows' problem.

'You're telling me, love,' he said at last, when she'd finished, 'that they've been married for twenty years, and have never consummated their marriage?'

'That's exactly what I'm telling you. Vanessa Bairstow is a virgin – her husband has never laid a finger on her. Won't, can't – I don't know. I don't really understand the psychology of it. All I know is that it's ruined her life.'

'But surely such a thing isn't possible!'

Lucy shook her head. 'It seems almost impossible to believe, but I've heard about such cases before. Apparently it's a lot more common than you'd ever think.'

David put his arm around her and drew her head on to his shoulder, stroking her hair absently. 'The poor woman.'

'From what she said, I think that the worst part of it is the damage it's done to her ego, to her self-esteem. I mean, people can live without sex, even without plain simple human contact. But to have a person – the person that you loved – telling you for years that you weren't attractive, that you repulsed them, and that there was something wrong with you for wanting a normal sex life – it's a wonder that she's managed to keep her sanity.'

David's mind leapt to the next conclusion before Lucy could tell him. 'She talked to Father Julian and Rachel about it, didn't she?'

She nodded. 'Yes. And now she's in a real state. Not just because her cat is dead. Not just because her husband won't touch her.' Lucy paused to give her next words their full impact. 'Darling, I'm sure that Vanessa Bairstow is terrified because she thinks that her husband killed them. So that they'd never be able to tell.'

'Good Lord,' said David, stunned.

CHAPTER 26

Behold, I was shapen in wickedness: and in sin hath my mother conceived me.
Psalm 51.5

Ruth worked her plan out carefully, taking into account all variables. The first problem, of course, was getting away from work without arousing anyone's suspicions. That meant acting in character, so it wouldn't very well do to try to appear helpful – to offer to run an errand for David's secretary, for instance. Nor could she pretend to feel ill – they would never send her back to Aunt Lucy's on her own. In the end she decided that the simplest solution was probably the best: she would just walk out and hope that no one would miss her or raise the alarm.

The second problem was finding Nicola Topping. That proved to be not at all difficult. While Mrs Simmons was away from her desk for a few minutes, Ruth borrowed her phone; ringing Directory Enquiries, she asked for a number for Norman Topping, which was readily supplied. All that was then required was to ring the number, and when Dolly answered, to ask for Nicola. For effect, and to be on the safe side, Ruth altered her voice by lowering it to what she reckoned to be an unrecognisable pitch.

In the event, Dolly was a more formidable obstacle than she'd anticipated, protecting her daughter from unwanted attentions. 'I'm afraid that Nicola's not very well. It's not convenient for her to come to the phone just now,' she asserted.

'It's very important,' Ruth insisted. 'I'm in her form at school,' she added in a burst of inspiration. 'I know that she's missed a few days lately, and I need to tell her something about . . . exams. Something she needs to know.'

Dolly paused. 'What did you say your name was?'

'It's . . . Sophie. Sophie King,' she improvised, thinking of Aunt Lucy's cat.

'I don't remember hearing Nicola mention your name before. You haven't been to the house with her, have you?'

'I don't really know Nicola very well, Mrs Topping,' Ruth replied ingratiatingly. 'But I admire her very much.'

'I'll call her to the phone, then,' Dolly relented.

Ruth was elated. This was easy – and fun.

'Hello?' came a cautious, expectant voice a moment later.

'Can your mother hear you? Is she right there?'

'Yes . . .'

'Then pretend that you know me. My name is Sophie. I'll explain as much as I can, if you'll just go along with me.'

Nicola was a natural. 'Oh, thanks for ringing, Sophie.'

'I need to see you. You don't know me, but it's about somebody important to you.'

'I'm not sure. When I'll be back to school, that is.'

'When can I see you? Some time today? It's important,' Ruth stressed.

'This afternoon? You're sure that there's an exam this afternoon?'

'I don't suppose it's any good me coming to your house, is it? With your mum there?'

'Well, if you'd like to stop by after school for a few minutes with the revision notes, I'm sure that it would be all right.'

Ruth looked over her shoulder to make sure that Mrs Simmons wasn't coming back; this was taking longer than she'd expected. 'And we can talk in private? Would three o'clock be all right?'

'No problem.' Displaying considerable ingenuity herself, Nicola went on, 'You've never been to my house before, have you, Sophie? Do you know the address?' She proceeded to give it. 'Just a little way along from St Margaret's Church,' she added for good measure. 'I'll see you later, Sophie. Thanks for thinking about me.'

Nicola was smiling as she put the phone down. 'Why haven't you ever mentioned this girl Sophie before?' Dolly interrogated her suspiciously.

'Oh, she's rather new. But she's really nice, Mum. You'll like her.'

'Is she coming round, then?'

'She offered to bring me some notes that I need for revision, after school this afternoon.' Nicola said it innocently, as though her mother hadn't been listening to every word.

'Well, then. You'd better go and lie down for a while, hadn't you? Before your friend gets here.'

'All right, Mum.' Docilely she went back to her room, hugging her secret knowledge to herself. This time she scarcely minded the sound of the key in the lock as she pulled the covers up to her chin. In a few hours Sophie would be here, bringing a message from Ben. She'd known all along that Ben hadn't forgotten her, and would manage somehow to get a message through to her, even though she was a virtual prisoner in her own house. The ingenuity of his method, using a girl who pretended to be from her school, surprised and delighted her. She couldn't wait to meet this Sophie, and to hear Ben's message of continuing love and support.

At half-past two, Ruth left her pile of documents for photocopying on the machine, extracting a few to serve as dummy revision notes, and calmly walked out of Fosdyke, Fosdyke & Galloway into Lincoln's Inn, and in a matter of minutes she was on the Piccadilly Line en route to South Kensington. After a short walk from the Tube at the other end, she rang the bell at three precisely, composing her face into an ingratiating smile for Dolly Topping. 'Hello, Mrs Topping,' she said sweetly. 'I'm Sophie King. Nicola is expecting me.'

Dolly looked her up and down. 'Haven't you just come from school? Why aren't you wearing a uniform?'

Ruth's dismay didn't register on her face, and she thought quickly. 'We don't have to wear uniforms on the days that we have exams. Didn't Nicola tell you?'

'I've never heard that rule before, I must say.'

Waving the papers in her hand – Dolly would have been surprised, had she inspected them, to discover that they were the middle section of a conveyancing document – Ruth gave a bright, perky smile. 'Here are the revision notes that I promised to bring for Nicola.' She held on to them tightly, lest Dolly should offer to take them.

'Well, all right,' Dolly capitulated. 'Nicola is in her room. I suppose you can go and see her there for a few minutes.'

'Thank you, Mrs Topping. I'll try not to tire her out.' Neither Lucy nor David would have recognised this mannerly and considerate child.

Dolly led the way upstairs to Nicola's room, tapped on the door, and turned the key in the lock on the outside. 'Your friend Sophie is here,' she announced. 'Not too long, now,' she cautioned Ruth. 'Remember, Nicola isn't very well.'

Then she was in the room, and she could hear the key turning in the lock on the other side.

The room was dark, with the curtains pulled and the lights out; it took a moment for her eyes to adjust to the dimness. She could just make out the bed, with a large form under the duvet.

'Come over here,' Nicola whispered in a state of high excitement, heaving herself up in bed.

Ruth moved closer. She could see Nicola now, and was surprised at her size, though perhaps she shouldn't have been, having met her mother.

Nicola seized her hands and pulled her down to her level. 'Tell me what he said,' she said urgently but quietly. 'Give me the message.'

The other girl's intensity startled Ruth as much as the unexpected demand. 'What message?' she blurted out stupidly.

'Ben's message, of course.'

'Who is Ben?'

'You don't have to pretend,' Nicola assured her. 'She can't hear, even if she presses her ear against the door. But if this will make you feel better . . .' She switched on her bedside radio, which was tuned to Radio 1, and turned the volume up. 'Now we can talk. Tell me what Ben said.'

'But I don't know any Ben,' insisted Ruth.

'If you don't know Ben,' Nicola said slowly, fixing her with feverish and rather beautiful eyes, 'then who are you? And what are you doing here?'

Ruth knelt down beside the bed; her voice matched the other girl's in intensity. 'I'm here because of Rachel – Rachel Nightingale. Miss Bright told me that you cared about Rachel.'

Nicola's eyes grew wider, and her mouth opened in a soundless 'O'. 'But she's dead,' she whispered. 'Rachel is dead.'

'Yes, and I'm trying to find out who killed her!' Ruth blurted out passionately. 'Rachel was wonderful, and I don't want them to get away with it! The police don't care. She didn't die by accident. I've got to find out who killed her!'

Nicola flung herself down on the bed and turned her back to Ruth. 'No,' she said, her voice muffled in her pillow. 'Just leave it.'

'I can't leave it, and neither can you. Not if you cared about Rachel.' There was no response, so Ruth leaned over the recumbent girl and added a little more loudly, 'And there was Father Julian, as well. Did you know Father Julian? Did you know that someone murdered him?'

Covering her ears with her hands, Nicola spoke stonily. 'Just go away. I won't listen to you.'

Roughly Ruth pulled a hand away and spoke close to the other girl's ear. 'And now someone has killed Miss Bright.'

'No!' Nicola turned to face her, her eyes huge in her paper-white face. 'You're making that up!'

'On Monday morning,' Ruth said deliberately. 'Someone went to her house, and killed her. So that she wouldn't tell what she knew about who murdered Rachel and Father Julian.'

'Oh my God.' Tears brimmed in the luminous eyes, spilling over and running down the full cheeks. 'It's true, isn't it? Mum didn't tell me.'

'It's true, all right.' For emphasis, or out of wilful cruelty, she told her, 'They went into her house and smothered her with a carrier bag.'

'Oh God.' Nicola covered her face with her hands. 'I liked Miss Bright.'

'So did I. Don't you see, then, that you've got to help me? You've got to tell me what you know!'

'Don't *you* see – you've got to get out of here, and don't ever come back.' Nicola's voice dropped to a whisper in volume but lost none of its vehemence. 'I'm cursed,' she said, with the extraordinary egocentricity of the young. 'All the people I talk to end up dead. Don't you see – it's all my fault! They'd all still be alive if it weren't for me!'

Ruth tried to take it in. 'What on earth are you saying?'

'It's God's punishment on me for disobeying my parents.' The tears trickled faster; she reached for a tissue.

'What a load of rubbish!' declared Ruth in a robust whisper.

'No – I promise you it's true! I talked to Father Julian, and he died. Then I talked to Rachel and *she* died. And now Miss Bright!'

'They didn't just die – they were murdered!'

Nicola gave her head a hopeless shake. 'It doesn't matter.'

'Of course it matters!' Ruth leaned down so that her face was only an inch or two from the other girl's. 'You've got to tell me what you know – you've *got* to. You owe it to Rachel.'

For a moment it hung in the balance, as Nicola stared into Ruth's eyes. Then she made up her mind. 'Yes, all right,' she said quietly. 'If you really want to know, I'll tell you.'

She did just that, concisely and unemotionally, over the next quarter of an hour, until the sound of the key turning cut her off in mid-sentence. Instantly she composed her face into a smile, which she turned towards the door as her mother entered.

'Don't you think that this gossip session has gone on long enough?' Dolly Topping said in a jolly voice. 'I, for one, think that it has.'

'Sophie's just been telling me about everything that's been happening at school while I've been . . . sick,' Nicola explained lightly. 'You wouldn't believe some of her stories.'

'Would you girls like a cup of tea?'

Ruth looked at her watch. 'Thanks awfully, Mrs Topping, but I really must be going. My mum will be expecting me.'

Dolly saw her to the door, then returned to Nicola's room with her daughter's tea. 'What a nice, polite girl,' she commented. 'You must have her round again, when you're feeling better.'

Bursting with her news, Ruth went straight to Lucy's house. She let herself in with her key, to find her aunt in the sitting room curled up on the sofa, feet up, sipping a cup of tea.

Lucy, who had been listening to Choral Evensong on Radio 3, looked up, startled at the girl's precipitate arrival. 'Ruth! Whatever are you doing here? What's wrong? Where's David?'

'Oh, never mind him,' the girl said impatiently. 'He's still at work, for all I know. Or care. But, Aunt Lucy – wait till you hear what I've found out!'

'Does he know that you've come home by yourself?' Lucy persisted.

'No, I just walked out. But that doesn't matter. I've just been—'

'He'll be worried sick, then. I'd better ring him and tell him that you're home safely.'

'All you care about is *him*.' Ruth's voice lost its excitement, became shrill and aggrieved. 'I've got something important to tell you, and you won't even listen to me.'

For once Lucy was firm. 'Whatever it is, it can wait until David gets home. I'm going to ring him now. And you'd better have a jolly good reason for doing what you've done, young lady!' she added with unaccustomed severity.

Unchastened and unrepentant, Ruth helped herself to Lucy's biscuits while her aunt went out to use the phone.

David *hadn't* missed her, he was chagrined to admit – to himself if not to Lucy. If he had been aware of the unusual tranquillity around the offices, he had accepted it gratefully – after all, if you went looking for trouble, you usually found it. So he'd stayed at his desk and enjoyed the brief if unexplained respite from Ruth's astringent presence.

After Lucy's call he came home straightaway, though; partly to propitiate his guilt and partly to assuage his curiosity. She had said that Ruth had found out something important: what on earth could it be?

The girl was in a fever of impatience by the time they'd all gathered in the sitting room. 'I've been to see Nicola Topping,' she burst out.

'Nicola Topping? Who on earth is she?' demanded David.

'Dolly Topping's daughter, of course.' She glared at him scornfully. If she'd dared, she would have added 'stupid', as she would have done with her brothers.

'How did you know that Dolly Topping had a daughter?' Lucy asked.

'Miss Bright told me. And she told me that she'd been close to Rachel, though her mum didn't know it. So when you said that Father Julian had had an appointment with someone called NT, I thought that it might have been Nicola instead of her father.'

David, though secretly impressed by her deductive powers, was not amused. 'Why on earth didn't you say?'

'Because,' she muttered rebelliously, 'you were keeping things from *me.* So I decided to investigate it on my own. Then you'd be sorry that you didn't tell me everything. *And,*' she went on, her level of excitement rising again, 'I managed to see her. I was really clever – I pretended that I was a friend from school, so that her mother would let me in the house to see her. And she talked to me! She told me everything!' Ruth paused momentously. 'So now I know who killed Rachel. And Father Julian, and Miss Bright.'

It was a poignant story, all the more heartrending for being narrated by someone who was still almost a child, as told to her by another who was very little older. Lucy and David listened, appalled yet fascinated, as Ruth related Nicola's tale.

In love with a boy of another race, against her mother's implacable – though not unexpected – opposition, Nicola Topping had confided in Father Julian Piper. Father Julian had been sympathetic, even to the extent of promising to marry the two young people when they reached eighteen and no longer needed their parents' consent. But after Father Julian's death, the girl had been without a confidante until the new curate had arrived at St Margaret's.

She'd lost no time in baring her soul to Rachel Nightingale. Rachel, too, had been sympathetic but cautious of becoming involved, given the virulence of Dolly's hatred for her. 'Wait until you're eighteen,' she had advised with prudence.

Desperate to take some sort of action, to seize the initiative from her mother, Nicola had deliberately become pregnant, believing that her parents would then have to allow her marriage. She had underestimated her mother. 'You're not marrying that wog,' Dolly had declared implacably. 'And you're not presenting me with a half-breed grandchild. It's out of the question.'

On the last afternoon of Rachel's life, a frantic Nicola had gone straight from school to see her, pouring out her fearful dilemma. Her parents hadn't relented, the marriage would not be allowed, and now there was the added complication of the baby to consider. What should she do? Her mother – that highly principled woman whose latest ideological involvement was with an anti-abortion group – was insisting that the pregnancy be terminated, secretly and at once. Nicola was resisting, and seeking support for her resistance. Rachel, feeling that her support would be counterproductive as far as the girl's parents were concerned, advised her to talk to Vera Bright, a woman to whom the senior Toppings might listen. On Nicola's return home from Rachel's there had been a terrible scene – the worst yet. She'd admitted her visit to Rachel; her mother had been livid.

And then Rachel was dead. Nicola, overcome with grief and guilt, had taken Rachel's final advice and had gone to see Vera Bright a few days later. There, in an emotional encounter, she had discovered why Rachel had sent her to that particular person.

She'd poured out her dilemma to the older woman, and had begged her to tell her what to do. 'Don't let them bully you,' Vera had insisted forcefully. 'Don't let them ruin your life.' Then, amidst tears on both sides, she had revealed her own story.

The Romeo to Vera's Juliet had been an American airman, in those long-ago wartime years. They had wanted to be married; her parents had been adamant in their opposition. 'No daughter of ours is going to marry a foreigner and go off to some foreign country to live,' Dr Bright had stated immovably. Like Nicola, young Vera had seen pregnancy as an escape route. It had seemed foolproof: in those days, unwed motherhood was a stigma too terrible to contemplate, and abortion was illegal. Her parents would have to consent to the marriage, or face public shame.

Vera had underestimated her father, as Nicola had underestimated her mother. Fate had played a role, as well: tragically, Gerry Hansen had been shot out of the sky before he even knew that he was to become a father. And Dr Bright had performed the abortion himself.

In the long years following, he had never let his daughter forget how she had disgraced him, or missed an opportunity to remind her of her indebtedness to him. 'You've made your bed, girl, and now you'll lie in it,' he'd been fond of saying, whenever making some particularly unreasonable demand. But the life had gone out of Vera with Gerry Hansen's death, and the loss of her baby. Her mother had died not long after – of shame, Dr Bright had insisted – and Vera had almost willingly embraced the life of servitude to a selfish old man's whims.

But she hadn't wanted to see Nicola take the same path; it was almost as if, in Nicola, she was being given a second chance to redeem her own folly. 'I've ruined my life. You mustn't ruin yours,' she'd insisted, adding, 'And that baby's.'

Galvanised into strength by Vera's support, Nicola had returned home to do battle for her baby's life. But over the nightmarish days that followed, locked in her room and on starvation rations, she'd been gradually worn down until, at last, crushed into submission by her mother's iron will, she'd had the abortion. Quickly, quietly. In a private clinic in the country, where the Toppings weren't known. Then back to her locked room for recuperation, insulated by her mother from the outside world, from news of Vera's death, from Ben. From everything, until a persistent girl who called herself Sophie had managed to penetrate the fortress and reach her in her misery and her guilt. Guilt upon guilt. Guilt about the baby, about Father Julian, about Rachel. And now about Vera Bright as well.

As Ruth drew near the end of the story, Lucy found that she'd been holding her breath. She let it out consciously in a sigh, then bowed her head, her hands still clenched.

'So did she actually tell you that her mother had killed them?' David demanded when she'd finished. 'Rachel, Father Julian, and Vera Bright?'

'Well, no,' Ruth admitted. 'She didn't have a chance to tell me – her mother came in the room before we got that far. She was just telling me that she'd heard her mother go out on Monday morning, when Miss Bright was murdered. And that her mother shops in Knightsbridge. But I'm sure that it was Dolly Topping who killed them, because they'd tried to help Nicola. And I know that Nicola thinks so, too – otherwise why would she feel so guilty?'

There were dimensions of guilt and variations of guilt that Ruth, in her youth and arrogance, couldn't begin to comprehend, David realised, feeling tremendously old. He took Lucy's hand and squeezed it, then addressed himself to her rather than to Ruth. 'Well, love. What do we do now?'

Ruth was furious. 'What about *me*? I'm the one who's done all the work! Why are you always trying to leave me out?'

CHAPTER 27

I will receive the cup of salvation: and call upon the Name of the Lord.
Psalm 116.12

'Two more days,' was the first thing that David said on Thursday morning, even before he'd opened his eyes. 'I think we're going to make it, love.'

Lucy wasn't quite awake yet. 'Hm?'

'I said that I think we're going to make it. We only have two days in which to restrain ourselves from wringing her neck. Forty-eight hours and a bit.'

'What a lovely thought.' She turned over and burrowed her face into her pillow, then remembered the day before and was suddenly wide awake. 'Seriously, darling,' she said in a completely different tone of voice. 'What *are* we going to do now? About the things that we've found out?'

'I'm not sure,' David confessed. 'We've never been in quite this position before, have we? We can't just go marching up to the police and tell them that we've solved three murders for them.'

'We haven't exactly solved them,' she protested. 'And anyway, I think that we should take it slowly and carefully, don't you?'

'There's no hurry, as far as I can see,' he agreed. 'I think we should definitely wait until Ruth is gone before we do anything at all.'

'That will make her furious.'

He smiled. 'I know.'

'You're terrible,' she giggled.

'I know that too, and you love me for it.'

'Or in spite of it.' There followed a few undignified moments in which tickling played a prominent part, but after they settled down and stopped laughing David returned to the subject again.

'At any rate, Lucy love, we're meant to be seeing Gabriel and Emily again on Saturday. Ruth will be safely out of the way by then, so that should be time enough to decide where we take it from here. After all, it was Gabriel who got us into this in the first place. So I think we'd be justified in throwing it back into his lap. Just tell him what we've learned, and let him deal with it. He's the Archdeacon, as he's so fond of reminding us.'

'Yes . . .' Lucy turned her back to him. 'Do we have to go?' she said quietly into her pillow. 'To see them on Saturday, I mean?'

'But why ever not, love?'

He had to strain to hear her answer. 'I hated it the other night. I hated the way that you were flirting with Gabriel.'

David was astonished. 'Me? Flirting with Gabriel? That's absurd!'

'All right, then. *He* was flirting with *you*, and you let him.'

'Don't be ridiculous!' He wasn't defensive, only puzzled. 'Why on earth would you think such a thing?'

'All that talk about old times, about Brighton and St Dunstan's. How was I supposed to feel, David?'

He leaned over so that he could see her face. 'I honestly don't know what you're going on about, my love. There was absolutely nothing in it, as far as I was concerned. And as far as Gabriel was concerned as well, I'm quite sure. He's a happily married man, and I'm a . . . well, what *would* you call me? Since you refuse to make an honest man of me?' He put on such a comically mournful expression that Lucy couldn't help giggling, and it soon degenerated into further tickling and other forms of intimate activity.

David had an idea over breakfast; he broached it to Lucy while Ruth was still in the shower. 'Were you doing anything special this afternoon?' he asked as a preliminary.

'Nothing in particular. I've got a commission that I should be getting on with, for Joan Everitt, but it's not pressing. Why? Did you have something in mind?'

'Well, I thought that it might be nice for you to take the *enfant terrible* out to lunch, on her nearly-last day.'

'Oh, yes?' Lucy sounded sceptical. 'In other words, you want to get rid of her.'

He gave her a shamefaced grin. 'Well, that *is* part of it, of course. And I've got an important client to see at lunchtime, which means that I'll have to lumber my secretary with her again, otherwise. But I *did* think that it would be a good idea – after all, love, you and Ruth haven't had much time together, just the two of you, since she's been here.'

'That's true,' Lucy admitted. 'She'd probably like to have me to herself for an hour or two.'

The idea developed further. 'You could take her shopping afterwards, if you liked.'

'So you'd be rid of her for even longer.'

'Well, yes. But she'd enjoy it, more than what she'd be doing at the office. Take her to Covent Garden and buy her something. I'll give you some money.'

'Oh, so now you're offering me bribes to take my niece off your hands.' Lucy tried to look cross, but a smile twitched at the corner of her mouth.

David was beginning to get enthusiastic about the plan. 'She should really buy something to take home to her parents,' he went on, developing it further. 'Something from F and M would be nice. Some special tea, or perhaps chocolates. I could meet you there at teatime, give the two of you a nice Fortnum's tea.'

'You've talked me into it,' Lucy laughed. 'I can never resist a Fortnum's tea.'

Lucy came by Fosdyke, Fosdyke & Galloway to collect Ruth as arranged, at about half-past twelve, stopping in only long enough to say hello to David. Things augured well for a less stressful afternoon than might have been expected: Ruth had actually expressed enthusiasm for the plan, and seemed to be looking forward to an afternoon of having her aunt to herself, at least until teatime. She had been almost pleasant that morning, perhaps still savouring her clever triumphs of the previous day.

Still, David wasn't sorry to see her go. His afternoon passed quickly, with two important meetings and a great deal of paperwork to be got through.

He took the Central Line to Bond Street and walked down towards Piccadilly; having allowed plenty of time to get through the early rush-hour traffic, he found himself in Old Bond Street with several minutes to spare. Suddenly he remembered his intention to call into Christie's to look at the catalogue for their sale of ecclesiastical items; it seemed a good time to do that.

There was only time to flick through it cursorily, but it looked interesting, so David bought a copy for a later, more detailed perusal, then progressed on towards Fortnum & Mason.

Lucy and her niece, laden down with carrier bags, were already waiting for him in the tearoom. They both seemed in high good humour; evidently their afternoon together had been a great success, and had gone a long way towards re-establishing the bond between them.

They were seated; David said grandly, 'I think we'll have the lot, don't you? Sandwiches, scones, and cakes.'

'Oh, yes,' agreed Ruth.

'Of course.' Lucy nodded. 'Now this is what I call civilised,' she added, indicating the string quartet.

'We've had such fun,' Ruth told him. 'We went to the Hard Rock Cafe for lunch – it was brilliant.'

'Oh, was it?' David glanced at Lucy; she resolutely refused to catch his eye. 'Had hamburgers, did you?'

Oblivious, Ruth rattled on. '*I* did. Aunt Lucy had a salad. And then we went to Covent Garden. That was super. There was a bloke there who was walking on his hands. And another one who was standing like a statue, dead still, and people tried to get him to move.'

'Did you buy anything?'

'Oh, yes. Aunt Lucy bought me some earrings, and then I found this wonderful hat. Didn't you notice?' She indicated the floppy black velvet which was perched atop her red curls.

'Very nice,' David acknowledged, realising to his shock that she was almost pretty when she smiled, in spite of the flashing hardware; it wasn't a phenomenon that he'd had very much chance to observe.

'And there was a cute teddy bear, but I decided against it. I thought that it was probably too babyish. But I bought some things for my brothers – some wooden toys. And in one of the shops I got some pipe tobacco for my father. And when we got here, I bought some special tea for my mum.'

The food arrived, and Ruth tucked in happily – appropriating all of the smoked salmon sandwiches, to David's secret sorrow.

'Aunt Lucy,' she said, 'I want your opinion about this hat. Now honestly, does it look better with the flower in the front, like this, or on the side, like that? What do you think?'

While Lucy gave careful consideration to the question and its ramifications, David picked up the Christie's catalogue and leafed through it casually. He turned a page, stopped, and went back. 'Good Lord,' he said. His voice was calm, but his mind was racing nearly as fast as his heart.

'What is it?' Lucy looked across the table.

'Here.' He held it up for her to see. 'For sale at Christie's. It's the chalice from St Margaret's.'

* * *

It was the one thing that they'd forgotten, David admitted to Gabriel later: the missing chalice. That it was no small omission he also admitted, with some chagrin. The chalice, it was to be assumed, had been taken at the time of Father Julian's murder to give the appearance of a burglary; it followed that the person who had taken the chalice had also killed Father Julian. And two other people as well. The chalice was the evidence they needed to catch the murderer – suspicions were all very well and good, but they needed something more concrete than suspicions to take to the police. They needed the chalice, or at least the name of the person who had taken it.

Admittedly, the police hadn't looked very hard for the chalice either. They had checked the usual outlets for stolen goods, Bermondsey Market and Portobello Road; they had circulated a vague description which might have applied just as well to a thousand other chalices.

Who would have thought that it would have turned up at Christie's? The catalogue description was admirably accurate. 'Silver gilt. Hallmarked John Hardman and Co., 1850. Thought to be a very early design by A. W. Pugin,' it said. The reserve price was £15,000.

Of course David raced back to Christie's as soon as they'd finished their tea. Not surprisingly, at the end of the day, there was no one there who could give him any information about the person who had put the chalice into the sale. 'I'm very sorry, sir, but you'll have to come back in the morning,' said a very junior functionary. 'You can check with our sales desk at that time. They may be able to help you.' He didn't sound very hopeful about the prospect.

CHAPTER 28

With the holy thou shalt be holy: and with a perfect man thou shalt be perfect. With the clean thou shalt be clean: and with the froward thou shalt learn frowardness.

Psalm 18.25–26

'I'm going with you,' Lucy said at breakfast on Friday morning, in a tone that would admit no argument. 'You're not leaving me behind.'

'Me, too.' Ruth's jaw stuck out at a pugnacious angle.

David wasn't sure that it was a good idea, but he could tell when he was outnumbered, and surrendered gracefully. 'Suit yourselves.'

They arrived at Christie's shortly after its opening, and went straight to the sales desk. An officious-mannered young man with more teeth than chin came forward to peer down his nose at them through hornrimmed spectacles. 'Can I be of help?' he enunciated in the most exaggeratedly self-conscious public school accent that David had ever heard.

David produced the catalogue along with his most imperious manner; this was not the time or the place for diffidence, he'd decided instantly. 'I do hope so. I'd like to know the name of the person who placed this item – the chalice – into your sale, please.'

'Out of the question,' the young man said with satisfaction. Saying no, and finding pretentious ways of saying it, afforded him his greatest pleasure in life. 'That information is of course classified.'

Briefly and fancifully considering whether he might not invite Ruth to sink her armoured teeth into the young man's tweedy leg, like the red-headed Rottweiler that she was, he decided to pull rank instead. 'We'll see what Sir Crispin Fosdyke has to say about that,' David stated, matching supercilious with supercilious. 'He *is* on your Board of Directors, I believe?' From his pocket he produced a business card and extended it with the 'Fosdyke, Fosdyke & Galloway' logo in prominent view.

It was the right thing to say. Instantly the young man's manner changed; he became almost fawningly obsequious. 'Oh, well of course if it's for Sir Crispin, that puts an entirely different light on things. I'm so sorry. You should have said.' He nearly bowed, backing off into the nether regions. 'I won't be a moment, sir.'

And indeed he was back quickly, with a card. 'Here's the information you require, sir. I've written it down for you.'

He'd been thorough. It was the name of an antique dealer, along with the address of his shop in Kensington Church Street. David knew the shop, though he didn't think he'd ever been inside: it was small but reputable, and not given, so far as he knew, to dealing in items of stolen church plate.

'Thank you very much indeed,' he said magnanimously. 'Sir Crispin will be pleased to hear that you've been so helpful. And so cooperative.'

'My pleasure, sir. And do convey my very warmest regards to Sir Crispin.' He ducked his head.

In a moment they were back in Bond Street; David thought hard as he hailed a taxi. 'Lincoln's Inn,' he told the taxi driver.

Ruth insisted on sitting backwards on the little fold-down seat. 'Why are we going to the office?'

'*You* are going to the office,' he stated firmly. 'Out of harm's way.'

Her face became a thundercloud. 'But I don't *want* to. I want to go with you and Aunt Lucy. You can't leave me out of this now. Now that it's getting exciting!'

David refused to discuss it. He folded his arms and leaned back, ignoring her tirade. When they reached Lincoln's Inn, he instructed the taxi driver to wait. 'You stay here,' he told Lucy. 'I'll be back in a minute.'

'You can't do this to me!' Ruth howled as he seized her arm and marched her into the offices.

'Don't make a scene,' he ordered; perhaps the rarefied atmosphere of Fosdyke, Fosdyke & Galloway had something to do with it, but for once she obeyed him. She clamped her lips together to suppress an outraged sob, pulled her arm away from his grasp, and stalked in front of him with her head held high.

'Keep an eye on her,' he instructed Mrs Simmons, who quailed inwardly at the assignment. 'Give her something to do. I've been called away on a matter of urgent business, but I'll be back as soon as possible.'

'You don't need to worry about me,' Ruth called after him with bitter dignity. 'I'll be just fine.'

At the tail end of the morning rush hour their progress was reasonable, but in David's impatient state it seemed to take an age to get to Kensington Church Street. Watching the meter, he had the money ready, paid the driver quickly, grabbed Lucy's hand and hurried to the shop.

He pushed the buzzer and the door opened in response by some remote-controlled magic, but it was some time before anyone appeared. Lucy inspected a tray of Victorian jewellery in a case, while David tapped his foot by the small desk in the corner. It was an old-fashioned sort of shop, with none of the appurtenances of modern commerce such as fax machines and cash tills – computerised or otherwise – and it contained an amazing quantity of items in a very small space. The shop specialised in decorative items, silver and jewellery rather than furniture. But everything in the shop, David apprehended quickly, was of the very highest quality, with prices to match. No junk, no knick-knacks, no jumble of dusty white elephants. Just a great many beautiful things displayed lovingly, if cheek-by-jowl. It told him something about the proprietor of the shop, and he realised even before the man appeared that the approach he'd taken with the young man at Christie's would not work here. Nor would the alternative approach that he'd considered during the taxi journey: veiled threats to report him for dealing in stolen goods if he refused to cooperate. A far more subtle touch would be required here. He slipped the Christie's catalogue back into his briefcase.

The William Morris tapestry curtains at the back of the shop parted and a face peered out, followed by a body. David expected it to be one of the dimwitted young twits usually employed in such places, seemingly with the sole function of screening out and dealing with casual browsers so that the proprietor could concentrate on the serious customers. But the man who appeared was on the verge of – though not quite – being elderly, small with a trim grey beard, and dragged one leg with a pronounced stiff-legged limp: clearly the proprietor himself. 'Oh, good morning. I'm sorry to have kept you waiting, but I was on the phone, and my assistant isn't in today.' His voice was courteous and precise, and he sized them up expertly without seeming to do so. 'Are you looking for something in particular? Some jewellery for the lady, perhaps?'

'Yes,' said David, inspired. Just the thing, he thought. 'I'd like to buy something special for her.'

'I can see that she's a very special lady,' the man said with a gallant little bow. He moved towards the case that Lucy was inspecting. 'I'm Mr Atkins, by the way. I like to be on a personal basis with my customers. And you're . . . ?'

'Mr Middleton-Brown, and this is Miss Kingsley.'

'Ah. Perhaps you were looking for a ring, Mr Middleton-Brown?' He raised his eyebrows in a significant way.

David looked at Lucy questioningly: not daring to ask, not daring to hope.

She didn't meet his eyes, but gave her head an infinitesimal shake.

'No, not this time,' he told Mr Atkins, unable to keep the disappointment from his voice. 'Could you suggest something else?'

The little man put his head to one side and gave Lucy the benefit of his professional consideration. 'With her beautiful colouring, and that lovely hair, I think that a nice cameo would be just the ticket.'

She smiled. 'I love cameos.'

'Then you shall have one, my love. Do you see any here that you fancy?'

Mr Atkins leaned forward and spoke in a confidential tone. 'I have something quite special in the back. Would you like to see it?'

David assented, and with painful slowness the man limped off to his curtained hideaway; he was away for several minutes, during which David had leisure to reflect on the advantages of cultivating patience. 'I can see that this is going to take all morning,' he muttered to Lucy.

'Here it is. I've found it.' The cultured voice preceded the corporal being in issuing from behind the curtain. 'I think, Mr Middleton-Brown, that you'll agree this was worth waiting for. I had it tucked away, waiting for just the right person to come along.' Eventually he reached the case, spread out a black velvet cloth, and arranged the cameo on it so that David and Lucy could see it to full effect. 'What do you think? Isn't it exquisite?'

It wasn't large or ostentatious, but it was beautifully carved, and surrounded by an intricate filigree of fine gold wires, suspended from a delicate gold chain. 'Oh, yes,' said Lucy. 'It's lovely.'

'Would you like to try it on?' Mr Atkins limped off in pursuit of a mirror, Lucy lifted her hair out of the way, and David carefully fastened the clasp at the back of her neck. 'Oh, it suits you very well,' Mr Atkins declared, nodding his approval. 'Just the thing, with your long neck, and that beautiful hair.' He held the mirror up for her.

Lucy smiled her pleasure, and David caught the other man's eye. 'Thank you, Mr Atkins. It's perfect.'

With admirable discretion Mr Atkins presented him with a slip of paper on which he'd written the price. David nodded and reached in his pocket for his chequebook.

'Is there anything else I can do for you today, Mr Middleton-Brown? Something for yourself, perhaps? I have a very nice set of cuff links that came in just yesterday.'

Uncapping his pen, David said casually, 'Actually, I'm rather interested in ecclesiastical silver. Do you have anything like that, perhaps in the back room? I don't see any pieces on display.'

Mr Atkins scratched his head and gave the matter some thought. 'I don't think I *do* have anything at the moment, actually. It's a rather specialised market, you know. There's never any problem selling candlesticks, of course – they walk out of the door as soon as I put them on display. And occasionally people buy incense boats to use as sugar bowls, if you can believe it. But things like thuribles and chalices have a very limited appeal to the average man in the street. I don't very often buy that sort of thing.' He lowered his voice to a confidential tone, though there was no one else in the shop. 'I *did* have a beautiful piece, not long ago. A Pugin chalice. Very rare. Quite early. Silver gilt.'

David effected to look just a bit more than politely interested. 'I would have liked to have seen that.'

'Actually,' said Mr Atkins, 'I've put it into Christie's. Perhaps you've seen the catalogue – the sale is coming up soon.'

'No, I haven't been into Christie's for a while.'

'I've got a copy of the catalogue here somewhere.' There followed another frustratingly extended interval wherein Mr Atkins disappeared behind the curtains and conducted a search. 'Yes, here it is.' Slowly he returned and held it open for David to see the photograph.

All of David's acting skills were called upon now. He looked, then started and moved in for a closer look. 'Do you mind?' he said, taking the catalogue from Mr Atkins and carrying it to the light.

'It's beautiful, isn't it?' the shop's proprietor asked rhetorically.

'Mr Atkins.' David looked up at the other man, a puzzled frown creasing his brow. 'Might I ask you where you obtained this chalice?'

Mr Atkins cleared his throat. 'I'm afraid I can't tell you that. My business depends on my absolute discretion in matters like this – I'm sure you understand.'

'What would you say,' David pressed him, 'if I told you that this chalice was stolen property?'

The other man choked; his voice came out in an uncharacteristic squeak. 'Stolen? But that's impossible.' He drew himself up to his full height. 'I can assure you, Mr Middleton-Brown, that this is *not* that sort of a shop!'

'Nevertheless, I'm afraid that this chalice is stolen property. It was stolen from St Margaret's Church, Pimlico, last December.' He paused to allow the full impact of his words. 'I know that you're an honest man, Mr Atkins, and I'm sure that you acquired this chalice in good faith. But I'm afraid that the police may not take that view.'

'Police!' It was the most feared word in Mr Atkins's vocabulary. 'This isn't that sort of a shop,' he repeated, but less forcefully, and beads of sweat had appeared on his forehead.

'Perhaps I might be of some help,' offered David. 'I'm a solicitor, and I've done some work for the Vicar and churchwardens of St Margaret's. That's how I happen to know about the stolen chalice. Perhaps this could be managed discreetly.'

He seized on the hope of reprieve with touching eagerness. 'You mean that the police might be kept out of it?'

'I'm afraid that the police will have to be told. But if I had a word with them, it could be done with no discredit to you. And no publicity,' he added.

'Oh, Mr Middleton-Brown! If you could!' He almost trembled in his relief. 'I'd be so very grateful if you could manage it. I can't have the police coming in here, with their great feet, knocking things about. This is a respectable shop – above reproach. I've never had any trouble before. I don't . . .' He was descending into incoherence.

'I'll deal with the police,' promised David. 'But you must tell me everything. How did you obtain the chalice, Mr Atkins?'

He pressed his fingers to his temples to calm himself; after a moment he spoke. 'A chap brought it in to the shop one day,' he said. 'A respectable chap – I can tell the other sort a mile off.'

'I'm sure you can.'

'He said that the chalice was a family heirloom – his grandfather had been a bishop, he said, and it had belonged to him.'

'Did he have any idea how valuable the chalice was?'

'Oh, yes. He knew that it was Pugin, and worth a great deal of money. I didn't try to cheat him,' Mr Atkins insisted, defending his professional integrity. 'I told him, quite honestly, that he'd do better putting it in the sale room himself. But he was in a hurry for a sale.'

'A hurry?'

'Yes, he said that his wife needed an operation, and he had to have the money right away. He couldn't wait to put it through Christie's himself. I felt sorry for the chap. It was hard luck for him, having to sell a family treasure for a reason like that. I was more generous with him than I might have been.'

'I'll need to tell the police how much you paid him.'

'I gave him seven thousand pounds,' Mr Atkins said reluctantly. 'In cash. It was rather a lot of cash, I know. I don't usually have that much right to hand, but I'd just had an American – a Texan – in that morning who bought several things. Pulled a roll of notes out of his pocket and paid in cash.'

'That doesn't happen very often, I imagine.'

'Not often enough! It was one of those lucky coincidences,' the man reflected. 'The American said that he wouldn't have even come down Kensington Church Street that morning, but an IRA bomb scare had closed the tube station – someone had been killed by a bomb at Victoria, I seem to remember. He walked past and saw something in the window that caught his eye. So he popped in, and ended up spending nearly ten thousand pounds.'

'What is it they say about an ill wind?' David remarked idly.

'Exactly. And so when the gentleman brought in the chalice, I was glad to be able to get rid of the cash – saved me closing the shop to go and bank it.'

It was time for the crucial question. 'You *did* get this man's name, I assume?'

'Of course,' said Mr Atkins indignantly. 'I always do things properly. I had him sign the book, just as the tax man requires me to do.'

'And may I see the book?'

David held his breath as the retreat behind the curtain was repeated for a third time. 'Yes, here it is.' He made his slow return, carrying a large book. He opened it on the desk, fumbled in his pocket for a pair of spectacles, which he settled on his nose with care, then flipped through the pages of the book. 'June, September, December. That's last year. I'm sure it was early this year. Yes, here. February. The eighth of February, this year.' He peered at the entry. 'That's right, I remember that he was a clergyman. So of course I dealt with him in good faith.' He paused to decipher the writing, then read it aloud. 'The Reverend William Keble Smythe, St Jude's Vicarage, Pimlico, SW1.'

'But what does it mean?' Lucy shook her head, baffled, as they took yet another taxi ride to Pimlico. 'I was expecting him to say Martin Bairstow, or Norman Topping. Not William Keble Smythe.'

'The Vicar.' David was rapidly readjusting his conceptions abou their investigation. 'I can't believe that it was the Vicar all along.'

'We eliminated him because he had an alibi,' Lucy pointed out 'Remember? He was the one person who wasn't at the church tha night, when they had the row.'

'That's not really an alibi, if you think about it. We know wher he *wasn't*, but that doesn't mean that we know where he *was*. If you understand me.'

'You mean that he could have been in his car, waiting for her t ride past?'

'Well,' David thought aloud, 'after all, he had asked her to take th service. He must have known what a kerfuffle it would cause.'

'He might have done it on purpose,' Lucy concluded slowly, touch ing her new cameo in an absent gesture. 'Asked her to take the servic knowing that there would be a row. And then waited for her to rid past. But why? Why would he want to kill Rachel?'

'The same reason that anyone else would, I reckon. What if she' found out something about him that was a threat to him in some way

'But I thought that Father Keble Smythe led a blameless life. That' what Dolly says, anyway.'

Something niggled at the corner of David's mind. 'I'm not so sur I've heard hints that he may not be all that he seems. I wish I coul remember.'

'Or maybe she found out somehow that he'd killed Father Julian Lucy suggested. 'That would be reason enough, I'd think.'

The taxi pulled up in front of the vicarage. 'Here you are, mate said the driver.

David paid him. 'I hope he's in,' he remarked as they marched u to the door.

Mrs Goode answered; she recognised David from his first visit though to her chagrin she couldn't remember his name, and Luc looked vaguely familiar to her as well. She looked back and fort between them, hoping for some clue.

'Hello, Mrs Goode,' David said smilingly, thereby endearing himself 'I don't expect you to remember me, but I'm David Middleton-Brown This is Miss Kingsley. I wondered if we might have a word with Fathe Keble Smythe.'

She returned his smile. 'Is Father expecting you?'

'No, but we'd be most awfully grateful if you could persuade hin to spare us a few minutes. It's important.'

'I'll see what I can do,' she promised, and withdrew in the direction of the Vicar's study, chuckling to herself. How romantic, she thought. They've just decided to get married, and they can't wait to talk to Father to set the date. What a lovely couple they make.

Mrs Goode returned more speedily than Mr Atkins had managed. 'Father is very busy,' she said, 'but I've persuaded him to see you.' She gave them a conspiratorial wink. 'I told him it was important.'

Father Keble Smythe was seated at his desk; he rose as they entered. 'Do come in,' he said courteously.

Lucy looked around with interest; it was her first visit to the Vicar's study. In a glance she took in the discreetly expensive furniture, the thick carpet, the silver-framed photo of the famed Miss Morag McKenzie.

'I apologise for the intrusion, Father,' David began, 'but it really is rather important.'

'So Mrs Goode said.' He gave them a genial smile. 'How much did you have to bribe her?' A modest chuckle at his own wit, then, 'Please, do sit down.'

David remained standing and wasted no time with preliminary chit-chat. 'I've located your stolen chalice,' he announced, watching carefully for the other man's response.

'My dear chap! How very splendid of you!' It was either genuine, or the man was a very good actor indeed. But Lucy remembered his star performance at Rachel's funeral, and determined to keep an open mind on the matter. 'But where is it? How did you find it? And when can we have it back?'

'At the moment,' said David, 'it's in Christie's sale room. But I expect you know that.'

The Vicar looked puzzled. 'I don't know what you mean. This is the first I've heard of it.'

'Or perhaps you thought that it was still in Mr Atkins's shop in Kensington Church Street.'

'What are you talking about?' The puzzlement was beginning to transmute into annoyance.

The room was still. For a long moment David sized up William Keble Smythe, then spoke deliberately into the silence, his words falling like stones between them. 'I'm talking about theft, Father. And murder. How else can you explain your signature in Mr Atkins's sales book?'

CHAPTER 29

As soon as they hear of me, they shall obey me: but the strange children shall dissemble with me.
The strange children shall fail: and be afraid out of their prisons.

Psalm 18.45–46

David sat at his desk, staring at without seeing the rather splendid view from his window. Spring was truly upon them, the yellow trumpets of the daffodils playing a symphony of their own in the newly verdant grass of Lincoln's Inn. For all that David appreciated it, though, it might still have been the dead of winter.

Father Keble Smythe had denied everything. All knowledge, all involvement. He had professed himself as baffled as they as to how his signature had appeared in Mr Atkins's book. And to say that he had not been amused at the accusation that David had levelled against him was something of an understatement. To call a man in holy orders – and the incumbent of a prestigious London parish to boot – a triple murderer was no small thing.

The worst of it was, David still wasn't sure whether the Vicar was telling the truth or not. If he *had* committed three murders to protect some secret, he certainly wouldn't admit it just because some solicitor strolled into his study and suggested that he might have done it. And he *was* a good actor, demonstrably so, with Rachel's funeral eulogy as an example.

In retrospect, David realised that their action in rushing straight to the vicarage to confront Father Keble Smythe might have been considered foolhardy. But at the time it hadn't crossed his mind, trusting instinctively in the proximity of the excellent Mrs Goode.

He'd realised, as well, that in their haste to get to the vicarage, they'd failed to ask Mr Atkins for a description of the man who had sold him the chalice – that might have gone a long way towards establishing Father Keble Smythe's guilt or innocence. An attempt to rectify their omission had failed: on their return to the shop, they'd been greeted with a notice on the door that the proprietor had gone for the weekend.

Frustrated, David put his mind to the problem. What could the Vicar be hiding? Ambition was one thing, and it was clear that Father Keble Smythe had that in abundance, but was there something else? What secret could he have that was worth killing to keep?

Suddenly he recalled the memory that had been on the edge of his consciousness: Alistair Duncan, in the musty, dusty sitting room of the clergy house in Brighton, suggesting that perhaps Father Keble Smythe might have one or two skeletons in his cupboard. At the time it had scarcely registered, but now it seemed overwhelmingly important.

He found the number quickly and dialled, holding his breath until the distinctive Scots burr said, 'Hello?'

'Oh, hello. This is David Middleton-Brown.' His mind worked rapidly. 'I've just realised that I walked off with Father Julian's diary when I saw you the other day, and wondered how desperate you were to have it back.'

'Not desperate.' Alistair's laugh was bittersweet. 'I don't think I've got much use for it at the moment. Keep it if you think it will help.'

'It just might.'

'You haven't found out yet who killed Jules?' The young man's voice held little hope.

'Not yet,' David admitted, 'but I may be getting close. And you might be able to get me a little further along, if you wouldn't mind telling me something.'

'Anything,' Alistair said promptly and without reservation. 'Anything that will help you catch the sodding bastard.'

David hesitated as he framed his next statement. 'When I saw you on Monday you mentioned Father Keble Smythe. You said that you knew a few things about him that you didn't think he would want his congregation to know.'

'Oh, aye.' Alistair laughed again, but without a great deal of amusement. 'He spent some time in Scotland, you see. At St Andrews, where he did his degree. He had rather a reputation north of the border.'

'What sort of a reputation?' David was afraid that he knew the answer already.

'Oh, you know. Wild parties. Men. There was a chap called Hamish Douglas that he was involved with for a while. But he put all that behind him when he came down south, or so it would seem.' He chuckled. 'Jules said that he was even claiming a fiancée nowadays. That's a pretty good one, given some of the stories I've heard about William Keble Smythe. Or Wendy, as he was known in those days.

Wendy Smythe – he seems to have picked up the "Keble" somewhere along the line.'

'So you mean,' David said slowly, 'that Father Julian knew about Father Keble Smythe's past.'

'Of course he did. There wasn't any reason for me not to tell him was there?' Alistair sounded slightly defensive.

David couldn't say what he was thinking: that perhaps that knowledge had led to Julian Piper's death. He adopted a reassuring tone hoping that Alistair wouldn't make the connection. 'No. Of course not. But thanks for telling me, and for all your help. And,' he added before ringing off, 'I'll let you know as soon as there's anything to tell I promise.'

It could have been, David said to himself, looking blankly at the phone. Father Keble Smythe. He could have done it – he certainly had motive enough, at least to kill Father Julian. And Rachel could have found out as well about his unsavoury past. If only he'd remembered to get the description from Mr Atkins. Nothing could be proved until they had that.

So much had happened in just a few hours – it was now only early afternoon. So much, but had it accomplished anything? They were still no closer to knowing the truth of the chalice than they'd been the day before.

The chalice. David was certain that its importance, ignored until so recently, could not be overestimated. For, as he had postulated earlier, the person who had taken the chalice had also killed three people.

The chalice. It had all begun with the chalice, and now it had come full circle. One chalice, three lives. David picked up a pencil and began doodling, sketching a chalice. One chalice, and then one more. And another.

He realised with a start that he was defacing a letter that he hadn't even read yet, part of the morning's post which had been opened by his efficient secretary and stacked on his desk for his attention.

A letter from the immigration office. Damn, he thought. Justin Thymme. Am I to be plagued forever by Justin Thymme?

The letter, from Mrs Hartman the immigration officer, was straightforward: a formal interview of his client, Mr Justin Thymme, had been scheduled for a date a fortnight hence, and he was being notified as a matter of course, since it was assumed that he would want to be in attendance. That was all, but it sparked something in his brain something that had been there all along lying dormant. Something that Pamela Hartman had said to him on the occasion of their initial interview.

Suddenly the pieces came together, like bits of coloured glass in a stained glass window: Pamela Hartman's offhand remark; something that Rachel Nightingale had said to Ruth after Evensong at Westminster Abbey; an entry in Father Julian's diary. In the space of time no longer than it took to draw breath, David knew why three people had died. There was only one piece missing: he didn't know who had killed them. Thinking rapidly, he reckoned that it almost certainly must have been one of two people. Two possibilities.

When Gabriel had told him about Father Julian, the death that had started it all, David had theorised that he and Rachel had both died because of the one thing that they had in common: the fact that they were both curates at St Margaret's Church. Now he realised how true that assumption had been, and how easily he and Lucy had been sidetracked – with Ruth's help – into quite the wrong conclusion, based on that assumption. They had thought that the significant thing about curates was that, as counsellors and recipients of confidences, they knew people's secrets – secrets that people would kill to keep that way. The truth was both simpler and more complicated than that.

The answer lay where the whole thing had begun: in the sacristy of St Margaret's Church. David was convinced of that. All he had to do was to get into that sacristy, on his own, and he would find the answer. The proof he needed was certainly there, and, with any luck, a pointer to the guilty person.

He thought for a moment more, then picked up the phone. But before he could dial the number, Ruth popped her head round the door. 'Would you like some tea?' she offered sullenly; she still hadn't forgiven him for excluding her that morning, but this was her own way of offering an olive branch.

'Yes, thanks. In a minute. I need to make an important phone call now – if you wouldn't mind shutting the door, please.'

Ruth didn't like being dismissed so peremptorily, especially when she'd been prepared to be nice to him. Then, with rising excitement, she realised that he'd said an important phone call. She was in luck – Mrs Simmons was still at lunch, so Ruth picked up the phone on her desk in time to hear Emily calling the Archdeacon to the phone.

'Gabriel,' said David after a moment, 'I've got a favour to ask you.'

'What's that?'

'Remember the other night, when you said that you would be available if we needed you to do something? Feel free to call on you, is what you said.' David paused. 'Well, you're about to be called upon.'

'What can I do for you, then?'

'I need the keys to the sacristy of St Margaret's. And to the safe.'

'You need what?' He sounded incredulous.

'Yes, I know that it's a strange request. But you'll have to trust me – it's important. And I need them as soon as possible,' he added.

There was a long pause. 'And how do you expect me to produce these keys?'

'I've thought it all out,' David explained. 'You're the Archdeacon. You have the right to make a visitation to any church at any time, don't you? Just ring the Vicar, or the Administrator, or one of the churchwardens, and say that you're coming this afternoon, to inspect the terrier. It's within your rights, Gabriel. They may think it's odd, but they can't really say no.'

'That's true,' Gabriel admitted cautiously. 'And then what am I supposed to do?'

'Pocket the keys somehow, when they're not looking. I know that you can do it,' he wheedled. 'And if you can get me those keys this afternoon – and a key to the church itself would be a great help, by the way – by tomorrow I ought to be able to tell you who killed the two curates and Vera Bright, and why.'

'Can't you tell me *now*?'

'I'm afraid that I won't know until I've been able to get into that sacristy. That's where the answer is to be found.'

'Well,' Gabriel capitulated. 'If it's that important, I'll see what I can do. I'll ring you later.'

'I won't leave my desk until I hear from you.' He gave Gabriel the number, adding, 'You promised, remember?'

As soon as she heard the click to show that the connection had been broken, Ruth put down the phone. Her mind worked furiously as she made the promised tea for David; she tapped on his closed door and, when he invited her to enter, delivered the tea with a smile.

'Thanks, Ruth,' he said abstractedly, then looked up at her. 'Do you have anything to do? I know that it's your last afternoon here – you could leave early, if you wanted. I could ring and ask your Aunt Lucy to come for you. I may have to stay a bit late today.'

'Oh, no. That's all right,' she assured him. 'Since it's my last day, everyone has come up with plenty of photocopying for me to do. Next week there won't be anyone here to do it!'

She was taking it in remarkably good spirit, he grudgingly admitted to himself. 'Well, if you'll be all right . . .'

'Yes. Don't worry about me. I'll be in the photocopier room.'

She went back to Mrs Simmons's desk, picked up the phone, and rang Directory Enquiries, asking for the number for St Margaret's Church. She wasn't sure whether there would even be a phone, and if there was, who might be there to answer it, but in due course it was answered. 'St Margaret's Church,' came a voice down the phone.

'Is this the Vicar?' she asked.

'No, this is the Administrator.'

'Oh, well, you'll do just as well,' she said sweetly. 'My name is Ruth Kingsley – I think that you know my aunt, Lucy Kingsley. You see, I'm doing a project at school for RE. We have to visit a church, and write something about it. And I'm afraid I've left it rather late. It has to be handed in next week. So I was wondering if it would be all right if I came to your church this afternoon.'

'Well, I don't know. I'm awfully busy. Isn't there any other church you could visit instead?'

'But your church is so beautiful,' Ruth said, though she'd never been inside it. 'I can't think of any other church that I like nearly so well as yours.'

The flattery was not without effect. 'What, in particular, would you like to see?'

She tried to think what was kept in the sacristy. 'The . . . um . . . silver,' she said. 'I'm sure that you could tell me some interesting things about it. My aunt says that you know ever so much about everything in the church.'

He sighed heavily. 'I'm a very busy man, young lady. The Archdeacon has just rung to say that he's coming by later to inspect the silver.'

'But if you have to get it out for him anyway,' she coaxed, 'it won't be any trouble for me to have a look at it as well.'

'All right, then,' he gave in. 'Perhaps the sacristan will be in a bit later, to change the frontals for the weekend, and he might be able to spare rather more time than I can. Will you be coming soon?'

'Oh, yes. Right away. I'll see you in a little while, then.'

Ruth put the phone down and turned to find Mrs Simmons looking at her, hands on ample hips. 'What do you think you're doing?' she demanded.

'Oh, I was just talking to Aunt Lucy.' Ruth gave her an innocent smile. 'Uncle David has said that I can go home early, as it's my last day, and I just wanted to tell her that I was coming.'

'By yourself?'

'Oh, yes.' Ruth waved her hand dismissively. 'He doesn't mind. He knows that I'm not a baby. I'm perfectly capable of getting to South Kensington by myself.'

'Well, if you're sure . . .'

She was already on her way. 'It's been nice knowing you,' she said over her shoulder. 'And remember – he's busy. Don't bother him.'

Half an hour later, Lucy rang David. As Mrs Simmons put the call through, she asked, 'Has Ruth made it home safely, then?'

Lucy was puzzled. 'Ruth? Why, no. She wouldn't come home on her own.'

'But she set off about thirty minutes ago. She said that Mr Middleton-Brown had told her to go home early. And she rang you to tell you that she was coming – I heard the end of the conversation.'

'No,' said Lucy, beginning to be alarmed. 'She *didn't* ring me. You'd better put me through to David right away.'

He sent for Mrs Simmons a minute later. 'Would you mind telling me what this is all about?' he asked. 'Where is Ruth?'

'She's gone home,' she repeated. 'She said that you told her to go.'

David frowned. 'Can you remember her exact words?'

'She said, "Uncle David said that I can go home early, as it's my last day." Or something quite close to that.'

He groaned. 'Are you sure that she said "Uncle David"?'

'Oh, yes. I remember that, because I've never heard her call you that before.'

Into the phone he said, 'Now I *know* that she's up to something, love.'

'You mean that you didn't tell her to go home?' queried Mrs Simmons, only beginning to understand.

'No, I didn't.'

'Then perhaps I should tell you that I thought it was a little strange. She said that she was talking to her Aunt Lucy on the phone, but part of the conversation was about churches and silver. She mentioned St Margaret's Church.'

'Good Lord.' David spoke into the phone again. 'I think that she's gone to St Margaret's. I'll go after her, Lucy. She'll be all right.'

'I'll meet you there,' she said immediately.

'I'd rather you didn't,' he protested, knowing that it would make no difference.

It should be all right, he thought as he walked rapidly to High Holborn and the tube station. Ruth wouldn't really be in danger, no matter how idiotically she had behaved. She didn't really know anything, and surely no one would harm her in a church, in daylight. There would be people around. Then he remembered who those people might be, and he quickened his pace. For a moment he considered whether it might not be faster to take a taxi, but decided that afternoon traffic in London would make the Underground the wiser choice, if speed were important. It wasn't just Ruth – Lucy was on her way as well, and no matter how quickly he managed to travel she would get there before he did. And he hadn't had the opportunity to tell her of his conclusions about the murderer. She'd be arriving at St Margaret's with only slightly more knowledge, and more wariness, than Ruth.

Would the Vicar be going to St Margaret's later to say Evensong? Or would he go to St Jude's, which was nearer the vicarage? And what time was Evensong, anyway? It could be important. David thought about the notation in Father Julian's diary, and he went suddenly cold as the last piece fell into place. He knew with a grim certainty who had killed three people – Father Julian had told him.

Would it be enough to convict? Probably not: they would need the evidence from the sacristy as well. And of course the testimony of Mr Atkins, who should be able to identify the seller of the chalice. As he hurried down the steps into the tube station, he remembered something that Mr Atkins had told him only that morning. It hadn't registered as significant at the time, but now it provided all the confirmation he needed to be sure that the information in Father Julian's diary was relevant. And that he didn't have any time to lose.

After her visit to the Toppings, Ruth had no difficulty in locating the neighbouring St Margaret's Church. The church was unlocked and seemingly empty, but after a brief exploration of the building Ruth found Stanley Everitt waiting for her in the sacristy. She had never met Stanley Everitt, though she'd seen him at Rachel's funeral – his death's head face was unmistakeable – but she wasn't sure whether he remembered her or not. 'Hello, Mr Everitt. I'm Ruth Kingsley,' she said with the ingratiating smile that she'd used to such good effect on Dolly Topping. 'I really do appreciate you taking the time to show me your silver.'

His peeved expression softened a fraction, and he unbent sufficiently to say, 'You're very fortunate that you came today. Friday is the only day I'm at St Margaret's – the rest of the week I'm at St Jude's.'

'Oh, what a lucky coincidence,' she gushed.

Everitt cleared his throat. 'Yes. Well.'

She saw that he had already taken the silver from the safe and set it out on the top of a vestment chest. That was a disappointment; she'd hoped to get a peek inside the safe when he opened it, but he had forestalled her. But she injected great eagerness into her voice as she said, 'So is this your silver, then?'

'Yes. I assume that what you're interested in for your school project is its liturgical use rather than its artistic qualities.' His tone was schoolmasterish, and indeed he had been an RE teacher himself before being made redundant and taking on the Administrator's job. 'This, of course, is a chalice. It is used to hold the wine during the Mass, referring to Our Lord's last supper.'

'Oh, so you have another chalice,' Ruth blurted out without thinking.

Everitt looked at her. 'What do you mean?'

'Oh, um,' she faltered. 'I just meant that of course everyone knows that the chalice was stolen in a robbery, when Father Julian was killed.'

'That was a terrible thing,' he intoned, furrowing his brow and wringing his hands. 'I was the one who found his body, you know. On the Saturday morning when I came in to prepare for a wedding. A great shock, it was.'

'Oh, it must have been.' She gained confidence in her information-gathering techniques. 'And an even greater shock to have another curate killed so soon after,' she added boldly.

The Administrator put the chalice down and took a closer look at Ruth. 'You were at the funeral.'

'Yes.'

'And at the vicarage after.' He leaned down and brought his face close to hers. 'You were a friend of Miss Bright, were you?'

'That's right.'

His voice was soft; it had lost its customary pedantic, self-important edge. 'You said that she knew who had killed Rachel. She didn't happen to tell you who it was, did she?'

Ruth decided to be cagey. 'Maybe she did, and maybe she didn't.'

He stared at her for a moment, as if weighing up her words, and she returned his stare coolly. It was at that moment that she saw, out of the corner of her eye, a green and gold carrier bag on the table in the corner, and she knew that she was confronting a murderer. 'It was you, wasn't it?' she said slowly. 'You killed Miss Bright. You killed them all.'

Things happened very quickly after that. Stanley Everitt reached for a penknife, left carelessly behind by the sacristan after cleaning the lumps of melted incense out of the thurible. Lucy appeared at the door, and Ruth screamed. 'Run, Aunt Lucy,' she shrilled. 'He killed them. Go and tell David. Tell him—'

Her shout was cut off by a hand over her mouth, and the knife blade was pressed to her throat. 'I don't think you'll want to do that, Miss Kingsley. Not unless you relish seeing your niece's throat cut.' His voice was chillingly calm; Lucy was transfixed with horror just inside the door.

It was only a few seconds later that David arrived, winded, having run from the tube station. He took in the situation instantly, pushing Lucy behind him and bursting into the sacristy.

'Stop right there,' Everitt warned. 'Don't come any closer, or I promise you that I'll kill her.'

All other circumstances aside, David was at a physical disadvantage, his heart pounding as he gasped for breath.

They were at an impasse. Everitt and his hostage, frozen in terror, faced David across the sacristy. 'Come inside away from the door,' Everitt commanded. 'You and the girl's aunt both. I don't want either one of you thinking that you're going to go for help. Over there.' He gestured with his head to the corner farthest from the door.

David knew that they had to obey. He took Lucy's hand and moved slowly around the circumference of the sacristy; Everitt backed round towards the door, continuing to watch them warily. 'Don't try anything, or I'll kill her,' he repeated.

'You would, too, wouldn't you?' David spoke at last. 'Just like you killed the others.'

Ruth gasped in pain as he nicked her throat with the knife. 'What do you know about that?' Everitt asked softly.

'I know that you killed them, and I know why.' David's voice sounded calm. 'But I'd like to know one thing. Why did you steal the marriage certificates? Was it just for the money?'

'Just for the money?' Everitt laughed. 'It was a great deal of money. More money than *you'll* ever see.'

'How did you get involved in it, then?'

'Do you really want to know?'

'Why don't you tell me,' David invited.

Everitt decided that there was nothing to lose; it was obvious that David knew something about it already, and he was actually quite proud of his own cleverness, welcoming a chance to share it. 'I was approached,' he said. 'The first time, it was just one that they wanted. One marriage certificate. A chap approached me and asked if I could get it for them. They offered me a thousand pounds for it. So I said yes.'

'They asked you because you were the Administrator?'

'Yes, of course. They knew that I'd have access to the certificates. It was no problem,' he boasted. 'Father Keble Smythe never checks the registers. He's always allowed me to fill them out and to do the reports for the registrar, so it couldn't have been simpler.'

'Then they wanted more?'

'As many as I could get for them, they said. They'd pay me a thousand pounds apiece for as many blank marriage certificates as I could supply.'

David knew that he had to keep him talking as long as possible. 'Then Father Julian stumbled on to your little . . . sideline?'

Everitt laughed. 'He was too conscientious by half. He decided that he wanted to fill out the register for the weddings he took, and he discovered that the numbers didn't match up. Fortunately he came to me instead of going to Father Keble Smythe.'

'So you killed him.'

'I had no choice – he would have exposed me. And there was an added benefit. Two, actually.' He chuckled softly to himself. 'I was able to take a whole book of certificates, as though it were part of the burglary. Later I reported them as stolen to the registrar, and was sent a whole new book. And of course there was the chalice.'

'But you didn't know how valuable it was when you took it, did you?'

'No, of course not. No one knew that the silver was worth anything. I took it just to add authenticity to the burglary, and put it at the back of my wardrobe at home. And then you came along and told me that it was worth thousands. I couldn't resist selling it.'

Lucy spoke for the first time. 'What about Rachel? Why did you have to kill *her*?'

Everitt frowned. 'They came back to me later, and wanted more certificates, only a few this time. She had weddings two Saturdays in a row. I'd taken the certificates during that week, and she noticed that the numbers were off. She was going to tell the Vicar – I was with him when she rang to say that she wanted to talk to him. I knew that she'd found out, so I took my chance.'

'And Miss Bright,' Lucy said. 'Did she really know that you'd killed them?'

His laugh was unpleasant. 'I don't know if she knew anything or not. But I couldn't chance it, could I? I don't think that she *did* know anything – she let me into her house quite happily, and made me a cup of coffee.'

Lucy shuddered; David squeezed her hand.

'What is the meaning of this?' The authoritative and outraged tones of the Archdeacon were heard at the sacristy door, triggering another rapid sequence of events.

Everitt turned his head sharply towards the door, for an instant slackening the pressure of the knife on Ruth's throat. She sensed her opportunity and sank her metal-encrusted teeth into the hand that covered her mouth; he shrieked in agony. And David, with a well-judged movement of his foot, kicked the silver choir cross which leaned against the wall, unbalancing it and causing it to topple over on to Everitt. It was over six feet tall and extremely heavy; the top of the cross caught him on the side of the head as it fell and sent him sprawling, unconscious. Ruth sprang clear, to be grabbed by Lucy with fierce protectiveness.

It had all happened so quickly, in a matter of seconds. Gabriel stood at the door, astonished.

Weak with relief, David grinned. 'Hello, Archdeacon,' he drawled. 'Well timed, though I confess I was beginning to think that you'd never get here. Why don't you make yourself useful and go ring 999?'

'Let me do it,' Ruth demanded, resilient as ever. 'Let *me* ring 999 – after all, I'm the one who discovered him.'

A few hours later they were all in the Archdeacon's drawing room. The ambulance had been and gone, and of course the police as well, who had taken their statements, collected certain evidence from the sacristy in consequence, and sent them home.

The shock was beginning to wear off, though Lucy still looked pale and was unusually subdued. Emily, the only one who had missed out on the excitement first hand, cosseted her with cups of strong tea and, when that didn't seem to have the desired effect, with brandy instead.

Of course David had to relate to Emily and to Gabriel the substance of Everitt's admissions of guilt, aided ably by Ruth's interjections. 'I still don't understand why he did it,' Emily said at the end, shaking her head in bafflement. 'Was there some reason that he needed the money?'

'I was just about to ask him, when your husband got round to rescuing us,' David put in with a wry grin.

Gabriel, who had been on the phone with the police, ignored David's jibe. 'He made a full statement to the police after he regained consciousness. They didn't want to tell me what he said, of course, but I threw my weight around a bit. Said that as Archdeacon I had a right to know, so they told me. It seems that his wife's a bit of a social climber. Keeping up with the Bairstows seems to be the chief concern – and that's where the problems began. Martin Bairstow is a successful businessman with more money than he and his wife between them know what to do with, and Stanley Everitt is – was – a Parish Administrator, making barely enough to survive. His wife doesn't work, and they have no additional income. So he thought that this would give him a little extra cash so that his wife would stop nagging him.'

'Everything she served at that meeting at her house a few weeks back came from Knightsbridge,' recalled Emily. 'I thought at the time that she seemed to be trying to out-do Vanessa.'

'And hence the carrier bag,' David added with a grim smile.

Lucy nodded. 'When she found out that Vanessa had commissioned a painting from me, she said that she wanted one as well. I wondered how on earth she could afford it, but at that meeting she said that she definitely wanted to go ahead with it.'

'Presumably,' David deduced, 'that was about the time that her husband went back to the well again, and stole the last few marriage certificates – the ones that made Rachel suspicious.'

'I think,' said Emily slowly, 'that there was more to it than that. More than just his wife, I mean. I think that, if anything, that was just an excuse for what he did.'

'What do you mean?' queried Gabriel.

'I think that it was his way of getting revenge on the Church. He was turned down by the Board of Ministry, wasn't he?'

'Yes,' Gabriel confirmed. 'Three times.'

'He wanted to be a priest,' remembered David. 'He told me so – and he was really bitter that the Church didn't want him, didn't value his talents.'

Emily nodded. 'That's what I mean. He had to be satisfied with being Administrator, always telling people how important he was. And surely it's significant that two of the people that he killed were curates. Something he'd never be, no matter how much he wanted it.'

'But what about Miss Bright?' Ruth put in. 'Why did he have to kill her too? When he wasn't even sure that she knew anything?'

'I think that by that time he'd got to like killing people,' Emily analysed shrewdly. 'I think he enjoyed the feeling of power that it gave him.' She shook her head. 'I think he's a real psychopath.'

Gabriel sighed. 'If only I'd been here that day when Rachel phoned. It was too late for Julian Piper, but two other deaths might have been prevented.'

'You mustn't think that.' Emily went to him, perching on the edge of his chair and putting a protective arm around his shoulders.

'Yes, well,' David put in quickly, in an attempt to forestall Ruth's breastbeating routine over Vera Bright. 'For a while I had the wrong end of the stick altogether. I was running round after Francis Nightingale.'

True to form, Ruth favoured him with an accusing glare. 'You never said.'

'Francis Nightingale?' Emily turned to him blankly. 'Colin's brother, you mean?'

'Yes.' David ignored Ruth. 'I don't think I ever told you about him. I was convinced that if anyone had killed Rachel, it had been him, because he was the one who benefited financially from her death. He needed money badly, I found out.'

'And after what Rachel said to me about him pulling the plug on Colin . . .' Emily surmised.

'Exactly. I think that he *did* pull the plug on Colin in the end, as it happens, but that's neither here nor there.'

Emily looked thoughtful. 'David, you still haven't told us how you figured it out about the marriage certificates. And how you knew that Stanley Everitt was the one who'd taken them.'

His mouth twisted in a self-deprecating smile. 'I should have known much sooner, actually. All of the evidence about the marriage certificates had been staring me in the face all along.'

'What do you mean?' Emily pressed him.

'I have a client called Justin Thymme,' he began, then paused at Emily and Gabriel's disbelieving looks to assure them, 'Yes, that's really his name. He's run into some trouble with the immigration office because he's married a Hong Kong Chinese woman. I won't bore you with the details, but for various reasons the immigration officer in charge of the case feels that the marriage might be a fraudulent one, entered into so that the wife can claim residency in this country, and eventually be eligible for a British passport, so that she can then bring all of her family in.' He took a sip of his whisky and went on. 'I happen to believe that she's right, but that's also neither here nor there. When I met the immigration officer, she was quite frank with me. She explained that some people will stop at nothing to get a British passport, and mentioned that there was a thriving trade in stolen marriage certificates going on. And where else would one steal marriage certificates, if not from a church? But I didn't make the connection, not then, and not till much later.'

Emily tried to make him feel better. 'But why should you have made the connection?'

'I knew about the burglary at St Margaret's, but as far as I was aware, nothing but the chalice had been stolen,' he acknowledged. 'I didn't even know, until you told me less than a week ago, that Father Julian had been killed in the burglary. But I *did* know that Rachel Nightingale performed a wedding on the Saturday before her death, because she told us so when we ran into her later that day at Westminster Abbey, and she mentioned that she had one the following week as well. And when I obtained Father Julian's diary, I also knew that he was to have performed a wedding on the Saturday after his death. But when I was looking for links, for connections, the weddings never occurred to me. And after Rachel had made a point of telling us that weddings were something that even deacons could perform!' He shook his head. 'I had a feeling all along that those two deaths had something to do with the fact that both of them were curates, but I was on completely the wrong track.'

Gabriel leaned forward. 'But once you'd figured out about the marriage certificates, how did you know that it was Stanley Everitt who had taken them?'

'Before I tell you that, why don't you explain to Lucy how the whole business of marriage certificates works?' David suggested, aware of her silence and mindful that she might be confused.

The Archdeacon nodded. 'Ordinarily,' he explained, 'the vicar is the one who fills out the register when a marriage takes place. Or the curate, of course. There are very strict rules about it, and it has to be done very carefully. Each entry is numbered, and the numbers in the register correspond to the numbers on the certificate which is given to the couple. Every quarter, each incumbent is required to fill out a form for the registrar, copying the information from the registers and supplying the numbers. A bit of a fiddle, because it has to be done just right, but one of those things that most clergy just get on with as part of the job. Apparently, though, Father Keble Smythe thought that it was a job which could safely be left to his Administrator.'

David took up the tale. 'So it seemed to me that it almost certainly had to be either the Administrator or the Vicar, as they were the only two people, apart from the curates, who would have had access to the marriage registers and the certificates. An inside job, in the vernacular,' he grinned. 'But which one? I had reason to suspect Father Keble Smythe, but I had no proof in either direction. And then, as I was on my way to St Margaret's, I remembered two things. I remembered that I'd run into Stanley Everitt in South Ken tube station, the day that there'd been an IRA bomb scare. And that, according to Mr Atkins the antique dealer, was the day that a man purporting to be Father William Keble Smythe had sold him a valuable chalice. Someone had been killed by a bomb – Mr Atkins and I both recalled it. And that was the day after I told the church-wardens and Everitt that the silver was worth a small fortune.'

'Hardly conclusive evidence,' Gabriel commented neutrally. 'But you said two things?'

'Oh, yes. The other thing that I remembered was Father Julian's diary.'

'You already mentioned that,' Emily pointed out. 'About the weddings.'

David shook his head. 'Not the weddings. Something else. You know that Father Julian's diary was in a sort of shorthand, so that he could fit everything in? Initials, and so forth?' He gave a dry laugh. 'That shorthand misled us more than once already, when we jumped to certain conclusions – remember VB and NT? Well, the mistake I made was even more unforgivable than that, for one who professes to know something about churches.'

Gabriel looked intrigued. 'What on earth are you getting at?'

Again David laughed. 'SE,' he said succinctly. 'The diary said SE on that last evening of his life. It meant Stanley Everitt, of course – he had planned to see him, to confront him with the discrepancies in the registers. Everitt always spent Fridays at St Margaret's, apparently. But – fool that I was – I just assumed that it meant Solemn Evensong!'

'Solemn Evensong – on a Friday evening in Advent?' Gabriel's laugh was rich and genuine. 'You must be joking! David, you do disappoint me!'

David shared in the general laughter at his own expense, knowing that he deserved it. But one voice that should have been the first to condemn his folly was strangely silent. He looked towards the chair which Ruth had appropriated – the most comfortable in the room, by virtue of her great ordeal. The girl's head had fallen to one side, her mouth was slightly open, and her eyes were closed. In sleep she looked peaceful, almost angelic, her red hair forming a halo around her serene face. Appearances can be deceiving, David said to himself.

CHAPTER 30

For in the hand of the Lord there is a cup, and the wine is red: it is full mixed, and he poureth out of the same.
As for the dregs thereof: all the ungodly of the earth shall drink them, and suck them out.

Psalm 75.9–10

'Well, I suppose this is it.' They were all thinking it, but it was Ruth who spoke the words as they stood on the platform at Euston Station. It hardly seemed possible, reflected David, that it had only been three weeks since the three of them had come together in this spot. Three of the longest weeks of his life – just as he had predicted that first night, he thought with a wry smile.

The train to Northampton would be leaving in just a few minutes. Ruth had allowed David to carry her case – now even heavier than it had been three weeks ago, with the addition of her Covent Garden purchases – and to heft it on to the train for her. Now it only remained to say goodbye.

Ruth stood squarely in front of David and thrust her hand out. 'Thank you for helping me with my work experience,' she said formally, almost as if on remembered instructions from her parents. 'And for everything else, too,' she added with a near-smile.

He took her hand and shook it. 'Have a safe journey.'

Lucy held out her arms to her niece; the girl went into them and hugged her aunt with an affection that even she couldn't hide. And she whispered something in her ear that made Lucy smile.

Then she clambered on to the train. Her face appeared by the window for a last wave and a moment later the train pulled out.

They stood for a moment as it receded into the distance. 'The poor kid,' said Lucy on a sigh.

'What do you mean, poor kid? Her parents are the ones to feel sorry for now, getting her back.'

Lucy shook her head. 'The other day when we had lunch together, she told me that her parents are having real problems with their marriage. That's why they packed her off here, instead of arranging for her to do her work experience in Northampton. She said that they row all the time, that life at home is pretty grim. It's no wonder she's mixed up, David. Being fourteen is quite bad enough without having to deal with hell at home.'

'Or maybe it's the other way around. Maybe *she's* the reason *they're* having problems.'

'Give the kid a break, David.' Lucy smiled. 'Don't you want to know what she whispered before she left?'

'I wait with bated breath.'

'She said that you're not too bad.'

'High praise indeed from the *enfant terrible*.' But he was touched in spite of himself. 'Just do me a favour,' he added.

'What's that?'

'If I ever suggest, in a moment of insanity, that we should have a child, just say "Ruth" to me. Or better yet, put a bullet through my head and put me out of my misery.'

Laughing, Lucy turned to him and put both hands over her abdomen. 'David,' she said, 'I'm afraid I have something to tell you.' For an instant she watched the welter of conflicting emotions struggling for supremacy on his face before she relented. 'Only joking, darling.'

David clutched his heart and gasped. 'Don't ever do that to me again.'

They walked back down the platform and into the station. 'Should we have coffee?' Lucy suggested, indicating the station café.

'Here? Surely we can do better than Travellers' Fare, love. Why don't we just go home?'

She turned her head away. 'There's something I need to say to you, and I'd rather do it here, on neutral territory.'

David had no presentiment of approaching disaster; he was merely puzzled. 'All right,' he agreed.

They went in and ordered coffee; it came in polystyrene cups, and they drank it sitting on red plastic chairs.

'So what did you want to say?' David prompted her.

Lucy took a deep breath. 'Something came in the post for you this morning. I opened it by mistake.'

'And what was it?' he grinned. 'Something terrible out of my past that's finally caught up with me?'

'Well, in a way it was. It was about Lady Constance's house. The will has been proved, and you can take possession at the beginning of April.' She added, 'The letter said that they'd sent some correspondence to you at the office but you hadn't replied, so they were writing to you at your home address instead.'

So the evil moment had come. 'Well?' he said cautiously. 'Does it have to make any difference?'

'I think that you should move into the house.' Lucy spoke rapidly in a voice that didn't sound anything like her. 'I think that perhaps it's time for us to live apart.'

It hit him like a painful blow to the solar plexus; for a moment he couldn't speak – couldn't even breathe. 'What are you saying?' he gulped finally.

Lucy cupped her hands round the polystyrene cup and looked down. 'I'll tell you,' she said. 'Please don't interrupt me, or try to argue – this is hard enough already. I just want to tell you and have done with it.'

'Go on.' David couldn't believe how calm he sounded, but now that the initial blow had fallen, he felt almost detached, as though this were happening to someone else.

She said it all quickly, without looking at him. 'I don't like what's been happening to us lately. It has nothing to do with Ruth – it has to do with me. And it's not that I don't love you, David – quite the contrary. Recently I've come to realise how much I *do* love you – much more than I've ever loved anyone before.'

He couldn't help himself. 'Surely that's good?'

'No, it's not. I don't like what it's doing to me. The other night at Emily and Gabriel's, I suddenly realised that I was jealous – jealous of you and Gabriel. I've never been a jealous person. I've never minded before – about what happened between you. But now I do mind – not because he's a man, but because you loved him – and I don't like that. And the other morning when I nagged you about it, I just couldn't help myself. I hated myself for it, but I couldn't stop.' She swirled the murky dregs around in the cup. 'I suppose what I'm saying is that I'm afraid of loving you too much.'

'But what is there to be afraid of?'

Lucy bit her lip. 'I suppose it's a sort of superstitious fear,' she confessed. 'That if I love you too much – invest too much of myself in you – you'll be taken away from me somehow. And I'd rather have that happen on my own terms.'

'You're going to try to stop loving me, then?' David's voice seemed to him to come from a long distance.

She replied obliquely. 'All of the things that have happened over the past few weeks, all of the misery that we've encountered, all of the unhappy people; when you think about it, it's all been about love. Casualties of love, every one of them. People who have loved too much, and look what it's done to them. Alistair Duncan loving Father Julian. Nicola Topping and her Ben. Vera Bright and her American. Vanessa. Rachel, too, in her way. And Ruth – damaged in the second generation by love that's gone wrong. And of course there was you and Gabriel.' She sighed softly. 'I don't want to be one of those casualties, David.'

David realised that what he said next could well determine the course of the rest of his life, and he'd better get it right. He fought the desire to reach across and touch her. Instinctively he knew that this was not the time for tears or impassioned argument, or for any sort of emotional blackmail; when he spoke his voice was calm and reasonable. 'Lucy, my own dear love, don't you realise that it's not possible to love too much – only too little? It's true that we've seen a lot of pain in other people, caused by love. Casualties of love, you called them, and that may be true. But I think that our love is something different from that – something strong and good, not constricting or limiting.'

He tore a piece of polystyrene from his cup. 'I'd rather think of it in terms of redemption, to use a Christian term. Redemption of the past. What we feel for each other doesn't cancel out what happened to either one of us before. But it can redeem it, if we let it. And in a sense it can redeem what's happened to all of those other unhappy people, if we can make it work. Our love is the only thing that makes it all worthwhile.' Unconsciously he was shredding the cup, reducing it to bits of polystyrene all over the table. 'I remember what it was like to be alone, before I met you,' he said. 'And nothing could be worse than that. I don't want to go back to that, and I don't really think that you do either. It seems to me that taking the risk of loving – loving too much, as you call it – is far better than not loving at all.'

At last she lifted her eyes to meet his; hers were swimming with unshed tears. That unnerved him at last. 'Please don't cry,' he said brokenly. 'I can't bear to see you cry, my love.'

She reached across the table and took his hand. 'Well,' she said, with a watery smile, 'it's still over a week until the first of April. It looks as though you've got a week to convince me.'

David grasped her hand and pulled her to her feet, leaving a mess of polystyrene behind. 'Come on, then,' he urged. 'A week isn't much time, and the clock is running. Let's go home, love.'

GRANTA BOOKS

NATIVE SPEAKER

Chang-rae Lee was born in Seoul, South Korea, in 1965, and emigrated to the United States when he was three. He was educated at Phillips Exeter, Yale and the University of Oregon, where he is now an assistant professor of creative writing. *Native Speaker* is his first novel.

NATIVE SPEAKER

CHANG-RAE LEE

GRANTA BOOKS
LONDON
in association with
PENGUIN BOOKS

GRANTA BOOKS
2/3 Hanover Yard, Noel Road, London N1 8BE

Published in association with the Penguin Group
Penguin Books Ltd, 27 Wrights Lane, London W8 5TZ, England
Viking Penguin, a division of Penguin Books USA Inc,
375 Hudson Street, New York NY 10014, USA
Penguin Books Australia Ltd, Ringwood, Victoria, Australia
Penguin Books Canada Ltd, 10 Alcorn Avenue,
Toronto, Ontario, Canada M4V 3B2
Penguin Books (NZ) Ltd, 182–190 Wairau Road,
Auckland 10, New Zealand

Penguin Books Ltd, Registered Offices: Harmondsworth, Middlesex,
England

First published in Great Britain by Granta Books 1995
This edition published by agreement with
the Putnam Berkley Publishing Group, Inc

1 3 5 7 9 10 8 6 4 2

A CIP catalogue record for this book is available from the British Library

Printed in Great Britain by Clays Ltd, St Ives plc

For my mother and my father

Acknowledgments

For much needed support during the writing of this book, I would like to thank the University of Oregon Creative Writing Program, the Jacob K. Javits Fellows Program of the U.S. Department of Education, and the Oregon Institute of Literary Arts.

For their expertise and perserverance and faith, I thank my truly wonderful editor, Cindy Spiegel, and the *über*agent Gordon Kato.

For their generosity and wisdom and friendship, my deepest gratitude to Fred Busch, Tracy Daugherty, and Terry Hummer, as well as a *mahalo nui loa* to Garrett Hongo.

For her love and care, my sister, Eunei.

And for everything, always, Michelle.

I turn but do not extricate myself,
Confused, a past-reading, another,
but with darkness yet.

—Walt Whitman

Native Speaker

The day my wife left she gave me a list of who I was.

I didn't know what she was handing me. She had been compiling it without my knowledge for the last year or so we were together. Eventually I would understand that she didn't mean the list as exhaustive, something complete, in any way the sum of my character or nature. Lelia was the last person who would attempt anything even vaguely encyclopedic.

But then maybe she herself didn't know what she was doing. She was drawing up idioms in the list, visions of me in the whitest raw light, instant snapshots of the difficult truths native to our time together.

The year before she left she often took trips. Mostly weekends somewhere. I stayed home. I never voiced any displeasure at this. I made sure to know where she was going, who'd likely be there, the particular *milieu,* whether dancing or a sauna might be involved, those kinds of angles. The destinations were harmless, really, like the farming cooperative upstate, where her college roommate made soft cheeses for the city street markets. Or she went to New Hampshire, to see her mother, who'd been more or less depressed and homebound for the last three years. Once or twice she went to Montreal, which worried me a little, because whenever she called to say she was fine I would hear the sound of French in the background, all breezy and guttural. She would fly westward on longer trips, to El Paso and the like, where we first met ten years ago. Then at last and every day, from our Manhattan apartment, she would take day trips to any part of New York City, which she loved and thought she would never leave.

One day Lelia came home from work and said she was burning out. She said she desperately needed time off. She worked as a speech therapist for children, mostly freelancing in the public schools and then part-time at a speech and hearing clinic downtown.

Sometimes she would have kids over at our place. The children she saw had all kinds of articulation problems, some because of physiological defects like cleft palates or tied tongues. Others had had laryngectomies, or else defective hearing, or learning disabilities, or for an unknown reason had begun speaking much later than was normal. And then others—the ones I always paid close attention to—came to her because they had entered the first grade speaking a home language other than English. They were nonnative speakers. All day she helped these children manipulate their tongues and their lips and their exhaling breath, guiding them through the difficult language.

So I told her fine, she could take it easy with work, that I could handle the finances, we were solid that way. This is when she professed a desire to travel—she hadn't yet said *alone*—and then in the next breath admitted she'd told the school people not to call for a while. She said she felt like maybe writing again, getting back to her essays and poems. She had published a few pieces in small, serious literary magazines early in our marriage, written some book reviews, articles, but nothing, she said harshly, that wasn't half-embarrassing.

She handed the list to me at the Alitalia counter at Kennedy, before her flight to Rome and then on to Naples and, finally, Sicily and Corsica. This was the way she had worked it out. Her intention was to spend November and December shuttling between the Italian islands, in some off-season rental, completely alone.

She was traveling heavy. This wasn't a trip of escape, in that normal sense. She was taking with her what seemed to be hundreds of books and notepapers. Also pads, brushes, tiny pastel-tinted sponges. Too many hats, I thought, which she wore like some dead and famed flyer. A signal white scarf of silk.

Nothing I had given her.

And maps. Here was a woman of maps. She had dozens of them, in various scales. Topographic, touristical, some schematic—these last handmade. Through the nights she stood like a field general over the kitchen counter, hands perched on those jutting hipbones, smoking with agitation, assessing points of entry and encampment and escape. Her routes, stenciled in thick deep blue, embarked inward, toward an uncharted grave center. A messy bruise of ink. She had already marked out a score of crosses that seemed to say *You Are Here.* Then, there were indications she was misreading the actual size of the islands. Her lines would have her trek the same patches of rocky earth many times over. Overrunning the land. I thought I could see her kicking at the bleached, known stones; the hard southern light surrendering to her boyish straightness; those clear green eyes, leveling on the rim of the arched sea.

Inside the international terminal I couldn't help her. She took to bearing the heaviest of her bags. But at some point I panicked and embraced her clumsily.

"Maybe I'll come with you this time," I said.

She tried to smile.

"You're just trading islands," I said, unhelpful as usual.

I asked if she had enough money. She said her savings would take care of her. I thought they were *our* savings, but the notion didn't seem to matter at the moment. Her answer was also, of course, a means of renunciation, itself a denial of everything else I wasn't offering.

When they started the call for boarding she gave me the list, squeezing it tight between our hands.

"This doesn't mean what you'll think," she said, getting up.

"That's okay."

"You don't even know what it is."

"It doesn't matter."

She bit her lip. In a steely voice she told me to read it when I got back to the car. I put it away. I walked with her to the entrance. Her cheek stiffened when I leaned to kiss her. She walked backward for several steps, her movement inertial, tipsy, and then disappeared down the telescoping tunnel.

I read through the list twice sitting in our car in the terminal garage. Later I would make three photocopies, one to reside permanently next to my body, in my wallet, as a kind of personal asterisk, I thought, in case of accidental death. Another I saved to show her again sometime, if I wanted pity or else needed some easy ammunition. The last, to historicize, I sealed in an envelope and mailed to myself.

The original I destroyed. I prefer versions of things, copies that aren't so precious. I remember its hand, definitely Lelia's, considerable, vertical, architectural, but gone awry in parts, scrawling and windbent, in unschemed colors of ink and graphite and Crayola. I could tell the page had been crumpled up and flattened out. Folded and unfolded. It looked weathered, beaten about her purse and pockets. There were smudges of olive oil. Maybe chocolate. I imagined her scribbling something down in the middle of a recipe.

My first impression was that it was a love poem. An amnesty. Dulcet verse.

But I was wrong. It said, variously:

You are surreptitious
B+ student of life
first thing hummer of Wagner and Strauss
illegal alien
emotional alien
genre bug
Yellow peril: neo-American
great in bed
overrated
poppa's boy
sentimentalist
anti-romantic
_____ analyst (you fill in)
stranger
follower
traitor
spy

For a long time I was able to resist the idea of considering the list as a cheap parting shot, a last-ditch lob between our spoiling trenches. I took it instead as one long message, broken into parts, terse communiqués from her moments of despair. For this reason, I never considered the thing mean. In fact, I even appreciated its count, the clean cadence. And just as I was nearly ready to forget the whole idea of it, maybe even forgive it completely, like the Christ that my mother and father always wished I would know, I found a scrap of paper beneath our bed while I was cleaning. Her signature, again: *False speaker of language.*

Before she left I had started a new assignment, nothing itself terribly significant but I will say now it was the sort of thing that can clinch a person's career. It's the one you spend all your energy on, it bears the fullness of your thoughts until done, the kind of job that if you mess up you've got only one more chance to redeem.

I thought I was keeping my work secret from her, an effort that was getting easier all the time. Or so it seemed. We were hardly talking then, sitting down to our evening meal like boarders in a rooming house, reciting the usual, drawn-out exchanges of familiar news, bits of the day. When she asked after my latest assignment I answered that it was *sensitive* and *evolving* but going well, and after a pause Lelia said down to her cold plate, *Oh good, it's the Henryspeak.*

By then she had long known what I was.

For the first few years she thought I worked for companies with security problems. Stolen industrial secrets, patents, worker theft. I let her think that I and my colleagues went to a company and covertly observed a warehouse or laboratory or retail floor, then exposed all the cheats and criminals.

But I wasn't to be found anywhere near corporate or industrial sites, then or ever. Rather, my work was entirely personal. I was always assigned to an individual, someone I didn't know or care the first stitch for on a given day but who in a matter of weeks could be as bound up with me as a brother or sister or wife.

I lied to Lelia. For as long as I could I lied. I will speak the evidence now. My father, a Confucian of high order, would commend me for finally honoring that which is wholly evident. For him, all of life was a rigid matter of family. I know all about that fine and terrible ordering, how it variously casts you as the golden child, the slave-son or daughter, the venerable father, the long-dead god. But I know, too, of the basic comfort in this familial precision, where the relation abides no argument, no questions or quarrels. The truth, finally, is who can tell it.

And yet you may know me. I am an amiable man. I can be most personable, if not charming, and whatever I possess in this life is more or less the result of a talent I have for making you feel good about yourself when you are with me. In this sense I am not a seducer. I am hardly seen. I won't speak untruths to you, I won't pass easy compliments or odious offerings of flattery. I make do with on-hand materials, what I can chip out of you, your natural ore. Then I fuel the fire of your most secret vanity.

I should have warned my American wife.

I met Lelia at a party given by an acquaintance of mine from college, a minor painter of landscapes. I bumped into him by pure chance in a trinket shop in El Paso. I was in the city on assignment, only my second one solo, and I'd just completed the job. It had been successful, but I was still jittery, the way you feel after a massive release of energy, my nerves on end and still working. I was planning to fly out that evening, but he invited me to a gathering of some of his artist-and-crafter friends and I decided to stay until the next morning.

That evening I went to his living loft and studio, which was on the second floor of a run-down hacienda in an old section of town. The party was crowded, mostly candlelit, the talk unfiltered, unwinding all over the single large room. People were sitting in groups on oversized floor pillows and on cane chairs turned backward, smoking grass and drinking tallneck beers. Nils—the painter—greeted me in the open kitchen.

"My good friend Henry," he said stridently, the strangeness of that notion hanging there for us.

I simply took his hand. He had a woman with him, or next to him, and he introduced us. She said hello to me and her voice surprised me with its pitch, clearer and higher than I was hearing those days. The women I knew back in New York grumbled from down low in the gut, in messy plaints, everything spoken in 2 A.M. arias.

It ended up that Lelia was the only person I spoke with. In fact Nils seemed to want us to talk, if only to keep her occupied while he entertained the other guests. He was probably figuring I wouldn't get in the way. He didn't say as much, they weren't lovers, but I could tell he desired her, the way he was ushering her around with his paint-splattered hand clinging to the small of her back. Make a gesture, he must have thought, let my Asian friend in the suit have a pleasant moment with her.

She was wearing a sand-hued wrap, a kind of sari, except it was looser than that, as if it had just been unwound and then only casually repinned. One shoulder was bared. I noticed she was very white, the skin of her shoulder almost blue, opalescent, unbelievably pale considering where she lived. When he left us she bid him goodbye using his surname, with neither irony nor derision. Then she told me to wait and she left. She came back after a few minutes with two beers pressed against her chest and a bowl of tortilla chips in her free hand. I took the bottles from her. They left winged damp marks on her wrap, which she didn't seem to notice. She led us to an open double window at the quieter end of the studio. She balanced the bowl on the wide sill and said to me, "I saw you right away when you came in."

"Did I look that uncomfortable?"

"Terribly," she said. "You kept pulling at your tie and then tightening it back up. I saw a little kid in a hot church."

"I'm usually better at parties," I told her.

"I'm usually worse," she said. "I guess tonight I feel social."

We clinked bottles.

She was looking at me closely, maybe wondering what a last name like Park meant ethnically. After a while our talk came 'round to it, so I told her.

"I knew," she said. "Or I was pretty sure. A friend in middle school taught me about Korean names, how Park and Kim were always Korean, the other names like Chung and Cho and Lee maybe Korean, maybe Chinese. Never Japanese. Am I getting this right?"

"You're getting this right."

"Aren't you going to guess what flavor my name is?"

She was about to remind me of it but I said *Boswell* aloud, very slowly as if in a recital or bee. I guessed somewhere in the Commonwealth.

"I'm too easy," she cried. "You even got the Massachusetts part without trying. It's so depressing. You don't know what it's like. An average white girl has no mystery anymore, if she ever did. Literally nothing to her name."

"There's always a mystery," I offered. "You just have to know where to look."

"I bet," she said.

I was immediately drawn to her. I liked the way she moved. I know how men will say this, to describe that womanly affect they find ineffable. I am as guilty as them all. There is a hurt that pinches your throat or chest when you look. But even before I took measure of her face and her manner, the shape of her body, her indefinite scent, all of which occurred so instantly anyway, I noticed how closely I was listening to her. What I found was this: that she could really speak. At first I took her as being exceedingly proper, but I soon realized that she was simply executing the language. She went word by word. Every letter had a border. I watched her wide full mouth sweep through her sentences like a figure touring a dark house, flipping on spots and banks of perfectly drawn light.

The sensuality, in certain rigors.

"So I work for a relief agency," she said, warming up. "I drive a pickup truck. I deliver boxes of canned food and old clothes to some neighborhoods around town. Many of the people there are illegals, Mexicans and Asians. Whole secret neighborhoods brown and yellow. Tell me, am I being offensive?"

"I don't think so."

"Okay. Anyway, they know my blue truck. They forget my face but they know my truck. I carry a box into a house. I check if the infants and children look healthy. The sick ones go on a list for the health service. I come back outside and people are always waiting there. They just want to talk. They know me as the English lady. All day I give lessons from the back of the truck. I sit there and they talk to me. I help them say what they want. *How much is this air conditioner? Does this bus go to Sunland Park Racetrack? Yes, I cook and clean and I can sew.* Now I teach a class at night. The same people and more. I try to turn them away, you know, because of fire codes. They look at me confused and don't move. Half of them end up standing. They bring their babies because they heard you can learn in your sleep. What can I do? I let them all stay. Everybody in this town wants to learn English."

I offered her what I could of me, inventing a story around the basic reasons why I was in El Paso. She didn't push. Nils finally came around but Lelia didn't say much and he said he had to step out for more crushed ice. We didn't see him again. For the next hour or so we took turns getting each other beers, until she came back the last time with a plastic cup full of tequila.

"It's still too hot in here," she said. "Let's go outside. There's a little park a few blocks away."

We sat on a bench among the sleepers. It was a clear night, the moon, a few high clouds. I'd given her my suit jacket. Some others were awake, talking and drinking like us. I heard them speaking Spanish, and I heard English, and then something else that Lelia said was called *mixup.* Its music was sonorous, rambling, some of the turns unexpected and lovely. Everywhere you heard versions.

"People like me are always thinking about still having an accent," I said, trying to remember the operation of the salt, the liquor, the lime.

"I can tell," she said.

I asked her how.

"You speak perfectly, of course. I mean if we were talking on the phone I wouldn't think twice."

"You mean it's my face."

"No, it's not that," she answered. She reached over as if to touch my cheek but rested her arm instead on the bench back, grazing my neck. "Your face is part of the equation, but not in the way you're thinking. You look like someone listening to himself. You pay attention to what you're doing. If I had to guess, you're not a native speaker. Say something."

"What should I say?"

"Say my name."

"Lelia," I said. "Lelia."

"See? You said *Leel-ya* so deliberately. You tried not to but you were taking in the sound of the syllables. You're very careful."

"So are you."

She took a sip from the cup. "It's my job, Mr. Henry Park. Unfortunately, I'm the standard-bearer."

A breeze rolled in. She wrapped herself tighter in my jacket and slid beside me. We sat like that for half an hour, in silence, listening to the voices from the edge of the dark. Finally I leaned and kissed her. She quickly kissed me back, though it was more like an answer than a statement. For a moment we were dumb to what was happening. We weren't drunk. I asked her if she had ever kissed an Asian before. She laughed and said she wasn't thinking about it that way, but no.

"You taste strange, but only because I don't know you. Hold on."

She kissed me again, lingering this time.

"Definitely Korean," she said, nodding. Then she stopped. "Hey, are you enjoying this?"

I smiled and said couldn't she tell.

She searched my eyes. "No," she said, now aroused, "I really can't."

I did something then that I didn't know I could do. It was strangely automatic. Instantly I was thinking of the lover she might want, the man whom she'd searched out but hadn't yet found in her life. I thought of the ways Nils was perhaps falling short. I put myself in her place and imagined her father and mother. Boyfriends, recent loves. I made those phantom calculations, did all that blind math so that I might cast for her the perfect picture of a face.

I embraced her firmly and kissed her.

"You can kiss me back, you know," I said. "I'm leaving tomorrow, so don't worry. I won't hold you to it."

I stayed another whole week. Later, and throughout our marriage, Lelia liked to speak of those first days. She would trace us back to that beginning time like some evolutionist. Maybe she thought certain clues would arise from the primordial pool to make sense of our eventual difficulties. Were there traits or habits of personality that we had too readily dismissed, too easily obliged?

But then marriage must be the willingness to walk the blind alleys. Maybe I know that now. You don't tempt fate, you ignore it completely. During the two months she was gone in the Italian islands I walked the streets of the city with my back blind. I was matching the steps of my soloist wife at the other end of the world. At times I found myself moving to her own ambling, driven gait, round on the heels, nearly race-walking, breasts forward in guidance, my life's ballasts. I mimicked her high, but never shrill voice. I felt the blush of an anger rise on my neck. I could even see myself, maddeningly centered as usual, hunched at the far end of our empty and too large apartment, sipping easy liquor.

Naturally, I came to see the list as indicative of her failures as well as mine. What we shared. It was the list of our sad children.

My eventual folly, played out in a bar in East New York, was that I came to know the list intimately as my own, as if I alone had authored it. I treasured the cheapest sort of vanity. I flashed it with a grotesque pride. Feigning shame, I showed it to some hard grunge types, to their even harder women, to red-faced professionals. I let them call me *The Yerrow Pelir.* They named a drink after this, some emetic concoction of Galliano and white wine, with which we toasted each other all night. Drunk, over-generous, I let them tack it to the wall with a dart. This the herald of our marriage.

The day after she left I asked Jack Kalantzakos what he knew about the places my wife would be, whether they were beautiful, striking, possibly dangerous.

"You mean will she take a lover there?" he said, his thick moustache spiced with strong oils. He was our office expert in affairs Mediterranean.

I must have nodded.

"I doubt she will," he answered himself, "unless she favors Asiatic, hollow-cheeked boys. Lean young swimmers. But then I look at you. . . ."

Of course he knew this was what I wanted to hear. I pressed him on it and learned only that the emperor Diocletian had built a resplendent palace on the shores of the Adriatic, for his retirement, of all things, as if he might escape the snarls of his Rome.

Jack was himself a cool-blooded demigod in a previous life. He had maybe twenty years in the firm. Any nobility resided in his powerful brow; his other features necessarily surrendered to it. He had massive, soft hands, which he pressed flat against his temples when he spoke. It often looked as if he had witnessed something disastrous.

"My advice," he said, "before you ask me for it, is that you go to her. Take the next boat." Jack was much older than you thought.

"Make short passage," he urged me. "Find her quickly."

"She wouldn't give me her address. She said she'd send it."

"Henry Park isn't one to follow his woman anyway," said Ichibata, who sat near him. "Henry Park sends a tail."

Pete Ichibata was gloomy, ironical, pale. I liked him immensely, his sullenness, his corpselike color, except when he was lodged in a good mood, when he became overbearing and megalomaniacal. He shelled peanuts obsessively. You crackled when you neared his desk—his early-warning system. My mother, in her hurt, invaded, Korean way, would have counseled me to distrust him, this clever Japanese. Then, too, she would have advised against my marriage to Lelia, the lengthy Anglican goddess, who'd measure me ceaselessly while I slept, continually appraise our vast differences, count up the ways.

"Go on, Pete," Kalantzakos said over his shoulder. "Do the drill for surveilling a woman. You stalk them, I know."

"You've got to be careful," Pete answered. "Women, especially in urban areas, are naturally defensive. They're sensitive to predation, men bearing gifts. They believe at all times that somebody is spooking them, though this mindset is also useful to the spook. You present yourself as a shield. The key is to walk with them, on their side, as the protector. You follow by leading."

"Pete's now a Muslim," spoke up Dennis Hoagland, our director. "This morning I caught him praying in the john. Moaning to some higher power. I think he was pointed straight at your desk, Grace."

Grace made a flourish with her hand, queenlike. She was working through a stack of papers and photographs. I knew she was hearing—and remembering—everything that was being said. Weeks later she might comment on the conversation, whether she had participated or not. Like the rest of us, over the years she had developed extremely keen powers of observation and recollection. I often wondered if she even liked us.

"I was puking, Dennis," Pete replied. "I thought you were, too."

Pete was a drinker, not too bad yet but maybe on the start to something tragic.

Dennis Hoagland I didn't know about. His colon was probably spastic. He was dyspeptic, fitful, an alimentary type. He often reeked of Maalox. He looked fine to the eye, ruddy, pumping, pink, but you sensed he was somehow on the brink of death.

Pete turned to Grace. "For the record," he said, "I save my prayers for after work. That's when I'm feeling contrite. Why not work on our guilt and shame together? What do you say, sweetheart?"

Grace tucked the pencil behind her ear.

She said, deadpan, "I don't know what you mean, Pete. I like the business. It's a good one. I make good money, meet nice people."

"You're murderous, Grace."

"Why, thank you."

We casually spoke of ourselves as business people. Domestic travelers. We went wherever there was a need. The urgency of that need, like much of everything else, was determined by some calculus of power and money. Political force, the fluid motion of capital. Influence on your fellow man. These basics drove our livelihood.

In a phrase, we were spies. But the sound of that is all wrong. We weren't the kind of figures you naturally thought of or maybe even hoped existed. Hoagland, who had recruited me, told me once that our job was simply to even things out, clear the market as it were, act as secret arbitrageurs. I pretended to believe him.

We pledged allegiance to no government. We weren't ourselves political creatures. We weren't patriots. Even less, heroes. We systematically overassessed risk, made it a bad word. Guns spooked us. Jack kept a pistol in his desk but it didn't work. We knew nothing of weaponry, torture, psychological warfare, extortion, electronics, supercomputers, explosives. Never anything like that.

Our office motto: *Cowardice is what you make of it.*

We chose instead to deal in people. Each of us engaged our own kind, more or less. Foreign workers, immigrants, first-generationals, neo-Americans. I worked with Koreans, Pete with Japanese. We split up the rest, the Chinese, Laotians, Singaporans, Filipinos, the whole transplanted Pacific Rim. Grace handled Eastern Europe; Jack, the Mediterranean and Middle East; the two Jimmys, Baptiste and Perez, Central America and Africa. There were a few others, freelancers who'd step in when we needed them. Dennis Hoagland had established the firm in the mid seventies, when another influx of newcomers was arriving. He said he knew a growth industry when he saw one; and there were no other firms with any ethnic coverage to speak of. The same reason the CIA had such shoddy intelligence in nonwhite countries. Hoagland oversaw the operation from our modest offices in Westchester County. He was the cultural dispatcher.

Our clients were multinational corporations, bureaus of foreign governments, individuals of resource and connection. We provided them with information about people working against their vested interests. We generated background studies, psychological assessments, daily chronologies, myriad facts and extrapolations. These in extensive reports.

Typically the subject was a well-to-do immigrant supporting some potential insurgency in his old land, or else funding a fledgling trade union or radical student organization. Sometimes he was simply an agitator. Maybe a writer of conscience. An expatriate artist.

We worked by contriving intricate and open-ended emotional conspiracies. We became acquaintances, casual friends. Sometimes lovers. We were social drinkers. Embracers of children. Doubles partners. We threw rice at weddings, we laid wreaths at funerals. We ate sweet pastries in the basements of churches.

Then we wrote the tract of their lives, remote, unauthorized biographies.

I the most prodigal and mundane of historians.

The intrigue. Always the intrigue. That certain sequence of unrelated events. Then bang. Dennis Hoagland said that in our time there were only two or three worth talking about, for complexity, fascination, depth of involvement: JFK, Watergate, the attempt on the Pope. Modern classics. He acknowledged outright that it was a personal matter, this choosing of one's mysteries. He said you could tell about a person not from what he believed, but by what worried him. Hoagland necessarily considered everyone a world-political creature, with a heightened persona, a neurotic cultural manner.

Of course, there were whole legions of adherents to his view. There were still, out there, handfuls of committed Pearl Harbor theorists. Devotees of the Hindenburg disaster. The UFO-Pentagon conspiracists. Amelia Earhart gurus.

Recently I received in the mail a handwritten pamphlet outlining the spread of HIV by the FBI. They were releasing infected mosquitoes by the billions.

This is the worry, alive and well everywhere.

It's people like Hoagland who call you up at odd hours of the night to tell you something you absolutely need to know, practicing on you the subtlest form of sleep deprivation. Half-conscious training. Two in the morning, three, he would ring. I'd get angry with him and he would apologize deeply but two nights later he'd start in again.

He did this after Lelia's return from the islands. I was spending less time up at the office in Purchase, doing whatever work I could from the apartment, mostly because I wanted to live there as much as I could, make it a home somehow, thinking this might draw Lelia back sooner than she was planning. But then Hoagland was complaining. Everyone else was out of the office and he had no one to spook or harass.

"So what are we putting you on, Harry?" Hoagland liked to call me Harry. It made him feel like an old-timer, venerable.

"John Kwang," I said, seeing the time on the clock. Four-fifteen.

"Right," he answered. He knew everything, certainly, but he just wanted me to do the drill. He said, "John Kwang. The rising star of the east. Prince of Northern Boulevard. What goes on?"

"You tell me," I said.

"We'll be placing you soon," he replied, typically confident. "I have a line on a position in his staff. Some public relations work. How do you like that?"

"Fine," I answered. "Jack asked me yesterday. What name will I use?"

"Whatever you like, this time. Bruce Lee, for all I care."

"Bigot."

"To hell with that. I know *Enter the Dragon* by the frame. I've had these dreams. I reach into people's hearts. I have *emow-tional content.* Ask me anything."

I knew he could recite the whole movie.

"I've got to go," I told him.

"Fine, fine. When are you going to show up here?"

"Not for a few days. I've got to work on some things."

"I heard," he said, thickly. "Where's Lelia? Grace said she finally came back."

I paused. "She's around."

"Good. I want my people happy. I want you happy, Harry. I need you that way, for all our sake. It's imperative."

"You're right, boss, I want to be happy."

"Fantastic. Good dreams. And come in soon. I mean it."

I hung up. But after twenty minutes of tossing I got out of bed. I usually couldn't sleep after his calls, not so much from anything he would say. It was mostly his tone that kept me awake, the lingering question of it, the brand of itch that was his voice. I could never simply ignore it, put it off, and I would rise and in half-sleep drift about the darkness of the large apartment, inexplicably checking the corners and the closets for things out of the ordinary, an unmatched shoe, a coat fallen from a hanger, a tie I didn't recognize, those tiny marks of what can go on while you sleep. Of course it was just my drowsy madness, though it dawned on me that I had become more like Hoagland than I would have liked to admit. My years with him and the rest of them, even good Jack, had somehow colored me funny, marked me.

But I knew Hoagland, in truth, was taking it easy on me. His phone calls were just payback for the recent cushion he had given me. For the only time in the last few months I had gone out on assignment, actually courted a live body, I had nearly blown cover.

It was when Lelia was away. He was a Filipino psychoanalyst, a Marcos sympathizer. Emile Luzan, Ph.D. I was one of his patients. I was a successful mortgage broker, married, seemingly poised at the sweet prime of my life. But I was troubled. I was drinking three or four cocktails a day. I wasn't making love to my wife. I couldn't sleep at night and I had sudden fits of anger and sadness. I was eating too much. I told him that a Dr. Hoagland had referred me. Depression, first episode.

"You'll be fine," Luzan said to me gently. "You'll be yourself again, I promise."

In the initial period everything was going well. Our sessions were becoming increasingly intense. I was elaborating upon my "legend" consistently and Luzan accepted my pathologies. The legend was something each of us wrote out in preparation for any assignment. It was an extraordinarily extensive "story" of who we were, an autobiography as such, often evolving to develop even the minutiae of life experience, countless facts and figures, though it also required a truthful ontological bearing, a certain presence of character.

In his earnestness, Dr. Luzan kept delving further into my psyche, plumbing the depths. I was developing into a model case. Of course I was switching between him and me, getting piecemeals of the doctor with projections in an almost classical mode, but for the first time I found myself at moments running short of my story, my chosen narrative. Normally I would have ceased matters temporarily, retreated to Westchester to reiterate and revise. But inexplicably I began stringing the legend back upon myself. I was no longer extrapolating; I was looping it through the core, freely talking about my life, suddenly breaching the confidences of my father and my mother and my wife. I even spoke to him about a lost dead son. I was becoming dangerously frank, inconsistently schizophrenic. I ceased listening to him altogether. Like a good doctor he let me go on and on, and in moments I felt he was the only one in the world who might comfort me. I genuinely began to like him. I looked forward to our fifty-minute sessions on Thursday mornings, enough so that we began meeting on Mondays as well. Hoagland assumed I was stepping up the operation. When I was in the chair across the desk from Luzan I completely lost myself. I was becoming a dependent, a friend. Hoagland, not hearing from me, sent in Jack Kalantzakos to retrieve my remains, my exposed bones.

I knew Hoagland was still wondering if he had done so in time.

He wanted me back with the program. John Kwang, the city councilman, was going to get me back to my old self. I had been vaguely following his career, out of my own interest.

John Kwang was Korean, slightly younger than my father would have been, though he spoke a beautiful, almost formal English. He had a JD-MBA from Fordham. He was a self-made millionaire. The pundits spoke of his integrity, his intelligence. His party was pressuring him for the mayoral race. He looked impressive on television. Handsome, irreproachable. Silver around the edges. A little unbeatable. Given my last assignment, I wouldn't have been surprised if Hoagland had given him to Pete Ichibata. But there wouldn't be a problem, he told me, not a problem for anyone. The job would be simple, uncomplicated. A brief background study. A primer. Just a collection of some personal items, arrived at slowly, from a distance. I might not even have to speak with the councilman. Hoagland almost promised as much. He said it was going to be titty. A walk in the woods. Pie.

But here I was, roaming the apartment again. Middle of the night. Trying knobs, the window locks. I never liked the place much. I never got over its main feature, that it really had no walls, just one built-in partition to set off the bedroom from the larger space. The one and only bathroom was by the front door, set into a corner. The place went very wrong for Lelia and me, at some point. It was one of those lofts you see in movies and at parties, the one cavernous nearly-empty room of windows and hardwood flooring, some exposed brick, steam pipes. The kind of place you see pictured in ads, where the bed lies beneath a basketball net and a Harley is parked beside the nightstand. A surprisingly dysfunctional space. It was often an inappropriate temperature. It was much too big. You felt you were living in the wrong scale. Our old cat, Boo, despised it, she was always nervous, riding the walls. To break her of this I put her dish in the center of the room. She would sneak up on it, take a few bites, shoot back. She lost too much weight so I stopped. But then I must remember how our son once loved the place: I can still see Mitt running wind sprints back and forth down the length of the room, hear the patter of his socked feet, see him sliding the last few yards, twirling to a halt, some beautiful kid.

Lelia and I tended to dwell in the corners, along the periphery. She inherited the apartment from her uncle Steven, who loved her and lived alone and died of AIDS. At first we thought we liked the place, the obscene white expanse of it. We even got into the adolescent notion of making love on every last coordinate of the space, thinking that these personal acts of colonialism would somehow help us acclimatize. But later the expanse and room were easy excuses for not seeing one another. The apartment became a little city with naturally separate habitats, her own private boroughs, and mine.

We did like the bath. Steven had installed an oversized waist-deep tub a few months before he died. I don't think he used it much. We did, almost nightly, during our first two winters. We used to scrub each other with a large sponge and a wiry padded mitten for our backs. Lelia didn't believe in bubbles. We used epsom salts if anything. We had a big block of brown soap from which we shaved slivers with an old cheese knife. We'd light six or seven candles so that there was plenty of light to see each other. We liked to squat in the hot water with me behind her and crossing my arms so that I wrapped her breasts like belts of ammunition. Sometimes she would grab the backs of my knees and lift me onto her shoulders and slowly walk me around the tub. She took pronounced, heaving steps, and hummed something low with the stammer of each step. I always feared we might fall.

After our son, Mitt, was born we all bathed together. He loved it. He was small enough that the tub was a pool for him. He learned to swim in it. When we finally coaxed him out, after all the splashing and laughter, he would sit on the edge of the tub and twist his knuckles into his eyes, which were red from the soapy water. Once, he slipped on the wet tile while horsing around and landed hard on his head and back; when we reached him his eyes jittered in their sockets and scrolled up into his head. I thought he was dead, but Lelia and I both yelled and his eyes dropped back down and he started moaning. We took him in a cab to the emergency room and he stayed overnight for observation. The next day he was perfectly fine. Once lucky, hard-headed boy.

Now that Lelia was back in the country I wondered if we would even keep the place. Still, I kept thinking she might stop by during the daytime, key in to the apartment, peek inside. She'd find me lone and innocent, waiting for her.

But this didn't happen. Instead I started loitering at the café across the street from our friend Molly's building where Lelia had been staying since her return, watching the entrance from a window table. I waited whole afternoons. Women of Lelia's shape would approach the door, buzz an apartment, look around, slip inside. A thickly bearded photographer had his studio on the floor above Molly's. Sometimes he would look down from his window and wave at them first, signaling something. Then they would step inside. Later in the day, handsome young men in blue-collar clothes would ring the bell. The men always came back down before the women did. Then they would all return, go upstairs, and then leave again. This sequence occurred throughout the day. I didn't know the particular nature of the work.

I kept wondering if Lelia had ever spoken to the photographer, or perhaps gone inside. I buzzed once and asked for her by name, but the gruff voice said I had the wrong place.

I drove up to the offices earlier than I'd planned. I wanted to see Jack. I loved the worn-down form of that handsome laughing Greek. To look at him was like reading a relic typeface, like the first letter-block of a book, maybe the letter Y, his frame bent a little sideways as though a mule had fought one arm, the wide shoulders set back, curiously askance, a physical assemblage that belied his uncowering nature. There was the head and brow, its mass like a forged bell, the thousand tiny pocks in his swarthy cheeks, his thick moustache, unvain and wild, the full, almost tortured lips, perennially split in the middle like he'd been punched or roughed up a little. His off-the-rack gray suits were always just a little too big for him, though he himself was a big man, six-two or -three, two-twenty but light on his feet, and the effect when he moved toward you with his jacket unbuttoned was that of a gargantuan moth, gliding, fluttering a bit, completely silent.

His wife, Sophie, a stunning Sicilian woman whose picture on his desk I had long been in love with, was dead nearly five years from cervical cancer. I saw her alive only a few times, the last time just before the diagnosis, when she dropped off his lunch in a brown bag and kissed him twice on top of his wiry-haired salt-and-pepper head.

"Yakavos," she called back to him lovingly, in her movie-star accent, moving those wide flat hips out past where I sat. "You ought to come home early tonight."

When I sat with him I'd pick up the brass-framed photograph of her and admire it. He seemed to like this.

"Our anniversary would have been next week," he said now. "The twenty-ninth of February. She wanted to get married on the leap year because she knew no other woman in her right mind would want to do it."

"You agreed."

"Of course."

I put the frame down, turning it back to face him. We were eating a lunch of ordered-in sandwiches at his desk, grilled Reubens, corn chips, pickles, hot coffee, fried honey cakes. The daily killing of ourselves. Jack, as always, had peeled open a tin of shriveled purple olives. We were building a pile of the pits on a file photo of one of his former subjects, a South American woman with a magnificently crooked nose. Mrs. Ochoa-Perez, an exquisite embassy wife, was very former, I knew, because Jack hadn't been on outside assignment in several years at least. Hoagland had retired him, plain and simple, after Jack requested a quiet exit. He'd had enough of our life. Normally that meant a two-week debriefing at the firm's house upstate in Greene County, a modest send-off here in the office (a few bottles of whiskey, some laughs) and then a good pension check every month, but Jack was an old salt if there was one, too observant, too wise—he'd taught Hoagland most everything—and he was too valuable for them to let go completely.

While Jack was on leave taking care of Sophie, Hoagland told me how Jack had been abducted in Cyprus by a red insurgent faction in sixty-four. At the time he was working piecemeal for the CIA. In Cyprus, Hoagland said, Jack's captors decided they were going to break every bone in his body with a small hammer, from the toes up. Then they would put a bullet in his brain. They started on the job but stopped when someone crashed a donkey cart into the bottom of the house. The way Hoagland tells it, when they went down to deal with the ruckus, Jack struggled with his guard, shot and killed him, then dragged himself onto the roof and flagged down a policeman from a prone position. But then you felt everything Hoagland said was apocryphal, always questionable. If it happened at all, Jack never mentioned it. Our mode at the firm was always to resist history, at least our own.

The floor was quiet while we ate our lunch; no one else was in the office this week, except for Candace, Hoagland's secretary. You could see the whole floor at once, because here there were no walls, not even those carpet-lined partitions many offices will use. Just the appropriate number of desks arranged more or less pentagonally about the floor with the secretaries positioned in the center. Only Hoagland had a private office, on the north side of the floor, and even that was walled by clear sound-proof glass, so that you saw him pacing around in there during the day, gesturing wildly as he spoke on the telephone, nervously jiggling handfuls of red Yahtzee dice like a cache of jewels. Hoagland wasn't in there now, though he was around, as always, lurking about, snooping somewhere on the grounds. He often took constitutionals with his dog, Spiro, an old gray-and-white shepherd mix that limped devotedly behind him on stiff arthritic hips. Or he could be just outside the door. You never knew. I always checked if he was in his office, kept one eye in his direction.

Our building was a five-story professional office, trapezoidal, contemporary, with smoked windows and a blush-red granite facade, the structure nestled in among other office buildings in a large, well-wooded corporate park in Purchase, New York, fifteen or so miles north of the city.

We occupied the top floor, under the name of Glimmer & Company. If you pushed us on it, if you were insistent, if you caught us alone in an elevator or on the back of an airplane or in a motel-bar lounge, we were consultants of ambient lighting to military installations. We said it exactly like that. And on the floors below us, in order of descent, were three small firms of computer dealers, attorneys, and real estate brokers. On the ground floor were two physicians' offices, a podiatrist and a psychiatrist. They enjoyed most of the building's traffic. You were always holding open doors for people either hobbling or hunched over, heads in their hands.

When you got out on the fifth floor you faced a flat cream-colored wall broken only by a metal security door with the company logo in plain block lettering. Beside the door was a mirror and a wooden table on which was placed a bouquet of artificial flowers. Orchids. No lobby, no receptionist. A camera had been installed behind the mirror. Hoagland always denied that it was his idea. Candace monitored a video screen on her desk. She had a button for the door by her foot.

Of course, no one had ever shown up unexpectedly.

"Did you always give Sophie what she wanted, Jack?" I said, picking through the olives.

Jack swallowed, wiping his moustache with the back of his hand.

"You have to, Parky," he insisted, his voice low, rumbling. "It is in the rules, a woman like that. There is no choice. With someone like Sophie, you are part of a greater agency, you make sure things are going right for her. If she is not mean-spirited or too selfish, you fall in love. You grow up, you become a man, you realize you have clear responsibilities. Then you are truly with her. You are partners."

"Tell me when this happens."

"Always too late," he said, settling back in his chair. He put his hands to his temples, as always. "Just tread lightly, Parky. Lelia will do the right thing. This is the time to let her think."

"What the hell were the islands for?"

"To run," he answered. Jack had a quieting directness.

"Right," I said. "I guess I know that."

"Knowledge is the least of your problems."

He lifted Sophie's picture and kept turning it, his eyes darting back and forth, as if he might steal something new from the shape of her face, another profile, an unwitnessed angle. I knew there had been lovers since Sophie, one of them Mrs. Ochoa-Perez, the embassy wife, whose husband found out about her infidelity and had her quickly dispatched back to Montevideo.

"Have you begun the workup of Kwang?" Jack asked me now. Hoagland had officially made him my wingman, to keep an eye on me, given my fiasco with Emile Luzan.

"Just a little bit. Jimmy's put together a sketch file but I haven't looked at it too closely. Why, what has Dennis said?"

"Nothing," Jack muttered, scratching his moustache. "I wondered if you were spending too much time on it but I guess not. That is good. John Kwang is not the end of the world."

"Dennis is acting otherwise."

"He is just softening you up. Just do your job, boy."

I always forgot that Jack had a certain inappropriateness in his expressions and gestures, as if he had learned them from an illustrated text. His parents came from a slum in Athens, no place near those magnificent columns of chalky rock, and I could imagine that his mother and father were just like him, thick-fingered people of the earth, human weeds, hardened and sad and always ready to burst from the drab husks of their lives with great quaking fits of emotion.

A person like my mother would have found it difficult to sit in the same room with them. They might have frightened her with their big bellying laughter and hot tears and full bear hugs. I could see Jack's mother attempting to embrace my mother in an act of solidarity. My mother would have stiffened and politely allowed her small body to be enfolded in those fleshy arms. She believed that displays of emotion signaled a certain failure between people. The only person who could upset her, make her cry or laugh in the open, was my father. He could always unsettle her face with a stern admonition or an old joke or pun in Korean. Otherwise, I thought she possessed the most exquisite control over the muscles of her face. She seemed to have the subtle power of inflection over them, the way a tongue can move air.

"But of course Dennis is a sick man. We know this. To him, information only has value if he has sole ownership. I wouldn't be surprised if there were small slips of paper with facts scribbled on them all locked away inside his safe."

"I didn't know he kept a safe."

"Beneath his desk. I only found out a few weeks ago. Candace accidently let it out." Jack now waved to her at the far end of the floor. She tilted her head to the side and made a sour face back.

"I bet he keeps little silver bullets in there," I said.

"Monkeys' thumbs," Jack added. "The dick of a hummingbird."

I nodded. "A first dub of the Zapruder film. One of a kind."

"Lady Bird Johnson's silk panties, circa 1969."

"An autographed picture from Rudy Giuliani," I said.

Jack liked that one. He said, "File photos of Sharon Tate, Squeaky Fromm. You will note the attached locks of hair."

"Long-lens photos of all of us," I said. "Grainy and flat."

"All in the buff," Jack said.

"With our women," I said.

"Them alone," Jack said.

Right. I pictured Lelia coming out of the shower in Molly's apartment, walking in front of the windows in a towel.

"Lelia has her own ideas about Hoagland," I told him.

"Lelia's the thing right now," he answered. "Does she know what you're working on?"

"No. I'm not going to bring this place up in conversation anymore."

Jack nodded. "I know she has never been comfortable with us."

"She adores you," I said. "Actually, she likes most everyone here, except for Hoagland."

"We're all very personable people." Jack laughed. "Not Dennis, of course. Dennis is a troublesome one."

"Dennis is a freak of man," I said, glancing down the floor to the empty office.

"That's right," Jack answered, chuckling. "Freak of man. But it's good you came in today. You ought to talk to him soon. Assure him. He is a worrier. You have become a subject for him. This is no good. I can see in his face that he thinks of you often. Here, take some of these to him later. Tell him I said olives are a Greek remedy for stress. Take them all and tell him."

He handed me the tub of olives, shooing them on me with his large brown hands. I sat back in the swivel chair and poked through the remainder. Jack was sliding the pits off the photo into his wastepaper basket. Then, after the briefest pause, he let go of the photo itself, the image of the woman still compelling, though smeared and oily. It had been a closed file for some time now, but I thought that even an old hand like Jack must have trouble with what he'd done in the past. I had begun to think that each of us was leading the life of a career criminal, in which the commission of acts was not by a single man but a series of men. One Jack killed the boy guard in Cyprus, another Jack seduced Mrs. Ochoa-Perez, and so on. Our work is but a string of serial identity. But then who was the Jack that loved and buried Sophie; was he just another version in the schema, or the true soul, or could he have been both?

I knew Lelia adored Jack because she always said so whenever he came up in our conversation. She always seemed to be hugging him throughout our get-togethers. At first her attention slightly annoyed me. I wondered what she found interesting enough that she always had to play it out, or where she might be leading with it. Hoagland, the human black cloud, had noticed this too, mentioned it sometimes as indicative of our good camaraderie. Then, and only recently, while she was gone in the islands, did it occur to me that her fondness for Jack might have something to do with me, a hope for what I did for a living. When I traveled to other cities on firm business for several days or a week, I called her nightly from where I was staying and we talked about everything but the very reason I was speaking to her on the telephone from another unspoken place. It didn't seem to matter then. We talked plenty anyway, talked her work, and other things, talked friends, did our talk of family, the talk of how much we missed each other, even the queer ironical talk of when I was coming back home.

"God," she would sigh deeply on the other end of the line, "I'm intensely horny. Will you do something?"

"What?" I'd say.

"Just say you're coming back soon. Say you're moving this way."

"I'm moving your way."

"Again, but just the moving part."

"I'm moving," I'd low, "moving, moving."

I could hear the driving tone to her voice. She was always surging ahead of where we were, never staying with one notion for too long, and I willingly followed her wherever she needed to go, off the real subject, maybe pushed her there myself.

But at some point you begin to see that you both come with open hands to this kind of practice, this mutual circling of speech. The movement is not so difficult. You updraft, you float. The urgency is gone. Somehow you've gotten onto the idea of conserving energy whenever possible. Asking after her is a drain; answering her is even harder. And it is only when you are willing, finally, to fly down and pick through the bones that you can check if the marriage is actually dead.

But with Jack we were fine. In summer days, Lelia and Mitt and I would go up to Jack's house and find him sweating in the garden in denim overalls, hoe in hand, wearing a huge sun hat of straw with a bright red band, one wide, sandaled foot resting up on a grass-plumed pile of overturned sod. He seemed happy enough. He told us about the sauce he was making, a *putanesca,* how he had prepared it the way Sophie taught him, shot full of capers, anchovies, olives, garlic, hot peppers. Jack would ladle it over your buttered linguine, your rounds of fresh bread. Then his Caesar salad, yolky, garlicky, rich. Everything with wine.

Jack's house was a classic split-level, the kind of house I knew best, the one immigrants must dream about, with a downstairs family room, another room called a den, cool linoleum floors, a double oven, two porches—the house laid out so that you and your new wife would sleep in a master bedroom built directly over the garage, the kids safely down the hall.

The neighborhood, Jack told us, was full of New York City cops, most of them retired. Their yards were small and well kept, landscaped with sprays of chipped bark and whitewashed trellises of huge yellow and pink roses. These burly red-faced men would see us on the deck and heartily shout "Jack-O!" or "Jack-Attack!" up to him, wave wide and furious like the marooned with their power shears and their Weedwhackers, flick them on with a zing or whirr whenever Lelia waved back.

Jack would laugh and hoot down something like, "You damn menace, O'Reilly!" and then pour us each another full glass of Barolo, the wine warm, its color deep purple, so that when he smiled you saw his teeth shadowed with its ink. The men below would keep at their work, steadily clipping away until dusk at the overgrowth—"man-a-curing" was Lelia's reprise—showing no mercy to the thorny shrubs, the crapweeds and wild grasses, the tiny shoots of anything that rose up between the cracks of their meticulously landscaped stones.

I thought Sophie must have despised this place, but Jack always said that she had seemed happy, that she had liked the neighbors, the brightly bedecked husbands and wives, the gregarious, delinquent, wise-ass children of cops who asked her daily to play tag with them after school. I imagined her donning big Jackie O glasses, a silk print scarf, white tennis shoes. She moved probably a little like Jack, a little unapparently, she probably just seemed to get from one place to another, floating majestically through her life until the day the internist informed them otherwise.

When Lelia was away I kept thinking how the same could happen to her. I thought Jack could wonder forever if he had looked at his wife hard enough while she was alive, if he had burned enough into memory of every last sensation of her bearing and presence, the heat of her long roped throat, burned enough her scent, the notes of her mind, burned all the things he needed now. I could see her there, the picture perched obliquely in his thick hands, her unanswered gaze dead on us both. How dark the eyes, how dark the mouth. Indelible, our last clues to a beautiful woman.

After lunch, Jack and I went to the microfiche room to look up press on John Kwang. Only three months earlier, Kwang had been on the cover of a Sunday magazine. He'd been elected to the city council two years before, on his second attempt, and there was rampant talk of a run against the mayor in the next Democratic primary. Already the mayor was feeling the heat; you could tell, because his surrogates on the council and the boards of Estimate and Education had begun quietly assailing Kwang for his interest in providing tax vouchers for bilingual education, to have English Only in the schools but subsidize native language study outside. The De Roos people were trying to get Hispanics thinking that Kwang wanted to cut the formal Spanish-English programs. They spoke in veiled attacks about his mediation of talks surrounding the black boycotts of Korean businesses across the city. They said Kwang was trying too hard to be all things to all people. Mayor De Roos himself was making a point of half-complimenting Kwang in the media whenever he could, just the week before calling him "a fervent voice in the wide chorus that is New York."

The mayor was a careerist, a consummate professional, and he knew how the game should be run against an ethnic challenger: marginalize him, isolate him, acknowledge his passion but color it radical, name it zealotry.

"The mayor is no slouch," Jack said, scanning film beside me. The room was a converted utility closet, with just enough space for two machines and their chairs. "He knows how hot Kwang is running. John Kwang is a media darling, he is untouchable right now, and there is no sense trying to attack him."

"The polls say the people are against bilingualism," I said. "They're against giving anything more to immigrants."

"They are more against the politicos," Jack answered. "The big players with interests and connections like the mayor. They love Kwang's style. He has a homemade sword and he is swinging it as hard as he can. He is the dragonslayer. It doesn't hurt to have that expression of his, all wisdom and sincerity. Sometimes I think you'll look like him, Parky, in fifteen years or so."

I stopped the microfiche at a photograph in the *Amsterdam News.* Kwang embracing leaders at an NAACP benefit. "Here he is with his wife, May."

"What did Joan find on her?" Jack asked.

I flipped through her part of the manila paper file. She hadn't found much. "Born Kwon So-jung, in Seoul. She's forty. Ewha Women's University, degree in English literature. Her father was a founder of one of the industrial conglomerates. He died three years ago. Her mother lives alone in Seoul. May has two brothers and a sister, all alive, all older, all living in Korea. She met Kwang in the States, but where and how we don't know yet."

"When did she marry him?" Jack asked.

"Fifteen years ago, the marriage license says in the county of Queens. They have two boys, named Peter and John Jr., ages eight and five. May does volunteer work. The family attends the Korean Presbyterian Church of Flushing. May also leads the children's Bible study class. Kwang has been an elder of the church for almost twenty years."

Jack nodded, his puffy lips extended. I could tell he'd already done some of his own work.

He said, "Kwang knows his base. He lives and dies on contributions from grocers and dry cleaners. It's said the congregation freely hands money to him after the service in envelopes. You'll have to see for yourself."

I imagined Kwang in a dark suit and white gloves, his parcels of tribute politely bundled behind him on the dais.

"I wonder if my father ever gave him money."

"Let's hope not," we heard, immediately behind us.

It was Dennis Hoagland. The grand never-knocker. He was wearing a red rain slicker and a canvas fishing hat pinned with wet flies and nymphs. As usual, Hoagland had waited to come at us from an unseeable angle. His dog, Spiro, unleashed, heeled behind him and yelped once in pain as he lowered himself to the floor.

"It's nice to see someone working around here," Hoagland said, rubbing warmth into his hands. He never seemed to address anyone in particular. "I can't do any work myself. February is the gloomiest month. It's never been this cloudy, never. The fucking sun must have died. Do you remember a time as dark and damp as this, Jack?"

"It's always sunny where I live."

"Damn, Jack." He stepped forward uneasily, then held his position on the threshold. "That sounds right. You live upstate. I live down here near the city, too close to the harbor. The water. It's like a lake effect."

"I know nothing about it, boss."

"Ha! Young Harry of the City knows. Did I tell you where we've got you placed?"

"I thought it was public relations."

"That too. We've gotten lucky. They're opening a new office in Flushing next week and they need volunteers. Everyone's talking about taking on the mayor. My opinion—Kwang will get squashed. Old man De Roos is too slick. Anyway, you'll do some phone work for John Kwang's second."

"How did you hook me?"

"Temp agency. Totally legit."

Jack said, "This is cake, Parky."

"No problemo," Hoagland pitched in. "Anyway, she handles the PR and media. Her name is Sherrie Chin-Watt."

Jack snorted. Sitting up straight in the chair with his thick legs bowed, he looked like a cossack dancer. He was mincing the floor with his feet. "Even a councilman has a PR man. Or woman."

"We all need one," Hoagland said. "My wife, Martha, is mine. She sends out weekly flyers to the neighbors that remind them that I'm a quantity. She includes the slightest hints that I'm an unstable personality. How I am an insomniac. That I still sometimes wet the bed."

"Is it working?" Jack asked.

"Damn right. No more dog shit on my lawn. It's clean. No more Girl Scouts at the door, either. No more Scientologists. We live in peace."

"Who is the woman?" I asked Hoagland, half-recognizing her name.

Hoagland did the drill on her, calling it out with a straight voice.

"Sherrie Chin-Watt. Chinese-American, born in San Francisco. Berkeley B.A. Did her law degree at Boalt. Law Review. Her parents run a small wig shop. Nothing special. She's around your age, Harry, thirty-three or thirty-four. Was married last year to your garden-variety investment banker, corporate finance. Her first marriage, his second. He works too much, sixty, sixty-five hours a week. Headed for the grave. Again nothing special, no real angle there for us. They own a co-op on Central Park West and a bungalow out in East Hampton. No children as yet. She suffers from endometriosis."

"Where'd you get that?" I asked.

"I'm friendly with a prominent gynecologist. Coincidence."

"Jesus."

"She had a successful laser surgery last year, though she's not pregnant yet. They sleep in separate rooms because he snores. Other items. They went to Morocco for their honeymoon. They usually eat out, though not together. She lettered in volleyball in high school. Solid setter. She still calls home twice a week. What else? Before signing on with Kwang last year, she was an attorney for the ACLU office in Los Angeles. She made a name for herself then. If you'll recall, she defended that Indonesian crank in Santa Monica who trained his goat to fart into a portable mike at political rallies."

"Free speech," Jack said.

"Sure, sure. The guy was saying they were only being silenced at Republican events."

"Republicans have the technology," Jack said.

Hoagland sneered at him. "But Kwang knew her even before that. Apparently she met him while she was in law school, after some talk he'd given there. She's been with him less than a year now, but things are heating up fast. What, the election's in two years? They're not involved yet. Big yet."

"I'm sure you would know," I said.

"Oh, I do," Hoagland belched out. He grimaced, knuckling the back of his thumb into his upper stomach. The doorway held him up. He quickly peeled away the foil wrapping from a roll of antacids.

"I know every rotten shit fucking thing going down in this hemisphere," he said.

"I keep forgetting."

"Ha!" He coughed. "You don't forget anything. That's why I love you so much, remember? Anyway, you're going to do Kwang right. Jack will be with you all the way. Do the full workup, certainly. We don't need anything unusual. Most of it you can do from here. Have you done any prep this week?"

Jack told him, "You're looking at it, boss."

"Fine."

Hoagland then motioned to me to walk with him back to his office. His way of telling you something was to stare at you for three seconds and then grin nervously like you've misunderstood each other. Spiro was trying to raise himself. When we got inside Hoagland's office he closed the glass door. Outside on the floor I saw Jack leave the microfiche room and walk back to his desk. Hoagland shed his slicker and hat. Spiro was waiting outside, whimpering. I sat down in the only other seat, a high metal stool on the other side of his desk.

"I take it you've been working things through with your wife. She's still your wife, right?"

"I think so," I said. I didn't want to give him anything. "We're still legal."

"Sure thing. We all love that girl, Harry. I know Jack does. Don't lose her. Martha, she's been nursing me toward sanity for a million years now. She's saved my sorry life more than a few times."

I said, "I guess that's their job."

"Damn right," he replied, pouring a carafe of cloudy water into the top of his coffeemaker. "That's job one."

He switched on the coffeemaker and lighted the butt of an old cigarette as he sat down. "Listen. I need you to work carefully through your legend with Jack before you come back to me with it. I've told him what I thought your angle might be. It's just a recommendation, you can take it or leave it. In fact, I want this to be left to you as much as possible. You're coming off a tough loss with that shrink and we're all pulling for you."

I told him I was hearing the cheers.

"You should. No one's sleeping at night because of you." He quickly finished the butt and was tapping out a fresh one. He was ignoring Jack's half tub of olives. Instead his fingers were jittering on the lighter. He was getting himself worked up, wanting to say something inspirational. He was the kind driven by the visions of certain men who'd come to occupy mythic sites in his life, scratchy visions of Rockne, Lombardi, visions of LBJ, Nixon. Then, the darker visions of Joe McCarthy, J. Edgar Hoover. Our American Hitlers.

"What happened to you has happened to all of us once. That shrink only got to you because he believed in you so fully. You were giving a fantastic performance. You were never better than in those sessions. You were a genius, Harry, you had that fat fuck squirming on his own couch. He was ready to ooze. You were in perfect position to stick him. He would have told you everything."

"If he had had anything."

"Immaterial. Anyway, we couldn't have known that."

"So I stuck myself."

"Doesn't matter," he growled. "You were there, in position. That's what counts. I listened to those tapes, Harry. You were fucking magnificent! I always knew you had it. Christ, *I* even wanted to help you with your problems. I kept forgetting why you were there. You were brilliant. Tony, Emmy, Academy-fucking-Award."

"He was a decent man," I said to him.

"The hell with that," Hoagland groaned.

I could see him, Luzan, sitting there in his brown suit and square black-framed glasses. He was a primary organizer of a small New York–based Filipino-American movement for Ferdinand Marcos' return to the homeland; he collected money for press notices, pro-Marcos picnics, anti-Aquino rallies. Nothing violent. This before Marcos finally died in Hawaii. I learned that Luzan himself had died, too, soon afterward, while attending a professional conference in the Caribbean. I didn't think Hoagland knew I had, but of course he did, keeping a bug even after he was dead, the s.o.b. I had called Luzan's office to apologize for suddenly quitting our sessions and disappearing as I did. I knew I shouldn't have. I was simply going to tell him that I was sorry for the breakoff, that he'd been helpful in what he had to say about my life, but his wife answered and told me he had drowned in a boating accident off St. Thomas. She was cleaning out his office when I called. At the last moment she had decided not to go with him. And I thought, *Lucky for you.* She wept a little, wheezing like she was sick in the chest, and thanked me for my concern. I could almost hear Luzan's bird-high voice, a bizarre pitch that like much else about him was a little silly, a dress of maudlin order on a man of such girth and weight. He could have been a bit player on a Saturday morning children's show. He kept his black hair damp and oily and combed straight down to his eyes. As a kid I would have said his was a fresh-off-the-boat look. Luzan smelled of milk and ground pepper and lemons. Over the seven weeks of sessions I grew fond of him. Once, he offered me macaroons his daughter had baked.

"Take one, my friend," he squeaked to me. "We shouldn't submit to the traditional doctor-patient relationship. It's not our psychology, anyway. Let them have their problems. We can share our own."

Hoagland said, "The doctor was veal, Harry, one huge medallion of sweet-ass veal. You were the wolf. You fed him cream, you fed him honey. You were holding the knife."

"No more knives," I said. "I swear, I'll bolt."

"Not a one," he assured me, his gaze and body now forward and bearing down on me. "This thing with Kwang should be quick and clean. This is a hands-off deal. I see you with his office for three, four weeks tops. All I want is that you do this right again, like I know you can."

He rose from his chair and stepped to the coffeemaker, pouring out a silty cup for me, and then one for himself.

He went on, different again, his voice calmer. "Remember how I taught you. Just stay in the background. Be unapparent and flat. Speak enough so they can hear your voice and come to trust it, but no more, and no one will think twice about who you are. The key is to make them think just once. No more, no less. I can see that this thing with your wife keeps you self-occupied. That's fucking great! Really! It happens. It's life. I just want you to write out a good legend for this and stick with it. When Jack had that awful thing with Sophie he decided to leave for a while. That's not the best course for you, in my opinion. I think you need to stay close."

"Jack's saying different," I told him.

Hoagland guffawed. "Don't listen to him. Jack's a romantic. What he means is protect what you've got. My view—your wife will leave you and come back and leave you for the rest of your natural life. It will go on and on. It's the bald-assed truth. It's nothing against her or you. Honest. I ought to know. Ask the last three generations of Hoaglands. We know the secret. Marriage is a traveling circus. We're the performers. Some of us, unfortunately, are more like freak acts. Maybe she likes certain towns, maybe you prefer others. She'll drop off somewhere every once in a while and stay for a bit. So what. She'll bore, she'll catch up, she'll be back."

I didn't answer him. I just kept thinking of his wife, Martha, nearly-poignant-if-not-for-her-feeble-will Martha, forever pale and small-shouldered and smiling, pulling uncomfortably at the strap of her sequined body suit, her tightrope fifty feet up in the air; Hoagland was down on the ground, in a cage, wielding a chair in one hand, a bullwhip in the other. Where's the beast? Crack. So it followed—I must be the Wolf-Boy. Lelia, the Tattooed Lady. Behold, their impossible love. We shared a wall between our sideshow tents, venally baring ourselves to the curious and craven. This is how we were meant for each other. How we make our living. The lives of frustrated poets and imposters. This, too, how the love works and then doesn't: a mutual spectacle of imagination.

"Harry," he said, "just do me one favor, will you?"

"What?"

"Promise me this—no, wait. I don't need promises."

"Dennis."

"Okay," he said, righting himself. He stole a sip of his coffee. "Don't mess your pants on this one. I mean it. Don't fuck this up. It won't be appreciated."

"What the fuck does that mean?"

"Back off, son. And give me a break. It's just good clean advice. Your scratch with Luzan cost us, and not just money. People are talking."

"It's good Luzan's not."

"Come on! I just read the notices in the paper," he said. He collected himself. "You ought to as well. That's all. People drown, politically involved fat analysts included. A bad thing can happen in the world. We do what we're paid for and then who can tell what it means? I flush a big one down the dumper and next week some kid in Costa Rica gets a rash. What the fuck am I supposed to do? And then everyone asks, who's to blame?"

"Go to hell," I said to him, getting up to leave.

"Don't be sore," he replied. "If it makes you feel any better, I probably will. You won't—you'll get to heaven, no problem. I just thought you knew the facts."

"I know enough."

He said, "Then you know that no matter how smart you are, no one is smart enough to see the whole world. There's always a picture too big to see. No one is safe, Harry, not in some fucking pleasure boat in the Caribbean, not even in lovely Long Island or Queens. There's no real evil in the world. It's just the world. Full of people like us. Your immigrant mother and father taught you that, I hope. Mine did. My pop owned three swell pubs but he still died broke and drunk. The Jews squeezed him first, then the wops, then people like you. Am I sore? No way. It doesn't matter how much you have. You can own every fucking Laundromat or falafel cart in New York, but someone is always bigger than you. If they want, they'll shut you up. They'll bring you down."

"Fuck you, Dennis," I said, closing his glass door on him.

But I could still hear him as I walked away, the hard twang of his answer, almost joyous, *When and where, Harry, when and where.*

My father would not have believed in the possibility of sub-rosa vocations. He would have scoffed at the notion. He knew nothing of the mystical and neurotic. It wasn't part of his makeup. He would have thought Hoagland was typically American, crazy, self-indulgent, too rich in time and money. For him, the world—and by that I must mean this very land, his chosen nation—operated on a determined set of procedures, certain rules of engagement. These were the inalienable rights of the immigrant.

I was to inherit them, the legacy unfurling before me this way: you worked from before sunrise to the dead of night. You were never unkind in your dealings, but then you were not generous. Your family was your life, though you rarely saw them. You kept close handsome sums of cash in small denominations. You were steadily cornering the market in self-pride. You drove a Chevy and then a Caddy and then a Benz. You never missed a mortgage payment or a day of church. You prayed furiously until you wept. You considered the only unseen forces to be those of capitalism and the love of Jesus Christ.

My low master. He died a year and a half after Mitt did. Massive global stroke. It was the third one that finally killed him. Lelia and I were going up on the weekends to help—it was practically the only thing we were doing together. We had retained a nurse to be there during the week.

He died during the night. In the morning I went to wake him and his jaw was locked open, his teeth bared, cursing the end to its face. He was still gripping the knob of the brass bedpost, which he had bent at the joint all the way down to four o'clock. He was going to jerk the whole house over his head. Gritty mule. I thought he was never going to die. Even after the first stroke, when he had trouble walking and urinating and brushing his teeth, I would see him as a kind of aging soldier of this life, a squat, stocky-torsoed warrior, bitter, never self-pitying, fearful, stubborn, world-fucking heroic.

He hated when I helped him, especially in the bathroom. I remember how we used to shower together when I was young, how he would scrub my head so hard I thought he wanted my scalp, how he would rub his wide thumb against the skin of my forearms until the dirt would magically appear in tiny black rolls, how he would growl and hoot beneath the streaming water, how the dark hair between his legs would get soapy and white and make his genitals look like a soiled and drunken Santa Claus.

Now, when he needed cleaning after the strokes, he would let Lelia bathe him, let her shampoo the coarse hair of his dense unmagical head, wash his blue prick, but only if I were around. He said (my jaundiced translation of his Korean) that he didn't want me becoming *an anxious boy,* as if he knew all of my panic buttons, that craphound, inveterate sucker-puncher, that damned machine.

The second stroke, just a week before the last one, took away his ability to move or speak. He sat up in bed with those worn black eyes and had to listen to me talk. I don't think he ever heard so much from my mouth. I talked straight through the night, and he silently took my confessions, maledictions, as though he were some font of blessing at which I might leave a final belated tithe. I spoke at him, this propped-up father figure, half-intending an emotional torture. I ticked through the whole long register of my disaffections, hit all the ready categories. In truth, Lelia's own eventual list was probably just karmic justice for what I made him endure those final nights, which was my berating him for the way he had conducted his life with my mother, and then his housekeeper, and his businesses and beliefs, to speak once and for all the less than holy versions of who he was.

I thought he would be an easy mark, being stiff, paralyzed, but of course the agony was mine. He was unmovable. I thought, too, that he was mocking me with his mouth, which lay slack, agape. Nothing I said seemed to penetrate him. But then what was my speech? He had raised me in a foreign land, put me through college, witnessed my marriage for my long-buried mother, even left me enough money that I could do the same for my children without the expense of his kind of struggle; his duties, uncomplex, were by all accounts complete. And the single-minded determination that had propelled him through twenty-five years of green-grocering in a famous ghetto of America would serve him a few last days, and through any of my meager execrations.

I thought his life was all about money. He drew much energy and pride from his ability to make it almost at will. He was some kind of human annuity. He had no real cleverness or secrets for good business; he simply refused to fail, leaving absolutely nothing to luck or chance or someone else. Of course, in his personal lore he would have said that he started with $200 in his pocket and a wife and baby and just a few words of English.

Knowing what every native loves to hear, he would have offered the classic immigrant story, casting himself as the heroic newcomer, self-sufficient, resourceful.

The truth, though, is that my father got his first infusion of capital from a *ggeh,* a Korean "money club" in which members contributed to a pool that was given out on a rotating basis. Each week you gave the specified amount; and then one week in the cycle, all the money was yours.

His first *ggeh* was formed from a couple dozen storekeepers who knew each other through a fledgling Korean-American business association. In those early days he would take me to their meetings down in the city, a third-floor office in midtown, 32nd Street between Fifth and Broadway, where the first few Korean businesses opened in Manhattan in the mid 1960s. On the block then were just one grocery, two small restaurants, a custom tailor, and a bar. At the meetings the men would be smoking, talking loudly, almost shouting their opinions. There were arguments but only a few, mostly it was just all the hope and excitement. I remember my father as the funny one, he'd make them all laugh with an old Korean joke or his impressions of Americans who came into his store, doing their stiff nasal tone, their petty annoyances and complaints.

In the summers we'd all get together, these men and their families, drive up to Westchester to some park in Mount Kisco or Rye. In the high heat the men would set up cones and play a match of soccer, and even then I couldn't believe how hard they tried and how competitive they were, my father especially, who wasn't so skilled as ferocious, especially on defense. He'd tackle his good friend Mr. Oh so hard that I thought a fight might start, but then Mr. Oh was gentle, and quick on his feet, and he'd pull up my father and just keep working to the goal.

Sometimes they would group up and play a team of Hispanic men who were also picnicking with their families. Once, they even played some black men, though my father pointed out to us in the car home that they were *African* blacks. Somehow there were rarely white people in the park, never groups of their families, just young couples, if anything. After some iced barley tea and a quick snack my father and his friends would set up a volleyball net and start all over again. The mothers and us younger ones would sit and watch, the older kids playing their own games, and when the athletics were done the mothers would set up the food and grill the ribs and the meat, and we'd eat and run and play until dark. And only when my father dumped the water from the cooler was it the final sign that we would go home.

I know over the years my father and his friends got together less and less. Certainly, after my mother died, he didn't seem to want to go to the gatherings anymore. But it wasn't just him. They all got busier and wealthier and lived farther and farther apart. Like us, their families moved to big houses with big yards to tend on weekends, they owned fancy cars that needed washing and waxing. They joined their own neighborhood pool and tennis clubs and were making drinking friends with Americans. Some of them, too, were already dead, like Mr. Oh, who had a heart attack after being held up at his store in Hell's Kitchen. And in the end my father no longer belonged to any *ggeh,* he complained about all the disgraceful troubles that were now cropping up, people not paying on time or leaving too soon after their turn getting the money. In America, he said, it's even hard to stay Korean.

I wonder if my father, if given the chance, would have wished to go back to the time before he made all that money, when he had just one store and we rented a tiny apartment in Queens. He worked hard and had worries but he had a joy then that he never seemed to regain once the money started coming in. He might turn on the radio and dance cheek to cheek with my mother. He worked on his car himself, a used green Impala with carburetor trouble. They had lots of Korean friends that they met at church and then even in the street, and when they talked in public there was a shared sense of how lucky they were, to be in America but still have countrymen near.

—

I know he never felt fully comfortable in his fine house in Ardsley. Though he was sometimes forward and forceful with some of his neighbors, he mostly operated as if the town were just barely tolerating our presence. The only time he'd come out in public was because of me. He would steal late and unnoticed into the gym where I was playing kiddie basketball and stand by the far side of the bleachers with a rolled-up newspaper in his hand, tapping it nervously against his thigh as he watched the action, craning to see me shoot the ball but never shouting or urging like the other fathers and mothers did.

My mother, too, was even worse, and she would gladly ruin a birthday cake rather than bearing the tiniest of shames in asking her next-door neighbor and friend for the needed egg she'd run out of, the child's pinch of baking powder.

I remember thinking of her, *What's she afraid of,* what could be so bad that we had to be that careful of what people thought of us, as if we ought to mince delicately about in pained feet through our immaculate neighborhood, we silent partners of the bordering WASPs and Jews, never rubbing them except with a smile, as if everything with us were always all right, in our great sham of propriety, as if nothing could touch us or wreak anger or sadness upon us. That we believed in anything American, in impressing Americans, in making money, polishing apples in the dead of night, perfectly pressed pants, perfect credit, being perfect, shooting black people, watching our stores and offices burn down to the ground.

Then, inevitably, if I asked hard questions of myself, of the one who should know, what might I come up with?

What belief did I ever hold in my father, whose daily life I so often ridiculed and looked upon with such abject shame? The summer before I started high school he made me go with him to one of the new stores on Sunday afternoons to help restock the shelves and the bins. I hated going.

My friends—suddenly including some girls—were always playing tennis or going to the pool club then. I never gave the reason why I always declined, and they eventually stopped asking. Later I found out from one of them, my first girlfriend, that they simply thought I was religious. When I was working for him I wore a white apron over my slacks and dress shirt and tie. The store was on Madison Avenue in the Eighties and my father made all the employees dress up for the blue-haired matrons, and the fancy dogs, and the sensible young mothers pushing antique velvet-draped prams, and their most quiet of infants, and the banker fathers brooding about annoyed and aloof and humorless.

My father, thinking that it might be good for business, urged me to show them how well I spoke English, to make a display of it, to casually recite "some Shakespeare words."

I, his princely Hal. Instead, and only in part to spite him, I grunted my best Korean to the other men. I saw that if I just kept speaking the language of our work the customers didn't seem to see me. I wasn't there. They didn't look at me. I was a comely shadow who didn't threaten them. I could even catch a rich old woman whose tight strand of pearls pinched in the sags of her neck whispering to her friend right behind me, "Oriental Jews."

I never retaliated the way I felt I could or said anything smart, like, "Does madam need help?" I kept on stacking the hothouse tomatoes and Bosc pears. That same woman came in the store every day; once, I saw her take a small bite of an apple and then put it back with its copper-mouthed wound facing down. I started over to her not knowing what I might say when my father intercepted me and said smiling in Korean, as if he were complimenting me, "She's a steady customer." He nudged me back to my station. I had to wait until she left to replace the ruined apple with a fresh one.

Mostly, though, I threw all my frustration into building those perfect, truncated pyramids of fruit. The other two workers seemed to have even more bottled up inside them, their worries of money and family. They marched through the work of the store as if they wanted to deplete themselves of every last bit of energy. Every means and source of struggle. They peeled and sorted and bunched and sprayed and cleaned and stacked and shelved and swept; my father put them to anything for which they didn't have to speak. They both had college degrees and knew no one in the country and spoke little English. The men, whom I knew as Mr. Yoon and Mr. Kim, were both recent immigrants in their thirties with wives and young children. They worked twelve-hour days six days a week for $200 cash and meals and all the fruit and vegetables we couldn't or wouldn't sell; it was the typical arrangement. My father like all successful immigrants before him gently and not so gently exploited his own.

"This is way I learn business, this is way they learn business."

And although I knew he gave them a $100 bonus every now and then I never let on that I felt he was anything but cruel to his workers. I still imagine Mr. Kim's and Mr. Yoon's children, lonely for their fathers, gratefully eating whatever was brought home to them, our overripe and almost rotten mangoes, our papayas, kiwis, pineapples, these exotic tastes of their wondrous new country, this joyful fruit now too soft and too sweet for those who knew better, us near natives, us earlier Americans.

For some reason unclear to me I made endless fun of the prices of my father's goods, how everything ended in .95 or .98 or .99.

"Look at all the pennies you need!" I'd cry when the store was empty, holding up the rolls beneath the cash register. "It's so ridiculous."

He'd cry back, "What you know? It's good for selling!"

"Who told you that?"

He was wiping down the glass fronts of the refrigerators of soda and beer and milk. "Nobody told me that. I know automatic. Like everybody else."

"So then why is this jar of artichoke hearts three ninety-eight instead of three ninety-nine?"

"You don't know?" he said, feigning graveness.

"No, Dad, tell me."

"Stupid boy," he answered, clutching at his chest. His overworked merchant heart. "It's feeling."

I remember when my father would come home from his vegetable stores late at night, and my mother would say the same three things to him as she fixed his meal of steamed barley rice and beef flank soup: *Spouse,* she would say, *you must be hungry. You come home so late. I hope we made enough money today.*

She never asked about the stores themselves, about what vegetables were selling, how the employees were working out, nothing ever about the painstaking, plodding nature of the work. I thought it was because she simply didn't care to know the particulars, but when I began to ask him one night about the business (I must have been six or seven), my mother immediately called me back into the bedroom and closed the door.

"Why are you asking him about the stores?" she interrogated me in Korean, her tongue plaintive, edgy, as though she were in some pain.

"I was just asking," I said.

"Don't ask him. He's very tired. He doesn't like talking about it."

"Why not?" I said, this time louder.

"Shh!" she said, grabbing my wrists. "Don't shame him! Your father is very proud. You don't know this, but he graduated from the best college in Korea, the very top, and he doesn't need to talk about selling fruits and vegetables. It's below him. He only does it for you, Byong-ho, he does everything for you. Now go and keep him company."

I walked back to the living room and found my father asleep on the sofa, his round mouth pursed and tightly shut, his breath filtering softly through his nose. A single fly, its armored back an oily, metallic green, was dancing a circle on his chin. What he'd brought home from work.

Once, he came home with deep bruises about his face, his nose and mouth bloody, his rough workshirt torn at the shoulder. He smelled rancid as usual from working with vegetables, but more so that night, as if he'd fallen into the compost heap. He came in and went straight up to the bedroom and shut and locked the door. My mother ran to it, pounding on the wood and sobbing for him to let her in so she could help him. He wouldn't answer. She kept hitting the door, asking him what had happened, almost kissing the panels, the side jamb. I was too frightened to go to her. After a while she tired and crumpled there and wept until he finally turned the lock and let her in. I went to my room where I could hear him talk through the wall. His voice was quiet and steady. Some black men had robbed the store and taken him to the basement and bound him and beaten him up. They took turns whipping him with the magazine of a pistol. They would have probably shot him in the head right there but his partners came for the night shift and the robbers fled.

I would learn in subsequent years that he had been trained as an industrial engineer, and had actually completed a master's degree. I never learned the exact reason he chose to come to America. He once mentioned something about the "big network" in Korean business, how someone from the rural regions of the country could only get so far in Seoul. Then, too, did I wonder whether he'd assumed he could be an American engineer who spoke little English, but of course he didn't.

My father liked to think I was a civil servant. Sometimes he asked Lelia what a municipal employee did on trips to Providence or Ann Arbor or Richmond. Size comparisons, Lelia might joke, but then she always referred him directly to me. But he never approached me, he never asked me point-blank what I did, he'd just inquire if I were earning enough for my family and then silently nod. He couldn't care for the importance of *career.* That notion was too costly for a man like him.

He genuinely liked Lelia. This surprised me. He was nice to her. When we met him at one of his stores he always had a sundry basket of treats for her, trifles from his shelves, bars of dark chocolate, exotic tropical fruits, tissue-wrapped biscotti. He would show her around every time as if it were the first, introduce her to the day manager and workers, most of whom were Korean, tell them proudly in English that she was his daughter. Whenever he could, he always tried to stand right next to her, and then marvel at how tall and straight she was, *like a fine young horse,* he'd say in Korean, admiringly. He'd hug her and ask me to take pictures. Laugh and kid with her generously.

He never said it, but I knew he liked the fact that Lelia was white. When I first told him that we were engaged I thought he would vehemently protest, again go over the scores of reasons why I should marry one of our own (as he had rambled on in my adolescence), but he only nodded and said he respected her and wished me luck. I think he had come to view our union logically, practically, and perhaps he thought he saw through my intentions, the assumption being that Lelia and her family would help me make my way in the land.

"Maybe you not so dumb after all," he said to me after the wedding ceremony.

Lelia, an old-man lover if there was one, always said he was sweet.

Sweet.

"He's just a more brutal version of you," she told me that last week we were taking care of him.

I didn't argue with her. My father was obviously not modern, in the psychological sense. He was still mostly unencumbered by those needling questions of existence and self-consciousness. Irony was always lost on him. He was the definition of a thick skin. For most of my youth I wasn't sure that he had the capacity to love. He showed great respect to my mother to the day she died—I was ten—and practiced for her the deepest sense of duty and honor, but I never witnessed from him a devotion I could call love. He never kissed her hand or bent down before her. He never said the word, in any language. Maybe none of this matters. But then I don't think he ever wept for her, either, even at the last moment of her life. He came out of the hospital room from which he had barred me and said that she had passed and I should go in and look at her one last time. I don't now remember what I saw in her room, maybe I never actually looked at her, though I can still see so clearly the image of my father standing there in the hall when I came back out, his hands clasped at his groin in a military pose, his neck taut and thick, working, trying hard to swallow the nothing balling up in his throat.

His life didn't seem to change. He seemed instantly recovered. The only noticeable thing was that he would come home much earlier than usual, maybe four in the afternoon instead of the usual eight or nine. He said he didn't want me coming home from school to an empty house, though he didn't actually spend any more time with me. He just went down to his workshop in the basement or to the garage to work on his car. For dinner we went either to a Chinese place or the Indian one in the next town, and sometimes he drove to the city so we could eat Korean. He settled us into a routine this way, a schedule. I thought all he wanted was to have nothing unusual sully his days, that what he disliked or feared most was uncertainty.

I wondered, too, whether he was suffering inside, whether he sometimes cried, as I did, for reasons unknown. I remember how I sat with him in those restaurants, both of us eating without savor, unjoyous, and my wanting to show him that I could be as steely as he, my chin as rigid and unquivering as any of his displays, that I would tolerate no mysteries either, no shadowy wounds or scars of the heart.

I thought it would be the two of us, like that, forever.

But one day my father called from one of his vegetable stores in the Bronx and said he was going to JFK and would be late coming home. I didn't think much of it. He often went to the airport, to the international terminal, to pick up a friend or a parcel from Korea. After my mother's death he had a steady flow of old friends visiting us, hardly any relatives, and it was my responsibility to make up the bed in the guest room and prepare a tray of sliced fruit and corn tea or liquor for their arrival.

My mother had always done this for guests; although I was a boy, I was the only child and there was no one else to peel the oranges and apples and set out nuts and spicy crackers and glasses of beer or a bottle of Johnnie Walker for my father and his friends. They used to sit on the carpeted floor around the lacquered Korean table with their legs crossed and laugh deeply and utterly together as if they had been holding themselves in for a long time, and I'd greedily pick at the snacks from the perch of my father's sturdy lap, pinching my throat in just such a way that I'd might rumble and shake, too. My mother would smile and talk to them, but she sat on a chair just outside the circle of men and politely covered her mouth whenever one of them made her laugh or offered compliments on her still-fresh beauty and youth.

The night my father phoned I went to the cabinet where he kept the whiskey and nuts and took out a bottle for their arrival. An ashtray, of course, because the men always smoked. The men—it was always only men—were mostly friends of his from college now come to the States on matters of business. Import-export. They seemed exotic to me then. They wore shiny, textured gray-blue suits and wide ties and sported long sideburns and slightly too large brown-tinted polarizing glasses. It was 1971. They dragged into the house huge square plastic suitcases on wheels, stuffed full of samples of their wares, knock-off perfumes and colognes, gaudy women's handkerchiefs, plastic AM radios cast in the shapes of footballs and automobiles, leatherette handbags, purses, belts, tinny watches and cuff links, half-crushed boxes of Oriental rice crackers and leathery sheets of dried squid, and bags upon bags of sickly-sweet sucking candy whose transparent wrappers were edible and dissolved on the tongue.

In the foyer these men had to struggle to pull off the tight black shoes from their swollen feet, and the sour, ammoniac smell of sweat-sopped wool and cheap leather reached me where I stood overlooking them from the raised living room of our split-level house, that nose-stinging smell of sixteen hours of sleepless cramped flight from Seoul to Anchorage to New York shot so full of their ranks, hopeful of good commerce here in America.

My father opened the door at ten o'clock, hauling into the house two huge, battered suitcases. I had just set out a tray of fruits and rice cakes to go along with the liquor on the low table in the living room and went down to help him. He waved me off and nodded toward the driveway.

"Go help," he said, immediately bearing the suitcases upstairs.

I walked outside. A dim figure of a woman stood unmoving in the darkness next to my father's Chevrolet. It was late winter, still cold and miserable, and she was bundled up in a long woolen coat that nearly reached the ground. Beside her were two small bags and a cardboard box messily bound with twine. When I got closer to her she lifted both bags and so I picked up the box; it was very heavy, full of glass jars and tins of pickled vegetables and meats. I realized she had transported homemade food thousands of miles, all the way from Korea, and the stench of overripe kimchee shot up through the cardboard flaps and I nearly dropped the whole thing.

The woman mumbled something in an unusual accent about my not knowing what kimchee was, but I didn't answer. I thought she was a very distant relative. She didn't look at all like us, nothing like my mother, whose broad, serene face was the smoothest mask. This woman, I could see, had deep pockmarks stippling her high, fleshy cheeks, like the scarring from a mistreated bout of chickenpox or smallpox, and she stood much shorter than I first thought, barely five feet in her heeled shoes. Her ankles and wrists were as thick as posts. She waited for me to turn and start for the house before she followed several steps behind me. I was surprised that my father wasn't waiting in the doorway, to greet her or hold the door, and as I walked up the carpeted steps leading to the kitchen I saw that the food and drink I had prepared had been cleared away.

"Please come this way," he said to her stiffly in Korean, appearing from the hallway to the bedrooms. "Please come this way."

He ushered her into the guest room and shut the door behind them. After a few minutes he came back out and sat down in the kitchen with me. He hadn't changed out of his work clothes, and his shirt and the knees and cuffs of his pants were stained with the slick juice of spoiled vegetables. I was eating apple quarters off the tray. My father picked one, bit into it, and then put it back. This was a habit of his, perhaps because he worked with fruits and vegetables all day, randomly sampling them for freshness and flavor.

He started speaking, but in English. Sometimes, when he wanted to hide or not outright lie, he chose to speak in English. He used to break into it when he argued with my mother, and it drove her crazy when he did and she would just plead, "No, no!" as though he had suddenly introduced a switchblade into a clean fistfight. Once, when he was having some money problems with a store, he started berating her with some awful stream of nonsensical street talk, shouting "my hot mama shit ass tight cock sucka," and "slant-eye spic-and-span motha-fucka" (he had picked it up, no doubt, from his customers). I broke into their argument and started yelling at him, making sure I was speaking in complete sentences about his cowardice and unfairness, shooting back at him his own medicine, until he slammed both palms on the table and demanded, "You shut up! You shut up!"

I kept at him anyway, using the biggest words I knew, whether they made sense or not, school words like "socioeconomic" and "intangible," anything I could lift from my dizzy burning thoughts and hurl against him, until my mother, who'd been perfectly quiet the whole time, whacked me hard across the back of the head and shouted in Korean, *Who do you think you are?*

Fair fight or not, she wasn't going to let me dress down my father, not with language, not with anything.

"Hen-*ry,*" he now said, accenting as always the second syllable, "you know, it's difficult now. Your mommy dead and nobody at home. You too young for that. This nice lady, she come for you. Take care home, food. Nice dinner. Clean house. Better that way."

I didn't answer him.

"I better tell you before, I know, but I know you don't like. So what I do? I go to store in morning and come home late, nine o'clock, ten. No good, no good. Nice lady, she fix that. And soon we move to nice neighborhood, over near Fern Pond, big house and yard. Very nice place."

"Fern Pond? I don't want to move! And I don't want to move there, all the rich kids live there."

"Ha!" he laughed. "You rich kid now, your daddy rich rich man. Big house, big tree, now even we got houselady. Nice big yard for you. I pay all cash."

"What? You bought a house already?"

"Price very low for big house. Fix-her-upper. You thank me someday . . ."

"I won't. I won't move. No way."

Byong-ho, he said firmly. His voice was already changing. He was shifting into Korean, getting his throat ready. Then he spoke as he rose to leave. *Let's not hear one more thing about it. The woman will come with us to the new house and take care of you. This is what I have decided. Our talk is past usefulness. There will be no other way.*

In the new house, the woman lived in the two small rooms behind the kitchen pantry. I decided early on that I would never venture in there or try to befriend her. Her manner unnerved me. She never laughed. She spoke only when it mattered, when a thing needed to be done, or requested, or acknowledged. Otherwise the sole sounds I heard from her were the sucking noises she would make through the spaces between her teeth after meals and in the mornings. Once I heard her humming a pretty melody in her room, some Korean folk song, but as I walked toward her doorway to hear it better she stopped immediately, and I never heard it again.

She kept a clean and orderly house. Because she was the one who really moved us from the old house, she organized and ran the new one in a manner that suited her. In the old Korean tradition, my presence in the kitchen was unwelcome unless I was actually eating, or passing through the room. I understood that her two rooms, the tiny bathroom adjoining them, and the kitchen and pantry, constituted the sphere of her influence, and she was quick to deflect any interest on my part to look into the cabinets or closets. If she were present, I was to ask her for something I wanted, even if it was in the refrigerator, and then she would get it for me. She became annoyed if I lingered too long, and I quickly learned to remove myself immediately after any eating or drinking. Only when a friend of mine was over, after school or sports, would she mysteriously recede from the kitchen. My tall, talkative white friends made her nervous. Then she would wait noiselessly in her back room until we had gone.

She smelled strongly of fried fish and sesame oil and garlic. Though I didn't like it, my friends called her "Aunt Scallion," and made faces behind her back.

Sometimes I thought she was some kind of zombie. When she wasn't cleaning or cooking or folding clothes she was barely present; she never whistled or hummed or made any noise, and it seemed to me as if she only partly possessed her own body, and preferred it that way. When she sat in the living room or outside on the patio she never read or listened to music. She didn't have a hobby, as far as I could see. She never exercised. She sometimes watched the soap operas on television (I found this out when I stayed home sick from school), but she always turned them off after a few minutes.

She never called her family in Korea, and they never called her. I imagined that something deeply horrible had happened to her when she was young, some nameless pain, something brutal, that a malicious man had taught her fear and sadness and she had had to leave her life and family because of it.

Years later, when the three of us came on Memorial Day for the summer-long stay with my father, he had the houselady prepare the apartment above the garage for us. Whenever we first opened its door at the top of the creaky narrow stairs we smelled the fresh veneers of pine oil and bleach and lemon balm. The pine floors were shimmering and dangerously slick. Mitt would dash past us to the king-sized mattress in the center of the open space and tumble on the neatly sheeted bed. The bed was my parents' old one; my father bought himself a twin the first year we moved into the new house. The rest of the stuff in the apartment had come with the property: there was an old leather sofa; a chest of drawers; a metal office desk; my first stereo, the all-in-one kind, still working; and someone's nod to a kitchen, thrown together next to the bathroom in the far corner, featuring a dorm-style refrigerator, a half-sized two-burner stove, and the single cabinet above it.

Mitt and Lelia loved that place. Lelia especially liked the tiny secret room that was tucked behind a false panel in the closet. The room, barely six by eight, featured a single-paned window in the shape of a face that swung out to a discreet view of my father's exquisitely landscaped garden of cut stones and flowers. She wrote back in that room during the summer, slipping in at sunrise before I left for Purchase, and was able to complete a handful of workable poems by the time we departed on Labor Day, when she had to go back to teaching.

Mitt liked the room, too, for its pitched ceiling that he could almost reach if he tippy-toed, and I could see he felt himself bigger in there as he stamped about in my father's musty cordovans like some thundering giant, sweeping at the air, though he only ventured in during the late afternoons when enough light could angle inside and warmly lamp every crag and corner nook. He got locked in once for a few hours, the panel becoming stuck somehow, and we heard his wails all the way from the kitchen in the big house.

"Spooky," Mitt pronounced that night, fearful and unashamed as he lay between us in our bed, clutching his mother's thigh.

Mitt slept with us those summers until my father bought him his own canvas army cot. That's what the boy wanted. He liked the camouflaging pattern of the thick fabric and sometimes tipped the thing on its side and shot rubber-tipped arrows at me and Lelia from behind its cover. We had to shoot them back before he would agree to go to bed.

When he was an infant we waited until he was asleep and then delicately placed him atop our two pillows, which we arranged on the floor next to the bed. We lay still a few minutes until we could hear his breathing deepen and become rhythmic. That's when we made love. It was warm up there in the summer and we didn't have to strip or do anything sudden. We moved as mutely and as deftly as we could bear, muffling ourselves in one another's hair and neck so as not to wake him, but then, too, of course, so we could hear the sound of his sleeping, his breathing, ours, that strange conspiring. Afterward, we lay quiet again, to make certain of his slumber, and then lifted him back between our hips into the bed, so heavy and alive with our mixed scent.

"Hey," Lelia whispered to me one night that first summer, "the woman, in the house, what do you think she does at night?"

"I don't know," I said, stroking her arm, Mitt's.

"I mean, does she have any friends or relatives?"

I didn't know.

She then said, "There's no one else besides your father?"

"I don't think she has anyone here. They're all in Korea."

"Has she ever gone back to visit?"

"I don't think so," I said. "I think she sends them money instead."

"God," Lelia answered. "How awful." She brushed back the damp downy hair from Mitt's forehead. "She must be so lonely."

"Does she seem lonely?" I asked.

She thought about it for a moment. "I guess not. She doesn't seem like she's anything. I keep looking for something, but even when she's with your father there's nothing in her face. She's been here since you were young, right?"

I nodded.

"You think they're friends?" she asked.

"I doubt it."

"Lovers?"

I had to answer, "Maybe."

"So what's her name?" Lelia asked after a moment.

"I don't know."

"What?"

I told her that I didn't know. That I had never known.

"What's that you call her, then?" she said. "I thought that was her name. Your father calls her that, too."

"It's not her name," I told her. "It's not her name. It's just a form of address."

It was the truth. Lelia had great trouble accepting this stunning ignorance of mine. That summer, when it seemed she was thinking about it, she would stare in wonderment at me as if I had a gaping hole blown through my head. I couldn't blame her. Americans live on a first-name basis. She didn't understand that there weren't moments in our language—the rigorous, regimental one of family and servants—when the woman's name could have naturally come out. Or why it wasn't important. At breakfast and lunch and dinner my father and I called her "Ah-juh-ma," literally *aunt,* but more akin to "ma'am," the customary address to an unrelated Korean woman. But in our context the title bore much less deference. I never heard my father speak her name in all the years she was with us.

But then he never even called my mother by her name, nor did she ever in my presence speak his. She was always and only "spouse" or "wife" or "Mother"; he was "husband" or "Father" or "Henry's father." And to this day, when someone asks what my parents' names were, I have to pause for a moment, I have to rehear them not from the memory of my own voice, my own calling to them, but through the staticky voices of their old friends phoning from the other end of the world.

"I can't believe this," Lelia cried, her long Scottish face all screwed up in the moonlight. "You've known her since you were a kid! She practically raised you."

"I don't know who raised me," I said to her.

"Well, she must have had something to do with it!" She nearly woke up Mitt.

She whispered, "What do you think cooking and cleaning and ironing is? That's what she does all day, if you haven't noticed. Your father depends so much on her. I'm sure you did, too, when you were young."

"Of course I did," I answered. "But what do you want, what do you want me to say?"

"There's nothing you *have* to say. I just wonder, that's all. This woman has given twenty years of her life to you and your father and it still seems like she could be anyone to you. It doesn't seem to matter who she is. Right? If your father switched her now with someone else, probably nothing would be different."

She paused. She brought up her knees so they were even with her hips. She pulled Mitt to her chest.

"Careful," I said. "You'll wake him."

"It scares me," she said. "I just think about you and me. What I am . . ."

"Don't be crazy," I said.

"I am not being crazy," she replied carefully. Mitt started to whimper. I slung my arm over her belly. She didn't move. This was the way, the very slow way, that our conversations were spoiling.

"I'll ask my father tomorrow," I stupidly said.

Lelia didn't say anything to that. After a while she turned away, Mitt still tight against her belly.

"Sweetie . . ." I whispered to her. I craned and licked the soft hair above her neck. She didn't budge. "Let's not make this something huge."

"My *God,"* she whispered.

—

For the next few days, Lelia was edgy. She wouldn't say much to me. She wandered around the large wooded yard with Mitt strapped tightly in her chest sling. Close to her. She wasn't writing, as far as I could tell. And she generally stayed away from the house; she couldn't bear to watch the woman do anything. Finally, Lelia decided to talk to her; I would have to interpret. We walked over to the house and found her dusting in the living room. But when the woman saw us purposefully approaching her, she quickly crept away so that we had to follow her into the dining room and then to the kitchen until she finally disappeared into her back rooms. I stopped us at the threshold. I called in and said that my wife wanted to speak with her. No answer. "Ahjuhma," I then called to the silence, "Ahjuhma!"

Finally her voice shot back, *There's nothing for your American wife and me to talk about. Will you please leave the kitchen. It is very dirty and needs cleaning.*

Despite how Ahjuhma felt about the three of us, our unusual little family, Lelia made several more futile attempts before she gave up. The woman didn't seem to accept Mitt, she seemed to sour when she looked upon his round, only half-Korean eyes and the reddish highlights in his hair.

One afternoon Lelia cornered the woman in the laundry room and tried to communicate with her while helping her fold a pile of clothes fresh out of the dryer. But each time Lelia picked up a shirt or a pair of shorts the woman gently tugged it away and quickly folded it herself. I walked by then and saw them standing side by side in the narrow steamy room, Lelia guarding her heap and grittily working as fast as she could, the woman steadily keeping pace with her, not a word or a glance between them. Lelia told me later that the woman actually began nudging her in the side with the fleshy mound of her low-set shoulder, grunting and pushing her out of the room with short steps; Lelia began hockey-checking back with her elbows, trying to hold her position, when by accident she caught her hard on the ear and the woman let out a loud shrill whine that sent them both scampering from the room. Lelia ran out to where I was working inside the garage, tears streaming from her eyes; we hurried back to the house, only to find the woman back in the laundry room, carefully refolding the dry laundry. She backed away when she saw Lelia and cried madly in Korean, *You cat! You nasty American cat!*

I scolded her then, telling her she couldn't speak to my wife that way if she wanted to keep living in our house. The woman bit her lip; she bent her head and bowed severely before me in a way that perhaps no one could anymore and then trundled out of the room between us. I suddenly felt as if I'd committed a great wrong.

Lelia shouted, "What did she say? What did you say? What the hell just happened?"

But I didn't answer her immediately and she cursed "Goddamnit!" under her breath and ran out the back door toward the apartment. I went after her but she wouldn't slow down. When I reached the side stairs to the apartment I heard the door slam hard above. I climbed the stairs and opened the door and saw she wasn't there. Then I realized that she'd already slipped into the secret room behind the closet.

She was sitting at my old child's desk below the face-shaped window, her head down in her folded arms. When I touched her shoulder she began shuddering, sobbing deeply into the bend of her elbow, and when I tried to coax her out she shook me off and dug in deeper. So I embraced her huddled figure, and she let me do that, and after a while she turned out of herself and began crying into my belly, where I felt the wetness blotting the front of my shirt.

"Come on," I said softly, stroking her hair. "Try to take it easy. I'm sorry. I don't know what to say about her. She's always been a mystery to me."

She soon calmed down and stopped crying. Lelia cried easily, but back then in our early days I didn't know and each time she wept I feared the worst, that it meant something catastrophic was happening between us, an irreversible damage. What I should have feared was the damage unseen, what she wouldn't end up crying over or even speaking about in our last good year.

"She's not a mystery to me, Henry," she now answered, her whole face looking as though it had been stung. With her eyes swollen like that and her high cheekbones, she looked almost Asian, like a certain kind of Russian. She wiped her eyes with her sleeve. She looked out the little window.

"I know who she is."

"Who?" I said, wanting to know.

"She's an abandoned girl. But all grown up."

During high school I used to wander out to the garage from the house to read or just get away after one of the countless arguments I had with my father. Our talk back then was in fact one long and grave contention, an incessant quarrel, though to hear it now would be to recognize the usual forms of homely rancor and still homelier devotion, involving all the dire subjects of adolescence—my imperfect studies, my unworthy friends, the driving of his car, smoking and drinking, the whatever and whatever. One of our worst nights of talk was after he suggested that the girl I was taking to the eighth-grade Spring Dance didn't—or couldn't—find me attractive.

"What you think she like?" he asked, or more accurately said, shaking his head to tell me I was a fool. We had been watching the late news in his study.

"She likes *me,"* I told him defiantly. "Why is that so hard for you to take?"

He laughed at me. "You think she like your funny face? Funny eyes? You think she dream you at night?"

"I really don't know, Dad," I answered. "She's not even my girlfriend or anything. I don't know why you bother so much."

"Bother?" he said. *"Bother?"*

"Nothing, Dad, nothing."

"Your mother say exact same," he decreed.

"Just forget it."

"No, no, *you* forget it," he shot back, his voice rising. "You don't know nothing! This American girl, she nobody for you. She don't know nothing about you. You Korean man. So so different. Also, she know we live in expensive area."

"So what!" I gasped.

"You real dummy, Henry. Don't you know? You just free dance ticket. She just using you." Just then the housekeeper shuffled by us into her rooms on the other side of the pantry.

"I guess that's right," I said. "I should have seen that. You know it all. I guess I still have much to learn from you about dealing with women."

"What you say!" he exploded. "What you say!" He slammed his palm on the side lamp table, almost breaking the plate of smoked glass. I started to leave but he grabbed me hard by the neck as if to shake me and I flung my arm back and knocked off his grip. We were turned on each other, suddenly ready to go, and I could tell he was as astonished as I to be glaring this way at his only blood. He took a step back, afraid of what might have happened. Then he threw up his hands and just muttered, "Stupid."

A few weeks later I stumbled home from the garage apartment late one night, drunk on some gin filched from a friend's parents' liquor cabinet. My father appeared downstairs at the door and I promptly vomited at his feet on the newly refinished floors. He didn't say anything and just helped me to my room. When I struggled down to the landing the next morning the mess was gone. I still felt nauseous. I went to the kitchen and he was sitting there with his tea, smoking and reading the Korean-language newspaper. I sat across from him.

"Did she clean it up?" I asked, looking about for the woman. He looked at me like I was crazy. He put down the paper and rose and disappeared into the pantry. He returned with a bottle of bourbon and glasses and he carefully poured two generous jiggers of it. It was nine o'clock on Sunday morning. He took one for himself and then slid the other under me.

"Mah-shuh!" he said firmly. *Drink!* I could see he was serious. *"Mah-shuh!"*

He sat there, waiting. I lifted the stinking glass to my lips and could only let a little of the alcohol seep onto my tongue before I leaped to the sink and dry-heaved uncontrollably. And as I turned with tears in my eyes and the spittle hanging from my mouth I saw my father grimace before he threw back his share all at once. He shuddered, and then recovered himself and brought the glasses to the sink. He was never much of a drinker. *Clean all this up well so she doesn't see it,* he said hoarsely in Korean. *Then help her with the windows.* He gently patted my back and then left the house and drove off to one of his stores in the city.

The woman, her head forward and bent, suddenly padded out from her back rooms in thickly socked feet and stood waiting for me, silent.

I knew the job, and I did it quickly for her. My father and I used to do a similar task together when I was very young. This before my mother died, in our first, modest house. Early in the morning on the first full warm day of the year he carried down from the attic the bug screens sandwiched in his brief, powerful arms and lined them up in a row against the side of the house. He had me stand back a few yards with the sprayer and wait for him to finish scrubbing the metal mesh with an old shoe brush and car soap. He squatted the way my grandmother did (she visited us once in America before she died), balancing on his flat feet with his armpits locked over his knees and his forearms working between them in front, the position so strangely apelike to me even then that I tried at night in my bedroom to mimic him, to see if the posture came naturally to us Parks, to us Koreans. It didn't.

When my father finished he rose and stretched his back in several directions and then moved to the side. He stood there straight as if at attention and then commanded me with a raised hand to fire away.

"In-jeh!" he yelled. *Now!*

I had to pull with both hands on the trigger, and I almost lost hold of the nozzle from the backforce of the water and sprayed wildly at whatever I could hit. He yelled at me to stop after a few seconds so he could inspect our work; he did this so that he could make a big deal of bending over in front of me, trying to coax his small boy to shoot his behind. When I finally figured it out I shot him; he wheeled about with his face all red storm and theater and shook his fists at me with comic menace. He skulked back to a safe position with his suspecting eyes fixed on me and commanded that I fire again. He shouted for me to stop and he went again and bent over the screens; again I shot him, this time hitting him square on the rump and back, and he yelled louder, his cheeks and jaw wrenched maudlin with rage. I threw down the hose and sprinted for the back door but he caught me from behind and swung me up in what seemed one motion and plunked me down hard on his soaked shoulders. My mother stuck her head out the second-floor kitchen window just then and said to him, *You be careful with that bad boy.*

My father grunted back in that low way of his, the vibrato from his neck tickling my thighs, his voice all raw meat and stones, and my mother just answered him, *Come up right now and eat some lunch.* He marched around the side of the house with me hanging from his back by my ankles and then bounded up the front stairs, inside, and up to the kitchen table, where she had set out bowls of noodles in broth with half-moon slices of pink and white fish cake and minced scallions. And as we sat down, my mother cracked two eggs into my father's bowl, one into mine, and then took her seat between us at the table before her spartan plate of last night's rice and kimchee and cold mackerel (she only ate leftovers at lunch), and then we shut our eyes and clasped our hands, my mother always holding mine extra tight, and I could taste on my face the rich steam of soup and the call of my hungry father offering up his most patient prayers to his God.

None of us even dreamed that she would be dead six years later from a cancer in her liver. She never even drank or smoked. I have trouble remembering the details of her illness because she and my father kept it from me until they couldn't hide it any longer. She was buried in a Korean ceremony two days afterward, and for me it was more a disappearance than a death. During her illness they said her regular outings on Saturday mornings were to go to "meetings" with her old school friends who were living down in the city. They said her constant weariness and tears were from her concern over my mediocre studies. They said, so calmly, that the rotten pumpkin color of her face and neck and the patchiness of her once rich hair were due to a skin condition that would get worse before it became better. They finally said, with hard pride, that she was afflicted with a "Korean fever" that no doctor in America was able to cure.

A few months after her death I would come home from school and smell the fishy salty broth of those same noodles. There was the woman, Ahjuhma, stirring a beaten egg into the pot with long chopsticks; she was wearing the yellow-piped white apron that my mother had once sewn and prettily embroidered with daisies. I ran straight up the stairs to my room on the second floor of the new house, and Ahjuhma called after me in her dialect, "Come, there is enough for you." I slammed the door as hard as I could. After a half hour there was a knock and I yelled back in English, "Leave me alone!" I opened the door hours later when I heard my father come in, and the bowl of soup was at my feet, sitting cold and misplaced.

After that we didn't bother much with each other.

I still remember certain things about the woman: she wore white rubber Korean slippers that were shaped exactly like miniature canoes. She had bad teeth that plagued her. My father sent her to the dentist, who fitted her with gold crowns. Afterward, she seemed to yawn for people, as if to show them off. She balled up her hair and held it with a wooden chopstick. She prepared fish and soup every night; meat or pork every other; at least four kinds of *namool,* prepared vegetables, and then always something fried.

She carefully dusted the photographs of my mother the first thing every morning, and then vacuumed the entire house.

For years I had no idea what she did on her day off; she'd go walking somewhere, maybe the two miles into town though I couldn't imagine what she did there because she never learned three words of English. Finally, one dull summer before I left for college, a friend and I secretly followed her. We trailed her on the road into the center of the town, into the village of Ardsley. She went into Rocky's Corner newsstand and bought a glossy teen magazine and a red Popsicle. She flipped through the pages, obviously looking only at the pictures. She ate the Popsicle like it was a hot dog, in three large bites.

"She's a total alien," my friend said. "She's completely bizarre."

She got up and peered into some store windows, talked to no one, and then she started on the long walk back to our house.

She didn't drive. I don't know if she didn't wish to or whether my father prohibited it. He would take her shopping once a week, first to the grocery and then maybe to the drugstore, if she needed something for herself. Once in a while he would take her to the mall and buy her some clothes or shoes. I think out of respect and ignorance she let him pick them out. Normally around the house she simply wore sweatpants and old blouses. I saw her dressed up only once, the day I graduated from high school. She put on an iridescent dress with nubbly flecks in the material, which somehow matched her silvery heels. She looked like a huge trout. My father had horrible taste.

Once, when I was back from college over spring break, I heard steps in the night on the back stairwell, up and then down. The next night I heard them coming up again and I stepped out into the hall. I caught the woman about to turn the knob of my father's door. She had a cup of tea in her hands. Her hair was down and she wore a white cotton shift and in the weak glow of the hallway night-light her skin looked almost smooth. I was surprised by the pretty shape of her face.

"Your papa is thirsty," she whispered in Korean, "go back to sleep."

The next day I went out to the garage, up to the nook behind the closet, to read some old novels. I had a bunch of them there from high school. I picked one to read over again and then crawled out through the closet to turn on the stereo; when I got back in I stood up for a moment and I saw them outside through the tiny oval window.

They were working together in the garden, loosening and turning over the packed soil of the beds. They must have thought I was off with friends, not because they did anything, or even spoke to one another, but because they were simply together and seemed to want it that way. In the house nothing between them had been any different. I watched them as they moved in tandem on their knees up and down the rows, passing a small hand shovel and a three-fingered claw between them. When they were finished my father stood up and stretched his back in his familiar way and then motioned to her to do the same.

She got up from her knees and turned her torso after him in slow circles, her hands on her hips. Like that, I thought she suddenly looked like someone else, like someone standing for real before her own life. They laughed lightly at something. For a few weeks I feared that my father might marry her, but nothing happened between them that way, then or ever.

The woman died sometime before my father did, of complications from pneumonia. It took all of us by surprise. He wasn't too well himself after his first mild stroke, and Lelia and I, despite our discord, were mutually grateful that the woman had been taking good care of him. At the time, this was something we could talk about without getting ourselves deeper into our troubles of what we were for one another, who we were, and we even took turns going up there on weekends to drive the woman to the grocery store and to the mall. We talked best when either she or I called from the big house, from the kitchen phone, my father and his housekeeper sitting quietly together somewhere in the house.

After his rehabilitation, my father didn't need us shuttling back and forth anymore. That's when she died. Apparently, she didn't bother telling him that she was feeling sick. One night she was carrying a tray of food to his bed when she collapsed on the back stairwell. Against her wishes my father took her to the hospital but somehow it was too late and she died four days later. When he called me up he sounded weary and spent. I told him I would go up there; he said no, no, everything was fine.

I drove up anyway and when I opened the door to the house he was sitting alone in the kitchen, the kettle on the stove madly whistling away. He was fast asleep; after the stroke he sometimes nodded off in the middle of things. I woke him, and when he saw me he patted my cheek.

"Good boy," he muttered.

I made him change his clothes and then fixed us a dinner of fried rice from some leftovers. Maybe the kind of food she would make. As I was cleaning up after we ate, I asked whether he had buried her, and if he did, where.

"No, no," he said, waving his hands. "Not that."

The woman had begged him not to. She didn't want to be buried here in America. Her last wish, he said, was to be burned. He did that for her. I imagined him there in the hospital room, leaning stiffly over her face, above her wracked lips, to listen to her speak. I wondered if she could ever say what he had meant to her. Or say his true name. Or request that he speak hers. Perhaps he did then, with sorrow and love.

I didn't ask him of these things. I knew already that he was there when she died. I knew he had suffered in his own unspeakable and shadowy way. I knew, by his custom, that he had her body moved to a local mortuary to be washed and then cremated, and that he had mailed the ashes back to Korea in a solid gold coffer finely etched with classical Chinese characters.

Our gift to her grieving blood.

I went to him this way:

Take the uptown number 2 train to Times Square. Get off. Switch, by descending the stairs to the very bottom of the station, to the number 7 trains, those shabby heaving brick-colored cars that seem to scratch and bore beneath the East River out of Manhattan before breaking ground again in Queens. They rise up on the elevated track, snaking their way northeast to the farthest end of the county. The last stop, mine.

Main Street, Flushing.

I liked the provincial pace of the local train. I could see the play of human movements on the streets below the track. I watched as people struggled to shift themselves forward in the bare morning light, gearing up for the work ahead of them, their ghostly forms drifting in and out of the cluttered maws of the storefronts and garages and warehouses.

The people were thin, even when they looked almost fat they were thin, drawn as they were about their necks and faces. Even this early they were smoking cigarettes and cigars. The steam of fumes, other fires. Breathing it in. They were always loading and unloading the light trucks and cube vans of stapled wooden crates and burlap sacks, the bulging bags of produce like turnips or jicama as heavy on their sloping shoulders as the bodies of their children still asleep at home. They were of all kinds, these streaming and working and dealing, these various platoons of Koreans, Indians, Vietnamese, Haitians, Colombians, Nigerians, these brown and yellow whatevers, whoevers, countless unheard nobodies, each offering to the marketplace their gross of kimchee, lichee, plantain, black bean, soy milk, coconut milk, ginger, grouper, ahi, yellow curry, cuchifrito, jalapeño, their everything, selling anything to each other and to themselves, every day of the year, and every minute.

John Kwang's people.

They must have loved him. Those first days I walked the streets of Flushing, I saw his name everywhere on stickers and posters, the red, white, and blue graphics plastered on the windows of every other shop and car along Kissena, Roosevelt, and Main. Downtown, near a subway entrance, sat a semipermanent wooden booth decorated with bunting and pennants and flags manned by neatly dressed youth volunteers in paper hats. They passed out flyers, pamphlets—*A Message from City Councilman John Kwang*—buttons, ballpoint pens, keychains, lapel pins, every last piece of it stamped with his perfectly angled script, simply signed, *John.*

The sight of his picture was equally evident. Those I saw were mostly modest five-by-sevens (I later learned they were gifts for contributions to his first campaign), plainly framed black-and-white portraits of him, often hung in a kind of sacred paper altar that mom-and-pop businesses tape up on the wall beside the cash register: John Kwang hung there with the first tilled bills of each denomination, a son's Ivy League diploma, a tattered letter of U.S. citizenship from the county clerk of Queens. You saw his face on the walls of restaurants, large-format color pictures of him standing arm in arm with the owners, the captured mood always joyous, celebratory.

One of his longtime staffers, an extremely tall, bitter-faced man named Cameron Jenkins, told us volunteers in a welcome meeting that it was decided the night he won the election that they would run a "permanent" campaign during the term.

"So we've only won the half of it yet," he shouted to us.

Now, Kwang's political machinery was just beginning to market him in the other quarters of the city. The local television stations never would have followed any candidate as much as they did John Kwang, out of fairness and protocol, but the election was more than two years off, and Kwang was denying at every instance his interest in running for mayor.

"But I wouldn't mind being the mayor," he would joke in interviews.

The news directors must have sensed that their viewers liked Kwang's youthful face, his grinning eyes, the tiny, new wrinkles.

Queens had seen a drop in violent crime since his election. The latest school test scores were up. You could think wise John Kwang was responsible. Sherrie Chin-Watt understood this and put him where the viewership wanted him, even outside of Queens. So you saw Kwang in news spots talking with Hispanic youths at a boys' club in Washington Heights, amongst the revelers in black tie at a plush Manhattan hotel party, playing miniature golf with union bosses in Staten Island, walking the streets with black church leaders in Bedford-Stuyvesant. Everywhere he went, what the staffers called a "mini-rally" seemed to develop, impromptu phalanges of citizens and reporters gathering about him on three sides, the fourth always kept open and clear for what the staffers called the "visuals."

This was the first of my jobs for John Kwang. I had been with the campaign for two full weeks and I wasn't getting near him. I was answering phones, photocopying, distributing newsletters on the street. I hadn't even actually met him yet, and had spoken just once in passing to Sherrie Chin-Watt. It was only after I had mollified a rowdy assemblage of twenty or so Peruvians who worked for Korean greengrocers (they were protesting low wages and poor working conditions) that Jenkins and some others identified me as being capable and motivated.

The Peruvians showed up outside the door of the converted storefront of the new office with their tall skinny drums and guitars and handmade placards that read: "Koreans Unfair." No permanent staffers were around to handle them. Sherrie was in Manhattan, Jenkins out of town. The group was becoming boisterous enough to attract attention on the street. I knew that someone in the neighborhood would eventually call a news crew, if they hadn't already. So I invited the men inside and showed them around the offices. I told them that Kwang didn't come in every day, but that when he did I would see that he was fully informed of their grievances. My face, perhaps appearing to them a little like his, seemed to assure them. I said he had some influence with the Korean businesspeople in the community, that he believed in fairness in pay and hard work, but that he could only do so much. What he could do was speak to the grocers in his next address before their business association.

The Peruvians seemed to accept this, if somewhat somberly. One of them, a very short older man with the squarest, broadest face of orange-brown I'd ever seen, said something to them and they all began leaving. At the door I handed each of them Kwang trinkets and souvenirs from a box labeled "Premiums."

Outside, a young reporter and her cameraman were waiting on the sidewalk, ready to capture a provocative scene, but all they got were pictures of the workers exiting the district office carrying *John*-inscribed pennants and bumper stickers, oven mitts and disposable lighters. The camera was running, and some of the Peruvians saw this and began to wave. The small crowd that had gathered in the street joined in, jumping at the lens. Encores of flags. Fingers saying *numero uno.*

The following Monday Jenkins informed me that some of my hours were being reassigned and that I was to work on a media advance team.

We went straight out to the streets. The leader of the team was Sherrie's protégé, another bright young civil attorney out of Boalt, Janice Pawlowsky. Janice was originally from Chicago, sharp-tongued, abrasive, ambitious, and sexy—you maybe thought—like your best friend's mean older sister. About fifteen pounds overweight, a bob of reddish, golden hair. She liked to wear a well-worn thrift-shop leather aviator jacket and black jeans, otherwise, smart dark suits tailored to make her look leaner than she was. All the hungrier. She would tell me in her maniacal westside of Chicago accent that she *really liked* me.

I stayed out of her way.

"Henry!" she yelled to me that morning (Jack and I had decided it was safe to use my own first name). "Stay with me!"

It was raining on us hard, loud. Only Janice had thought to bring an umbrella.

"Don't take your eyes off me! I'm only doing this once, goddamnit!"

Janice Pawlowsky was the Scheduling Manager. It was one of her many jobs. Her mission in this one was to fill every moment of Kwang's waking time with events and meetings and meals. Get him out there at all costs. For a public appearance, she would take me and the other man, a squat, burly college student named Eduardo Fermin, to scout out the area the day before. For the Bedford-Stuyvesant gathering, Janice had already confirmed her plans with church representatives as well as the local Democratic district chairman, who would be on hand to "host" the gathering.

We were practicing a walk-through of the exact paces Kwang would take the next day. For his half-block "tour" of the neighborhood, Janice began on the steps leading up from the subway, her umbrella madly spilling rainwater, and then counted out the twenty seconds that Kwang would stand there and converse with the ministers. She tried to measure all his talking and stops in that same interval, so if they ran a clip of him on the news they'd be pressed to play the whole thing. If she let him talk for minutes and minutes whenever he wanted they'd just pick and choose quotes to suit their story, and not necessarily his. She made him speak in lines that were difficult to sound-bite, discrete units of ideas, notions. You have to control the raw material, she said, or they'll make you into a clown.

Now she stepped down to street level and turned east, moving down the exact middle of the sidewalk. She chose east because there were tidy storefronts and an elementary school playground in that direction, and in the far background—if you were looking head-on at Kwang, as the cameras would—the shape of the Manhattan skyline. She paused after fifteen paces; they would stop here for ten seconds, in front of a Turk-owned deli, enough time for Kwang to make a comment about ethnic fellowship and shake the proprietor's hand. Then they would move on to the end of the block.

Eduardo and I had a simple task: don't let anything or anyone get between Kwang and the cameras. As she walked his steps, Janice indicated places of potential complication, points where foot traffic might impede the track of the small parade, checking to make sure of enough space for the newspeople covering the event. This was free advertising, and although there was a danger in having little or no control over the coverage or commentary, Janice could at least set up the shots by making them striking and obvious for the cameramen.

"TV people are lazy!" she shouted to us over the rain from beneath her umbrella. "You gotta help them out!" Eduardo and I both nodded, our hands shielding our heads.

Janice bought us breakfast in a coffee shop across the street. We sat in a window booth. After the rain stopped we'd do the drill a few more times. Eduardo ordered eight links of sausage and buttered toast, spraying all of it with hot sauce. He sat next to Janice, eating methodically. He looked older than twenty-three. He wore brand-new horn-rimmed glasses and he adjusted them at the corners after each swallow. He was studying political science at St. John's at night, working afternoons for a caterer and volunteering whenever he could for John Kwang. He wanted to go to law school. Janice had obviously chosen him for his bulk; our job, I soon learned, required the ability and willingness to push around bodies, even shove some. Direct the traffic. He'd worked for her nearly a year. He was ideal for the job, centered low as he was in his fireplug body, a plow of well-muscled forearms in front of him, a pulling guard for a sweeping Kwang.

I wasn't as apt as he. My glory years as a physical, athletic presence were at least twenty years behind me, when, in the seventh grade, I was generally the same height and weight as everyone else; I had excelled in football, basketball, baseball, tennis. I eventually grew, but grew skinny. I realized at some point that only my head could compete. I'd always wondered what might have been had I grown to six-foot-three and two hundred pounds. Now, I had been given to Janice's advance team by Jenkins, an ex–basketball star at CUNY, once the kind of kid I could dribble circles around before he grew ten inches and wised up enough to realize he didn't have to chase me, he could hang back near the basket and wait for my approach. Jenkins thought I might prove effective as a kind of herald for John Kwang. Calm the crowd with my amenable Asian face.

At breakfast, Janice wanted to know what I did for money. In the rest of my life. "You seem a little old for this," she said, sculling out spoons of flesh from her half melon. "You don't seem to be one of those I'll-take-the-bullet types."

"You never know."

"Doesn't look that way to me. I'm sure. So what's your deal?" she asked. "What do you really do?"

I cracked the lid of my legend.

"I'm a freelance writer," I said to her. Eduardo glanced up from his plate. "I write for magazines."

"Yeah?"

I picked at the scrambled eggs. "Nothing too exciting. My aim is to do profiles. This is the first big one."

"Yeah, yeah, but there's something else, right?" she said, aiming her spoon at me. I looked straight at her and didn't say anything. There was almost an ugly pause. I raised the corners of my mouth, the way Hoagland taught me. The confidence grin. Then she said: "You're doing something on the side, right?"

I didn't answer.

"You're writing a book or something. A true-crime novel."

"Sort of."

"Of course you are. This is a city of novelists. What's it about?" she said, sitting up in the booth seat. "Wait, I know, it's about John. I mean, it's about someone like John, an ambitious politician."

"I thought John Kwang wasn't ambitious."

"He doesn't want to be the fucking President," Janice sneered. "But then neither do I."

"That surprises me," I said to her.

"Did that surprise you?" she asked Eduardo. She put her arm around his back. "I mean come on, Eddy, was I such a hard-driving bitch right off?"

"I thought you were going for Czar," Eduardo answered. He ordered us more coffee.

"We're getting off the subject," Janice said, pulling the tight dark curls of hair above his ear. "Anyway, we were talking about Henry's secret literary career."

"It doesn't exist," I replied. "I don't have the imagination."

"You're just in need of my help," said Janice, sculling again through her cantalope. "It's one of those stories of corruption and scandal."

"So keep going," I told her.

"This is easy," she answered. "A rising politician with nowhere to go but the top, that's clear, everyone loves him. He's someone like John, a decent, kind, good man and father and husband, like you can't believe he's actually a politician."

"Except?" Eduardo said.

Janice repositioned herself, elbows astride her plate, her round shape pitching forward. She turned to him. "Except, Eddy, there's some slut who knows a dirty fact about him. Maybe it's her, or his mob ties, or that he's secretly a drug kingpin, and she's blackmailing him. He stupidly strangles her one night after a whole lot of kinky sex. He has a devoted staffer—we'll call him *Jenkins*—dispose of the body. Trouble is, Jenkins is a self-hating closet homosexual. He's a raging psychopath. His secret love for John compels him to hold on to her body for horrible acts of mutilation and necrophilia. And cannibalism, of course. All for John. I mean all. But he's soon caught because of the awful smell coming from his apartment. John's afraid that he'll talk, so he has the captain of the precinct, who owes him a favor for covering up his wrongful shooting of a black kid ten years before, make it look like Jenkins commits suicide in his holding cell. Soon after, the captain gets himself killed in a car wreck. Meanwhile, a sharp city reporter—you—who'd heard rumors of the liaison between Kwang and the bimbo, starts adding up the bodies. You enlist the help of the savvy, sensual ADA—yours truly—and begin your own undercover investigation."

"I see where this is going," I said.

"You can with good stories," she answered. She put a hand on Eduardo's bulky shoulder. "A good story will always sell, book or movie or man. Political lesson number one."

Eduardo shrugged. "I like a nice love story."

"Christ," Janice complained. "You Dominicans are so fucking romantic! I don't understand tropical Catholics. We original ones don't believe in love ever after. That's for someone else. Evangelists."

"So what are you?" he asked her.

"Polish, what do you think? You don't need smarts to get into heaven."

"My mother and father are good Catholics," Eduardo said, brushing her off him. "My sisters are Jesuits and my little brother I don't know yet. I'm nothing in particular."

"You're a Democrat," Janice told him.

"I'm a Democrat like John Kwang is a Democrat."

"Which means one who's going to win everything," she said. "You're the only real thing, Eddy," she answered. She looked at me. "Henry and I, we were secretly Reagan Democrats. Selfish cowards. Admit it, I will. I know you Koreans."

"Never," I said.

"See?" Janice told him. "You're the best thing we have. Our party loves you, Eduardo. To death."

"I love the party," he answered, tepidly. "I love the party."

The heavy rains suddenly stopped. Janice was already up at the cash register paying the check. She pointed outside. "Let's do it, guys," she called to us.

We spent the rest of the morning choreographing steps around fire hydrants and mailboxes. At Janice's request I played John Kwang. Eduardo cleared the way. We must have looked like a small troupe of performance artists staging an imaginary event. People on the sidewalk stepped back into doorways to watch us, not knowing what they were looking at. Mostly they were focused on me, whispering, nodding, conjecturing on who I was. Someone important, maybe. Known. Powerful. I was unaccustomed to this scope of attention. With Janice and Eduardo orbiting me like flitting moons I felt like the emperor of a secret world. I put myself in the onlookers' places and considered the scene: here is an Asian man in his early thirties. He could pass for twenty-four. He's pleasant of face, not so much handsome as he is gentle-looking, and pink of cheek; he only shaves in spots. His gait is casual and patient and straight. He's not looking at anything in particular, his gaze too fair. Too fair all around, as though he couldn't offend anybody. So he looks friendly, he looks like he'd be willing to talk to you, but really because of the way his gaze circles about you, gets at your outline instead of your live center, you think he's really stepping back as he approaches, stepping back inside and back away from you so nothing can get around or behind him.

People gathered in the street around us. Janice simply ignored them, directing us instead, figuring in her head the positions of the preachers, the crowd, Kwang, paletting their various skin tones into an ambient mix for the media. She asked that I remind her to bring along a young blonde who temped at the office to be in the throng the next day. "It's like flower arranging," she said to me. "You've got to be careful. Too much color and it begins looking crass."

After Eduardo left for other work at the office, Janice and I drove around Queens. She had me at the wheel. The clouds were clearing, and it was getting warm in her old Datsun. The vinyl seats smelled stale and moldering and were littered with bits of caramel popcorn and skeins of hair and dried-up splatters of soda. The backseat was crammed with cardboard file boxes full of papers and documents and photographs. This was her rolling, touring office. We were taking a local route through the neighborhoods of south Queens so that she could scout appearance locations for John Kwang. She was drinking from a plastic liter bottle of mineral water.

"You never really said anything about what you Koreans believe in," she said.

"Staying out of trouble," I said.

"I can see that," she replied. She penciled some notes on the next day's schedule. "John's been fantastic at that. Everyone seems to love him. He can draw hordes, you know. He has that gift. Not all politicians do. Most have to learn how to do it. Anyway, I want you to expect a lot of media. Another grocer boycott started in the Bronx."

"That must make about six so far this year," I said.

Janice nodded. "It's not so awful, actually. They've been making all his meetings with black groups newsworthy. I'm not being cynical. John's a genuine peacemaker. He does good work and influential people trust him. I think the electorate is really beginning to understand that about him."

"Eduardo admires him," I said. "Maybe loves him."

"I love him," answered Janice. "We all love him. He's genuinely kind. You know he's sexy."

"Really?" I asked.

"Definitely," said Janice. "It's his skin."

I asked, "His skin where?"

"Just his skin," she said, smirking at me. "Anyway, there's such a beautiful glow to it. It looks soft. Like a woman's skin."

"So that's it?" I asked.

"I think so. He has a nice color."

"Pale yellow like silk or pale green like jade?" I said to her.

She smiled with surprise. "Henry, are you giving me shit?"

"No," I said.

"Good," she answered. "You wouldn't have the right. There were so many Asians at Berkeley. In fact all of my friends were Asian. There wasn't anyone else. All my three boyfriends in college. Actually, they were, in a row, Chinese, Japanese, and Korean."

"What were their names?"

"God! Wait, there was Bobby Feng. Ken Nakajima. And John Kim."

"So which one did you like best?"

"How come every Asian man I mention this to has to ask that?"

"We're competitive."

She beamed anyway. "I guess I liked them all. I liked John a hell of a lot. He was the last one. He was an art student. He made collages from magazine pictures and then painted over them. He had long coarse hair."

"What happened?"

"Nothing," she said. "We broke up just before graduation. My parents wanted me back in Chicago before starting law school. They have a pastry shop and bakery. They even said he could come back with me. John didn't want to live in our house and decided to go back to Los Angeles. We had a huge fight. Actually, I mostly yelled at him. He wouldn't say anything back. I called him later from Chicago but he wasn't home and his mother answered. She had no idea who I was. She never knew I existed. He never told them."

"Maybe it only seemed like she didn't recognize your name. Korean parents don't say too much."

"Oh, she did. I told her I was his girlfriend for the last year and a half. She said very politely that I shouldn't call back. Then I told her I was white and Polish. She started shrieking for her husband, I think."

"Probably just shrieking," I said.

Janice frowned. "So I hung up," she said. "I haven't spoken to him since before that. I never understood how he could just drop me like that. Is it a Korean thing? I mean, what kind of person does that? Except for the very end, everything was great between us. We had great sex, too, and that doesn't happen a lot in college. But now I have to think none of it was very good. It was like he'd done his time with me, with a white girl, and then it was over. I almost still hate him. Asshole."

We drove for the next two hours in stops and starts through tight car-jammed streets lined with old row houses. Archie Bunkers. Janice stopped us every now and then and got out and surveyed a corner or a building with her arms crossed tight. We were at an elementary school. She wasn't talking much anymore. I didn't mention to her that I had known at least six John Kims in my life. Kim is a prevalent Korean surname, and the name John is still popular among immigrant parents because they think it's very American, although of course it was more popular twenty-five or thirty years ago, after the wars. I knew I could have tried to comfort her, perhaps telling her how John Kim was probably just as hurt as she was and that his silence was more complicated than she presently understood. That perhaps the ways of his mother and his father had occupied whole regions of his heart. I know this. We perhaps depend too often on the faulty honor of silence, use it too liberally and for gaining advantage. I showed Lelia how this was done, sometimes brutally, my face a peerless mask, the bluntest instrument. And Janice's John Kim, exquisitely silent, was like some fault-ridden patch of ground that shakes and threatens a violence but then just falls in upon itself, cascading softly and evenly down its own private fissure until tightly filled up again.

I watched Janice head away from the car to talk to some people loitering outside the school building. I remembered a day when I visited a Korean friend's house in New Jersey. It was during a winter break from college. We entered Albert's house from the garage and the sweet scents of broiled beef short ribs and spicy codfish soup and sesame-fried zucchini made me think of my own house before my mother died. Then Albert's mother called happily to him in Korean, "Now you've come home!" and although her accent was different, too breathy, nearly Japanese, the inflection of the words was just that of my mother's, so much so that I nearly dropped my duffel and went to the strange-faced woman standing there in the busy kitchen in her soy-sauce-and-oil-splattered apron. And while sitting at dinner listening to her and Albert's father asking their son questions about school, his health, worrying as they were in the very words, in the very tone and gesture of my own growing up, a familiarity arose that should have been impossible but wasn't and made me feel a little sick inside. It wasn't that Albert and I were similar; we weren't, our parents weren't. It was something else. That night, lying in the short bunk bed above snoring Albert, I wondered if anything would have turned out differently had a careless nurse switched the two of us in a hospital nursery, whether his family would be significantly changed, whether mine would have been, whether any of us Koreans, raised as we were, would sense the barest tinge of a loss or estrangement. If I-as-Albert in the bottom bunk were listening to Albert-snoring-as-Henry, would I know the huge wrong that had passed upon our lives?

Janice pranced back to the car all smiles. She pulled in her door with a slam.

"Drive, man, drive," she told me. I accelerated. She'd come upon some information about Mayor De Roos. She said that apparently the tabloid rumors of his extramarital affair with a young black woman were true. The woman worked for the Transit Authority. De Roos was supposed to have seen her at a news conference last year on subway crime, held down inside the station where she sold tokens. Her name was Kiki and she had grown up and still lived in the neighborhood. The people hanging out in front of the school knew her and said she was flashing new clothes and jewelry around the neighborhood, and that a call car could be seen at all hours of the night in front of her apartment building.

Janice sat quietly, spinning doom inside her head. I drove on without direction from her, weaving the noisy four-speed through the nameless streets.

"What are you going to do?" I then said.

"I don't know yet," she answered softly, almost reverently, as if in awe of an angle she might now have. "But you've got to swear, damn it, that you don't know anything about this. I only told you because I had to tell somebody. I trust you, anyway. I might not even tell Sherrie."

"Okay. But why not Sherrie?"

"Sherrie doesn't need to know this. Believe me. I'm protecting her. She'll thank me later. I'm protecting everybody."

She didn't say anything more than that. She flipped to a new page on her legal pad and began scribbling half-sentences. She quickly filled two sheets. I thought at first that she might be trying to hide something from me, bending over the page so, to use somehow the hard fact for her own direct gain. But then she straightened and what I could read glancing over at her notes made it clear that she was plotting for John Kwang alone. She was being a good soldier. She was brainstorming ideas on how to leak something that wasn't hers in the first place. The ideas ranged wildly in practicality and sensibility: call a television news station or a newspaper with a tip; hire a photographer to take pictures of them together; take the pictures yourself; offer the girl money to talk; get some neighborhood kids to slash his call car's tires, trip the fire alarm in her building when he's there; set a real fire; get her arrested; tell De Roos straight out that we have dirt on him and will use it if he ever plays rough.

I figured, too, that what she meant by protection was to put up what staffers called a "Chinese wall" between a release of the information and anyone else high up in the Kwang office, Sherrie Chin-Watt or Jenkins. John Kwang, without mention, would never know of it. I would soon learn that this was typical, that any political life was made up of minor battles and skirmishes, opportunities on the edge of the front discovered or sometimes created by people like Janice Pawlowsky. John Kwang, evidently, had come to trust her judgment and loyalty and willingness to sacrifice herself. It was only later that I fully understood the depth of his trust in the people working under him. I, finally, would prove his trust wrong. And that was the strangeness for me, that someone like Janice, with all her attendant cynicism and ambition, could believe in another person so singularly, that she could shelter her candidate, her man for office, and step in front of angry bullets shot from his opponents or the press.

We kept on scouting neighborhoods for homeless shelters, community centers, training schools, drug rehabilitation clinics, halfway houses. Sites where he might be seen in the coming months. Photo ops. She made me stop several more times. Our last stop, toward dusk, was an abandoned tenement building beside an elevated ramp of the Brooklyn Queens Expressway. She had me get out and stand on the crumbling steps. Then she rambled across the street and peered back at me through her palm-sized director's viewfinder.

"Hold your hand out, like you're shaking with somebody!"

I extended both, like Kwang in our file photos at the office.

"Good! Now go inside the archway and come out!"

I stepped back into the entrance. The walls of the lobby were badly damaged, unsheathed layers of wire and wood and corrugated paper hanging out of gouges in the plaster. The tiled floor was mostly shattered and broken through in places down past the joists. I could see into the basement where mangled parts of children's bicycles lay in dusty heaps.

"Come on out! Slowly, slowly."

I walked out in the light of breaking clouds. I lifted my face to the sky, as commanded. She told me to raise my arms in victory. So I did.

"Freeze," she said. "Awesome."

Our boy, Mitt, was exactly seven years old when he died, just around the age when you start really worrying about your kid. Then, you look long at his tender arms and calves and you wish you could keep him inside the house for the next ten years, buckled up and helmeted. But all of a sudden, more than you know, he's outside somewhere, sometimes even alone, crossing the streets, scaling rocks, wrestling with dogs, swimming in pits, getting into everything mechanical and combustible and toxic. You suddenly notice that all of his friends are wild, bad kids, the kind that hold lighted firecrackers until the very last second, or torment the neighborhood animals. Mitt, the clean and bright one—somehow, miraculously, ours—runs off with them anyway, shouting the praises of his perfect life.

From the time he was four we spent whole summers up at my father's house in Ardsley, mostly so Mitt could troop about on the grass and earth and bugs—the city offering only broken swings and dry swimming pools—and Lelia and I seemed to share an understanding of what would be safest and most healthful for him.

My father would call me each year a few days before Memorial Day and say as if he didn't really care, *Ya, oh-noon-guh-ya?* and I would answer him and say yes, we were coming again this summer, and he could get things ready for us.

The city, of course, seemed too dangerous. Especially during the summer, the streets so dog mad with heat, untempered, literally steaming with possibilities, none of them good. People got meaner, stuck beneath all that hard light and stone. They worked through it by talking, speaking, shouting and screaming, in every language on earth. And the cursing: in New York City, summer is the season of bad language. It shouts at you from propped-up windows, it hangs on gold chains out of cars, it lingers at phone booths, peep booths, in every standing line for movies and museums and methadone.

And then there were the heat waves, the crime waves. The clouds of soot and dust. In the evening it all descended unseen, an invisible ash of distant fires, soiling us everywhere.

So escape. Rent a car, pack it up, drive right into the heart of dreamland. Here, it went by names like Bronxville, Scarsdale, Chappaqua, Ardsley. The local all-stars.

We wanted our boy to know a cooler, softer ground. On the expansive property of my father's house stood high poplar, oak, the few elm not yet fallen with disease. They didn't appear much different to me than they did twenty years before; they looked just as tall, as venerable, the capital of my father's life. And there would wend Mitt, the child of ceaseless movement, leafy stick in hand, poking beneath the shady skirts of the trees for the smallest signs of life.

Lelia and I would watch him from the back patio. My father slept in the sun with a neon-orange golf cap pulled down over his eyes. Sometimes he spoke from beneath it, his weary Korean mumbling, and I could only read the embroidery of the word *Titleist* in place of actually understanding him. Mitt would shout for us from the trees, holding up something too small to see. My father would groan in acknowledgment, lowing the refrain of my youth. *Yahhh.* Mitt, unconcerned, hopped a little dance, his patented jig, waving madly, legs pumping. We waved back. I shouted to him, too loud.

He brought back rocks to us. Dead insects. Live slugs, green pennies, bits of faded magazines. Every kind and condition of bark. Stuff, he said. He arranged them carefully next to my father's chaise like trinkets for barter, all the while recounting to himself in a small voice the catalogue of his suburban treasure. He offered the entire lot to my father.

"I give you a dollar," my father said to him.

"Two!" Mitt cried.

"Lucky silver dollar," the old man countered, as if luck had meant anything in his life.

"The one on your desk?"

"You go get it now," he said, pointing up to the top window of the house.

Mitt liked to carry the coin with him. I knew because he would produce it wherever we were and start rubbing the face with his thumb. My father must have advised him so, told him some Bronze Age Korean mythology to go with it, the tale of a lost young prince whose magic coin is sole proof of his rightful seat and destiny.

A week after the accident, when the nurse at the hospital desk gave me the plastic bag of his clothes, I found the coin in the back flap pocket of his shorts. The coin was warm—the bag must have been left near a window—and I wondered how long the shiny metal could hold in a heat, if it could remember something like the press of flesh.

He loved the old man, adored him. Whenever you looked, Mitt was scaling the wide bow of that paternal back, or swinging from his shoulders, or standing on the tops of his feet so that they walked in tandem, with ponderous, doubled soles.

There were certain concordances. In profile, you saw the same blunt line descend the back of their necks, those high, flat ears, but then little else because Lelia—or maybe her father—had endowed Mitt with that other, potent sprawl of limbs, those round, vigilant eyes, the upturned ancestral nose (like a scrivener's, in my imagination), his boy's form already so beautifully jumbled and subversive and historic. No one, I thought, had ever looked like that.

The kids in my father's neighborhood gave him trouble that first summer. One afternoon Mitt tugged at my pant leg and called me innocently, in succession, a *chink,* a *jap,* a *gook.* I couldn't immediately respond and so he said them again, this time adding, in singsong, "Charlie Chan, face as flat as a pan."

They're just words, I then told him firmly, confidently—in the way a father believes he should—but mostly because I didn't know what else to say. And after the same kids saw Lelia and me play with him in the front yard they started in with other things, teaching him words like mutt, mongrel, half-breed, banana, twinkie. One day Mitt came home with his clothes soiled and said that they had pushed him down to the ground and put dirt in his mouth. He proudly told my father that he hadn't cried. Lelia, who up to now had been liberal and assured, started shrieking angrily about suburbia, America, the brand of culture we had to live in, and packed Mitt up the stairs to scrub his muddy face, telling him all the while how wonderful he was.

That evening my father and I went around the neighborhood to talk to the parents. We walked stiffly in silence on those manicured streets, and it seemed a repetition of a moment from many years before, when an older boy named Clay had taken away my cap pistol. I remembered how my father had spoken to Clay's mother in a halting, polite English and how he had excused her son for taking advantage of my timidity and misunderstandings.

"My son," he explained, "is no good for friends." The woman hardly understood what he said, and Clay—grinning to himself behind her and looking more menacing than ever—only temporarily handed over my toy gun.

Now, as the first front door opened, I spoke calmly and severely, explaining the situation as one of gravity but not crisis. But then, at the sight of the offending boy, the old man behind me inexplicably exploded, chopping the air with his worn fingers, cursing red-faced like a cheated peasant in our throaty mother tongue until the bewildered child began to cry. His mother protested meekly (you could tell she knew my father) and I, too, wanted him to stop yelling, to shut up and let me speak. Instead I allowed myself to sacrifice this boy and his mother, perhaps even myself, and let the old man yell this one bloody murder, if only for Mitt.

I know this: a child doesn't forgive or forget—he works it out.

By that last summer Mitt was thick with them all. Friends for life, or so it must have seemed. I knew their names once, could place them with their well-fed faces. After he died they all seemed to get hidden away somewhere, like sets of precious china, and eventually I forgot everything about them.

But for a long time the little arms and legs and voices were part of my nightly ritual before sleep. Like a cinematic mantra, a mystical trailer of memory, I replayed the scene of all those boys standing in the grass about the spontaneous crèche of his death. Lelia knew I did this with the night. She would grasp my hand until she couldn't wait any longer for me to say something, and finally she would fall asleep. When her hand went limp, I would let myself wander over the ground of what happened. I could only see it when she slumbered. I needed her right next to me, I thought, bodied up, but off in another world.

I was just coming back from the store with more soda and candy for the birthday party. A boy came running out toward the car, leaping and waving his hands. He was sick-looking, half-smiling and jumping. As I turned the car into the driveway I heard nervous, confused shouts echoing from the backyard through the tops of the trees. I ran around the side of the house without turning off the ignition. All the boys were standing there lock-kneed. In the middle of them was Lelia, sitting on the grass, cradling his dead blue head in her arms and lap and rocking on her knees. She was wailing nothing I could understand or remember now, and she sounded like someone else, an anybody on the street. A boy to my side was crying fitfully and telling me between gasps how they didn't mean to stay on him as long as they did. *It was just a stupid dog pile,* he kept shouting, *it was just a stupid dog pile.* And then my father came out from the sliding porch door and saw me, a cordless phone in his hand, and he yelled in Korean that the ambulance was coming. But before he made it to us his legs seemed to fold under him and he sat back unnaturally on the matted lawn, his face so small-looking, arrested, so short of breath.

I bent down and started blowing into Mitt's mouth. Lelia cried that she'd tried already. She kept screaming about it and I had to tell her to shut up. I didn't know what I was doing. I pulled open his mouth and blew anyway, a dozen times, a hundred, pumping down on his chest with all my weight, eventually pounding on him as if he were solid ground. I shudder to think that I might have injured him, hurt his delicate breastbone or his ribs, or worse, that his last thought was to ask why his father was harming him. I've read the dying feel no pain but sense everything that goes on around them. They view the scene from a brief distance above and no matter who they are or how old, they gain a wisdom from that last vista. But we are the living, remaining on the ground, and what we know is the narrow and the broken. Here, we are strewn about in the lengthy expanse of an archipelago, too far to call one another, too far to see.

During certain nights, I pulled a half-sleeping Lelia back onto my body, right onto my chest, and breathed as barely as I could without falling faint. I could see her wake, flutter a moment, look for my eyes. She let herself balance on me until she was no longer touching the bed. She knew what to do, what to do to me, that I was Mitt, that then she was Mitt, our pile of two as heavy as the balance of all those boys who had now grown up. We nearly pressed each other to death, our swollen lips and eyes, wishing upon ourselves the fall of tears, that great free anger, that great obese heft of melancholy, enough of it piling on at once so that sometimes whether we wanted to or not we made love so hard and gritty we had to say fuck to be telling the very first part of the truth. In the bed, in the space between us, it was about the sad way of all flesh, alive or dead or caught in between, it was about what must happen between people who lose forever the truest moment of their union. Flesh, the pressure, the rhymes of gasps. This was all we could find in each other, this the novel language of our life.

Mornings brought sober hope, then the usual imperatives. Look for Lelia (she was most often gone before I woke, already off somewhere in the city working with students). Now, keep thinking. Think for keeps. Then, isolate the wonderments, the curiosities of his death; they will help you to see. Shed sentimentality. Stop this falling in love with fate. Reside, if you can, in the last place of the dead.

Maybe this way:

A crush. You pale little boys are crushing him, your adoring mob of hands and feet, your necks and heads, your nostrils and knees, your still-sweet sweat and teeth and grunts. Too thick anyway, to breathe. How pale his face, his chest. Blanket his eyes. Listen, now. You can hear the attempt of his breath, that unlost voice, calling us from the bottom of the world.

Lelia and Mitt used to play around with a tape recorder I sometimes brought home from the office. It was a palm-sized model, voice-activated, that I used in the beginning for making notes to myself about work. I didn't need to use it much later on. Mitt especially liked the microcassettes the machine used. He would peer at their miniature opaque housings, twist them around in the light, and he was always holding them up to his ear and shaking them, as if trying to rattle loose their secrets. He said to me once that these little ones could hear you even when you whispered, so that you had to be extra careful of what you said.

I knew he sometimes watched me speak into the machine. Later I saw him mimicking me; he would recline on the sofa with his little legs propped on pillows, speaking intermittently into the recorder as though he were taking drags on a cigarette. He'd talk about imaginary people in an aimless, child's way. After a while he expertly put in another tape, pretending to mark the old one with a name or note. When he was a little older, he would actually make recordings of himself and sometimes of us, the machine being small enough that he could hide it easily. Of course I feared his perceptiveness, what he might have seen of me, or even possibly thought in his young mind.

But I knew, too, that he got the notion of being careful of what you said mostly from being with us, his father and his mother, how we were beginning to speak to one another during the course of a day with more waiting and quiet than any real noise or talk. I remember him playing in the park one weekend when he was five, tumbling as he would on the black rubber beneath the playground ladders and nets, with Lelia and me sitting on a bench a few feet away. We were arguing quietly, or at least I was. I kept looking around to make sure that the other parents couldn't hear us. Lelia didn't seem to care. She wasn't yelling but her voice was clear enough that when she raised it in the crisp autumn air I thought all of downtown could hear our trouble.

We were discussing the question of another child. I knew Lelia herself wasn't fully sold on the idea, but she kept making the argument that for her it was getting to be now or never. I told her we could have one in a few years, that she'd only be thirty-three. She argued that things can happen after a certain age. Complications. We'll be careful, I said. And wiser, as well. Then why not wait until I'm forty, she said. We'll be absolutely brilliant when I'm forty-five. At sixty we'll be goddamn geniuses. I asked her not to make a scene of it, and I could see that she was about to shout out but then just as quickly she quelled herself—a trick perhaps that she had gleaned from me—and whispered sharply that if I wanted to wait I had better be willing to talk about adoption again.

Of course she knew my feelings. Adoption, I know, is a noble and mostly happy practice. No doubt an advancement for a culture. And yet for me, the prerogative is that you should still bestow your blood whenever able. You grow your own. For although your offerings of unconditional love and respect and devotion will make good of most any child, what you cannot give or else substitute is that tie unspoken and unseen, the belief in blood, that unbreakable connection telling your boy or girl that hers will never be a truly solitary life.

Mitt then shouted and ran to us, thrusting himself face first into Lelia's chest and arms. She opened her wool coat and wrapped him up. She kissed his head. His rosy face just now untucked itself, the whole moment marsupial, strangely wondrous that way, and I thought if I had tasted a family hunger all my life that this should be my daily bread. What else is there to behold? I watched her kiss him again. But I said coldly to her anyway, "You know there's really no chance for that."

She didn't say or do anything that might disturb Mitt. She was always too protective that way. She wouldn't look at me. She just kept combing his hair with her fingers, kissing it in the spots where it was irritated with the psoriasis he often had. Sometimes he even got little patches of baldness on the back of his head, and she checked for them now, sifting through his dark brown strands with slow method. When she found one she made a tight face, touching the bare skin softly with her thumb.

"It's not possible," I said again.

"We'll talk about this later," she answered stiffly, still examining him.

"You wanted to talk before," I pointed out to her.

"I changed my mind."

"Well, too late."

"Henry," she said weakly. "Stop this now."

Mitt had slipped back down into her coat, out of sight. There was some struggling inside. She unzipped her front and he bolted away immediately. He found his friends again near the concrete monkey barrels and started playing with them like he hadn't missed a beat. Normally this would have been when Lelia started something, shook up the embers, but sitting there on the end of the bench she looked all frozen and chipped. No chance of fire. Then I didn't know what I wanted. I got up to walk around the playground. I thought to look at all the children, the many colors of them, listen to the shouting music of their mixed-up voice, inflections of a hundred home languages. As I came back around I looked all over for Mitt. I didn't see him. Lelia was still sitting on the bench, and this panicked me, made me angry that she wasn't keeping a close eye on him. I felt angry with myself. Then I heard his voice among the others. I bent down to look in one of the concrete barrels on its side, and inside were Mitt and two other boys, the three of them crouched like commandos around the micro-recorder. I stepped back a little. They were too busy to notice me. He was showing them how it worked, that you turn it on and just talk, you press this button and wait and then listen. They tried this back and forth, taking turns saying things, making gun sounds, fart sounds, their yabba-dabbas, and when he rewound the tape and played it back our voices spoke instead from the hollow barrel, the tight grim interchange. Mitt said he didn't want to play and skipped out the other end. I watched as he picked up speed and ran toward his mother, who saw him and opened wide her arms.

Now that Lelia was back from the islands for a few weeks I called her at Molly's and I asked if I could have the tapes for a while. She took them whenever she settled somewhere semipermanently. I said I wanted to hear his voice. She was quiet and then told me she would leave them with the super downstairs. She said it was a long time since we had seen each other and that there was no sense in doing anything before the meeting we had already planned. I wondered if she realized that it was her voice, too, that I wished to hear. Her responses to our son, their laughter, the simple, ambient noise of that time. Back at the apartment I rigged the micro-recorder up to our stereo.

"Hey," I listened to her say on a tape, "what happened to the dinosaurs Daddy gave you? You had so many in that box."

"I think they died," he answered. Mitt must have been three.

"How?"

"I dunno," he said. "See my Gobot, laser guns come out of his chest and shoot. See? Pht-pht. Pht-pht-pht."

"Swell."

"Too bad you don't have guns there, too, then you could shoot dumb Alex."

"I thought Alex was your friend."

"Nope," Mitt answered.

"Did something happen when he came to play? You were playing, weren't you, with the dinosaurs?"

"Uh-huh. He wanted to see them. He said dinosaurs were dumb. He said they were no-brains."

"Well, to be honest, they weren't very bright."

Mitt made the shooting sound again. "Alex said they were dumb. He said his Godzilla was smart and my T-rex was dumb and had no brains so he took my bat and smashed its head."

"That wasn't very considerate of him," she said.

"He was right."

"What do you mean?"

"No-brains. We smashed the other ones, too. All of them. They're under my bed. Nothing in them. He was right."

"They're just plastic toys, sweetie. Real dinosaurs had brains, very small ones, but they did have them." Pause. "I wish you hadn't broken them like that."

"Alex said that's why they're *a-stink*. Dumb-dumbs."

"That's not necessarily true. And the word is *ex-tinct.* When an animal completely dies off, every last one of its kind, then you say it's extinct."

"Will people get a-stink?"

"Extinct. We can, if we're not careful."

"Will you and Daddy?"

"That's different, but no, sweetie, I hope not, not us. We'll try our best."

"Good," Mitt said.

I went through and listened to the whole box of tapes. It was only the second time I was hearing them, and I noticed again how much care Lelia took while talking with him, not just with the words, but with her manner, so unstudied, calm. I thought how lucky he was to have had a woman like her directing his life. It struck me, too, how she spoke to him as though they had all the time in the world.

She did get angry with him on some of the later tapes, when he was older and his own quick temper (an inheritance from my father) overcame him. On one he called her a "jerkface," and she must have hit him hard on the ass because there was a pause and he said it didn't hurt but then he began to cry. Lelia cried a little with him. Sometimes they seemed to forget about the tape recorder, especially Lelia, who had a habit of talking to herself if she was short on cigarettes. One entire tape was Mitt saying every bad word he knew. I had to wonder about his expensive private-school yard. The worst bad word, he whispered, was "motherfucker." Some tapes had them singing Christmas carols, singing Michael Jackson, singing the teapot song. The last one I listened to was an extended birthday card to me. Mitt said I love you four times. Lelia, three.

I compared these to some of the other moments that I remembered her saying it, the night we decided to live together, the morning after Mitt was born, the time drunk in a bar when she thought I had been sleeping with another woman.

I never felt comfortable with the phrase, had a deep trouble with it, all the ways it was said. You could say it in a celebratory sense. For corroboration. In gratitude. To get a point across, to instill guilt in your lover, to defend yourself. You said it after great deliberation, or when you felt reckless. You said it when you meant it and sometimes when you didn't.

You somehow always said it when you had to.

I sorted the tapes and went out in the streets. It was late, warm for February, and I called Molly's apartment from a pay phone but hung up before anyone could answer.

Molly was a filmmaker and a performance artist. She was smart, generous, her looks unquestionably homely, queer, egregiously frank, hip to the bones. Her swaddling clothes must have been black. Sometimes I thought she could have been a very beautiful Jimmy Durante. She was becoming mildly famous. She enjoyed a renown in Europe. I saw in a store once some German posters for retrospective festivals of her work. Years before we would go to some blacked-out converted garage or artists' space to watch her latest show. Now she played places like the Ritz, and her short films were shown at the MOMA and Angelika.

Molly would sometimes call me from the pay phone outside in the street, to tell me what was going on with my wife. She thought I should know. We both acknowledged how painfully adolescent and insipid we were being with these third-party phone calls—we'd joke harshly about zits, menstruation, jerking off—but then over the line I could hear the street behind her, the din of a thousand hurried movements, my wife maybe becoming just one of them, hidden and indistinguishable.

I walked a few more blocks and then telephoned again. No one this time. I walked to Molly's building anyway. She lived on the second floor. When I got there her windows were black. I wondered if they were asleep. I entertained an urge to find a pebble and throw it up against the panes but then there weren't pebbles in the streets of New York, nothing small enough for anything cute, just hunks of broken brick, quart beer bottles. I would have to effect something in between. I flanked my hands to my mouth and said her name. I was whispering. I said it again, this time loud enough to feel it in my throat. I was ready to say it again, maybe yell it, but a light went on and the window opened and Lelia peered down at me. From her silhouette I could tell she had cut off all of her hair. The naked line of her head and neck reminded me of Mitt.

"Henry," she said in a rough, sleepy voice, "is that you?"

"Yes," I answered.

"God," she said. "You better come up, then."

In the doorway, she was wearing a white cotton nightgown that fell to her thigh. I could see the darkness of her nipples. She looked skinny to me, even gaunt, but I probably thought that because of her hair. Nothing left. The color seemed darker, what had been traces of a reddish hue were now gone, and only her roots were left, the fine nubs rich and brown. I beat down the idea that her cutting of it was a statement intended for me. Women, I know, sometimes have themselves shorn at those watershed moments of their lives, like discarding the memory of a man.

"I thought we had a plan," Lelia said, rubbing her eyes.

"I'm sorry."

"I know, I know."

Lelia was sleeping in the sofa bed. On the lamp table were her reading glasses and a high pile of books. She slumped into one of Molly's leather beanbags. I sat below her on the rug with my feet out. Her knees were bony, white. Now she stretched the nightgown over them.

"Your hair looks good short," I said. "It hasn't been that way since El Paso."

"Oh, c'mon, it looks terrible. I cut it myself. Thus I discovered another talent I don't have."

"Why didn't you let Molly cut it?" Molly always cut our hair.

"She wanted to. She was watching me and crying the whole time. I told her to go away. I didn't mean to be cruel."

"Is she here?"

"Nope. On a date. Looks like she won't be back tonight."

She looked for a cigarette, but didn't find one. I thought for a moment that the tenor of her voice sounded like mine in those many months of our trouble, clipped, almost dead.

"I listened to the tapes tonight," I said, trying not to sound sentimental. "I decided to wander over."

"I bet," she said, crossing her arms. "Though I doubt you've ever really wandered."

"I wander a lot."

"Oh, that's good," she replied. "But only in the place and time of your choosing. The word for that is *invasion.*"

"So shoot me."

She cocked her thumb and aimed right between my eyes.

"Pow."

I could see she wasn't in a horrible mood.

She said, "Anyway, you're here. I guess I don't mind, Henry, but you're always doing this."

"Doing what?"

"What?" she laughed. "You preempt! Our supposed meeting next week, for starters. We had it all planned out, remember? What we've been talking about for the last month. Take it slow, gradual. Just like you said we should. I was heeding you."

"I know."

"Since I've been back you're always calling just as I'm getting into bed, or stepping out of the shower, or just when I've locked the door behind me. I rush to the phone and then of course it's you. Now I wait five seconds before bolting the lock. It's crazy. You always want to talk when I can't."

"I know."

"Well, please please please cut it out."

"I'll try."

"Okay." She took a deep breath. "How is Jack? I think I truly miss Jack."

"He's fine. He misses you. He wants to hear about the islands. I want to hear about the islands."

Her expression dimmed. I knew the time was wrong. The trip to the islands would be off limits. I was promising myself that I wouldn't make it painful, whatever she told me. Anything.

But of course I knew that certain events must have occurred.

"How did Mitt sound?" she asked, sensing my silence.

"Great. Really great. It's amazing."

She shifted in the mass, sitting up. She said, "I haven't listened to the tapes in a long time. I don't think they would depress me anymore, but I know I still couldn't do anything afterwards. I'd just stop moving for a few days."

"He rings in your ears."

"Maybe," she answered, playing with the tiny pink flowerets at the base of her collar. "I keep remembering how I sat in the window with my feet hanging out and the tape machine between my legs. The volume on high so the people would look up. I didn't mind looking a little suicidal."

"You scared the shit out of me."

She chuckled. "You only saw me on the weekends. You had a place to go at least. You could hide up there with Jack. You could do what you do. What you still do. Oh my god, do I not want to talk about that now."

"Let's not, then."

She let her head fall over the back of the beanbag. "You know I listened to everybody about getting back to my life. Back to my life. *As if.* I even listened to my mother! You don't know, but at school I worked those poor kids to the bone. I'd end up yelling all the time. They'd cry and cry. I kept telling myself they were just little grown-ups, that they could handle anything."

"It got you through."

"Sorry, but I was a low-down bitch."

"No you weren't."

"Damn it, Henry!"

She got up. "Shit. I'm sorry. Do you want a drink? I'm having one."

She went into the kitchen and came back with two lowballs of ice and a bottle of scotch. She poured for us. We were silent for a few minutes. She was drinking with both hands around her glass. She was going at it. As usual I was trying to keep up with her, wanting to get to the same page, and I was suddenly reminded of the fact that she always drank a little too much and that I never drank enough.

She finally said, "Where were we?"

"You were hurting."

"There's a phrase."

"So was I," I offered.

"You did a great job hiding it," she said sharply. "I'm sorry, Henry, I don't want to be no fun but I'm not going to let you step into the middle of my night and start revising our history. History is clear here. You were solemn and dignified. Remember? That's who you were for about a year. The bowing, the white-glove bit. You're the one who calmly explained to everyone how well we were doing. Of course I was the mad and stupid one. The crazy white lady in the attic."

"I did what I could."

"Yeah?"

"That's right."

"And I didn't?"

So we'd traveled back to square one.

"I'm such a dope," she said, taking a deep sip. "Say I'm a dope."

"I'm a dope."

"Good," she said. She was rolling the glass against her cheek. "Why did I ever let you in tonight?"

"I guess you're just kind and good."

"I am *not* good," Lelia said. "Ask Molly."

"She hasn't said anything to me."

"Oh, so is she your spy now?"

"Sometimes."

"Not all the time?"

I said, "Only when I'm really desperate."

That seemed to soften her. She said, "I always knew Molly liked you better. I should have stayed with Mother. I'd be absolutely crazy, of course. I went to Boston last week. You probably know that, right? I should have stayed with Mother. But being there is like having another conscience knocking around. I hate what I hear but I listen. Why is it that when I'm up there I wear lipstick to breakfast and wrap up my used tampons in newspaper? It's like I'm giving the garbageman a present. And I think she's getting worse and worse. She's so frightfully scared of everything and everyone but Lord knows she's become the most awful snob on earth. I've begun to think those conditions are related. Of course, like everyone else, she completely adores you. She says you're old-style charming, like back in 1957."

"My kind didn't exist for her then."

"You should have. I think it's a crush for life."

"I'm her exotic," I said. "Like a snow leopard. Except I'm not porcelain."

"The things she doesn't know," Lelia said. She half-tilted her glass, in truce. "But maybe she sees something."

I made an act of toasting her mother, which made Lelia laugh. I said, "Has she gone outside at all?"

Lelia shrugged. "Does the sunroom count? Otherwise, no. She's stopped seeing her therapist. After all these years she's suddenly scared of him, and I'll tell you the man looks like Walter Cronkite. Frankly, I don't know what's going to happen to her. The house smells like death. Perfume of old-lady-death. Lilacs and cat piss. I never thought my mother's house would get to this. And she looks so old all of a sudden. What should I do, Henry? I'm sick."

"What about Stew?" Stew was her father.

"His line's always busy. She won't call him, anyway. I think out of everything she's definitely most afraid of Stew. In that way I guess I'm no different."

I didn't answer. I knew that I was afraid of him, too. And what it was about Lelia that I desired and feared came partly through his bloodline running through her, the openness and exuberance and all that hard focus she could sometimes call up. She got the drinking from him, too. Her father was one of those tall, angular, self-embalming types. All balls and liver. His kind predated the notion of alcoholism. Groton, Princeton, Harvard Business School. His neatly clipped silver hair and tailored suits and unmitigating stare of eyes and trim old body said it all over in simple, clear language: Chief Executive Officer. Do not fuck with this man.

He generally liked me, tended to treat me, I thought, as he might some rising young VP in his Boston-based holding company, alternatingly coddling and browbeating me. His talent didn't necessarily reside in a wisdom for capital and markets but rather in an expert and unflinching opportunism, the hunch for the big kill. I could imagine him regarding a long shiny table of company directors with the savor of some poor bastard's blood lolling like an unguent in the back of his mouth.

During the first year of our marriage Lelia and I went up for a month to his beach house in Maine, and I remember how he'd have a glass in hand all day and evening, a lead crystal tumbler of scotch and ice. He possessed a certain grace with the glass in his hand, the way he'd hold himself with it thrust toward the ocean like one man's saving beacon, the dying yellow light hitting it from behind him and sparking the amber. He drank only scotch, only one brand, and when I went down once to the cellar to fetch us more booze I stumbled on dozens of empty case boxes of it, their sleeves flattened and the bottoms punched out, the cardboard neatly stacked about the cellar like hay piles as high as my thighs. I liked drinking with him partly because it was something I didn't do with my father, who never learned to enjoy the taste of liquor or the casual slip of conversation that alcohol made possible between people who would never otherwise be friends.

"I'll say it right now," Stew said to me the night we arrived, "when I first found out that Lelia was dating you I didn't like it one bit. I'm showing my cards here. Put yourself in my place. I'm saying, who in the hell were you? Sure, some bright Oriental kid. And then when she told us you were getting married, I nearly yanked the phone out of the wall. I said some things to her that night I now regret. Did she ever relate them to you?"

"I think she said you weren't 'thrilled.' "

He let out a shout, his booze spilling over the edge of his glass, now over the salt-bleached wood of the deck. I could see Lelia and Bimma (Stew's companion at the time) through the small kitchen window, drying and putting away the dishes. He was leaning against the rail. "Typical of her. So I wasn't so happy. I said some things about you. Heat-of-the-moment variety. But I didn't know you then."

"You hardly know me now."

"Of course I do." He jiggled his drink, as if to reset himself. "I can see you now, and that makes all the difference. Before that you were just a bad idea. I can see now why Lelia chose you. She's always been a little too unsteady. I like to say she's a Mack truck on Pinto tires. She needs someone like you. You're ambitious and serious. You think before you speak. I can see that now. There's so much that's admirable in the Oriental culture and mind. You've been raised to be circumspect and careful. It's no wonder we're getting our heads handed to us. It's a new world out there. Different players now. Different rules. Say, Lelia tells me your father is a fine businessman."

"Absolute best," I said, taking a long sip.

"He had to be," he replied. "No one was going to help him if he failed. I wish I had spoken to him more at the wedding. I saw a man who didn't have to make a display of himself. You knew he walked every inch to where he is. He owes no one, and he can't conceive of being owed something. That's the problem with us right now, it's that we have a country here of people, both rich and poor, who think they're entitled to everything good in life. I read a newspaper article about a young couple with two small children. You know the story. Hot-dog gumbo for dinner. Of course, neither of them is working. They're on welfare and food stamps but they still somehow have enough money for cable and long distance. They tell the reporter they *need* them."

"They probably do."

"Balls! We've grown into a spoiled culture. Japan, thank God, is going the same way, the first signs are there. I go there a half dozen times a year and I can see things are on a downswing. You Koreans are really doing a number on them, in certain areas. You're kicking some major butt around the world."

"I'm not kicking anyone's butt, Stew."

"You're young," he said encouragingly, now sitting down next to me. He refilled my glass with two gurgling splashes from the bottle. "Listen. No more bullshit. I know what you do for a living. Wait, wait. Just hold on. Lelia never says anything, she refuses up and down, if you know what I mean, but I know. No shame necessary. I take one look at you and *I know.* A year ago we had to send a man into our Brussels R and D facility. Someone was leaking a new manufacturing process to a German competitor. The guy did a bang-up job. Deep deep throat. We were able to clean out the whole traitorous mess. Two shitheads are now in the cooler, including the manager of the lab. Even better, we're still royally screwing the Germans over it. Icing *pour moi.*"

"*Beaucoup* icing *ici,*" I said. I was officially drunk.

"So here's the moral of the story. The mole did the job, is what I'm saying. Truth? I love him. He exposed everyone's ass. Now the facility is running cleaner and tighter than ever. I'll tell you, we have plans to send a man into every single business we own."

"Someone is always stealing something."

"You read my mind," Stew said, clinking my glass.

By the end of the evening he grew quiet. "So tell me, Henry, are you two thinking about kids?"

"We're still thinking," I answered. I realized Lelia hadn't told him that she was already—unexpectedly—pregnant. It had happened almost immediately after the wedding. Our tiny not yet Mitt.

"If money's the issue. You know. We don't have to tell our little girl. Just say you got a big bonus."

"Our money's okay."

"Fine then. You know, I'll admit I'm looking forward to having grandchildren. You never think about it until the opportunity arises. Suddenly, the idea has a true appeal to me. My only child's children. I'm going to retire in a few years. I don't golf or fish. Has my ex-wife talked this way?"

"Not to me," I told him. "I think we're going to see her Labor Day weekend. I don't know what she's said to Lelia."

"Right. Anyway, I don't care what they look like. No offense. I thought about it and I don't really give a damn if they look like a goddamn UNICEF poster, though I think they'll probably be damn nice to look at. You two think about it. A little baby granddaughter, or grandson. Anyhow, just make some babies, for the old folks. Make some babies for us."

It was late, past two in the morning, and Lelia and I lay down on the sofa bed. She left the reading light on. Although we weren't avoiding it, we weren't touching each other. I was still in my street clothes, on top of the blanket. Somehow she'd slipped beneath the covers. Molly finally called to say she wasn't coming home, so it would just be us tonight.

I wasn't consciously thinking it at the time, but I know that part of me was patiently waiting to get to this point in the evening. We were past the first full sprint of drink and talk and the pace was easing, settling in. Where the runners exchange positions. Hoagland would say that now was the time for playing certain finesses, that in the wake of the activity arose those moments that could be manipulated. Carefully you marked out the openings; then you took one boldly, as if it didn't matter what people could see. For him even your wife could be a subject.

"Have you been writing since you've been back?" I asked.

"Not really," she said.

"No poems?" I asked.

"Nothing besides letters."

I had noticed a few blue airmail letters stuck between her books.

She went on, "Frankly, I'm on the brink of really quitting. I'm sick of it. No more poems, no more reviews, nothing. What do you think?"

"You've tried to do that before."

"I'm more sure now," she said, turning to me. "Believe me, I'll live. It's not dire. I decided that I'm not going to be one of those tortured anemic women who despite all signs believes in her micro-talent to the bitter end. It's all too tacky and righteous, even for me. Is it possible to be resolved about not having much resolve?"

"It's possible."

"Good. I guess I'll have to stick with teaching speech. Truth is, Henry, I'm a schoolmarm, just like Mother before she exited real life. I'm destined for black knee-highs and pleated skirts. My life will be about hoping against hope for other people's kids. Maybe my breasts will finally get big."

"I think you'll be writing again soon."

"No, I won't," she said finally. "Just add it to the list of everything of mine that's dead."

I said, "I'm not keeping lists."

She looked at me with some pathos. "I'm sorry. That was very passive-aggressive of me. Very unfair. I'm not proud, Henry. You don't know how many times I tore it up in my mind."

"Before or after you got on the plane?"

"I said I was sorry."

I could see she was willing. It was there in her face like an invitation. A different kind of opening. But suddenly I felt the urge to make something else of the moment.

"At least you still write letters."

"Sure," she said, pulling on the covers. "Letters being letters."

"Easy come easy go," I said.

She looked unsettled. "Are you saying something?"

"I wish you would write *me* a letter sometime."

"Why should I? We talk between every meal, remember? That's what we do. The premise of the movie about us is that we spontaneously combust if we don't talk every six hours."

"We still have too many gaps," I said. "Absolutely nothing about the last couple months."

Lelia was shaking her head. "I'll give you a story for your gaps. Girl is married to boy. Boy makes girl crazy. Girl also makes girl crazy, so girl leaves for a while. Girl goes to island in the sun. Girl returns shiny and new."

I rolled off the bed. "What makes the girl shiny and new?"

"You want me to say it?"

"I want you to say it."

She rubbed at her temples with the insides of her wrists. That familiar exercise of hers, half rumination, half anxiety.

She said, "I take it back. I'm not saying anything."

"Give me a name."

"You're not serious."

"I need to know."

"No," she insisted, kneeling up to face me. Her voice was strong. "You don't need to know! What would you do with his name anyway? Would you run a background check? Find out if he's planted bombs for the Red Brigades? You could get a list of the books he has out from the library. Maybe you could nail him for something good."

"Sleeping with another man's wife."

"I think here we must use 'wife' technically."

"Then let's. Did he please the wife?"

She laughed. "God, I'd forgotten how much I love your language. I'm not answering your question except to say he isn't important. Not to us, anyway."

"I'm noting the present tense. Letters being letters."

She hissed, "That's the Henry I know!"

"Fine. What did you say about us?"

Lelia looked around for a cigarette but couldn't find one. She was anxious herself. Beneath that amazingly capable, resilient shell I knew she was reeling, completely sick inside. Once, we got into a fairly serious car accident once going to her mother's house. I was too dazed to do much except sit on the side of the road with Mitt; Lelia was fine, and she was doing all the right things, setting up a flare, rerouting traffic, getting names and addresses of drivers and witnesses. But as we started driving away in the towman's truck she asked him calmly to pull over. She threw open the door and ran to bushes and vomited until she dry-heaved. We had to stop two more times before we got to the garage.

Now she said, "I told him we were separated. He thought I meant divorce but I said that wasn't it. I told him how I still felt love, but that I didn't trust you anymore. That I didn't know how you really felt about anything, our marriage. Me. You. I realized one day that I didn't know the first thing about what was going on inside your head. Sometimes I think you're not even here, with the rest of us, you know, engaged, present. I don't know anymore why you do things. What you really want from me. I don't know what you need in life. For example, do you need your job?"

"I'm not understanding what you mean by *need.*"

"See what I mean?" she shouted. "You know, I really honestly thought about it for the first time in Corsica, I mean really thought about what you do up there with your friends."

"We've talked about this."

"We haven't talked about anything. Maybe it doesn't matter to me anymore that we talk about it. I just see it as something *not good.* It's as simple as that. I'm not going to invent things anymore for what you do. You think you can leave in the morning and play camera obscura all day and then come home and get into bed and say you're glad to see me. Well, buster, people aren't like that. I hope to high heaven you're not really like that. You just can't do that, turn it on and off. Not forever."

"This job isn't forever."

"Fine. I don't even think I'm asking you to quit. I'm not sure that your quitting tomorrow would make things different anyway. Maybe it's a condition with you. I just know you have parts to you that I can't touch. Maybe I figured out I didn't want to get to them anymore. Or shouldn't bother."

I tried to answer but I couldn't. I wanted to explain myself, smartly, irrefutably. But once again I had nothing to offer. I had always thought that I could be anyone, perhaps several anyones at once. Dennis Hoagland and his private firm had conveniently appeared at the right time, offering the perfect vocation for the person I was, someone who could reside in his one place and take half-steps out whenever he wished. For that I felt indebted to him for life. I found a sanction from our work, for I thought I had finally found my truest place in the culture.

Lelia got up and checked the drawers of a desk. This time she found a cigarette. She got back into bed and lit the cigarette and took a quick, red-hot inhale. She'd been a pack-a-week smoker since high school, never more, never less. She stopped smoking while she was pregnant with Mitt and then until he started nursery school. I tried once or twice to pick up the habit, in sympathy with my wife, so we could sit together by the windows in the heat and not talk and not always have to look at one another, to have those tranquil moments true smokers seem to share and secretly count on. But I never could master it, I was overconscious of this thing burning down between my fingers, of its spew of smoke, the way Lelia would hunch over her knees with the butt in her right hand cast up by her head, and I simply ended up making her nervous.

It was in those moments that you might have heard the first scant formalities arising between us, that careful polite mildly acidic phrasing Lelia grew up with and that I so naturally adopted, maybe even took advantage of, the kind of things Stew and Alice must have plied each other with, the *I'm sure I don't know what you mean,* or the *I must not have heard you correctly, darling.*

How similar it was with me, with my father in our house. Even the most minor speech seemed trying. To tell him I loved him, I studied far into the night. I read my entire children's encyclopedia, drilling from aardvark to zymurgy. I never made an error at shortstop. I spit-shined and brushed his shoes every Sunday morning. Later, to tell him something else, I'd place a larger bouquet than his on my mother's grave. I drove only used, beat-up cars. I never asked him for his money. I spoke volumes to him this way, speak to him still, those same volumes he spoke with me.

I said, "You're the only one for me. You know that's what I want."

"I'm not sure," she answered softly. "Sometimes I think you just do things to get what you want. Tonight, for example, you listened to the tapes. Why?"

"Isn't it obvious?"

"It ought to be," she answered. "But it's not obvious, not to me. When you asked me for the tapes, I almost didn't want to think about it. I wasn't sure why you really wanted them."

"Christ, Lee, you must think I'm a real shit."

She didn't answer. Then, "Just think about it. You haven't said his name more than four or five times since it happened. You haven't said his name tonight. Maybe you've talked all this time with Jack about him, maybe you say his name in your sleep, but we've never really talked about it, we haven't really come right out together and said it, really named what happened for what it was."

"What was it?" I said softly, hearing the sudden quiver in her voice.

"It was the worst thing that ever happened to us," she said, her fist knuckling down on the bed with each word. "It was the worst thing we ever did together. Our utterly lowest moment. All backward, all wrong. Just so dumb."

"It was a terrible accident."

"An accident?" she cried, nearly hollering. She covered her mouth. Her voice was breaking. "How can you say it was an accident? We haven't treated it like one. Not for a second. Look at us. Sweetie, can't you see, when your baby dies it's never an accident. I don't care if a truck hit him or he crawled out a window or he put a live wire in his mouth, it was not an accident. And that's a word you and I have no business using. Sometimes I think it's more like some long-turning karma that finally came back for us. Or that we didn't love each other. We thought our life was good enough. Maybe it's that Mitt wasn't all white or all yellow. I go crazy thinking about it. Don't you? Maybe the world wasn't ready for him. God. Maybe it's that he was so damn happy."

She was crying a little now, her sobs coming evenly, almost controlled, as though she'd cried enough over the years that this is what was left to her, to both of us, just trickles and weariness.

We lay down together but we weren't touching. Her eyes were closed, though just barely, the lids frail and milky and almost transparent in the dim light. The heat of her face, her throat, drew me closer to her and the tiny hairs on my cheeks and brow tingled from the nearness. For it was nearness and not touch that had always compelled me. I have only known proximity. She didn't move away. I didn't try to touch her. I knew I shouldn't. I just closed my eyes, and I slid to her until I could feel the warmth of my own face play back against hers, the reflection like an instant map of heat. I thought I could read every contour of her skin and bone, every relief of her flesh. What it all said. As if I could ever read her mind.

I finally met Kwang a week after the scouting. I was charting out with Janice his April and May schedules of meetings and speaking engagements in the expansive war room of his Flushing headquarters. His own small office was set in the back of the war room. The activity ceased for a few seconds as people near the door greeted him. He was alone, which I thought peculiar, because I had assumed that there would be someone beside him at all times feeding him information and strategy and advice. He was only a councilman, but as Jenkins told us our efforts were already acquiring the shape of a campaign, a full-blown interborough enterprise. It was usually Sherrie Chin-Watt or Cameron Jenkins who was with him, less often Janice or some underling like Eduardo or me.

Today he was supposed to be working quietly at home, but here he was, come in for an unexpected visit to his staffers. They seemed to appreciate his presence, which they rightly sensed was solely for them, particularly the younger volunteers, who I could see wanted to say something to him but didn't and stayed back, nervous and excited.

But everyone took notice of him. From the moment he stepped into the room, I thought each of us was suddenly oriented toward him. Janice and I were standing at the chalkboard in the middle of the room. She didn't say anything but smiled and turned to the board casually; I would have thought she was generally accustomed to his entrances, but I noticed that her posture had shifted in acknowledgment of the man approaching at her back. She continued chalking times and places on the slate, but I saw that her eyes weren't following the motion of her hand. I thought she had it the way everyone else did, the way she was waiting for his touch on her arm or his voicing of her name. It made me think that she was a little in love with him, the same way Eduardo and the other people in the room were. The same way, perhaps, that I would be. Somehow you felt for him a pin-ache of unneeded love on top of the respect and hope and plain like of him, that little bit of extra feeling that must separate even a good man and politician from a natural leader of people.

I moved toward the channel made by the desks and chairs. He was joking now with Eduardo. The two of them stood close to each other feigning the movements of boxers, their heads weaving, bobbing, tucked tight behind ready hands. Kwang was around my height, maybe five-ten or so, way above Eduardo, but giving away at least thirty pounds to him. Eduardo had been a junior boxer, as had Kwang. They first met at a boys' club visit of Kwang's where Eduardo was coaching. Now Kwang reached out and jabbed gently at Eduardo's temple and Eduardo took a step back as if stunned and then staggered onto the edge of his desk. Kwang leaned into him with a flurry to the midsection. Eduardo doubled over, protecting himself. They were both grimacing, grinning, swinging.

Janice shouted through her hands, "Someone stop this massacre!"

A handkerchief landed at their feet. Technical knockout.

He put his arm around Eduardo. He nodded to Janice. Then he noticed me. I wanted to look away but didn't dare. It wasn't that I was afraid of him, or worried by what he might somehow be able to see. A beginner thinks this, despite many hours of painstaking preparation. It is unavoidable. For the first few assignments you feel perfectly transparent, as if the man or woman in question can witness every leap of your heart. You think they can sense every false move. But in successive turns you grow an opacity, a pearl-like glow whose surface can repel all manner of heat and light.

What I saw now was the face of a recognition, the same face that Emile Luzan offered me that first day, too, in his cluttered third-floor office in Babylon, Long Island. The good doctor from Manila. From the very start he took my hand and said simply that I should not worry. I didn't know what to make of his gesture save its unorthodoxy, its colloquial and unprofessional tone. I thought immediately that he was treating me differently from his other patients and rather than feign an ignorance that might alert his suspicions I asked if this was his usual method.

"Certainly it is not," he said to me, chuckling in his ho-ho way. "But my feeling after speaking with you now for half the session is that perhaps only a small part of your difficulties is attributable to biochemical issues, if at all. I don't think medication is in order, although you seem to feel it necessary. Were you someone else I'd probably just follow your wishes. I shouldn't tell you that, but I will. Certainly like all of us you have traditional issues to deal with. Parentage, intimacy, trust.

"But hand in hand with all that is the larger one of where we live, my friend, and who you are within that place. Or believe yourself to be. We have our multiple roles like everyone else. Now throw in an additional dimension. A cultural one. Cast it all, if you will, in a broad yellow light. Let us see where this leads you and me."

For now, I must say to the good doctor, it led to John Kwang.

Kwang certainly didn't know who I was but he regarded me as if he were seeing a memory. He seemed to light up as he moved past in his pressed, clean-smelling suit, grazing my shoulders and arms with his. I thought that this was how he moved through a crowded room of his loyal cadre, baring his tiny perfect hands, him looking at each of us at least once, connecting and lighting up.

"Eduardo!" he said into the air.

"Yes, boss!"

"All your work done?"

"Yes, boss!"

"Let's see it then."

Eduardo stepped behind his desk and pulled a manila folder from a drawer. He laid it open on the conference table and he and Kwang went over it.

I said John was my height. He was actually shorter than I was, two or three inches at least. Maybe it was the kind of light that emanated from him, or the way his figure bent the light to a crucial incidence, but from any distance at all he appeared to me as though he were ascending an invisible ramp that magically preceded him. His warm-hued face was square, owing its shape to the eminence of his angular jaw, which carved out two perfect hollows on either side of his chin. He still had those shadows of youth upon him. He was clean-shaven, as always.

I think I will forever see him with that smooth face, almost aglow, almost pubescent, despite my memory of those final days of his shortened career, when his true age seemed to besiege him all over and at once.

His neatly clipped black hair, silvery about the temples with scant patches of grayness, reminded me of my father's head ten years before, those dense shines of hair. Though it ultimately wasn't true, my father appeared to be the most vital of men. He seemed to understand that it was his hair which lent him his attractiveness and authority, and so it became, strangely enough, the one and only vanity of his life.

He used to stand before the bathroom mirror, dabbing all sorts of conditioners and dressings on it in a time when there were only products like Vitalis and Brylcreem. Without any shame he would faithfully apply my mother's sundry ointments each morning and each night, slowly working into his scalp the brightly tinted gobs without romance or fuss.

I suppose I always envied that brush of his, how wavy it was. I remember how proud he was of it. He used to say to me when I was young that his *gohpsul muh-rhee* showed the great vigor of the blood running through him. Then he'd grab at my own skull, roll the fine straight strands of my hair between his fingers, and gravely shake his head.

Look at this, he'd scoff, *just like your mother's.*

How worn and weak. He was forever there to let me know every disadvantage I would have to overcome. I knew I would never enjoy his stern constitution. I have my mother's thin blood, the kind so easily forayed by a chilly draft, an unexpected rain. She and I were always sick with something. In certain periods my mother seemed to live from her bed, rising only to clean the tub or cook dinner for my father and me, which she would do in any condition. The climate was never quite suitable for her. In truth, she could only stand up to the harshness of people and their words, a native tenacity that I can only hope someday to uncover in myself.

My self-conception was that I was frail. I would sometimes affect similar ailments to my mother's and try to mimic her, stay in my room whole weekends with a pile of picture books or puzzles, never changing out of my pajamas. Or I would slip into her bed while she napped and fall asleep in the warm curve of her belly.

My father might come in and stand before the bed with his arms crossed and savagely complain about us. He enjoyed ranting about how she and I were living lucky in this life, resounding his personal lore of how merciless and dangerous it was in this land and that he could only do so much to protect us. Certainly it was the emptiest of his threats, for he was nothing if not a provider and a bulwark. He was the kind of man who subscribed to that old-fashioned idea of nation as personal test—and by extension, a test of family—and not only because he was an immigrant. What kept him toiling and working through his years was that he bore that small man's folly of sometimes seeing himself in terms historical, a necessary evil, as if each apple or turnip or six-pack he was selling would be the very one to catapult him toward a renown he could only with great difficulty imagine for himself. He watched too much television. I remember how he would make fun of Joe Namath in those old cologne commercials, remark that he was too ugly a man to have so many beautiful women surrounding him.

What a nose! he'd cry in Korean at the television set. *It looks like a big dried daikon.*

But then there it was, invariably, the little green bottle of musky potion that Joe also used, ready for him on my mother's dresser. My father could splash it on blithely before he went to the city for work. He could leave the house with a fresh confidence. But when he came back late at night, the magic had all but abandoned his face and his step, the aura was gone, the lilt, and I could smell the animal of him as he walked past my bedroom door in the short hall, the stink of sweat and ruined vegetables and the ashen city penetrating me like an epochal sickness.

He would have probably admired John Kwang—at least for his appearance. Though not openly, of course. That kind of admiration between men was either effeminate or disrespectful, and then a little shameful, if the object was a younger man. No, my father would likely never have approached him if he had come upon the chance. He was still alive when John Kwang first appeared on the city political scene, but the old man was at that point too ill and self-absorbed with his own decline to notice anything extramural, Korean-American or not.

John Kwang dressed like a power broker. His taste for colors and fabrics was impeccable. His wife, May, didn't dress him or buy his clothes. Later, I would note that whenever he had the opportunity he'd duck into a clothier in Manhattan and buy a French-cuffed shirt and several ties. He had every kind of shoe for his occasions, brogans, oxfords, wing tips, Loafers, patent-leather pumps, deep-treaded boots. With his suits he mostly stayed to the conservative, what the people expected of him, Paul Stuart and J. Press, the American executive look, but at more internationally flavored events and certain parties you could see him working the room in something silken and double-breasted, the lines rakishly cut down to hug his youthful waist. When he took meetings around the borough, he wore a wool flannel three-piece. The jacket of the dark charcoal suit fit him perfectly, as did his trousers, which must have been retailored from their lanky western proportion to flatter his short Korean legs. I know those limbs. I remember Mitt pointing at the gnarled trunks of my father's tanned bowlegs bared beneath his shorts and saying, "Grandpa's a bulldog." I laughed, thinking how right Mitt didn't yet know he was, and figured, too, that with so much of Lelia in him, with so much of her drawnness and length, Mitt would be a greyhound when he grew up, a wispy thing, gentler and more tender of step than we who would course through him like trickling old rivers.

Kwang himself exhibited a different grace: he didn't sport the brief choppy step of our number, but seemed instead to stride in luxurious borrowed lengths. He almost loped, not after the six-foot-three-inch bound of a Stew Boswell, but like a man who understood the true stamp and limit of his gait. As if he rode on those legs. A primed athlete among the unlimbered mass of men. And then there he was, on his way back out, holding Janice firmly by the shoulders in his customary way, as if he might lay a deep kiss upon her brow or warmly pull into his chest her solid cocksure body now offering up its last slack to his womanly hands. She was a little stunned with him. He glanced back at me once more and then moved on to the rest of the people in the room, spreading himself among them wide but never thin.

This proved what appeared to me to be his great talent: his seeming resistance to dilution. This despite the fact that everyone he met, each one of us he encountered inside and outside his office and circle, even and perhaps especially strangers, the curious citizenry of the streets, Kwang made feel as though he were bequeathing a significant part of himself. And I thought that no matter what skin you were, no matter what your opinion of him, when you met him in person you somehow felt that you understood the subtle pressure of his grip, that it said or meant that you were the faintest brother to him, perhaps distantly removed by circumstance or blood but a brother nonetheless.

I had ready connections to him, of course. He knew I was Korean, or Korean-American, though perhaps not exactly the same way he was. We were of different stripes, like any two people, though taken together you might say that one was an outlying version of the other. I think we both understood this from the very beginning, and insofar as it was evident I suppose you could call ours a kind of romance, though I don't exactly know what he saw in me. Maybe a someone we Koreans were becoming, the latest brand of an American. That I was from the future.

Kwang was certainly arresting to me. Not so much paternally, in that grim way my father always impressed himself on me, which eventually built up in my chest a resolve that told me I would never yield to him or surrender. I would come to share a different difficulty with John Kwang.

I suppose it was a question of imagination. What I was able to see. Before I knew of him, I had never even conceived of someone like him. A Korean man, of his age, as part of the vernacular. Not just a respectable grocer or dry cleaner or doctor, but a larger public figure who was willing to speak and act outside the tight sphere of his family. He displayed an ambition I didn't recognize, or more, one I hadn't yet envisioned as something a Korean man would find significant or worthy of energy and devotion; he didn't seem afraid like my mother and father, who were always wary of those who would try to shame us or mistreat us. When Hoagland first mentioned Kwang's name I only saw his ready image, what everyone else had at hand. In media photographs and video he appeared to me as an ambitious minority politician and what being one had always meant—the adjutant interest groups, the unwavering agenda, the stridency, the righteousness. A lover of the republic. An underdog champion. I thought I could peg him easily; were I an actor, I would have all the material I required for my beginning method. This is what Hoagland meant when he promised the assignment would be simple, that I'd just have to lurk close enough and witness the play of the story as we already knew it. For ours, finally, were just acts of verification. I would tick off each staging of the narrative, every known turn and counter-turn. The what and the what and the what.

I would tell a familiar story. The ones we recite in our sleep. I remember how Mitt liked to have the same book read to him each night for two or three weeks, how he would sit rapt with the tale and eventually murmur the words along with me, though on the first reading he would hardly listen and climb all over the bed and my shoulders and laugh frantically at the suspenseful moments, which for him began with the first *Once, long ago.* There is something universally chilling about a new plot. And I could see how my boy needed time and space for a story to bloom in his mind, because at any age what comes before sight is a conjuring. A trope, which is just a way to believe.

My necessary invention was John Kwang. This must sound funny, I know. He had always existed in his own right, and he lives at this very moment in a distant land that must seem to him like a great vessel of strangers. I do not know what he does now. I do not know the first or last iota of him. I do not know whether he has taken up a vocation or an art to pass the solemnity of the hours. I know only that I will never see him again, and that anything I can say or offer by way of his present life might well be taken as reductive and suspect. So be it. I intend no irony or special mode. The fact is I had him in my sights. I believed I had a grasp of his identity, not only the many things he was to the public and to his family and to his staff and to me, but who he was to himself, the man he beheld in his most private mirror.

I will say again that none of this was my duty. My job, which I executed faithfully, was never to spy out those moments of his self-regard, it was not to peer through the crack of the door and watch as he bore off each successive visage. My appointed plan was just to give a good scratch to the surface, come away with some spice or flavor under my nails. As Hoagland would half-joke, whatever grit of an ethnicity. But then all that is a sham. Through events both arbitrary and conceived it so happened that one of his faces fell away, and then another, and another, until he revealed to me a final level that would not strip off. The last mask. And what I saw in him I had not thought to seek, but will search out now for the long remainder of my days.

Every morning Eduardo tipped his head to me and said in a convincing accent, *Ahn-young-ha-sae-yo.* I greeted him back in Spanish, but his accent was much better than mine. John Kwang had taught him the words so that he could properly greet the large number of Korean constituents and visitors to our Flushing office. Most everyone on the staff seemed to have at least a rudimentary knowledge of the language and customs, how to say *hello* and *goodbye* and *please wait a moment,* how to bow down low enough and speak in a tone of respect with eyes cast at a deferential angle. Sherrie and Janice conducted hit-and-run seminars on the practice, usually after a new crop of volunteers came on. We had to be careful not to speak Korean to every Asian person who arrived, and because I was Korean I was regularly stationed to work at the greeting desk.

All of northern Queens seemed to pass through that door. Although Kwang's power base was every last Korean vote in the district, and then most of the Chinese, he did exceedingly well with the newer immigrants, the Southeast Asians and Indians, the Central Americans, and blacks from the Caribbean and West Indies. Some Eastern Europeans. The native whites didn't seem to pay much attention to him, either way. African-Americans didn't seem to trust him. He was a Democrat in name, in the party of Mayor De Roos, but he drew little from that machinery, the strong-arm cadres of unionized workers and tradespeople, white ethnic old New York.

Instead, he had made his the party of livery drivers and nannies and wok cooks and seamstresses and delivery boys, and his wealthiest patrons were the armies of small-business owners through whose coffers passed all of Queens, by the nickel and dime.

Before the last campaign he had voter-registered literally thousands. That's all his staff still did, and it was why John Kwang retained so many volunteers and such a large staff for just a city councilman, why he paid extra for their salaries and their lunches and their late-night call cars. He gave cash bonuses for the top five people registering the most voters each month, bonuses for pledged future votes, bonuses for signing up immigrants for naturalization. It was like a church drive but at all hours, the whole body of us spread through the district, jammed into cars and sent out to find them.

This his daily order: do the good duty, go out into the street, go into the stores, stop them in the alleyways. Just get in a word. In ten different languages you say *Kwang is like you. You will be an American.* You have a flyer with his fine picture and his life story beneath. Show them that. If you tell them the story of their lives they will listen. Peel a dollar from the stack that Jenkins gives each of us in the morning, the bill clipped to an envelope so they can send in their name and address and family and occupation. *Have a dollar so we can help you.*

The mood in the office was messianic. We felt like his guerrillas. Some weekends we'd come in for extra work, stay out all day Saturday and then have a big dinner with him at an all-night Korean restaurant, ten or fifteen of us sitting on the floor with him at the head, pouring for each other from double-sized bottles of Korean ale. He'd teach us old songs in Korean, drinking songs, school songs, whatever we could learn. I was usually the only Korean in a room of young Jews and Chinese and Hispanics.

Eduardo Fermin was his favorite. He would make him stand up and sing a Dominican island song, or a hymn. Eduardo would rise without a word. He'd sing beautifully, his high choirboy voice hitting every note like a bell. When he finished we'd all clap and hoot and then John would give him the business, all joking, bulling, asking if he'd ever learned anything from anyone besides the good Sisters of the Virgin of Guadalupe.

"What other schmaltz do you want me to sing?" Eduardo would yell back, and John would laugh and tell him the name of another song.

I tried to sit at the far end of the table, so that if he were in one of his high, manic moods he wouldn't pick me out in front of the group. This way, too, I could observe the entire table, the faces, take the run of the evenings.

He seemed to understand this, and sometimes he would catch my eye from across the room when other people were heatedly talking or arguing and nod affirmingly. Only afterward, on the way out or in the street, would he take me aside—almost without exception—and ask how I was doing with the office work, and if my other work as a magazine writer weren't being compromised. Rarely did he pursue me in front of the others, and then only if he were in the foulest humor, sometimes asking in a dramatic voice for me to speak on behalf of *Koreans everywhere.* If we were talking about some thorny issue like welfare reform or affirmative action he would say like a reporter both unctuous and angling, "Mr. Park, if you would tell us the *Korean-American* position on this please." He liked to linger on the hyphenation. Then he'd deliver some below-the-belt follow-up: "Do you think a single black mother with six kids should be rewarded for having any more?"

I never had a good response, and neither did anyone else. In truth, I thought he couldn't help but sometimes punish us with the same notions and language that daily confronted him. He might snap at you with a comment from the last press conference.

Some problems were dogging him. For months he had been talking to Chinese and Korean gang leaders, in an effort to halt their street extortion and violence, negotiate some kind of settlement. But the dialogues ceased after a surprise arrest by police immediately following the last meeting at Reverend Cho's church, several weeks before. An arrested Korean gang chief named Han had been publicly threatening him, spreading the word on the street that Kwang had betrayed them.

With this first real trouble, I noticed that he was getting caught up in his moods. I began to see the whip of his temper. One afternoon I watched him shout at his wife, May, for what seemed ten straight minutes as they sat inside their white sedan. He was shaking his fist so close to her face, which had gone white. I was across the street in front of the office so I couldn't hear him, but I was certain that he was yelling in both Korean and English. She sat perfectly still and took it all. Then he stepped from the car and spoke softly to her from the open door, shutting it gently before she drove off.

He usually treated me with genuine warmth. Perhaps to him I was someone he ought to look out for, a Korean-American, well educated, solitary-looking, seemingly jobless. He often asked about my wife, freely offering his aid in finding her more speech work with the city. She could work in a Flushing district, he said, nodding to say that he could do that. What threw me most, however, was that he would sometimes misremember whether I had children—this seems improbable, given what I would learn about his amazing feats of memory—and while talking about child-rearing he might refer to how I must know this thing or that, the way a child can be joyous and harrowing, ask of what I imagined in life for my daughter or my son. When he overdrank he wanted to see pictures. I had to tell him I didn't carry any. He would open his wallet and show me snapshots of his own children, Peter and John Jr., in matching blue suits.

He also carried a picture of May, though it dated to the sixties (her hair, her dress) and was nearly faded of all color.

I want to say that he was a family man, that being Korean and old-fashioned made him cherish and honor the institution, that his family was the basic unit of wealth in his life, everything paling and tarnished before it. But then I would be speaking only half of the truth, and the most accessible half at that, the part that had the least to do with him. Certainly, he loved his family. He loved May and he loved Peter and perhaps most he loved little John. Like any good father, I thought, he would have died for them, a thousand times.

But then he loved the pure idea of family as well, which in its most elemental version must have nothing to do with blood. It was how he saw all of us, and then by extension all those parts of Queens that he was now calling his. All day and all night we worked without stopping, knowing we'd get to be with him at the end of the day. *Oo-rhee-jip,* he'd say then, just before the eating and drinking, asking for our hands around the table, speaking *oo-rhee-jip* for *Our house.* Our new life.

Since the beginning I was writing down everything and thus committing—if I so wished—all of our movements to an official and secret memory. I had a long queue of files on a disk waiting to be wired to Hoagland's terminal in Purchase. I was sending him various items, of course, brief profiles of Kwang at various events around the city. These were overly precious entries, and I knew they were written too much in the mode of a fanciful reporter-at-large: appraisals of Kwang from the back of a crowded room, the point of view through the glass of a fancy cocktail, my prose full of handsomeness and brio. Lively perhaps, but exactly what Hoagland couldn't use, material any spy would read and crabbily say was *inedible paper.*

I seemed to be waiting for something to happen before I could send to Hoagland what he needed from me. In previous assignments, even the one with Luzan, I had always been able to follow through with my initial transmissions despite feeling a moment's pang of remorse. Jack told me from the start that this would happen. The first incision is always the hardest. Only then can you get down to business, work yourself elbow deep. With John Kwang I wrote exemplary reports but I couldn't accept the idea that Hoagland would be combing through them. It seemed like an unbearable encroachment. An exposure of a different order, as if I were offering a private fact about my father or mother to a complete stranger in one of our stores.

Perhaps this was because John Kwang constantly spoke of us as his own, of himself as a part of us. Though he rarely called you a brother, sister, son. He was prudent with his language. If anything, he called you friend. He said looking right into your eyes that he trusted you with his life. He said he loved you for what you did. He made it seem as if he couldn't believe any of our devotion or duty.

Once I saw him drop to one knee before a young volunteer for having stayed an extra shift. He was seamless in the act, he made no show of it, and bent small like that he looked as if he had been that way all his life, bent before this half-terrified girl to lay a kiss on her hand. In horror the girl buckled and knelt down with him, and in answer he rose and lifted them both. I didn't know then if I had witnessed the gravest humility or conceit. What does it matter which? He was a man who could do such a thing. But then John Kwang was also American. Maybe he simply wanted what any newcomer like him wanted and would will for himself, a broader foreground from which he might naturally emerge. Family who would make up events in the lore of his life. The girl he kneels to. Eduardo his boxer. Janice, keen Sherrie. Now a latecomer by the name of Henry Park. But I can imagine my father saying his no, no, it was clearly Kwang's Confucian training at work, his secular religion of pure hierarchy, his belief that everyone is at once a noble and a servant and then just a man. Its adherents know no hubris. Instead this: you simply bow down before those who would honor you. You honor them back. For you are but ash to their fire. All spent of light.

On the morning of his meeting with the black ministers, Eduardo and I drove out a few hours early to the site in Brooklyn and walked it through once again. We brought other volunteers to help us plan the movement of the principals on the street, the expected crowd, all the starts and stops where the press would have obvious positions for video. We held the procession. Janice reminded us that everything had to be perfect. She was trusting us. She and Sherrie were too busy dealing with the mayor, and would only arrive with him.

De Roos was on the offensive again, trying to spoil Kwang's show with the same questions about his role in the boycotts, suggesting that he was obstructing the efforts of the police and community groups. His hard line was also meant to draw attention from the more pointed talk of his alleged adultery with a woman whose name was now public, rumors he was saying were the work of certain political opportunists. Janice wasn't saying anything to anyone. She'd look at me hard if the subject came up in the office and casually draw a finger across her throat. The mayor would then want to talk about John Kwang and his methods of registering voters, the excessive use of street money and underage volunteers.

"This isn't the Third World," De Roos said on the news, standing in the heart of downtown Flushing. "Americans make up their own minds."

When Kwang's car arrived he got out and we immediately led him up the steps, inside the church. There would be a closed meeting between Kwang and the church leaders for the first hour, and then they would all speak before a gathering outside. The private talk would actually be more a negotiation, Janice told me the week before, about what everyone would be saying before the cameras. Sherrie would be sitting in then, though she was to leave unseen afterward, before they all stepped outside. Janice had convinced them both that having Sherrie in the shots would just confuse the viewers; they'd think she was his wife, or his girlfriend, and only make the story of the day more difficult to tell.

I waited in my position. I was nervous. I don't know why. The crowd was much larger than we'd expected, an even mix of Koreans, blacks, Hispanics. The press was there in force, but I sensed that they understood, too, that the occasion wasn't particularly momentous or crucial to the disposition of actual events, the real violence and tension, even if they would portray it as such on the evening programs.

I suppose I wanted to watch him work the crowd. I wanted to take in his every move among the people, to witness the telling presence that I'd seen glimpses of but on a much smaller scale, at the office, on building stoops, inside restaurants. I didn't know if he could tread with the same proportion here.

When they came out, he stood on the rise of the church steps among the four enrobed ministers. He didn't look nervous. A line of microphones was set up. Eduardo and I were on either side of the group, a few steps down, half-facing the crowd. The men were all smiling and shaking hands with each other. The lead minister, the Reverend Benjamin Shavers, hushed the crowd. He spoke for a few minutes about the tragedy of strife between the communities. The reverend then asked John Kwang to speak.

John stepped forward into the tightening space of the steps. The sky was clear. He wore a dark wool topcoat over his suit and white shirt and tie. He held no speaking notes or cards.

"My friends," he said, his accents on the syllables of his words unlikely, melodic. "I have something to tell you today. An incredible bit of news. Black and Korean children, as some in this city would have you believe, aren't yet boycotting one another's corner lemonade stands."

There was scattered laughter in the throng.

"It's true, it's true," he answered. "I have this from reliable sources. You know how my people have been roaming the boroughs."

"Where are the mayor's people?" a voice yelled from the back. I thought it sounded like Janice's.

"Oh please, please," Kwang pleaded in her direction. "Let us show compassion for the mayor's position in this. He just found out what's on this side of the East River."

A chorus of cheers went up. The crowd had been steadily growing and was now spilling back out into the street. Police were setting up barricades blocking one whole lane of cars.

"But let us not think about the mayor today. Let us not think about the inaction of his administration in the face of what he says is a 'touchy situation.' When he casually tells the newspapers that 'it's getting wild out there in Queens and Brooklyn,' let's not simply nod and agree. Let's not accept that kind of imagery. Let's think instead of what we have to bear together.

"A young black mother of two, Saranda Harlans, is dead. Shot in the back by a Korean shopkeeper. Charles Kim, a Korean-American college student, is also dead. He was overcome by fumes trying to save merchandise in the firebombed store of his family. I was in the hospital room when he died. I attended Miss Harlans' funeral. And I say that though they may lie beneath the earth, they are not buried.

"So let's think together in a different way. Today, here, now. Let us think that for the moment it is not a Korean problem. That it is not a black problem or a brown and yellow problem, that it is not a problem of our peoples, that it is not even ultimately a problem of our mistrust or our ignorance. Let us think it is the problem of a self-hate.

"Yes," he said, starting to sing the words. "Let us think that. Think of this, my friends: when a Korean merchant haunts an old black gentleman strolling through the aisles of his grocery store, does he hold even the smallest hope that the man will not steal from him? Or when a group of black girls takes turns spitting in the face and hair of the new student from Korea, as happened to my friend's daughter, whose muck of hate do they ball up on their tongues? Who is the girl the girls are seeing? Who is the man who appears to be stealing? Who are they, those who know no justice, no fairness; do you know them? Are they familiar?"

There were random calls from the crowd. Then a man heckled something but was immediately shouted down. There was a brief scuffle and the heckler cursed them and slipped away.

"Yes," he said. "Yes. Let us think differently today. The problem is our acceptance of what we loathe and fear in ourselves. Not in the other, not in the person standing next to you, not in the one living outside in this your street, in this your city, not in the one who drives your bus or who mops the floors of your child's school, not in the one who cleans your shirts and presses your suits, not in the one who sells books and watches on the corner. No! No, no!"

He started pointing, gesturing about the crowd, picking out people. "This person, this person, she, that person, he, that person, they, those, them, they're like us, they are us, they're just like you! They want to live with dignity and respect! They want a fair day of work. They want a chance to own something for themselves, be it a store or a cart. They want to show compassion to the less fortunate. They want happiness for their children. They want enough heat in the winter so they can sleep, they want a clean park in the summer so they can play. They want to love like sweet life this city in which they live, not just to exist, not just to get by, not just to survive this day and go home tonight and tend fresh wounds. Think of yourself, think of your close ones, whom no one else loves, and then you will be thinking of them, whom you believe to be the other, the enemy, the cause of the problems in your life. Those who are a different dark color. Who may seem strange. Who cannot speak your language just yet. Who cannot seem to understand the first thing about who you are.

Who must certainly hate you, you are thinking, because of the constant frustration of your own heart turning hard against them.

"If you are listening to me now and you are Korean, and you pridefully own your own store, your *yah-cheh-ga-geh* that you have built up from nothing, know these facts. Know that the blacks who spend money in your store and help put food on your table and send your children to college cannot open their own stores. Why? Why can't they? Why don't they even try? Because banks will not lend to them because they are black. Because these neighborhoods are *troubled, high risk.* Because if they did open stores, no one would insure them. And if they do not have the same strong community you enjoy, the one you brought with you from Korea, which can pool money and efforts for its members—it is because this community has been broken and dissolved through history.

"We Koreans know something of this tragedy. Recall the days over fifty years ago, when Koreans were made servants and slaves in their own country by the Imperial Japanese Army. How our mothers and sisters were made the concubines of the very soldiers who enslaved us.

"I am speaking of histories that all of us should know. Remember, or now know, how Koreans were cast as the dogs of Asia, remember the way our children could not speak their own language in school, remember how they called each other by the Japanese names forced upon them, remember the public executions of patriots and the shadowy murders of collaborators, remember our feelings of disgrace and penury and shame, remember most of all the struggle to survive with one's own identity still strong and alive.

"I ask that you remember these things, or know them now. Know that what we have in common, the sadness and pain and injustice, will always be stronger than our differences. I respect and honor you deeply."

Kwang then bowed and thanked the crowd and they applauded loudly as he hugged each minister in turn. I was pushed toward him as they shrank inward to get closer to him. I tried to hold those nearest to me back, but it was useless. I couldn't find Eduardo or Janice. Kwang himself was talking, laughing, pointing, taking every hand he could, slowly roping through the crowd down the church steps toward the street as if carrying himself on a human vine. I could see he wanted to get out, maybe the crowd was getting too fervent. But he was going to move past them by moving through their very heart.

A dull pop went off, followed quickly by another. People ducked where they stood, half crouching, covering their heads. Quiet. Then screaming. They all started to run. I saw Eduardo dive toward John Kwang and grab him hard by the shoulders. He looked all right, but Eduardo had him quickly tucked under his arms. Eduardo saw me and shouted, "Henry! Henry!" He jerked his head desperately toward the car. I understood what he wanted. I hurled myself through the mess of people, shouting as Janice had instructed me, "Aide to Councilman Kwang! Aide to Councilman Kwang!" and I led a path for Eduardo to follow. John was still hidden away, but he was walking down low, keeping up. There was suddenly heavy smoke and we moved through a thick white screen of it, the smell sulfurous, burnt.

Janice appeared, kneeling in her skirt on the trunk of his sedan. She was yelling at a cop and pointing back toward the steps of the church. "Over there!" she screamed. "Over there! There! It's a kid!"

They were holding down somebody to the side of where John had been speaking. Immediately the camera crews were trying to get there. We were still jammed in twenty yards or so from the car by all the people on the wide sidewalk. It was difficult to move. The traffic had stopped in the street. I didn't see any police except for the young cop Janice had berated, who was making his way to the spot she had been pointing to.

Eduardo and now another volunteer from the office were covering Kwang. He motioned for me to take his position and I cuffed John at the elbow, his head still covered beneath Eduardo's outercoat. Eduardo shouted for us to wait and then ran the long way around, halfway down the block and back. He finally got behind the wheel of the car and started it up. He was maneuvering it to and fro, trying to back it onto the sidewalk so that they could get to us. I could see Janice in the backseat urging him to keep moving. I thought they were going to roll over people, crush somebody. But a seam opened and Janice pushed out the door when they neared us. I shielded his head and slid him into the backseat. When Janice saw him she screamed but he assured her in a calm voice, "I'm okay, I'm okay. No worry. I'm okay." He looked shaken but fine. I shut the door. He looked up at me through the window and gave a weak thumbs-up. His lips said, I was sure in Korean, *Thank you.* There were cameras behind me and I was careful not to turn directly around. I rapped the roof of the car twice and Eduardo moved it slowly through the crowd before squealing off north, through the red lights, for Queens.

Jack and I spoke regularly. I called him from various payphones in Flushing or from the flat in Manhattan our firm rented. Sometimes, when we were both in the city, we met there. The apartment was nothing special. It was in the East Thirties, an alley-side studio on the third floor of a shabby rent-control building. The tenants were mostly older folks who'd lived there since *before the war,* and then all the illegal subletters. A lot of them were time-sharers like stewardesses or nursing students, or guys running dispatch for gypsy cabs and escort services or telephone rigs like astrology or phone-sex parlors. The kind of people who generally didn't hang out in the halls or make conversation. It was the perfect setup for Dennis Hoagland, who himself had background-checked all thirty-six apartments. He paid the super $50 a month for any changes and names.

"The scared and the scamming," he liked to say, "always give the best cover."

You got in with a plastic key, the kind big hotels use. The door had a brushed brass plate with a slot and heavy-duty handle. You inserted the key and heard a plush click. A green pinlight went on. It was fully automated. This way, Hoagland could change the code at will from the Westchester office, then have Candace cut the appropriate keys. He readily admitted it was completely unnecessary. He said he was American and so reserved the right to flagrant displays of technology. Every few weeks he would distribute new keys to us. Jack immediately threw his away.

The place had two windows, a large, many-paned one in the main area that faced the alley, and then another in the bathroom. Both were blacked out with matte spray paint. There was an air conditioner for cooling and ventilation. Hoagland had furnished the place with a three-bay sound partition, each bay fitted with a dedicated phone line and laptop with fax/modem. There was a shared printer and a coffee machine. A blobby gesture at a sofa near the door, and his trademark fake orchids in the corners. The idea, in his words, was for the place to be a kind of "work lounge" for those of us on assignment in the city, or for "associates" of ours having unexpected layovers. Of course, it didn't get much use.

Jack said it was the wet-dream version of the treehouse Hoagland never had as a boy.

"You're all fucking over me," Dennis answered him. He grinned. "But you're wrong. It's the one I burned down."

I myself didn't mind the place. I almost liked how cramped and lightless it was, so unlike our windy, too bright apartment. Sometimes I spent nights there after particularly depressing fights with Lelia, which were really more non-fights, those bleak evenings in which we sat crossly at different ends of the loft, smoldering with voodoo.

Lelia couldn't have known where I stayed all those nights, and because she never once asked, I felt I was allowed to let her stew in her imagination. Let her think. An ugly fancy, I thought, might do us both some good, snap us into clarity, though how and when I had no idea. For although I have spent ample hours of my adult life rigorously assessing and figuring all sorts of human calculations, the *flesh math,* as we say, I retain an amazing facility for discharging to hope and dumb chance the things most precious to me.

When real trouble hits, I lock up. I can't work the trusty calculus. I can't speak. I sit there, unmoved. For a person like Lelia, who grew up with hollerers and criers, mine is the worst response. It must look as if I'm not even trying. Unless I drink too much I'll eventually recede. I go into my "father's act," though she only knows this from what I've told her. It's the one complaint she'll make about him, though she always ends with something fond. And this is the primary gripe she has with me—she's even said as much, despite her list—but with us it's ever urgent, the big one.

I don't have any deep problems with her. I know this must sound spiteful. She has her shortcomings, certainly, but I won't go into them because once you start ticking things off they just keep going until they take on a life of their own, which neither truth nor good intention can withstand.

What will I say? Lelia is mostly wonderful. And lovely. She has a prominent nose that seems just right and slightly off kilter at the same time. Her eyes are wide-set. She doesn't much fuss with her hair. When you hand her a football she instantly spins it to the laces and says, "Go out." Each morning she rises at 6:30 and stretches in her underwear and makes a good pot of coffee. She always scalds the milk. I go in the kitchen and believe I will never see a more perfect set of hipbones. Or uglier feet. I know how her voice will sound with the first word of the day, not as low as it should be and as spare and clean as light. That effortless pitch. When she play-acts, horses around, she is silly and awkward, completely unconvincing. She must be the worst actor on earth.

And perhaps most I loved this about her, her helpless way, love it still, how she can't hide a single thing, that she looks hurt when she is hurt, seems happy when happy. That I know at every moment the precise place where she stands. What else can move a man like me, who would find nothing as siren or comforting?

When I asked her to marry me we'd been together for only three months, the entire time she had been in the city since moving from El Paso. Although she had her own apartment we were pretty much sharing house (she'd already moved over most of her clothes), and I knew we were heading for something serious when we stopped by her place to use the bathroom and I didn't even see a toothbrush.

One evening I took us both by surprise. I hadn't thought at all about the literal act, the moment of asking, though of course the idea of being married to her was something I'd considered since the beginning. I had gone over the trodden middle-class ground, moving through the necessary business, how our *personalities* complemented each other, what our sex life was like (and might become), our money situation, what our fathers would say, the fact that she was white and I was Asian (was this one question, or two?) and then what our children might be like. Look like. Ironically, these were all the things that my father forever wanted me to consider, and to what as a teenager I had disingenously cried, "What about love?"

Old artificer, undead old man.

Before me, Lelia had come off a string of men who made her feel steadily sorry and confused and burgled. Each relationship was ending up a net loss. It struck her how a man could seem to gain a little bit of magic or grace or virtue with every woman he was with, but that a woman—though she said maybe she should be fair and just speak for herself—relinquished something each time, even if it ended mutually and well. One night in bed she said, "The men I've been with have this idea to make me over. I feel like a rock in some boy's polishing kit. I go in dull, scratched up, and then rumble rumble whirr, I'm supposed to come out precious and sparkling again."

"Does it work?"

"They seem to think so."

"How do you feel?" I asked.

"A little smaller."

Among other things, I took this as complimentary. The implication, of course, was that I wasn't trying the same number on her. This was true enough. I have no business improving others, much less buffing up Lelia, who has it over me in spades. Perhaps part of our trouble was that in the course of time there arose moments when I should have taken measures, done something, if only for what the actions would have said about my feelings for her.

I never envisioned myself in that kind of white hat, though, astride some fine horse, galloping into the main street of town. I mostly come by the midnight coach. If I may say this, I have always only ventured where I was invited or otherwise welcomed. When I was a boy, I wouldn't join any school club or organization before a member first approached me. I wouldn't eat or sleep at a friend's house if it weren't prearranged. I never assumed anyone would be generous to me, or in any way helpful. I never considered it my right to expect approval or sanction no matter what good I had done. My father always reminded me that neither he nor the world owed me a penny or a prayer, though he left me many millions of one and braying echoes of the other. So call me what you will. An assimilist, a lackey. A duteous foreign-faced boy. I have already been whatever you can say or imagine, every version of the newcomer who is always fearing and bitter and sad.

It's my brand of sloth, surely, that I could fail my wife so miserably but seem to provide all the necessary objects and affections. On paper, by any known standard, I was an impeccable mate. I did everything well enough. I cooked well enough, cleaned enough, was romantic and sensitive and silly enough, I made love enough, was paternal, big brotherly, just a good friend enough, father-to-my-son enough, forlorn enough, and then even bull-headed and dull and macho enough, to make it all seamless. For ten years she hadn't realized the breadth of what I had accomplished with my exacting competence, the daily *work* I did, which unto itself became an unassailable body of cover. And the surest testament to the magnificent and horrifying level of my virtuosity was that neither had I.

When I got to the flat Jack was waiting inside. He was set deep in the sofa, reading one of the magazines Hoagland had on subscription for us. We periodically told him not to bother but he didn't listen. Hoagland said it was part of our job to keep up with current issues, though none of us could figure out what he was getting at with the selections: *Redbook, Guns & Ammo, Town & Country,* some airline magazines, and then a few sundry *zines,* including a softcore glossy called *Dirt World Nation,* which was what Jack was reading. When he saw me he removed his delicate half-glasses from his bridgeless boxer's nose.

"I didn't see you outside so I came up," I said, shutting the door behind me. "How did you get in?"

"Grace gave me her key," he said.

"She doesn't need it?"

"She's off somewhere with Pete."

"Not for fun?"

"Those two? No way, Parky. All business, all business."

"Everything's *all business,*" I said. "Even with us."

"I know," he answered, putting down the magazine. He held out his big hands. "Now I can finally get out of this damn couch. You better pull."

It was his first real visit. He'd seen schematics Hoagland had drawn up, pictures he'd taken. I showed him around the flat. I turned on all the lights for him, ran the shower in the bathroom until it was hot, opened the doors of the refrigerator and the microwave. I showed him the listening devices Hoagland had installed in the drop ceiling. I could cut power to them whenever I wanted. I did it now. He was unimpressed but he didn't seem to mind.

He seemed a little tired. He kept coughing and complaining about the rainy weather. It was the end of March, he figured, so the rains would stay at least one more month. I noticed he was a bit slow in his talk. A place like this should have seemed too small for him, like a shallow hole in the ground, but he sat in a desk chair in one of the carpet-lined cubbies and listened while I harshly joked and grab-assed. Hoagland was the target, always the mode Jack and I favored.

He asked after Lelia, how the two of us were doing. I told him we were meeting often, almost twice a week. There were lunches, mid-evening drinks. We sat closer to each other now. We had gone to a few parties together. She even slept at our apartment one night—on the sofa—after a late dinner I'd made.

"Candles and wine?" Jack asked.

"A little of each," I said, pulling over a chair. "I kept the lights on high. I didn't want to make her nervous."

"It sounds like you are doing right."

"Am I? I'm not running on instinct."

"Yes you are," he said, tapping on the laptop in front of him. "You just don't know it."

"What are the signs?" I asked him.

"Fear and confusion."

"What else?"

"You need more than that?" he said, coughing again.

"I guess not."

"Parky," he said, leaning forward. "I have no worries about you and Lee. Twice a week you meet already! What more can you ask? Tell me, you touch each other?"

"Hellos and goodbyes."

"Naturally. Nothing else?"

"We're working up to something," I said. "But I don't think either of us is too keen on being the first to make a move. We've planned to go up next week to my father's house. We're going to spend the weekend finally cleaning it out. Maybe something will happen. Somehow, though, the consequences seem awesome. I realize it's pure junior high. I'm beginning to think we need Seven Minutes in Heaven."

"I don't know what you're talking about," Jack said, knitting his brow.

"Don't bother," I told him, waving it off. "I always forget you're not American."

"I don't see how," he replied, spreading his arms wide. His moustache twitched. His big voice suddenly came back. "Great are the gods I'm not. If I were American, there would be much hell to pay. I would have strangled Dennis many times over. That I can view him as a curiosity has saved both of us."

"That's your excuse," I said. "Your heart's just too big."

"My *Greek heart* is too big. My American one is still composed of delicate halves. They call them *gonads.*"

I said, "My hearts must be about to burst."

He bellowed in his way. He told me, "Just keep on meeting her. Don't try too hard. You have time. Don't think otherwise. She is your wife and she still loves you. At least Lelia's the easy one. She's not half the trouble you are."

"I try to be easy," I said.

"Naturally," Jack answered. "You were well raised. You have a keen sense of accommodation. This is clear. You understand respect and distance and separateness. Fine things. But someplace in your life you let them go too far. Too far for any more good to come of them. The result is foregone."

"You see the trail?"

"I don't know." He got up and paced. "Maybe this. *This.* Why you find yourself here in this silly room with a man like me, rather than at home in bed with your beautiful wife. Why you are one of us. I look at you and see someone who could have done whatever he wished in life. Any career."

"Yet I'm here."

"Yet you're here."

"Stuck."

"Yes. Maybe yes." Jack leaned on the blacked-out window, trying to scratch it with his thumb. "You have made your bed, as they say."

When Dennis Hoagland and I first met, outside the career services office of my alma mater, I thought it would be a brief affair. I was a few years out of school and beginning to think I ought to do some graduate study, though in what I didn't know. I was running out of money. But I had promised my father I'd look into serious work first, a career, and I drove to the campus to see what was being offered. It was the boom time, and the Wall Street banks and management consultants and insurance conglomerates were crowding the bulletin boards looking for talent.

I was looking at the various flyers and notices when he approached me. He wore a moustache then. He looked like one of those consumptive snooker players on cable. He said he was with a "research services firm." They were hiring new analysts. Competitive salaries, excellent benefits. We spoke for a few minutes, and because I wasn't really seriously considering a job, I was loose, sarcastic. He seemed to like me and said I should come to Westchester the next week to talk with his associates. I told him I didn't know. He said what could I lose? They would even pay me a stipend for my time. A simple interview. No strings. I asked what his company researched. "The one thing worth researching," he casually replied. "People."

I now asked Jack why he was in our line.

"I have good reasons," he said. "My excuse is that I was poor and dumb but hardy as an ox. I was not you. I needed any job that would have me. One day in Athens an American talks to me on the street. He says I look like a strong boy and he will give me fifty dollars to remove some papers from an office. No problem. The next week I get a hundred and fifty for setting fire to the same building. I drive a truck of coffins filled with rifles and grenades to the Albanian border. Next I help kidnap a man. Then another. One man I kidnap tells me that I work for the asshole CIA. I beat him badly for that. But why should I care? Soon I traveled the world doing dirty deeds. Who needed to like it? Who cared who employed me? I have done more or less the same for thirty years. This is where I will retire. I have only two months to finish. Then Dennis will give me my full pension. This firm was by far the easiest. But then I had Sophie to make right what I had done. Sophie was my life. I thought she was forgiveness for not doing those things anymore. She was to be God's gift to me, a blessing for having changed my ways."

"She's still a blessing."

"No no. She is gone."

Jack lightly rapped the glass with his knuckles. "You are kind. But you know a blessing so beautiful should not die. You and Lelia know this. Your boy. Your boy was a perfection. Was his life so that you might taste true wonder and happiness? Could it be that arbitrary? Please, no. Sometimes I suspect of us living that we are marred. The unspoiled must take leave of the world. I think they must bear the ills of their loved ones. I am not speaking as a Christian here. You know how I am not a Christian. But in my heart I fear they are the vessels for our failures. We make it impossible for them to live in this place. One day they fill up. Then they sink. They disappear."

He hacked into his fist and pulled a handkerchief from his back pocket to wipe his hand and his mouth. I asked him if he wanted some tea. He nodded. I put on water. When I came out he was sitting inside one of the bays, examining its laptop computer. He was trying to figure out how the screen opened. I folded it out and he made play of typing, his index fingers too big and thick for the cramped keyboard. He typed too hard, as if the keys were manual. I turned it on for him and brought up a program in which he could draw pictures. I showed him the mouse. The kettle was whistling and when I called back to ask what flavor he wanted he said something about my *register.*

I let it pass for a moment. I didn't answer him immediately and let his tea steep. I brought him his mug. Now he wanted to get to the place in the computer where he could type a message for Dennis. I switched him over. Then he asked me how often I was sending word.

I said to him, "What is Dennis saying? I don't think about these things anymore, so you better tell me."

"You know it, my friend," he spoke grimly. "I don't have to."

"What am I doing?" I said. "Why are you here, Jack?"

"My friend."

I said, "What am I doing?"

His shoulders softened. "Dennis wants more word. Simple. He deserves more contact. You could come up to Westchester sometimes."

"I'm not going up there again."

"Fine. You could make a gesture, however. For example, he said he has heard nothing from you about what happened at the church. He is very agitated, you know. Patiently he has been waiting. What do you have to say about this?"

"I've been processing it," I told him.

"What is there to process?" he cried. "It should be so simple. You see it and you write it down. A prank by schoolboys!"

"You know what those boys' lawyers are saying."

"Ah!" he groaned. "They will say anything. Do you really believe somebody would trust two eleven-year-olds to disrupt an event? With smoke bombs, no less? Sheer insanity. Who would pay fifty dollars, or five dollars, to little boys to do a man's job?"

"I know a man who might."

"Ah!" He threw up his hands. "You are becoming a very fine neurotic, my friend."

"I have good training."

"Perhaps," Jack said, his feet and hands restless. "Dennis might not agree at this point. He is agitated. I should tell you he looks ill. He is saying the firm is not getting enough business lately. He wants all our present work to get done by the numbers. No more playing around. He is serious. He made a speech to us."

"I'm sorry I missed it."

"I mean it. For your sake you should know. You know how he wears his anxiety on his sleeve. You can see how terrible he would be out in the field. And he has been privately lecturing the others. Reminding them about the great investment he has made in the business. He passed out a listing of all that he has given up for them. Of course he hates being a technocrat. Pete and the others are so bored with him. They joke and whisper *old fart Lear* behind his back. I haven't asked them yet what this means."

"It means we're headed for family trouble," I said. "The meanest kind."

Jack answered, "Not necessarily."

"Then why are you here?"

Jack snorted. "I am too old. I am tired. I just wanted to see your face. If that is a crime. What Dennis wants I won't quarrel with. You know how I felt at the start of this business. You were not in the right state of mind anymore. Luzan made certain things difficult for you."

"Luzan, Luzan."

"No jokes. I want to be serious now. Let me be serious with you." He took a last sip of his tea. "Listen to me. Be quiet and listen. You should have left us then but you started this thing. I suppose it cannot matter now. You are on the assignment. So now I say, see it through. Present your man Kwang. Give Dennis what he is paying you for. Find something he can use. What about these rumors of a money operation? People sending him money. That Spanish kid you name, corner him."

"No angle there," I said. "He's just a good kid. He's a mascot. There isn't anything." So far Kwang was clean, as far as I knew. There was the street money, certainly, but that was nothing out of the ordinary. And the constant rumors about massive secret contributions to Kwang were nothing I could see.

"Then perhaps you should go straight home," Jack said. "Go home to your wife if there is nothing."

I said, "Help me, Jack."

He waited, opening his arms.

I asked him, "I want to know if he can be put in danger."

"You sound like a rookie," he said. "This is a rookie interest."

"I don't give a shit."

He frowned a little, his melancholic Jack-face. "What can I say? He is a very public figure. Luzan was not. This is not to say I know anything. This is not a nuance. But people think of John Kwang. He is in the language now. The buildings and streets there are written with him. In this sense he exists."

I said, "It ought to mean something."

"Yes."

"You don't seem convinced."

He looked away from me. "Well, then perhaps you should operate as if he is in danger."

"That's not an answer."

"You know as well as anyone that we are not an answer business."

"Jack."

"What are you going to do, Parky, hold me down and pummel me?"

"I may. You have seventy-five pounds on me but I may."

Suddenly he looked hurt.

"I'm sorry," I told him.

"I have been tortured before," he said gravely. "By more persuasive people. Not a sweetheart like you. And they got nothing."

"I'm sorry."

"Forget it," he said, but I knew his quick answer, if anything, was just an American convention, an easy idiom. He got up to put on his raincoat but I asked him to stay a little longer. There must have been something desperate or pitiable in my voice, for he slung his coat back over the partition. He said while he was here I might as well go over a few things. Show him the protocol.

I was supposed to come here every few nights and write out the daily register. As trained, I would follow the journalistic method, naming the who, the what, the where, when, and then very briefly interpret it, offer the how and why of what Kwang did or said. I would then by modem transmit my pages directly to the main-office computer, from which only Hoagland could download files with his password. Jack, being my assignment operator, my wing, was seeing whatever Hoagland let him, which was likely everything. Jack probably knew that the registers I'd been sending were useless. And even they had been growing infrequent. My coverage wasn't daily anymore, as it had been for the first few weeks. It was more like every other day, or every third, that I sent something.

I could probably assume that there was the onset of a worry again, concern at the office about good Henry, good Harry, Parky. All my good names. Hoagland had always let everyone there know how good I was at writing the daily register. I wasn't slick Pete with the subjects, or Jimmy Baptiste when things got rough, or Grace with her nose for the potential mistake or breakdown. I simply wrote textbook examples of our workaday narrative, veritable style sheets that Hoagland even used to remind the other analysts of how it ought to be done. He'd periodically tape them on the wall near the coffeemaker and I'd see graffiti markered across the pages in Pete's or Jimmy's laughing hand: *Teacher's pet,* and *Korean geek,* and *Oh what talent.*

For a brief time, I even harbored a little pride.

And sometimes I will write them out now, again, though for myself, those old strokes, unofficial versions of any newcomer I see in the street or on the bus or in the demi-shops of the city, the need in me still to undo the cipherlike faces scrawled with hard work, and no work, and all trouble. The faces of my father and his workers, and Ahjuhma, and the ever-dimming one of my mother. I will write out the face of the young girl I saw only yesterday wearily unloading small sacks of basmati in front of her family's store, a baby wrapped tightly to her back with a sheet of raw cloth, the very sheet being her shirt, the warm hump now her back, her brother or sister the same thing as her weight.

Jack and I talked a little while longer before he left. I mentioned how much I had been encountering Kwang. Jack didn't seem too interested or concerned. He just asked if I liked him. The question struck me as strange, but he spoke in a tone that said it would be natural if I did. I told him as far as I could tell. He brought up nothing else specific. In the sudden quiet I showed him the electronic way I sent in the reports. How we printed them out. He nodded. He clapped my shoulder with fondness and lightly boxed my ear. Perhaps if I had grown up with a father like him I would be a more physical person today. I would have made my answer with a nudge. The smallest pitch of my weight. I would have assured him as I truly wanted, made the necessary offering.

But I did not. I celebrate every order of silence borne of the tongue and the heart and the mind. I am a linguist of the field. You, too, may know the troubling, expert power. It finds hard expression in the faces of those who would love you most. Look there now. All you see will someday fade away. To what chill of you remains.

I steadily entrenched myself in the routines of Kwang's office. When I wasn't out working with Janice, I was the willing guy Friday. I let the staffers know through painstaking displays of competence and efficiency that I was serious about the work however menial and clerical, and that I was ready to do what anyone of authority required. I was just the person they were looking for. I answered phones and made plasticene overheads and picked up dry cleaning and kids from day care. I had to show the staff that I possessed native intelligence but not so great a one or of a certain kind that it impeded my sense of duty.

This is never easy; you must be at once convincing and unremarkable. It takes long training and practice, an understanding of one's self-control and self-proportion: you must know your effective *size* in a given situation, the tenor at which you might best speak. Hoagland would talk for hours on the subject. He bemoaned the fact that Americans generally made the worst spies. Mostly he meant whites. Even with methodical training they were inclined to run off at the mouth, make unnecessary displays of themselves, unconsciously slip in the tiniest flourish that could scare off a nervous contact. An off-color anecdote, a laugh in the wrong place. They felt this subcutaneous aching to let everyone know they were a spook, they couldn't help it, it was like some charge or vanity of the culture, à la James Bond and Maxwell Smart.

"If I were running a big house like the CIA," Hoagland said to me once, "I'd breed agents by raising white kids in your standard Asian household. Discipline farms."

His Boys from Bushido.

I told him go ahead. Incubate. See what he got. He'd have platoons of guys like Pete Ichibata deployed about the globe, each too brilliant for his own good, whose primary modes were sorrow and parody. Then, too, regret. Pete makes a good spook but a good spook has no brothers, no sisters, no father or mother. He's intentionally lost that huge baggage, those encumbering remnants of blood and flesh, and because of this he carries no memory of a house, no memory of a land, he seems to have emerged from nowhere. He's brought himself forth, self-cesarean. If I see him at all it is the picture of him silently whittling down fruitwood dowels into the most refined sets of chopsticks, the used-up squares of finishing sandpaper petaling about his desk amid the other detritus of peanut shells and wood shavings and peels of tangerine, the skins of everything he touches compulsively mined, strip-searched.

His friendly advice on how to handle Luzan was that I actively seek out his weaknesses, expose and use them to take him apart, limb from limb, cell by cell. Pete was a kind of anti-therapist, a professional who steadily ruined you session by session. He was a one-man crisis of faith. He was skilled enough in our work that he didn't simply listen, watch, wait; he poked and denuded and uncovered secrets while still remaining unextraordinary to the subject, making the subjects dismantle themselves through his care and guidance without their ever realizing it.

As part of my initial training I watched him work a Chinese graduate student at Columbia. The student was starting a doctorate in electrical engineering. He also organized rallies against the hard-liners in Beijing in the flag plaza of the UN.

Pete and I were supposedly working with a Japanese daily, the something something *Shimbun,* Pete the reporter and me in tow taking pictures. Wen Zhou, our subject, his face fleshy like a boy's, sat quietly for us in his tiny, orderly studio apartment in Morningside Heights. As my rented Nikkormat clicked and whirred, Pete plied him with the expected questions but then in a filial tone smattered with perfect Mandarin asked after his family and his studies and the long way he must feel from home. Pete then smoked a cigarette with him. I kept working the shutter, getting angles we didn't need, even though I'd long run out of film. The two of them joked about American girls. Pete tried to get me involved but I just grunted when he asked what I thought. Wen shyly said he didn't know any well but wouldn't mind meeting one. A date would be fun. He confessed to a fancy for those with reddish hair. Pete laughed and told him he knew a few and they ought to go drinking together and have a fun time, and then he asked Wen if he wasn't concerned for the safety of his loved ones back in China, with his face and name in the news. Wen said no one immediate, they were all living in Kowloon now, or some other place, but that yes there was one person, a young woman he'd befriended at the national university, a bright and ambitious girl from the southern provinces. He said he had stopped writing to her, so she wouldn't have any trouble.

Pete kept on him, talking so gently and sweetly that he seemed all the more furious in his discipline, and I thought he had to be murdering himself inside to hold the line like that. We had been there nearly an hour. In the second hour Wen broke. He opened like the great gates of the Forbidden City. Pete led us inside the walls. We got whole scrolls of names, people both here and in China, and even names of contributors (all of them minor, not even the stuff of trivia) who helped the students by paying for flyers and banners and the renting of meeting halls.

I was enjoying myself. I was thrilled with what we were doing, as with a discovery, like finding a new place you like, or a good book. I felt explicitly that secret living I'd known throughout my life, but now for the first time it took the form of a bizarre sanction being with Pete and even Wen. We laughed heartily together. We three thieves American. Wen was soon talking without prompts from Pete about his giant China, about the provinces, and poverty, the backwardness of people and leaders. It was both stony and nostalgic, the whole messy text of his homesickness. He liked New York City. The only other place he had been was West Lafayette, Indiana, doing a term of research at Purdue. "I guess I am a Boilermaker."

He spoke the sweetest, halting English. Caesurae abounding. He kept saying, "America and Japan strong, but China is the future place." He retrieved an album from below his sofa bed and showed us pictures of a collective farm where his father grew up, a full page of his grandmother, a shrunken woman with three teeth and skin the color of chestnuts, his mother and father and sister in the middle of Hong Kong harbor on a tour junk, overdressed, looking sea-green. And I thought I heard Pete say to him, "And you'll be back someday."

But then Wen said the name of the girl he loved. I knew immediately that she was doomed. I don't remember her name, maybe I forgot it instantly when he volunteered the thing. Rather what I recall exactly was Pete's face, which I caught reconfiguring, lamping up with the day's first piece of truly useful information. There was a joy there, if oblique, left-handed, and Wen probably thought here was a man with whom he could share a longing. I noticed earlier that Pete hadn't asked after her when Wen first brought her up. Of course he wasn't missing anything. Not a step. It's the simplest finesse, Dennis Hoagland lesson number one, and only effective with virginals like Wen, who would never imagine anything beyond a simple polarity to the world. Positive and negative. You couldn't fault him, for why would an immense China ever need a third party to reach a person like him, the tiniest of the tiny, so easily forgotten, whom no one ever listened to anyway?

The Kwang job was different. Nobody in the office was a cherry. This was street-level urban politics, conducted house by house, block by block, the work sweaty and inglorious. You could get mugged or beaten up if you strayed down an alley, or knocked on the wrong door. Bravery didn't matter. Nor raw smarts. You had to be tactical. Suspicious. Ready to admit your losses. Careful with the tongue.

And as Hoagland always said, "Brave like the gazelle."

In truth the setup was perfect for me. I had to agree with Dennis on that one. I didn't have to manufacture the circumstances in which I could ask questions that would get worthwhile answers. I didn't have to push too hard. Each day brought scores of regular people and visitors through the offices, and with all the lesser meetings and speeches Kwang attended to weekly, the countless minor moments, I witnessed what ertswhile observers—anthropologists and pundits alike—might have called his *natural state.*

His human clues. I'd sit in one corner of his office during the three hours on Wednesdays that he opened his door to speak with "walk-ins," the sundry visitors and neighborhood groups. By noon they'd be lined up in skeins outside the building, all kinds of people, people holding bags and children, people in suits, in smocks.

I sat in on the meetings with him and took notes. He wanted a record of each person and his or her concerns, and afterward I had to quickly interview them myself for their personal and biographical information. The office kept an electronic database of every voter and potential voter we encountered, and then those that it reached through regular mailers. With this body of files we could sift and sort through the population of the district by gender, race, ethnicity, party affiliation, occupation. We had names and birthdates of their children and relatives. Data on weekly income, what they paid in rent, in utilities, if they were on public assistance, how long. If they had been victims of crime. Their houses of worship. The languages they spoke, in rank of proficiency. The list always growing, profligate. Almost biblical.

On Fridays, John Kwang took home a stack of double-wide green-and-white printouts to commit to memory. It was something you eventually learned when you worked here: John Kwang was a devotee of memory. I thought it strange, first on the obvious level of why a busy and ambitious politician would devote any amount of time to memorizing lists of people he'd never need to know. Then I wondered if he wasn't simply odd, nervous. An uptight Korean man. What I eventually saw was that he never intended to know each live body in the district, his purpose wasn't statistical mastery, although that certainly happened. The memorizing was more a discipline for him, like a serious craft or martial art, a chosen kind of suffering involving hours of practice and concentration by which you gradually came to know yourself.

Late in the afternoon one Friday I was printing out the newest records in the war room. Kwang must have heard the whine of the machine and looked in. He caught me scanning the sheets. I was always good at memory games, and as a boy I annoyed my father by beating him if he slipped just once. But now, serene with Hoagland's method, my memory is fantastic, near diabolic. It arrests whatever appears before my eyes. I don't memorize anymore. I simply see.

When the printing was done I folded the sheaf in half so it would fit inside his briefcase. He took it graciously. He said nothing as I helped him with his light overcoat. I was ready for him to ask me what my interest in the printout was but instead he said if I wasn't busy he would like me to come have drink and good food with him. That was how he said it, *drink and good food.* Certain things he still expressed with a foreigner's simplicity. May and the boys were upstate for the week at their house on Cayuga

Lake, and he said he wasn't in the mood to eat by himself. It was a strange thing to hear from a Korean man, and I wondered what circumstance would have had to arise for my father to profess openly a feeling like that.

"Learning the business, I see," John finally said, affably. We were walking outside. "In past times, a person's education was a matter of what he could remember. It still is in Korea and Japan. I must assume in China as well. Americans like to believe this is the great failing of Asia. Why the Japanese are good at copying and not inventing, which is no longer really true, if it ever was. I had a teacher who made us memorize scores of classical Chinese and Korean poems. We had to recite any one of them on command. He was hoping to give us knowledge, but what he actually impressed upon us was a legacy. He would smack the top of your head if you hadn't perfectly prepared the assignment, but then later in the class he could be overcome after reading a poem aloud."

He stopped to unlock the door for me. He drove a new Lincoln Continental. I noticed that he drove several different cars as well, and then only American models; a politician, especially an Asian-American one, doesn't have a choice in the matter. He had interests in car dealerships and a local chain of electronics stores, in addition to his core business of selling high-end dry-cleaning equipment.

"Young Master Lim," he said. "He was becoming a respected writer when the war broke out. We later heard that he was killed in the fighting. Sometime before the school was closed he said it was our solemn duty to act as vessels for our country and civilization, that we must give ourselves over to what had come before us, as much to literature as we did to our parents and ancestors. You look like him, I think. Around the eyes. Thick lidded."

"My mother's," I said.

"Ah. You know, Henry, why they're so? They're thick to keep the spirit warm and contented."

"I don't know if my mother would have said they worked," I told him.

"How about for you?" he asked.

I laughed a little bit and said, "They work perfectly."

We joked a little more, I thought like regular American men, faking, dipping, juking. I found myself listening to us. For despite how well he spoke, how perfectly he moved through the sounds of his words, I kept listening for the errant tone, the flag, the minor mistake that would tell of his original race. Although I had seen hours of him on videotape, there was something that I still couldn't abide in his speech. I couldn't help but think there was a mysterious dubbing going on, the very idea I wouldn't give quarter to when I would speak to strangers, the checkout girl, the mechanic, the professor, their faces dully awaiting my real speech, my truer talk and voice. When I was young I'd look in the mirror and address it, as if daring the boy there; I would say something dead and normal, like, "Pleased to make your acquaintance," and I could barely convince myself that it was I who was talking.

We hit the Friday night street traffic on 39th Avenue going west toward Corona. The restaurant was a dozen or so blocks farther than that, near Elmhurst, a new Korean barbecue house. He talked steadily through the stop and go, freely using his hands to punctuate his speech, the movements subtle but stylized, what I recognized as Anglo. The boycotts of Korean grocers were spreading from Brooklyn to other parts of the city, to black neighborhoods in the Bronx and even in his home borough, in the Williamsburg section, and then also in upper Manhattan. Though he wasn't having trouble in his own neighborhoods, he was being hounded by the media for statements and opinions on the mayor's handling of them, particularly the first riot in Brownsville, where a mostly black crowd, watched over by a handful of police, looted and arsoned a Korean-owned grocery.

"De Roos has positioned himself in the situation very skillfully," he said. "He denounces the violence but has Chillingsworth nearby to take the heat for letting things get out of hand. He has his lieutenants leak his concern about Chillingsworth's decision-making but then in public says he stands behind 'the commissioner's expertise and judgment.' "

Roy Chillingsworth was the police commissioner. He'd worked in New Orleans and Dade County, Florida, before being hired by De Roos early in the present term. He was a prosecuting attorney by training. He had a reputation for being tough on drug dealers and gangs and illegal immigrants. And he was black.

"No one ultimately faults the commissioner," Kwang said. "There weren't any deaths or injuries. Given that, it's almost acceptable that he didn't order in more police to arrest his own people. The mayor himself didn't lose any black confidence or votes. Perhaps he even gained some. All along, he offered himself as a model of liberal reaction, which is initially fascination and disdain, but then relief. It's a race war everyone can live with. Blacks and Koreans somehow seem meant for trouble in America. It was long coming. In some ways we never had a chance. But then, Henry, I imagine that you know these difficulties firsthand."

He knew my father had run vegetable stores in the city. I knew that Kwang might hear of this when I told Eduardo, given how close they seemed to be. I wasn't overly concerned in the beginning—nor were Dennis and Jack, for that matter—that I was employing my own life as material for my alter identity. Though to a much lesser extent, a certain borrowing is always required in our work. But this assignment made it, in fact, quite necessary to allow for more than the usual trade. When the line between identities is fine (and the situation is not dangerous), it's preferable not to build up a whole other, nearly parallel legend.

This, Jack had once told me, was the source of my troubles with Emile Luzan. Inconsistencies began to arise in crucial details, all of which I inexplicably confused and alternated. From the soft stuffed chair of his office I told the kind brown-faced doctor that my son had suffocated while playing alone with a plastic garbage bag, or that my American *girlfriend* was conducting extended research in Europe, or that my father had recently taken *a second wife;* and then in another session, in another week, I might tell him another set of near-truths, forget my conflations and hidings and offer him whatever lay immediately within my grasp.

Luzan himself was afraid I was unraveling. He held my hand to comfort me. He eventually recommended a course of medication. But for me it was simply loose, terrible business. The kind of display my father would not have tolerated in any member of his family. It would have sickened him.

Nobody give two damn about your problem or pain, he might say. *You just take care yourself. Keep it quiet.*

I didn't have to tell John Kwang the first thing about my father and our life, at least in relation to what he was talking about. I told him what my *ah-boh-jee* had done for work. Simply, it felt good not having to explain any further. To others you need to explain so much to get across anything worthwhile. It's not like a flavor that you can offer and have someone simply taste. The problem, you realize, is that while you have been raised to speak quietly and little, the notions of where you come from and who you are need a maximal approach. I used to wish that I were more like my Jewish and Italian friends, or even the black kids who hung out in front of my father's stores; I was envious of how they'd speak so confidently, so jubilantly celebrate the fact with their hands and hips and tongues, letting it all hang out (though of course in different ways) for anybody who'd look and listen.

As we passed the rows of Korean stores on the boulevard, John could tell me the names of the owners and previous owners. Mr. Kim, before him Park, Hong, then Cho, Im, Noh, Mrs. Yi. He himself once ran a wholesale shop on this very row, long before all of it became Korean in the 1980s. He sold and leased dry-cleaning machines and commercial washers and dryers, only high-end equipment. He expanded quickly from the little neighborhood business, the street-front store, for he had mastered enough language to deal with non-Korean suppliers and distributors in other cities and Europe. Other Koreans depended on him to find good deals and transact them. Suddenly, he existed outside the intimate community of his family and church and the street where he conducted his commerce. He wasn't bound to 600 square feet of ghetto retail space like my father, who more or less duplicated the same basic store in various parts of the city. Those five stores defined the outer limit of his ambition, the necessary end of what he could conceive for himself. I am not saying that my father was not a remarkable and clever man, though I know of others like him who have reached farther into the land and grabbed hold of every last advantage and opportunity. My father simply did his job. Better than most, perhaps.

Kwang, though, kept pushing, adding to his wholesale stores by eventually leasing plants in North Carolina to assemble in part the machines he sold for the Italian and German manufacturers. He bought into car and electronics dealerships, too, though it was known that some of the businesses had been troubled in recent years, going without his full attention. The rumor was that he'd lost a few million at least. But he seemed to have plenty left. At the age of forty-one he started attending Fordham full-time for his law and business degrees. I have seen pictures of the graduation day hung about his house, Kwang and his wife, May, smiling in the bright afternoon light, bear-hugging each other. He passed the bar immediately, though I know he never intended to practice the law or big corporate business. He wanted the credentials. But that sounds too cynical of him, which would be all wrong. He wasn't vulnerable to that kind of pettiness. He was old-fashioned enough that he believed he needed proper intellectual training and expertise before he could serve the public.

"Henry," he said, "over there, on the far corner." There were two men talking and pointing at each other in the open street display of a wristwatch and handbag store. The lighted sign read H&J ENTERPRISES, with smaller Korean characters on the ends. He pulled us over and I followed him out.

The owner recognized Kwang immediately, and stopped arguing with the other man and quickly bowed. The man was shaking a gold-toned watch: it had stopped working and he wanted his money back. The Korean explained to us that he only gave exchanges, no refunds, he seemed to say again for all, pointing continually at the sign that said so by the door. Besides, he told Kwang in Korean, this man bought the watch many months ago, during the winter, and he was being generous enough in offering him another one. He added, *You know how these blacks are, always expecting special treatment.*

Kwang let the statement pass. He introduced himself to the man, telling him he was a councilman. He asked the man if he had bought other things at the store.

"I stop here every couple weeks," the man answered. "Maybe pick out something for my wife."

"One time a muhnt!" the Korean insisted.

The man shook his head and mouthed, "Bullshit." He explained he'd originally come to get an exchange, but the owner was so rude and hard to understand (intentionally, he thought) that he decided to demand a full refund instead. He wasn't going to leave until he got one. He showed us the receipt. Kwang nodded and then gestured for the storekeeper to speak with him inside the store. I waited outside with the customer. I remember him particularly well because his name, Henry, was embossed on a tag clipped to his shirt pocket. When I told him my name he smiled weakly and looked in the store for Kwang. I didn't say anything else and he coughed and adjusted his glasses and said he was tired and frustrated and just wanted his money or an exchange so he could get on home. He was a salesman at the big discount office furniture store off 108th Street.

"I don't know why I keep shopping here," he said to me, searching the wares in the bins. "It's mostly junk anyway. My wife kind of enjoys the jewelry, though, and it's pretty inexpensive, I suppose. Buying a watch here was my mistake. I should know better. Thirteen ninety-nine. And *I know* I wasn't born yesterday."

We laughed a little. Henry explained that it was easy to stop here on

Fridays to buy something for his wife, a pair of earrings or a bracelet. "She works real hard all week and I like to give her a little present, to let her know I know what's going on." She was a registered nurse. He showed me a five-dollar set of silver earrings. "I was gonna buy these, but I don't know, you don't expect anybody to be *nice* anymore, but that man in there, he can be cold."

I didn't try to explain the store owner to Henry, or otherwise defend him. I don't know what stopped me. Maybe there was too much to say. Where to begin?

Certainly my father ran his stores with an iron attitude. It was amazing how successful he still was. He generally saw his customers as adversaries. He disliked the petty complaints about the prices, especially from the customers in Manhattan. "Those millionaires is biggest trouble," he often said when he got home. "They don't like anybody else making good money." He hated explaining to them why his prices were higher than at other stores, even the other Korean ones, though he always did. He would say without flinching that his produce was simply the best. The freshest. They should shop at other stores and see for themselves. He tried to put on a good face, but it irked him all the same.

With blacks he just turned to stone. He never bothered to explain his prices to them. He didn't follow them around the aisles like some storekeepers do, but he always let them know there wasn't going to be any *funny business* here. When a young black man or woman came in—old people or those with children in tow didn't seem to alarm him—he took his broom and started sweeping at the store entrance very slowly, deliberately, not looking at the floor. He wouldn't make any attempt to hide what he was doing. At certain stores there were at least two or three incidents a day. Shoplifting, accusations of shoplifting, complaints and arguments. Always arguments.

To hear those cries now: the scene a stand of oranges, a wall of canned ham. I see my father in his white apron, sleeves rolled up. A woman in a dirty coat. They lean in and let each other have it, though the giving is almost in turns. It's like the most awful and sad opera, the strong music of his English, then her black English; her colorful, almost elevated, mocking of him, and his grim explosions. They fight like lovers, scarred, knowing. Their song circular and vicious. For she always comes back the next day, and so does he. It's like they are here to torture each other. He can't afford a store anywhere else but where she lives, and she has no other place to buy a good apple or a fresh loaf of bread.

In the end, after all those years, he felt nothing for them. Not even pity. To him a black face meant inconvenience, or trouble, or the threat of death. He never met any blacks who measured up to his idea of decency; of course he'd never give a man like Henry half a chance. It was too risky. He personally knew several merchants who had been killed in their stores, all by blacks, and he knew of others who had shot or killed someone trying to rob them. He had that one close call himself, of which he never spoke.

For a time, he tried not to hate them. I will say this. In one of his first stores, a half-wide fruit and vegetable shop on 173rd Street off Jerome in the Bronx, he hired a few black men to haul and clean the produce. I remember my mother looking worried when he told her. But none of them worked out. He said they either came to work late or never and when they did often passed off fruit and candy and six-packs of beer to their friends. Of course, he never let them work the register.

Eventually, he replaced them with Puerto Ricans and Peruvians. The "Spanish" ones were harder working, he said, because they didn't speak English too well, just like us. This became a kind of rule of thumb for him, to hire somebody if they couldn't speak English, even blacks from Haiti or Ethiopia, because he figured they were new to the land and understood that no one would help them for nothing. The most important thing was that they hadn't been in America too long.

I asked Henry instead if he had known of Kwang before. He didn't, not caring much for politics or politicians. "But you know," he said, "he's not like all the other Koreans around here, all tense and everything."

When they returned, the shop owner approached Henry and nodded very slightly, in the barest bow, and offered him another watch, this one boxed in clear plastic. "I give you betteh one!" he said, indicating the higher price on the sticker. "Puh-rease accept earring too. Pfor your wifuh. No chargeh!"

Henry looked confused and was about to decline when John Kwang reached over and vigorously shook his hand, pinning the jewelry there. "This is a gift," he said firmly. "Mr. Baeh would like you to accept it."

Henry shook our hands and left for home. As we waited for the traffic to pass so we could pull away from the curb, I saw Baeh inside his tiny store shaking his head as he quickly hung handbags. Every third or fourth one he banged hard against the plastic display grid. He wouldn't look back out at us. Kwang saw him, too. We drove a few blocks before he said anything.

"He knows what's good for us is good for him," Kwang said grimly. "He doesn't have to like it. Right now, he doesn't have any choice."

At the time I didn't know what Kwang meant by that last notion, what kind of dominion or direct influence he had over people like Baeh. I only considered the fact of his position and stature in the community as what had persuaded the storekeeper to deal fairly with Henry. I assumed Baeh was honoring the traditional Confucian structure of community, where in each village a prominent elder man heard the townspeople's grievances and arbitrated and ruled. Though in that world Baeh would have shown displeasure only in private. He would have acted as the dutiful younger until the wise man was far down the road.

But respect is often altered or lost in translation. Here on 39th Avenue of old Queens, in the mixed lot of peoples, respect (and honor and kindness) is a matter of margins, what you can clear on a $13.99 quartz watch, or how much selling it takes to recover when you give one away. I knew that Mr. Baeh would stay open late tonight, maybe for no more of a chance than to catch the dance club overflow a full five hours later, drunk and high kids who might blow a few bucks on one of his gun-metal rings or satin scarves or T-shirts. The other merchants on the block would do the same. The Vietnamese deli, the West Indian takeout. Stay open. Keep the eyes open. You are your cheapest labor. Here is the great secret, the great mystery to an immigrant's success, the dwindle of irredeemable hours beneath the cheap tube lights. Pass them like a machine. Believe only in chronology. This will be your coin-small salvation.

The Korean restaurant had two floors. The main floor was for casual diners, lone businessmen and couples and families. The upstairs was reserved for quieter meals and private parties. The tables were all large enough for a small metal hollow to be fitted in their centers. When you order *kalbi* or *bulgogi,* a man brings a tin of red-hot coals to set inside the pit of the table. He then places over it a cast-iron grill. The waitress brings a platter of the marinated meat and starts cooking it. She leaves and then comes back with a huge tray of side plates, prepared vegetables and shellfish and seaweed and four or five kinds of kimchee. A basket of fresh lettuce, hot bean paste. Covered metal bowls of rice. She brings Korean beer. A bubbling stone crock of fish stew. She brings more plates, none larger than a hand, and soon the table is completely covered. There must be almost twenty plates. The Korean table is a lesson in plates. You finish the grilling yourself, the way you like it, and then wrap the sweetened meat with rice and paste in leaf lettuce, and eat quickly with your hands.

The hostess appeared from the coat room and greeted us with bows. She took our coats. John Kwang walked a few steps with her and said something I couldn't hear, but she nodded and then led us to an upstairs room.

She was very lovely. Beautifully colored, if this can be said, the blackness of her hair, the faint blush of her cheek, her lips. And there was a serenity to her expression which I could not decide on, whether it was the face of someone simply a little tired or quelling a sadness. It must be the obvious keeping of secrets that I find so attractive. I watched her as she ascended. Her hair was pulled back and held in a tight bun. She wore a traditional Korean costume, the shortened brocade vest and billowing long skirt in bright yellow and red silk and rainbow bands around the oversized sleeves. It wasn't an outfit for working, by any means, though the woman moved easily in it.

The hostess pushed open a wood-and-paper sliding screen to the private room, and inside there was a low Korean-style table and sitting mats and a central ceiling vent for the grill smoke. She bowed again and took away our shoes. I realized she had not spoken a word to us.

Soon afterward a man wearing a suit came in, speaking effusively in Korean. He carried a tray of porcelain shot glasses and a small bottle of *soju,* clear liquor made from potatoes. The man, who I realized was the manager and owner, was saying how honored he was for *Master Kwang* to have come in to his fledgling establishment. He wanted the *Master and his protégé* to be special guests of his tonight, and hoped the house cuisine would be to our taste.

Kwang tried to protest but the manager insisted by pouring out two glasses of *soju* for us. Kwang then leaned forward to offer one to him, but I interceded and poured a third shot from the bottle. We toasted each other and drank. We made several more toasts and it wasn't until the arrival of the first course of *gochoo pajun* (hot pepper and scallion fritters) that the manager rose to leave.

Master Kwang, he said before sliding shut the screen, *may your presence here be a blessing to this house as you have been a blessing to our brethren in New York.* He bowed several times and backed out and shut the screen.

Kwang seemed relieved to have him go. He must have had two dozen conversations a day like this. He loosened his tie and rolled up his sleeves to eat.

"You have a family, yes?" Kwang asked, placing a strip of *pajun* on my dish with his chopsticks.

"I have a wife."

"Is she Korean?"

"No," I said.

"Ah. Any children?" he asked, sounding hopeful, like my father once had.

I shook my head. Then I said, "Once."

He looked at me gravely. "I'm sorry, Henry. I don't mean to pry. You ought to tell me if I am."

"You're not," I said.

"Well, I won't ruin your meal. I didn't invite you for that." He poured me more *soju.* "I just wanted to meet you. Janice gave me a copy of your résumé. You must be smart to have gone to such a good school. I hope the same for my sons. You were born where?"

"Here."

"Yes. As you've seen, there aren't many Koreans working for me aside from the students from CUNY. No *adults,* as it were, except for you."

"I guess I should be an investment banker or lawyer."

Kwang laughed. "I'm happy you're not! Ah, I know that is what all the young Korean-Americans are doing. Some in medicine, engineering. Good for them. We need them all to succeed. My wife's niece, Sara, is already a vice-president in mergers and acquisitions. She's only twenty-eight. Whenever I see her she asks if I'm thinking of selling my business. 'Is there a buyer?' I asked her last time. 'Give me eighteen hours,' she said so seriously. I had to tear away her cellular phone. All she'd have to do is talk half a minute with my accountant to know there's nothing to interest her. She thinks I'm much bigger than I am. Much bigger. She says if I run for mayor she wants to be comptroller, of all things."

"Is she electable?"

"Eminently," he answered, smiling. "She's dynamite."

I took the obvious opening. "The real question," I said to him, "is whether you're going to run."

He replied without looking up from his dish. "The papers seem to think so."

This was true. I had read numerous editorials in the last few months that had questioned De Roos' interest in genuinely improving the city, suggesting that he had grown comfortable and cynical and out of touch with his job, being now in his second term. Assuming a third. But the feeling was that the city was beginning to buckle under its burdens. Businesses were relocating to New Jersey because of high taxes and crime. There was a string of deadly subway accidents. Some schools were spending more on metal detectors than on lab equipment. There were no neighborhoods—even on the Upper East and West sides of Manhattan—that were safe. De Roos, suddenly, was looking as if he had been asleep at the wheel. The editorialists suggested John Kwang, among others, as someone who could bring a fresh face to confront the city's ills, a politician who could better understand the needs of the rapidly changing populace.

Mostly, it was the season's language. Kwang, it was easy to see, was already running into his first real troubles. The press was having a field day. They had multiple boycotts to cover. Vandalism. Street-filling crowds of chanting blacks. Heavily armed Koreans. Fires in the night. The pictures were the easiest 11 P.M. drama. Nothing John Kwang could say or do would win him praise. His sympathy for either side was a bias for one. He couldn't even speak out against the obvious violence and destruction, after black groups had insisted they were "demonstrations" against the callousness of Korean merchants and the unjust acquittal of the Korean storeowner who'd shot and killed Saranda Harlans. The papers and television stations were starting to go back and forth with "information" and "statements." Reporters talked to anyone on the street. What I was noticing most was the liberty they took with the Koreans. A reporter cornered some grocer in an apron, or a woman in the door of her shop, both of them looking drawn and weary. The lighting was too harsh. The Koreans stood there, uneasy, trying to explain difficult notions in a broken English. Spliced into the news stories, sound-bited, they always came off as brutal, heartless. Like human walls.

"Sometimes I have serious thoughts about running," he said, pausing now from the eating. He leaned forward on the table with his forearms. "But I'm suspicious. It's usually after some round of clamor. That's not a good sign, obviously. I find myself getting caught up. When others construct and model you favorably, it's easy to let them keep at it, even if they start going off in ways that aren't immediately comfortable or right. This is the challenge for us Asians in America. How do you say no to what seems like a compliment? From the very start we don't wish to be rude or inconsiderate. So we stay silent in our guises. We misapply what our parents taught us. I'm as guilty as anyone. For instance, this talk that I'm the one to revitalize the Democratic party in New York."

"That's the mayor's secret mission," I replied. De Roos had been pushing this angle since the last campaign. He had an idea to remake the image of the local party machinery. He himself had mentioned John Kwang as a part of that vanguard, though his implication was then cast only in terms of *succession.* "But people think that the shoe fits better on you."

"In theory," John said, "all in theory." By the tone of his voice I thought he was going to drop the subject, but he downed his *soju* and filled both our cups again. His voice cracked with the fume of the liquor. "But the fact is, Henry, that it's a one-party system. We only need one party."

"What party is that?"

"It's the party of jobs and safe streets and education. These are the issues. Are you for them or against them? Please nod. Good. Of course you are. Every politician in this city wants the same things. And the people know very well any one politician can only do so much. So what's left is that we set out to capture their imagination. We let them think that change will come to their lives. How many politicians have walked through the Carver housing projects in the last twenty-five years? How many rallies and speeches have been made there? How many words of hope have been spoken? And what does it still look like? Would you live there for any price? Generations have been lost in those buildings. Thousands of people. A black mayor couldn't change that. What can a Korean do for them?"

"Still, black groups should be supporting you," I said. "I can't think of any other prominent officials who are minorities."

"Some of the organizations do," he answered. "The church community seems open to talking. That's why I'm going to meet *them* next week, and not with more political groups. The NAACP has invited me to certain forums but I feel token there. Everybody is hesitant, cautious. They study me carefully. I can see they're not sure if I'll promote an agenda that suits them. I can support social programs, school lunches, homeless housing, free clinics, but if I mention the first thing about special enterprise zones or more openness toward immigrants I'm suddenly off limits. Or worse, I'm whitey's boy. It's a grave reaction. I don't think I'll ever get used to it."

"It's still a black-and-white world."

"It seems so, Henry, doesn't it? Thirty years ago it certainly was. I remember walking these very streets as a young man, watching the crowds and demonstrations. I felt welcomed by the parades of young black men and women. A man pulled me right out from the sidewalk and said I should join them. I did. I went along. I tried to feel what they were feeling. How could I know? I had visited Louisiana and Texas and I sat where I wished on buses, I drank from whatever fountain was nearest. No one ever said anything. One day I was coming out of a public bathroom in Fort Worth and a pretty white woman stopped me and pointed and said that the Colored in the sign meant black and Mexican. She smiled very kindly and told me I was very light-skinned. 'Orientals' were okay in those parts, except maybe the kind from the Philippines. I remember saying thank you and bowing. She gave me a mint from her purse and welcomed me to the United States. What did I know? I didn't speak English very well, and like anyone who doesn't I mostly listened. But back here, the black power on the streets! Their songs and chants! I thought *this* is America! They were so young and awesome, so truly powerful, if only in themselves, no matter what anybody said."

I told him how I was too young to understand any of it. How my father never bothered with what was happening. He got passionate only once, when he got angry that a young teacher let us out early the day they arrested Bobby Seale. My father was like Mr. Baeh. So focused on his own life. He couldn't understand anything about *rights.* "What a big noise," he'd mutter at the television. *Egoh joem ba, tihgee seki-nohm mehnnal nah-wandah. Look at this, every day these black sons of bitches show up.* He'd shake his head slowly, as if to say, *Useless.* The sole right he wanted was to be left alone, unmolested by the IRS and corrupt city inspectors and street criminals, so he could just run his stores.

Kwang nodded, beckoning me to eat and drink. I noticed that his gestures were becoming tighter than before, that somehow he appeared more calm and ordered, which seemed to me unusual, given how we were drinking.

"Who can blame him?" he said loudly. "Your father's world was you and your mother. He didn't have time for the troubles of white and black people. It was their problem. None of it was his doing. He was new to the situation. The rights people could say to him, 'We're helping you, too, raising you up with us,' but how did he ever see that in practice?"

"He wouldn't have looked if they had," I said.

"Don't be so hard on your father," he quickly answered. He cleared his throat. "Likely, I know, you are right. But I understand his feeling more than I ever have. Everyone can see the landscape is changing. Soon there will be more brown and yellow than black and white. And yet the politics, especially minority politics, remain cast in terms that barely acknowledge us. It's an old syntax. People still vote for what they think they want; they're calling on a bright memory of a time that has gone, rather than voting for and demanding what they need for their children. They're still living in the glow of civil rights furor. There's valuable light there, but little heat. And if I don't receive the blessing of African-Americans, am I still a *minority* politician? Who is the heavy now? I'm afraid that the world isn't governed by fiends and saints but by ten thousand dim souls in between. I am one of them. Lately I've been feeling like the great enemy of the oppressed. You look knowledgeable for your years, Henry. You have a kind face. You should know, how there must be a way to speak truthfully and not be demonized or made a traitor."

"Very softly," I said to him, offering the steady answer of my life. "And to yourself."

Steadily the other dishes were brought in, a half dozen or so of them, one varied and progressive course. Koreans like to taste everything at once, have it all out on the table, flagrantly mixing the flavors. Sashimi, spicy soup, the grilled meat, fried fish. More *soju.* He poured as I grilled. He obviously wasn't a drinker, I mean a drinker in the way I'd seen real drinkers, which is to say the liquor was beginning to affect him in a manner I couldn't predict or call. Old Stew might rant, he might take you by the collar, become belligerent, even stumble on the stairs when going to sleep, but none of it was a surprise. A man like that was eminently navigable. From the first glass you could see the whole dark trip of his evenings, every black jetty, every cove.

But John Kwang was affecting me. A good rule of thumb when you drink with a subject is that you keep yourself twice as sober as he is. Jack calls it the Taxi Rule. This means that you can get drunk, for the sake of building ambience and camaraderie (and for your own taut nerves), but still keep in mind that you haven't done right if you don't eventually bear him home. Call a taxi and tuck him in. Tonight I was working unscrupulously. I usually abstained completely on the job, much less matched a subject shot for shot. But soon I found myself pouring the drinks, too, joking with him for no other reason but to share a simple pleasure. We flirted with our two waitresses, making them stay a moment and have a drink with us. I rapped on the table when one of them downed three quick shots in a row. I thought I saw Kwang nip the other waitress' ankle with his finger and thumb. She sat next to him on the floormat and drank with him. After a while they both scolded us and thanked us and curtsied before they left, laughing. Somehow we got on to the idea of making a toast to our absent wives.

"To Lee," I said first, clinking Kwang's cup too hard. "The person who taught me how to curse out loud. And mean it."

"To my perfect May," he responded. "Who has never cursed or sworn, even in her mind."

We grew quiet then. There is always the slenderest remorse after any fanfare. We ate the food in near silence, the Korean family way, bent over the steaming crocks and dishes like scribing monks.

I can see this only now, reinvent it in this present time, for in some moments then, I don't know how long, exactly, I forgot the entirety of what I was doing. I lost—or better, misplaced—the very reason why I was there, in that papered room, sharing food with him. I could look at him and see little save his movements, expressions, the mundane sounds of his eating. The unburnished, happy surface of a man. Unmysterious. There was nothing to report, certainly, nothing worth commentary. But Hoagland would have wanted me to continue pushing him, to extend the evening's narrative to its logical and fitting end. I know where and how a story should go, for I have been educated and trained at the greatest expense;

though even a novice could see that John Kwang was in a vulnerable position, the way Wen had been for Pete. It's as simple as picking a ten-dollar bill off the street. Act like it's yours. Now propel him toward the finish.

A good spy is but the secret writer of all moments imminent.

There was a light tap at the door. The paper-and-wood screen slid open and the hostess in the formal dress stepped inside the room. *Master Kwang,* she said softly in Korean. Then she ushered in Sherrie Chin-Watt.

"I should have known you'd have company," Sherrie said to him matter-of-factly, not yet looking at me. She curled each foot back to remove her shoes.

Kwang said, "Where's Eddie?"

"I told him to go home. I said he could take your car."

"Why didn't you tell him to come and eat?"

"Because quite frankly I'm sick of him," she answered. "He's always around. Besides, you treat him too well as it is."

"Too bad," Kwang replied, carefully turning the *bulgogi* on the grill. "We shouldn't send the boy home unfed. Hey, you sit down and eat."

Sherrie was a tall woman, certainly tall for a Chinese woman, and to her credit there was no sign of that adolescent high-back slouch in her stance. That night she wore a dark gabardine suit and a silk blouse, the top two or three buttons undone. She touched there, in the space, the skin soft-looking, faintly hued. Her hair falling lush and straight, riding just above her shoulders.

She gave the hostess her raincoat but kept her briefcase. She sat down across from me, next to Kwang.

"It's not all volunteer work with us," she said to me. "We pay the Asian way around here."

I just nodded. She looked oddly at me, as if surprised by my reticence. Normally I would have launched into conversation, swiftly conducted her, as it were, into the piece I should have been orchestrating, but instead I only wanted her to drink something, and I began to pour her a cup of *soju.*

But she immediately winced, shaking me off, saying, "Oh, no, no. I despise that stuff. It tastes like rotten vodka. Just some water for now."

I kept myself quiet. I let the two of them talk about the coming week, plans in the schedule, minor things I already knew. Just facts, times. It would have been easier if Eduardo had come up to be a natural buffer for me, a screen, and perhaps also to provide the pretext by which I might depart. I know my compulsion was flawed. It was the perfect situation, the two of them together, in so congenial a setting. And with Kwang in the careless state he was. We could have talked all night. But I was sensing that Sherrie now wanted me to leave them alone. And I myself wanted very much to leave. I had enjoyed the time with John Kwang, but there was something about Sherrie that had from the start greatly unsettled me, even during our first interview. If I must do justice to my own apprehension then I will say it was the nature of her familiarity that drew me to a halt. She regarded me as if she were seeing me for the thousandth time but was still unconvinced. That somehow she knew better.

I gradually wound myself out of their conversation. They didn't appear to notice. Though I often stumble, I can be a most careful speaker when I wish. Ask Lelia. She knows my method. My sentences will dwindle, darn, steadily unravel themselves. Up and collapse. But all the while the ready manner of my face and hands and body will say, "Yes, I am here, enjoying your company, so let us go on, please." I can be positively Edwardian. Lelia would always call me something else. Thank God, for her sake. She deserved to hurl whatever was available, to keep us moving, to speak in counterpoint to the deadening strings of my pyrrhic feet.

I was preparing for Sherrie to try to corner me. To what end I could not have imagined. But she didn't. After a while she didn't breathe a word my way. I sat across from them, slowly eating. I noticed they were sitting very close to one another. Sherrie wanted to talk about the disposition of certain *funds,* but John kept joking with her, stalling her with odd cracks and silliness. She glanced coldly at me and he told her, "Good man." She gave him a hard look. He asked what she wanted to drink, maybe she'd like some plum wine. She finally agreed. Then in a small voice she said the situation was *getting serious now.* He groaned a little. He said he would cover whatever was needed.

"That's not the point."

"It'll have to do."

"It won't do, John."

"Make it."

She seemed exasperated. I felt the moment was right to run a finesse play and leave them so they could have a full-blown talk about it, if just for the time I was off in the bathroom. Let them "release," Jack would say, directly from your action. And leaving right then would also serve to quell any suspicions, at least at the level we were working. I figured, too—and rightly—that I'd soon learn all the significant details. John would bestow on me the whole of what I needed.

But then he touched her. Just barely. Just the flat of his hand low on her back, slipped beneath her blazer. It looked natural at first, tender and friendly, but his hand stayed there. He wasn't trying to lurk, steal. His face softened, as if he were trying to make up for his curtness. And though it wasn't much, she gave away absolutely nothing. You can tell with some: she would have been the same if he'd held a lighted match to her. She just kept talking about the office, personnel and scheduling, holding up the beat. I thought of how much Hoagland would have liked to get his hands on her, for a dozen reasons. And while she continued, I thought John was working her there, inching lower, inside the band of her skirt, where maybe the blouse was riding up.

I averted my gaze just as Sherrie looked over at me.

I decided then to leave them for the evening. I told John that my wife would be worrying and that the dinner was very good. He said we would come back again sometime. He didn't try to dissuade me, though I knew I could have easily stayed longer. Perhaps they would have relented. Shown me what I knew.

In hindsight, one could view my actions as solid textbook. Inelegantly executed, perhaps, but effective. I wasn't employing a technique so much as my own instant live burial. It's the prerogative of moles, after all, which only certain American lifetimes can teach. I am the obedient, soft-spoken son. What other talent can Hoagland so prize? I will duly retreat to the position of the good volunteer, the invisible underling. I have always known that moment of disappearance, and the even uglier truth is that I have long treasured it. That always honorable-seeming absence. It appears I can go anywhere I wish. Is this my assimilation, so many years in the making? Is this the long-sought sweetness?

I have tried to heed Jack. I go faithfully to the flat to write out my reports. For the first days since the beginning I can write three or four pages on my subject and then another page of breezy analysis in less than an hour. I am supposed to do it this way, precisely but fast, checking off the day hour by hour the way a bright-eyed kid might reel off what he just got for Christmas. If I pore over the events too long, Hoagland always reminded me, I might get the proportions wrong, lend an act or word a note of too much significance and weight.

I am to be a *clean writer,* of the most reasonable eye, and present the subject in question like some sentient machine of transcription. In the commentary, I won't employ anything that even smacks of theme or moral. I will know nothing of the crafts of argument or narrative or drama. Nothing of beauty or art. And I am to stay on my uncomplicated task of rendering a man's life and ambition and leave to the unseen experts the arcana of human interpretation. The palmistry, the scriptology, the rest of their esoterica. The deep science.

I will simply know character. Identity. This is the all. I am to follow like a starved dog the entrails of any personal affect. I will uncover and invoke inclinations and aversions. Mannerisms of mind. Tics of his life. His opinions, prejudices, insecurities, vanities. Even the piques of his palate, if they speak to anything. What I am paid to do is to observe him in a rigorous present tense, as a subject dynamically inhabiting a scene, as a phenomenon of study.

And I will build all these up into the daily log of his life, into a secret book of personality that I care nothing for except that I necessarily remember everything in it, every voice and detail, and then remember again all of the books before, of Luzan and the others, those inalienable texts the blocks of a cruel palace of memory in which I now live.

But one night last week, after a full day of escorting him to district meetings and fundraisers, I realized that Kwang presented a profound problem for me. I couldn't write the usual about him, at least in that automatic, half-conscious way. I had trouble again. I could not picture him. It seemed I had no profile from which to work. I was prolific, however, I wrote other pieces, entire tracts on him, tones and notes of him, but nothing I could use. I transmitted what I had on hand, two or three pages of vague and aimless reporting, and on the following nights I'd have the replies waiting for me and I'd print them out, mostly blank pages typed with terse messages like: *Get with it, son,* and *You know better than this.*

For Hoagland's is a constant prerogative: You know better, Harry. Be the scribe. The eye. Just point and pull the trigger. You'll hit something.

Certainly, a strange thing is happening. My recollection and sight are focusing elsewhere now. I am seeing a different story. As I flesh out the day's register, as I am tonight, I feel as if I am desperately prospecting for an alibi, one mine more than Kwang's. The teller, I know, can keep his face in the shadows only so long. We want him to come out, step into the light, bare himself. This is the shape of our era.

And what—if I recall correctly—did Dr. Luzan say to me at one of our meetings, in his wheezing singsong voice, but *Who, my young friend, have you been all your life?*

The good doctor knew the story. He could immediately see. A close look into my face and he could read the insistent question. He always spoke to me of my development. I remember his asking if I had had any heroes growing up, figures actual or imagined that I cherished, admired. *Besides your father,* he added. I laughed. So I told him of my invisible brother with no name.

"Why didn't your invisible brother have a name?" Luzan asked me, sitting placidly as always behind his metal office desk.

I told him how I didn't know the subtle nuances or meanings of Korean names, even though I knew quite a few, that it would have been like naming someone purely by sound. And he wouldn't want an American name, because everybody else had one, because it was all so ordinary, even if convenient. I described him for the doctor, his walking before me in the schoolyard, stamping the blacktop, announcing our presence with his swagger, his shout. He knew karate, kung fu, tae kwon do, jujitsu. He could beat up the big black kids if he wished, the tough Puerto Rican kids, anyone else who called us names or made slanty eyes. The white boys admired him for his athleticism, how far past the fence he could send a kickball. The white girls were especially fond of him. He often kissed them after school, in front of everyone. He knew all about science, about model rocketry, chemistry sets, baseball cards, about American history. He was the lead in the school play. He spoke a singing beautiful English. He made public speeches. My mother and father were so proud of him. He was better than anyone. He was perfect. In my imagination these blinding halos of terror and beauty rung him, or maybe they were the same, as though he were limited somehow by his own unbearable preeminence and in that way given over to a doom in his life. In the daytime I could feel him near me, sense not so much his friendship but his vigilance and guidance, the veil of his cover. But at night, alone in my bed, my stomach would burn, ache anxiously for his well-being. I feared he would perish in some accident wherever he was (when he didn't need to be with me), that he was going to die tragically, drown in a lake or slip and fall off a cliff; it wouldn't be his fault, it wouldn't be anyone's, just that it would happen without warning or reason. And soon I'd find myself knotted into a hard coil in the bed, the points of my knees jabbing back the stabs of worry in my stomach and chest, and I wondered if in the morning after I left the house for the long walk to school he would be there for me, at my flank again, that comely wall of him, talking his trash and his resplendence, talking me up, too, talking my story.

Luzan always preferred that I speak to him in skeins such as this; he urged me to take up story-forms, even prepare something for our sessions. His method with me was in fact anti-associative, and he asked me to look at my life not just from a singular mode but through the crucible of a larger narrative. He said he could learn much about me from the way I saw myself working in the world. Is this what I have left of the doctor? That I no longer can simply flash a light inside a character, paint a figure like Kwang with a momentary language, but that I know the greater truths reside in our necessary fictions spanning human event and time?

I know that on this one Hoagland would agree: to be a true spy of identity, he often said, you must be a spy of the culture.

On what turned out to be my last meeting with Luzan I went over the appointed fifty minutes. He did not stop me. He instructed his secretary through the squawky intercom that she clear the rest of his afternoon. He calmed me, patting my hand like an old woman. He wondered why I seemed unusually agitated today, and asked if anything was wrong.

"No," I told him, "but next time will be my last session."

"Why so?" he asked, adjusting on his nose his thick, square black frames.

"My job is being relocated," I said. "We're being moved upstate next week."

"I am sorry to hear it," he said, obviously surprised that I hadn't mentioned it to him. He leaned forward, his buttery dark skin wrinkleless from the great flesh of his cheeks.

"Tell me, my friend," he said warmly. "Are you concerned about this? Will you find someone to talk to up there? I may be able to refer you."

I told him no, that I hadn't planned on going to anyone for a while. There would be house moving to do, changes at work, enough important matters to consume me for the coming weeks. I felt stronger anyway—because of his kindness and efforts I was sure—and should be of no worry to him. There I was again, being a good son, good boy, good citizen, assuring authority. But what I wanted to tell him was that he had saved my life in ways he never imagined, or ever could. He knew a hundredfold of me compared to what I had filched from him. Though that was plenty for Dennis Hoagland, who had called me the night before. *You're off, Harry,* he said grimly. *Don't go in tomorrow, stay in bed, you're relieved.*

A few weeks earlier I had revealed to Luzan the single infidelity during my marriage, a brief episode very early in my career with a Chinese woman whose importer husband I was attempting to encounter and track. The importer was extremely unpleasant, friendless, and I had no other avenue to get to him. I told Luzan what I could; for years I felt disordered by it, sickened, until I released the secret to him. The woman's husband regularly beat her, and I used this to my advantage, terribly, as I was the retailer who would extend her warmth and tenderness on his buying visits. Of course I didn't love her, I hardly liked her, but she was so pitiable and I so fearful and ambitious for my new career that we made love on several occasions in a washroom of their Brooklyn warehouse. But it didn't help any, I was still shut out, and I stopped going to the display store altogether. I eventually reached her husband through his importers' association, which would later blackball him for undercutting his fellow members.

But the woman, his wife, somehow crept back into my thoughts. I didn't want to meet her, even speak to her, but I drove to her store and parked across the street, to wait for her to come out. Near the end of the day she finally did, quickly turning to lock the door, and when she turned to the street I saw the large fresh bruises about the side of her face and one eye, her head color unbalanced, like a soft yellow apple that has fallen off a counter, steadily rusting under the skin. She got into her car and I followed her for a dozen blocks, watching the back of her head, her signal lights, until I accelerated beside her to get another look at her face. She glanced over and saw me. It was her good side. She didn't slow down or speed up and it was as if we were running on side-by-side tracks. She looked at me as if I were already dead, and then she turned her gaze back to the avenue and where she was going, the long way home to her husband.

In the second hour I turned the conversation back on Dr. Luzan. He asked me then if I would call him Emile. Emile. He said his great-grandfather was a French missionary who had been beaten senseless by a mob in his family's village. His great-grandmother's father saved him from being killed, and took him in and nursed him back to health. He spoke of his eight brothers and six sisters, how every one of them had eventually come to America, though a few had already passed away. He spoke of his beloved wife, and then of his teenage daughter, and of the new house they were building in Massapequa with a heated greenhouse in back for his wife, who wished to grow her native fruits and herbs. He was considering finally taking up golf. His practice was healthy, built up now for many years, and I could tell it was all adding up to the prime of his life, that noble time, a period that my father seemed to squeeze down to a few scant minutes around midnight, sitting with a beer in front of his projection TV, absently chuckling at wrestlers and clowns.

Into our third hour I got up to get a drink of water. I said when I got back I would be telling something about him and about myself and the greater circumstance of our new friendship. I felt I should leave him a gift. Honor him with some fraction of the truth. He nodded and said he would wait. I had already decided that I was going to advise the doctor to be careful in his future dealings, that he should be wary of unfamiliar invitations, strange visitors to his home or office, as well as chance meetings with other Filipinos, especially when he vacationed or traveled. I was prepared to reveal whatever was required for him to take me seriously, which would have probably been significant given how tattered and desperate he thought I was. I didn't know anything at the time; Dennis had been as cryptic and evasive as ever, Jack professing nothing. But my suspicions and fears for the doctor were keen, not so much because of his political activities but from my simple fondness for him. I never dreamed that anything could actually happen to him, though theoretically, of course—and this in Dennis' language—many events can take place.

I stepped out into the hall to go to the fountain and standing there in business suits were Jack and Jimmy Baptiste. Jimmy said hiya and put out his cigarette.

"Let us go now, Parky," Jack said, his arm curling around my shoulders. "It is time."

I looked back at Luzan's door and started to speak but Jimmy swiftly approached from the side and pressed a bandanna around my mouth and nose. The cloth was laced with something like ether, though weakly, so that I wouldn't fully lose consciousness, and they walked me out of the building affably telling people and security that it was my birthday and I was drunk. From the back of the car I desperately searched the windows of the three-story building, my thoughts clouded, somehow joyous, perverse, thinking of a moment long past when my mother and father both rode with me on a carnival ride of cups and saucers, and in my vision I thought I spotted him up there, everything twirling but him, his fleshy face, the old-style glasses, the greasy cut mop of hair, and then his roundish hand, bluntly pressed against the glass, more like a paw than an instrument, happily fingerless, bidding me goodbye.

And now I have Kwang. There are scores and scores of his versions scattered about the room, myriad trunks of him, thistling branches, specied and catalogued, a thousand stills of him from every possible angle.

But there is one more version I want to write for Hoagland, for the client, for the entire business of our research. The greater lore that I can now see. I want to tell them that what they have here is a man named John Kwang, born in Seoul before the last world war, a boy during the Korean one, his family not mercifully sundered or refugeed but obliterated, the coordinates of his home village twice removed from the maps. That he stole away to America as the houseboy of a retiring two-star general. Where he saved enough money to leave the general's house in Ohio and go to New York. Where he named himself John. Where he was beaten nearly to death and robbed of all his savings. Where he worked in a Chinatown noodle shop and slept outside next to the steam vent and awoke one morning to see that his feet had turned almost black with the cold. Where he knew hunger again, that unforgettable taste of his other country. Where, desperate as he was, he took to stealing from others, one of them a young priest who saw something to salvage and took him to a Catholic orphanage. Where he first went to a real school and learned to read and write and speak his new home language. And where he began to think of America as a part of him, maybe even his, and this for me was the crucial leap of his character, deep flaw or not, the leap of his identity no one in our work would find valuable but me.

So I followed him. I wrote what I could. He knew I was near. I believed he wished me so. For how do you trail someone who keeps you so close? How do you write of one who tells you more stories than you need to know? Where do you begin, and where are you able to end?

Lelia came in on the 5:13 at the Ardsley station. I got there early, or the train was late, and I watched her as she stepped from the doors. It was raining lightly, and she wore a red silk scarf. Everywhere else was gray. This will always be the color of Westchester for me, that wan gray, the kind of gray that speaks of an impenetrable wealth, never too fancy. What my father so belittled and envied. You see it in the slate gray of a pristine Mercedes-Benz, the gray-white fumes funneling out the back, the gray mop of hair of the unsmiling woman at the wheel. Lines all over her face, her hands. She's always driving alone.

The platform was nearly empty as it was Sunday and she looked around for me until she spotted our car across the tracks. I flashed the high beams. She didn't wave, but just started walking, taking her time, marching up the stairs to the overpass and then back down to the street. As she approached the car I leaned over and pushed the door out to her. She angled herself in.

"It wasn't raining in the city?" I said to her, my grand greeting.

"I guess it was," she said, pulling the scarf off her head. "Why?"

"No umbrella."

"Shit!" she said, her hand wiping the fogged window. The train was already rolling north. "My third this week!"

I started driving. "Was it a good one?"

She sighed lightly. "I don't know. It cost two dollars. I've been buying them like candy from those guys on Broadway, you know, the ones who suddenly appear on the corner with huge boxes of umbrellas at the first drop of rain."

"The Nigerians?" I said.

"I guess so." Then she was quiet, as though taking care in her head. "Not that it matters. But does it even rain in Nigeria?"

"In certain parts, I think. I think a lot. Maybe I'm wrong."

"I guess it makes sense," she said, relaxing now.

I looked at her.

"Desert peoples being sensitive to rain," she said.

"That's right."

Two hours later she was stirring a pot of her lamb stew. I sat at the kitchen table, which I had set with my mother's good service and cloth napkins and glasses for water and wine. Lelia took her usual care preparing the dish, parboiling the meat first and then adding chopped vegetables to its simmering stock, and then dropping a clove of garlic in the pot and then one more clove after some deliberation, then the herbs, the aromatics, and then letting the whole thing stew, at first covered, later not. The soup was on from the moment we arrived at the house—she called ahead so that I could buy the ingredients—and now she tippled in a final splash of sherry, a few drops of Worcestershire, and then took a taste of the gravy from a wooden spoon.

"Not bad," she said, wiping her mouth with the back of her hand.

It was my favorite dish. She made it often when we first were married. We even got into a habit of making love toward the end of its cooking so that when we were done and spent and a little famished it stirred thick enough to ladle into deep bowls and eat at the foot of the bed. My crotch smelled salty and sharp with her and bleached with me, and the rich pungent meat of the lamb was an offering passing between us. Somehow the tastes held an inner logic. Then, we fed each other with big spoons; somehow hers always tasted different from my own. When we finished we crawled back into bed and belched and joked and curled up and slept it off. Lelia always worried that in ten years we would be fat and dull and maybe by then even have a big-screen TV. I remember telling her no, there would be a kid or two or three to keep us slender, jumping forever.

Lelia said she was working out again with Molly. With her sleeves pulled up I saw the new bands in her arms as she chopped and minced. I noticed the muscles running along her forearms and the tightness in the tendons of her hands. She kept unkinking her neck like it was stiff. She and Molly went to one of those health clubs down in the financial district, the rooftop of a glass-and-steel number, where the bankers and lawyers went at lunchtime to sweat off breakfast and look for that night's action at the juice bar. It's for my heart, they would say, unstrapping sopped Rolexes from their hairy wrists. I could see Lelia and Molly humoring one of them until he suggested the three of them go somewhere; then they might work him over before he even knew what happened and he had to go back to the speed bag with a malice to figure it all out.

With all the chopping and peeling we weren't talking much yet, but it didn't seem to bother her. The stew was almost done and there was nothing left to do so I opened the bottle of burgundy and started pouring.

"Not too much for me," she said from the sink, her long back sort of slow-dancing. "I've been getting headaches lately. I think it's those sulfites."

"You never had a problem before," I answered, giving her a little more than half a glass.

"I didn't know about sulfites before," she said, looking back and grinning. "Molly has literature on it."

She wiped her hands in a dish towel and sat down next to me. "Besides, we've got a lot of work to do tonight."

"Tonight? We've got all tomorrow off."

"I want to get started, Henry. You know me."

"Okay, but let's not get crazy."

"We won't get crazy." She carefully sipped her wine.

The house had lain pretty much fallow since my father died. Lelia had already worked on the house once, this a while ago, after his funeral, so we could sell off the things we didn't want or need. We were actually planning to move up there for good, to leave the city, which neither of us was actually enjoying much anymore, if we ever truly had. But then the strangeness between us began, the feelings of oddness and misplacement, and our move never happened. If we still had had Mitt, of course, we probably would have moved anyway, so he could go to a better public school, have some grass to play on, and we'd have figured out our problems later. Or maybe another baby might have helped us. Another try. Of course, that's the worst reason to have a child, anyone on the street can tell you that, because no one can handle being an attempt at something from the very start.

I couldn't help her with the house that first time. I was on assignment in Miami and had to return there immediately after his funeral. I asked Lelia to take care of the place—I didn't think I could do it anyway—and she said sure, she'd do it, she could live there for the week and commute to work until I got back. In truth, she didn't like staying for too long in our apartment alone. The place was too breezy, had too many echoes.

In my father's house she felt safe. I think the place reminded her of her childhood home in Brookline, Massachusetts, though that one was much more expansive than my father's house, to a point palatial, with separate living wings for her mother Alice and Stew. Lelia's parents needed that kind of space. They fought a lot; Alice wasn't so afraid of things then. They'd start hollering somewhere in the middle of the house, assail each other furiously, then retire to their corners and start drinking.

Lelia liked houses that you could go all the way up and hide yourself in, high stretching houses with garrets, widow's peaks, secret attics. That's why she loved our garage so much, with its secret room. It didn't matter to her if the rest of a house were empty and creaky and dark as long as she was lodged above it all, in a nook with a pitched ceiling and a lamp, her books and a writing pad ready on a table. In the same spirit she liked to climb trees, could still ramble up the bark of one with complete ease and confidence, though she had a deep, running scar on her lower back from falling through the branches of an oak tree when she was nine.

And just last week, on one of our brief visits together, while we were picnicking in Central Park, I made her angry with some stupid comment about Stew or Mitt or something, and after we fought a little she got up without saying anything and climbed the tree we were sitting under. I wanted to go up after her, grab her in the branches and shake her, I was burning to drag her back down, tussle and overcome her, but then I could never bring myself to climb beyond that first large branch, not from the height, but somehow I could never abide the subtle sway of living limbs, stake anything on their pliant strength. I just watched her until she reached the smallest branch that would bear her weight. She gazed straight down at me from almost twenty feet, unquivering, wordless, her hair rubbing against the branches, hanging those narrow bare feet out into the air.

The week after my father's funeral Lelia slept in the room Mitt occupied his last summer, when he decided he was old enough to live by himself in the big house. My father—who could display amazing properties of emotional recovery—had long before cleared it of any signs of our boy, removing not just his few toys and summer clothes but all the furniture and wall hangings. He'd even painted the room, from its sky blue to a barren, optic white. *Now done,* I can still hear him thinking.

Lelia immediately dragged a mattress and a floor lamp in there and went to work on the rest of the house. The place had become overfurnished and cluttered since my mother's death. My father habitually bought sundry pieces of furniture whenever he stepped into a store; he showed little judgment in his choices. Much of the furniture in our house was garish and oddly colored and overpriced. His penchant was for textured synthetic fabrics, often featuring some geometric design like diamonds or pentagons. He would ask Ahjuhma to place each new piece, despite the fact that she would generally leave it where the delivery men happened to put it down, just making sure the new chair or side table was kept clean for him and in good condition. From this stuff Lelia separated what we would keep and what we would sell or donate to Goodwill.

I remember a poem she wrote about a woman who cleans out her father-in-law's house after his death, dispatching his possessions and effects with only her imagination to guide her in what she will keep or discard. As she moves through the house in the poem, the speaker begins to realize how few of her father-in-law's possessions are actually personal, intimate in nature, and she feels as though she's sifting through the material of a time-share bungalow, a house strangely unpossessed. She wonders, in turn, if this dead immigrant had ever reconsidered the generic still-life of apples he'd hung in the upstairs hall, had ever touched again the bouquet of wooden roses placed on the tank of his toilet, had ever comfortably worn the reams of clothes in his closet, the rack filled with the suits and shoes he would buy on his days off but never wore anywhere. There are a few things that tell of his mortal presence: in his bedroom, the woman carefully bundles his dark socks and underwear in an old yellow raincoat; she finds a pornographic magazine in a drawer of his night table, from April 1978, and a few odd condoms; she smells his toothbrush—peppermint and dust; she discovers in the attic a brick-sized wad of $20 bills rubberbanded inside a shoebox, probably the first large sum of cash he salted away from the IRS in the beginning years of green-grocering, money that he'd long forgotten about and never needed; and she finds faded sheets of lined notebook paper in his desk, completely written over with the American name (I had once told her) he'd given himself but never once used: *George Washington Park.*

He was practicing the writing of his signature.

And then, the woman begins to shift her consciousness from the dead father to the absent son, her husband. *Is it the coldness of objects,* she wonders, *that persists?* She considers her own apartment, the bed she shares with her husband; she tries to think of the things there that might signify him, call his real name. A certain paperback book, an old comb with broken teeth. And then she considers herself, wonders if a stranger could understand who her husband was by looking at her, imagines the scrolls the stranger might read on her face and body, what that writing would say: *Are you at all in love? What was it then between you, in the first place? What's left now?*

After we finished dinner I took out the chocolate mousse cake with mocha icing that I'd bought from Patisserie Lind, a fancy sweetshop near the station, Lelia's and Mitt's favorite old place. I'd buy treats there for Mitt for being good on the train ride up. He liked best the dark chocolate hazelnut truffles, and didn't seem to mind the slight bitterness of the hard chocolate shell. He'd put a whole one in his mouth and sit quietly and deal with it for the next quarter hour, his tongue wrestling the sticky orb. Lelia taught him not to bite through it: a good lesson in restraint. Sometimes it dropped out and he'd just pick up the slimy mass from wherever it was and mouth it again. We still have stains all over the backseat of my father's car. When Mitt finally dissolved the outside and got to the soft center he'd mumble, "Oooh baby" to me and Lelia, and we'd oooh baby back, and then he'd mash it between his tongue and palate and stretch his messy mouth open and show us the sweet whipped guts.

As Lelia cleared the table I cut her a big slice and a smaller one for myself. Then I made the coffee, like I always used to after dinner, throwing in an extra scoop of grounds tonight for the work ahead of us. It's the routines you follow and count on when you start something again, the way of simply doing an activity together. I used to think you ought to have sex after trouble; I got Lelia to believe this, get right back and all over each other, reaffirm your presence immediately and directly. But now I think the best way to resolve a fight is to clean the house or cook together, do something simple like that, take the energy out on a mutual project that you can share and look at when you're done and not have to wonder what else has gone on.

When we were ready we carried the cake and mugs of coffee to my father's study. There we found the entirety of the pictures of my family in the same cabinet where my father kept the liquor. Lelia removed the dozen or so shoeboxes of pictures from the top shelves and lined them up between us on the white shag carpet. Many of the pictures had been sent to us over the years from relatives in Korea, many of these very old, and no one had ever organized them or placed them in albums. Even my mother, who was obsessive about order and neatness in her house, chose to let the photographs of the two families get commingled and confused. When she received a photo with a letter she would immediately go and slip it inside one of the boxes, as if she didn't want any images or faces of her old country haunting about the house.

"These are wonderful pictures," Lelia said, shuffling a stack above her face as she lay on her back. She was wearing old jeans and a loose black zip-up turtleneck. Her long shape lurking beneath. "Look at these. I think they're silver-prints. I think it's your mother as a little girl."

"How do you know?" I said, sitting back against the foot of the sofa. I was looking through some shots of my father during his military service. He was startlingly smooth of face and slim and handsome, so much so that it looked as though he would always be that way, like you might have thought of a young Sinatra.

"I've been comparing her to ones of you at the same age. It's pretty incredible."

"We're dead ringers," I said.

"Definitely. Look at the eyes, the mouth. The jaw. Anyway, it's not just your features. I think the expressions are exactly the same. The way you hold your mouths. So straight across and firmly set. It looks as if you've both just spoken something awful but true. But the expression isn't really of sadness."

"What is it?" I asked.

She paused, holding the photos side by side. "It says, 'You won't get to me. Don't try. I'm immune.' "

I snorted. "We're difficult people. My mother was the worst. She was an impossible woman. Of course she was a good mother. I think now she treated it like a job. She wasn't what you'd call friendly. Never warm."

I was sorting quickly through the boxes, making piles of people of my mother's side of the family, then my father's, and then one of faces I didn't know, a growing stack of strangers.

"When I was a teenager," I said, "I so wanted to be familiar and friendly with my parents like my white friends were with theirs. You know, they'd use curses with each other, make fun of each other at dinner, maybe even get drunk together on holidays."

"It's not so goddamn wonderful, you know," Lelia said.

"I know. Of course it's not. But I wanted just once for my mother and father to relax a little bit with me. Not treat me so much like a *son,* like a figure in a long line of figures. They treated each other like that, too. Like it was their duty and not their love."

Lelia was quiet to this. "It's incredible, isn't it," she then said, "that it's so clear what we get from them?"

"Maybe incredible isn't the word."

Lelia handed me a picture.

"I do have her blood," I said, looking now at a young girl standing before the gate of a Buddhist temple in a dark velvet suit. My mother's face.

Lelia rolled over and rested her head on my leg. "You should watch yourself, those cancers run in families. You told me once how your mother bit down on her lip whenever she was angry, just like you do. It's crazy."

"What are you going to get from Alice and Stew?" I asked her.

Lelia laughed harshly, turning on her side. "Let's see," she said, propping her head up. "Frailness and oversensitivity from my mother. A fat liver from Stew. And all those old rugs."

"How are the old people?"

"Okay," she said. "Mother seems better. She's been going out shopping lately with a friend. She's feeling lonely. Actually, I think it's a sign of improvement. She won't admit to me that she's horny as hell. I reminded her that it's been four years since her last boyfriend. She said *three and a half,* and then she broke down crying. I told her to put an ad in the paper but she didn't want to because she thought all of Boston would know who it was, particularly my father. She finally placed one a few weeks ago, and of course the day it appeared Stew called her out of the blue just to say hello. He can be such a shit."

"He saw the ad?"

"Of course not," she said. "That's just my father. He's lucky that way. He asked about you the last time I spoke to him. He wants you to call him sometime."

"I don't know why," I answered. "With our troubles."

Lelia shook her head. "Don't worry, he blames me for everything."

She tucked down her chin and made a stern face. " 'Henry's a kind and respectful man,' " she gruffed, doing him from her throat. " 'What the hell's the matter with you?' I think things haven't been going well with Katie but he won't say."

"Katie's the one with the legs?"

Lelia shook her head. "Katie is the younger woman, the curator. Maybe you haven't met her. Did you? I don't know. I like her, actually. She doesn't go for his captain-of-industry routine. They were both in New York last month and we had dinner. Katie had this one long streak of gray in her hair. She didn't have it the first time I met her, and I thought, oh shit, Stew's ruining another good woman."

"I never understood that kind of grayness."

"It comes from grief," Lelia said. "When I got her alone I asked if anything was wrong and she said nothing and laughed and said you mean with the hair? She told me she had it done, that she had a streak of color bleached out."

"What for?"

"I guess Stew wanted her to look more distinguished or something at his functions. Less artsy-fartsy. So she decided to go gray."

"Bride of Frankenstein."

Lelia laughed and said, "Of course Stew hated it. He didn't say anything, though. I think for the first time in his life he's afraid of losing a woman."

"Your old man isn't afraid of anything."

"It just *seems* that way," she said. "He's getting old. What am I saying? He *is* old. He's been old for twenty years."

"So what's different now?" I asked. "Is it Katie?"

"Mostly," Lelia said, looking through more photos. "I think he's finally catching up to my mother. He's just begun to feel the sadness of growing old, if that's what it is. Decrepitude, obsolescence. There's no good cure."

"He's the semi-immortal type," I said. "A Titan."

"Give him a break," Lelia said. "When you're sixty-four we'll see if you're not feeling a little desperate."

I got up to take down more shoeboxes. "We Parks don't let it get to that," I told her. "No one in my family actually survives his fifty-fifth birthday anyway."

"I don't think you've got to worry about that," she said. "You'll make it."

I sat back down on the littered floor. "A minute ago you were talking cancer."

"I changed my mind. I'll make sure to take you to the internist twice a year."

"I would like that."

She stretched her neck and vigorously massaged her head with both hands. "Anyway," she said, messy-haired, "you don't work like them. You don't drive yourself to exhaustion like your father or mother. The problem for them was stress. That's not the thing that's going to kill you."

"What will kill me?"

Lelia shifted toward me on her knees. When she touched my cheek with her open hand we got the shock of static she built up from the carpet.

"You obsess, Henry," she said, her hand still trembling. "You live in one tiny part of your life at a time."

"I'm trying not to."

"How is work going?" she suddenly asked, words I hadn't heard from her since before Mitt was born.

"Okay," I said.

"Really?"

"Yes."

She bit her lip, but then said, "Jack didn't seem to think so."

I slowly unlidded the next shoebox.

"I talked to him a couple days ago," she said. "Actually, Molly wanted to meet him. She was intrigued by his picture. She loved his big features. I thought what the hell. Jack, as usual, wasn't sure if he was ready to meet anyone. So we just talked. Then the more we talked the more it seemed that he was worrying about you."

"What did he say?"

"He didn't say anything. He just kept mentioning you. *Parky this,*

Parky that. You were steadily becoming the point of the conversation. Finally I called him on it and he said nothing was wrong but I better talk to you. He knew we were coming up here."

"I told him."

"I figured," she said. "Come on, sweetie. What's going on? You should say. You should tell your only wife. Isn't that how your father always said it? *She is your only wife.* I promise not to get angry. Say anything. Promise. It's most of the reason I came up, you know. Cleaning we can do any old weekend."

"You were oddly insistent."

She smiled again. "I've picked up a few things in ten years with you."

I nodded, looking away from her. Then she reached for my cheek, her cool fingertips on my skin. I leaned into them. I took her hand and held it to my face, against my mouth. At that moment I almost wished for something like smothering myself with her.

"You're so warm," she said. "You're flushed."

"It's the wine," I said. Then I whispered, "I'm sinking a little, Lee."

"Henry," she said, wrapping her arms around me. She hugged me tightly, her arms shaking. "You better tell me what's wrong right now, right now, because I have the feeling I may start bleeding internally."

"I wish you hadn't talked to him."

"I'm glad I did. He cares, you know."

"I'm not sure that he does," I said. "But I can't really blame him. I won't. This is a business, Lee. Research and reports are fine. But if we don't generate certain *material* there's no operation. The thing doesn't work. It seizes."

"What do they want from you?" she asked.

"Something damning."

She let go of me and stood up. She asked, "Do you have something?"

"No."

"Then tell Dennis that. Tell Jack. Look, I'm going to the phone. I'm calling Jack right now. I'm going to tell him and then give him a piece of my mind."

"It won't matter," I said. "What Jack says doesn't matter. It's Dennis. Are you willing to talk to Dennis? He will say it's the nature of things that you can always find what you need."

"Then please quit," Lelia begged. She was kneeling on the carpet again, stiffly shuffling together the loose photographs.

I explained to her that I couldn't quit, at least not until the assignment was done. It was bad form to cut loose in the middle, and then also perhaps hazardous; Jack had once told me no one had ever done that before to Dennis Hoagland. Nobody could say what he might try.

She stopped what she was doing. "Then give him what he wants."

"Someone could get hurt," I said.

"Why do you care all of a sudden? Why now when we're just getting things straight?" She swung her arms back and accidently knocked over the rest of her coffee onto the white rug. "Oh shit! Shit!"

"It's okay, just leave it."

She tried to mop it with her sleeve but the stain was spreading. Suddenly she looked exhausted, sodden in the face. "As long as you don't get hurt, I won't care. I promise, Henry, I promise. I won't say a word to you. I won't even think it."

She got up and left the room and came back with a hand towel from the hall bath. She carefully blotted the dark patch, staring down at the spill. "Am I an official bad person now?"

I took her and we lay down on the carpet. Before I could do anything else to stop myself I told her his name. John Kwang. I could almost see her turning the words inside her head. Of course she knew who he was, that he was Korean. He was appearing on the broadcasts almost nightly because of the boycotts. She didn't say anything, though, and I could see that she was trying her very best to stay quiet, to think around the notion for a moment instead of steaming right through it. Ten years with me and now she was the one with the ready method. She turned into me, eyes shut. Her breath warm like a priest's. And now her voice brooking in my ear, in a voice I hardly recognized. "You just say what you want. Please say what you want."

No trace of light outside, the night ink, and suddenly the sky raining hard again. The roof chattering. I lay on the small bed in Mitt's old summer-time room. I had left her downstairs with the pictures. I was absently putting clothes in shopping bags, and I felt tired and lay down for a moment.

All over the house things were still in piles. The amount of the work was beginning to overwhelm us. Neither of us was much of an organizer. Picture albums, address books, receipt-keeping, these were the happy tasks of people completely staked to one another, so that they could produce a chit on demand, order and reorder their memories for a future day. We used to enjoy those legions of collectibles, and we were glad for them, their happy messes. Bulging photo albums, corks of wines we'd drunk at restaurants in overcoat pockets. Boxes of mostly useless paper. Trails of frayed odd ribbons and precious bits of gift wrap and other junks of the past. Loose tapes of Mitt.

And if I remember everything now in the form of lists it is that these notions come to me along a floating string of memory, a long and lyric processional that leads me out from the city in which I live, to return me here, back to this place of our ghosts.

I didn't notice her come in. She curled in beside me. I began stroking her. Her shoulder down her arm to the rise of her hip, with one hand. I was being slow. I wanted to be slow with her. She wasn't responding to the graze of my fingers but she wasn't ignoring it, either, and just as I was about to cease my movement and fall back I heard her breathe, once, heavily, through her mouth. She whispered, *Easy.* Tucking my face into her hair, I kept going, stroking, holding down my rhythm to the slowest ache I could bear. She broke the seam of her legs and scissored one back and hooked my ankle with her instep, pulling my knee between hers. Rub of old jeans. I smelled her soap on the back of her neck. I kissed there, the lightest way I knew. So she wouldn't jump or freeze. I kissed her again, this time my lips on the pale soft hairs of her neck, and she craned so that the white skin inched up past the cover of her shirt fabric. Bone white, purple white. I felt a heat anyway. Her mouth was open. She was trying to stay herself and I understood. I was doing the same. I was watching my hand stroking and watching my face closing in against her. I pushed myself up on the bed and tugged her to roll and face me and she did. I kissed her neck and the bone between her breasts and I pressed my face maybe too hard against her belly. She pulled me by a beltloop of my trousers and then I slipped my thumbs into two of hers and the bed suddenly seemed too small and fragile and I started to take her with my head up against the angled ceiling painted dead flat white by my father in a long fit of mourning and she said, *No, sweetie, not here,* and she swung her legs to the floor and led us out of the room and then down the back stairs to the kitchen.

She asked if it was locked up out there.

I shook my head. We'd never locked the garage. Even my father, who safeguarded his possessions with a military order and zeal, never bothered with it, considering it a colony of junk that was mine. I looked around for something to put on my feet but I didn't see anything. I started for the front door where I'd left my shoes.

"Just take off your socks," Lelia said, already undoing her feet in kind.

I did what she said. She slid open the glass door and we walked out gingerly onto the slick deck and down steps to the slatestone path leading to the garage. It was raining hard enough that we were already wet to the skin by the time we reached the side door to the apartment. I was shivering. When we got upstairs Lelia stripped me of my clothes and then she stripped herself. She walked naked to the far wall and knelt and turned the dial on the baseboard heater. She stood up. I watched the straightness of her as she moved, her long belly, the dark collapse below that. I felt a melancholy before her nakedness. She gripped at my breast and collarbone and tore me down to the carpet.

I had forgotten how to make love to my wife.

Five months, since I had seen her body, maybe eight or nine since I'd really touched her. My low and narrow hips wanted to be lost in her width, the chute of her sternum my sole guide to the one place where we came in the same basic size and shape and flavor: that good piece, the mouth.

We were always oral. We were forever biting, we bit hard, we spit and shined each other, we licked each other, we slobbered, we gorged, we made elaborate meals of ourselves, we made holiday feasts Scotch and Korean, the cold strange meal of tongue, of ankle, of toe, we made a mess. She was given to anything vampiric, went wild for Blacula, Christopher Lee, Lugosi, bats, Venus's-flytraps, and she said it was the best way, to use your mouth, that this was it, this was the thing that made us human. Not the thumb but the mouth.

"Hey," she said, gripping me, breathing like there wasn't enough air. "Hold me now."

"Okay."

She fell back on the floor and winged her arms wide. I asked her if she wanted to get on the couch. She shook her head.

I rolled on top of her and grabbed her at the wrists. The old carpet was threadbare against her back, my knees were scraping the rope webbing. I kissed her, and she nibbled at my lips as I pulled away. I pushed her hands together above her head and held them there tightly with one hand, my free one searching the scallops of her ribs, her taut neck, now unfolding inside her needy mouth. She was tasting herself on my fingers and wet nose and my chin. The room was still freezing. She kept eating. I kept eating, too, wanting every last fold of her, the taste brand new to me, or, at least, a reconfection of what I knew.

She wanted me to push down on her harder. I couldn't, so then she turned us around and pushed down on me, the slightest grimace stealing across her face. Her body yawed above me, buoyed and restless. I held on by her flat hips, angling her and helping her to let me in. Mixed-up memory, hunger. It was like lonesome old dogs, all wags and tongues and worn eyes. This was the woman I promised to love. This is my wife.

We live again in our loft on Jane Street. I help Lelia move back in. An untidy suitcase of clothes, a carton of books. Not much else. Molly waves goodbye to us from the window of her apartment as we flag a cab. She wears dark sunglasses, she tells us, to cover her tears of joy.

We have to leave moving to my father's house in Ardsley for later. When later is we're not certain. Soon, perhaps. We've cleaned up there as much as we could, held a garage sale, given away much of the rest, and the house stands nearly empty. The house is ready for us. But we decide—or more, understand—that what we need is to live together again before moving off anywhere else. The apartment is where the trouble started, and like most couples we gravitate toward our private sites of pleasure and pain. It's like you're looking at a serious wound scarring over, wondering how it ever actually happened, that you survived, that it even hurt you as much as it did although you know damn well it nearly killed.

Lelia is working again, but now only freelancing. I'm at home two days during the week, working the weekends because Kwang and Janice Pawlowsky need me for the trips, for the talks and luncheons, for meeting the press. If Lelia's busy in the studio with a student I'll answer phones for her and schedule appointments and make lunches of soup and sandwiches for all of us.

Children visit us daily. They're young, ages three and up, and on the whole they're funny in the face, not so much in proportion as in use. Or ill use. The little chins, the lips, the eyes, they're tentative organs on these kids, almost as if they're optional equipment. Lelia greets them at the door and they shuffle in on the legs of their mothers, and then they quickly walk to the speech studio Lelia's set up at the alley end of the loft, where there's a soundproofed sliding wall to push back.

Lelia decorates the studio with colored butcher paper and animal posters and cutouts her students make. You see her hand-drawn illustrations of the human mouth, the tongue, the upper and lower palates, the uvula. Her strokes are broad and gentle, the colors muted; Lelia says anatomically correct pictures give the kids nightmares.

Maws, I say. She says don't let them hear you joke and pinches me, but she knows my own history with speech therapists. She knows how I was raised by language experts, saved from the wild.

Lelia has cookies and juice ready for the kids and coffee for the adults, who usually leave after five minutes. They'll return in an hour and a half. The children remain. Sometimes, when the door shuts, I hear some of them cry. They can all do that.

Presently three of her dozen or so students are Asian. One has a problem with her ears. Her words come out all blunted, edgeless. She sounds as if she's speaking behind a wall of water. *Mahler,* she will say, meaning something else we can't figure out.

The other two are Laotian boys who as far as anyone can tell are perfectly fine. They come today, their fathers bringing them this time. The public school has to farm them out to Lelia because it doesn't have enough staff. The boys seem happy. They keep slapping each other about the head, pinching noses, pulling ears and eyebrows. They speak a rudimentary English—*milk, pee-pee, cookie*—but have trouble with words like onion and union. They don't seem to care. They want to play. Lelia recognizes this, too, and they all gallop on broomsticks while they recite an old nursery rhyme. Maybe this will work, Lelia says to me, hopping in her turn. Sing, she tells them, let's all sing the song.

Will they remember the verse? I still know the one that ancient chalk-white woman taught me with a polished fruitwood stick. Mrs. Albrecht was her name, her bony hands smelling of diapers.

"Henry Park," her voice would quiver. "Please recite our favorite verse." I'd choke, stumble inside myself. And this was her therapy, struck in sublime meter on my palms and the backs of my calves:

Till, like one in slumber bound,
Borne to ocean, I float down, around,
Into a sea profound, of ever-spreading sound . . .

Peanut Butter Shelley, I'd murmur beneath my breath, unable to remember all the poet's womanly names. It was my first year of school, my first days away from the private realm of our house and tongue. I thought English would be simply a version of our Korean. Like another kind of coat you could wear. I didn't know what a difference in language meant then. Or how my tongue would tie in the initial attempts, stiffen so, struggle like an animal booby-trapped and dying inside my head. Native speakers may not fully know this, but English is a scabrous mouthful. In Korean, there are no separate sounds for L and R, the sound is singular and without a baroque Spanish trill or roll. There is no B and V for us, no P and F. I always thought someone must have invented certain words to torture us. *Frivolous. Barbarian.* I remember my father saying, Your eyes all *led,* staring at me after I'd smoked pot the first time, and I went to my room and laughed until I wept.

I will always make bad errors of speech. I remind myself of my mother and father, fumbling in front of strangers. Lelia says there are certain mental pathways of speaking that can never be unlearned. Sometimes I'll still say *riddle* for *little,* or *bent* for *vent,* though without any accent and so whoever's present just thinks I've momentarily lost my train of thought. But I always hear myself displacing the two languages, conflating them—maybe conflagrating them—for there's so much rubbing and friction, a fire always threatens to blow up between the tongues. Friction, affliction. In kindergarten, kids would call me "Marble Mouth" because I spoke in a garbled voice, my bound tongue wrenching itself to move in the right ways.

"Yo, China boy," the older black kids would yell at me across the blacktop, "what you doin' there, practicin'?"

Of course I was. I would rewhisper all the words and sounds I had messed up earlier that morning, trying to invoke how the one girl who always wore a baby-blue cardigan would speak.

"Thus flies foul our fearless night owl," she might say, the words forming so punctiliously on her lips, her head raised and neck straight and her eyes fixed on our teacher. Alice Eckles. I adored and despised her height and beauty and the oniony sheen of her skin. I knew she looked just like her parents—lanky, washed-out, lipless—and that when she spoke to them they answered her in the same even, lowing rhythm of ennui and supremacy she lorded over us.

Alice used to sneer at me when I left our class for my special daily period upstairs. The class was Remedial Speech, and I accepted my own presence there if only because of the very trouble I had pronouncing it. The other students were misfits, they all seemed to have dirty hair and oversized mouths and shrunken foreheads and in my estimation were as dumb as the dead. By association, though, so was I. We were the school retards, the mentals, the losers who stuttered or could explode in rage or wet their pants or who just couldn't say the words.

In truth, the fact that you were in the class likely meant you came from a difficult background, homes where parents fought or took drugs or beat their kids or maybe spoke a foreign language. A few had genuine problems with their mouths or their ears, but the rest of us, we were sent there by the grace of either too much institutional frustration or goodwill.

The teacher was a young woman in her early twenties, straight brown hair, freckles, with a name like Miss Haven or Havishaw. She never struck us like Mrs. Albrecht did, she was actually very quiet, seemingly shoeless, unmatronly, vigilant, gentle. She'd give each of us a small hand mirror so that we might examine our mouths as we spoke, and then she'd come around and practice with us. She would go from one student to the next, sit herself squarely before him or her, and say, *Now put your hand on my throat.* She wanted us to understand the vibration certain sounds required. If the kid wouldn't do it—most of us would automatically reach for her neck—she'd take the hand and move it up there herself and say something deep and thrilling like *vampire,* and you thought, this is a teacher, a person who can show, her mottled milky skin still damp with the sweat of other palms, her breath sweet.

The boys' names are Ouboume and Bouhoaume. Such beautiful names. I think Laotian should be our Esperanto. After some more romping Lelia sits them down with picture books. They keep gazing over at me through the break in the wall, maybe thinking I'm next. Lelia never likes to close the sliding door and so she gives them headphones, and then puts one on herself. She waves me over anyway so they won't stare off and I get up and join them. They listen to a tape of consonant sounds, and then practice what they hear for ten minutes. It sounds like a rookery. Lelia has them drill with their mouths like they're playing scales on the piano. Finally she clicks off the tape. They remove the headgear.

"Press your lips together," she now tells them, squeezing her own between her fingers. "We're going to do the sound for P again. This time so we can hear ourselves. Remember P. For P, blow through your lips, like a puff of smoke."

They repeat after her, as do I: *Papa, pickle, paint, peep, pool.*

"Great. Let's do F now." She uses a rubberized half-section model of the mouth. She pushes the white upper teeth against the inside flesh of the lower lip.

"Do it this way," she says, helping Ouboume. I show Bouhoaume. She tells us: "Now push air through and say after me."

Father, finger, food, fun, fang.

We sing the words in unison and then take our turns. Bouhoaume has trouble. He uses his fingers to make himself work like the model, and he tries so hard a slick of drool icicles from his mouth. Ouboume shrieks with delight. Lelia regards him crossly, and he gently pats Bouhoaume on the back. We all try again. We move on to V, which is similar to F, except that you hum a vibrato, which the boys enjoy.

They eat their sandwiches without talking. Egg salad with diced celery. The Asian and Hispanic kids rarely complain about what we give them; the black kids and white kids often do, they act entitled, though in different ways. I don't know what this means, maybe something about the force of fathers, or the Catholic God.

As I look at the boys I keep thinking of Romulus and Remus, wayward children, what they might say now about their magnificent city of Rome and its citizenry. At their height, the Romans lived among all their conquered, the outer peoples brought to the city as ambassadors, lovers, soldiers, slaves. And these carried with them their native spice and fabric, rites, contagion. Then language. Ancient Rome was the first true Babel. New York City must be the second. No doubt the last will be Los Angeles. Still, to enter this resplendent place, the new ones must learn the primary Latin. Quell the old tongue, loosen the lips. Listen, the hawk and cry of the American city.

The boys are first cousins by way of their fathers, who run a dry-goods business from the back of a beat-up Ford van. When they return to pick up their children, they enter and remove their mesh baseball caps. They are bearing gifts for us. Lelia gets a miniature wooden rack for earrings and rings; a striped silk tie for me. Lelia gets the boys ready to leave. I ask if this is their business and they somehow understand and gesture for me to come down and take a look. Ouboume's father unlocks the back doors and shows me their rolling stock. They sell off-brand cassette tapes and ladies' scarves and 99¢ hardcover books and a dozen other items. They keep trying to give me whatever I look at, and finally I accept a celebrity cookbook. The boys are jostling for a seat inside. When I take out my wallet the two men start hollering excitedly in some dialect and push my money away.

As he shuts the van doors Ouboume's father takes a long look at me.

"Japan? Japan?" he asks.

I shake my head.

"Korea? Korea?"

I nod. He smiles wide and gives me two thumbs-up.

"I like Korea," he says, I think meaning Koreans. "Tough tough. Hard work." He points upstairs. "You wife?"

"Yes," I answer.

"No Korea!"

"No Korea!" I say.

"Ha!"

My answer seems to confirm something for him. Bouhoaume's father calls him from the front seat.

"You like *Kwan?*" he says, moving around to the front.

"What?"

"Kwan, Kwan."

"Kwan," I say.

He stands erect, as if stepping into a stature. "Big man, *Kwan.* Big man, big man!"

"Yes," I tell him. "Big man. I like *Kwan.*"

He hops in shotgun and flips thumbs-up again. The boys do the same from the back. They lean against a gross of cigarette cartons. Winstons, Marlboros. Gray-market goods. They'll drive around the city—there won't be any more schooling today—and search the ordered blocks for a good spot in the stream of people, and then set up for a few hours, or until an inspector asks to see their license to sell. One of the fathers will stall in broken English while the others hastily pack the merchandise into the van. *No trouble, no trouble,* he'll say, shouting it, bowing, shaking his hands, seeming to beg, and as the van starts rolling away he'll slip in the passenger door and all four of them will call it, breathing it out like a necessary song: *No trouble.* The boys know it, too, they've learned this well, and they'll all wave goodbye with it, stridently, strong-armed, father-son, with the bombast of Americans, not yet knowing that this is the last language they will share.

Upstairs Lelia is cleaning the mess the boys leave in her studio. No speech until Monday. I restack picture books and place the toys back in wooden bins while she sweeps for cookie crumbs, egg splots, cracklings of hard candy.

"Little-boy droppings," she says, examining whatever is stuck to her broom.

As she kneels with the dustpan, I can already see the coil in her back that says she is her mother's daughter. The waiting rheumatism. The soft bones. I have to remind her to drink more milk. I can see now, too, how she used to pick up after Mitt, the way the day's weariness would fold upon her body, how she'd almost collapse on her legs to pull off his socks or wipe his chin. Then he'd jump up again, bare-assed and wild, and shout, "Come on, Mom!" and off they'd go across the apartment, chugging like locomotives, never any stops.

Mitt always spoke beautifully, if I remember anything. Lelia read to him every night since he was a year old. She wanted me to read him stories, too, but I never felt comfortable reading aloud, even when I was in high school and college, and I didn't want to fumble or clutter any words for the boy just as he was coming to the language. I feared I might handicap him, stunt the speech blooming in his brain, and that Lelia would provide the best example of how to speak. My silliness. I should have watched and listened. When Mitt played with my father their communication was somehow wholly untroubled, perfect in its way, and if there were questions between them the boy would simply repeat what the old man said, try to echo his pidgin, his story, learn that talk, too. I suppose they could build a bridge because they needed one. I was too close to the old man, we were always within striking distance of each other. We were intently inarticulate, competitively so. But I thought that Mitt was beginning to appreciate the differences in the three of us; he could mimic the finest gradations in our English and Korean, those notes of who we were, and perhaps he could imagine, if ever briefly, that this was our truest world, rich with disparate melodies.

"Come on, Henry," Lelia says, tossing the sponge into the bucket. "We've cleaned enough. Let's go outside. Let's go to the park. It's too pretty a day to waste."

"Okay, but downtown. I'd rather ride the ferry."

"Fine. Anything. To Staten Island, then." She was already changing, loose slacks and a blouse. Muted greens on muted greens. "Let's just move."

The ferry, everyone knows, is the city's cheapest vacation. For fifty cents you can escape Manhattan by boat, crossing the waters of the harbor and bay past all the famous islands, Governor's, Liberty, Ellis. It used to be a quarter, before that a dime. Lelia and I must have taken the trip over fifty times, not once setting foot on Staten Island itself. We always stand against the railing, whatever the season, whatever the weather, making sure to get a good spot on the Manhattan side of the boat so we can watch the skyline both ways. How it looms, unlooms, looms again. In the daytime, most of the traffic is commuters, some school kids, always a few tourists, many more in the summer.

But after eight or nine at night, it's a different crowd. You hear the portable music, the boat is full of dressed-up kids, Italian and Irish kids, Hispanic kids, laced up in silk, all the youthful couples, the lovers. They are journeying to Manhattan to dance. To drink and maybe fight and make a little love. To act old. Play with their hard-earned money.

We leave the big island with crowds of office workers going home early for the weekend. They're weary. They stay inside where it's warm and undrafty, where they can sit down and finally read the day's paper. We're in our spot next to the wide gangway, standing among the traders and workmen and a pack of youthful Japanese, everyone waiting for the launch and the black billows of diesel. The sun is dipping below the rim of clouds, a sudden last brightness. Lelia pulls my hand around her and tucks it inside the lapel of her blazer. My palm is cold on her breast, and she jumps a little. Although it's balmy, we're not dressed for the sea wind, even the one of this harbor, which reeks of long-dead water. As we push off the dock, Lelia reminds me that whenever a boat departs the land a hundred hearts are broken.

"That sounds like a saying of immigrants," I say.

"My mother told it to me," she replies. "I think it's for sailors and their girls."

"Was Stew a sailor?"

"Double-u double-u two," Lelia growls, turning into me. It's funny how she can never just speak for her father. Certain voices you have to honor. They're unassailable. "Backed the landing at I-wo Ji-ma," she says, "and then Ko-RE-a."

"No kidding. He never mentioned that to me."

"I don't think he likes to talk about it. I think some of his friends got killed."

I kiss the softness between her eyes. People watch us. "My father never talked about the war," I say. "He tried once. I had to write a report for social studies. I got the bright idea to do something on the Korean War. I asked him what it was like. He almost smiled and started to talk as if it was no big deal but then he choked up and left the room."

"How did you do the report?"

"I read my junior encyclopedia," I tell her. "The entry didn't mention any Koreans except for Syngman Rhee and Kim Il Sung, the Communist leader. Kim was a *bad* Korean. In the volume there was a picture of him wearing a Chinese jacket. He was fat-faced and maniacal. Bayonets were in the frame behind him. He looked like an evil robot."

"The Mao lover's Mao," Lelia answers.

"Exactly," I reply. "So I didn't know what to do. I didn't want to embarrass myself in front of the class. So my report was about the threat of Communism, the Chinese Army, how MacArthur was a visionary, that Truman should have listened to him. How lucky all of us Koreans were."

"You really felt that way?"

"More or less, when I was little. Sometimes, even now. You know, it's being with old guys like Stew that diminishes you."

"But I thought he never said anything to you. You didn't even know."

"It doesn't matter," I tell her loudly, holding her close. The boat is powering up to speed, throwing its wake. "It's that coloring those old guys have about the face and body, all pale and pink and silver, those veins pumping in purple heart. It says, 'I saved your skinny gook ass, and your momma's, too.' "

"I never understood that word," she shouts into the wind. *"Gook.* I sometimes hear it from the students. I thought it was meant for Southeast Asians. I don't get it."

"Everyone's got a theory. Mine is, when the American GIs came to a place they'd be met by all the Korean villagers, who'd be hungry and excited, all shouting and screaming. The villagers would be yelling, *Mee-*

gook! Mee-gook! and so that's what they were to the GIs, just gooks, that's what they seemed to be calling themselves, but that wasn't it at all."

"What were they saying?"

" 'Americans! Americans!' *Mee-gook* means America."

"That's perfect," Lelia says, shaking her head. "I better ask Stew."

"Don't harass your father," I tell her. "He won't know anything. It's funny, I used to almost feel good that there was a word for me, even if it was a slur. I thought, I know I'm not a chink or a jap, which they would wrongly call me all the time, so maybe I'm a gook. The logic of a wounded eight-year-old."

"It stinks," she utters, turning to the waters. Her hands are white on the rail. "If I had heard that one redheaded kid say even one funny word to Mitt! God! I would have punched his fucking lights out! I would have made him scream!" Her chest bucks, and she almost starts to cry, strangely, as if she's frightened herself with a memory that isn't true.

The redheaded boy lived in my father's neighborhood. He was older than Mitt, maybe nine or ten when Mitt was six, and we often saw him at the town pool. Mitt would always step behind us when he approached. He used to tell us how the kid, named Dylan or Dean, had "the hugest muscles," and when I see that kid now I understand the proportion Mitt's eyes must have been measuring, I can see the creamy flesh of a nine-year-old bully, the brutish, magical pall he must have cast. Of course, he was also a kind of friend. Dylan or Dean would teach Mitt and the other kids the run of bad words; he'd teach them how to trash-talk Mitt and then teach Mitt how to trash-talk them back. It was our boy's first formal education. But the other kids would have more ammo against Mitt, they were all just Westchester white boys, some of them Jews. Maybe Mitt could say "kike" (which he did once in the house, until Lelia cracked him hard on the ass) or else pretty much nothing, maybe something lame like "paleface" or "ghost," unless the kid had big ears or was plainly slow. Because there isn't anything good to say to an average white boy to make him feel small. The talk somehow works in their favor, there's a shield in the language, there's no fair way for us to fight.

We're nearing the dock. Lelia suddenly wants to get off the boat. She wants to stay on Staten Island tonight. I tell her it's haunted, spooked, that it's the isle of brutes and bigots.

"Who's the spook?" she says, though gently.

She knows it will only be a few more weeks with Kwang. This is the promise that hangs between us. She'll go back to the school district, and I'll stay at home for a while, keep my head low.

When the boat docks we step off the gangway and ask a cabdriver to take us to any nearby motel. He drops us off at the Grey Island Inn, a long rectangular three-decker with a view of the ship docks and the Jersey shoreline. We order in hamburgers and beer from the Greek diner next door and pay for the in-room movie, though we can't watch much of it. It's a new technothriller stocked with laser-guided weapons, gunboats, all flavors of machismo. Muscular agents. Give us *The Third Man,* we decide, give us *The Manchurian Candidate* and *The Spy Who Came in from the Cold.*

Lelia switches the wall heater to high and we take off our clothes and slip into bed. We try to take a bath but the water doesn't clear of its rust; the shower is the same. The pay movie is finally ending. We first muted the sound, but there's no remote so we let it go on, silent. Now, the flickering lights of the finale wash over us, spectacular explosions, muzzle flashes, the steady glow of reactor fires. Only a movie can color your lovemaking like a movie's.

We know the hero won't die. He can't. There's too much blood on his face, he's too pummeled and wrecked to perish, his bedragglement is the sign to us that he is safe, actually immortal. The gunmen who sport $200 haircuts and Italian suits take bullets to the head. Lelia winces each time they fall. I imagine Jack in Cyprus, both knees broken, blood gluing his teeth, taking aim and shooting his young captor in the eye while lying on the ground. In our fictions, a lucky shot saves your life.

Lelia sits up to go to the bathroom, waits for a second, then runs through the dark. I hear her pee and then flush. The creak of the mirror. Then she's still for a moment.

She calls out.

"Henry," she says, sounding worried. "I think I'm getting old. Fast."

"Not so fast," I say.

"That's not the right answer," she calls, singing the last word.

She creeps out, runs back. After certain movies we rent, a sniper waits somewhere in the room, a strangler or rapist lurks. She used to check on Mitt during the credits, making sure he hadn't been stolen. She still insists on renting slasher films, demon movies. She wants to get stuck in her imagination. I saw her carry a marble paperweight through our apartment after we watched *Jaws.*

But I think the rest of her is becoming dauntless, even with our years and troubles. Mitt. Her trip of escape, the brief love affair. My treacheries. None of these are written on her face, none of these can be read on her body. History, it turns out, is not a human expression. Age is, time is. And she's right; the oldness is now just appearing about her lip, her temples, in the tide of her voice, which is steadily deepening, broadening. In fact she is beginning to sound a little like her old man, but without all the heady blow and bellow. These days, I notice, she likes to hum her songs, prefers this, when once she would only sing pristine notes, ring them out like clarions around the apartment.

"Try to find the weather for tomorrow," she says to me, nodding toward the television. "If it's nice, maybe we should stay another day."

I get up and flip around until I find the local news station. Another cabbie is dead, shot in the back of the head, this time a Cuban driver in the

Bronx. They show the blood-soaked seat, the shattered windshield, a dashboard scent infuser tagged with a religious inscription in Spanish.

"Christ," Lelia whispers.

The man is the fifth or sixth driver murdered in the last two months. The cabbies are threatening a one-day strike of all New York. They want something done, more police protection, swift justice, but no one has any good idea of how to get it done. The news shows Mayor De Roos venerably bowing his head at a press conference. The reporter speaks to several drivers at the company garages, and though all of them are concerned and scared there's nobody who can speak for the drivers as a group, who even wants to, they're too different from one another, they're recently arrived Latvians and Jamaicans, Pakistanis, Hmong.

What they have in common are the trinkets from their homelands swaying from the rearview mirror, the strings of beads, shells, the brass letters, the blurry snapshots of their small children, the night-worn eyes. I wonder if the Cuban could even beg for his life so that the killer might understand. What could he do? *Have mercy,* should be the first lesson in this city, how to say the phrase instantly in forty signs and tongues.

The next story is about a small freighter that runs aground off Far Rockaway in the middle of the night. The boat carries around fifty Chinese men who have paid $20,000 each to smugglers to ship them to America. Men are leaping from the sides of the boat, clinging to ropes dangling down into the water. Rescue boats bob in the rough surf, plucking the treaders with looped gaffs. The drowned are lined up on the dock beneath canvas tarps. The ones who make it, dazed, soaked, unspeaking, are led off in a line into police vans.

The last big story is a fire. It is burning even now. A two-alarm blaze at the main offices of City Councilman John Kwang, and the building next door. The cause is suspicious. Witnesses say there was a small explosion around 9 P.M. There are no official reports as yet of injuries or fatalities. It happened too late, authorities think, for anyone to be inside. The witnesses saw two men in ski masks running from the alley. Then the windows blew out. The pictures show the street in chaos, the burning frame of a car parked out front. The back part of the building is ferociously spewing smoke and a girl on the street is crying and pointing at something and covering her mouth. I know Kwang was in Washington, D.C., this afternoon, and we now see him stepping from the shuttle gate at La Guardia, rushing out to his car, Jenkins rushing with him, and then Sherrie Chin-Watt. None of them will comment.

We stop watching and lie back and wait for the weather forecast but we don't hear it. There is a perfect calm in the bed, and then Lelia gets up and shuts off the television. When she comes back she is looking up at the plastered ceiling, her arms folded, pinning the sheet tight against her chest. I turn off my light. Then she clicks off her side. It's pitch dark. We've made love just a little before but now I notice how conscious I am of touching her. She is perfectly still. I can't even hear her breathing.

"God," she says, the awe quieting her voice. "Good god. You could have been there."

"Maybe," I say.

She rolls into me, nearly on top of me. She whispers close, "He's safe."

"Yes."

"Who did this?" she asks.

"I don't know," I say, the possibilities firing in my head, though most of them involve Dennis, and now even Jack, the two of them watching the blaze from the periphery.

"Do we need to go back now?"

"No," I tell her. "We'll go in the morning."

"I feel ill," she says, getting up. She stumbles to the bathroom. I follow her and hold her shoulders as she gets sick into the toilet.

"I'm sorry, Henry," she says, turning on the tap. "I'm all right now."

I don't say any more. I can't. I walk her back through the dark room to the bed. We lie down and in a few minutes she's so quiet that for a second I think she's dead. I put my fingers near her mouth to check. She's just breathing faintly, not yet asleep.

Now I'm scarcely breathing myself. This is wont with my training in the face of sudden turns or shifts in events. But I'm square in the fear. If you're skilled you don't try to steel yourself, you actually do the opposite, you let yourself go, completely, Hoagland told me once, like you are sitting on the toilet, you loosen a certain muscle. It's a classic NKVD trick, and if you're careful and practiced it works without disaster. Old Soviets know. You are serene as Siberia.

Once, I do it perfectly. Maybe for years. A child of mine is somehow dead. He is no longer inhabiting our life. I watch my wife go out every morning to wander about the grounds of my father's house, poking in the bushes and the trees for hours at a time, as if to follow his last tracks. One morning she returns with objects in her hands, pretty rocks and twigs and big oak leaves, and she sits down silently at the small table in our garage apartment to construct a little house. She works slowly. I watch her from the corner, where I often read. Eventually, the rocks show a path, she raises walls with the twigs, and the canopy of leaves she blows gently with her breath, to make sure its utility. She peers inside, expressionless. She blows harder and then leaves it. Then she crawls back into bed.

The twig house sits there for days. Lelia cries on and off. She seems to live in the bed. I don't speak to her then. I try my best to ignore her. This, I think at the time, is best for us both. I will attempt to eat at the table, or read the newspaper there, but it's so small and rickety that any wrong movement endangers the house. Finally one day I find it outside, at the far end of my father's lawn, perfectly intact right down to the rocks. I look back to the garage, to the big house. I don't see anyone in the windows, including the small oval of the secret room, but I think she is watching me, to witness what I might do. I kneel down before it. Pick it apart, leaf by twig, stone by rock, until I have orderly piles of the material. I stand up and shout out his name. I shout it again, as loud as my meager voice can. Then I fling it all in the woods, dismantled piece by piece. I turn back, ready for her, but even with all of my hope she still isn't there.

Now I cannot see her face and she cannot see mine. Though I think even if it were light I would not effect my oft-drilled calm, which I have done for her a hundred times but will not do now. I will not rid my expression of the sudden worry and weight. I will not hush or so handle my heart. I will put my hand in her hair. Kiss her ear. Now whisper a speech with my smallest voice. She whispers back, this blessing we share. Now I think we will both dream of fire.

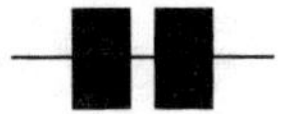

The front windows are blown out. A large crowd is already formed behind the barricade. The fire marshals and bomb squad pick through the burned-out section in the back that serves as an annex for the office, where we keep voting registration and contributor records. Minor devices, one of them says. I hear Janice Pawlowsky cursing, but from where I can't see. Her wails and epithets carry out from the broken windows, down the fire-stairs.

The staff is allowed to go inside in shifts to retrieve records and personal items. John Kwang hasn't arrived yet, but he's expected and the media are thick on the ground. They wait outside the yellow police tape, stopping everyone and interrogating them. All of them want to know if we personally knew the dead. I pretend I don't speak English.

But these are ours: an office janitor, an older, always cheery woman named Helda Brandeis, and the college student, Eduardo Fermin. Both were working after hours; they were found in the back war room, huddled together, trapped, overcome by fumes. They weren't burned. Nothing in that room burned. Janice didn't see them but heard they were covered in a film of ash, as if they'd slept through a gentle, black snow.

Eduardo's family has been holding a vigil in front of the office since last night, his mother and father, his grandmother, his two sisters and his baby brother. The coroner removed the bodies hours ago for autopsy, but Eduardo's family still remains, unable to leave, as if waiting for his ghost to return to the place he was last alive.

When it's my turn to go in, I gather the things in his desk next to mine and place them in a file box. I fill it with everything I can find, but I keep for myself an embossed 3×5 note card he had printed with the phrase John Kwang always said: "Honor your family."

I leave my own things alone. There is nothing I wish to salvage. Better that it's thrown away. I come back out and place the box of Eduardo's things near them. His mother gasps something in Spanish, she's short of breath, and Eduardo's young brother immediately pulls off the cardboard lid. It smells of smoke. On top of his papers and framed photographs is Eduardo's goldtone ballpoint pen, obviously a family gift, maybe from high school graduation, and here's the little boy taking it, writing slowly in the air. Now they gather up his things and finally go home.

Sherrie walks the site with the authorities. She has me follow them and take notes. Apparently, there are two accelerants: the first, the lethal one, is meant for fire, hurled through the windows in front and back in the alley. Probably just Molotovs. The other is a device, timed and set inside the front reception room of the office. Maybe it was wrapped as a package. Now they're piecing together how the fire spread through the offices full of paper fuel, pinning in Eduardo and the woman. The explosion is nothing to speak of, nothing special, they believe no plastique was used, no deep electronics, just a stick or two of dynamite, a model airplane battery for detonation, a few rounds of duct tape. Common materials.

"So it could be anybody who works on a construction site," Sherrie says to the group of men. "Or has access to one." They stare at her. She wearily asks them, "What are you going to tell the press?"

"Crude explosive," one of them says. "I wouldn't let it get in your hair, lady. Just because it's a bomb doesn't mean we're dealing with a terrorist. It's probably just some crank who's sore at Kwang."

Everyone mostly agrees. Nobody wants a situation. The tabloids are already screaming for one, they're suddenly calling the start of a terrorist race war, American-style. I realize that the men and Sherrie want to quell the notion. But no one is acknowledging what at least is clear, that someone took a little trouble with this one, that it's not a drive-by situation, it's not the work of vandals or addicts.

When we finish with the investigators I slip away and call Jack from a deli down the block. He isn't at home or at work. I call his house again and leave a message saying it's just me needing some wisdom. That I'll try again. Then I call the office and the phone picks up.

It's Dennis.

"Good to hear your voice, Harry," he says. "You say hello in the nicest way."

"Where's Jack?"

"Out to lunch."

"Bullshit. He eats later."

"So you caught me."

"Where is he?"

"Gone," he says.

"Come on," I say.

"Okay, Harry."

"What?"

"He's dead."

All stop.

"I'm kidding," Dennis says. Not even a laugh. "Jesus, I'm kidding."

"Fuck you forever."

"Okay," he then says, "have it your way, sore-sport, I'm passing the phone."

Jack gets on. He sounds all out of breath. I ask him what's going on. He says the elevator's out. But now I want to know what he knows.

"The fire?" he asks.

"The two guys in ski masks."

"Who can say? I will look into it, if you wish. But I think it is nothing."

"People are dead."

"I am sorry," he says. "The Spanish boy, and a woman."

"Does it matter to you?" I ask him.

"I guess not," he answers.

"Then tell me you don't know anything," I say. "Tell me you just saw the news. Otherwise don't say a word. Say goodbye and hang up."

"Don't worry, Parky. It's nothing. Nothing. I would know."

"Would you?" I say. "There's the bomb to consider."

He's quiet. "What kind was it?"

"Something simple. Sticks of dynamite."

"See? Proof. This is nothing. Nothing. Nobody uses dynamite."

"I wish I could believe you."

"Damnit, you should," he says, almost finally. "But be crazy if you like. Crazy! This is not what we do. I know. Tell me, Parky, tell a stupid old man. What would be our interest?"

"I don't see any," I answer. "He was just a kid. He didn't know anything."

"Then it is just another act. You are losing it, boy. You must be forgetting this is New York City. Random murder and violence."

"What does Dennis have to say?" I ask. "He must be listening to us. I'm talking to you, Dennis."

"He does not have to listen," Jack cries. "I will tell him everything anyway. You know this. I will say you are concerned. That is enough. Not crazy, like you are."

"Thanks so much, Jack."

"Let me say something before I go, Parky. Sometimes you should look closer to home. If something is funny then look there. This is my advice to you. And I will tell you one more thing. If you cannot trust me there is nobody."

"God bless me then, Jack."

"Bless you then," he says.

I walk quickly back to the ruined building. "Hey, Henry," Sherrie says, calling me over to her car. "I need you to write a summary of this for John. Not right now, just give it to him by tonight. We need everyone now to move the essentials over to his house in Woodside. We're going to work out of the basement. I've sent Janice over already. You know where the house is?"

I shouldn't know, but I do.

"Good," she says. "You know, I'm sorry. I know you worked with Eduardo. I liked him a lot."

I nod.

"Here," she says, reaching into her bag. She hands me a thick white envelope bound with a red sash. "John wants you to give this to his family. This is important to him. He trusts you with doing this."

"Don't worry."

"Thanks," she says. "John wants to bring it himself, but the papers might take it the wrong way if they found out, you know what I mean?"

"I understand," I say.

"Good," she says, squeezing my arm. "I appreciate this. It's good to work with other Asians, you know? You don't have to explain yourself."

"Right."

"Right," she says. "Oh, and you better call home, too. I know it's Saturday, but we're probably going to work all night. Help pack up here and then ride over with Jenkins in the van. I'll see you there later."

Sherrie smiles and handles my arm again, the ball of my shoulder. I put the money away inside my jacket. She goes back to directing the mess, managing the people traffic. They all listen to her, heed her. The whole office likes her. But I find the touching strange. From someone else, for instance Janice, the contact would simply be casual, friendly, just a kind of parlance, formless, easy talk. But from Sherrie the touch is different. It's not sexual and not sisterly. It calls on that very minor power we can have over each other, that exercise of influence and duty which we know from our families, our fathers. Our cousin blood. That age-old weakness of brethren you always root out and you always use.

The Fermins are caretakers of their tenement building. They live on the ground floor next to the elevator, and even inside their apartment you can hear the tired heave of cables running in the shaft, the up and down shouts of little kids who need to pee. Mrs. Fermin recognizes me immediately and opens the steel door. I tell her my name, who I am. She cups my hand and tries to smile. She leads me through a dim half-corridor and gestures to the sofa. She says *cerveza* and I say yes. Her husband sits on one end of the frilly sofa, half asleep from the long night, half mourning. He's too weak to acknowledge my presence. He's not crying, he's not doing anything. I sit down on the other end. They've drawn the blinds and it's almost completely dark. Mrs. Fermin comes back from the kitchen and hands me a can of Budweiser and sits in a dining chair with a can for herself. We drink in silence. The other children aren't here, even the young boy, but the grandmother is. She's chopping in the kitchen and the apartment air is oniony, sharp, and she's speaking to herself over and over in a rhythm that sounds like the Lord's prayer.

The whole room is set up with pictures of Eduardo. Seeing his parents,

I realize he was a very handsome young man. Sometimes you have to meet the parents to figure out what someone really looks like. In their many pictures Eduardo is a baby, he's a black bear for Halloween, he's a bristling Golden Glover, he's in a suit that's too big. He sports a downy prideful adolescent moustache. He stands arm in arm with John Kwang. And what I see is that most of the pictures are already hung, part of a permanent collection, that this room has always been a kind of family chapel to their son.

Mrs. Fermin smiles at me and says very softly, very gently, "What d'you wan, Mr. Park?"

I say I've come on behalf of John Kwang, that I've brought something for her family from him. I tell her that he doesn't want his gift to be publicly recognized, that she should accept it and use it for her family, but then Mrs. Fermin waves her hands and shakes her head saying, "Slow, slow." She tries to say something to me, but she's being too careful and nothing can come out. She speaks quickly to her husband in Spanish but he just responds, "Ay, Carmelina," and buries his head in the crook of his arm.

I stop talking and take out the envelope. I give it to her, for some reason, in the formal Korean way, with my eyes down and my free hand guiding my extended wrist. Maybe I think Kwang would do it like this, want it done like this.

She steadies her can of beer on the carpet and places the envelope in her wide lap. I get up to go but she wants me to stay. The grandmother comes out to look at the package. Mrs. Fermin slowly unties the red ribbon, lifting the folds of the heavy paper until they petal out to show the bright color of the neatly stacked money. Mrs. Fermin can't touch the money. She lifts up the bundle by the paper and carries it to me. She can't speak, she doesn't know what to do. I count it for her. There are a hundred $100 notes in the stack, and the bills are brand new, they rustle on touch and stick to one another.

The grandmother rushes up and snatches the money away from me and disappears to the back end of the apartment. We can hear her madly opening closet doors, drawers, boxes. She's hiding all the money. Mrs. Fermin starts weeping in her chair. Her husband still hasn't moved.

"You know, he helpin Eduardo always," she now says, wiping her eyes with her sleeve, rocking. "Mr. John Kwang. He helpin Eduardo go law school. Before Mr. Kwang, Eduardo doin too many jobs, this and that, this and that. Now, me Eduardo, he gon make everyone happy. Jus like Mr. Kwang. Eduardo gon make everyone happy and rich. He's a beautiful boy."

She brings me an album of pictures. We look at pictures together, and she keeps talking about him. I know what she means, despite her tenses. She's not acting out, acting crazy. I know this Mrs. Fermin. Half the people in Queens talk like her. Half the people I knew when I was a child. And I think she's saying it perfectly, just like she should. When you're too careful you can't say anything. You can't imagine the play of the words in your head. You can't hear them, and they all sound like they belong to somebody else.

Mrs. Fermin gestures for me to follow her to the back of the apartment, to his bedroom. We pass a closed door, behind which the grandmother waits for me to leave. Eduardo shared a small one-window room with his little brother, Stevie. They each have a twin bed with matching bedspreads that Stevie picked out, full of space shuttles and star stations. There are two of the same chipboard desk, the size too small for Eduardo and maybe too big for Stevie; Eduardo's boxing trophies, a line of aluminum baseball bats, posters of Latin pop groups and singers. Mrs. Fermin shows me a picture frame inset with Eduardo's ninth-grade report card. Straight A's.

"After some more times, we don' do agayn," she says. "No more frames."

She shows me pictures of his girlfriend, Arabel, who likes the color pink and carnations and who said she was going to be his wife. She shows me his ribbons and medals from Lucky Meier's Gym of Champions, and she shows me three shoeboxes stuffed with commendations, certificates of merit, honorable mentions, a plaque from the Latino League of New York's Father-Son Day, for what I can't tell, she shows me a dozen other mementos of her three men, whom she has all known as boys and will forever love that way, their first charm and vulnerability, and she shows me a yellow silken bird of the islands, the one that augurs mercy and good tidings, which now falls off its perch on the post of Stevie's tidy bed.

Mr. Fermin calls out for her from the living room. He calls her name, and then in a voice drunk with sadness he calls for his sons, his daughters, he doesn't want to be left alone.

"I go now," she says to me politely.

She leads me out. Mr. Fermin is stretched out on the sofa. His slack arm covers his face. She says to him in Spanish, *The man is leaving.*

He grumbles. She repeats herself.

And so he answers, trying hard, "Goodbye, Mr. Kwang."

Sherrie and Janice have called the entire office in, all the volunteers, the part-time canvassers, even the high school kids who station the sidewalk kiosks. His large row house is trafficked by us rushing in and out, depositing papers, carrying file cabinets, computers, lamps, makeshift desks. Sherrie says he wants everybody together today. This is important. He wants everyone near. He doesn't need to see us or hear us. Just have us close.

When something bad happens, you gather the family and count heads.

He hasn't slept, Sherrie tells us. He's hurting badly. He has been weeping all night for his friend Eduardo, and then Helda Brandeis, praying for them with old Reverend Cho from the Flushing Korean Church. He hasn't come down from his office on the third floor of the house since he returned from D.C., now a few days. His wife and his boys go up and visit with him for a while and then leave him alone, and only the minister has been allowed up. Every hour Mrs. Kwang gives Sherrie a new message of what he wants said or done.

For the last few hours the communiqués have ceased coming down. It's nearing five o'clock and the stations need something new for their first evening broadcasts. The reporters have begun clamoring for him, shouting their questions up to the third-floor window. There are enough reporters and cameramen on the narrow sidewalk that the police have set up barricades to keep them from flowing out into the street and obstructing traffic. The neighbors have been complaining about some of them, who want to use their upstairs to look in on Kwang's house, some even asking if the basements might be connected. His immediate neighbors, though, are loyal, the whole block stays vigilant over Kwang, and they have started hurling garbage and buckets of water at those trying to sneak up the sides and back of the property. Sherrie and Janice instruct us again and again not to speak to the press as we move things inside.

But as we work all the talk is about who did this to us. Everyone is exchanging rumors, theories.

It's the Black Muslims. They can't accept Yellow Power. No, someone else says, *they'd never do something like this. Who is it, then? The Man, stupid, it's always the Man. No shit, but who's that? De Roos. Who else?*

I hear the talk from all his people. They offer each other the spectrum of notions; the bombers are North Korean terrorists, or the growing white-separatist cell based on eastern Long Island, or even the worldwide agents of the Mossad—you can always lay blame on them—who will never forget Kwang's verbal support of the children of the Intifada. The late money says it's the Indians, who so despise Korean competition, it's the Jews envious of new Korean money, Chinese hateful of Korean communality, blacks who want something, anything of justice, it's the uneasy coalition of our colors, that oldest strife of city and alley and schoolyard.

If you beat your brother with his stick, I heard Kwang once say to a crowd, *he'll come back around and beat you with yours.*

The customary lessons, the historical formulas.

But now I hear a low whisper: it was *Eduardo* they wanted.

I look toward the stair but there are too many bodies trundling through the house, too many unknown faces to pick one out. And the idea is one I've been turning over in my mind. Aside from his family and blood, if you wanted to take someone away from John Kwang, if you simply desired to hurt him, exercise true malice, Eduardo would figure near the top of the list. But how did they know he'd be working that late? Or were he and the cleaning woman just caught in the smoke and the flames?

Near the kitchen Sherrie spots me and eyes me to come over. She's talking with May. Sherrie towers over her. They're holding each other's hands like schoolgirls. May is glassy-eyed. They've been talking about Helda.

Besides the office, Helda also cleaned the Kwangs' house once a week since she started about a year ago. She left her family back in what was the old East Germany to make enough money to send for her husband and three grown children. She was planning to bring them over one at a time. Helda was living with another German family in the Bronx, sharing a bedroom with two other boarders five nights a week. The other nights the boarders had to stay elsewhere because of an after-hours club the owners ran on the weekends. For the first month or so, Helda would shuttle back and forth between all-night diners, drinking coffee to stay awake. Jenkins found her asleep one night during her cleaning shift at the office and wanted to fire her, but John learned what was going on—Eduardo, who often worked at night, told him—and he invited Helda to sleep in his family's guest bedroom on the weekends. She could look after the boys if he and May went out. If guests came, she chose to sleep on the floor in the boys' room.

"The boys liked it," May says. "They said she was nice and pretty and old."

"They're good boys," Sherrie tells her.

"They've been crying with their father. I don't think they really understand but they see him and do the same."

"Did you go and see the Fermins, Henry?" asks Sherrie.

I tell her yes and look at May, her face as yet wrinkleless, so round, her full cheek pinching her narrow eyes, the color and curve so durably Korean. I now notice, too, the faintest patch of redness high on her cheek, between her left eye and ear, like she'd been sunburned just there, or was slapped once, very hard.

"They accepted your gift," I say to her.

"It's from all of us," May answers. "I hope you told her that. John wanted to present something on all of our behalf. My family as well as our office."

"I think Mrs. Fermin understood." Then I say, "She seemed a little overwhelmed by the amount."

"Funerals are expensive," Sherrie says.

May lowers her eyes. She's from *yangban* stock, her people are the Korean landed gentry, and she finds this open talk of figures awkward, unnecessary. The money, her eyes tell me, is simply an acknowledgment of our dead. I understand this. Even a poor cabbage farmer's son like my father knows the custom. But I wonder who in our office delivered Helda's honor, if there was one at all, whether it was air-posted to Germany in a handsomely twined bundle of vellum and silk.

May says, "My husband wants to speak with you, actually. Not today. Tomorrow, maybe. He wanted to ask you about how Eduardo's family is doing. He said he hasn't seen you in a few weeks."

After May goes upstairs Sherrie pulls me aside. We stand in the arch of a small powder room beneath the riser.

"I might not be around tomorrow so I'll tell you right now. Don't take too much of his time."

"Sure," I say. "What's wrong?"

"He's just not responding well to this and we've got to come out and make an appearance. He's got to come out strong. We're starting to suffer, people are starting to think he doesn't care. The damn papers aren't helping either."

This is true; the late edition headline of one of the tabloids reads, *Wherrrre's Johnny?*

"I don't want you to slow the process," she warns me. "He's vulnerable. You'll see that. Help him get his act together so he can get his face out there. He's looking like a coward."

"To some."

"He's not to me," she says harshly. "But the situation is getting critical. You can be a lifelong saint, but in politics you've only got a few days of disaster. Any more of this and we could be finished. He likes you and I think you can help him."

"I'm not sure I'm the one," I tell her.

"What does that matter?" she cries, her eyes sparkling, dark. "You've become important to us. That Peruvian thing you handled like a pro. And then the immigration mess with the six Haitians. You made it possible for John to help. Everyone he talks to in the office gives you a good report. Even Jenkins."

She suddenly turns quiet, inches closer. Touches my shoulder as she talks. I don't move.

"You know, now with Eduardo gone you'll have to do more. I know you're some kind of freelancer, but we're thinking about putting you on, full-time, if you need it that way. You relate well to strangers and constituents. People immediately trust you. You seem to understand what they need. That's a valuable asset in our work. You could work with me and John more closely. He likes the idea. We talked about you last week."

"What about Janice?"

"I already spoke to her," Sherrie says intently. "You're being wasted with her. She really only needs bodies, bulk. Let's face it, that's not you. This would be a great opportunity. You're not twenty-five anymore."

"You mean like you and Janice."

"Ha, ha," she groans, showing her straight teeth. Just now I can hear the scantest inflection of her Chinese, that rampant *hyawr* sound.

"Janice might be. I'm almost thirty-five. Ancient. God, I can't even imagine kids. I'm just saying, you don't seem to have a career you desperately love. I don't know how much you can make with your work writing bit articles."

I tell her, "I'm already past the time I should have left."

Sherrie frowns. "So what? One article you've got. Big deal. If we can get over this, John's going to be around for a long, long time. I don't have to tell you, you're smart, you think about it. We can all go right to the top. Even two Koreans and a Chinese. See what John says. And you better tell me soon if you're going to leave."

"I will."

"Good," she says, stepping away. "Don't make a mistake with your life, Henry Park."

I leave the house late in the evening. John hasn't made a statement yet and he's threatened to fire anyone who makes one for him. Outside the house a few reporters are still lingering. I walk quickly down the street before they can catch up to me, and flag a cab to take me to the subway station. The car stops and before the driver unlocks the doors he leans over and checks me. Yesterday a few Asian men were arrested for cabbie murders in Queens. Through the window glass I tell him the subway station at 45th Road but he shakes his head at me and so I say Manhattan instead. He nods. As I get in I notice a snub-nosed revolver shoved next to him in the seat. On any night someone in this city could put a bullet in his head for $30. So he drives with a gun, though I think he must know no weapon can save him. Maybe the pictures of his children on the dash can, maybe God can. The scent infuser is gushing lavender and bougainvillea, so heavily that I can almost see the flow, and on the radio someone is speaking a kind of French, though more grandly Latinesque, the beat honeyed and calyptic; this is a Haitian ship. The driver checks me in the rearview mirror and I hold up my hands so he can see. He laughs big and turns up the music, half relieved, half embarrassed, and I think with him, *One less good fare to get tonight.*

He takes us west at an amazing speed. We almost clip everything, hurtling by a hundred near-disasters. Somehow I think I'm safe in this vessel, though I wouldn't mind actually hitting something, as if that might confirm the real dangers in the world. All evening I've been locked inside myself, playing these hypothetical games of confidence and chance, thinking of the firebomb and why it happened and who could have left the scene with a light burning in his hand. There are always untenable events, freak happenings like someone recognizing you, or at worst, the trouble results from a foolish and negligent spy, like my time with Luzan.

But here a bomb goes off, crude as it is. A bomb means that there's too much care involved, even if you mean to kill. Jack himself always said that when you make a bomb you are also constructing a statement, employing a more complicated grammar than is required. It's the way civilized man now encumbers his territory, not with great walls or stretches of wire but with a single well-placed device, a neat bundling with the workings of a mind. It reads time, speaks volumes. Long after the flash, the concussive burn, it will speak to you again, at your fine desk, in your fine bed. Saying these are your certain ruins.

The next day the older boy, Peter, is upstairs in the office. He sits at his father's desk, scrawling away importantly on the office stationery with a fat black fountain pen. I stay in the doorway.

"Hello," I say.

"Hello," Peter replies, still writing, not looking up. The young man of the people. He says, "Please feel free to sit down, anywhere you want. Is the councilman expecting you?"

"Yes, I believe so."

"Very good."

He finally finishes his work and sighs. Looks up, Kwang-style, the face wholly open, as if he's about to smile, but he sees me and bounces up from the seat. He bows his head sharply and fumbles out, *"Me-yahn-ney-oh, ah-juh-shih." I'm very sorry, sir.*

"Gaen-cha-nah," I mutter, chuckling, telling him it's okay. I put out my hand. *"Yuh-gi ahn-juh." Come here and sit.*

He comes around the desk and sits upright in the wing chair beside mine. His straight black hair is bowl-cut. The bridge of his nose hasn't yet pushed out. The arms at attention, the eyes ever lowered, a venerating bend to his head. He waits for me to address him. From his earliest moments he knows to be like this before an elder.

He is so much like me when I was ten, so unlike our Mitt, whom Lelia and my father and I let raucously trample over all our custom and ceremony. Our Mitt, untethered. He'd tug at my father's pant legs during church sermons, roam the shadows of restaurant tables, publicly address his mother by her given name: all these spoils of our American life. And despite Lelia's insistence that he go to Korean school on the weekends, I knew our son would never learn the old language, this was never in question, and my hope was that he would grow up with a singular sense of his world, a life univocal, which might have offered him the authority and confidence that his broad half-yellow face could not. Of course, this is assimilist sentiment, part of my own ugly and half-blind romance with the land.

Peter and I possess a similar command of Korean, though perhaps his grasp is slightly better, his *bah-rham* or accent, or, literally, "breeze," is more authentic, still deeply redolent of the old country. Perhaps in twenty years his Korean words will creep out like mine, the notes uncertain, tentative. When I step into a Korean dry cleaner, or a candy shop, I always feel I'm an audience member asked to stand up and sing with the diva, that I know every pitch and note but can no longer call them forth.

We talk baseball, the opening of the new season. The Yankees finally have some pitching. The Mets are sliding fast. We hate, hate Boston and St. Louis. Out of respect he tries to speak as much Korean as he can, and I don't let him know his rapid speech is variously lost on me. I listen and keep nodding, and ask in English what position he likes to play. He says he plays second base. What do you *want* to play, is the question. He curls one foot behind the other, bites his lip, and whispers: shortstop.

"Ah," I say, "why don't you play it then? Someone isn't better at it?"

"No way!" he answers stridently. "Dad wanted me to play second this year. The coach wanted me to be the shortstop but Dad said I had to learn how to play second base first. Next year I'll be at shortstop." His eyes concentrating. "You must learn how to be a good corporal before you can be a great general."

"Sounds like good advice," I say.

"Sure," Peter says. "This season, I'm paying my dues." He stands up.

I stand up with him. John walks in. He addresses his son by his Korean name and the boy leaps up and hugs him. His father kisses him on the temple and deep in the hair and says he wants him to fetch us some drink, some food. *Mother will know.* Peter turns but then stops and quickly bows to me before running downstairs.

He motions to my chair and we both sit. He wears a pressed white oxford shirt, new blue jeans, loafers. His hair is still wet from the shower, the silvery gray shining brightly through the black strands. His cheeks brushed red by steam and water. But he looks much older with his hair flat and matted, his head an orb more dully drawn, as if diminished. I see his posture as somehow broken, there's not his familiar pliancy and spring at a public appearance, his steely poise among the crowds, the drive pooled up in his fists, the huge voice, the miracle forcefulness. I have witnessed him shake fifteen hundred hands in the space of a city block, Q & A for five hours with an assembly of greedy malcontents, kneel whole mornings in Reverend Cho's cavernous church praying for a rookie cop shot up in

Hunt's Point. In the afternoons, when Eduardo and I escorted him from the office to the subway, which he sometimes liked to ride home, we heard him greet his citizens in Spanish, Hindi, Mandarin, Thai, Portuguese, him lilting forth with a perfection unborrowed and unstudied: *Keep on, keep faith, we know how you feel, you are not alone.*

"He's not like his younger brother, you know," he says, his head resting in the seam of the high chairback. "Peter's never been too aggressive. Not Johnny's way. Johnny already gets into scuffles in nursery school, you know, he has trouble, he doesn't talk too much yet. He prefers contact. For example, he loves those Ninjas."

"Peter's very thoughtful," I say.

"Yes, very much," he answers, almost beaming. His color seems to come back. "For some time I felt somewhat disappointed by this. I couldn't understand why. The boy is sensitive and intelligent. Clearly there's deep warmth in his heart, a deep compassion, even at his age. I watched him once in front of his school, his mother and I were waiting in the car to pick him up. Some older boys were calling him names, a fairy, whatever, and also making fun of me, saying his father wasn't a 'real chink' like he was. Peter was quiet. I could tell this approach of theirs confused him a little. He had so much to respond to, and in different ways. He kept staring at them, though without malice. May wanted me to go and stop it but I admit I couldn't. I didn't want to. Sometimes you want to see what will happen with a boy on his own. I feared for him but I did nothing. Sometimes you must wait and see."

"What happened?"

He remains hunched over. Now he closes his eyes to remember; it's a habit of his, he'll often shut them for three, four seconds, as he gathers what he'll say.

"Suddenly, Peter punched the loud boy in the mouth. He knew tae kwon do. His blow drew blood right away, and the boy fell down. The others scattered and the boy was left there, below Peter, holding his bleeding lip. You could see he was a tough kid, or that he considered himself tough. He got up and swung wildly at Peter but kept missing. Peter would wait, he was well trained, and then strike out when there was an opening. It happened in a matter of seconds. May was getting very angry at me and I had to hold her elbow to keep her inside the car. Peter kept landing blows, and the boy, he must have been all of ten or eleven, finally fell down again and then completely broke. He wailed like his age. He was afraid. I went for them then. As I approached I watched Peter bend down on his knees and put his face in front of the boy's. I heard him say, 'Hit me back.' But the boy couldn't, or wouldn't. He thought Peter was just baiting him. The teachers arrived and helped the boy get up. When we got back to the car May was silent, and then Peter began to cry. He didn't stop for an hour. He wouldn't look us in the face. He was sick in bed for two days afterwards. I let him stay sick, I understood this reaction, I accepted it."

We hear patters ascending the steps. It's John Jr., carrying in a tray of rice crackers wrapped in roasted nori, salted nuts, strips of dried squid. Peter follows him in with another, a bottle of Chivas and a small tin pail of ice. His father greets them heartily and takes the tray from Peter, who knows to retrieve glasses from the low shelf beneath the window. John Jr.'s got a crew cut, the thickest little hands. His head is still too big for him. He slaps his hands up and down to say he's finished his work. He stares up at me and says to his father in Korean, *What did uncle bring us?*

Peter tells his little brother to be quiet. John Jr. asks again and I say I left the present at home and will bring it tomorrow, which I will. Peter grabs him by the back of the neck and veers him toward the door. John Kwang calls them to come to him first; he kisses them both, and smacks John Jr. hard on the rear, which makes the boy shriek with happiness.

He tells them in a low Korean as they stand like soldiers before him, *You two behave tonight while I'm out. Be good to your mother. She has perished many times for you. Honor her with your obedience.*

Yes, Papa, they answer. They bow low before us, John Jr. checking so he can bow lower than Peter, who bends as if alone in prayer, his eyes shut tight.

John pours the whiskey and I find myself holding my glass to the bottle in the formal manner, the way I held the envelope for Mrs. Fermin. Then I pour for him, again with two hands. By custom with an elder, I look away while I sip. John doesn't seem to notice. For a long time I disliked this etiquette. When I was with my father and his friends I wouldn't drink, simply so I could avoid it. I understood only that my father enjoyed my practicing the motions, that it was an exercise of my servitude to him, the posture he desired. But I never fathomed the need of the culture even for the smallest acts.

"You know, I never drank before I became a councilman. Never thirty-dollar scotch. But it's amazing, Henry, how much people want to give to you and share with you. I must have received over a hundred bottles of liquor and champagne already this year. How many neckties does a man need? How many boxes of fruit? At dinners, they want to share a drink or two, and I always oblige. This one," he says, checking a chit taped to the neck of the bottle, "was from Kim Young-Ju last Christmas. He owns several convenience stores near Crown Heights. One of them was burned down last week."

"I know," I answer. "I sent him a note from the office. His merchants' association and the churches have been helping him."

"Good. Which church does he attend?"

"Port Washington Glory. Reverend Lee."

"Will you send something from us, too?"

"I'm not quite sure how to do that."

"Speak to Sherrie. Tell her that we spoke about you handling that from now on. She'll help you get started and introduce you around. Perhaps she's already spoken to you about staying on with us."

I drink at this. "I never considered staying in politics."

"Who says your work with us is in the realm of politics?" he says, throwing back his head. His face reddens slightly with the alcohol. "That's not what you've been doing, Henry. That's not what we're doing. Everyone speaks of politics as if it's some kind of sentence. This is a fundamental misunderstanding."

He points out the window.

"Down there, all those people from the media, those people snooping around for the mayor, that's what they believe we're all doing. Politics! We're 'politicians.' So we cut deals and make compromises and hope our constituents will look favorably on us. We act appropriately outraged and righteous. We are champions of causes. We are concessionists. We are public servants. This is how we are marketed and so this is how we end up marketing ourselves."

"No one says those things cynically of you."

"They all do," he says, clicking his glass on the side table. "I have been every one of those politicians. But it makes no matter, finally. Not to us. That's not why we're here. That's not why I'm here."

He delicately brushes his hair with his hand, as if it were strands of ash. All over he looks fragile, the model of someone grieving. I am conscious of how right he appears to me, how perfect, every one of his tones and gestures dead on, not simply what I expect but what I want desperately to see.

He says low, "Eduardo's family. You saw them?"

"Yes."

"When is the funeral?"

"The day after tomorrow."

"Will you go for me?"

"You're not?" I say.

He is silent. "He was easy to be with," John whispers. "He was so bright-eyed, ambitious in the good way, for his mother and father, for his family who had given him the chance. They sacrifice for him and he returns their gift as best he can. What else is there? When I see a boy like Eduardo, working so hard for those behind him, I want to weep. For me, there is nothing else, our life is made only of hope and melancholy. I asked him to watch the boys a few times so they could be with him and learn. Imagine, I wanted them to learn from him. He had a natural will, a genuine confidence you rarely see in anyone."

"I thought it was the boxing," I say.

"No way," John cries, reminding me of how my father would say the words, he thought, like an American. "He could box because he had the confidence. I know. You can't let someone pound on your bare skull unless you have a very clear and strong sense of self. Everything begins with that. Everything. No matter what happens, you crouch down, protect yourself as best you can, and you concentrate on what got you there."

"Even with bombs?"

"I don't give a damn about bombs! God Almighty! Do you really care about bombs, *Park Byong-ho shih?*"

I stop. I always freeze for a second on hearing my Korean name.

He yells, "Do you really care about who did this to us? That's what everyone out there wants to know."

I say, "They want to know what you believe."

"That's right," he answers. He rises and walks behind the desk, taking hold of the back of his chair. "They want me to make a statement. They want me to respond to their theories of who's responsible, whether it's blacks, whites, the Asian gang leaders I've been trying to negotiate with, they want me to shade my suspicion toward one party or another."

I say, "What if evidence comes forth? What if you have to?"

"There is no good evidence. You were there with Sherrie, yes? And even if there is I won't let myself be their fire. This should strictly be a criminal investigation. What they want from me is a statement about color. Whatever I say they'll make into a matter of race. Yellow man speaks out."

"Or yellow man stays quiet," I say.

"Perhaps. But the more racial strife they can report, the more the public questions what good any of this diversity brings. The underlying sense of what's presented these days is that this country has difference that ails rather than strengthens and enriches. You can see what can happen from this, how the public may begin viewing anything outside mainstream experience and culture to be threatening or dangerous. There is a closing going, Henry, slowly but steadily, a narrowing of who can rightfully live here and be counted."

He moves to the window shaded by venetian blinds, pulls the cord to open the slats. Almost twilight. He looks out. I hear shouts rise from the street, peppering the house. White camera light jumps up through the slats. They are trained on us. More shouts, and the window brightens further. Now it is the media keeping a vigil. They will stay all night, drinking hot coffee in the street, joking bitterly, working the video and microphones in shifts. This is their kind of hope, a Kwang Watch.

John peers down into the lights, unflinching.

"What is the mood downstairs, Henry, I mean, of our people?"

"Nothing bad," I tell him. "They're expectant, too, like the whole city. Haven't you talked with Sherrie?"

"Yes. But I want to know what you see. I believe I can trust you," he says, smiling easily, the manner still casual. "You seem already to move well among us," he tells me. "You've made everyone forget your reason for being here, the article, what not. At times I've forgotten, too, and I think you're here because you believe in what we're doing. I hope that's a little true."

I grunt in assent, sipping the liquor. I can't offer anything more. It is in these moments that I wish for John Kwang to start speaking the other tongue we know; somehow our English can't touch what I want to say. I want to call the simple Korean back to him the way I once could when I was Peter's age, our comely language of distance and bows, by which real secrets may be slowly courted, slowly unveiled.

"Sherrie," he says, sitting down now at his desk, "she's the best at many things, but I know people tend to hold their tongues around her. She's so intelligent and attractive. Most people don't handle that package well. Even some reporters cower a little with her. They get awed and start asking questions they think she'd like to answer."

"They do the same with you," I say.

"I believe that ended as of last week."

"Don't worry about our people," I offer. "We're just wondering like everyone else why this happened. Everyone is devastated. We can't see any good reasons."

John laughs bitterly, his head in his hands. "What are the bad ones, my friend?"

After a moment of quiet he pulls the bottom drawer and retrieves a folded green and white computer printout markered in Eduardo's hand. I take it in my hands. Somehow it's been retrieved from the fire, though I notice that it doesn't at all smell of smoke. He pushes it to me. It is a listing of names and addresses, names and ages of children, occupation, name and address of business or businesses, estimated yearly income, nationality, year-to-date dollar figures, percentage changes. Then, to the far right, double-underlined, the dollar amounts.

"What Eduardo was working on," John says softly, his voice lower, honorific. "What I ask you to do for us now. Before you look too much you must say yes or no. Say yes, my friend. Say yes to me tonight."

I tell them cash is acceptable. Please nothing else. Checks, lottery tickets, diamond stud earrings, cases of fruit, VSOP cognac, tubs of fresh tofu, and all other wares will be returned or donated or else thrown away. The money comes in weekly, some of them giving as much as $250 and $500, others as little as $10. Most give fifty. We welcome them all. Ten dollars a week is what it takes to start, ten dollars for the right of knowing a someone in the city for you who are yet nobody. But then no one, no matter the amount, has his ear over another. It matters only that you give what you can. You give with honor and indomitable spirit. You remain loyal. True. These are the simple rules of his house.

He knows all the givers. He continually memorizes and re-memorizes the entire listing of contributors, every one of the nearly two thousand, the feat itself awesome, and then he learns the names of newcomers every Monday morning, so that if just one of them were to bump into him at a dumpling cart or street festival he'd know something about them, that they own a wholesale fabric store or a wig shop, that they have a boy and a girl and a brand-new baby, that they are doing well, better probably than they hoped, just a little better every year.

The Korean money funnels in mostly through the dozens of churches across the metropolitan area. We have connections to most of them, not just from Queens and the other boroughs but from Nassau and Westchester and Bergen counties. The network isn't so good yet in Connecticut. Maybe Connecticut Koreans are too distant, perhaps they think they have more money or class than other Koreans. They send their kids to private day schools and drive expensive 4X4s and they belong to country clubs that have no blacks and no Jews. They're too far away from the city, the grimy little shops, the sweat merchants they used to be and know. They think they've escaped. They think they don't need John Kwang.

The church money arrives in bundled manila envelopes from Christian congregations called Presbyterian Glory, Heaven on Earth, Korean Fellowship of Devotion, Building Up The Christ, from Korean Catholics, Methodists, Baptists, Evangelicals, even Lutherans. The only missing variety is Episcopalian, the C of E never reaching us, or else never trying. They will never know the devotion they missed.

The rest of the money comes addressed directly to me, to a name of my choosing. Eduardo used his own name, but John wants me to have an alias. So I decide they should write care of a Mr. Dennis. I receive hundreds of small white envelopes each week, some delivered by hand, and there is extra money inside them lately, money for *Mr. Fermin. Rest in peace, Eduardo,* a handwritten note reads, a five-dollar bill stapled to it. Other bills clipped, bills taped, money falling out to the floor. The writing is in pidgin English and Spanish and Mandarin and then languages I have never seen. I collect this and other monies to bring to his mother, who asked at the funeral that they receive no more from us. She feels funny, she tells me. I will take it to her anyway, jam the money under their steel door.

I use Eduardo's spreadsheets on the notebook computer John bought him last Christmas. I work alone in the Kwangs' basement late at night. I black out the basement windows with thick muslin. I leave on one dull light in the corner. I work mostly in silence. The one bug silence. Then the hum of the machine. The phone rings and I stop everything. I pick it up and it's Janice. She wonders how I've been. No one sees me anymore. Have I gone up and died?

I do the same thing every night. I enter the giving in vertical rows. I have the machine sort the figures into two dozen categories. Every way it comes out I add it up, recompiling every bit of information we have to date. I have steadily become a compiler of lives. I am writing a new book of the land.

Like John Kwang, I am remembering every last piece of them. Whether I wish it or not, I possess them, their spouses and children, their jobs and money and life. And the more I see and remember the more their story is the same. The story is mine. How I come by plane, come by boat. Come climbing over a fence. When I get here, I work. I work for the day I will finally work for myself. I work so hard that one day I end up forgetting the person I am. I forget my wife, my son. Now, too, I have lost my old mother tongue. And I forget the ancestral graves I have left on a hillside of a faraway land, the loneliest stones that each year go unblessed.

Near morning, I print out what I have done in one long continuous sheet, the way he prefers to read the thick stack of names. He says it doesn't seem right all broken up. *This is a family,* he reminds me, grasping it with both hands.

He models our program on the *ggeh.* A Korean money club. Small *ggeh,* like the one my father had, work because the members all know each other, trust one another not to run off or drop out after their turn comes up. Reputation is always worth more than money. In this sense we are all related. The larger *ggeh* depend solely on this notion, that the lessons of the culture will be stronger than a momentary lack, can subdue any individual weakness or want. This the power lovely and terrible, what we try to engender in Kwang's giant money club, our huge *ggeh* for all. What John says it is about.

My father would have thought him crazy to run a *ggeh* with people other than just our own. Spanish people? Indians? Vietnamese? How could you trust them? Then even if you could, why would you? If my father had possessed the words, he would have said the whole enterprise was bad hubris. But in his own language, the one of fruit stand and cash register, he'd simply make his face of disbelief, then throw up his hands and try hard not to think of it again, the idea that someone as smart as Kwang would so waste his time.

In our *ggeh,* if you give a few dollars you can expect to receive a few hundred. The more you give, the more you can ask for; everyone comes to learn what's a fair amount. You send a letter. Then you come at night and you make your request. You spoke with Eduardo, who in the beginning spoke to John. Now you will simply speak to me. Bring an interpreter or phrase book. Everything is in private, we deal like family, among ourselves, without chits or contracts. This is why I must see your face, hear your voice, make certain that you live how you say. It doesn't matter what your color is, whether your breath reeks of garlic or pork fat or chilis. Just bring your wife or your husband, bring your children. If you want a down payment on a store, bring the owner of the store you work in now. Bring your daughter who wants to attend Columbia, bring her transcripts and civics essay and have her bring her violin. Bring X rays of your mother who needs a new hip. I want to see the fleshed shape of the need, I want to know the blood you've lost, or that someone has stolen, or tricked from you, the blood you desperately want back from the world.

Now I spend my days helping Lelia with her speech kids, then nap for a few hours after an early dinner until I leave at nine for the nightly work with John Kwang. Lelia seems to understand. Before I leave she makes certain to pull on my arms, pull on my ears like she used to do to Mitt before he would go outside. I take her tugs as little warnings, reminders that she is here, staying in our life, and choosing to let me go to his house in Woodside. Sometimes, she'll crawl up next to me on the sofa after dinner, interrupt my brief sleep with a garlicky mouth pressed down around my nose. Throttling my breath. Then I'll struggle, she'll lean into me with all her weight, press her flesh, and then somehow the clothes start coming off. The world skips into rhythm.

My strange hours are somehow revamping our sexual life. We hit-and-run each other at odd junctures, off hours. There is a sense of our stalking each other through the day and the night, each of us waiting for the other to fall asleep, to step out of the shower, hold a hot pan at the range, not expecting a touch. It's the first second of contact that sets her off, that almost criminal moment. For me, it's the idea that she's been considering us through her day, circling the notion of an act, picturing something while I've been away sorting through Kwang's papers, filing, adding figures. At home I turn the corner and suddenly there she is, lurking in some old crepe de chine. Here, she will say, a little story complete in her head, are you ready. So please let's go.

At other times we're on the move. It seems to us right now that if we stop moving, we die. We take the subway to parts of the city we've never been to and walk the neighborhoods for hours, combing through the sidewalk clearance bins for important pieces, amulets, future totems of the city. What we cherish most are the specialty items from far away, what the people have brought with them or are bringing in now, to sell to the natives: Honduran back scratchers, Polish mothballs, Flip Flops from every nation in the Pacific Rim, Statuettes of Liberty (earrings and pendants), made in Mexico City.

Yesterday we're in Ozone Park. We're talking the whole way on the train, talky talk, chattering at each other across the aisle of the swaying car like edgy ball players. At a deli we buy stuffed grape leaves and hot wings and Burmese beer and eat quickly with our hands on someone's overheated stoop. Half the time venturing down the streets is dangerous, certifiable behavior, and at least once each day I wish for the gun I always thought I should buy for living here; but there's something about the two of us that puts off the hoodlums and muggers. We're too unlikely a sight to be harmless, pluckable; it's Lelia's deadly-looking elbows and knees, it's my special street face (learned working with my father) looking already cheated and intolerant, and in a pinch we do instant run-throughs of her speech lessons, the most bending diphthongs, to ward off the especially hostile and brave.

Lelia grabs my hand and we run.

From Ozone Park we head to Flushing. She wants to go back to the places we used to explore, with Mitt on one of our backs or swinging between us like a monkey, back to certain streets where you can look down the block and see nothing but Koreans working the storefronts, speaking their language like it's the only one in the world. Lelia used to say that this must be like the old country, this is how it must be there, but one day in front of his store my father explained to her how if she looked carefully at the people she'd see the extra spring in their steps, the little boost everyone had, just by the idea of where they were. "Look, look," he implored her, crouched, slapping the pavement with both hands. "This is an American street."

Lelia said that she did see. I thought she was just romancing him, kindly playing to his mostly self-promoting immigrant lore, but later she'd showed Mitt, too, kneeling down beside him to watch the men and women busy in the street. They're just like you, she'd whisper.

Now I realize we're near the burned-out office. In a past day I might say anything to steer us in the other direction, but I walk us by the ruined building. There's fresh litter in the entrance, cola cups and newspaper. The metal frame of the once-lighted sign of his name has melted, and it sags down limply over where the big front windows used to be. We stand in the street, as close as the police tape lets us.

"Where did you work?" she asks.

"In back, by the alley."

"I think I need to see."

We duck under the tape and walk around to the side door. The opening has been boarded up with a piece of plywood, but someone has already kicked it in; in this city, every fire means a shelter. We step through the debris of charred cabinets and chair legs used as firewood, and move through the offices skylighted by gaping holes punched through the ceiling and roof by the firefighters. The major beams have all held, but whole walls have crumbled. We can still reach the war room, which is stripped but mostly intact. I walk to the small, windowless office where Eduardo and Helda were found, half expecting to see the ashen outline of their bodies, but nothing is there. Lelia calls and asks me who I am here and I don't understand.

"Your name," she says, not ironical. "Who do they think you are?"

I'm not sure how to answer. Then I say a man named Henry Park.

"What else do they know about him?" she says.

"He has a wife named Lelia," I tell her. "They once had a beautiful boy."

She is quiet, her arms snugly crossed. "Are they still happy?"

"Yes," I say. "But not as much as they want."

She turns around and stands before the blackboard, examining what's left. It's still somehow scribbled with target numbers and dates, Janice's writing, Sherrie's. For a moment I think Lelia is trying to map out for herself what might have gone on here, to imagine a version of me and what I would do on a particular day, and I begin to think this is a terrible mistake, a horrible conflation. Now, with a piece of chalk, Lelia starts writing out my name, over and over, as if she's kept herself after school to work a lesson into her head. She starts in the corner and writes steadily across, my name and my name traversing everything else.

At home, she makes other signs. For the last week now I've been taking the green-colored pills again, honoring our longtime agreement that when she is on the Pill, I will take the fourth week of placebos, out of fair play and sympathy for her and womankind. I forget to take a pill one morning and she peppers me with comments about my preternatural plotting to burden our life. These days, trading places is our necessary mode. Then I wonder aloud that perhaps I shouldn't take the pills anymore, and Lelia knows I mean another thing entirely. She doesn't jump, she doesn't stop. Later, at dinner, she laments the fact that she'll be thirty-five in a couple of months. She says her hair is drying out, her skin and nails, she shows me all over how she's dying on the vine.

Implications, again.

There's some desperation, of course. Worry and fear. Would we be trying to fill myriad holes in our life? Was that our attempt the first time? No, I think, but even if it were, it turned out to be Mitt, some wondrous thing, who will forever annul any of our regret. But he is gone, I have to keep telling myself. Eternally lost.

Lately I keep seeing him in Lelia's arms, the way he looked so different from her when he was just born, the shock of his black hair, the delicate slips of his eyes. His face would change soon enough, but he looked so fully Korean then (if nothing like me), and Lelia, dead exhausted and only casually speaking, wondered aloud how she could pass him so little of herself. Of course it didn't concern her further. Though I kept quiet, I was deeply hurting inside, angry with the idea that she wished he was more white. The truth of my feeling, exposed and ugly to me now, is that I was the one who was hoping whiteness for Mitt, being fearful of what I might have bestowed on him: all that too-ready devotion and honoring, and the chilly pitch of my blood, and then all that burning language that I once presumed useless, never uttered and never lived.

It is twilight again, and Lelia sits on the bed as I dress. My nightly departure. When we get to this point in the evening I suddenly forget the happy, earlier hours. I'm too live. I think I can see danger everywhere, the way it used to be around here. After Mitt died, it was like we were wading knee-deep in kerosene. Suddenly your speech is a match. A wrong word from either of us and whoom! Now, Lelia rises and helps me with my tie, tucking it beneath the back of my collar. She smooths the material with her fingertips. Her lips are pursed, though not tight, and they can work well enough to say *be careful* and lightly kiss my ear. From the bed she picks up my jacket and walks with me across the length of the apartment, to the front door. She holds the coat out for me and I take it. She says love you and I say love you back. No fuss or romance. We've long tired of goodbyes.

Soon I see Jack again, this time at a diner around the corner from Hoagland's flat. He is sick with the last of the season's flu, running a low-grade fever, body aches. He says he's having crap attacks. No one is taking care of him. We sit in a booth near the washroom. When the waiter comes he orders a gyro platter and a side of pepperoncini and coffee. I just want tea.

"You look very chipper, Parky. What, have you eaten already?"

"With Lelia," I answer. "You look like shit."

"I feel like shit. Why not? This is a good time for it. I hate this transitional weather. Is that what Dennis calls it?"

"You're delirious. Go home."

"No," he says, holding a glass of ice water to his head. "I am here already. I am hungry, finally. You will not eat with me? I am buying the food tonight."

"No."

"Ah, the chipper young man says no. You are looking very chipper," he says, now drinking the whole glass in one pull. He calls the waiter in Greek and his glass is refilled. He drinks it all and calls the waiter again, who grumbles something to Jack and just leaves the pitcher.

"What did he say?" I ask.

"That he was not my whore tonight. He also suggested I was a faggot. Also likely a cheapskate."

"He hardly said three syllables."

"Greek is a very special language," Jack answers. "You understand these are rough translations."

The waiter comes around with our coffee and tea. He acts as if nothing has happened and goes away.

"I love the service in this city," Jack says, his forehead sweating now. He wipes his face with a napkin. "Very special all around. I must tell you, my friend, that you are being appreciated again. The talk is good."

"This must mean Dennis."

"Yes," he says, smelling his coffee. "I love seeing you, Parky, but in truth you are right. I should be at home, in bed. But Dennis, he is so urgent with things. He is like a human bladder. One can always go if one wants, yes? The question is timing, appropriateness, convenience . . ."

"Jack, go home."

"Dennis would have my head," he says, coughing a little. "I promised I would meet with you. It is fine. I knew that when I refused any more of his field work, this would be my job until retirement."

"Tailing unreliables."

"Parky. Listen to me. Everything is fine. Dennis is satisfied again with the registers," he says, his voice hoarse. "I read your stuff myself. Professional material. Very excellent. I made Dennis admit it. And your analysis of the bombing, at least, was inventive. You understand he cannot use it in his final reports. He says it is not written after our style. Nothing like our style. But he is not angry about it."

I tell Jack that finesse is not a concept that agrees with him. He nods in admission. In that day's register, I'd written that in the absence of actual events, it was likely that Glimmer & Company itself was involved in the manufacturing of happenings, creating intrigue and complication for the sake of extending funded research. Certainly, I knew that Hoagland would strike out that part of the day's entry, but it didn't matter because I had meant it only for him; it was true insofar as it was possible, which is enough for anyone in our line. More than anything, I was sending a personal note to Dennis, to say that whatever I was giving him should be considered, for his purposes, to be suspect, mistold prose. Perhaps you can't trust Henry Park, I wanted him to think, you can't abide anymore what he now sees and says.

Jack tells me, "There could be more material in Dennis' view, but I am telling him you are doing your best."

"He'll get two more weeks," I say. "That's the schedule. Then it's over."

"Dennis thinks you will come back."

"Dennis is wrong."

"This is the hope, of course," Jack answers. "But then I have never known him to be. He is mad, Parky, a brilliant liar and a cheat and a fool, but he has also never been wrong. I have known him for many years. He always wins the game, if only because he knows how large and wide it truly is. People like us can see just a small part of things. This is inescapable. We are just good immigrant boys, so maybe we don't care. What you and I want is a little bit of the good life. If we work hard, and do not question the rules too much, we can get a piece of what they have."

"What is that, Jack?"

"Are you kidding?" he cries. "Just look at yourself. Look at your beautiful American wife. Look at the many things you have, how you can go anyplace you want and speak your mind."

"But I don't," I say. "I've forgotten how, if I ever knew. Then, when someone like Kwang attempts anything larger, there's instant suspicion. Someone must step up and pay to send in us hyenas. We'll sniff him out. We eat our own, you know."

Jack shakes his head. "You are difficult, boy. Okay. So listen to me anyway. Listen to me on the matter of these two weeks, Parky. There is still some concern."

"It doesn't matter to me anymore. Listen, Jack. This is my mind finally speaking."

"Come on," he says. He clears his throat. "The question is, what is Parky going to do now. You are a grown man. You must want control back, yes? This began as your task and it should be yours to the end."

I don't answer.

"You can have the knowledge of ending cleanly," he says. He coughs, hacking away from the table. "I had the chance once. Now I will retire with too many memories."

I am not certain of the virtue of what he says, but I don't disagree. For some time now I have been operating under the thesis that Jack is under extreme pressures of his own—whether because of me or not doesn't seem to matter—and that he is working without regard to my best interests. No illusions for us. I don't blame him, for I would do the same. I am fond of Jack, and to the end I will strictly believe that he has much feeling for me. It does not matter what he does to me, or I to him, for what other friends can we hope to have? With strange souls like us, who must have opposite hearts from you, treachery is more sweetly served by our dearest than by archstrangers we never see.

His dinner comes. He folds the shaved meat and peppers into the pita and takes huge bites of the roll. He slurps at his coffee.

"Dennis requests one thing," he says, still chewing his food. "Hear m out before you say anything. I will do my job tonight for Dennis if it kill me. He wants the remaining registers, of course. Do this please. But thi thing that you are working on. This money club. This is important."

"I've made my report on it. He already knows what it is and what i isn't." I had written that Kwang took no profits and made no interest, tha he just redistributed funds at the end of every week, like any *ggeh.*

"Yes, I know, Parky. Now Dennis would like an additional item. Yo have offered some useful facts and analysis but he requires material. Yo say you regularly make printouts of the list of club members for Kwang Good. Now make one for us. You will do this?"

I think of the list of Kwang's people. His best and most loving. In som way I see it as the expression of the past seven years of his life, who he ha been at the camp meetings and rallies, at the picnics and races and hig school wrestling matches. I almost hear their voices as I open the en velopes, the stiff new bills that rush in to us in even greater tides now tha he is publicly troubled, sounding out in marginal English their love fo him, their devotion.

"Why does he want it?" I ask Jack.

"I do not ask such things," he answers, already nearly finished with hi meal. "I am happier with limited knowledge."

"Propose something," I ask, to push him into saying anything, which can always reveal. "For your friend."

Jack wipes his mouth and sighs. "Okay, friend. Last week, two mer were waiting for the elevator on our floor when I got out. I did not recog nize them. I asked Candace who they were. She said they were Dennis friends, from Arizona."

"Dennis has no friends."

"Right," Jack replies. "So I assumed they were clients. But I tell you Parky, I can smell that type right away."

"What?"

"Cheap cologne and cheap shoes," Jack says. "I noticed one of them was filling out an expense book. Of course I didn't ask Dennis. But it was clear. Baptiste thought so, too. You can ask him. *Federales.*"

"Government people?" I say.

"You add it up," Jack says. "Now, if they were visiting Dennis because of Kwang, which I am not saying, then why? You say he is legitimate, except there is a minor fact of thousands of dollars coming in through the basement of his house every week."

"I described every stage for you. I saw everything. It's clean."

"Of course you did," Jack says, waving his finger at me. "But look at this. This could be of keen interest to the revenue service. You say you redistribute almost all of the money. But maybe you don't know. He has lost a lot of money in some businesses, yes, since becoming a councilman? A small fortune. Maybe he thinks the people owe him something back. Maybe you are running just one of his money clubs, of which there are a dozen, or two dozen."

"You and Dennis have all the angles."

He laughs at me. "Dennis and I cannot fool you. Whatever you wish to believe about what happened at Kwang's office is your right. So remember this. *I* am the one who has been an arsonist and murderer, Parky, not Dennis. Dennis is not a man in that way. He is not a *doing* creature. He will falsely take credit whenever he can, big talker he is, but that is all. Now, I am seeing what you write of Kwang, the way you present him with something extra. It is evident that you cannot help yourself. Something takes you over. You must see how this is a ripe condition. So could it be that the honorable John Kwang is deceiving you, Parky, and not just the other way? Is it possible that through all of your genuine respect and admiration, he is using you?"

Jack spreads his hands on the table, his favored stance rhetorical. Of course I can't reply. He snorts and goes back to the rest of his plate of pepperoncini, taking them neatly like candies, one by one. When he's done he calls for more coffee and tea.

"I did not come to make trouble for you, Parky," Jack tells me, taking my hand. "You can think I am right or I am crazy. Either way it will not hurt us, I hope. We are brothers, yes, Greek and Korean? Like it or not, Parky, ours is a family. Pete, Grace, the Jimmys. Me and you. I know it is a sad excuse for one, but what else do we have?"

"It's an orphanage, Jack," I say. "And there's a Fagin."

He shakes his head. "Whatever you say. I am not schooled. What I know is that America is not so open. People like you and me can only do what is necessary. We are not the ones who have the choices. Maybe we feel outside of things, and are smart enough, and we also know our own. So what is better, Parky, for who we are?"

"Nothing better," I tell him.

"Right," he says. "So you will please give us the list. Soon, yes? Dennis will probably like to send someone down for pickup."

"I'm not sure what I can give you," I answer.

"Well, you figure it out," he says, with some finality. He takes out some bills to pay for dinner. He calls the waiter, who slowly walks over. Jack points up at him with his finger and says something, his tone suddenly sharp, raspy, and vicious. The waiter carefully takes the money and goes away without speaking.

We rise to leave. He folds up his wallet with his big hands.

"He spit in my coffee," Jack says, watching the man walk every step to the register. "I told him I loved it. Now he will always wonder when this crazy Greek will come back for him."

When you are someone like me, you will be many people all at once. You are a father, a dictator, a servant, the most agile actor this land has ever known. And all throughout you must be the favorite chaste love of the people.

John Kwang tells me this. He tells me this at night when I work in the basement of the house. He tells me this when we walk the lovely empty 4 A.M. streets of Flushing, and in the all-night Korean restaurants full of taxi drivers and dry cleaners, where we share plates of grilled short ribs and heated crocks of spicy intestine stew and lager imported from Seoul. He tells me these tips of survival as if preparing me for his rank, his position, his singular place in the city that he is letting slip from his grasp.

He is no longer moving in his customary way. He looks old and weary, like he's standing still. He decides to make a brief appearance for the media in the foyer of the ruined offices (against the repeated warnings of Janice, who hates the shot—all that shadowy wreckage and defeat), and with the barrage of questions and arc lights and auto winders he actually falters. Perhaps for the first time in his public life he mumbles, his voice cracks, and even an accent sneaks through. He doesn't seem to be occupying the office, the position. He gazes listlessly at the cameras and responds like a man stopped on the street, dutifully answering each part of each question, answering the follow-ups, searching through the mess of his emotions for reasons this could happen.

Total amateur hour, Janice grumbles to me. The only good thing, she says later, is that he finally steps down from the microphones before the volleys of questions about that morning's still unconfirmed news, which is that Eduardo Fermin was renting his own apartment in Manhattan. Otherwise, she adds, it might have been official, a complete meltdown. But they shout after him anyway as he makes his way out: how did a volunteer and night student afford $1,000 a month? How come even his parents didn't know? Who was he, and what was he doing, to have this other life?

In the next staff meeting, Janice gives us the official last word, come directly from John. He knows nothing about it. By my longtime habit and practice I put myself in Kwang's place, and I know it must be something with the *ggeh,* his paying of Eduardo, the apartment being a generous gift, what he thought his protégé deserved. I would have offered good Eduardo the same. There is, however, another notion, another idea steadily working itself through my thoughts: that perhaps Eduardo was taking money from John Kwang, stealing from him and his people, the very ones we are working for all day and all night.

I check what I can. I go back over Eduardo's records of the *ggeh,* the daily cash flows, every line of the ledgers. I check the rest of our political contributions. Nothing seems to be off, and what I'm beginning to realize is that Eduardo Fermin kept magnificent records and files. All this confounds me even more. I know that if there is complication in every assignment, a shift or turn that can newly show events in either shadow or light, this is the way our world has always been written. You must sail an expectedly treacherous course.

And yet for me, the mystery of a happening has no magic anymore, no natural draw. It is the graver thing I must seek, the dire constant, which I thought at first was simply John Kwang. It is him, too, for certain, but it's also the condition Jack has suggested. Revelations are not to be found in the far bend of the river, darkly hidden in the trees. There are no ready savages there, and never were. We make angels and devils of our own want and regard, improvising from ourselves along the way.

Though I cannot see that my business has directly brought Kwang to his trouble, I know that Hoagland is now busy recompiling my daily work, preparing it for his secret reader, who will do with it what he wishes. In my weaker moments, I imagine the client as a vastly wealthy voyeur, a decrepit, shut-away xenophobe who keeps a national vigilance on eminent agitators and ethnics. Of course he's more a collector than anything else, loving the pursuit too much, easily bored. But then I allow myself to see, and I flush with regret. I picture another client, the kind more numerous. I dread him, for he lives in the very mouth of the world; he knows its sweet and its stink, how to read any talk, and he will sift through my troubled affection for John Kwang with the soberest eyes.

Out in the world, John Kwang is falling. His name is diving in the polls; not just in one poll but across the board, the news-organization polls, the radio call-in polls, the 900-number talk show polls which you can call into and vote on what he should do. We know he still has plenty of supporters, but they're mostly silent, and the scope of the questions keeps growing. Reporters call everyone on the staff, phone us at the office, suggesting unceasingly how it must involve money, it must involve money.

You click them off as fast as you can. There's only a skeleton crew working, even during the day, when the hourly barrage of calls comes in. Requests and repeated requests, reporters at the basement door posing as utility men, utility women, they're at the point where they simply want to get inside the walls. Suddenly this has become enough for them, the new low standard, just to see where he's hiding, get the feel of the cell, the bunker.

I stay close to him, as Janice asks. Practically no one else sees him, sometimes Sherrie, though even she has begun to distance herself, drop away. More and more it is Janice who is directing the daily operations, actually there at the house urging the rest of us on. He has sent May and the boys and a helper to their other house, upstate. They don't have a television up there, they don't have a radio. They don't need to see their father like this.

I think John Kwang would be a man to keep his boys close, keep May even closer, that he would collect the four of them in one shut-away room and have them sleep and eat and bathe all together until the tempests subsided. His move is more what my father would do, what I have learned, too, through all of my life. To send people away or else allow them to go, that what is most noble to me is the exquisite gift of silence. My mask of serenity and repose.

Tonight, while I'm working in the makeshift rooms of his basement, he comes down the stairs in his plaid pajamas and white robe, with his hair pressed to a funny shape by sleep, and sits in the corner armchair with two goblets and a bottle of scotch.

"Byong-ho," he now calls me, his voice like a bassoon. And he says in satori-accented Korean, *Hey you, arrogant youth, stop doing all that work and come drink with an elder.*

I rise and wheel the desk chair to the corner, take my glass, let him pour. I don't really drink, just let the liquor sting my tongue. I sit for him. His thick white robe is monogrammed, JK, in light blue stitched above his left breast, and for a moment, with the heavy drink in his hand, he almost looks like those men who lounge for hours in the locker room of a midtown university club and scratch their bared balls and watch FNN and pop cashews and snicker about black athletes and fool colleagues and all the fat-assed women they have loved. But John doesn't feature the polished ivory potbelly, the connected nests of body hair, a booming pepper-grinder voice; he'll sing instead. He always jury-rigs a folk song onto his stories. I don't know any of his songs, but it's the same register my mother used to hum while doing the housework, a languorous baritone, the most Korean range, low enough for our gut of sadness, high for the wonder of chance, good luck.

"Don't you know any Korean songs?" he asks.

"The only one is *Arirang,* " I tell him. "Then only the tune, and the first few words."

John nods, rocking ever gently.

"Listen to the melody," he says. He hums a few bars, to the first refrain. The tune, somehow, is immediately wrenching, its measures plead in near arpeggios, and like any good folk song it makes the voice of its singer sound lost, or forlorn, incomplete. "Imagine," he goes on, "that *that* could be the spirit of an entire country. You do it."

I sing the words until the second stanza, when I can't remember them.

Ah, yes, John intones, his Korean accent getting thicker and heavier. I have some trouble understanding him. He leans back now, his slippered feet bobbing, the drink maybe getting to him, and he says, *You've almost got it, there, but something is still missing. You're cheating its sweetness. Let me show you. A different song now. A very old one I know.*

He sings with his eyes shut tight, the way I would see old Koreans praying in the front pews of Minister Cho's huge church, their fearsome bouts of concentration on display, ferociously willing. His grace to wash over them. He sings about a young man who decides to leave his family's farm and go to the city to make his fortune. He weeps as he sings, the whiskey and the late hour and the watery sound of his own voice taking him back to a place far from this one. He drinks deeply and tells me the full story of the song.

"The young man hates the tenant farming, you know, its dull work, the fact that they will always be poor. The young man's mother begs him to stay—they have no other children—saying that his father will be heartbroken. But the father, prideful, refuses to speak to him, and the young man departs before sunrise. The young man arrives in the city after the full day's journey and finds work at an old silk-weaver's. He works hard for nine years and then buys the business, and in nine more years he becomes prosperous and wealthy. He has his own family. One day he overhears one of his clerks take an order for a death shroud and robe in his old village. He asks the buyer who needs these things, and is told the wife of old farmer Yee. His mother. The man breaks down and weeps, asks himself how he could have ignored them so, and decides to make the journey back, to deliver the death garments himself. Perhaps, he thinks, he will finally settle the difficulty with his father. When he arrives at the house, his mother's body is being prepared by other relatives in one of the rooms. Old friends are there, talking and weeping quietly among themselves. But he can't seem to find his father. He asks a girl where he is, and she bows to this rich silk dealer and leads him to the back of the house, where the fields begin.

Where is he? he asks, *I don't see him.*

She points to the face of the cleared hill to the east. *Up there,* she says, *where all the poor in the village are buried. Does the dead woman owe money to your family as well?*

No, he answers after a moment. He asks, *Do you know when the old man died?*

Oh, no, she tells him, *he must have passed ages ago, before I was even born.*

I say to him, "Korean stories always work like that. Everybody dies but one. And the one has little to live for."

"But somehow he lives," John says. "The one goes on. We're too stubborn."

"I think we're too brave and too blind," I answer, drinking seriously now. "I read that Korean nationals are the most rescued people from the world's mountaintops."

"Is that true?"

"I'm not sure, but I believe it. We're too willing to take risks before we're fully prepared."

"What about us Korean-Americans?" he asks me.

I say, "We're the most rescued from burning malls."

We both half-snort at this, half-groan, and I can see we're in the mood for talk that will only hurt and sting. Perhaps he's actually thinking about Eduardo, as I suddenly am, the bitter sleep he must have had. But I look at Kwang now, hunched over in his robe, his posture softening.

Then, another idea suddenly hits me: that I am searching out the raw spots in him, the places where he appears open, where the wounds are still fresh. I can't help myself. The last days have worn him down. It's enough to see the frail line of his calf, bare old bone, to want to lean in a little.

I ask him how May and the boys are doing.

He stops his humming. He drinks stiffly and without looking at me, says, "What do you think?"

"I think they must miss their father."

"Oh yes," he says, pushing up the loose terry sleeves. The old boxer again. "What else, *Park Byong-ho shih?*"

"They must wonder if he's all right," I answer.

"Ah. And is he? What would you tell them? Is their father being himself?"

I don't answer him.

"Well, come on! You sound like you want trouble tonight. Why don't you ask me about Eduardo and his apartment? You are the only one left who hasn't! Is it because you actually respect my grief or are just afraid of what you will hear?"

"I am not afraid of you."

John cries, "You sound so formal! Even with a little hate you are so respectful and Korean."

"What do you want me to sound like?"

He says, in a laughing Korean, *Ah, you, I want it just like that!*

"Aayeh!" I yell.

He yells, *That's much better, you! Why not yell at me? I'll allow it. Don't think of me as elder; come, strike out at me with your words, or something else. This is America, we can do this. Say it in English if you have to. Get it out in the open. You want this. I am not your father. I am not your friend. Come on, I will survive.*

He steps toward me, his hands balled into fists. We're not two feet apart. I don't move. Something in me wants to crush him but I don't move. I think I can't bear his inaction. His weeks of strange silence. I think I can bear silence from anyone but him. I want him to stand up and show his face and say something for Eduardo. And for a moment I feel that hot ore of my father's rage, what would sometimes drive him like disease or madness to hack like a demon at wet sod in the backyard. I am still silent, but I know not for long. I think, let him come at me. I'll shout him right down.

He says in Korean, *Watch out, boy.* Then he slowly backs away and sits down again. He pours more whiskey for himself and then puts down the bottle between us. I roll my chair forward, stretch out my arm, take it up. I can see that he is hurt, the instant hang in his expression. How his American life shows through so clearly. Another Korean man of his generation would not forgive the moment so quickly, if ever at all.

We sit for at least an hour saying nothing else. Yesterday, he canceled another news conference at the last minute—or rather, I canceled it for him.

Sherrie and Jenkins refuse to make the phone call to pull him out. They counsel fiercely against it. They practically shout at him while he sits mutely at his desk, moving a crystal paperweight inside a splash of light and then out again. Like everyone else, they want him to speak. They want him to go on television and eulogize his dead, to make a statement to the city with his best public face and deny any involvement with what

Eduardo Fermin was allegedly doing after hours; that he had no idea of his running whatever's been rumored, a pyramidal laundering scheme, a people's lottery, an Asian numbers game. That he knew the boy and liked the boy but neither all that well. They want to get him some distance from the fire and bombing, from anything of that scenery which enforces the idea of John Kwang as a man losing control over his people, weak and vulnerable and somehow deserving.

Earlier, the news stations run competing evening stories profiling Eduardo, and in the hastily set up video room we watch him painted as an overly ambitious student who was treated like a son by the councilman: he worked like a religious fanatic for the man, who in turn, according to the reporter, was steadily building an "empire" from his "ethnic base" in northern Queens. They show the ground-floor apartment the Fermin family inhabits, the lethal scene of the office, the procession of black cars rolling through the famous cemetery in Queens, the immense necropolis below the highway, distant spires of Manhattan against the stone monuments, the last one Eduardo's.

"Perfect," Janice screams at the monitor. "Drop a cherry on top."

Next they get De Roos on videotape, saying with a straight face how much he has admired the councilman in recent years, how he wished he had some of that "amazing mystical energy" for himself, but adding, too, in response to the rumors, that "everyone in this town has to follow the rules."

Kwang isn't present for any of this. He remains at the top of the house until everyone has gone home. Then maybe, if she's even here, Sherrie climbs up, stays for a while; I think I can hear the chant of their voices conducting through the iron pipes. Sometimes edgy laughter, raised voices. When she leaves through the side door of the kitchen, I know it's just the two of us, two Korean men at opposite ends of a stately Victorian house.

The place feels borrowed to me, unlived in. There are no strange smells, no lingering aroma of cooking oils. The house is a showplace for the Kwangs' many guests and visiting dignitaries, trimmed in heavy damask and chintz, with freshly cut flowers. There's too much ornate woodwork here, and the precious layerings of molding and mullion and balustrade and apse, all those thousands of genteel decisions, the studied cuts, just unsettle me.

I prefer it here in the mostly unconsidered rooms of the basement, the stone walls rough-hewn, damp, ill lighted like any memory. Helda, on May's orders, kept the Korean foodstuffs down here, the earthenware jars of pickled vegetables and meats, the fermented seasoning pastes and sauces, strips of dried seafood. All of it was scrupulously sealed and double-wrapped but it didn't do any good. The smell is still Korean, irreparably so, cousin to that happy stink of my mother's breath. When we moved here after the fire, I noticed that some staffers balked when they first reached the bottom of the stairs. Once I saw Jenkins suspiciously tap one of the jars with his size sixteen wing tip, checking for signs of life.

Now John finally rises to go upstairs, teetering a little, pulling his robe tightly around him. It's almost four in the morning. He says to me stiffly, "You are done with your work?"

"Almost."

"Finish up quickly. I'll be back down in half an hour. You will drive me somewhere?"

I say I will.

He sits quietly in the back of the sedan. When I pull the car in front of his house, he immediately goes to the rear where the windows are tinted black. He says to drive to Manhattan by the bridge. I take us west down Northern Boulevard to the Queensboro. This late at night there's no real traffic and the lights let us run almost all the way.

When we finally stop at a light a half mile from the bridge he says we're going to the Upper East Side, on Park Avenue. In the mirror I see him gazing out at the shops and lots of the boulevard, the rows of bulb and neon stretching west before us like a luminous trail to the island. Manhattan was going to be the next stage, the next phase of his life. He wasn't going to be just another ethnic pol from the outer boroughs, content and provincial; he was going to be somebody who counted, who would stand up like a first citizen of these lands in every quarter of the city, in Flushing and Brownsville and Spanish Harlem and Clinton. He would be the one to bring all the various peoples to the steps of Gracie Mansion, bear them with him not as trophies, or the subdued, but as the living voice of the city, which must always be renewed.

The place, he once told me, where no one can define you if you possess enough will. Where it doesn't matter if no one affords you charity, or nostalgia for your memories. Where you know your family is the one thing without price. He has also spoken this in public, with fire and light in his eyes. He has sung whole love songs to the cynical crowds, told tall stories of courage and honor, doing all this without any mythic display, without savvy, almost embarrassing the urban throng. They would look up at him from their seats and see he was serious and then quietly make certain to themselves that this was still the country they grew up in. They had never imagined a man like him, an American like him. But no one ever left.

He was how I imagined a Korean would be, at least one living in any renown. He would stride the daises and the stages with his voice strong and clear, unafraid to speak the language like a Puritan and like a Chinaman and like every boat person in between. I found him most moving and beautiful in those moments. And whenever I hear the strains of a different English, I will still shatter a little inside. Within every echo from a city storefront or window, I can hear the old laments of my mother and my father, and mine as a confused schoolboy, and then even the fitful mumblings of our Ahjuhma, the instant American inventions of her tongue. They speak to me, as John Kwang could always, not simply in new accents or notes but in the ancient untold music of a newcomer's heart, sonorous with longing and hope.

We cross the bridge to the city. The streets are empty. I drive uptown on Third and then cut across to Park. I ask him exactly where we're going on the Avenue.

He tells me the address and street, then says low, "It's Sherrie's. Have you ever taken me there? I can't remember now."

"No," I say.

We don't talk after that. When we get there I go inside the marbled foyer of her building and have the night doorman ring up. It's past three in the morning. The night man is a young Chino-Latino. He regards me another moment and then says into the receiver, "He here, ma'am." He nods and then offers me the handset.

"John?" I hear her say.

"No."

"Who is this?"

"It's Henry."

"Shit."

I tell her he's in the car.

"Christ. Go outside then. Don't let anyone see you. I'll be down in a few minutes."

When she comes she rushes from the awning in a long slicker, her head covered with the hood. They don't kiss. They don't touch. They sit upright and John says to go to an after-hours club on lower Broadway, near all the Korean restaurants and shops. No one will trouble us there.

Some of the clubs are known as "stand" bars, where the bartenders are all women and will have a drink with you. The women aren't prostitutes. They won't have sex. They'll hold your hand and flirt and maybe even kiss you if you show enough politeness. They'll sing popular songs and tell racy Korean jokes. Nothing pornographic or even that vulgar. This is the club pretense, the etiquette. They are ready companions, and their job is to soothe the lonely feeling of these men for a woman and a homeland. The patrons are mostly businessmen from Korea, but there are others, some whites, and then some young Korean-Americans dressed in conservative suits, speaking perfect English, red-faced, drunk. Investment bankers and lawyers. This is how I come to know these places, from the last stops of several bachelor parties I went to after college. After the fancy restaurants, the serious drinking, after the tall white strippers in a suite of a midtown hotel, we would arrive here arm in arm and weary with drink, sporting an almost sorrowful obedience, not even knowing that we were searching for a familiar face pale and wide and round.

We enter a second-floor "salon" bar, basically a stand bar but one with private rooms as well. I am here because in the street John insists that all of us go upstairs. Sherrie is too tired for arguments. She just winces; obviously, they've been here before. They haven't said but a few words to each other. As he shepherds us inside, I think she's expending whatever energy she has toward an idea of John Kwang in irretrievable fall. She stares off like she's deciding on something, promising to herself that she'll get out while she can. But she accedes to his wishes, as do I. As long as you can, you will please the father, the most holy and fragile animal.

Our private room has two leather loveseats and a smoked-glass coffee table. The walls are paneled with paper screens lighted from behind. On the table is a bottle of vodka and a bottle of scotch and lowball glasses and four cans of Sprite. John sits with Sherrie. A young woman soon enters with a tray of ornately sliced fruit and a bucket of ice. She carefully prepares the drinks, whiskey on the rocks for the men, vodka and soda for Sherrie. She bows slightly as she presents each drink, the dark eyes held down.

I can smell her perfume. It's the kind pre-teenage girls wear, that ultrasweet, virginal scent. She is exceedingly pretty, exceedingly young. Her hair is pulled up in a French twist, and her body shows clearly through her silken dress, her breasts more like fleshy rises than mounds, her hips framed low, feet and hands of a pixie. I could crack her fingerbones with a handshake, dislocate her shoulder with a stiff pull.

She picks up the tray and bows before leaving. I watch her go out. I'm tired, too, like Sherrie, and my concentration flags. It settles on sights like the girl. Her shape is easy, uncomplicated. Watching John and Sherrie work toward each other in my presence is more difficult, not for their awkwardness but for how lonely they seem.

After a few minutes the girl reappears in the doorway. She's changed. She's let her hair down and her new dress is loose like a slip, short, the color matte black. She looks me in the eyes. She asks John something in Korean slang, something about "being okay," and he grunts back. The girl sits down with me. Pours herself a big drink.

John has energy. He wants to talk, but Sherrie just drinks and broods against his shoulder, slumped like a young girl in the backseat of the family wagon. We sit and drink for a while, not talking, and I watch them. I know from Janice that Sherrie's husband is away most of the time, he's in Tokyo right now working on bridge financing for an industrial complex in Bangladesh. Janice says he's a looker, tall and lean and impressive, that he speaks fluent German and Japanese, and that he hasn't slept with his wife for more than a year. I ask how she knows and she says, "Take a good look at Sherrie when someone mentions him. All dried up and dead." I push her and she admits Sherrie told her, too.

Now I realize that Kwang has contrived that the girl is here for me.

"Ah-ggah-shih," he calls her, his talking slowed, an octave lowered. Then he says, *Young lady, please earn your money tonight.*

She tips her brow. She takes her drink in several deep gulps and motions for me to pour more for her. I do. She touches my hand, plucks at the skin of my wrist. She can't be any older than seventeen. She obviously speaks no English, and although my Korean is lacking I know the accents enough to know that hers isn't educated. Her speech is unclipped and loose, full of attitude even when speaking to John in the formal constructions.

I ask her where she's from and she answers with practice a certain fancy neighborhood in Seoul, and then offers other facts I might want to hear: she's twenty-two, a college graduate, a good cook. I'm waiting for her to say she's not yet an American citizen. She begins to steal closer to me, pulling her legs onto the sofa. She's not wearing hose. She calls me *Ah-juh-shih* and rests her head on my shoulder. I look over and see John and Sherrie embracing.

The girl begins massaging my neck, then curls her cool fingers about my ear. John starts talking, but only in English: he is narrating what he sees, in the tone of a reporter. He tells of me, the girl. My stiffness. "The young man of integrity," he says. "Look at the clear principle, the control. He reminds me of another Asian figure in city politics we used to know and love. Where is he now? How I wish I could recall his name. But see here, how it begins."

The girl lifts herself and straddles one of my legs. She starts moving. She dips down and rubs herself on my knee and thigh. The pressure and length of her strokes steadily increase with his talk, which is now Korean. It sounds as if he's berating her, but he's telling the girl what to do. I don't hold her back. He wants it this way. I am just flesh for this room. She holds me with a hand to the back of my neck, the other on my free leg. I'm waiting for her to kiss me, show me her tongue, slip her tiny hand between my legs. But finally she's chaste, or, better, she treats me as if I am. This is her service to us, her honoring.

"Tell her that's enough, John," Sherrie says, pulling away from him. "John, he's not Eddy. He doesn't like it."

"Quiet!"

"This is making me sick," she answers, putting down her drink. "I don't get you two. Is this Korean? You're so brutal. Why don't you just ask the manager for a knife and then see how much of your blood you can offer each other?" Now she glares at me. "What are you doing here?" she screams. "What the hell are you doing here? What do you want?"

"Enough!" John shouts, slamming his open palm on the table. The girl stops what she's doing and holds on to me. He stares at Sherrie, his cheeks mottled red with anger.

"Maybe you will leave the room for a while!" He's yelling at the top of his voice. His accent is somehow broken, it comes out strained, too loud. "Maybe you leave! Take the goddamn car key! *Park Byong-ho shih,* it will please me if you will drive her home, right now!"

"Forget it, I'm taking a cab," Sherrie says, scrambling for her purse so she can get to the door. She almost stumbles as she rises, steadying herself on the corner of the coffee table. She tries the knob but it's locked from the outside. She slaps at the panels. John swiftly goes to her, his hands raised. He wraps her from behind.

"Someone open this fucking door!" she yells, pushing him away. But John makes her stop. He takes her by the forearm and pulls her toward me on the sofa but she's resisting, leaning away from him. They tug-of-war for a moment. He's only toying with her, using just one hand and a dug-in foot, almost taunting her with his strength, and Sherrie's starting to cry and get angry. She's about to scream. She starts chopping at his grip. He slaps her hard and she crumples. The girl beside me is half-crying now. She has slid off me and sits on the floor with her legs still on the sofa, trying to crawl away. Now John lifts Sherrie by the elbow and raises his hand to slap her again.

I tackle him beneath one shoulder and pin him against the wall. The whole room shakes. His expression when he turns is full of contempt, as if any of this business is mine. I shout at him to stop. He tries to push me off but I stay with him. A waiter suddenly opens the door and Sherrie is able to get up on her feet and run out. This angers him, and he wants to follow her, but I hold him by hooking my arms around his front, though he drags us out to the doorway. His strength surprises me. Sherrie is wobbily descending the stairs to the street. John yells after her in Korean, calling her something I don't understand. The waiter tells him to calm down and

John shouts for him to leave his sight. He finally shakes me loose and wheels and pushes me hard with his knuckles against my breastbone.

"Who do you think you are?" he shouts, his voice louder than I've ever heard it. "Get your mind in order! Don't you ever get in my way!"

"You were hurting her," I answer.

He shakes his head in disbelief. "That woman? She has been hurting me! Do you know that? She and that dog Jenkins would have me bow down before every cheat and beggar in this city. Who is left? You? Should I get on my knees to you, too?"

He throws up his hands. The manager is here and asks if Master Kwang needs anything. John curses at him to leave us alone, going to the table to pour himself another full glass of whiskey. The manager calls to the girl but John tells him she will stay. She is slumped into the corner with her knees up against her chest, crying a little, too drunk to move.

"Have some drink," he says to me, short of breath.

I stay clear of him.

"Do what you want," he gasps, drinking swiftly, swallowing it all down. "You have a chance, Henry Park. Stay with me for a while. The rest are becoming nothing to me. They don't know who I am. Even Eduardo. Eduardo. He didn't understand what we are doing. But then I misjudged him, too."

"He was stealing," I say.

"What? Of course not!" he shouts, incredulous. "You think he could get away with that? You think I would allow him to cheat me that way?"

"I don't know," I say. "But the apartment."

"I didn't give him any money!" he yells, slamming his glass on the table. "How many times do I have to repeat myself? He worked for me for nothing, the same as you. For *nothing,* except for what I might show him about our life, what is possible for people like us. I thought this is what he wanted. Was I crazy? I would have given him anything in my power. But he was betraying us, Henry. Betraying everything we were doing. To De

Roos, I must think! Reports! You see, there is horror in your face. Think of mine when I found him out. I loved him, Henry, I grieve for him, but he was disloyal, the most terrible thing, a traitor. I left it to Han and his gang. I didn't know it would happen like that, and with Helda. You are the only one who knows now. You are the world. I am telling you so the world can know. I would bring him back if I could. Bring him back right now. Say the world knows this. Say it knows, Henry, for me."

I won't speak for him now, not a breath or a word.

He tells me, "Then you can go to hell."

He leans over and lifts the girl by her underarms onto the sofa. She speaks, apologizing to him. She says she is very sorry, that he must know she usually works afternoons and is not accustomed to the liquor and then the lateness of the hour. He tells her she does not need his forgiveness. She parts her lips. He strums her hair with the back of his hand until she smiles again. She clutches him around the neck. The size of her hands and wrists makes his head and back look giant. He brushes her cheek. He waits a second, and then he kisses her gently on the mouth. He holds her beneath her thigh. The girl glances up at me. He sees this, but doesn't move an inch. My presence won't concern him. I leave his car keys on the arm of the sofa and go out of this place. He believes I am a necessary phantom in his house. I am a lantern to him, constant, unwinking. But I am gone.

I am to meet with Grace and Pete.

I keep making false sightings of them through the day. In one, they appear to me in baby form, wrapped in saris of pearl-hued silk and winged. They hover about the downtown streets of Flushing, spying out usable souls. All the while Pete keeps trying to rub up against Grace when she isn't looking, but he is an infant and he doesn't have the equipment yet and ends up just peeing on her leg and her wing. She pats him on the head, kisses his cheek. One way or another, Pete always gets what he wants.

Lelia swears she does not see them. I nod toward the end of the street, across the subway platform. She strains to look, but of course it's strangers, just another couple combing their way through the city. We move on. There is enough to worry us in the real world, she says. She knows that tonight I will be handing over the member listing of the *ggeh,* my remaining official duty before I leave them all forever: Hoagland, and Jack, and even John Kwang.

I don't tell Lelia who is behind the bombing. In another time, if I felt it unavoidable, I would have presented the fact solely to mitigate the ill sweep of my own activities. Perhaps I will tell her in a future day, but presently this is dangerous knowledge, capital material, which can only serve to place her within the reach of hazard, even more than she is now. In exchange for the list and—if necessary—myself as sacrifice, I have already made Jack and Hoagland agree to keep her clear of any action or trouble. In the old narratives that Dennis practices, he might well involve a wife or lover to use against a troublesome operative; but with me he understands that he can forever count on my Confucian upbringing, press it to my brow like a tribal lodestone, a signet of the culture, which he knows can burn deeper than even love or fear.

But Dennis, I have promised myself, will not learn of the crime from me. This is my final honoring to Kwang, my last offering, which is the sole way of giving I have known in my life: an omission, solemn and prone. So let Dennis hear the words from someone else. Let another mole push up blind from the depths and speak. I have always known it possible that he could have many minions and pawns surrounding a case, a swarm invisible even to the spy. How else could Dennis have tolerated my writing almost nothing in the weeks before the bombing? Or given me any assignment after my debacle with Luzan, much less one with a man like John Kwang, with whom I might so easily identify? I could regard events in such a way as to see that Dennis has been patiently availing me of the elements with which I might effect my own undoing, all along contriving to witness and test my discipline and loyalty. As if his design were to watch me steadily unravel from the inside out, to record in my fraying mesh of self the hidden hazard of all traitors and spies. For even Dennis Hoagland understands that in every betrayal dwells a self-betrayal, which brings you that much closer to a reckoning.

—

It is raining tonight, again. The springtime won't end. Queens has minor flooding. Some of the sewers are clogged, spitting up refuse from the grates. The air is almost tropical. I think the soaked concrete of the borough must smell a little of Venice, or what I imagine of Venice, a redolence consumptive, intestinal. I go anyway through the ankle-deep water of flooded street corners, the brown pools slicked with spectral emulsions of engine oil and cooking grease, soot and sweat.

The Korean noodle shop is near 41st and Parsons. I am to meet them here sometime after midnight. We don't have to be exact. The restaurant is part of a whole block of Korean businesses lodged in converted row apartments dating from the fifties, when the population was still Italian and Irish and Jewish. Now the signs are all in Korean. The only English words in the windows are SALE and DISCOUNT and SHOPLIFTERS BEWARE. The walls of the restaurant are papered with legal-sized sheets with the house specials in Korean characters. The woman with the kindly face brings me a glass of water, a spoon, and chopsticks. I come here enough that she recognizes me. She thinks I am Chinese or Japanese because I always order in English or by number or by pointing to what I want on another table.

There are other regulars here tonight, sitting in their customary places. There is the vegetable store worker in the fatigue jacket, the call car driver, the delivery men. Everyone eats alone. The waitress brings me a bonus: two silver-dollar patties of beef and pork, dipped in egg and fried. "Korean ham-bah-gah," she says, smiling, offering it with a small bowl of flavored soy. "Sauce-su." She seems to want to stay and watch me taste it but she hurries back to her work in the open kitchen preparing the *bahnchahn,* the savory half dishes of vegetables and fish. She peers over the stainless-steel counter. I bow my head low to her. I want to thank her, too, with a surprise of saying something in our language, but there is nothing in my throat to call up. I am half afraid of disappointing her with some fumble of poorly accented words. If I had the sentence, the right words, I would ask her about her family and she could tell me about her daughter and her son. If I were able with my speech, maybe her feeling would turn and she could confide in hushed tones that her husband who brought them here too late in his life died one morning of a heart attack and was simply gone, that that's why she was here and not at home, sound asleep near her good children.

Grace and Pete arrive, shaking the rain from their coats in the doorway. The woman greets them in English and Pete immediately points and answers in fine Korean that they'll sit with me. She smiles at him. He is a prodigy with languages. He orders two bowls of *on myun* and some barley tea and asks for the bathroom. Grace comes over and kisses me on the cheek.

"Harry! Long time no see!"

"You look healthy," I say.

"Do I?" she answers, sitting across from me, squeezing the water from her dark hair. "I've been working too much."

"You're tan."

She looks slyly around for signs of an enemy. She whispers, "The Bahamas. The story is this. We're buyers of precious stones. Pete's the Japanese dealer, I'm his translator. The client wants a who's who of the island's middlemen and suppliers. You know, we make the list, check it twice. As usual, nothing special. But you don't really want to know, do you?"

"No," I say. "What I want to know is how you fended off Pete."

"Don't ask."

"But I'm asking."

"Badly," she answers.

"You're kidding."

She looks at me like the dead. "Okay. Very badly."

Pete sits down next to her, having heard everything.

"Hiya, Harry."

"I've never seen you this dark," I tell him. For some reason I want him to feel vulnerable, laid open, though I know it will be completely useless. I say to him anyway, "You do well in the sun. It's nice. Now you're almost the color of concrete."

"He doesn't tan," Grace says. "He tarnishes."

"What color do you get?" Pete says to me, whittling off fine splinters from the ends of his chopsticks.

"I turn splotchy," I say. "Banana."

Pete laughs appreciatively, everything tight and from the throat, his grin still familiar to me, shit-eating, larcenous. He picks at the kimchee as though it might leap up at him, but then lifts a rolled bunch into his mouth.

"I don't know how you eat that," Grace says. "I think it's pure torture."

"So do I," Peter answers as he chews, wiping the tears from his eyes. "Slide me some of your water, Harry, quick. Good, good. This kimchee is fine, very fine. Nothing is better than this. Nothing better in the whole world."

I watch them eat. Grace twists her noodles around the chopsticks and then lifts them stiffly to her mouth. Pete makes fun of her, tells her she eats like a white woman. Grace says she is a white woman. She lets the thick tendrils of rice noodle hang for a moment before slurping them up. She sips spoons of broth in between. Pete shovels back the noodles as fast as he can bear their heat. All the while Grace nudges him to slow down. They bicker and flirt and handle each other. They even kiss.

I make sure to be careful. Though always routine and uneventful, these meetings tend to follow a certain thespian formality. I could always drive up and deliver the material in person, but Dennis doesn't want it that way. And he doesn't trust the mails. We are serious in the spook play, playing as we are. So he sends a courier or two. They'll display an edge, some suspicion. Sometimes I don't even recognize the people who come (they'll simply say, "Dennis"). Sometimes we won't even speak.

"We're shocking him, Pete, we better stop this silliness."

"Harry doesn't care," he answers her. "He likes it. Look, he's getting misty."

"Go on and eat," I say. "Grope if you like. I'll talk."

"What about?" Pete asks, about to slurp his broth.

"What I'm paid to talk about."

"Then don't bother. I'm bored with work."

Grace says, "Go ahead, we're listening. Tell us something we don't know. Tell us about the big guy. Mr. Kwang."

Pete breaks in. "What's to tell? He's in it this high," he says, his hand at his chin.

"Just like us," I say.

Pete says, "Speak for yourself."

"We're all trying," I tell him.

Grace says, "I thought we were going to have a few laughs tonight."

"So we will."

Pete offers me a toothpick. "You know, Harry, Dennis wants you to know he thinks you're doing a beautiful job this time."

"Fuck you, too, Pete."

Grace says, "I heard him myself, Harry."

"Of course you did," I say. I push my bowl to the side. The woman comes around to take my plates and refill our water glasses but Pete waves her off. Catching my eye, she looks a little scared for me. I say *'gaen-chanah,' it's all right,* but she doesn't seem to hear me, as if not understanding, and she goes.

Pete stares at me and says in the most even voice: "You brought what you were supposed to?"

I nod.

Grace quietly finishes her soup. We are friends again, after a fashion. She and Pete will enjoy my company, and I will enjoy theirs. We are friends in the way people in an unprovisioned lifeboat are, chance consorts who are sure that they'll be picked up soon, any day now, but not exactly how or when.

Pete pays the check and leaves a big tip. The waitress smiles at him. He and Grace climb into his German coupe, my manila envelope safely in the back. They will drive across the Whitestone Bridge to his condo in Stamford. Before they go Pete describes the islands where they've been, the snorkeling he did under the glassy water, showing with his hands how his body knifed through the pools of coral inlets, Grace looking on from the shore.

They pull away. Grace waves. She is too young, even for us. She must be only twenty-five, and I remember Dennis bragging about how he recruited her outside a downtown temp agency with the promise of working in a multinational business. He had his choice of a dozen Ivy Leaguers, but he wanted her, he said, for her "Iron Curtain look," the angular temples and jaw, the heady alto speaking voice. She was obviously smart and trainable.

And as I flag a taxi to go back home, I wonder what any of our parents would think, if they knew the whole truth. And would they even disapprove? If anything, I think my father would choose to see my deceptions in a rigidly practical light, as if they were similar to that daily survival he came to endure, the need to adapt, assume an advantageous shape.

My ugly immigrant's truth, as was his, is that I have exploited my own, and those others who can be exploited. This forever is my burden to bear. But I and my kind possess another dimension. We will learn every lesson of accent and idiom, we will dismantle every last pretense and practice you hold, noble as well as ruinous. You can keep nothing safe from our eyes and ears. This is your own history. We are your most perilous and dutiful brethren, the song of our hearts at once furious and sad. For only you could grant me these lyrical modes. I call them back to you. Here is the sole talent I ever dared nurture. Here is all of my American education.

They have flash pictures of him leaving a downtown precinct house after his bail is posted. It's all in time for the morning edition. They have him in the bricked alley behind the building, the shots dark and grainy. They have him walking away in half-profile, from the back, from the side, his suit jacket unfurled, suggesting flight. No one is with him. His tie is unknotted and his hair is dampened and mussed and he has a gauze patch taped above his left temple where his head glanced the ceiling of his sedan when it crashed. His body must have popped up when he hit the concrete divider of the bridge on-ramp, his suit shoulder become caught and torn on some window trim. The white batting is fluffed out, exposed, the whole effect of him vapid and dislodged. His left eye is black, closed almost to a squint by the swelling. The right one, mulish, untouched, stares back dead at the lens.

The shots are nearly criminal.

The accompanying text reads as if it is compiled rather than written. There seem to be several points of view embedded within the article, though each of them is indignant and righteous in tone. The words merely serve the pictures of the subject in question, employing the facts for the tabloid polemic of how a city should be run, justice served.

Evidently, he had an airbag. The girl didn't. They don't yet have pictures of her. Maybe tomorrow. She still lies in the ICU at Beth Israel Hospital with the tube of an air pump taped inside her mouth to make her lungs work. She is still in a coma. Her skull hit the windshield and jerked her neck to the side with a freak snap. They say her face is hardly even scratched, just a small bruise on the side of her cheek, one mark on the pretty sleeper. Councilman Kwang tells the officers on the scene—who arrive at the accident immediately and then in swarms—that he wasn't even traveling very fast, maybe thirty-five miles per hour. The police verify this by the crumple pattern and damage to the divider and where the car comes to rest. There are no skidmarks. They also verify his blood alcohol level, which is still above the legal limit two hours after the crash.

The police don't know the identity of the girl right away because no one can read the ID card in her purse; they send a copy of it to a language department at Columbia. Her name comes back as Chun Ji-yun. It's difficult for the police because no one where she works wants to talk, and everyone's English is poor. They know she is sixteen years old, born in Seoul. She shares an apartment with some other girls who work at the bar. The police believe that she is a "hospitality girl," which the newspaper says is a type of Asian prostitute. They quote the police quoting the councilman as admitting to meeting her at the midtown club, drinking a little, agreeing to drive her home. He tells the police the two of them were alone the whole time.

Janice is going crazy. We are at her apartment in Astoria because no one is at his house, where both of us headed when we learned the news. She's cursing now, wringing her hands, stomping her feet. This is it, she keeps saying, this is it. It's over now, it's fucking over. We're done.

I was thinking the same when I rushed over to Woodside in the morning. We were done. The whole thing, literally out of my hands. And yet, on seeing his face, his spelled-out name, I immediately began to get ready to go. Lelia had already left the apartment for a freelance job, though she'd clipped a note to the front page of the paper: *You don't have to go.* We both knew that with the list in Hoagland's care I had been finally taken off, that there was no official prerogative anymore, no high man or custom to heed. I felt alone, alarmingly so. And washing the sleep from my face, I remembered how for a time in my boyhood I would often awake before dawn and step outside on the front porch. It was always perfectly quiet and dark, as if the land were completely unpeopled save for me. No Korean father or mother, no taunting boys or girls, no teachers showing me how to say my American name. I'd then run back inside and look in the mirror, desperately hoping in that solitary moment to catch a glimpse of who I truly was; but looking back at me was just the same boy again, no clearer than before, unshakably lodged in that difficult face.

No one has seen John since he was released late last night, four or five hours after the crash. The night before that, he and I and Sherrie were at the bar. He must have gone back, or stayed a whole day longer with the girl. But he has disappeared. The print and TV people already seem to know this because they've assigned skeleton crews to wait around at the house. Janice calls Sherrie but no one answers. She's turned off her machine. Janice finally reaches Jenkins, but he tells her he can't come meet us. He says he needs some time and can't talk and hangs up.

May and the boys are on their way down from upstate. Janice has already asked her where he might have gone. She doesn't know. We have to find him to know what we can say and do, if anything. I can see that Janice senses it's all her ship, but the waterline is rising and she needs to make decisions. The question isn't damage control. It's no longer about containment or what we can spin. He can't hide now, he's not a victim of some bombing anymore; he's a player, a principal. We need to find him and just survive.

If she wanted, she could start trying for distance like Jenkins or maybe Sherrie, to get away from him now before it's too late. A figure in scandal is like a heavy metal, the closer and longer you stay near, the more lasting the effects. Janice tells me this, thinking she's warning me about a career I might want in politics.

She herself keeps calling the precinct house, the lawyers, the hospital, she will say anything to get information on the chances for the girl, what we should expect. She even puts me on the line to pretend I am a cousin. I have to speak choppy English to talk to a doctor but he keeps asking who I am and when I'll come see her. I don't have the heart and hang up.

I help her make calls into the evening. She has every bike messenger and private driver she knows looking for him. We phone the airlines and the buses. We know it's useless. He's probably in a soup monger's somewhere in Flushing, sipping corn tea. Now we're just waiting for the late news. In the meantime Janice is attempting to spirit him back. She lights blunt red sticks of Korean incense he gave her for Christmas and paces in circles, cutting slow butterflies in the smoke with her arms. She's joking some, of course. But I can tell she is a little jumpy, she can't hide all of her anxiousness. She doesn't seem to realize how she keeps touching me, grabbing onto my forearm and my shoulder. She walks through her apartment inspecting things, picking up the same framed photographs of her family. She watches the wall clock.

She doesn't want it to end. Not this one. It's the job that showed her she could have a vocation. She grew up with him, found out how her eye could quickly level on a scene, instantly figure the possibilities, aggressively fight and broker the way they'd want to shoot him. She is a natural at being an anti-director, an anti-producer. Without her John would never have been safe.

She's nervous so she wants to eat. She wants to order Chinese but her place can't deliver tonight. She thinks they are saying that a few of their delivery boys have caught something and didn't come in.

"I'd better just go," she says. "I've got to go down there to order. He didn't speak enough English. It's ten blocks. I've got to burn something off before I eat anyway."

"You've been burning all day."

"You don't know how many moo shus I can eat."

"I'll go with you."

"Someone should stay near the phone."

I tell her again that he's not going to call.

"Come on, then, hurry," she says, pulling on a light jacket. "I'm ravenous. The woman said it's crazy down there tonight. There's a huge line."

We walk the night streets of Queens. It does not seem strange that we go hand in hand. Nothing meant. She takes my hand as we step out of her building and I leave it there because I know there is a true feeling of loneliness that comes from waiting together. It's like two people still standing at a bus terminal after all the passengers have been met, the instant shared feeling almost enough to make them intimates.

We pass by newsstands. He is papering their displays, their walls. I wonder if he has seen his own face in the papers. Will the people see just another politician in trouble, just another scandal? Will they see an American there? I think of him wandering somewhere in the streets of this city. I know he hasn't left. Where would he go? He is somewhere in Queens, I want to believe, lodged safely among any of those strangers whose names so people his mind. He'll knock on a door and they will see him and cry out. Hustle him in. They will seat him at the head of their table. Listen as he blesses their children and their health.

But can you really make a family of thousands? One that will last? I know he never sought to be an ethnic politician. He didn't want them to vote for him solely because he was colored or Asian. He knew he'd never win anything that way. There aren't enough of our own. So you make them into a part of you. You remember every one of their names. You are the model by which they will work and live. You are their hope. And all this because you are such a natural American, first thing and last, if something other in between.

We now walk west. Always you end up going west. Janice picks up the pace. We're on a broader street now, it runs straight into the distance, and you can see a few of the lights of Manhattan. There is a small crowd milling outside the Chinese takeout, which Janice says is the neighborhood's best. People are waiting for their orders. It's warm tonight, the warmest spring night so far, and no one seems to mind. Tomorrow's Friday and work will stop. We go inside and give our order, get our slip. They're out of scallops, also out of shrimp and squid, the girl at the register says. Some of their deliveries didn't come today. We order twice-cooked pork and chow fun and steamed *gailon,* semi-bitter greens. I know I'm American because I order too much when I eat Chinese. We stand outside with everyone else, the crowd mixed, Jews and Hispanics, Asians and blacks. Everyone gets along. There's cross-talking and joking. Easy laughs. It's something enough, I suppose, when you know you will soon eat the same food.

It's almost ten o'clock, and we're one of the last orders they take. They actually have to send a cook to one of their stores a few miles away for ingredients. They say to customers sorry it's so early, but they have to close sooner tonight. They didn't get their cooking oil delivered either, other things as well. No more ginger, no more scallion. Very please you come back tomorrow. Thank you very much.

A brief rain pours down and the few of us still waiting come inside. There are a few chairs along the walls, the space not ten feet square. The kitchen is tiny. An old color TV is set high in a corner opposite the register. Everyone quiets for the final story of a weekly magazine show. They're interviewing several of the men from the cargo ship that ran aground in Far Rockaway. The young men are in their twenties, rice-water skinny, unshaven. They wear light blue coveralls that the detention center has provided them. They have very white, bad teeth. They describe the conditions on the ship, the lack of plumbing, how some of the passengers died during the 12,000 mile voyage and were wrapped in plastic and cast into the ocean. They try to keep smiling and downplay the hardship.

I listen closely to what they say. Or at least, how they are translated by a woman who sounds Chinese-American, her tones over-round and bulky like Sherrie's. She imparts a formality and respect to their statements, and they seem to be interviewing for a position rather than telling their story, unceasingly nodding and bowing and grinning exuberantly with the joy of their good fortune. They keep repeating the words *America* and *new life.*

Luck, like most everything else, must be a Chinese invention. We Koreans have reinvented the idea of luck as mostly bad, and try to do everything we can to prevent it. We fear leaving anything to chance. So with John Kwang, in whatever he did. But how will he come back to the world now? A part of me doesn't want him to show up again. Not only for the television, for the public, but for me and Janice and the rest. Whoever is left. It is not that I don't wish to face him. I think we can both bear that burden. What I dread most is the feeling that might come out in him on his return, the expression of self-loss and self-doubt on a face that I have known as almost unblemished, resolute, magically unweathered by strife and time. For so long he was effortlessly Korean, effortlessly American. Now I don't want him ever to lower his eyes. I don't want to witness the submissive dip of his brow or the bend of his knee before me or anyone else. I didn't—or don't now—come to him for the occasion of looking upon this. I am here for the hope of his identity, which may also be mine, who he has been on a public scale when the rest of us wanted only security in the tiny dollar-shops and churches of our lives.

We get our cartons of food but now the 10 P.M. news comes on. Mostly they report the same facts and allegations as earlier in the day, trying to talk to girls who work at the club, hounding its owner as he gets into a car. They show the outside of the hospital where a reporter files her story. They run old footage of John Kwang from various points during his career, almost a retrospective as though he has died, and as the reporter conjectures on what effect this accident will have on his council seat they splice in frames of the salon room where we sat, the interior of his sedan, the spidery crack on her side of the windshield. The mayor refuses to comment but his commissioner of police is suddenly everywhere talking tough about equal justice under the law. The commissioner promises that his force will conduct a full and zealous investigation, and that the district attorney has accorded this case his highest priority.

Janice groans and sits back down.

Now another related report, an exclusive. There is hard evidence of a community money club that John Kwang oversees. The club is like a private bank that pays revolving interest and principal to its members, many of whom are Korean, lending activities that aren't registered with any banking commission and haven't reported to tax authorities. The information, oddly, originates from the regional director of the Immigration and Naturalization Service.

"What the fuck is he talking about?" Janice cries. "What the hell is going?"

But I am silent.

They now hook the director in live.

He is an average-looking man sitting behind a wide gray desk. He is pale, severely balding, with a trimmed moustache and round wire-rim eyeglasses. He speaks from the back of his mouth; the sound of his talk is sticky. He rests his hand on a stack of papers. A good number of them, he says, touching the printouts, are not documented.

"How many exactly?" the news anchor asks.

He answers that the INS has no records of birth or entry or naturalization for nearly three dozen of them and their families. Maybe it's about a hundred total. The illegals are of all nationalities—some Koreans, of course, but mostly other Asians, West Indians, various Africans, and "most whatever else you can think of," he says, adding that aliens are coming now from everywhere. He speaks all this without any outward alarm unanimated, not unconcerned but as if the situation is already too fa gone.

He says further that a check unrelated to this listing showed that th Korean girl involved in the accident with John Kwang is also an illegal.

"Isn't it unwise to air this information," the anchor suggests, "give that these aliens might now go into hiding?"

"No, sir," the director answers, matter-of-factly. He almost smiles. "O course the girl is in serious condition and immobile. We'll talk to her i and when she is able. But we have hit all of the suspected illegals and thei families at their residences early this morning. It should be pretty muc over by now. We have them all."

Now the people want him out. They march to his house down the middle of the street, impromptu parades of them, husbands and wives and crying toddlers on shoulders, angry white people and brown people and black people, and now even some yellow, a few faces I think I recognize from past rallies and events, yelling together for his ouster in the simple rhyme of the picket: *Hey, ho, Kwang must go!*

It is past noon. Warm. You can't see the sun through the thin buffer of cloud cover but the light is fully diffused, almost too bright to see.

They surround the house in bands. Two, maybe three hundred people. I can see only a few police cars parked on the periphery, their number scattered about the crowd. One of the groups is made up of unemployed toy and light-metal workers. They are well organized, passing out pamphlets and addressing the crowd through bullhorns. Their literature asks how many of John Kwang's money club members have stolen their jobs. They curse him for helping them after they sneak into the country. They chant that they want to kick every last one of them back to where they came from, kick him back with them, let them drown in the ocean with "Smuggler Kwang." Next to them, in front of his driveway, people stand behind two sewn-together sheets spray-painted with the words: AMERICA FOR AMERICANS. They are generally younger, white, male, mostly talking and laughing and pointing to the house. They are drinking. Several of them intermittently wave a huge flag. One of them raises his fist and jumps up and down and shouts, "We want our fucking future back."

The rest of the throng are those of us hoping and waiting for Kwang to come back. There are enough of us to cause friction with the protesters. Someone keeps hollering over to us the question, *How many of you swam here?* Our numbers seem to hold them back from physical assaults, but more shouting matches are starting to break out along the border that is quickly forming. A few police stand in the buffer zone but not enough of them, it seems, if any real trouble flares up. Shouts of "white trash" and "Spanish niggers" and "greasy gooks" fly back and forth over their heads, though they don't seem to hear them.

He has not surfaced for nearly thirty-six hours since the accident. Then, the surprise dawn sweep by the INS. We hear rumors that he has been taken in for questioning by federal agents in Manhattan. That he will be here soon. One reporter seems able to confirm this, but no one else is certain. Janice, who arrived here early this morning, is now inside the house with May and the boys. May won't let anyone else in. When I finally get through the busy line from a pay phone Janice says May is losing it. She keeps sending the boys away to play and right away asks where they are.

Janice figures there is no longer anything to do except stay with May and wait. She won't draft a statement for him or make any more phone calls to confuse or delay the press. It is up to him to appear imminently and explain himself on all the counts. If he is alive and breathing he knows this.

She is afraid for him. Over the phone, she couldn't say the word she was thinking. But I told her she was wrong. I know he is alive. Koreans don't take their own lives. At least not from shame. My mother said to me once that suffering is the noblest art, the quieter the better. If you bite your lip and understand that this is the only world, you will perhaps persist and endure. What she meant, too, was that we cannot change anything, that if a person wants things like money or comfort or respect he has to change himself to make them possible, because the world will always work to foil you.

I will hear her voice always: *San konno san itta.* Over the mountains there are mountains.

She would have called John Kwang a fool long before any scandal ever arose. She would never have understood why he needed more than the money he made selling dry-cleaning equipment. He had a good wife and strong boys. What did he want from this country? Didn't he know he could only get so far with his face so different and broad? He should have had ambition for only his little family. In turn, she'd proudly hold up my father as the best example of our people: how he was able to discard his excellent Korean education and training, which were once his greatest pride, the very markings by which he had known himself, before he was able to set straight his mind and spirit and make a life for his family. This, she reminded me almost nightly, was his true courage and sacrifice.

And when I consider him, I see how my father had to retool his life to the ambitions his meager knowledge of the language and culture would allow, invent again the man he wanted to be. He came to know that the sky was never the limit, that the truer height for him was more like a handful of vegetable stores that would eventually run themselves, making him enough money that he could live in a majestic white house in Westchester and call himself a rich man.

I am his lone American son, blessed with every hope and quarter he could provide. And yet I am bestowed only with the meager effect of his hard-fought riches, that troubling awe and contempt and piety I still hold for his life. This, I am afraid, will endure. If he would forgive me now. For what I have done with my life is the darkest version of what he only dreamed of, to enter a place and tender the native language with body and tongue and have no one turn and point to the door.

I should have seen that Dennis never really wanted any other material. The monographs, the reports. The daily registers. For him it was all trivial prose. John Kwang, I can hear him saying with a pop in his voice, is not so important a man. At least not individually, as a single human possibility. No one is. If a client is interested at all it is because there is activity going on behind the man in question, because the man exercises an influence or maybe even grace on some greater slice of humanity. Or most simply, he is representative, easily drawn and iconic, the idea being if you know him you can know a whole people.

To Dennis, and to the reporters that are here, I could explain forever Kwang's particular thinking, how the idea of the *ggeh* occurred as second nature to him. He didn't know who was an "illegal" and who was not, for he would never come to see that fact as something vital. If anything, the *ggeh* was his one enduring vanity, a system paternal, how in the beginning people would come right to the house and ask for some money and his blessing. He wasn't a warlord or a don, he had no real power over any of them save their trust in his wisdom. He was merely giving to them just the start, like other people get an inheritance, a hope chest of what they would work hard for in the rest of their lives.

When I listened to their requests for money, I wondered if I could ever desire as much from this land. My citizenship is an accident of birth, my mother delivering me on this end of a long plane ride from Seoul. In truth, she didn't want me to be an American. She didn't want any reasons to stay. By rights I am as American as anyone, as graced and flawed and righteous as any of these people chanting for fire in the heart of his house. And yet I can never stop considering the pitch and drift of their forlorn boats on the sea, the movements that must be endless, promising nothing to their numbers within, headlong voyages scaled in a lyric of search, like the great love of Solomon.

Yet, in the holds of those ships there is never any singing. The people only whisper and breathe low. Not one of them thinks these streets are paved with gold. This remains our own fancy. They know more about the guns and rapes and the riots than of millionaires. They have heard stories of bands of young men who will look for them to beat up or murder. They know they will come here and live eight or nine to a room and earn ten dollars a day, maybe save five. They can figure that math, how long it will take to send for their family, how much longer for a few carts of fruit to push, an old truck of wares, a small shop to sell the dumplings and cakes and sweet drinks of their old land.

Last night, I come right home after seeing the news with Janice. All the lights in the apartment are out, and Lelia is already in bed. I take off my clothes and sit beside her. I try to whisper to her, but she's asleep. I put my hand on the rise of her hip. She moans, and I say I am here.

"You're home," she says, still half asleep.

"Yes."

"Henry," she says, suddenly waking up. "So many. They got so many."

"Yes," I whisper.

She turns on the lamp. She sits up, squinting at me. "Do you know them?"

"Only a few," I say, my head in my hands.

"What's going to happen now?"

I tell her, "They'll each have a hearing. Most of them will probably be declined asylum, and there will be appeals, and it will take many months until in the end they're sent back."

She looks sick for me. "But you didn't know this would happen."

"What does it matter," I answer. "Something bad was going to happen. I always knew that. All those years should have told me. Dennis has a use for everything. Even throwaways, like a list of immigrants. On the way home, I kept putting my father in their place."

"No one would be sending your father anywhere," Lelia says. "He would have slipped away."

I say, "Maybe I would have found him."

"If he let you," she says.

I know Lelia is right. My father was a kind of trickster all his own. He'd keep me guessing with his storefront patois. Any moment I had him square in my sights, he'd surprise me with a dip, a shake, a move from the street that I'd never heard or seen.

I say to Lelia, "Imagine, though, if they told my father he really had to leave. If they put him inside a plane and it took off. Can you see his face? It would be a death for him. Or worse."

"Nothing's worse," she says to me, her voice sad and low. "Nothing. You remember that, Henry. No matter what happens, damnit."

"Okay."

"It's over," Lelia now says. "You don't work for Dennis anymore. You can help those people if you want."

"It's too late," I say. "They need lawyers."

"Then you can work here," she says, taking me by the shoulders. "I have too many kids. I need another set of hands."

"Another mouth," I say.

She brushes my hair, gently kissing me now. "Yeah."

We can't sleep. Instead, we sit for a long time in the open windows, looking down on the intersection. On the far corner is the all-night Korean deli; two workers, a Korean and a Hispanic, are sitting on crates and smoking cigarettes outside. There's no traffic, and when the wind is right, their voices filter up to us. We listen to the earnest attempts of their talk, the bits of their stilted English. I know I would have ridiculed them when I was young: I would cringe and grow ashamed and angry at those funny tones of my father and his workers, all that Konglish, Spanglish, Jive. Just talk right, I wanted to yell, just talk right for once in your sorry lives. But now, I think I would give most anything to hear my father's talk again, the crash and bang and stop of his language, always hurtling by. I will listen for him forever in the streets of this city. I want to hear the rest of them, too, especially the disbelieving cries and shouts of those who were taken away. I will bear whatever sentence they wish to rain on me, all the volleys of their prayers and curses.

In the morning, Lelia already knows where I am going. She wants to go with me but I ask her to stay home. One more trip to him, that is all. She looks sick, worried.

"Nothing will happen to me," I promise.

"You better be right, Henry," she says, her voice breaking a little. "Or I'll come find you and kill you, I swear."

I have her snap all the bolts on the door. Don't answer the phone, don't answer the door.

I go out into the street and look for a cab. An old silver Pontiac pulls up. It's Jack's car.

"Let me give you a lift," he says. "Come on, now."

I get in. I say, "What, Jack, you want to go inspect the ruins?"

"No, Parky," he says, pulling away. "I came to see you."

We drive for a while without talking. He takes the tunnel, and when we come back out and pass the toll plaza he takes the first exit. He drives the smaller streets to the house in Woodside.

"Parky," he says softly, "what is there to say?"

"Not much," I answer. "You won. I guess this is my concession ride."

"I won nothing," he says firmly. "Dennis has, perhaps. But then he wins all the time."

"You knew the play, didn't you, Jack?"

He shakes his head. "Dennis would never tell me that. He knows I would prefer not to lie to you."

"You knew about Kwang and Eduardo."

"I knew we were not responsible for the bombing. That was not us. I told you that from the start."

"But the other matter."

"Okay," he says, not looking at me. "I did. But only after he was killed. I swear I did not know him. Dennis has other stations at his disposal, you know. He can bring in people when he wants. He was very angry that day of the bombing. Very angry. He let it slip. He wanted payback for his investment."

"And I gave it to him."

"It worked out that way, yes? Dennis put you in for your own sake. A refresher course. No one knew but him. Not even Eduardo. Each to his own world. But things changed, as they always do. You were in place. As Dennis says, *in situ.*"

"Eduardo was good," I say, picturing him play-boxing with Kwang.

"He got caught," Jack says. "Like you, he let himself get too close, but then he also got himself dead. In my book these are two big strikes against him."

"So I have just one."

Jack snorts. "You know, I would still take you on my team, Parky, any day of the week."

He stops the car a block from the house. It's early, but there are already people milling about in the street in front of the house. "Maybe you should go home, Parky. I will take you back home now. This is pointless. You owe him nothing."

"Don't tell me what I owe, Jack," I say to him. "Don't tell me anything like that."

I get out and stand beside the car. His hands are heavy on the steering wheel.

"This must be the moment," I say. "Now you get to retire."

"Yes," he answers. "So what will I do?"

"Garden," I tell him. "You can work on the house."

"But who will come up?"

I can't answer him then. I don't like seeing the picture of him, all sweaty and muddy, trudging into a silent house. His hands full of harvest, his kitchen shining and bright. But there's no one to show the sauce tomatoes to, no one to smell his rosemary and sage. He takes his time, pulling the fragrant leaves. There. He will cook a beautiful meal tonight.

"You'll be okay," I say.

"That is right," he says, weakly. "You are kind to let me drive you, Parky. You are a kind man."

"I don't mean to be."

"What does it matter?" he says.

"Goodbye, Jack."

"Henry," he suddenly says, the sound of it strange. "Try hard to forget us. It can be done. Forget what you can."

The crowd is growing loud again. Some of the people are arm in arm, drinking from beer bottles wrapped in small brown bags, not only men but women, too. If I were one of the people they were protesting, fresh off the boat, I would be sure I had just happened upon some community celebration, a festival of the culture.

Americans, one of them would say, are a wonderful and exuberant people. They dance, they play-fight, they puff up their lips and blow out their chests. They enjoy using their hands. They seem to live always at a football match. They stand in broken columns and flurry with both arms and both legs and they are not afraid to make a mess of themselves. They don't so much sing as they do chant. Chanting is more satisfying, at least how they do it. Their calls first start all together and slow and then pick up speed and volume until they finally dissipate to separate voices and rounds of hand clapping and cheers. They slap hands in the air. Everyone leaps up and down. The sight is a most pleasing thing. They are every shape and color but they still share this talk, and this is the other tongue they have learned, this must be the special language.

We see flashing lights in the distance. Soon a line of six or seven squad cars turns the far corner and heads up the block toward us. The cars reach the edge of the throng and then slowly pull their way through the crowd, the lead car trying to move everyone to the sidewalks with sharp barks of its siren. It doesn't work. People excitedly rush the vehicles, trying to see if he is inside one of them, checking all the back windows. From their motions you can tell he doesn't seem to be there and this makes everyone even more anxious and edgy. People are beginning to shout at the squad cars, drum on the window glass and the trunks. The cars finally park and the cops angrily push their way out. There is some shoving, and finally they force people out of the way, using their nightsticks as blocking bars.

With all the commotion, I find I can get closer to the house, right up against the blue barricades that bar the short driveway. I notice that none of the officers manning them seems too concerned when the squad cars pull up, which tells me he probably isn't with them. The extra cops are now aligning themselves along two yellow tapes they string in the form of a corridor that leads from the street to the house just past where I am.

The mass returns quickly, filling in the spaces on each side of the narrow cordon of police. I am hemmed in. The cameras are already pushing for the best angles, and the reporters are mostly ignoring the crowd, trying to get the officers to tell them what is going on; they complain that they need to know if they should be feeding live.

Two maroon four-doors somehow pull up without attracting much no-ice. Men in dark suits get out of the first one and then the doors of the other car open. Now other men exit, squinting in the light. They all look in this direction. Then one of them leans down and nods into the cab. Says something.

And then we see him. He steps from the car. In the distance of thirty yards, he looks small to me. Or maybe thinner. I half expect them to help him, but he pulls himself out, his hands free. He holds his suit jacket with one hand and shields his eyes with the other. He still has the bandage on his forehead, but the bruises around his left eye look almost healed.

They walk him up from the middle of the street. The people who are angry with him are hollering and pointing at him, stretching the police tape as far as they can. They scream at him like he is a child. They are calling him every ugly Asian name I have ever heard. A woman leans out and spits on his shoulder. Some others try to touch him but the plainclothesmen push them away.

I notice some others who are standing very still with their hands at their mouths. Most of these are Asian women. They look like the older women you see working in the alley behind a restaurant, pouring out buckets of dirty dishwater. They are tired, expressionless. But now they gaze at him as if he were their son, one maybe gone bad though now finally home, and the numbed speech on their faces seems to say how sad he must be and hurt enough and how he should be forgiven.

He is moving too slowly. He seems to tempt the mass. The men walking him try to speed him up, but he stays his pace. He shrugs them off. Now, he even stops. The people are screaming. An arm's length away from him they shout with everything they have. But nothing registers in his face. It is as if he is deaf. He seems to look only at a window of his house, but I look up and no one is there.

He is already in another world.

But some part of him will taste this last crowd. He is willing to suffer their angry medicine. Perhaps he sees something meaningful, how this might be a test and a recompense. If you must walk the white-hot stones, touch each one.

I think that he wants to defy them, too, with this deliberation, each of his steps a careful word to break down the ready meter they have built, each halting a kind of instant deliverance.

The people seem to sense this, that there is some part of him they're not getting to, not even touching, that he isn't there for them. They start heaving forward on the other side of the path and snap the tape on their side.

Suddenly I can't see him any longer. I can bear anything but I will not bear this. The bodies behind me respond and we push forward. I break the tape myself. I rush toward where he is and I see him at last. I fight my way. I can finally see him, three bodies deep, barely protected by the plainclothes cops, who are busy holding people and cameras back.

People are grabbing his shoulders, his hair. His bandage is torn from his head. Everyone is shouting. A hundred mouths shouting for him.

And when I reach him I strike at them. I strike at everything that shouts and calls. Everything but his face. But with every blow I land I feel another equal to it ring my own ears, my neck, the back of my head. I half welcome them. And at the very moment I fall back for good he glimpses who I am and I see him crouch down, like a broken child, shielding from me his wide immigrant face.

This is a city of words.

We live here. In the street the shouting is in a language we hardly know. The strangest chorale. We pass by the throngs of mongers, carefully nodding and heeding the signs. Everyone sounds angry and theatrical. Completely out of time. They want you to buy something, or hawk what you have, or else shove off. The constant cry is that you belong here, or you make yourself belong, or you must go.

Most of my days begin the same. In the morning I go out in the street and I search for them. I rarely need to go far. I look for the rises of steam from pushcarts. I look for old-model vans painted in matte, their tires always bald. I look for rusty hand trucks and hasty corner displays, and then down tenement alleys strung with fancy laundry and in the half-soaped windows of basement stores. I stop in the doorways of every smoke shop and deli and grocer I can find. They are all here, the shades of skin I know, all the mouths of bad teeth, the speaking that is too loud, the cooking smells, body smells, the English, and then the phases of English, their grunts of it to get by.

Once inside, I flip through magazines, slowly choose a piece of fruit, a candy. The store will grow quiet. The man or woman at the register is suspicious of my lingering, and then murmurs to the back, in a tone they want me to understand and in a language I won't, to their brother or their wife. A face appears from a curtain, staring at me. I finally decide on something, put my money on the counter. I look back and the face is gone.

My father, I know, would have chased someone like me right out, stamping his broom, saying, *What you do? Buy or go, buy or go!*

I used to love to walk these streets of Flushing with Lelia and Mitt, bring them back here on Sunday trips during the summer. We would eat cold buckwheat noodles at a Korean restaurant near the subway station and then go browsing in the big Korean groceries, not corner vegetable stands like my father's but real supermarkets with every kind of Asian food. Mitt always marveled at the long wall of glassed-door refrigerators stacked full with gallon jars of five kinds of kimchee, and even he noticed that if a customer took one down the space was almost immediately filled with another. *The kimchee museum,* he'd say, with appropriate awe. Then, Lelia would stray off to the butcher's section, Mitt to the candies. I always went to the back, to the magazine section, and although I couldn't read the Korean well I'd pretend anyway, just as I did when I was a boy, flipping the pages from right to left, my finger scanning vertically the way my father read. Eventually I'd hear Lelia's voice, calling to both of us, calling the only English to be heard that day in the store, and we would meet again at the register with what we wanted, the three of us, looking like a family accident, gathering on the counter the most serendipitous pile. We got looks. Later, after he died, I'd try it again, ride the train with Lelia to the ame restaurant and store, but in the end we would separately wander the isles not looking for anything, except at the last moment, when we finally ncountered each other, who was not him.

Still I love it here. I love these streets lined with big American sedans nd livery cars and vans. I love the early morning storefronts opening up ne by one, shopkeepers talking as they crank their awnings down. I love ow the Spanish disco thumps out from windows, and how the people ropped halfway out still jiggle and dance in the sill and frame. I follow the trolling Saturday families of brightly wrapped Hindus and then the black-lad Hasidim, and step into all the old churches that were once German nd then Korean and are now Vietnamese. And I love the brief Queens unlight at the end of the day, the warm lamp always reaching through the vestward tops of that magnificent city.

Vhen I am ready, I will flag a taxi and have the driver take only side streets or the three miles to John Kwang's house, going the long way past the big nansions near the water of the Sound, where my mother once said she vould like to live if we were rich enough. She wanted for us to stay in Queens, where all her friends were and she could speak her language in the treet. But my father told her they wouldn't let us live there for any mount of money. All those movie stars and bankers and rich old Italians. *They'll burn us out,* he warned her, laughing, *when they smell what you cook n a house.*

Once, I get inside the Kwang house again. I call the realtor whose name s on the sign outside and we tour the place. As she keys the door she asks what I do and I tell her I am between jobs. She smiles. She still carefully hows me the parlor, the large country kitchen, the formal dining room, ll six of the bedrooms, two of them masters. I look out to the street from he study at the top of the stairs. We go down to the basement, still equipped with office partitions. When we're done she asks if I'm interest and I point out that she hasn't yet mentioned who used to live in such grand place.

Foreigners, she says. They went back to their country.

By the time I reach home again Lelia is usually finishing up with her la students. I'll come out of the elevator and see her bidding them goodb outside our door. She'll kiss them if they want. They reach up with bo arms and wait for her to bend down. The parent will thank her and th pass by me quickly to catch the elevator. Then she is leaning in the emp doorway, arms akimbo, almost standing in the way I would glimpse h when I left her countless times before, her figure steeled, allowing. Sl wouldn't say goodbye.

Now, I am always coming back inside. We play this game in which I a her long-term guest. Permanently visiting. That she likes me okay a bears my presence, but who can know for how long? I step inside and wa to the bedroom and lie down and close my eyes. She follows me and sa that this is her room. I usually sleep on the couch.

Usually? I murmur.

Yes, she says, her voice suddenly closer, hot to the ear, and she's alrea on me.

After a few hours of lying around and joking and making funny soun she'll get up and drift off to the other end of the apartment. It's a hap distance. She'll prepare some lessons or read. Maybe practice in a ha mirror being the Tongue Lady, to make sure she's doing it right for t kids.

I make whatever is easy for dinner, tonight a Korean dish of soup a steamed rice. I scoop the rice into deep bowls and ladle in broth and bri them over to where she is working. We eat by the open windows. She lik the spicy soup, but she can't understand why I only seem to make it on t hottest, muggiest nights. It's a practice of my mother's, I tell her, how if you sweat and suffer a boiling soup in the heat you'll feel that much cooler when you're done.

I don't know, Lelia says, wiping her brow with her sleeve. But she eats the whole thing.

She has been on her visits around the city. The city hires people like her to work with summer students whose schools don't have speech facilities, or not enough of them. She brings her gear in two rolling plastic suitcases and goes to work. Today she has two schools, both in Manhattan. One of the schools is on the Lower East Side, which can be rough, even the seven- or eight-year-olds will carry knives or sharp tools like awls.

We decide that I should go with her. Besides, I've been an assistant before. Luckily, the school officials we check in with don't seem to care. They greet her and then look at me and don't ask questions. They can figure I am part of her materials, the day's curriculum. Show and tell.

Lelia usually doesn't like this kind of work, even though it pays well, mostly because there are too many students in a class for her to make much difference. There are at least twenty anxious faces. It's really a form of day care, ESL-style. We do what we can. We spend the first half hour figuring out who is who and what they speak. We have everyone say aloud his or her full name. When we finally start the gig, she ends up giving a kind of multimedia show for them, three active hours of video and mouth models and recorded sounds. They love it. She uses buck-toothed puppets with big mouths, scary masks, makes the talk unserious and fun.

I like my job. I wear a green rubber hood and act in my role as the Speech Monster. I play it well. I gobble up kids but I cower when anyone repeats the day's secret phrase, which Lelia has them practice earlier. Today the phrase is *Gently down the stream.* It's hard for some of them to say, but it helps that they can remember the melody of the song we've already taught them, and so they singsong it to me, to slay me, subdue me, his very first of their lyrics.

Lelia doesn't attempt any other speech work. The kids are mostly jus foreign language speakers, anyway, and she thinks it's better with thei high number and kind to give them some laughs and then read a tall tale i her gentlest, queerest voice. It doesn't matter what they understand. Sh wants them to know that there is nothing to fear, she wants to offer up pale white woman horsing with the language to show them it's fine to mes it all up.

At the end of the session we bid each kid goodbye. Many freelance rotate in these weekly assignments, and we probably won't see them agai this summer. I take off my mask and we both hug and kiss each one. Whe I embrace them, half pick them up, they are just that size I will foreve know, that very weight so wondrous to me, and awful. I tell them I wi miss them. They don't quite know how to respond. I put them down. sense that some of them gaze up at me for a moment longer, some wonde in their looks as they check again that my voice moves in time with m mouth, truly belongs to my face.

Lelia gives each one a sticker. She uses the class list to write their name inside the sunburst-shaped badge. Everybody, she says, has been a goo citizen. She will say the name, quickly write on the sticker, and then hav me press it to each of their chests as they leave. It is a line of quiet faces. take them down in my head. Now, she calls out each one as best as she ca taking care of every last pitch and accent, and I hear her speaking a doze lovely and native languages, calling all the difficult names of who we are.